Praise for Tracy Wolff's Crave Series

#BookTok

"*Covet* is a fun and addictive read, with a plot
that will have you hooked."
—**CaitsBooks** on *Covet*

"Damn. That was good."
—**Xenatine** on *Covet*

"It's 3 AM and I'm an emotional wreck."
—**samsreading.addiction** on *Covet*

"Tracy Wolff needs to apologize bc it's been almost 5
months and I'm still crying."
—**Jena.loves.books** on *Covet*

"Yeah. Started this at midnight. Finished at 6:00 AM.
#nosleep #noregrets"
—**MunnyReads** on *Crush*

"A book ending that left me shook."
—**Theemmarae** on *Crush*

"Hudson is a blast. He's a sass master."
—**Twilight_Talk** on *Crush*

"Twilight in Hogwarts with dragons."
—**books_and_crafts** on *Crush*

"Twilight meets Harry Potter meets CW Drama."
—**Heybiancaj** on *Crave*

More praise for Tracy Wolff's Crave series

court

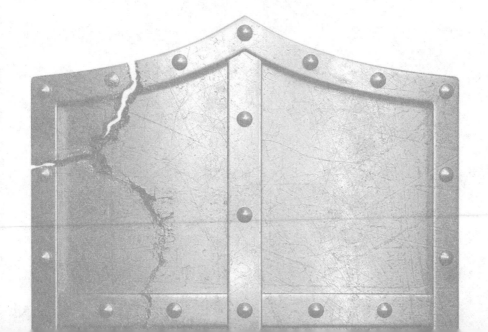

ALSO BY TRACY WOLFF

court

NEW YORK TIMES BESTSELLING AUTHOR
TRACY WOLFF

Entangled Publishing, LLC
10940 S Parker Road
Suite 327
Parker, CO 80134
rights@entangledpublishing.com

Entangled Teen is an imprint of Entangled Publishing, LLC.

Visit our website at www.entangledpublishing.com.

Edited by Liz Pelletier
Cover design by Bree Archer
Cover artwork by
koya79/GettyImages, Renphoto/Gettyimages, and Envato Elements
Interior Endpaper Design by Elizabeth Turner Stokes
Interior design by Toni Kerr

ISBN 978-1-64937-060-0 (Hardcover) ISBN 978-1-64937-180-5 (B&N)
ISBN 978-1-64937-181-2 (BAM) ISBN 978-1-64937-182-9 (TARGET)
ISNB 978-1-64937-183-6 (INDIE) ISBN 978-1-64937-061-7 (Ebook)

Manufactured in the United States of America

First Edition February 2022

10 9 8 7 6 5 4 3

entangled teen
an imprint of Entangled Publishing LLC

To Stephanie
Thank you for saying yes

At Entangled, we want our readers to be well-informed. If you would like to know if this book contains any elements that might be of concern for you, please check the back of the book for details.

Fake It Till
It Breaks You
—Hudson—

O

We are totally fucked.

And if Grace's terrified expression is any indication, she knows it, too.

I want to tell her everything is going to be okay, but the truth is, I'm terrified, too. Just not for the same reasons she is, though I'm not ready to go there yet.

Right now, she's sitting on my couch in front of the fire, her hair wet from her shower, her curls glistening in the flickering light. She's wearing one of my T-shirts and a pair of my sweatpants all rolled up.

She's never looked more beautiful.

Or more defenseless.

Fear threatens to overwhelm me at the thought, even as I tell myself she's nowhere near as defenseless as she looks. Even as I tell myself that she can take anything our fucking world can throw at her.

Anything but Cyrus.

If I've learned one thing about my father, it's that he'll never stop. Not until he gets what he wants and fuck the consequences.

The thought turns my blood cold.

I've never been afraid of anything in my whole miserable life—not of living and definitely not of dying. Enter Grace, and now I live in constant terror.

Terror I'll lose her and terror that if I do, she'll take the light with her. I know what it's like to be in the shadows—I've spent my whole bloody life in the dark.

And I don't want to go back.

"Can I—" I clear my throat and start again. "Can I get you a drink?" I ask, but Grace doesn't respond. I'm not sure she even hears me as she continues to stare at her phone, not wanting to miss a word on Flint. The specialist arrived ten minutes ago to look at him, and the wait to hear if he'll be able to keep his leg has been interminable. I know she wants to be in the infirmary with him—we all do—but when he asked for privacy, we couldn't say no. "Right. Okay. I'll only be a few minutes," I tell her, because she wasn't the only one in desperate need of a shower.

She still doesn't answer, and I can't help wondering what she's thinking. What she's feeling. She hasn't said more than a few words since we got back to school and realized Cyrus had tricked us and kidnapped all the students while we were fighting on the island. I just wish I knew what I could do to help her. To reach her before everything goes to hell again.

Because it will. Cyrus's terrifying new alliances are proof of that. As is his bold kidnapping of the children of the most powerful paranormals in the world. There's nowhere for him to go from here, nothing for him to do but destroy *everything*.

Not wanting to leave Grace sitting all alone in silence, I walk over to my record collection and riffle through the albums until my fingers land on Nina Simone. I pull the vinyl from the sleeve and place it on the turntable, click a button, and wait as the needle swings out and lowers with a crisp bite of static before Nina's whiskey voice fills the quiet space. I adjust the volume so it's more background music, and with one last look at Grace's still frame, I turn and head to the bathroom.

I take the fastest shower on record, considering the amount of blood and gore and death I need to wash away. I get dressed nearly as fast.

I don't know why I'm rushing, don't know what I'm afraid I'll find when—

My racing heart slows as I see Grace right where I left her. And I finally admit the truth to myself: the reason I haven't wanted to let her out of my sight is because I'm afraid she'll realize she made a mistake in choosing me.

Is it an irrational fear, considering she told me she loves me? That she chooses me, even with everything going on, even knowing what a burden my gifts are? Absolutely.

Does that make it go away? Not even close.

That's the power she holds over me, the power she'll always hold.

"Any word on Flint?" I ask as I grab a bottle of water from the fridge in the corner and carry it over to her.

"Nothing on the group chat yet."

I try to hand her the water, but when she doesn't take it from my outstretched hand, I walk to the other side of the couch and sit beside her, set the water on the table in front of us.

She turns from the fire then, slays me with her wounded gaze, and whispers, "I love you." And my heart pounds again.

She looks so serious, too serious, and even a little bit desperate. So I do what I always do to pull her out of her own head: I tease her, this time with our favorite movie line. "I know."

When a slow smile touches the edges of the shadows in her eyes, I know I made the right choice. I reach out and pull her onto my lap, relishing the feel of all of her against all of me. I glance down and run my finger along the promise ring I gave her, remembering the vow I made that day, the trembling conviction in my voice as I said those fateful words, and my chest tightens.

"You know," she says, pulling my gaze back to hers, "you said if I ever guessed what promise you made, you'd tell me. I think I've figured it out."

I raise one eyebrow. "Do you now?"

She nods. "You promised to bring me breakfast in bed for the rest of my life."

I snort-laugh. "Doubtful. You are a brat in the mornings."

The first real smile I've seen from her in what feels like forever lightens her face. "Hey, I *resemble* that." Then she laughs at her own joke, and I can't help myself from joining her. It's *so fucking nice* to see her smiling again.

"I know…" she continues, pretending to ponder alternatives. "You promised to let me win every argument?"

I give a full belly laugh at that ridiculous suggestion. She loves arguing with me. The *last* thing she'd ever want is for me to roll over and just let her have her way. "Not likely."

She stills then, blinking up at me. "Are you ever going to tell me?"

She's not ready to hear what I promised before I even knew she would ever love me back. So instead I joke, "Now where would the fun be in that?"

She fake punches me in the shoulder. "I *will* get it out of you one day." She runs her soft hand along the stubble on my jaw, her eyes turning serious again. "I have forever to keep guessing, mate."

And just like that, I'm on fire.

"I love you," I whisper and lean down to brush my lips across hers. Once, twice. But Grace is having none of it. She reaches up and holds my head between her palms, her lashes fluttering across her cheeks just before she demands everything from me. My breath. My heart. My very soul.

When we're both breathless, I lean back and hold her gaze. I could get lost in the depths of her warm brown eyes for an eternity.

"I love you," I tell her again.

"I know," she teases, repeating my words from earlier.

"That smart mouth is going to be the death of me," I murmur and start to kiss her once more, thoughts of picking her up and carrying her over to my bed dancing through my head. But she stiffens, and I know my thoughtless comment about dying reminded her, reminded us both, of everything we've lost, could still lose.

My heart nearly stops when I see the tears filling her eyes. "I'm sorry," I murmur.

She gives her head a quick shake, like I shouldn't be beating myself up over my slip, but, well, not going to happen. Then she bites her lip, her chin quivering as she tries to hold all the pain she's feeling inside, and for the billionth time, I want to kick myself for always speaking first and thinking second when she's near me.

"Babe, it's going to be okay," I tell her even as everything inside me turns to liquid. Bones, arteries, muscles, all of it just dissolves in the space from one breath to the next, and all I'm left with is what I'd be without Grace. An empty, bleeding shell.

"What can I do?" I ask. "What do you need—"

She cuts me off by placing her small, cold fingers against my mouth.

"Luca died for nothing. Flint's leg, Jaxon's heart, everything… It was all for nothing, Hudson," she whispers.

I pull her back into my arms, hold her while the anguish of what we've survived works its way through her system, her shaking now becoming my own as I know I'm out of excuses.

In this moment, while I hold the girl I love—the girl I would do anything to save—I know my time has run out. The cold hard truth I've spent the last hour doing my bloody best to ignore slams into me and steals my breath.

It's all my fault.

Everything. Every agony, every death, every moment of pain Grace and the others felt on that island—it's all my damn fault.

Because I was selfish. Because I didn't want to give her up yet. Because I was *weak*.

I've spent my life running from a destiny my father always wanted for me, but I realize now I have no choice. It's coming for me whether I want it to or not, and there isn't shit all I can do to avoid it. Not a second time. Not with Grace's happiness at stake.

And when I finally surrender to my fate, I'm afraid it will destroy us all.

1

Sometimes Two Rights
Make One Very Big Wrong

I want to be anywhere but here.

Anywhere but standing right here, in the middle of this too-cold room that all but reeks of pain and misery and a heavy dose of antiseptic. I send Hudson a quick smile before turning to face the rest of the gang.

"What do we do first?" Macy speaks softly, but my cousin's question echoes through the destroyed clinic, bouncing off the empty walls and broken beds like a gunshot.

It's the million-dollar question, the *billion*-dollar question. And right now, in front of Macy and our friends, I don't have a clue how to answer it.

To be fair, I've been in shock since we showed up at Katmere and found it ransacked, with blood-spattered walls, wrecked rooms, and every single student and professor missing. And now to find out that Flint's leg couldn't be saved? I'm devastated, and the fact that he's trying so hard to be strong only makes it a million times worse.

Now, an hour later, I may be cleaner after my shower, but I am still reeling from the devastation of it all.

Even worse, as I look from one friend's face to the next—Jaxon, Flint, Rafael, Liam, Byron, Mekhi, Eden, Macy, *Hudson*—it's clear they're as shaken as I am. And no one seems to have any more clue than I do about what happens next.

Then again, what is there to do at a time like this, when the entire world as you know it is ending and you're caught in the middle, watching it crumble brick by brick? At a time when every wall you shore up just leaves an opening for everything else to collapse around you?

It's not the first time we've suffered loss these last few months, but it is the first time since my parents died that everything feels truly hopeless for us all.

Even when I was alone on the Ludares field, I knew things would be okay—if not for me, then for the people I cared about. Or fighting the giants with

Hudson—I always knew he would survive. And when we were on the Unkillable Beast's island, fighting the vampire king and his troops, I still felt like we had a chance. Still felt like we could somehow find a way to defeat Cyrus and his unholy alliances.

And in the end, when he fled, we thought we had done it.

Thought we had at least won the battle, if not the war.

Thought the sacrifices—the so very, very many sacrifices—we had made had been worth it.

Until we got back here, to Katmere, and realized we hadn't been fighting a war at all—or even a battle. No, what had been life-and-death for us, what had brought us to our knees and sent us sinking into an abyss of despair, hadn't been a battle at all. Instead, it had been little more than a playdate, one meant to keep the children occupied while the adults took care of winning the *real* war.

I feel like a fool...and a failure. Because even knowing Cyrus can't be trusted, even knowing he has a plethora of tricks up his sleeve, we fell for it. Worse, some of us even died for it.

Luca died for it, and now Flint has lost his leg.

Judging from the looks on the faces of every single person in the infirmary, I'm not the only one who feels like this. A bitter mix of agony and rage hangs heavy among us. So heavy that there's barely room to feel anything else—barely room to *think* anything else.

Marise, the school's nurse practitioner and only surviving person left at Katmere, rests on one of the hospital beds, bruises and cuts still visible on her arms and cheek, which is testament to how hard she must have fought that her vampire metabolism hasn't healed her yet. Macy brings her a bottle of blood from the nearby fridge, and Marise nods a thank-you before drinking. Helping out the specialist with Flint obviously took what was left of her strength.

I glance at Flint sitting on a hospital bed in the corner with what's left of his leg propped up, at the pain etched on a face normally stretched wide with a big, goofy grin, and my stomach pitches. He looks so small, shoulders hunched in pain and grief, that I have to fight the rising bile back down my throat. Sheer will is the only thing keeping me upright at the moment—well, that and Hudson as he wraps an arm around my waist, like he knows I'd fall without his support. His hold, his obvious attempt at comfort, should reassure me. And maybe it would, if he wasn't currently trembling as badly as I am.

Silence stretches taut as a heartstring among the group of us, until Jaxon clears his throat and says in a voice as rough as we all feel, "We need to talk about Luca. There isn't much time."

"Luca?" Marise asks, heartbreak evident in her raspy words. "He didn't make it?"

"No." Flint's answer is as empty as his eyes. "He didn't."

"We brought his body back to Katmere," Mekhi adds.

"Good. He shouldn't be left on that godforsaken island." Marise tries to say something else, but her voice cracks in the middle. She clears her throat, tries again. "But you're right. There isn't much time."

"Time for what?" I ask, my gaze going to Byron as he pulls a phone from his front pocket.

"Luca's parents need to be notified," he answers as he scrolls. "He has to be buried within twenty-four hours."

"Twenty-four hours?" I repeat. "That seems awfully fast."

"It *is* fast," Mekhi answers. "But if he's not sealed in a crypt by then, he'll disintegrate."

The harshness of his answer—the harshness of this world—has my breath clogging in my throat.

Of course, we all turn to dust in the end, but how awful for it to happen so quickly. Maybe before Luca's parents can even get here to see him. Definitely before any of us can wrap our head around the reality that he is really gone.

Before we can even say goodbye.

"Byron's right," Macy says quietly. "Luca's parents deserve the chance to say goodbye."

"Of course they do," Hudson agrees in a voice that turns the sudden silence into a pulsing wound. "But we can't afford to give it to them."

No one seems to know what to say to that, and instead, we all stare at him, nonplussed. I can't help wondering if I heard him wrong, and judging from the looks on the others' faces, they feel the same.

"We have to tell them," Jaxon states, and it's clear he's in no mood to debate the topic.

"What do you mean?" Macy asks at the same time. She doesn't sound mad, though. Just concerned.

"They need time to take his body to the family crypt," Byron says, but he has stopped scrolling on his phone—either because he finally found Luca's parents' number or because he can't believe what he's hearing. "If we don't call them now, there won't be anything left of him."

Hudson eases his arm from around my waist and steps away, and I can't help but shiver at the loss of his warmth. "I know that," he replies, crossing his arms. "But they're vampires, from the Vampire Court. How do we know we can trust them?"

"Their son is dead." Flint's voice crackles with indignation as he struggles to stand. I can't believe he's up and moving already, but shifters heal fast, even under the most dire of circumstances. Jaxon turns to help him, but Flint throws his hand out in a silent *back the hell off*, though his gaze never leaves Hudson's. "You can't really think they'll take Cyrus's side?"

"Is the idea truly that surprising?" Hudson's face is blank when he turns to Jaxon. "You barely survived your last encounter with our *own* father."

"That's different," Jaxon snarls.

"Why? Because it's Cyrus? You actually believe he's the only one who thinks that way?" Hudson arches a brow. "If he was, there wouldn't have been so bloody many people to fight on that island."

Silence stretches until Eden says, "It pains me, but I think Hudson's right." She shakes her head. "We don't know if we can trust Luca's parents. We don't know if we can trust *anyone*."

"Their son is *dead*," Flint repeats emphatically, his gaze narrowing on Eden's. "They need to know while they still have time to bury him. If you're all too chickenshit to do it, I will." He nails Hudson with a heated glare. "Ever think we wouldn't have to notify them at all if you had done your job?"

I gasp as the words ricochet through my body like a physical blow. It's obvious he means Hudson's ability to disintegrate our enemies with a thought, and I want to rage at Flint that he'd even *suggest* such a thing, let alone expect it, but I also know he's hurting, and now isn't the time.

Hudson's gaze darts to mine, and instead, I try to reassure him with a look that it's not his fault. But quick as lightning, he focuses back on Flint and throws his arms wide in disbelief. "I was there fighting, same as you."

"But it's not the same, now, is it?" Flint raises a brow. "You act like you gave everything you had to that fight, but we all know that's not true. Why don't you ask yourself: If it had been Grace about to die, would we be having this conversation at all, or would Luca still be alive?"

Hudson's jaw clenches. "You don't know what the fuck you're talking about."

"Yeah, you keep telling yourself that." And with that, Flint uses the edge of the bed to hop over to a pair of crutches in the corner. He shoves them under his arms and shuffles out without another word.

Hudson doesn't say anything. No one does.

My chest squeezes tight at the choices he has to make, the expectations placed on his shoulders. Expectations too heavy for *anyone* to carry. And yet he does. Always.

But that doesn't mean he has to do it alone.

I pull him back into my arms and lay my head against his chest, close my eyes, and listen to his steady heartbeat until his shoulders start to relax, until his lips brush a faint kiss against my hair. Only then do I sigh. He's going to be okay. *We're* going to be okay.

But when I open my eyes, my gaze lands on our friends, and my breath catches.

Regret. Anger. *Accusation*. It's all there—and directed at Hudson and me.

It's then that I recognize Cyrus's real victory today.

We're divided.

Which is just another way of saying we are completely screwed. Again.

2

Standoff and Deliver

With those dark emotions flashing over their expressions, the Order shifts so that they're all standing at Jaxon's back as he faces off against Hudson. My stomach does a quick, unpleasant flip. This is shaping up to have all the makings of an Old West showdown, and I have no interest in getting caught in the crossfire. Or watching anyone else get caught, either.

Which is why I step into the empty space between Jaxon and my mate. Hudson makes a displeased sound low in his throat, but he doesn't try to stop me. I consider defending Hudson's choices on the battlefield, but in the end, I figure what we need to do first is focus on Luca. The minutes are counting down until he turns to dust.

I promise myself we *will* have this conversation about what everyone expects Hudson to do in a fight, but not today. We have enough issues as it is.

"Look, Jaxon, I get it." I hold a placating hand out to the boy who once meant everything to me. "This sucks. It *really* sucks. But you have to see how risky it is to invite Luca's parents here."

"Risky?" He shoots me a disbelieving look as he holds his arms out in a very similar gesture to what Hudson just did. Apparently, blood really does tell. "What else do you think they can do to this place? In case you haven't noticed, it's gutted."

"Not to mention the fact that if they want to attack us, they don't have to wait for an engraved invitation," Byron chimes in. "We're not exactly fortified right now."

"Yeah, but they don't know that we're here," Eden says as she walks forward to stand beside Hudson. "For all they know, we showed up, saw this destruction, and took off for parts unknown. Which, I have to admit, feels a little bit like what we *should* be doing."

"I can notify Luca's parents." Marise sits up in the hospital bed, and though she is still pale, her wounds are finally starting to heal. "While you guys go somewhere safer, somewhere off campus."

"We're not leaving you, Marise." Macy sounds firm as she walks over to Marise's side near the Order. "If we leave, you're coming with us."

"I'm not strong enough for that just yet," the vampire healer tells her.

"Which means we're not going anywhere until you are," Macy replies. "Besides, they left you for dead, so they obviously know you're on our side. They're just as likely to come after you when they know you're alive as they are to come after us."

"They won't hurt me," Marise says, but even she doesn't sound convinced.

"We're not leaving you," I reiterate and cross to the fridge and get another bottle of blood for her. She takes it, drinking a healthy amount before she sets it on the table beside her bed.

"Luca's parents have the right to know," Jaxon says again, but the latent aggression drains from his stance a little more with each word. "Whether they're traitors or not, they deserve the chance to bury their child. Whatever comes from inviting them here, whatever problems it causes, we'll deal with it. Because denying them that..." He closes his eyes, shakes his head. "Denying them that—"

"Makes us no better than Cyrus," Hudson finishes, sounding as resigned as Jaxon looks.

"Some things are worth the risk," Mekhi says. "Doing what's right is one of them."

Eden bites her lip, and it looks like she's going to argue, but in the end, she just shoves a frustrated hand through her hair and nods.

Jaxon waits to see if anyone else wants to chime in, glancing from one of us to the other. Thankfully, Hudson's acquiescence seems to have convinced everyone. When no one says anything, Jaxon turns to Marise. "I'll make the call."

Then Jaxon takes out his phone and fades across the room to the door and the hallway beyond.

"Now what?" Macy asks in a voice that sounds as shaky as I feel.

"Now we wait," Hudson answers, his eyes on the door Jaxon just disappeared through. "And hope we're not making a huge mistake."

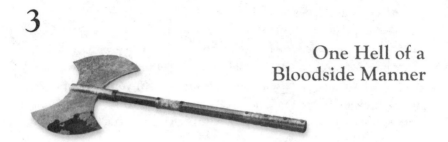

3

One Hell of a Bloodside Manner

Twenty minutes later, Flint is back on his hospital bed and pissy as hell as Marise prepares to start his wound care as the specialist instructed.

"Wait right here," she tells him. "I need to get more bandages."

"And here I thought I was going to climb Denali," he answers in a strained attempt at irony. She just shakes her head as she walks haltingly to a cabinet in the far corner of the infirmary—a sure sign that she's still not feeling nearly as good as she'd like us to believe.

Jaxon and the Order left to deal with Luca, and she'd insisted I bring Flint back so she could check on his leg. I figured Hudson would leave, too, once Flint shot him a death glare as soon as he reentered the infirmary. But to his credit, Hudson stayed. Of course, he's currently leaning against a wall and pretending to scroll through his phone, but he is here, being as supportive as Flint will let him.

Watching Flint trying to be brave in the face of everything he's lost, an all-too-familiar panic twists my stomach, and I drag a slow, deep breath into my lungs. Exhale. Then breathe in again.

Marise unlocks the glass cabinet and shuffles several pill bottles around until she finds what she's looking for. "Here, it's time for more pain medication," she tells him, walking back and handing him two blue pills.

After Marise cleans the wound and starts the tedious process of re-bandaging it, Macy and Eden ask her questions about the attack.

"I'm sorry, girls," Marise says after offering no new information to yet another volley of questions. "I wish I had more answers for you."

Macy and Eden exchange a look before Macy replies, "No, no. It's fine. You were fighting for your life—we understand. Not the best time to ask questions. We just wish you knew *something* that would help us figure out our next move."

"Well, I think you kids should just stay at Katmere where you're safe," Marise answers as she scoops up the used bandages. "No sense getting caught and giving

Cyrus an opportunity to steal your power, too."

"Wait, Cyrus kidnapped the kids to have leverage against their parents, force them to do his bidding," Eden says, her eyebrows shooting up. "Didn't he?"

I lean forward. Have we all gotten it wrong?

Marise shrugs and looks back down at Flint's leg. "I don't know anything about that, but I overheard one wolf talking about needing young magic to power something."

I gasp and shake my head at no one in particular. *No, no, no. That can't be right.*

"He kidnapped them to steal their magic?" Macy's voice breaks on the last word, her eyes widening in terror. "But our magic is tied to our soul. If Cyrus is trying to siphon it, he'll end up killing them!"

I glance over at Hudson to see if he's hearing this as well and am not surprised to notice him staring intently at the older vampire, his eyes narrowed in thought.

"I'm sorry," Marise says as she turns to drop Flint's bandages in a nearby medical waste bin. "That's all I know."

Macy asks something else, but I can't hear anything over the roaring in my ears. When we got to school and realized Cyrus had kidnapped the entire student body, it horrified all of us. But still, in the back of my mind, I think we all figured he wouldn't actually kill them. I mean, it's hard to use them for leverage against their parents if they're dead, right?

But now, realizing he might only want them for their magic, that he has no need to keep them alive after he's taken what he wants from them, I can't believe I took the time for a shower. Or—oh my God—actually *made out* with Hudson while students might be dying.

I glance up at my mate, then wish I hadn't because I know my thoughts are written across my face. The remorse. The shame. The *horror.*

His jaw tenses before he catches himself, but then his face goes completely blank as he registers how upset I am. Regret settles in my stomach, making it twist and churn. Because no matter how devastated this realization makes me, it's nothing compared to what Hudson is certainly feeling. Not after everything Flint accused him of earlier.

Oh, he tried to pretend like it was no big deal, tried to pretend that Flint's words rolled right off his back. Which might not have bothered me so much if he was just fronting to the others. But he's doing it with me as well, and that, more than anything else, tells me just how devastated he is.

Hudson and I don't pretend with each other—we never have. Not when I first unfroze us, when he was locked in my head and it was impossible for us to hide stuff from each other. And not now that he's out, either, because that's not who we are together. We tell each other the truth, even when it's hard. So if he's so far gone that he's hiding from me, things are bad. Really, really bad.

Fear turns my blood to ice, and I begin to make my way across the room to him. He needs to know this isn't his fault, needs to understand that none of this can be laid at his door. But before I can, Marise starts giving Flint a litany of instructions about his leg.

As she does, we all crowd around the bed, wanting to know what—if anything—we can do to help. Even Hudson puts his phone down, though he doesn't make a move to get closer to the bed or Flint.

Eventually, though, there are no more questions to ask. There's only the knowledge that regardless of how much we wish this isn't happening, there's nothing we can do but support Flint.

Because the truth is, no matter how much power you have, sometimes broken things have to stay broken, even though we might wish otherwise.

"I'm so sorry this happened to you," Macy tells him as she rubs a soothing hand down his arm. "But we'll do everything we can for you. We can take you to the Witch Court; the healers can make you a prosthetic—"

"Are these the same witches who just tried to kill us?" he answers caustically.

"I'm sorry," she whispers, tears blooming in her eyes. "I didn't mean—"

Flint mutters under his breath, shakes his head. "Ignore me. I'm in a foul mood."

"Yeah, well, if anyone has the right to be..." Macy blinks back her tears. "It's definitely you."

I feel a little voyeuristic to just be standing here watching Flint suffer, so I turn my back as Marise tells him, "And on the plus side, you're healing well, even faster than shifters normally do. Your wound is already nearly sealed, and I expect the skin to finish healing completely in the next twenty-four hours. In the meantime, you'll need an antibiotic and some extra bandages."

Eden moves closer and bumps his shoulder with her own. "You're going to be okay," she says fiercely. "We'll make sure of it."

"Yeah, we will," Macy agrees.

"I can't believe this is happening," I whisper to no one in particular, and then Hudson is beside me, his hands turning my shoulders so I face him.

"Flint *is* going to be okay," he says. "*Everything* is going to be okay."

I raise a brow at him. "It would be really nice if I actually thought you believed that."

Before he can think of something else to say, Jaxon comes back in the room, stopping on the other side of Flint's bed.

"Luca's parents are leaving now." His face is grim, his eyes infinite pools of grief. "They'll be here by morning."

4

"**Y**our dad is draining the kids of their magic and could be killing them," I blurt out. Probably not the best way to deliver the news to Jaxon, but, well, it definitely chases the grief from his eyes fast. What is burning there now is a white-hot fury that sends a chill down my spine.

"I will kill him with my bare hands," Jaxon bites out, and he looks like he means to do so right this minute.

"Let's play Who Gets to Kill Father Dearest First in the morning," Hudson drawls. "I think what we all need is sleep, or no one is going to be getting killed except us."

Everyone grumbles, but we know he's right. I feel like I'm about to fall over from exhaustion. Marise makes a few attempts to get us to promise not to do anything rash, but the best Jaxon will agree to is not to leave before morning. He waits until Flint is back up on his crutches, and then he and the Order head to their rooms.

As we all file out the door behind them, Hudson wraps an arm securely around my waist and fades us to the stairs leading to his room in a blink. I have to admit, sometimes the whole fading thing really comes in handy—especially since we were moving so fast, it made it impossible to catalog all the damage Katmere Academy sustained in the attack. I know I'll have to look eventually, but right now, I'm not sure I'm up for seeing just how much Cyrus's minions managed to destroy of this place I've come to call home.

Hudson sets me gently on my feet beside the bed, his gaze bouncing around the room, looking anywhere but at me. "You need to get some sleep. I'll take the couch so I don't disturb you."

"Disturb me? As if you ever could." He might be standing in front of me, but I can't help noticing the elephant wedged between us. "Hudson, we should talk about what happened in the infirmary."

"What's there to talk about?" he answers grimly. "It is what it is."

I lay a gentle hand on his arm. "I'm so sor—"

"Grace, stop." He sounds firm but not angry. And not nearly as wrecked as I feel.

"Why are you acting like this?" I ask, hating how needy I sound. Hating even more how needy and uncertain I *feel*. "What's wrong?"

He gives me a *seriously?* look. And I get it—*everything's* wrong. But that's nothing new. That's not us. That's just everything around us. Except...

Except when he's acting like this, it feels an awful lot like it might be us after all.

I'm not okay with that, not after everything we've been through to get here. And I'm definitely not okay with him just pulling away to lick his wounds, instead of sharing his concerns with me.

"Hudson, please," I say, trying to reach for him. "Don't do this."

"Don't do what?" he asks.

It's my turn to give him a look. And it must hit home because his jaw tightens, and suddenly he's very, very interested in the wall directly behind my head.

"Talk to me," I whisper, moving closer and closer, until our bodies are nearly touching and we're breathing the same air.

He stays where he is for one second, two, then takes a deliberate step back. And it slices like a knife. "I don't have anything to say."

"I guess there really is a first for everything," I try to tease, hoping to get a reaction out of him. Hoping to bring back the Hudson who's too sure of himself, too cocky for his own good.

He looks at me then, finally, and as I look back, I feel myself drowning in the endless infinity of his oceanic gaze—the endless infinity of him.

But the closer I look, the more aware I become that he's drowning, too. And no matter how hard I try, he won't let me toss him a life preserver.

"Let me help you," I whisper.

He gives a sad little half laugh. "I don't need your help, Grace."

"Then what *do* you need?" I grab on to him, burrow close. "Tell me what it is, and I'll find a way to give it to you."

He doesn't answer, doesn't wrap his arms around me, doesn't so much as move. And just like that, fear is a snarling beast deep within me, desperately clawing at my insides to get out.

Because this isn't my Hudson. This is a stranger, and I don't know how to bring him back. I don't even know how to find him under all that ice. I just know that I have to try.

Which is why when he begins to move back again, I hold on tight. I clutch his shirt in my hands, press my body against him, keep my gaze locked on his. And refuse to let go.

Because Hudson Vega is mine, and I am not going to lose him to the demons buried inside him. Not now, not ever.

I don't know how long we stay like that, but it's long enough for my throat to tighten. Long enough for my palms to go damp. More than long enough for a sob to rise in my chest.

And still, I don't look away. Still, I don't let him go.

And that's when it happens.

Jaw clenched, throat working, he slides his fingers around the back of my neck and fists his hand in my hair. Then tugs my head back, eyes still locked with mine, and says, "Grace," in a voice so raw and anguished, it has my whole body tensing in anticipation and despair.

"I'm sorry," he tells me. "I can't— I don't—"

"It's okay," I answer even as I cup his cheek in my hand and pull his head down to mine.

For a moment, I think he's going to pull away, that he doesn't want to kiss me after all. But then he makes a sound low in his throat, and just that easily, all the fears and the failures slip away in the frantic, frenzied crush of his lips against my own.

One moment I'm trying to crack him open, and the next I'm drowning in sandalwood and amber and hard, solid male.

And nothing has ever felt so good. Because this is Hudson, *my* Hudson. My mate. And even when things go wrong, *this* is so, so right.

As if to prove it, he nibbles along my lower lip, his fangs scraping the sensitive skin at the corners of my mouth, and I can't help but lose myself in the heat of his dark and desperate heart.

"It's okay," I murmur as his fingers clutch at my back and his trembling body strains against my own. "Hudson, it's okay."

He doesn't seem to hear me—or maybe it's just that he doesn't believe me— as he deepens the kiss and breaks the world, and me, wide open.

Lightning strikes, thunder crashes, and I swear all I can hear is him. All I can see or feel or smell is him, even before he slides his tongue along my own.

He tastes like honey—sweet, warm, dangerous. It's addictive, *he's* addictive, and I moan, giving him everything that I can. Giving him everything that he wants and begging him to take more. So much more.

We're both gasping when he finally pulls away. I try to hang on a little longer, try to keep the connection between us from slipping away. Because as long as he is wrapped up in me—in us—then he's not locked in his head, destroying himself for something he can't, and shouldn't, change.

Eventually, he pulls back, but I'm not ready to let him go. I keep my arms locked around his waist, my body pressed against his. *Just a little longer*, I plead silently. *Just give me a few more minutes of you and me and the oblivion I feel when we're touching.*

He must feel my desperation—and the fragility I'm working so hard to hide—because he doesn't move.

I wait for him to say something witty or sarcastic or just plain ridiculous in the way that only he can, but he doesn't say a word. Instead, he just holds me and lets me hold him.

And—for now—it's enough.

We've been through so much in the last twenty-four hours. Fighting giants, escaping prison, that horrible battle, losing Luca and nearly losing Jaxon and Flint, finding Katmere wrecked. Part of me thinks it's amazing we're still standing. The rest of me is just grateful that we are.

"I'm sorry," Hudson whispers again, his breath hot against my face. "I'm so sorry."

A powerful shudder rocks his long, lean frame.

"For what?" I ask, pulling back so I can see his face.

"I should have saved him," he says as our gazes collide and his voice breaks. "I should have saved them all."

I can see the guilt eating him alive, and I won't allow it. I can't. "You did nothing wrong, Hudson," I tell him firmly.

"Flint was right. I should have stopped them."

"By *stopped them*, you mean disintegrated hundreds of people on the spot?" I ask, brows raised.

He tries to turn away, shamefaced, but I hold him tightly. I've carried this kind of guilt and pain ever since my parents died, and it's not exactly fun. No way am I going to stand here and let Hudson do the same. Not if I can help it.

"What were you supposed to do?" I ask him. "Make Cyrus and everyone else against us just"—I shake my head, searching for the right words—"disappear into thin air?"

"If I had, Luca would still be alive. Flint would still have his leg. And Jaxon and Nuri—"

"Could you have done it?" I ask, because I felt his confusion at the beginning of that battle, felt him struggling to get control of himself and the situation as mayhem rained around us. "In the beginning, when everything was such a mess, could you have done it?"

"Of course I could have—" He breaks off, runs a hand through his hair. "I don't know. Everything was so close and chaotic. And when Jaxon threw himself right in the middle of it all…"

"You threw yourself in the middle right with him. Because you couldn't take the risk of missing and hurting him or the others. And you would rather have died yourself than let anything happen to Jaxon."

"Well, you saw him," Hudson drawls, and for a moment, he sounds like his old self. "The kid obviously needs protection. The second I turn my back, he goes and gets his heart ripped out of his chest."

"I'm not sure that's quite what happened," I say with a snort. "But I know you would do anything to protect him and me. I also know you would do anything to protect the others, too. You didn't disintegrate everyone at the beginning because you couldn't be sure you wouldn't get one of us. And once you were sure, once you did figure things out, you threatened to do so and would have, I'm sure."

He stares at the wall over my shoulder again. "You don't understand. No one does. It's not that simple." He sighs. "I hate this thing inside me."

"I know you do." I slide my hands from his waist and cup his face, wait patiently until his eyes meet mine again. "But I also know if Cyrus and the others hadn't left when you warned them, you would have made every single one of them cease to exist, and you would have done it for us. I have no doubt that you would have done it if it meant keeping us safe."

His gaze holds mine as he admits, "To keep *you* safe, I would have done anything."

But I'm not buying it. Hudson loves me, I know that, but I don't think even he realizes how much he would sacrifice for everyone else, not just me. "To keep *everyone* safe."

He shrugs, but I can feel him relax just a tiny bit this time. So I wrap my arms around him again and hug him even tighter, do my best to show him that I have faith in him even when he doesn't have faith in himself.

"Either way…" Hudson coughs and adds, "Before we go up against Cyrus again, I need to talk to Macy about how to counteract a sense spell."

"A sense spell?"

"That had to be what Cyrus used," he continues. "Cyrus had the witches do something to the whole group of them—I'm almost sure of it. Which is why, when I tried to persuade his troops to back off, they didn't so much as acknowledge me. It was like..."

"They didn't hear you at all?" I finish for him.

"Yeah." He shakes his head in disgust—whether at himself or his father, I don't know. "I should have expected him to do something like that."

"Because you're omniscient?" I ask sarcastically. I get why he's blaming himself—he's Hudson, and he takes the weight of the world on his shoulders whether it belongs there or not—but enough is enough. "Or because you're a god?"

His turbulent blue eyes narrow just a little in annoyance. "Because I know my father. I know how he thinks. And I know he'll stop at nothing to get what he wants."

"That's right," I tell him. "*He'll* stop at nothing. Which means everything that happened on that island is because of him, not you."

Hudson starts to argue with me but quiets again at the arch look I give him. This time he knows I'm right, whether he wants to admit it or not.

We stay that way for what feels like an eternity, eyes locked, bodies pressed together, everything we've seen and done settling like wet cement between us. I just wish I could be sure it was binding us together and not forming a wall.

Because this war is far from over. We've got a long road ahead of us if we hope to save the kids before Cyrus kills them, and there are no guarantees that it will end the way we want it to.

No guarantees that anything will ever be okay again.

Which is why I take a deep breath and tell him the fear that's been plaguing my mind since we got back to Katmere. "I don't think the Crown is what we thought it was."

5

Dream a Little Scream of Me

Hudson looks at my palm, and I can all but see a million different thoughts and scenarios running through his head as he tries to figure out how to respond. In the end, he only says, "Just because you haven't found its power yet doesn't mean it doesn't exist."

"Maybe not," I agree doubtfully. "But I'm pretty sure I would feel *something* if I had a new power."

"Just like you knew you were a gargoyle when you first arrived at Katmere?" he asks with a raised brow.

The question makes my stomach hurt, so I shove it—and any potential answers—down as deep as I can manage. It's far from the best solution, but until the Unkillable Beast decides to wake up and answer some questions for me, I'm pretty much stuck. No use freaking out for the next several hours if I can avoid it. Especially not when I really, really need to sleep.

"We've got time to worry about the Crown later," Hudson says. He loosens his arms around my waist and turns me toward his large bed that looks like heaven to my tired eyes. Hudson presses a kiss to the top of my head. "Why don't you crawl in?"

I'm too exhausted to do much more than follow his suggestion and climb into the bed, pulling the sheet and comforter over me as he heads toward the bathroom. Almost immediately, I find my eyes closing despite my determination to wait for Hudson. It only takes a minute before I'm drifting in a kind of fog, pictures of the battle we've all lived through flashing in my head in what feels like a never-ending montage of half memories and half dreams.

I shift as images of Luca dying mix with memories of being trapped in prison. Blood from Flint's leg covering my hands, Remy's swirling silver eyes telling me he'll see me again soon. I twist around, trying to figure out where I am. My heart is racing. Am I still in prison? Did I dream we got free, that we saved the

Unkillable Beast—*no, a gargoyle*, my groggy mind reminds me.

Worried, Grace. So worried.

The older gargoyle's voice slides into my mind, slipping between the images that are still flashing in my brain. I slog through my consciousness, but each second pulls me further under, like I'm stuck in quicksand.

No time, no time. His voice is more frantic than ever, punching through the fog. And then more clearly than he's ever spoken to me, like he's concentrating on every word: *Wake up, Grace! We're almost out of time!*

6

Snap, Crackle,
and Pop-Tart

The command in his voice has me shooting upward in bed.

My heart is beating fast, my blood roaring in my ears, and it almost feels like I'm waking up in the middle of a full-blown panic attack. Except my brain is clear, and the adrenaline coursing through my body has everything to do with urgency and nothing to do with fear.

I glance at Hudson, but for once, he's actually asleep. His breathing is even, the faint bruises on his cheek a stark reminder of everything he's been through the last couple of days. Most of the marks from his fights in the prison have faded already, but it's going to take more than just blood to erase the exhaustion under his eyes. I reach out, trace a tender, trembling finger along his cheek. His eyes flutter for a moment, and I'm afraid I've woken him. But then he rolls over with a sigh and falls straight back to sleep.

Too bad I'm not going to be able to do the same.

A quick glance at my phone tells me that I've been asleep a little more than seven hours—which means I've got a handful of hours left before morning. As I roll out of bed, the sun is beginning to peek over the top of Denali. It's the middle of the night, but in Alaska in spring, sunrise comes at four a.m.

Shades of red and dark purple paint the sky and mountains visible through the half windows in Hudson's room. It's beautiful, no doubt, but the shadow of what looks to be an approaching storm also feels ominous as fuck. Like the sky is bleeding onto the mountains, washing the whole world in blood and regret and fear.

Then again, that could just be me transferring my own feelings. God knows, it feels like my whole world is washed in blood right now.

I think about going back to bed, trying to get some more sleep. But that ship has sailed. And since I have no desire to put my dirty clothes back on, I need to get to my room and grab an extra change before we leave.

My stomach shimmies as I head up the stairs and into Katmere's battered main halls, remembering the first time I walked through this school, wandering these halls because my whole life had changed in the blink of an eye and I couldn't sleep.

It feels like I'm on the edge of another precipice, one that's crumbling a little more with each step I take. So much has changed since that first night—my gargoyle, Hudson, Jaxon, even Katmere itself—and yet it feels like some things haven't changed at all.

Like the chances that a couple of homicidal wolves show up and want to toss me in the snow again really aren't that low.

Telling myself I'm being ridiculous—Cyrus is unlikely to send the wolves after us now that he's got the students—I nevertheless take the stairs two at a time on my way up to my room. If the enemy is somehow going to invade, I'd at least like to be wearing pants when I face them.

Macy's sound asleep when I get to our room, so I creep in as quietly as I can. I use my phone light to see, once again cursing the fact that, gargoyle or not, I don't have eyes like the vamps and wolves and can't see in the dark.

I keep my light pointed down—showing just enough that I don't trip and land on Macy's sleeping form by accident—as I head to my closet.

I grab my black Katmere backpack and stuff it with a few things I'll need if I'm staying in Hudson's room. A pair of jeans and an extra T-shirt, some underwear, my toiletry bag, a handful of elastic hair bands, and—surprise, surprise—a box of cherry Pop-Tarts. If I've learned nothing from the last seven months of hanging out with vampires in unpredictable times, it's that if I want to make sure I don't starve, I should always pack a snack.

Once I've shoved it all inside the bag, I throw on a hoodie as well before plopping down on the floor and pulling on socks and my favorite pair of boots.

I get back up and take one last glance around the room to make sure I'm not forgetting anything important, then remember two things I would never want to leave without. I creep over to my jewelry box on my dresser, tilt the lid open, and grab the diamond Hudson gave me as well as the necklace from Jaxon. I shove both treasured items into the front zipper pouch as well as a tube of pink lip balm Macy gave me and sling the backpack over my shoulder before tiptoeing toward the door.

As I'm leaving, Macy stirs a little bit and whimpers in her sleep. I freeze, waiting to see if she needs me, but after another soft sound of distress, she settles back into the snuffle snores I've grown used to over the past several months.

The sound makes me long for the time when I first arrived at Katmere, before everything got so crazy and my biggest worry was just how loud my cousin could snore—which was very. The feeling has me glancing between Macy and my bed, wondering if maybe I *could* steal a few more hours of rest...after all, it might be the last chance any of us can get for a real night's sleep in who knows how long.

I don't even bother kicking off my boots—just curl up on top of the covers, snuggle into the pillow, and let the rhythm of Macy's snores lull me asleep.

No time!

A voice in my head startles me awake. I check my phone—I slept another two hours. Macy is still snoring softly, but I know sleep is no longer possible for me.

Maybe if I'm lucky, I can slip back into Hudson's room without waking him up, either.

I've barely gotten to the top of the stairs before the Beast's voice is in my brain again. *No time. No time. No time.*

No time for what? I ask in the back corner of my mind. *Are you all ri—*

I break off as I round the landing and find the gargoyle in human form sitting at the broken chess table at the bottom of the stairs, one of only a few surviving chess pieces in his hand.

A sickening wave of déjà vu slides through me as I realize that the piece he's holding is none other than the vampire queen herself.

7

Say What?

I state the obvious. "You're human again."

He nods as I take my time walking down the last couple of steps between us. I'm trying to get my head around what's going on here, but I'm lost. I have no idea what to say to the Unkillable Beast, no idea how to treat him. He's a gargoyle, the only other living gargoyle in existence, which means we should have some things in common.

But the truth is, I've never felt further apart from anyone—which is beyond strange, considering I can actually hear him inside my head.

"Are you okay?" I ask, sitting down in the chair on the other side of the chess table.

"Worried. So worried," he says out loud, and I'm startled to hear his voice. I mean, he spoke to me on the island, but I'm so used to hearing him in my head that it takes a moment to adjust.

I nod. "Yes, I know. I heard you while I was sleeping. And when I woke up."

"Sorry." He looks sheepish. "Must hurry."

"Don't apologize," I tell him with a shake of my head. "But why do we need to hurry? What's going on?"

"Out of time."

I can't tell if he's talking about us, himself, or someone else. I really hope he's saying Cyrus is out of time, but I doubt I'm that lucky. "Who's out of time?"

He doesn't answer, just leans forward in his chair to emphasize the urgency of his message. "Out of time."

Which tells me exactly nothing that I didn't know before. He keeps saying the *out of time* thing, and it's beginning to freak me out—especially when I think about all the different things going on that could have us running out of time. Are we almost out of time to save the kids? Is Cyrus coming back for us? Is the Crown about to self-destruct on my hand?

"*What* is running out of time?" I ask, frustration evident in my voice. "What's going to happen?"

But he doesn't answer. Of course he doesn't—he's always been good at getting me all worked up over a warning but not providing any details to back up that warning. From the tunnels when I first got here to that weird-looking tree out on the Katmere grounds to the prison cell Hudson, Flint, and I were locked in with Remy and Calder, he's given me a bunch of advice. He just never tells me what the advice is for or what I should do instead of whatever it is he's advising against.

Which is helpful in some ways, I guess, but definitely not helpful in others.

Like now, when he holds the chess piece of the vampire queen out to me.

"You want to play chess?" I ask, ignoring the piece that I now realize bears a marked resemblance to Delilah. Thanks but no thanks. Been there, done that, so not interested in a repeat performance. Particularly since playing with the remaining vampire pieces means having to pick up the vampire king as well. And no way am I voluntarily going near Cyrus, even if it is just a marble likeness of him. "If so, I call dragons."

The Beast shakes his head.

"You don't want to play chess?"

"Out of time." He jabs the air with the vampire queen chess piece.

"The vampire queen is out of time? That doesn't exactly make me feel bad, you know?"

This time the gargoyle sighs, like he's so disappointed that I don't understand what he wants from me. And I feel bad, I do. But it's not like his disjointed manner of communication makes things easy. Of course, who am I to talk? If I spent a thousand years chained up in a cave with paranormal creatures from all over the globe regularly trying to kill me, my grasp on language—and reality— would probably be pretty tenuous, too.

But knowing that only makes it harder for me to try to figure out his advice, not easier. Because if a thousand years in isolation has driven him mad, how can I trust what he's trying to tell me anyway?

It's my turn to sigh. This whole mess keeps turning into a bigger and bigger nightmare.

"Grace."

He says my name with such urgency—and authority—that I automatically snap to attention. "Yes?"

"Careful. Be careful."

Tell me something I don't know. "I know. I'm being careful. Believe me, we're all being careful as fuck of the Vampire Court. Cyrus—"

"No!" He stares at me with narrowed eyes, then slams the vampire queen down so hard, I expect the piece to shatter. But it doesn't. In fact, it doesn't so much as chip an edge.

Like that isn't even more ominous. All I need is Delilah to be as indestructible as Cyrus is turning out to be.

"The queen?" I ask, reaching for the piece. "Are you warning me about Delilah?"

I expect him to let go of the piece now that he's made his point, but he holds on to the cool marble even as I wrap my hand around it. Which is how our fingers brush and how a strange electricity zings its way straight through me, causing me to instinctively reach for my platinum gargoyle string in a rush. Before I can grab it, though, a jolt of power zaps me so hard, it steals my breath.

At first, I think it's just a shock, just static electricity as two people touch. But I haven't been shocked since I turned into a gargoyle the first time by accident.

I go to pull my hand away with a nervous laugh and try to make a joke, but it's too late. He's turning back into stone, and a quick glance down at my body shows that I am, too, with both our now-stone hands still firmly holding the vampire queen.

8

A Full-Court Mess

I know this feeling.

It's like turning to stone, only not. When I become a gargoyle, there's a strange kind of tingling that starts in my feet. Fast, so fast that I barely feel it happening, the tingling moves up my legs and arms. It takes over my whole body, tiny pinpricks of electricity all over me, heightening my senses instead of dulling them, exacerbating the feel of my heart beating, lungs breathing, blood rushing through my body. Sharpening my mind so that it's like I see everything, feel everything, as time slows, as my reactions speed up.

This is most definitely not that.

This is just as fast, but I'm aware of every cell as the electricity moves up my body, crawling along every nerve ending like needles stabbing into my flesh instead of mere pinpricks. My feet, my legs, my hands, my chest, my shoulders, the pain is almost too much to bear. By the time it reaches my head, I open my mouth to scream in agony, but it's too late. My body is already solid stone, suffocating the scream in my chest under its heavy weight.

My senses are so overwhelmed—*I'm* so overwhelmed—that it takes a second for me to catch my breath and several more seconds for me to get my bearings. If you can call it that, considering I have absolutely no idea what just happened and if I'm even still *here*. As I look around, trying to answer at least one of those questions, I realize that I can barely see three feet in front of my face.

Everything else is encased in mist.

At first, I think I'm alone, and panic kicks in as a million different scenarios race through my brain. Like maybe this is all some terrible trap that Cyrus has laid for me with this man's help. Like maybe he wanted us to free the Unkillable Beast all along—just to get me here.

But as I turn around and see the older gargoyle in his human form several feet away, reason comes back to me. The Beast *hates* Cyrus—at least as much as

Hudson does. The vampire king kept him imprisoned in a cave for a thousand years. No way would he get in bed with him now that he's finally free. I don't believe it.

Moreover, I *won't* believe it.

It's that thought more than any other that has me taking several steps toward the gargoyle, who is currently crouching on the ground.

As I get closer, I realize he looks as shocked as I feel—maybe even more so. His eyes are wide, his mouth slightly open as he reaches down to touch the shiny stone floor beneath our feet.

"Is this real?" he whispers as he moves left and right, touching the floor all around him.

"I was about to ask you the same question," I tell him, watching as a smile takes over his worried face for what I'm pretty sure is the first time since I've met him.

It's an incredible smile, and it absolutely transforms him. It makes him look younger, handsomer, stronger, prouder.

It's an image that is reinforced when he finally stands up. No longer is he the worn down, broken, confused Unkillable Beast we've been dealing with ever since we first found his island. No, this man is something else entirely.

Something regal.

Something powerful.

He stands about six foot six, taller than Hudson and Jaxon and broader around the shoulders, too. His heavily muscled arms are enclosed in a tight black shirt, over which he is wearing a long gray-and-black tunic that goes down to mid-thigh. His legs are encased in black tights, his feet in black boots, and as he smooths a hand down the fine velvet fabric, I realize what I'm staring at.

This is the gargoyle in his heyday, before Cyrus tricked him into that cave and turned him into the Unkillable Beast.

And like a hit to the chest, I know who he is. Who he has to be. This handsome, noble man in thousand-year-old finery is none other than the gargoyle king.

The true ruler of the Gargoyle Court I laid claim to during that game of Ludares.

The true owner of the Crown currently emblazoned on my palm.

And suddenly, I don't have a clue what to say to him. Or if I should bow.

Thankfully, he doesn't seem to be suffering from the same problem. After he finishes inspecting himself—and straightening his tunic just the slightest bit—he takes another look around. "Well done, Grace," he says. "Well done."

The words are heavily accented, but I'm not sure from where. It's a familiar-sounding English accent—not British like Hudson, not Australian like some of my favorite actors, and definitely not American, but familiar all the same.

"I don't think I can take any credit for this," I tell him truthfully. "Considering I have no idea where we are or how we got here."

Somehow, his grin grows even wider. "Do you really not know where we are?"

I look around, trying to see beyond the mist, but nearly everything that's more than a couple of feet away is shrouded in mystery. "I have absolutely no idea."

"What a shame it's come to this." He shakes his head a little sadly, then waves an arm, and the fog clears, letting me finally see what the mist was hiding. "Welcome, my dear Grace, to the Gargoyle Court."

9

Does Google Translate Speak Gargoyle?

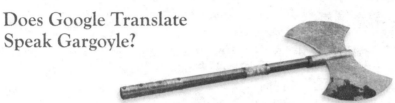

H oly shit.
I mean, *holy shit.*

He has to be kidding, right? We can't actually be at the Gargoyle Court.

Except, as I look around at this opulent courtyard, I can't help but think that he's telling the truth. The floor is made of marble, as are the pillars on either side of a tall, intricately woven, gold-and-jeweled fence. And the courtyard is the front entrance to what looks like a very large, very ornate medieval castle.

Which makes sense, considering the gargoyle king has been imprisoned for more than a thousand years. According to Flint, the Dragon Court has changed and adapted through the years, currently in one of the most expensive skyscrapers in New York. With the king imprisoned and the rest of the gargoyles dead, the Gargoyle Court didn't have the chance to evolve at all.

We must be in a dream in his mind somehow, experiencing the majesty of this Court he remembers. Thinking of what the Gargoyle Court could be, should be now if not for Cyrus, makes my heart ache.

"It's beautiful," I tell him, looking up at a castle that is easily twice as big as Katmere, and so majestic my fingers itch to paint it.

We're standing in the courtyard in front of the main structure, but as I turn in a circle to take everything in, I realize there's a lot more behind me as well as in front of me. The castle is surrounded by a huge, real-life moat with a large wooden drawbridge. And around the whole property is a giant stone wall that has to be a good seventy-five feet tall—I assume to combat the fact that most paranormal creatures can jump pretty damn high.

The castle itself is incredibly imposing, built from stone, with huge, crenelated battlements at the top of the main structure and four large, round towers that stand at each corner.

There are more windows in all shapes and sizes than I expected based on my very limited knowledge of medieval castles. But the stained glass of the windows is a lot more rudimentary in design than I'd have guessed. Of course, it's not like I have any idea when stained glass became a thing. Maybe this was as sophisticated as it got a thousand years ago.

The rest of the castle certainly seems to be top-of-the-line.

"This is your Court?" I ask, still spinning in a slow circle in an effort to take it all in. "You are the gargoyle king and built it?"

"I am, and I did. My name is Alistair, by the way," he says in that smooth and cultured voice that is so different from anything I have ever heard from him before. "But you're mistaken as to whose Court it is." He grins at me as he holds up my hand with the Crown tattoo. "This is your Court, my dear Grace, not mine. Not anymore."

My knees go weak at the thought. When I imagined building the Gargoyle Court with the money I got from the Wyvernhoard, I'd imagined something a little smaller, less intimidating. More...beachy. A place a born-and-raised San Diego girl could feel comfortable in.

I look up, up, up to the top of the castle. There's nothing comfortable about this place. Everything I've seen here screams opulence and pure intimidation.

"But you're the king," I tell him, doing my best to ignore the way the Crown is burning against my palm. "This belongs to you."

"I *was* the king." His smile is more rueful than sad. "You rule the Gargoyle Court now, which means this castle—this Court—is yours to do with as you will."

The thought makes my already aching stomach twist even more. This whole ruling thing is getting real, too real, even though we're the only two gargoyles left. If we actually manage to defeat Cyrus, I'm suddenly terrified that I really am going to have to take my place on the Circle.

"Is that why you brought me here?" I ask as I try to get my head around the magnitude of all this. "To show me what I rule?"

Alistair laughs. "I'm sorry to disappoint you, Grace, but I didn't bring you here. *You* brought *me* here. And I am so glad you did. It's..." He pauses to look around as he runs his hand down the fine velvet of his tunic once more. "It's nice to be here again, even if it is just for a few stolen moments."

"I don't understand. What do you mean, I brought you here? I didn't even know this place existed—"

"And yet you got us here nonetheless. It's very impressive, my dear. Very, very impressive. Especially considering how young you are." He shakes his head, an awed look on his face. "You're so much more powerful than I imagined, and

I imagined quite a lot."

I must look as confused as I feel, because Alistair waves a hand in front of us. "Let's walk, shall we, and I'll try to answer all your questions."

"There are a lot of them," I warn him as we begin to stroll across this giant, ancient courtyard like we're having an afternoon tea party instead of waiting in the early morning for Cyrus and his army to try to destroy everyone and everything we care about. "Starting with, how can you talk here so easily? Usually when you speak to me, it's obvious that it's an effort." He raises one imperious brow at that, and I quickly hold my hands up in apology. "No offense meant."

"No offense taken," he answers. But his face remains stern, his eyes narrowed.

And can I just say how truly bizarre the differences in him are? I mean, I get that he was locked up for a thousand years and that did really terrible things to every part of him. And I'm not saying he wasn't scary as hell as the Unkillable Beast. He absolutely was. But there's something about the gargoyle king, something about *this* Alistair, that is a million times more daunting.

We walk for several more yards in silence, the heels of Alistair's boots clapping against the polished marble with each step we take. I'm just beginning to think he isn't going to answer my question, despite what he promised, when he says, "Leading our people isn't easy. It comes with many responsibilities— to the world and to our people. One of those responsibilities is being open to them, always."

He sighs and takes a long, slow breath before continuing. "Gargoyles were created to be the perfect peacekeeper, to bring balance back to the world of humans and paranormals. One of those gifts to aid us, as I'm sure you've figured out by now, is that gargoyles can all speak telepathically to one another. It's how we can coordinate attacks and better patrol areas."

What he's saying makes complete sense, based on the story the Crone told us, yet I can't help my heart from speeding up, as I'm finally learning more about what it means to be a gargoyle—*from* a gargoyle.

He continues. "Everyone can communicate telepathically within a short distance. A unit can easily stay coordinated that way. There are a few lieutenants who can communicate over much larger distances, of course. And then there's the royal line…" He turns to look me in the eyes as he explains. "The royal line can speak to everyone, regardless of distance. They're our people, and we can always hear them when they need us. It's both a gift and a burden."

Okay, in theory, that sounds lovely. A king so connected to his subjects that they can reach out to him anytime and have his attention in an instant. In practice, however, I can only imagine it's more troublesome being able to hear those thousands and thousands of voices every minute of every day, if the king chooses.

"Can you never silence the voices?" I ask.

He nods. "We can filter as we need. But being trapped in gargoyle form for a millennium, well, I've slowly lost that strength and control in the real world. Slowly lost the ability to quiet the voices, much less reply to them. Thousands of voices speaking simultaneously in my head at all times, begging me to help, to save them, to free them. Crying out in pain and wondering why I haven't come, why I haven't answered their pleas." His voice turns to gravel. "So many voices..."

It sounds horrible, beyond horrible really.

And then another thought comes to me. A thought so overwhelming, so tempting, it has my heart beating wildly in my chest.

Because there wouldn't be thousands of people preventing him from thinking clearly if we are the only two remaining gargoyles...

I'm about to ask him as much, but then he lifts a brow and says something that makes my heart drop to my toes even as it sends my brain spinning in a million different directions.

"Surely you know what that's like, granddaughter. You must be inundated with voices from the Gargoyle Army as well, yes?"

10

Rock My World

There is so much to unpack in that statement that I don't even know where to start.

Granddaughter? Gargoyle Army? I should hear the voices, too? Of creatures everyone believes are dead? Just the thought makes me feel like I'm going to throw up.

I mean, what exactly am I supposed to say to any of this? And how am I supposed to chill my stomach out when it's been in free fall ever since he said the word "granddaughter"?

Which I guess tells me exactly where I need to start. I mean, having a Gargoyle Army talk to me at all hours—even having a Gargoyle Army at all—is a pretty big thing to have dropped on you out of nowhere. But for me, personally, it's nowhere near as big as the fifteen-thousand-pound elephant that the gargoyle king—that my grandfather?—just brought into the room.

"Granddaughter?" I ask, nearly choking on the word for a lot of different reasons. To begin with, I've never had grandparents—my own parents said mine died years before I was born.

And secondly, how can the gargoyle king—*the gargoyle king*—be my grandfather? He's been chained in a cave alone for a thousand years, and my parents were only in their forties when they died. The timing doesn't make sense.

Then again, nothing makes sense right now, including Alistair's insistence that I'm the one who brought us to the Gargoyle Court.

"Not my immediate granddaughter, of course. But you're definitely of my line. Several greats down that line, if I had my guess, but your power is unmistakable."

Okay, being his great-great-great-whatever-granddaughter makes a little more sense. But how does he know that we're related? It's not like I have his very aquiline nose or his gray-eyed coloring. The more I think about how commanding the gargoyle king is, how regal, versus how absolutely clueless I usually feel, my skin itches beneath my wrinkled hoodie as adrenaline rushes in my veins.

We're strolling along the edges of the courtyard now, where there is a ring of dirt and rosebushes every few feet. They look dormant, but as we walk past the first, it springs to life the second my too-many-to-count-great-grandfather passes by. It's incredible to watch, and I can't help wondering if this is an extension of the earth powers I'm just beginning to understand.

Which reminds me... "What did you mean?" I ask as yet another rosebush comes alive—this one a bright, cheerful coral that makes me smile despite the seriousness of this whole situation. "About my power being unmistakable?"

"I've been mated to your grandmother for nearly two millennia. I would recognize her power anywhere, and you, my dear, definitely have it inside you." He winks. "Plus, you're a fighter. You've got my grit."

I'm not sure about that, considering my fights tend to choose me instead of the other way around. I don't run from them, but it's not like I look for them, either. It's just that there are a lot of people in this new world who seem to want me dead. And since I don't want to be dead...fighting is pretty much the only option open to me.

But now doesn't exactly feel like the time to debate my fighting instincts, not when my grandfather has dropped yet another bomb. "I have a grandmother, too?"

"Of course you have a grandmother! And she is one hell of a woman—definitely the bravest, stubbornest female I've ever met." He looks me over. "Up until now, that is."

He acts like he wants to say more, but instead he pauses, and his eyes go blank, like he's searching deep inside himself for something. As silence stretches between us, I can't help thinking about what he said when he gave me the Crown and the woman he spoke so adamantly about. Was it my grandmother all along? And if so, how can she be alive when Alistair and I are the last two gargoyles in existence?

I'm about to ask, but he chooses that moment to sigh in relief as his eyes come back into focus. "She's still alive. I knew she must be, but since you didn't know about her, I was afraid..." He shakes his head as if clearing it of thoughts he'd rather not talk about. "But she's fine and is definitely still kicking. You really should go meet her. Maybe you can take me with you. She's been angry with me for a millennium, but I know she's missed me, too. And I've missed her very, very much."

"She's alive?" I ask, excitement zipping through me despite my still-churning stomach. "There's another gargoyle out there? I thought we were the only ones."

Now it's Alistair's turn to look incredulous. "First of all, your grandmother would bite you—or turn you into something very, very slimy—if she even imagined that you would mistake her for a gargoyle. She loves me, but she definitely has a little bit of a superiority complex about the stone thing."

He rolls his eyes with a laugh, and for a moment, he looks so boyish—so not the poor, tortured Beast we fought to free—that I can't help but laugh along with him.

But then he grows serious. "Your grandmother is my mate, the love of my life."

My heart breaks at what he doesn't say: that he's been separated from his mate for a thousand years. I think of Hudson, of how safe and happy and right it feels to be in his arms, and then I think about what it would feel like to be away from him. Not for a day or two but for what feels like an eternity.

It hurts, more than I could have imagined it would. It makes me ache for Alistair and for his mate, whoever she is.

And that's before he tries to blink away the tears in his eyes, looking like he hopes I won't notice. "Do you think you could bring her here to us? Just for a little while? I miss her so much."

"I—" My voice breaks, and I clear my throat, even as I try to figure out what to say. I would love to bring her here, if I knew where *here* was. Or where she was. Or how I even brought the two of us to this place that I've never seen before, that I never even imagined still existed.

"I would really like to do that," I finally settle on, because it's true. "Do you know where your mate is?"

"I don't know. I just assumed she would have found you—" He breaks off with a heavy sigh. "Well, that's a shame, then. I was really hoping to see her sooner rather than later. She quieted the voices in my head when no one and nothing else could. I was hoping she could do that now, so I could be of some help to you in planning a strategy for the coming battle."

The words are another punch to my already shaky gut. "She's the only way you can quiet the voices?" I ask.

"For now, yes," he answers gravely.

"Even though they're dead? They still speak to you?"

"Dead?" He looks half confused, half affronted.

"I mean gone." I change tacks quickly, as the last thing I want to do is offend him. "Even though they're gone?"

This time he just looks baffled. "The gargoyles aren't gone, dear. They're all around us, and they never stop talking."

Now I'm the one who's confused. "What do you mean, they're all around us?"

Maybe those years in isolation have done even more damage to his psyche than I thought.

"They're all around us," he repeats, waving an arm to the side, like he's the barker at some paranormal carnival.

As he does, he reaches for the huge wooden doors at the front of the castle we've been walking toward and swings them open, revealing an even larger grass courtyard. Spread out around the courtyard are dozens upon dozens of gargoyles, and each one is carrying a massive sword and an even more massive shield.

11

Light as a Feather, Hard as a Stone

This time, I'm the one whose mouth is wide open in astonishment, but I don't think anyone can blame me. For months now, I've thought I was the only gargoyle left, and now—right in front of me—are so many that they fill an entire courtyard that's almost the size of a football field.

"Are they—are they real?" I ask, barely able to get the words past my suddenly too-tight throat. It's overwhelming—in an entirely good way—to realize I'm not alone in the world. That there are more people out there who are just like me.

I love Hudson and Jaxon and Macy and Flint—not to mention the rest of my friends. I really do, and I know that I'll always have a place with them. That I'll always fit in with them. But that doesn't mean I haven't wished I could be like them sometimes, so sure of who and what they are in a world that continuously turns me upside down. Yes, they all have their own worries and problems, but at least they aren't also struggling with the core identity of who they are. Hudson is a vampire through and through. Everything about Flint screams dragon. And Macy is definitely a witch.

More importantly, they know what that *means*. What they can do, what they can take—what they can survive.

As for me...up until a few months ago, I would have said I know exactly who I am. And for the most part, I do. I'm Grace. I like art and old movies, history and Harry Styles, Dr Pepper and dancing for hours. Before my parents died, I planned on going to UC Santa Cruz and studying marine conservation. And now I live in Alaska—at least for a little while longer anyway. I don't know what is going to happen in the next ten minutes, let alone the next four years. And I'm a gargoyle.

Which is cool. It really is, for so many, many reasons. I love it. But as I stand here looking at a courtyard full of paranormals who are just like me on a fundamental level, I realize that there's a part of me that has been lonely through all of this. A part of me that wants someone to compare notes with, someone to talk to about all the wild stuff going on inside me, someone who understands what it feels like to be a gargoyle.

And now, right in front of me, are a whole lot of people who *do* understand. Who *do* know our history and our powers. I don't know them yet. I may never know them, but realizing that they exist makes me feel a little less alone.

"They're real, my dear girl." Alistair grins down at me indulgently. "And this group is just a drop in the bucket of how many gargoyles are out there, an entire army just waiting for their chance to reclaim their honor. To reclaim their place in the world under the direction of their queen. Their general."

My stomach does a complicated series of backflips at his words. I'm getting used to being a gargoyle, and maybe even getting used to being the head of the Gargoyle Court, with a seat on the Circle. But that was when I thought there were no gargoyles left. Now, to find out that there are a lot of gargoyles in the world, and I'm supposed to be their queen—and even more shocking, *their general*—is more than I can wrap my head around. At least none of them have spotted us yet. I need time to process.

"Would you like to meet some of them?" Alistair asks me.

"I can meet them?" My heart rate ticks up another several notches. "I mean, I can talk to them?"

"Of course. You are the gargoyle queen, after all."

"But if I'm the queen," I say as I allow him to propel me through the ornately carved doors, "what does that make you?"

My words give him pause, and at first I think he isn't going to answer. But then he glances at me out of the corner of his eye and says, "A trusted adviser, I hope."

The massive doors close behind us with an ominous *thud*, and I can't help thinking that Alistair isn't the only one longing for his mate. It would be pretty nice to have Hudson here with me, watching my back as I enter into a situation I never even imagined, let alone prepared for.

Alistair takes several more steps into the space, and I follow him, my eyes jumping from one group of gargoyles to the next.

Though they are all armed and in their animate stone form, nobody has a weapon raised. Instead, they're all milling around the courtyard in groups of two, and sometimes three or four. Everyone is tall and muscular—much bigger than I am—but none of them is quite as large as Alistair. Of course, even in his regular old gargoyle, non–Unkillable Beast form, he stands head and shoulders above most people.

There's only one other person in the room in human form—a tall, bulky man positioned at the front of the group. He's dressed like Alistair, in tights and a tunic, though his clothes are in shades of emerald green and gold instead of Alistair's black and gray. He's also the only one in the group not carrying a weapon.

Still, when he shouts, "Ready!" everyone else in the courtyard springs into action. They lower themselves into defensive crouches with their shields held high or go on the offensive, their gigantic swords raised to attack.

I wait for the sound of steel striking against steel, but several *long* seconds tick by before the man shouts, "Ionsaí!"

I have no idea what the word means, but it's obviously the command the other gargoyles are waiting for. His shout is still ringing all around us when swords begin to arc through the air.

I watch in awe as the gargoyles spar, swords meeting other swords or shields as they jump, spin, even somersault in midair. These gargoyles are huge, heavy, and yet they move like they are made of feathers rather than stone.

A tall, sturdy girl shouts something in a language I don't understand as she slams her sword down on her opponent with all her might. He meets her with the edge of his shield, but she's pivoting even as the weapons connect, doing a jump-spin combination that ends when she brings her sword around in a sweeping arc, the broad side of it hitting her opponent right between the shoulder blades.

He goes flying ass over teakettle and ends up sprawled out on the ground, shield raised defensively as she swings her sword back around one more time.

At the last minute, she grins and tucks her sword back into the scabbard at her waist before reaching a hand down to help him up. He rolls his eyes and says something in that language I don't understand that makes her throw back her head and laugh. Seconds later, they both transform into human forms.

She's Black, with rows of gorgeous braids, and he has short dark hair and golden-brown skin.

"Still think I fight like a girl?" she taunts.

"Damn straight," he answers with what sounds like an Indian accent. "I just wish I did, too." He moves his sword in a complicated pattern, then breaks off mid-swing. "Hey, show me how you did that wrist thing earlier?"

"Of course."

As she moves to show him, I glance at another group. This one is made up of all male gargoyles, and I'm not exaggerating when I say they are massive—

like *two football players each* massive—with swords and shields built to match.

Right now, they're fighting two-on-one, with the biggest of the three playing defense against the others. And he is still kicking both their butts.

Alistair and I stand to the side and watch as the training continues. The guy in green, who has been in human form all along, walks from group to group, offering advice and critiques: "watch your back," "turn your wrist when you make that move," "don't drop your shoulder," "pick your foot up and pivot on the ball of it." The comments go on and on, as nothing seems to escape his eagle eye.

Every gargoyle he talks to hangs on his every word, and I can see them trying to implement his suggestions as soon as he walks away. It's fascinating.

"Who is that?" I finally ask Alistair once the guy in emerald green begins his third circle of the courtyard.

"That's Chastain. He's been my lieutenant general for as far back as I can remember." Alistair pauses, a contemplative look on his face as he watches his old friend. "And now I guess he's yours. Would you like to meet him?"

Wow. This is getting real, fast. I blow out a long breath and say the only thing I can. "Yes, of course. I'd love to."

After all, a queen really does need to know who she can trust. Right?

12

A Whole Lot of Rock and a Little Bit of Roll

"Chastain!" Alistair calls, raising a hand to beckon the other man over. The commander offers a few more quick instructions to a group, this time in that language I don't understand, then turns to Alistair—and his eyes widen in shock.

"What language are they speaking?" I ask as we wait for Chastain to make his way over to us.

Alistair raises his brows. "English?"

I laugh. "I know they're speaking English. But they're also speaking something else. What is it?"

"Oh, that's Gaelic, child. You don't recognize it?"

"Gaelic?" I look around in wonder. Even as I repeat the word, Alistair's familiar-sounding accent clicks into place. No wonder he sounds so much like Niall Horan. He's Irish. "Are we in *Ireland*?"

"Yes," Alistair answers, his gaze holding Chastain's as the other man's long strides eat up the space between them. "County Cork, to be precise."

"Cork?" I call up my very rudimentary understanding of Irish geography. "That's near the sea, isn't it?"

"You can't hear it?" Alistair asks. "We're right on the edge of it."

At first, I'm not sure what he's talking about—I can't hear anything—but before I can say that, a couple of new gargoyles walk into the courtyard. And the second they open the heavy wooden doors, I know exactly what he's talking about. I do hear it—the sound of water hitting against rock over and over again.

We're on the ocean! Or, if not the ocean, then at least the edge of a sea. It's the closest I've come to a beach in months, and it takes every ounce of energy I have not to race out of the castle and run for the water. It's been so long, and now that it's right here, close enough to stand on—close enough to touch—it's all I can think about.

Except just then, Chastain reaches us. I watch as the two men give each other a very masculine, *pat on the back* kind of hug before Chastain says, "My king, I thought—we all thought—the worst may have happened to you. It's been too long, but we never lost hope."

My eyes widen as I realize everyone must not have known what happened to Alistair, that he's been hunted for a thousand years and chained up on a deserted island, unable to return to his people. I can't even imagine what it must feel like to see him now, know that he is alive and returned, wonder what kept him away.

The smile dims in Alistair's eyes. "I am so sorry I was gone for so long. Especially after what my mate did to you all. Just know there was no other way. I see that now. Everything that has happened, happened for a reason. And now there is much to do to prepare for what is to come, my friend."

"We are ready, my king. We have not missed a day of training since..."

A look passes between the two men that is heavy with meaning. "Yes, well, we have this young lady to thank for my rescue and return." Alistair turns to me. "Chastain, this is my great-great-great—" He laughs. "You know what? I'm just going to forget how many greats there are between us and call her my granddaughter. This is my granddaughter, Grace, and now the queen of the Gargoyle Court. Grace, this is Chastain, my oldest and dearest friend. For centuries, he was my second-in-command of the greatest army to ever walk the earth. You should feel free to call on him anytime you have questions about your army."

Chastain's eyes widen as Alistair speaks, though I don't know if it's because he's surprised I'm Alistair's granddaughter or if it's because he's as shocked to find out there's a new ruler of the Gargoyle Court as I am to find out there are actually gargoyles to rule.

Either way, he covers his surprise by bending his head and dropping into a deep bow.

As one, the entire courtyard of gargoyles stops training and turns to Alistair and me—and drops to their knees in matching bows.

And that doesn't feel weird at all.

13

Time's Not the Only
Thing That's Warped

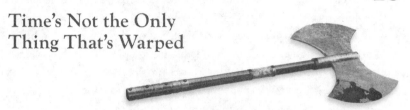

"**I**t is an honor to meet you, my queen."

"It's an honor to meet you, too?" It comes out sounding like a question, but that has more to do with me feeling awkward about being called *queen* than it does not being honored to meet him.

He holds out a hand to me even as he continues to bow. Mystified, I go to take his hand, but Alistair stops me with a shake of his head.

I give him a *what do I do?* look, and he smiles as he holds up his own hand for me to see.

For the first time, I notice that he is wearing an ornate gold ring set with a square-cut emerald the size of a large die. It's beautiful—a deep, clear green that looks very, very expensive—and I watch in horror as he slips it off his finger and holds it out to me.

"What—" My voice cracks for the second time in the last hour as I ask a question whose answer I am very much afraid of. "What are you doing with that?"

He shoots me a reproving look, one that tells me I'm right to be afraid, just before he takes my right hand and slides it onto my ring finger.

I expect the ring to be too big—Alistair's hands are much bigger than mine—and instinctively clutch my fingers into a fist to keep it from falling off. But it turns out that, somehow, the ring fits perfectly. It's heavy as fuck and big enough to take an eye out, but it definitely fits.

Which causes my already shaky stomach to pitch and roll as violently as the waves crashing against the cliffs below us. I may not have had a formal coronation yet, but something tells me this is more than just symbolic—and that there's no going back now.

This can't be happening. I'm not ready for this to be happening. This can't be happening. The phrases leapfrog through my brain over and over as Chastain takes my newly beringed hand and kisses the ring. My ring.

I don't think anything in my life has ever terrified me as much as this moment. Not being on the Ludares field alone, not being locked in that horrible prison, not even doing battle on the Unkillable Beast's island. Because this whole queen thing...it's a lot.

It was a lot when it was just me. Now that I find out I'm supposed to be in charge of all these gargoyles, being responsible for keeping them safe when I can barely keep *myself* safe, is nearly unfathomable.

And yet the ring is on my finger, which means I have to fathom it.

Finally—*finally*—Chastain lets go of my hand and rises from his bow.

He appears to be waiting for me to say something, but I have no idea what the custom is. I settle for, "Thank you?" which makes Alistair laugh and Chastain give me a slightly bewildered look.

I cast around for something else to say, but before anything comes to me, Chastain glances at Alistair and says, "So, old man. Shall we show her how it's done?"

At first, Alistair looks like he's going to refuse the request, whatever it's for, but then he grins wider than I've ever seen and says, "By all means, *older* man."

From the space of one quick breath to the next, swords and shields appear in their hands. I barely have time to process what's happening, let alone duck out of the way, before Chastain strikes the first powerful blow.

Alistair brings his shield up to block the attack, then somersaults—actually *somersaults*—through the air, shifting instantly into his gargoyle form, to land on his feet behind Chastain. This time, it's his sword that arcs through the air.

Chastain dodges at the last second and shifts just as quickly, kicking out with his left stone foot even as he whirls around. And then it's on, the two of them striking steel upon steel over and over again. Both are determined to win, and both are excellent swordsmen, which means neither can quite get the jump on the other. And "jump" is definitely the right word as they roll, tuck, jump, fly, all with the hopes of catching the other by surprise.

It doesn't take long before a crowd of the other gargoyles gathers around us, swords at their hips as they cheer on Chastain and Alistair. I'm surrounded by gargoyles two times bigger than I am, all of whom are laughing and whistling and placing bets on who will win.

I end up standing next to the kick-ass girl I watched win her match earlier, and she is grinning ear to ear as she says, "They're fantastic, aren't they?"

It takes me a moment to realize she's speaking to me. "Yeah, they are." My eyes go big as Alistair delivers a blow with his sword that has Chastain flying backward out of the impromptu practice circle the two created. He's moving so fast that I'm certain he's going to take out a gargoyle or three, and I brace myself for the impending crash.

They manage to scramble out of the way at the last second, and he ends up landing several yards back, at the base of the gold fence. For a second, he looks confused, and then another emotion flits across his face—annoyance or embarrassment, I can't quite tell. But then he's springing into action again, firing himself into the air fast and hard, like a bullet from a gun, before crashing back to earth on top of Alistair.

I expect Alistair to spin aside, but he braces himself instead and absorbs the impact, right before he uses Chastain's momentum against him and sends him flying in the other direction. This time, Chastain hits the fence hard enough to leave a dent in it and knock the air out of his lungs, which has everyone in the crowd chanting Alistair's name.

Apparently, that last takedown makes him the winner.

Chastain looks like he wants to object, like he wants to get up and knock Alistair into next week. But as the chanting gets louder and louder, Alistair takes a bow. The other gargoyles rush toward him, and one grabs his arm and lifts it in the air in the manner of champions everywhere.

Chastain, in the meantime, gets up slowly, brushes himself off, and waits for the crowd around Alistair to die down a little before walking over to congratulate him.

He's got a wide smile on his face, but there's something in his eyes that makes me nervous, even before he turns to me with an arched brow and asks, "So, do you want to try it?"

"Try what?" I ask, baffled.

Another gargoyle hurries up to us, a sword and a shield in his hands. "Here." He extends them out to me. "Why don't you try these on for size?"

Everything inside me recoils at the thought of picking up that sword and shield. Because if I do, it means I'm planning on using them to hurt—maybe even to kill—someone. Or be killed. "I'm not..." I trail off as I try to figure out how to explain my hesitation to a general who has obviously seen many battles.

Chastain is clearly interested in an explanation, because he asks, "Not what?"

"I don't—" I break off a second time, still not sure what I want to say here. Not sure what there is to say, except, "I'm not that kind of queen."

"And what kind is that exactly?" Chastain asks. His voice is mild, but he doesn't look impressed. In fact, for a second, I would swear he looks flat-out disgusted.

Still, the expression disappears as fast as it came—as do the sword and shield being held out to me when the young man pulls them back and scurries away.

As though the question were rhetorical, Chastain turns away and joins the crowd of gargoyles around Alistair. I wait patiently for their enthusiasm to wane, not sure what I'm supposed to be saying or doing besides lurking on the sidelines.

Chastain puts up with the chaotic well wishes for a few minutes before ordering the other gargoyles back to training. I watch as the men and women do as instructed, pulling out their swords and shields and diving in for another set of mock battles.

The tall girl with the braids is back in action, knocking her partner onto his butt in less than thirty seconds.

"Keep that up and I won't be able to walk tonight, let alone take over your watch," he warns her as he climbs back to his feet.

"Hey, it's not my fault you show me what you're going to do a good three seconds before you do it," she answers with a shrug.

"I do not!" he squawks indignantly.

"Oh yeah?" She lifts her sword back into position. "Then why do I keep knocking you down?"

He says something else, but I don't catch it because, all of a sudden, Alistair half shouts, "That isn't what we talked about!" to Chastain.

Chastain tries to say something else, but Alistair walks away from him mid-explanation.

The gargoyle king looks disgruntled and more than a little upset as he makes his way toward me. "Come on, Grace. We need to get going."

"Is everything okay?" I ask, even as I follow him back out through the courtyard.

"It'll be fine once—" He cuts himself off with a sigh. "It's fine."

"Are you sure?" I ask as we walk outside the castle gate to the land beyond. For the first time, I can see the sea down below. It's wild and wind-tossed, and as it smashes against the bottom of the cliffs, I feel a longing deep inside me—a homesickness for California, for the beach, *for my parents*—that I haven't let myself feel in a long, long time.

It's so strong that it makes my hands shake and my stomach hurt. I do my best to breathe through the pain…and to blink away the tears that come out of nowhere. Over the last few months, I've learned that grief is a strange and awful thing. You never know when it's going to catch up with you or how hard it will hit. Just that it will.

"Do you hear them yet?" Alistair asks.

I'm confused at first, thinking he means my parents. "Hear who?"

"The gargoyles. I hoped that being here, in the Court, might help you find them."

"Oh." I shove the grief down and do my best to listen deep inside my mind, but I don't hear anything except my own thoughts. "I'm sorry, but I don't."

He looks so disappointed that I can't help feeling guilty, which just gives me one more emotion that I don't know how to deal with roiling around inside me.

But before I can think of a way to apologize for what he clearly thinks is a failing on my part, Alistair continues. "No matter, dear girl. I'm sure you'll figure things out once you go see your grandmother." He grabs my hand, looks deep into my eyes. "There is much to do to prepare and very little time. You must let your grandmother help you. Cyrus will stop at nothing to kill you, Grace. You're the key to everything. Promise me you'll go see her."

He drops my hand before I can tell him that I have no idea who my grandmother is. And then it feels like we're falling, falling, falling, even though my feet never leave the ground.

Moments later, I'm back at Katmere, the chess piece in my hand and Alistair sitting across from me. But gone is the gargoyle king, and in his place is the very confused, very upset Unkillable Beast.

"No time," he grinds out as he climbs to his feet. "I must find mate."

And then he rushes to the entrance, throws open the door of the school, and flies away.

I gape after him. Well, *that* wasn't what I expected. Not him flying off and certainly nothing before that. Maybe I'm still asleep. Or maybe this was all some kind of bizarre hallucination on my part. I mean, it makes more sense than the idea that I somehow transported the Unkillable Beast—scratch that, *Alistair*, the former *gargoyle king*—and myself to the Gargoyle Court first thing in the morning.

At least until I look down and realize I'm still wearing the green-and-gold ring.

I stare at the empty seat in front of me, at the abandoned chess pieces, and my stomach twists. There are others like me, other gargoyles. But now?

Now I feel exactly like I did when I was told I'm the last gargoyle—all alone.

14

We Have to Stop Bleeding This Way

I may be alone, but there's still a lot to do, so I grab my bag from the floor and head back to Hudson's room. If he woke up while I was gone and couldn't find me, he's probably freaking out. And, more than likely, has all the others freaking out, too.

Not that I'd blame him. If he—or any of the others—disappeared right now, in the middle of this current mess, I'd be the first one turning over every rock in the place to find them. These are dangerous days we're living through, and I really do feel bad about getting lost like that in the Gargoyle Court.

Determined to calm Hudson down if he's currently scouring Katmere to find me, I pull out my cell to text him that I'm okay...only to realize that Alistair and I were only gone for about five minutes. Which doesn't make sense when I think about all the things we saw at the Gargoyle Court. I mean, Alistair's fight with Chastain alone took way longer than five minutes. And yet, according to my home screen, it's only been eight minutes since I snuck out of Macy's and my room.

Weird.

Again, I glance down at my finger. And again, the giant emerald winks up at me in the light cast by the black dragon sconces on the walls all around me.

So. Freaking. Weird.

I'm about to text Hudson anyway—better safe than sorry—but my phone goes off with a series of texts. Expecting it to be Hudson asking if everything is okay, I'm a little startled to find the texts are from Jaxon on our group chat, letting all of us know that Luca's parents have arrived hours ahead of schedule, and I feel short of breath.

Once again, it hits me that this is really happening, that this newest nightmare is one we can't wake up from, no matter how much we might wish it so.

I may not know exactly what Luca's parents are going through, but I know something of it, and it makes me sick. Makes me ache that after everything that's happened in the last seven months, it feels like I'm right back where I started. Where all of this started.

Still, this isn't about me. It's about them, about Luca. And standing here on the verge of a panic attack isn't going to help any of them. I need to get my shit together and go out there—for Luca, for Jaxon, for *Flint*.

With that thought in mind, I head toward Katmere's main entrance and arrive just as a man and a woman walk through the door, their faces carefully blank but their eyes alive with pain and disbelief.

Jaxon is already in the foyer, as are Mekhi, Byron, Rafael, and Liam. Not that that surprises me—the Order has always had a kind of preternatural ability to know where the others are at all times and when they are needed.

One thing that does surprise me, though, is how steady Jaxon looks as he steps forward to greet Luca's parents. For a guy who nearly died less than twelve hours ago, he looks pretty damn solid—even taking into account the ability to heal quickly that most paranormals have.

The circles under his eyes that seemed to have grown worse every time I saw him for weeks are suddenly absent. His skin has gone from the sickly gray it was when he was losing his soul to a warm color that makes him look more vibrant. And even his body, which started to go from lean to gaunt, has begun to fill back out in the last twenty-four hours.

As he holds a hand out to first Luca's father and then his mother, a small spurt of relief cuts through the sadness and sickness inside me because, for the first time in what feels like a very long time, it looks like Jaxon might actually be okay. And that means everything to me.

"I'm so sorry," Jaxon tells them. "I failed to protect him—"

"We *all* failed," Mekhi interrupts, sorrow shining out of his dark-brown eyes. "He was our brother, and we couldn't save him. From the depths of my soul, I am sorry."

Each member of the Order steps forward and individually echoes the sentiment. Luca's parents respond to each apology with a nod, and though his mother has thin trails of tears running down her cheeks, she shows no other emotion—and neither does Luca's father. I don't know if that's a vampire thing or if it's just them, but the tight stranglehold they have on their emotions makes everything about this a little better...and a little worse.

They don't say anything else to accept the Order's apologies, but they don't scream at them, either. Instead, they simply stare at the five vampires with sad but assessing eyes. I don't know what they're looking for, and I definitely don't know if they've found it. All I know is that their silence is making me very, very nervous, and it's making all of Hudson's concerns about them from earlier flood back into my mind.

Hudson arrives just as Liam finishes making his apology, and I feel him before I see him. The air in the room changes, and I turn toward him a second before he wraps an arm around my waist. "You okay?" he murmurs, his eyes cataloging my change in wardrobe as well as the backpack draped over my shoulder.

"As okay as I can be," I answer, sinking into his body as I turn back to Luca's parents.

"Where is he?" Luca's father finally asks, and I realize it's the first time he's spoken since he arrived. He's a tall man and lean like his son was. It's easy to see where Luca got his looks from, even though his father appears exhausted, his eyes sunken and skin drawn too tight over his cheekbones.

"We put him in one of the study halls," Jaxon answers, turning to lead the way down the hall.

"A study hall?" his mother echoes, a quiet horror in her voice.

And I get it, I do. Taken at face value, it doesn't sound like the most respectful place to put him.

But look around. Katmere is a disaster, and Jaxon's choices were obviously limited. Plus, this is a school, not a government building. It's not like there were many choices of what to do with a body even when Katmere was in good shape. Especially since the entire staff, minus Marise, has been kidnapped. Or worse.

Jaxon knows all this, but he doesn't defend his choice, even as his shoulders slump at their words. In my mind, it's just more proof that he really is a class act.

Eventually, Luca's parents move to follow Jaxon, which frees the rest of us to do the same. First the Order, then Hudson and me. We walk in solemn silence until we're joined by Eden and Macy about halfway down the hallway.

Eden whispers, "Where's Flint?" from behind us.

"I don't know. Do you think he's sleeping?" Macy asks.

"I don't think oversleeping is his problem," Hudson answers grimly. "More likely he can't get down here. I'll go see if I can—"

He breaks off suddenly as Flint, in dragon form, comes flying straight down the hallway, his crutches clutched in his front talons and his wings tucked in tight so as not to hit the walls around us. It's such an unexpected sight that all of us freeze.

Except Luca's mother, who gives a startled scream as he races over our heads, then flips a quick U-turn and lands right behind us.

15

Et Tu, Marise?

Flint shimmers for a moment before his dragon form disappears in a shower of beautifully colored sparks. Seconds later, he's standing in front of us in human form.

Though *standing* might be a bit of a stretch, considering he's wobbling a little as he balances on his one good foot while also trying to squat to get his crutches. He mutters a string of curses under his breath, and I move to him, determined to keep him from falling on his face in the middle of what is already a terrible time for him.

Jaxon beats me, though, scooping up Flint's crutches in one hand while he uses the other to steady him.

Flint ducks his head as he takes the crutches, but not before it becomes obvious that his cheeks are burning with embarrassment. I want to go to him, to tell him it's okay, but every single thing about him is screaming for us to leave him alone. So I do, as do the others.

Eventually, he gets himself situated on the crutches and walks forward, toward Luca's parents. We scramble out of the way—anything to make it easier for him—but once he locks eyes on Luca's mother, I don't think he even notices us anymore.

She seems to feel the same way, as she stares back just as intently. But her focus isn't on Flint's eyes. It's on Flint's mangled leg.

The look on his face is terrible, heartbreaking, as he negotiates his way down the hall to stop in front of her. Once there, he bows his head, much the same way that Jaxon did.

"I'm sorry," he whispers. "I'm so sorry we couldn't save him."

At first, I don't think she's going to say anything to him, but eventually she puts her hand on the back of his lowered head and whispers, "As are we."

A world of meaning—and accusation—hangs in those words, and I see it hit

Flint and Jaxon and the others, an avalanche of grief and pain that they don't even try to dodge. Which isn't fair to them—at all. They fought hard against Cyrus, risked life and limb to keep him from getting the Crown.

Yes, Luca died, and yes, it is horrible and tragic and senseless. But that doesn't make it Flint's fault. It doesn't make it any of our faults when we were right there with him, doing our best to keep one another safe. After all, where exactly were Luca's parents during the battle that killed their son?

A glance at Hudson tells me he's thinking the same thing I am. That he's likely been thinking it all along. Either way, he's in full defensive mode right now—hands loose by his sides, weight forward on the balls of his feet, eyes laser focused on Luca's parents, waiting for them to make a wrong move.

I really hope they don't.

Jaxon clears his throat, and Luca's parents reluctantly pull their attention away from Flint and back to him. He doesn't say anything, though. Just turns and continues to lead the way down the hall to the only study room on the first floor.

When we finally reach it, he takes a moment, as if he's bracing himself for what's within…or for whatever is going to happen next. Then he pushes the door open and steps back so that Luca's parents can go inside first.

Luca's mother gasps as she looks through the open doorway, and for a second, I think she's about to go down. But Luca's dad grabs on to her, wrapping an arm around her for support. Then the two of them make their way through the doorway into the room that holds Luca's remains while the rest of us follow quietly behind.

I brace myself, expecting it to be just like those moments when I had to identify my parents' bodies.

But it turns out there's nothing cold or sterile about the study room. Sometime while I was with Hudson—or Alistair—the Order has transformed it into a proper place of mourning.

Luca is laid out on a table in the center of the room, a sheet draped over him so that only his face is exposed. All around him burn hundreds of black candles—they must have raided the witches' tower to get this many—and beyond the candles are container after container of Alaskan wildflowers.

This time it's Luca's father who gasps as he stifles a sob. Luca's mother simply sinks to her knees beside her son's body.

"We'll give you a few minutes," Jaxon says into the agonized silence while the rest of us nod like puppets—then he backs toward the door.

"Thank you," his mother chokes out.

"Yes," his father echoes. "Thank you for taking care of our son."

"Luca was our brother," Byron tells him, voice aching. "There's nothing we wouldn't have done for him."

"We can see that." Luca's father clears his throat. "He always swore—"

He breaks off as Marise sweeps into the room in full dress robes. She's still a little pale, but other than that, she looks much better than she did earlier. "Vivian, Miles. I'm so sorry that we're meeting under these circumstances. We all loved Luca here at Katmere, and his death weighs heavy on us all."

Luca's parents don't turn from their son, so Marise pivots to the rest of us, her striking face filled with compassion as she whispers, "I've made health draughts for you. They're in the main common room, along with several bottles of blood. Drink them now and I'll make more later. We don't know what's coming, and you need them to regain your strength."

We definitely need all the help we can get, so I nod as Flint murmurs, "Yes, Marise," and we turn to shuffle out of the room.

But just then, Luca's father whirls around. His voice rings through the room as he orders, "Don't!"

Marise reaches for him. "What's wrong, Mi—"

She never gets to finish her sentence, because Vivian chooses that moment to spring up from the ground...and rip Marise's throat out with her teeth.

Macy screams as Luca's mom drops Marise, who is gurgling and gasping for breath with only half a throat, to the ground and steps back so Miles can drive a dagger right through the nurse practitioner's heart.

"You need to go!" Miles warns as Vivian grabs on to Luca's lifeless hand. "Marise alerted Cyrus that you had returned, and he's coming for you. We were to be the distraction."

It takes a second for his words to register for any of us. I know I'm too busy staring at Marise's lifeless body, too busy trying to figure out what just happened, to internalize his warning.

I mean, Marise helped me so many times since I've been at Katmere. She saved my life when a broken window nearly killed me. She helped me begin to accept the idea that I'm a gargoyle, took care of me after the fight with Lia.

How could she be on Cyrus's side? It doesn't make sense.

Apparently, I'm not the only one with doubts, because Eden demands, "You think we're just going to believe you? You killed her!"

"It makes no difference to me if you believe us or not," Vivian snaps. "But it's obvious you took care of my son the best you could. It seems only right that we do our best to look after those he called friends, as he would be doing if he still could."

"By killing Marise?" Macy asks, tears shining on her cheeks.

"Yes, and by warning you to get out before it's too late," Miles answers.

"Marise is no friend to you," Vivian snarls. "Didn't you ever wonder why she was the only one left here alive? Because she has always been loyal to Cyrus." She looks down at Luca. "As have we, until now."

"You have to go," Miles repeats urgently. "Cyrus wants Grace, and he'll stop at nothing to get her."

With that, he leans forward to wrap one arm around Vivian and one arm around his son. Seconds later, all three of them vanish, fading in a blink out of the room to the portal outside they'd arrived through and leaving the rest of us standing over Marise's body.

As her blood pools around her limp form, I can't help the shiver that races along my spine at how violent and unforgiving this world is—and that it's coming for me next.

16

Every Wolf
Has Their Day

"What do we do now?" Mekhi asks into the deafening silence that follows their departure.

Hudson is already at the window, scanning the early-morning horizon. "I don't see anything, but that doesn't mean they aren't out there."

"Oh, they're out there," comments a lightly accented voice from the doorway behind us. "And pretty soon, they'll be in here."

I whirl around so fast, I nearly trip over Jaxon, who has positioned himself in front of me even as Hudson fades to the door.

"Who are you?" Hudson demands of a young boy, probably fifteen or sixteen years old, with deep brown eyes and brown skin. His hair is black and just long enough that it brushes against his shoulders. At only a couple of inches taller than me, I'm oddly happy he's not another giant of a paranormal for me to crane my neck to look at. He's also super skinny, something that his too-big science T-shirt makes painfully obvious. If it wasn't such a terrible day, I'd laugh at the slogan on it, though.

You matter, unless you multiply yourself by the speed of light. Then you energy.

I'm also pretty sure that he's a wolf.

It's that realization that has me crossing the room at a run so that I can back Hudson up—as does everyone else in the room.

The boy doesn't even flinch. He skims his eyes over each of us, as if trying to decide who the biggest threat is. He must decide it's Hudson, because he's the one he's looking at when he answers, "My name is Dawud. I'm from the Den of the Desert Sun in Syria."

So I was right. He's a wolf. "What are you doing here?" I ask, Luca's parents' warning fresh in my mind.

"I'm here because I didn't think the Court vamps had it in them to betray

Cyrus," he answers. "And to deliver the same warning they did. Wolves from all over the world are descending on Katmere to capture you—including the best soldiers in my den. I ran ahead to warn you, but they should be here soon, en masse."

"You *ran ahead*?" Eden asks skeptically.

"I'm fast. And motivated." Dawud picks something up off a table and examines it, then stuffs it into his pocket. "As you should be, unless you all want to die—or get captured. They really will be here soon. My guess is five minutes, ten if you're lucky."

He makes getting captured sound like the worse option of the two, and frankly, I don't blame him. The idea of being at Cyrus's mercy—of Hudson and Jaxon being at his mercy—has my heart stumbling in my chest.

"Why should we trust this guy if his alpha is in league with Cyrus?" Flint demands. "Maybe he's here as a decoy."

"They, actually," Dawud clarifies. "And the vampire already admitted they were supposed to be the distraction. I'm here for the most obvious reason of them all. I need you."

I have a hard time believing that.

"Need us for what?" I ask even as I consider reaching for my platinum string. Every nerve I have is on red alert, and if I need to fight, I want to be in gargoyle form to do it.

"My younger brother's name is Amir. He's a freshman at Katmere, and he was taken with the others. I have to get him out."

"I know Amir!" Macy exclaims. "He's a Padres fan, and we bonded one day over his vintage Tony Gwynn jersey." Her shoulders sag. "My dad has one just like it."

"That's Amir." Dawud's throat works convulsively. "Our parents were killed two years ago, and I've been in charge of him ever since. I sent him to school expecting it to be the safest place for him, but… You're the only chance I have to save him, and that won't happen if I let Cyrus kill or capture you."

Their voice rings with truth, and I can't help believing them. A glance around shows me my friends believe them, too. God help us all.

"We've got ten minutes?" Jaxon asks, and I can practically see the wheels turning in his head.

"At the most."

"So what do we do?" Eden asks.

"What do you think we do?" Byron growls. "We get the fuck out of here."

Hudson wraps an arm around me. "Come on. Let's fade to your room and pack what you need."

"I already packed a bag to bring to your room. It's got everything."

"Well then, the rest of you pack a bag," Hudson tells us as we walk back toward the foyer. "Grace and I will stand watch until you're ready to go. But hurry, will you? Something tells me Cyrus won't be waiting much longer."

"Five min—" Flint starts, but he breaks off mid-word as a growl echoes from the staircase above us.

My blood turns to ice at the sound, and I look up in time to see a pack of fifty or so wolves—teeth bared and claws out—leap over the banisters at the exact same moment. Even worse, most of them seem to be heading straight for me.

Hudson and Jaxon both lunge in front of me at the same moment. But then more growls sound from the front door behind us, and we're surrounded. There's no way we can fight them all, from every direction.

One minute they're thirty feet away, and the next they're only a breath from me. The shock of it has me frozen before I can reach for my platinum string.

I recover quickly, but before I can shift, just like that, they're gone. Snarling for my blood one minute—nothing but dust the next.

My stomach twists, and this time, it's not from mere nerves. Because I know what just happened and, even worse, exactly what it cost him.

17

Not All Dogs Go to Heaven

Hudson staggers back, nearly falls on his ass, but catches himself with a hand on the wall, his body doubled over.

"Dude, what the hell just happened?" Liam demands, spinning in a circle as if expecting the wolves to jump out at us at any moment.

"I don't know," Eden answers as she turns to Dawud. "Did you—"

"I didn't do anything," the wolf answers, hands up. "I didn't think they'd get here this fast."

Hudson bends over farther, as though even leaning on the wall is too much effort for him, and instead braces his hands on his knees as he takes a couple of deep breaths. Then, sounding more defeated than I've ever heard him, he admits, "I did it."

My heart stutters in my chest as I rush to Hudson's side.

Rafael apparently hasn't caught up with the program, though, because he has a confused look on his face as he asks, "Did what?"

Still, it must only take a couple of seconds for the truth of who he is talking to—and what Hudson is capable of—to hit him, because his eyes suddenly go wide. "Wait a minute. Are you saying that you…" Rafael's voice trails off as he searches for the right verb to describe Hudson's power.

"Poofed." Mekhi fills in the missing word. "You poofed the wolves?" This time when he says it, he uses his hands to mimic something exploding.

"Are you really that surprised?" Hudson asks, dragging in breaths. "I *did* bring down a stadium."

"Yeah, but that's not that hard," Liam interjects. "Even Jaxon could have done that—"

"Thanks for the vote of confidence," Jaxon deadpans at the same time Hudson quotes, "Damning with faint praise."

But Liam's mind is too blown to apologize to my former mate…or my current mate, for that matter. Instead, he continues to turn around, searching the room, as he says, "He poofed the wolves, Jaxon. He just—" This time, he's the one who makes the hand gesture for exploding. "Poofed them."

When Hudson doesn't straighten back up, I get on my knees in front of him, lift his bent head to look into his eyes, and what I see nearly breaks my heart wide open. It's not the pain etched in the grit of his jaw, the anguish in the depths of his oceanic eyes that wrecks me. It's the fact that in the next instant, he blinks—and the agony is gone like it never existed. In its place is a cold, dark wall that I know isn't just Hudson trying to hide the pain from me. He's hiding it from himself as well.

"They were going for Grace," Hudson murmurs, like that explains everything.

For as long as I've known him, he's tried not to use this power against anyone. To destroy a building? Sure. To blow up a forest? Absolutely. To eviscerate an island? Yeah, if he absolutely has to.

But today he murdered those wolves in the blink of an eye—not one, but dozens and dozens, maybe more. And he didn't hesitate...*to save me.*

The realization wrings the breath from my chest. I feel awful. Awful that so many people have died in this horrible war of Cyrus's and even more awful that Hudson had to be the one to do this—and that he did it to protect me.

And I've absolutely failed to protect *him.* Which is pretty much my most important job as his mate.

Killing all those wolves shattered him and, in doing so, shattered me as well.

As though no one can tell Hudson and I are grappling to put the pieces of our souls back together, the rest continue the debate around us.

"They were definitely going for her," Flint agrees with narrowed eyes. "But the question is, why her specifically?"

"Luca's dad said Cyrus wanted her dead," Eden reminds him.

"Of course my father wants Grace dead," Jaxon snarls. "When has he ever been okay with someone having power he can't control? And now that she's got the Crown? He'll be gunning for her double-time with everything he's got."

"Which is nothing new," I tell them, hoping to calm everyone down just a little so I can focus on Hudson. "He's always had it out for me."

"There's having it out for you, and then there's wanting to crush you for the specific purpose of sucking every drop of power from your dead body," Jaxon shoots back. "The first is normal. The second is sociopathic and means you have a giant target on your head."

"Which makes me wonder why exactly we're still standing here," Mekhi comments, brows raised sardonically. "Considering Cyrus probably has a second wave on the way."

"He definitely has a second wave on the way." Dawud glances at the stairs where the wolves were standing less than a minute ago.

"Were they from your den?" I ask quietly.

"No," they whisper.

Knowing that doesn't make me feel any better—and it doesn't make Hudson feel better, either, judging from the look on his face.

"Screw packing a bag," Flint says, even as he scans the horizon for signs of more paranormals. "We need to get the fuck out of here."

"Whatever we need, we can buy when we get someplace safe," Eden agrees as she moves to one of the windows on the south side of the castle and begins to watch the area for any sign of an incoming attack.

"Is there any place safe we can go at the moment?" Byron asks quietly. "If Cyrus could turn Marise against us, then who's left we can trust?"

It's a terrifying question, one that doesn't bear thinking about. Not when we have nowhere to call home. Everyone chooses to use our last few minutes to debate where we can go next. I decide to let them sort that question out themselves so I can take a moment and focus on Hudson. I reach up to cup his cheek.

"I'm fine," Hudson tries to assure me and stands to his full height again, turns to look out the window. But the hand he runs through his hair is shaking.

"No, you're not. But you will be," I whisper as we stare out at the gray Alaskan sky. It's as empty of activity as Katmere's halls this morning, but that doesn't mean much, considering any witch who's ever been to Katmere can open a portal up right in the middle of the common room—or anywhere else, for that matter. Not to mention the fact that an entire pack of wolves somehow got in here, and we never even saw them coming.

How that happened is a question for later, though, because right now I'm focused on my mate.

"I'm fine," Hudson repeats, but he's trying to convince himself more than me this time.

"You look like hell," I say bluntly. "And I know what you just did wasn't easy for you."

His face closes up. "That's where you're wrong. It was *extremely* easy for me." He gives a harsh laugh. "Isn't that the problem?"

"I know *exactly* what the problem is, Hudson."

When he looks away, jaw working, I know I've struck a nerve.

More concerning to me, though, is he actually looks sick. I know he just expended a shit ton of energy, and I'm sure that's part of it, but that isn't the main part. I've seen him use his power before, seen him use more power than even this took on the Unkillable Beast's island, and he never broke a sweat.

So the way he's currently got his hands in his pockets so I won't see them shake isn't normal. Neither is the way he's locking his knees to make sure he doesn't go down. Something is really wrong with Hudson, and I'd bet breakfast it has more to do with the fact that he just killed a whole lot of people than it does the fact that he used too much power.

"Hey." I wrap an arm around his waist for support. "Can I help?"

I expect him to pull away, maybe crack one of those ridiculously dry jokes of his like he always does. Instead, he sinks into me, and I can tell his hands aren't the only things that are shaking. His entire body is trembling like he's in shock.

And maybe he is. He's wrestled with using his power for so long, and then to have it happen like this—so fast and almost out of his control—has to have freaked him out.

I snuggle in a little closer and whisper, "I love you, no matter what."

A shudder runs through him at my words, and his eyes close for several long seconds. When he opens them, they're filled with the same resolve I usually see from him. Which is pretty much all I can hope for at this point.

But I have to do something. Anything to help him move past this. So I tilt my face up to his and say, "I think I finally know what promise you made with my ring."

At first, he doesn't respond. Doesn't even acknowledge what I've said. But then, ever so slowly, his gaze meets mine, and one eyebrow goes up. "Do you?"

I'm so relieved he's going to play along that I squeeze his waist before answering, "You promised to always do all the dishes for me."

He can't help the chuckle that escapes as he asks, "Why would I ever promise to do dishes when I don't *use* dishes?"

Then his gaze slides down to my neck, and a blush steals up my cheeks. Oh man, I walked right into that one. But as heat thaws the ice in his gaze, I sigh. There he is. My Hudson is coming back to me. Relief washing over me, weakening my knees, I lean into his strength.

His lips brush the top of my forehead before he whispers in my ear, "Thank you." And it sounds an awful lot like *I love you.*

Before I can respond, someone's cell dings, and the moment is gone as we both turn to see what's happening.

"My aunt just texted that we can hide out at the Witch Court with her," Macy says from the other side of the main common room, where she and Eden have positioned themselves to watch the school's back windows. "It'll only take me five minutes to build a portal."

"We don't have five more minutes," Hudson says grimly. "They're coming."

18

Everybody Needs a Little Push Sometimes

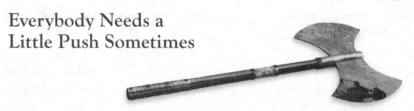

"**W**here are they?" Jaxon's at the window before I can turn around to look. "Fuck."

"I don't see any—" I break off as my human/gargoyle eyes finally notice what their vampire eyes picked up on seconds ago.

Hundreds and hundreds of wolves racing across the mountainside and clearing to get to Katmere. To get to us.

"Let's go!" Hudson orders, and the rest of us don't have to be told twice. "Head to the back of the school!"

I grab on to him, and he fades us through the narrow corridors, Jaxon and the others hot on our heels. With no room to change into their dragons as we dash through the school, Flint and Eden are struggling to keep up, so Jaxon takes hold of Flint and pours on the speed.

Byron does the same with Eden, and though both dragons curse at the insult of being carried by vampires, neither pulls away. Right now, every second counts, and we all know it.

Shockingly, Dawud has no trouble keeping up with the fading vampires— apparently, they really are as fast as they say.

We make it to the giant rear doors less than a minute later—which is a really good thing, considering it would normally take me several minutes to get there.

Mekhi is manning the door, ready to tear any intruders apart. "It's all clear out here," he says after a quick look outside.

"Everyone, head to the art cottage across the field," Jaxon commands. "Macy can build a portal there. I'll stay and hold them off."

The Order starts to protest, but Hudson interrupts. "I'll stay with him."

"No!" I exclaim, panic racing through me at the thought of anything happening to Hudson or Jaxon. "We all stay or we all go."

"Grace, you have to trust me," Hudson says as he grabs my hands. "Jaxon and

I can handle these assholes. We'll be right behind you as soon as the portal opens."

"The Order will stay as well," Mekhi volunteers, but Jaxon shakes his head.

"You need to protect Grace. If Marise is right and Cyrus is stealing magic to power something—and the only thing that can stop him is Grace—we have to keep her safe."

"I can keep myself—"

"The Order will protect her with their lives," Jaxon interrupts, tapping his chest with a closed fist, and the Order answers with the same gesture, as though that decides everything.

Annoyance snakes through me, and I'm about to protest the massive display of *you don't get a vote* when there's a loud crash from the cafeteria. It's followed by the snarls of wolves so close that a shiver races along my spine.

"Jaxon's right, Grace. Cyrus himself came to that island to try to keep you from getting the Crown. We don't know how it works yet, but I agree with Jaxon—if he's afraid of you having it, there must be a reason." Hudson rushes through the words. "You need to get the hell out of here. We'll be right behind you. I promise."

"I can't—" I begin before Hudson interrupts.

"Grace." This time there's more bite in his words. "I fought an entire prison population. I can survive some mangy wolves. But if you don't leave now, I'll have no choice but to disintegrate them instead of just maiming the fuckers."

My chest feels like it's going to crack wide open. I'd do anything for Hudson to never have to use his gift again, but the idea of leaving him and Jaxon to fight an army of wolves alone makes me sick. Not when there's strength in numbers. We've always been at our best together...why can't Hudson see that?

Then again, maybe he can. Hudson would never keep me out of a fight for fear I couldn't hold my own. Which means he really does think he has this and needs me out of the way so he doesn't use his gift to kill again the second a wolf gets close to me.

The realization only worries me more—he must be even worse off than I thought if he's that afraid he might lose control.

Which is why I nod and take a step back even though it's the last thing I want to do.

Relief flashes across his face as he throws me a half smile that doesn't reach his eyes. "I swear, I've got this, Grace."

And he does. I know he does. But that doesn't mean leaving him here to fight an army of wolves who want to rip him apart is any easier. My chest tightens, and I lift my gaze to his.

I take a moment to memorize the high cheekbones framing his deep blue eyes, the hard line of his jaw, the rich brown hair still perfectly styled in its usual pompadour.

Then I whisper, "You better," before giving him a quick, hard kiss. I promise myself this won't be the last time I see my mate as I turn and shout, "Let's go!" to the rest of the gang.

They spring into action, and I grab my platinum string as Flint kicks open the doors. I hit the skies, my giant wings eating up the short distance to the cottage in mere seconds.

Macy immediately gets to work opening a portal while Flint insists he should go back and crispy-fry Cyrus's army.

Mekhi shakes his head. "That's Jaxon and Hudson up there. They'll hold them off."

"You don't know that," I say, upset because everyone thinks Jaxon and Hudson are so invincible. But they aren't. I've seen them both struggle, and I've seen them both bleed. They can get hurt—they can *die*—just like the rest of us. My stomach twists, and suddenly I'm afraid I've made a terrible mistake.

"We never should have left them," Flint says, and he sounds as freaked out as I feel.

Rafael was the last to fade to us, and his eyes find mine. "Like Hudson said, they've got this," he assures me. "Don't worry."

"How many are there?" Flint demands.

Rafael just shakes his head. "They'll be fine," he repeats.

He might be more believable if he didn't look so shaken—and if a new series of snarls wasn't coming from the school. Snarls that are followed immediately by a handful of loud thuds, crashes, and then, finally, high-pitched animal whines.

"What can we do?" Eden asks Macy, who is swirling fire between her hands as the very beginning of a portal emerges.

"Just be ready to jump through as soon as I get it open," Macy says, her hands a blur of movement as she works through the intricate portal magic.

"I'm with her," Dawud says, speaking for the first time since they slid to a stop next to the cottage. "I didn't risk everything to warn you so that you'd die here anyway."

Mekhi agrees, though he sounds as desperate as I feel when he says, "As soon as Macy gets that portal open, we need to go through it."

"They'll be right behind us," Byron adds, his eyes steady on mine. "I promise,

Grace. I wouldn't leave if I thought they couldn't do this alone."

I glare at him. "You would if *Jaxon* ordered you to get us out of here."

He looks away, jaw working. I've hit closer to home than I thought.

But before I can even begin to process that, the ground shakes and the whole building rumbles. I forget how to swallow as I figure out what's happening.

Jaxon is using Katmere itself to fight them off—which means there must be a hell of a lot more wolves than we imagined.

I turn to Macy. "We're almost out of time."

Macy nods, moving her hands in an intricate pattern that has the portal changing shape and color before her. With one final movement, she exclaims, "I've got it!"

"Get going!" Byron shouts. "We don't have any more time."

I feel like I'm being wrenched apart. They don't actually expect me to leave Hudson and Jaxon here. I can't do that. I can't just walk away from my mate and hope he makes it. How could any of them even think that I could?

There's no time to tell Byron that, because Katmere shakes right in front of us. The whole structure literally *trembles* as large cracks slash through the walls, causing stones at the top to tumble to the ground with a thundering crash.

"Holy shit," Flint breathes, eyes wide with the same horror tearing through me. "They're really going to do it. They're going to bring it all down."

Just the idea is a knife to my gut. Then again, the thought of losing Hudson or Jaxon is a full-on rocket launcher.

"You go ahead," I tell the others. "I'm going to wait for—"

I break off with a gasp as Eden pushes me straight toward the portal.

19

Taste the Rainbow

I stumble, pinwheeling my arms until I feel like a wind chime on a stormy day in a desperate effort to regain my balance.

But it's too late. Eden's push was too deliberate and too well-placed. I fall backward straight into the portal, which turns out to be even worse than my normal method of diving headfirst because I have even less control over my body in reverse.

I spend what feels like forever but is probably only a few seconds tumbling through Macy's psychedelic rainbows. Every witch's portal looks and feels different—hence the variations in portals on the Ludares field—and my cousin's are always made up of giant sparkling rainbows. Which isn't exactly a surprise and which I normally don't mind. But somersaulting backward through them against my will feels like I'm on a sugar high gone wrong.

When the portal finally spits me out onto a cold, hard, white marble floor, I get flipped over and land flat on my face.

Note to self: never complain about landing on my butt again, because hitting the ground face-first and then having the rest of me do a giant belly flop is absolutely no fun.

I take a few seconds to catch my breath, then roll over with a groan, only to find myself staring at a white carved ceiling filled with swirling wildflowers and ornate curlicues.

I only have a few seconds to wonder where the hell I am before Eden lands right next to me—on her feet, of course. It's all I can do to keep from snarling.

Another note to self: never trust a dragon with attitude problems and a freakishly good sense of balance.

"What the hell was that for?" I demand, pushing aside the hand she offers to help me up. "You had no right—"

"I had every right," she shoots back. "You weren't going to go through the portal, and you needed to."

"Hudson and Jaxon—"

"Hudson and Jaxon are two of the most powerful vampires in existence. They can handle this—as long as they're not distracted worrying about *you*." She steps out of the way as Mekhi comes through the portal. "Getting you out of there made it easier for them to do what they need to do."

"She's right," Mekhi agrees as he, too, offers me a hand up. This time I take it, ignoring the roll of Eden's eyes as he pulls me to my feet just as the others come through the portal, one after another.

"They can do this, Grace," he continues. "We just have to—"

He breaks off as the sound of walls collapsing echoes through the room. We whirl around just in time to see Macy flying through the portal opening. She lands on her knees but is up in seconds, holding her arms out high and wide.

Her eyes are wild and her face is smudged with dirt, but her focus never wavers from the portal that is growing ever wider as we stand here.

Usually Macy is the last one through and the portal closes as soon as she exits. But not this time. This time, she's using every ounce of power she has to hold it open from this side—something I didn't even know was possible.

Judging from the looks on the others' faces, they didn't think it could be done, either. But if I've learned anything over the last few months, it's that my happy, bubbly cousin has immense magic inside her. I really believe she can do anything she sets her mind to—including this.

Please, God, let her be able to do this.

"Holy shit," Dawud breathes, and I get it. I really do.

I've never looked at the back side of an open portal before, and as I do, I realize that beyond the swirling rainbow colors, I can still see the grassy field spanning between the cottage and Katmere. Except, even in the small amount of time it took us to get through the passage, everything has changed.

The walls and tower on the west side are completely gone, lying in a pile of rubble and dust, and I gasp, my hand covering my mouth to stop the scream balancing on my tongue. Because the rest of the school is not far behind, if the earsplitting groan of stone and wood and everything I used to call home is anything to go by.

I'm both happy and terrified of that shaking—and the way the walls are literally being cleaved into pieces. Happy, because it means Jaxon and Hudson are still alive. Terrified, because what if they don't get out in time? What if they end up trapped beneath Katmere's tumbling walls along with everyone else?

"I can't hold it much longer—" She breaks off with a small scream, her face pained as she struggles to hold the portal open.

Please, please, please. The word is a mantra in my mind as I position myself next to Macy, one hand on her shoulder. A plea to the universe to save Hudson and Jaxon against what feels like all the odds. I don't have magic the way my cousin does, but I can channel power. I've done it before—with Macy and with Remy.

Holding my arm in a straight line out in front of me, I close my eyes. Take a deep breath. And open myself up to the power all around me. The earth, the trees, the stone. There's power there, but not enough. "I need more power!" I shout.

A hand lands on my shoulder as Flint says, "Take mine." And I understand immediately, tossing him a grateful smile as I reach for his string and channel his magic into the portal.

The Order and Eden step forward next, so many hands on my arms and shoulders. So many different-colored threads to juggle, so many different fears and hopes and abilities to navigate through, and so little time in which to do it.

In the end, I give up on trying to distinguish one power—one person—from the other. And instead, I reach out and scoop up every string I can with my left hand.

Power—huge, unimaginable, *unmanageable* power—rips through me so fast and hard that it nearly knocks me off my feet. I lock my knees, ground myself, and somehow manage to stay upright even as what feels like massive bolts of electricity course through me.

There's no time to absorb it, no time to learn how to finesse it. Katmere is falling before my very eyes, and the only two guys I've ever loved are right in the middle of it. So, without a second thought, I take all the power I have and throw it straight at the portal. Macy might not be able to hold it open alone, but together—with all the power in my friends—maybe, just maybe, we can buy Hudson and Jaxon the time they need.

20

Bringing Down
the House

Macy gasps as the power I'm channeling hits her magic, but she manages to hold on—we both do—pouring everything we can into that portal. Into holding it open just a little bit longer.

And it works, because even as we start to shake, the portal grows wider. And wider.

It grows so large, we can see everything. The entire school. The fields on either side. The cottages. Even the ominous thunderclouds covering the sky above.

But that's not what has my attention, has every breath almost too painful to draw into my aching lungs. What I can't take my eyes from is the last section of Katmere still standing, the last tiny portion—where I know Hudson and Jaxon are still fighting.

"Come on, come on," Mekhi mutters, as fixated on the open portal as we are.

And then we see them. Both Vega brothers fade to a stop just outside the doors into the rear courtyard, the remaining walls of the school still surrounding them.

"Stop showboating and get the fuck into the portal," Flint growls as Jaxon raises a hand and slashes it downward, a huge section of wall tumbling to the ground. Hudson pivots and faces another section of wall, and the middle portion instantly turns to dust, causing the upper bricks to tumble down around him.

And from the debris and dust...hundreds of wolves emerge, surrounding them. I don't even wonder for a moment why Hudson hasn't disintegrated the remaining wolves. I know why. I saw what killing that way did to him earlier, and he'd only do that ever again as a last resort—or if he were too weak.

Fear claws at my insides, but I tamp it down, determined not to let it take hold of me. Determined not to let it interfere with the power I'm currently channeling, the power still growing in my veins and making my muscles tremble.

Jaxon lifts a hand, and another wall splits in half and topples down on the closest wolves.

But that means rocks are falling on Hudson and Jaxon, too, and watching it happen is truly terrifying.

Yes, they're vampires.

Yes, they're powerful.

Yes, it takes a lot to kill them.

But everyone in that castle is a paranormal, and it's going to take a lot to stop *any* of them. Maybe even more than Hudson and Jaxon can safely give.

It's that thought that has my hands shaking and my knees knocking together.

Even the Order watches the portal with narrowed eyes and clenched fists.

Eden screeches, "Get in the damn portal!"

But they can't hear her any more than they can hear the silent screams deep inside me. Not that it matters. I know both of them well enough to know that they wouldn't listen even if they could. They'll die to protect us, and if that means bringing Katmere down on top of themselves, I have no doubt they'll do it.

That fear propels me to reach deep inside myself, reaching for power like it's the air I breathe, and taking it in, letting it consume me, feed my cells and heart and lungs, gathering every ounce of power I can find and pouring it into helping Macy hold open the portal as it narrows and wavers.

But then a loud creaking sound fills the air. And everything falls apart.

The last thing I see is thousands of pounds of rubble pouring down on Hudson's and Jaxon's heads.

21

Never Bite the Vamp
Who Feeds You

"It's gone!" Macy screams, staring into the portal.

"What's gone?" Liam shouts. But the look on his face says that, like the rest of us, he already knows.

It's Katmere.

Katmere is gone. And with it, Jaxon and Hudson?

Just the thought has my knees buckling, and I almost hit the ground, probably would have if everyone weren't still holding on to me.

"Macy!" I shout as the skies finally unleash their fury, drenching the rubble in pelting rain and shaking the ground with frightening thunder and lightning. As if the universe is just as upset as I am that my school, the last symbol of my childhood, is truly gone.

Suddenly, the magic I'm channeling causes the portal to wobble as I lose a bit of control.

Before Macy can answer, the portal burns bright, electric blue for one second, two—and then it explodes as Jaxon and Hudson burst out of it.

Relief swamps me, but it's short-lived because the second the portal snaps closed, all the energy I've been channeling to hold it open rebounds and slams into me so hard that I go flying—straight over Mekhi's and the rest of my friends' heads.

I brace myself for impact—it happened so fast, I can't even find my platinum string, let alone grab it—but just as I'm about to hit the ground, Hudson plucks me out of midair and pulls me straight into his arms.

He's filthy—covered in rock and dirt and God only knows what else—and his heart is beating so fast and hard beneath my cheek that it kind of feels like I'm being smacked in the face over and over again. But I don't care, because right now, there is absolutely nowhere I'd rather be.

"Holy shit!" Rafael exclaims. "I really didn't think you two were going to make it this time."

"You're not the only one," Jaxon answers. He's standing in the center of the room, hands braced on his knees as he pulls in a series of long, deep breaths.

"It's all good," Hudson says, shrugging off his very-near-death experience in typical Hudson fashion. I swear, he could be bleeding to death right here and he would still be completely nonchalant. "We were just biding our time, waiting for you to get settled. You know how much my baby brother loves making a grand entrance."

Jaxon doesn't even bother looking up from where he's still gasping for air— but he does take a second to flip Hudson off and snort. "So says the guy who thinks the entire world's a stage."

"I swear, that boy will say anything to get me to give him an encore," Hudson tells him even as he settles me back on my feet and strokes my wild curls back from my face.

"Why was I even worried?" I ask, exasperated.

His grin is wicked, but his eyes are filled with tenderness as he gazes down at me. "I have no idea."

"Yeah, me neither." Still, I bury my face against his chest and take a few seconds to breathe him in. To let the terror go and give myself a chance to come to grips with the fact that he's okay. That they both are. They made it out against all the odds, and that is what matters.

Eventually, though, reality intrudes on my relief as Macy asks, "Katmere?"

The hope in her voice is painful to hear, especially when Hudson stiffens against me. "I'm sorry," he says, voice aching. "We had to bring it down."

"There were too many of them," Jaxon adds. "They were everywhere. There was no other way."

Macy nods, but she still looks like she's been punched in the stomach. Not that I blame her. Her father's been kidnapped, maybe killed, and now the only home she's ever known is gone. I know what that feels like, and I wouldn't wish it on anyone, let alone my sweet, kind, amazing cousin.

"It's going to be okay," Eden tells her as she rubs a comforting hand up and down Macy's back.

"We'll find a way to fix it," I agree, pulling away from Hudson so I can go to Macy and hug her. "I don't know how, but we will."

"*After* we free my brother," Dawud interjects, their voice like steel.

"You aren't the only one with family there, you know," Macy shoots back. "Cyrus has my father. Believe me, no one wants to get to the Vampire Court and free them more than we do."

"But we can't just go storming in there," Byron says. "Or he'll kill every single one of them—starting with the people we care about most."

Just the thought of losing Uncle Finn and Gwen and everyone else sends ice skating down my spine. "To be honest, I don't get why every parent with a kid at Katmere isn't storming the Vampire Court," I say with a shake of my head. "Why aren't they demanding that Cyrus release their kids?"

"The dragons can't," Flint says grimly. "I talked to my dad after I left the infirmary, and he said things are a mess at Court. We lost a lot of dragons in the fight on the island, and the ones who are left are questioning my mother's leadership because she—" He breaks off, throat working.

"Because she gave up her dragon to save me," Jaxon finishes flatly.

Flint doesn't answer. In fact, he doesn't even look Jaxon's way as tension—taut, slippery, dangerous—simmers in the air between them.

"The wolves won't go against him," Dawud contributes. "They have his word that he won't hurt any of their children."

"So why do they think he kidnapped them?" Mekhi asks, his tone rife with skepticism. "I mean, holding people against their will is pretty much the defining characteristic of someone with bad intentions."

"I don't disagree," Dawud answers with a shrug. "But they just keep drinking the Kool-Aid. They can't see the truth—or maybe they won't let themselves. Either way, there's no convincing them that he's anything other than what he tells them he is."

"Which is what exactly?" Jaxon asks, his voice so distant, it's like he's talking about some stranger and not his father.

"You mean, besides a monster?" Hudson asks archly.

"He's the king who will save them from obscurity, of course. The one who will bring them into the light and make it so they don't have to hide who they are anymore." Dawud shakes their head. "I mean, anyone with a brain knows it's bullshit. But they're eating it up like it's ice cream with a cherry on top. There's no way to convince them otherwise."

"And dying is what? An unfortunate side effect?" Hudson's voice drips sarcasm, but there's something in his eyes—a mixture of regret and resolve—that has me reaching for the blue string deep inside me.

I run a hand down our mating bond, pouring all the love and comfort I can into my touch. I know he doesn't want anyone else to know just how tormented he is over what happened with the wolves earlier, and this is the only way I can think of to offer support at the moment.

If it works.

Moments later, I have the satisfaction of watching my mate's eyes go wide. His gaze meets mine across the room, and the sudden warmth there makes me smile. As does the relief ripping through him, burning away the pain and the regret. At least for now.

"Especially then," Liam answers quietly. "There's nothing quite like dying for something you believe in."

The horror of his answer echoes through the room, along with the knowledge that he's right. And so is Dawud. How many times have we been willing to die to stop Cyrus over the last several months? How many times have we almost sacrificed everything because we know that stopping him is the right thing—the only thing—to do?

But what if we were on the other side? What if we believed in him as fiercely as we despise him and everything he stands for? What if we really thought that he was doing the right thing, and anyone who opposed him was trying to hurt us, our children, and the world we were working so hard to build?

The thought makes me shudder—partly because it's so awful to think of so many wolves and vampires buying into Cyrus's horrible agenda and partly because I'm really beginning to understand what we're up against. And it is overwhelming.

"What do we do?" I whisper, the horror of my realization evident in my voice.

"First step?" Rafael asks from where he's leaning against the wall, knee bent and face impassive. "I say we figure out exactly where we are and whether or not we're safe here."

"Oh, that's easy," Macy tells him. "We're at the Witch Court. And of *course* we're safe—"

She breaks off as the door crashes open and what looks to be half of what must be the Witch Guard, given their uniforms, pours into the room, wands raised and ready to fire.

22

"**Y**ou need to leave," the witch leading the guard says. She is tall and menacing and, judging from the insignia on her purple uniform robes, also one of the top members of this army. "Now."

"Leave?" Macy asks, mystified. "But we just got here, Valentina."

"And now you can go somewhere else." Valentina's eyes are icy as she waves her wand between Hudson, Jaxon, and me. "The Witch Guard has no room for the likes of you here."

"The likes of us?" My cousin is beginning to sound like a pissed-off parrot, fury turning her voice more than a little squawky as she repeats Valentina's words back to her. "I'm a witch, and these are my friends. We're here for sanctuary."

As she speaks, she moves between Valentina's wand and Jaxon, Hudson, and me. I don't like Macy using herself as a shield for us, and it's obvious the guys don't, either, but when we step to move out from behind her, she shoots us a warning look that has all of us freezing in place.

Who knew Macy could be so intimidating when she put her mind to it? There's a part of me that's very impressed—or will be, once these witches put down their damn wands.

"You'll find no sanctuary here—for you or your friends," Valentina snarls.

"Yeah, well, the *Witch Guard* doesn't get to make that decision. Only a king and queen can deny sanctuary," Macy shoots back.

"That's what I'm trying to tell you." Valentina twists her thin lips into a smirk. "They already have."

Jaxon stiffens at that revelation, but a glance at Hudson shows me that he isn't the least bit surprised. And truth be told, neither am I. If what Dawud has been telling us is true, it's almost impossible to know who stands with Cyrus and who doesn't. If the Witch Court has fallen to him, then we're lucky that all they're doing is denying us sanctuary and ordering us to leave.

It could be so much worse.

Macy apparently hasn't gotten that memo, though, because she steps forward until she is nose to nose with Valentina. "I don't believe you."

Valentina lifts a brow, but she doesn't back down an inch as she answers. "I don't care if you believe me or not, little girl. All I care about is that you and your friends leave the Witch Court. *Now*."

"Or what?" Macy demands, a question that has me wincing, because now is definitely not the time to issue ultimatums or call bluffs.

Not when the guard is this annoyed. And definitely not when, behind the guard leader, her troops are growing restless. I mean, we're doing the same over here, anxiety and exhaustion combining to make us all a little volatile. Of course, we aren't the ones wielding deadly weapons. I mean, unless you count six pairs of fangs and two fire- and ice-breathing dragons...which they probably are.

"Do you really want to find out?" Valentina queries.

"Not even a little bit," Macy replies as she reaches into her fanny pack for her wand. "But I guess I'm going to have to, because one way or another, I will speak to the king and queen."

And there it is, the ultimatum I've been dreading. Hudson and Jaxon obviously recognize it, too, considering they're shifting beside me, their hands clenching and eyes narrowing as they focus on their targets. Which makes me reach deep inside myself and grab hold of my platinum string. I don't know why Macy is so adamant about seeing the king and queen, but I'm willing to go along with it. Even if it means fighting the entire Witch Guard.

I pull my platinum string and shift to my gargoyle form in the space between one breath and the next. At the same time, Jaxon lets loose with a tremor that shakes the whole room.

This time it's Valentina's eyes that narrow at the threat. Behind her, wands sweep through the air, and we brace ourselves for an incoming attack. But just as the wands begin to lower, a woman in elaborate purple robes appears in the doorway.

"Enough!" she snaps, and immediately the guard stands down. "I will not condone violence against a fellow witch." Her strange violet eyes cut from the guards to Macy as she continues. "A child claiming sanctuary at that."

"My orders were clear—"

"Yes, well, I'm changing your orders. Bring them to the main hall. If my sister is choosing to deny this child sanctuary, she owes her—and the entire Court—an explanation. So let's get to it."

The queen's sister whirls around, disappearing from the doorway as quickly as she appeared.

For a second, nobody moves. But then wands are lowered and Valentina steps grudgingly back from Macy, who gives her a surprisingly sunny smile in response. The smile obviously gets on Valentina's last nerve, because this time she's the one who gets in Macy's face. "If one of you so much as *looks* at the king or queen the wrong way, I will cut out your organs and use them in the most heinous spell I can find."

As far as threats go, it's a pretty good one—especially because none of us wants our organs cut out but also because she says it with a *lot* of sincerity. And since I have no desire to set her or her torture-happy wand off, I change back to my human form. Considering how on edge everyone at the Witch Court is right now, it seems best to appear as nonthreatening as possible.

I want to tell Hudson to do the same thing, but who am I kidding? Even standing there in a pair of worn jeans and a black button-up shirt, he radiates strength, confidence, power. Everything that Cyrus is afraid of…and everything that he covets.

"Follow me," Valentina orders. "And don't even think about stepping one foot toward anything but the main hall."

Then she turns on her heel and walks out of the room at a fast, steady clip. When we don't immediately fall into line and follow her, the Witch Guard starts rounding us up, herding us inexorably toward the door.

"I'm sorry," Macy whispers as we pour into a long, wide hallway. "I didn't know where else to go, and I really thought we would be safe here."

"Just because Valentina woke up on the wrong side of the cauldron doesn't mean we're not safe," I tell her as I wrap an arm around her shoulder for a quick hug. "What's the worst thing they could do to us?"

"Were you not listening?" Dawud asks, eyes wide in an obvious *duh* expression. "Rip out our hearts and use them in a love spell."

"She's all bark," Macy says.

"Yeah," Mekhi agrees with a snort. "If by *all bark*, you mean even more bite. That woman is more than capable of feeding us to her favorite familiar and then setting that familiar on fire just to make a point."

"And what point would that be exactly?" Rafael asks with a lift of his brow.

"That you're not as special as you think you are," Valentina snaps over her shoulder. "And my favorite familiar is an octopus. So good luck with that."

She doesn't say another word as we continue down the hallway—and neither do the rest of us. But there's not a lot to say about that.

Except, *Octopus?* Eden mouths.

Macy gives a little shrug. "Better than an emu."

"Do you actually know someone who has an emu as a familiar?" Jaxon asks, his disbelief obvious.

"I know someone who has a *vampire* as a familiar," Macy shoots back.

"And we know emus are smarter than that," Flint jokes.

It's pretty obvious he's trying to get a rise out of Jaxon. It doesn't work, of course, but the rest of the Order squawks their objections while Hudson just laughs.

For the first time since we got back to Katmere from the island, I feel like I can breathe. Like maybe, just maybe, the world won't come crashing down on us this very second. Ten seconds from now is a different story, of course, but for now, I'll take this very, very brief reprieve and the chance to laugh with my friends before everything goes to hell yet again.

Maybe because I'm not completely terrified at this exact moment, I take the chance to look around for the first time. And what my initial glimpse shows me is that the Witch Court is absolutely nothing like the Dragon or Gargoyle Courts—which are the only other Courts I've been to.

Whereas the Dragon Court is all sleek, Manhattan sophistication, and the Gargoyle Court seems to have gotten stuck back in Medieval times, the Witch Court is stately elegance with an emphasis on elaborate art and even more elaborate architecture. The hallway is lined with carved walls highlighting the elements, as well as the sun, moon, and stars. In between the carvings are giant, fanciful picture frames made of real gold. Inside are paintings of sky-blue-clad witches forming magic circles and landscapes featuring wooded scenes. And there are candles everywhere. Red, purple, black, white, gold, they fill the sconces carved into the walls every few feet.

Half of them are lit and half of them aren't, I realize at the same time I notice two witches—one on either side—walking the hallway several yards in front of us. Each is holding a long, ceremonial-looking lighter, which they use to light the candles.

"They don't use magic?" I whisper to Macy, who shakes her head adamantly.

"We're taught from an early age that magic shouldn't be squandered. It comes at a cost—to us, to the natural world, to the very universe around us—so to use it for something as mundane as lighting non-ceremonial candles just isn't done. Especially since they have to be lit every day at this time. The queen insists, despite the fact that we have actual lights that work perfectly well."

She starts to say something else but stops abruptly as we approach two giant French doors. Like so much of this castle, they are made of real gold engraved with garlands of flowers. But each of these flowers is inlaid with different-colored semiprecious and precious stones—rubies, emeralds, sapphires, lapis, quartz, turquoise, and a bunch more that I recognize but can't name.

It doesn't take a genius to figure out that we're about to enter the hall where the king and queen receive guests. Even if the ridiculously expensive doors didn't all but scream that to the world, the fact that Macy is standing at attention for pretty much the first time ever would have tipped me off. Every member of the Witch Guard is doing the same thing—especially Valentina.

"Treat them with the respect they are due," she warns as she straightens her cape. "Or I will make you wish you had never been born."

Then, before we can even process her warning, she steps forward, and the big, heavy gold doors begin to swing open. "Welcome," she says through gritted teeth, "to the Great Hall of the Witch Court."

23

All the Show, None of the Tell

Several seconds pass before the doors swing open completely, and I can't help but get a good look at the Great Hall as we wait. And can I just say, "Great Hall" is the perfect name for this place? "Throne Room" also works, as does "Ostentatious Display of Wealth."

It seems strange, because based on what I know of Macy and Uncle Finn, I never would have expected the Witch Court to look like this. The Vampire Court? Hell yes. Absolutely. But the witches I know at Katmere are more down-to-earth. Less consumed by flaunting their power and their money.

Then again, it is Court. Based on what I know of old-time kings and queens, flaunting your power is pretty much the whole point of holding court.

Still, as we walk into the Great Hall, I realize I only *thought* the hallway was elaborate. It's actually quite plain when compared to this room with its massive frescoes on the ceiling, gigantic chandeliers, and floor-to-ceiling paintings that cover every part of the walls that aren't a giant, silk-bedecked window.

The floor itself is made of gold-veined marble to match all the gold around the room, and even the furniture is extravagant and oversize. Especially the thrones, which are made of pure gold inlaid with gemstones the size of my fist and have purple satin cushions on the seats and backs—my guess is they are a concession to the fact that solid gold is probably not that fun to sit on.

At the same time, anyone who wants a solid-gold throne probably doesn't care if it's hard to sit on as long as it looks powerful and important.

I'm a little surprised that the king and queen aren't actually sitting on the thrones. I didn't get to know them when they came to Katmere, but they totally seem the type to lord it over an entire room of their subjects. But this space is filled with people laughing, talking, eating from the fancy buffet laid out against the entire side wall, and nobody is being particularly obsequious.

At least not until the door closes behind us, and the hollow clap of the locks snicking back into place echoes through the room. It seems like everyone in the hall turns as one to stare at us, even before the guard surrounds us and forces us to accompany them to the front of the room as they march in a *very* complicated formation.

A man in a fancy military jacket over dark slacks steps forward and announces to the room, "King Linden Choi and Queen Imogen Choi."

Only when we are all in front of the thrones do the king and queen appear, walking out of the crowd with their dark-purple velvet robes swirling around them. The king is wearing his dark hair buzzcut short, his doublet a little tighter than the last time I saw him at Katmere, the dark vest stretching taut beneath the violet cape. The queen towers over her mate, her strawberry-blond hair flowing in waves above her diamond-studded lavender dress that shimmers with her every movement.

Each of them is also wearing a crown, and as they settle themselves on their thrones—the king on the left, queen on the right—the entire guard drops down into bows so low that they're practically kissing the floor.

What surprises me even more, though, is that my friends do the same thing. Macy, Eden, Dawud, Jaxon, Hudson, and the members of the Order all bow down in front of the witch king and queen. Seconds later, the rest of the room follows suit, so that the only person who is currently standing straight up is...me.

I move to bow down, too, but Jaxon and Hudson reach out at the same moment, each of them latching on to one of my elbows to urge me to remain upright. That's when it hits me. Of course they are bowing. Each of them is a prince in his own right but still lower station than the king or queen. No wonder Hudson and Jaxon seem so adamant that I don't bow. I squeeze my fist, and the ring on my finger, and remind myself I am a queen as well.

The Crown tattoo on my hand itches a little at the reminder, and I shift uncomfortably.

Still, I remain standing. Better to meet the witch king and queen as equals, I suppose, than to meet them as some underling begging for I don't know what. Help? Information? Sanctuary, as Macy claimed earlier?

They survey my lack of supplication in front of them, eyes half closed and lips twisted into annoyed scowls. I don't know if they're pissed that I refuse to bow or if they're pissed that the whole group of us had the nerve to come here at all. Either way, I guess it doesn't really matter. Not when the end result is the witch king and queen looking like they've spent the last hour sucking on a bunch of really sour lemons.

"You may rise." The queen's voice, light and melodic, rings through the Great Hall, and finally the bowing ends.

She waits until everyone in the room has done what she says before narrowing her focus on Macy, who shifts uncomfortably under the scrutiny even as she holds her queen's gaze.

"Why did you come here?" the queen asks, though it sounds more like an accusation than a question.

"I didn't know where else to go," Macy answers, and her voice never wavers. She is shaking like a leaf, though, and I want nothing more than to step forward and offer her my support. But something tells me that doing so would be the wrong move this time, so I stand my ground and try not to glare daggers at the queen. "Katmere is—"

"We know exactly what happened at Katmere," the queen snaps. "Just as we know that the lot of you are responsible for it."

Macy swallows hard. "We had no choice but to destroy the school. Cyrus's allies—"

"I'm not talking about that ridiculous temper tantrum the vampire princes just threw," the queen snaps. "I'm speaking of the taking of our children. That never would have happened if—"

"If what?" Flint demands with a growl. "If we had let Cyrus murder us?"

"More like if we had just rolled over and let him own us," Hudson interjects, "the way the Witch Court is letting him own them now."

The king's eyes narrow to slits at Hudson's accusation. "Do you really think insulting us is the way to gain our help?"

"No," Hudson answers with a negligent shrug. "But you've already decided that you won't help us. All the rest of this is just for show."

"There is nothing we can do for you here." The queen's words slice through the already tense air. "Valentina will escort you out."

"You mean there's nothing you *will* do for us," Macy counters. "I just don't understand why, when we are pleading for sanctuary."

"You aren't pleading for anything," the king snaps. "You are demanding, and that is not your place."

"I'm sorry." Macy lowers her head in obvious supplication. "That's not our intention at all—"

"It is precisely your intention," the king tells her. "But your arrogance—and the arrogance of your friends—is not why we are denying your request."

"We have already done all we can for you," the queen says. "We should have notified Cyrus the moment you tripped our alarms by portaling in here with your non-witch friends."

"Cyrus?" I ask, so incredulous by her defense that the word flies out of my mouth before I register that I'm going to say it. "You're working with Cyrus now?"

"We are not working with him!" The king's voice rings throughout the Great Hall as his gaze finds Hudson's. "But you know, better than most, what he has done."

"You're going to have to be a little more specific," my mate drawls, flicking an imaginary speck off his shoulder. "Of late, my father has been a very bad boy."

"That's one way to put it," Flint mutters under his breath.

"Do you think you're the only ones worried about what happened at Katmere?" The king bites off each syllable like it tastes bad. "Do you think you're the only ones frantic about the people he has taken? He has more than a hundred witch children from our Court and our most powerful covens. We must keep them safe until we can negotiate for their return."

"And you think the way to keep them safe is to kick us out?" Macy asks, eyes wide and voice small.

"We cannot harbor you, nor can we provide any aid. As long as we do not do those two things, the vampire king assures me our children will be safe." The queen swallows. "My daughter will be safe."

And then I remember—the king and queen's daughter was a freshman at Katmere this past year. Emma, I think her name is. Macy pointed her out in the halls once, but I've never actually met her.

Part of me understands why they're being so unhelpful now. Of course, there's another, bigger part of me that thinks they're fools. They should know by now that trusting Cyrus—about anything—is a huge mistake. If he wants to hurt Emma, he'll hurt her, and absolutely nothing will change his mind about doing so.

Apparently, I'm not the only one who thinks like that, because Hudson gives an incredulous—and insulting—laugh. "You can't really believe that," he snaps when they turn to look at him. "Your children aren't safe now. I know my father, and he's never kept an agreement in his life. He wouldn't even know how."

Macy lifts her chin and says, "He's hurting them. He's hurting the kids."

The queen leans forward. "How would you know this?"

"Marise told us she overheard the wolves talking about needing the kids for their young magic, not for hostages." Macy doesn't mention Marise ended up betraying us, which makes me wonder if Macy doubts what she told us.

At this, the king and queen exchange a long glance, and I almost think they might give in, might see that they can't trust Cyrus and need our help. But then the king turns back to us and shakes his head. "While it's true young magic is easier to steal, to consume, Cyrus has assured us that no harm will come to our children, and we see no reason to doubt him."

"See no reason?" Hudson rolls his eyes. "Have you not been paying attention? He *kidnapped your kids*. What in that action implies honesty?"

"And who is this Marise?" the queen asks, ignoring Hudson's comment, one haughty brow raised so high, it nearly reaches her hairline. "How do we even know *she* can be trusted?"

Macy starts to explain but barely gets out the first words, "She was our—" before the king slams his fist down on the edge of the arm of his throne.

"Enough! We will not listen to your lies anymore. You will leave this place immediately or face the consequences." His gaze narrows on Hudson and Jaxon. "And don't think we can't stop one of your tantrums from tearing down our Court."

Hudson snorts. "Yeah, I'd like to see you try."

"In kicking us out," Jaxon adds, "all you're doing is abandoning the one group of people who might actually be able to help save your daughter."

This time, it's the queen whose laugh is insulting. "You really think you have a chance against Cyrus and the coalition he's assembled? The eleven of you against his army of thousands?"

"If Cyrus himself didn't consider us a threat, then why is he going to such lengths to hunt us down, to stop anyone from helping us?"

Hudson makes a very good point. Why *is* Cyrus going to such extreme lengths for the eleven of us? For me?

I glance down at the Crown on the palm of my hand and think I might know the answer.

24

It's Not a Deal if You Don't Want It

"**I** have the Crown," I announce, and the room stills as I hold my right hand up to show the king and queen the tattoo on the palm of my hand. They both rear back, staring at me with a look of both horror and fear, then lean as far away from my hand as they can while remaining on their thrones. Honestly, their reaction would be comical if I could see the humor in anything right now.

The king seems to catch himself, though, and sits taller, then reaches out and pats the queen's hand. "Do not worry, my dear. The Crown is worthless without the Gargoyle Army."

Now it's my turn to rear back like I've been slapped. My grandfather hadn't gotten around to telling me what the Crown was exactly *or* how to use it that day in the Gargoyle Court, but he definitely didn't mention it was worthless without the Army.

Thanks, Gramps.

Regardless, I can't help but wonder what the Crown does that the witch king and queen would be so afraid of it. I mean, we all already guessed it must be powerful, given the vampire king himself came to fight on the island to stop us from getting it. I'd begun to worry that it was me, that I wasn't strong enough to wield it or worthy enough to bear it, and that's why I sensed no change since the gargoyle king transferred the tattoo to me.

I sigh. I really need to stop underestimating myself. Beginning now.

With a blink, I flip my hand over. The ornate ring my grandfather gave me is now facing the king and queen, its giant emerald apparent for everyone to see. "Then I guess it's a good thing I have that army, eh?"

I hold my breath, waiting for their reaction. And it comes swiftly as everyone in the Great Hall gasps, even Macy.

I haven't had a chance to tell Hudson, or anyone, about my trip to the Gargoyle Court yet, let alone the ring or the Gargoyle Army or that I'm actually related to the Unkillable Beast. But I'll have to catch them up later. This feels like our only chance to convince the witch king and queen to help. It's clear they fear what the Crown can do—with the Army, of course—and that's all the confirmation I need that this is the right move.

Hudson shuffles beside me, and I give him a quick look and mouth, *Later*, before turning back to the royals before me. We are going to need the help of the Witch Court, whether they want to give it or not, and that means convincing them I have the power to wield the Crown—whatever that means and whatever it can do.

"It can't be," the queen whispers. "The Gargoyle Army disappeared more than a thousand years ago."

"Who gave you that ring, young lady?" the king demands, his subjects now crowding around us for a look at what has everyone freaking out. "You stole it," he declares.

I bristle. "I most certainly did not steal this ring. My grandfather gave it to me." I pause, noticing for the first time the eerie quiet in the hall as everyone hangs on my next words. And I decide two can play to an audience as I narrow my eyes and state, "You know, the gargoyle king?"

Pandemonium breaks out as everyone whisper-shouts to one another. "The gargoyle king is alive?" "The Army is alive?" "She's in charge of everything?" And my personal favorite, "This girl is supposed to lead an army against Cyrus?"

The witch king glances over the crowd of people, listening to them question their future, *my* future, then assesses me. "You think you can lead this army against Cyrus? Get our children back?"

No. Absolutely not. But if that's what it's going to take, I'm damn sure going to try.

I take a deep breath and say, "Of course." I shoot a quick glance at Hudson, who nods, urging me to go on. "But I'll need your help."

The queen shakes her head. "The rules have not changed. No matter whose ring you wear. We cannot help you as long as the vampire king has our children held hostage."

And with that, my shoulders sag, my hand with the ring falling to my side.

But Hudson isn't so easily defeated. "So you're saying if we can rescue your kids from Cyrus's clutches, the Witch Court will agree to help us defeat Cyrus?"

"Now, I didn't—" the king starts to say, but his wife interrupts him.

"Yes." And her tone is final. "If our kids are safe, I pledge the Witch Court to your cause."

Before she changes her mind, I quickly reply, "Deal." And the hundreds of candles lining the walls of the Great Hall burn a brilliant blue for several seconds, the whole hue of the room shifting to blue tones, before the color flickers out and the candles' flames return to their normal orange-yellow.

"A deal has been struck," the queen states. "Now leave."

Guards suddenly swarm us from every angle and usher us out the door of the Great Hall, shoving us into a large anteroom to the left of the main doors. As far as dismissals go, I guess this one could have been worse. I mean, at least we're all still standing and even a little hopeful the Witch Court might end up helping us in a war against Cyrus.

That thought lasts until Valentina waves a hand, and Macy and the rest of my friends vanish into thin air.

25

No GPS for the Not-So-Wicked

"**W**hat did you do?" I demand as horrible thoughts crowd my brain. "Where are they? What did you do to my friends?"

"I forgot gargoyles are immune to magic." She sighs heavily, then waves a hand toward a guard. "Do something with her, will you, please?"

"With pleasure." The guard's eyes gleam with dislike as he makes a grab for me.

I consider avoiding him, consider reaching for the platinum string deep inside me so I can fight him off, but in the end, I don't do anything. I don't want to be here without my friends any more than they want me here. Besides, with any luck, he'll take me to wherever they are, and we can work out what to do next. And where to go.

We need to find a way to rescue the kids, but we need a really good plan before we try to attack Cyrus in his own Court. Otherwise, we'll end up trapped with everyone else...or worse.

Which is why I don't fight the guard when he grabs on to my arm or when he starts marching me out the door in front of him. Valentina laughs a little at my lack of fight, but I ignore her. The last thing I want is for her to decide to throw me in a dungeon somewhere just for kicks.

In the end, she allows the guard to march me back through the long hallway with the wall carvings and the paintings, then down a flight of stairs. We don't stop walking until we get to the side doors out of the Witch Court, which swing open with a wave of Valentina's wand.

"Good luck out there," she tells me, and for the first time, she doesn't sound mean or sarcastic. In fact, I can't help but think she sounds sincere—even as she ushers me straight through the solid-gold doors, through the black candle–lined courtyard, and out the wrought-iron gate onto the rough cobblestone street beyond.

Except I'm not really on a street, I realize as I look around. Dusk is setting in, so it's harder to see than it might be during the day, but it's still light enough that I can get a basic idea of where I am.

I'm obviously in an urban area, because wherever I am looks a lot like some kind of city square, and the street signs aren't in English. Plus it was morning when we left Katmere, so obviously I'm in a foreign country at least partway around the world.

I pull my phone out of my backpack and take a quick video of the area, turning 360 degrees as I do. Then I send it to my friends on our group chat along with a text that reads:

Me: Where am I?

And another one that reads:

Me: Where are you?

I stay put, wanting to be in the same spot where I took the video if they come looking for me. As I wait, I glance around, trying to get a better idea of what city—or at least what country—I'm in. I start by taking a photo of the closest sign and then blowing it up until I can actually read the words.

La Piazza Castello.

Huh. So the Witch Court is in Italy. It's not what I expected, which honestly makes me feel kind of silly. I mean, how could I have roomed with Macy for this many months and not have asked her where the Witch Court is? And how could she have never mentioned it?

I shoot off another text to my friends, letting them know where I am, then take stock of the area. "Piazza" means "plaza" or "square" in Italian, if I'm not mistaken, and looking around at this place, I understand how it got its name. The whole area is a rectangle, with dead-end stone streets forming a kind of border around a large, rectangular patch of grass.

The streets are lined with beautiful white buildings with a distinct Italian flair, and the number of street signs implies that it can be a very busy area. At this time of night, though, it's completely empty. Like, so empty that to the best of my knowledge, I am the only person in the entire piazza—which feels eerie as fuck, to be honest.

Just as quickly as I think to myself that I do not want to be on this street alone, Hudson fades to directly in front of me, pulling me into his arms.

"Hey there," he says, running his hands along my arms. "You okay?"

I offer up a half smile. "Sorry about that. Valentina forgot magic doesn't work on gargoyles." I glance over his shoulder at the still-empty piazza. "Where is everyone?"

"We split up. I got here first."

He shrugs like this is obvious. And I suppose it is, because he always finds me.

"That was some bomb you dropped in there." He's grinning now as he lets me go. "Loved every minute of it. Especially when the witch queen almost fell off her throne trying to get away from the Crown."

I shake my head and chuckle. "Yeah, that was odd. Of course, it doesn't help me figure out what the Crown actually *does*."

"True. But we know it terrifies powerful creatures. And likely is why Cyrus is hunting you down. He wants the Crown."

I shiver, and he pulls me into his arms again. It's as natural as breathing to snake my arms around his waist, rest my head on his chest, let the even beats of his heart sync with mine. I don't know how long we stand like this, but I'm grateful that Hudson isn't asking questions, even though I know he must have a dozen. Or a million. The biggest likely being how we've been together almost every waking—and sleeping—minute and yet I managed to discover not only that the gargoyle king is my grandfather, of some generation, and that the Gargoyle Army is alive, but I've also managed to get the ring that means I'm now leading them.

But he doesn't ask anything, just holds me, listening to me breathe and reassuring me with his warmth that no matter what, I'm not alone.

Eventually, I lean back to look up at him, and he just raises one brow and says, "So the Unkillable Beast is the gargoyle king, eh?"

Of course Hudson would figure it out. I nod.

"And you're a direct descendant, somewhere down the line." This last is a statement, not a question.

Again, I nod.

"And he gave you the ring to lead your people."

This time when I nod, I can't help holding my breath, waiting for his reaction.

He smiles down at me, pushing a few strands of hair behind my ear, before saying, "Well, that was smart. He's not in any condition to lead anyone to the bathroom, much less to war."

And I can't help it. I crack up laughing.

"What's so funny?" Jaxon asks as the Order and the rest of my friends skid to a stop around us.

They must have finally caught up while I was anxiously focused on my mate's response to learning I was now in charge of a mythical army. But just because

I told Hudson doesn't mean I want to discuss it with the rest of the group yet.

Instead, I try to deflect any questions by teasing Hudson. "Oh, I just discovered the promise Hudson made me with my promise ring is to paint my toenails every night for the rest of our lives."

Everyone laughs as Hudson plays along and rolls his eyes with a grin. "You wish."

"We all do, my friend." Mekhi slaps him on the shoulder. "I'd pay good money to see that. And post it. Everywhere."

"Hey, I'm comfortable with my masculinity. I'm happy to paint anyone's toenails, including my own." He turns to Flint. "Well, except your talons." Turns to Jaxon. "And your toes." Turns to the entire Order. "Okay, none of yours, except maybe Byron's. He looks like he puts a fair bit of time into cuticle care."

And with that, everyone busts out laughing, and I love this guy so much, my heart feels near to bursting. I know what he's doing, and it means the world to me. He knows everyone has questions, but he's giving me a chance to tell them what's going on, what happened with the gargoyle king, in my own time. Which is not now.

Because right now, a very familiar witch is heading straight for us.

26

A Long Game of
Hide-and-Weep

"Viola." Macy's voice trembles as we turn as one to find the witch in the gorgeous purple robes who was responsible for us getting our so-called audience in front of the queen. "What are you doing out here?"

"I felt all the commotion and decided to come investigate. Imagine my surprise and consternation when I realized my dear sister had set a child down in the middle of La Piazza Castello without an ounce of light or direction." She waves a hand, and the entire square is illuminated by a bright, otherworldly light.

"Some of us were doing just fine in the dark," Liam grinds out, clearly done with all witches in general.

Macy glances at him nervously before rushing in. "Well, I'm not a fan of the shadows, so thank you, Viola."

"It was no trouble at all," Viola answers. "But there are a few witches especially good at dispelling shadows, my dear, and you happen to be one of them."

"What does that mean?" I demand at the same time Macy asks, "I am?"

Viola tilts her head to the side as she studies Macy. She looks contemplative, like she's trying to decide what or how much to say. But that doesn't make sense, considering she's the one who came to us. Shouldn't she already know what she wants to say?

The others must be as anxious for her to speak as I am, because none of them says a word until, finally, Viola speaks. "I only know of one witch who can send even the fiercest shadowdweller running in fear, and I think you might need her before your journey is over."

"Why is that?" Byron asks. "And how do we find her?"

"She's not lost—you don't have to find her. She's at the Vampire Court. As for who she is..." She turns to Macy. "I thought you would have figured that out by now."

"What do you mean?" Macy asks, confused. "I don't know anyone who deals in shadow magic."

"Of course you do, darling. Your mother is a wiz at it."

Her words hang in the air like a lit firework in the moments before it explodes—powerful, incendiary, irrevocable.

"My mother?" Macy whispers as color drains from her cheeks. "My mother is gone. She's been gone for years. No one knows where she is."

"That's not precisely true." Viola sighs. "I didn't want to be the one to have to tell you this, but...she's in the same place she's been for eight years. At the Vampire Court, serving Cyrus."

If possible, Macy loses even more color. "That's not true." Her voice is flat, her eyes frantic. "My mother wouldn't do that. She *couldn't* do that. Not Cyrus. My mom may have left us, she may have disappeared off the face of the earth, but she and my father have always despised Cyrus. She would never work for him."

Viola gives a little shrug in an *I guess we'll see who's right* kind of way. "Remember, my child. In Cyrus's world, things are very rarely what he says they are. And never what they appear to be."

"You're defending him?" Macy's voice cracks with indignation.

"I would never defend that animal," Viola snaps, and this time there is real anger on her face. "And make no mistake about it—if he touches one hair on our children's heads, he will suffer in a way that makes the gates to Hell look like a child's playground."

"Then who—"

"I'm defending your mother. It's a dangerous world out there, and sometimes the most unsavory of alliances must be made if one has any hope of survival. And sometimes, you have to do things like that regardless of choice."

"You always have a choice," Dawud says, shoving their fists deep into the pockets of their jeans.

"Maybe." Viola looks down her long, slender nose at the werewolf. "But sometimes there are no good choices—only the choice that won't get you or the people you care about dead. Anyone who thinks otherwise is a child."

Macy goes quiet after that—not quiet like she's run out of things to say, but quiet like she doesn't know *what* to say. Or what to feel. It's going to take more than five minutes for her to absorb the news that her mother is alive and living in the Vampire Court, let alone everything else we've been talking about.

A thought occurs to me. It was clear in the Witch Court that the king and queen knew exactly what the Crown could do. "Viola, can I ask you a question?"

The older witch pierces me with her violet eyes, one eyebrow raised. "You can ask, certainly, although I'm not sure I can guarantee an answer."

"Fair enough." I nod, then take a deep breath, wrap my shaking hands around my waist. I'm not sure why I'm so afraid to ask, but I finally lift my chin. "Do you know what the Crown does? Why the king and queen—and Cyrus—are so afraid of it?"

Viola's eyes go wide, as though she thought I would ask any question but that one. "No one told you when they gave it to you?"

I shake my head.

"Well, that's...unusual." She pauses, seeming to weigh whether to tell me or not, but then she must decide I need to know because she leans forward like she's sharing a secret. "Gargoyles were the law and order of the paranormal world for a thousand years. The Gargoyle Army would surround those who committed egregious crimes against another—and the gargoyle king would lay the Crown on their chest and decide their punishment."

And now it's my turn to be surprised someone said the exact opposite thing I was expecting. "Well, that doesn't seem a helpful power in a war." I can't help the bitterness and disappointment from coloring my words. "I thought the Crown was supposed to give the wearer infinite power. Isn't that why Cyrus wants it?"

But Viola makes a *tsk*ing sound. "You don't understand, child. The person who wields the Crown can take away a paranormal's powers, some or all of them if they choose. For a day. A week. Forever. Whatever befits the crime the Gargoyle Army has found them guilty of. With just a touch of your hand. Do you not think the ability to render any enemy powerless to be 'infinite power'?"

"Holy hell," Flint says, then whistles long and hard. And takes two steps away from me. Everyone does, actually. Except Hudson.

My stomach churns at the idea of removing anyone's powers. I whisper on a ragged breath, "I know what it's like to not have my gargoyle, from my time in prison, and I wouldn't wish that on anyone. I don—" My voice breaks, and I have to try again. "I don't want this Crown. How do I get rid of it?"

But Viola just stares at me, and something like admiration slowly sharpens her gaze. Her eyes flick to my feet and back up again before she says, "I imagine a lot of people underestimate you, don't they, Grace? That's good. They'll never see you coming."

Okay, well, I guess that's a compliment? "I don't need the Crown for that. Do you know how I can get rid of it?"

"The only way to pass the Crown is to abdicate the throne to another gargoyle in the royal line," she says, and each word feels like the swing of a hammer against my battered soul. I like to think I understand what Hudson goes through, the choices he has to make about others' fates and how he agonizes over making the wrong ones, but I don't think I truly understood until this moment. Until I literally held the power in the palm of my hand to strip someone of their basic right to *be* who they were meant to be. To continue their lives as they choose. Could I give that burden to someone else to carry so easily?

But I haven't even used this power yet, and I want it gone, this tattoo off my hand now. I'm fighting the urge to claw at my palm when Hudson reaches down and takes my hand in his, pulls me against him. "It's going to be okay," he whispers in my hair, and I try to believe him.

Viola continues. "Are you saying, if you had the chance to strip Cyrus of his powers for the crimes he's committed, you wouldn't do it?"

I shake my head. Because no, I wouldn't. Or at least, I don't think I would. "I would have to believe, without a shadow of a doubt, that he would never stop harming others, killing others, but even then, I think it would be very hard to do."

"And this is why you hold the Crown, Grace. A decision such as this should never be easy. But sometimes, there is no other way."

Thinking of what Cyrus is capable of, it's hard not to believe her, not to realize I have no choice but to see this through for now rather than give up what may be our only chance at stopping him before he hurts more people. I'm just about to agree with her when her mouth turns down as she admits, "Of course, the question is moot because, as the king said, the Crown does not work without the Gargoyle Army. Something Cyrus must think he's found a way around, if what you say about him wanting the Crown is true."

"So what do we do now?" Byron queries.

He's asking the rest of us—and specifically Jaxon—but Viola is the one who answers. "Now?" She lifts a brow. "Now you get as far from the Witch Court as you possibly can."

"I definitely think that's our plan," Macy agrees. "But we don't know where to go if we can't stay—"

"Why?" Hudson's voice burns with urgency. "What haven't we figured out?"

Viola studies him, her eyes searching his face like she's looking for something, though I don't know what it could be. She must find it, though, because she answers, "If I know my sister, you've got about ten more minutes before all hell breaks loose."

"You think she's going to turn us in?" Now Jaxon is all urgency, his eyes darting around the piazza as he waits for her answer.

"I think Imogen feels like she doesn't have a choice." Her voice is deliberately bland as she repeats the words—or at least the sentiment—that she and Dawud just disagreed on. "In fact, I think a lot of us feel that way right now. Including you."

"That doesn't mean we shouldn't try to find a better choice," Flint tells her. "Just going along because we're scared of what might happen isn't an answer. Or, at least, it's not a good answer."

This time, when Viola lifts a brow, there's respect in her eyes. Along with something else. My gut tells me it's that something else that has her bending down out of the blue and pressing a palm to Flint's injured leg.

"What are you—" He breaks off with a startled cry as another explosion of light comes from beneath her hand.

"Silence," she hisses, but it's an impossible demand when—seconds later—a smooth, polished prosthetic appears where the bottom half of Flint's leg used to be.

"Oh my God," Eden breathes. "How did you do that?"

Viola raises both brows, even as she looks down her nose at Eden—and the rest of us. "Magic, of course."

She turns back to Flint, who looks both shocked and overwhelmed as he gazes at his new prosthetic. "I don't— I can't— Thank y—"

"It should shift back and forth when you move." She deliberately cuts him off before he can thank her fully. "Obviously, it won't be as good as your leg, but it should work well enough to let you get rid of those things." She looks at his crutches with disdain.

"Why did you seek us out?" I ask, because no way did this woman come down here just to see what the "commotion" was about.

She gives me a measured gaze before replying. "Whatever you do, Grace, you cannot allow Cyrus to capture you. Death would be better than what he has planned for you."

I gasp.

"And what is that exactly?" Hudson bites out.

"He's going to—" she begins to reply, then startles suddenly at a noise in the distance. Her eyes widen before she shouts, "Run! Now!" just as her light goes out and the piazza around us is plunged into total darkness.

27

Country Roads
Take Me *Where?*

For a second, I'm completely disoriented. But then Hudson pulls me against him, and we fade straight out of the piazza. I don't know why Viola told us to run—because the Witch Guard is coming or because Cyrus's troops have shown up to capture us. Maybe both.

Probably both.

Either way, I'm all for getting out of this dark and twisted piazza and taking all my friends with me. I glance behind me to make sure they're with us, and they are. The Order is together, with Macy holding on to Byron for dear life as they fade through the streets. Dawud is right behind them, and lagging a little behind are Eden and Flint, whose new prosthetic is working almost as well as his old leg. There's a slight hesitation every few steps, but it isn't slowing him down.

It's pretty obvious that he and Eden want to shift into their dragon forms, but it's just as obvious that they are waiting until we're in a place where two dragons flying overhead won't make a million views on YouTube. Too bad we don't have a clue where that less crowded place is.

And so we keep running, putting as much distance between the Witch Court and ourselves as we can manage. Eventually, the densely populated city streets crowded with buildings and fountains and parked cars give way to more greenery, fewer houses. But it's not until it finally seems like we've left the city behind and are heading straight into the Alps that stand over the city like snow-capped sentries that we finally pause to take a breath.

"Thank God!" Eden says, falling face-first into the grass the second we stop. She's drenched in sweat, her clothes sticking to her body as she pulls in long, shuddering breaths.

Flint—whose prosthetic held up incredibly well—follows her down, as does Dawud, though they fall on their back rather than flopping flat onto their face. All three look like they've been ridden hard and put away wet.

As opposed to the vampires, none of whom seem any worse for wear. Yeah, the Order is a little winded, but that's about it, while Jaxon and Hudson look like they've been out for a midnight stroll. Big shock. I'm doing fine and so is Macy, but that's because Hudson and Byron carried us the entire way. Otherwise, I'm pretty sure we'd still be several miles back.

"So," Flint says when he finally catches his breath. "What do we do now?"

"Lay here and wait for death," Eden answers with a groan. The words are muffled, as her face is still planted firmly in the ground beneath her.

Dawud sits up, rolling their eyes. "Charming as that sounds, my vote is for raiding the Vampire Court."

"It's not safe," Rafael answers.

"It's never going to be safe," they shoot back. "And the longer we wait, the more time he has to fortify himself inside that damn fortress."

"He's already fortified himself," Hudson says. "He's always been hypervigilant when it comes to security, and nothing about this situation will change that. Rushing in there like lambs to the slaughter isn't going to save your brother. Or anyone else."

"Neither will running around the globe begging for help from people who won't give it," Eden counters.

"You're right about that," Jaxon agrees. "But that doesn't mean we just attack Cyrus and to hell with the consequences."

"Too much is riding on getting into the Vampire Court to just rush in without a plan," I tell Dawud. "We need to take a few days and figure out the best way to infiltrate without getting caught, and then I'll be the first one in line to help you tear the damn thing down brick by brick."

"My brother may not have a few days," they object.

"I agree. Our family is in there, our friends, and who knows for how much longer." Macy's voice is rough, strained.

Mekhi shakes his head. "I'm with Grace. We need a foolproof plan or we're just going to end up locked away with the others—and there won't be anyone left to rescue us."

"So what do we do?" Byron asks as he sinks down onto the ground beside Flint. "I mean, where do we even go to make this plan? Katmere is gone. The Witch Court won't take us—"

Flint rolls onto his side and props his head in his hand. "The dragons are in total disarray."

"Our families are probably being watched." Liam settles down on the ground between Byron and Dawud.

"They're definitely being watched," Hudson agrees. "And even if they aren't—"

"They are," Macy interrupts.

"They are," Jaxon affirms. "But if they weren't, do we really want to risk getting them involved? Cyrus isn't exactly known for his restraint when it comes to people who get in the way of what he wants."

"Is that what they call being a psychopath these days?" Hudson's voice is amused, though his eyes are anything but. "A lack of restraint?"

"Takes one to know one," Flint accuses, and Hudson goes stiff, his jaw working as he looks into the distance.

"Seriously?" I tell Flint, fighting the urge to punch him right in his big, fat mouth. I get that he's still pissed off at Hudson—and that he might always be—and pissed that Hudson was willing to use his gifts to save me but, to Flint, not to save Luca. But now is not the time for us to take potshots at each other. And especially not at my mate, who gave us a chance to escape Katmere to begin with...and has been tormenting himself ever since.

"It's fine—" Hudson starts.

"No, it's not!" I tell him. "We're all each other has. This group is made up of the only people in the world we can actually count on, and the last thing we need is to be swiping at one another."

"She's right. You're better than this," Jaxon says and holds Flint's gaze for so long, it makes me squirm.

Flint lets out a long-suffering sigh and says, "I'll try not to be a dick. No promises, though."

"Which means he'll definitely still be a dick," Liam says with a grin.

"Look who's talking," Rafael counters with a friendly shoulder bump, to which Liam gives a little *touché* tilt of his head that makes everyone laugh.

It loosens the tension just enough that I *almost* let go of my anger. But knowing that Flint still hasn't forgiven Hudson keeps me from getting all the way there.

"What about the Bloodletter?" Eden suggests once the boys quiet down again. "She has an entire ice cave to herself. Surely we could take a breather and figure out our next steps there."

"No." The answer comes from deep inside me as my entire being recoils at just the thought of seeing her again. "We can't go back to her."

"Why not?" Jaxon asks. "It's not actually that bad of an idea."

"It's a horrible idea. That woman—" I break off, reminding myself that I never told Jaxon about what she did to him. To us. And now, in front of everyone, is definitely not the time to spill the beans.

I finally settle on saying, "I don't trust her. She's never once told us everything we needed to know. I don't think we need any more wild goose chases or half-truths."

"You can say that again," Macy agrees. She looks sadder and more lost than I have ever seen her—even after Xavier died. Not that I blame her. Finding out that her mother left her to go to the Vampire Court and work with Cyrus...there are no words. Especially not since her father is currently being held against his will in that very Vampire Court.

I give her a hug, and at first, she resists. I persist, though—if anyone in the world ever needed comfort right now, it's my cousin—and eventually she hugs me back.

The others talk quietly among themselves, throwing out ideas of where we can go. Eden keeps glancing at us, clearly upset Macy is upset, but I give her a thumbs-up behind Macy's back that I've got her covered. She nods and turns back to the group, adding another suggestion of a possible refuge for us.

No one hits on anything that's really going to work, though, and an idea begins growing in the back of my mind. It's absurd, utterly bizarre, and fantastical, which is why it just might work.

Eventually, Macy pulls away. "Sorry," she whispers as she searches her backpack for something to wipe her face.

I pull a small pack of tissues out of the front pocket of my backpack and hand a couple to her. "Don't apologize. You've had a lot thrown at you in the last twenty-four hours."

"We all have," she says.

"Yeah, but this isn't a contest. And honestly, if it were, I'm pretty sure you'd win. At least the rest of us know where our parents are."

"We do," Hudson agrees, dropping down behind us. "More's the pity."

Macy's laugh is a little bit teary, but it's still a laugh. "I can see how knowing where Cyrus is could be a bummer."

"Not as big a bummer as *not* knowing where he is," Hudson counters.

"True that," Flint chimes in as he scoots over, wraps an arm around Macy's shoulder, and squeezes tight.

Soon, all the others are stretched out on the grass around us. They look as exhausted as I feel. Then again, it's been a chaotic couple of days. Any one of the things that happened seems unimaginable. Add them all together and it feels like the end of the damn world.

Or maybe that's already happened, and we just don't know it yet.

It's a lot to think about when we're in the middle of the Italian countryside with nowhere to go. Reaching into my backpack, I pull out the box of Pop-Tarts and pass it around to all the non-vampires in the group, then follow it with the two bottles of water I shoved in there at the last minute.

Everyone takes a couple of sips, and somehow that—along with a cherry Pop-Tart—makes everything feel not quite so unmanageable. Like maybe we actually have a shot here.

A shot is all we've ever had, and somehow we've made it work. Maybe, just maybe, this time won't be any different.

It's that hope that spurs me to share the thought that's been growing in the back of my mind since the Witch Court. "I have an idea."

28

Irish Luck Be a Lady Tonight

I t takes a second for my words to get through, and I wait patiently for everyone to stop talking and turn to me.

"What is it?" Jaxon asks after everyone grows quiet.

I take a deep breath as I try to figure out the best way to explain what happened with Alistair and the Gargoyle Court. In the end, I decide to start by showing them the same thing that convinced me—the emerald ring I'm still wearing on my right ring finger.

"I got this at the Gargoyle Court," I tell them, turning on my phone's flashlight so they can see the gleam of the stone in the darkness as I quickly fill them in on everything that happened.

I finish with, "I thought maybe I'd hallucinated the whole thing, but I still have this, the ring that Alistair gave me and Chastain kissed…so it has to have actually happened, right?"

"Of course it happened." Hudson reaches for my hand and kisses both the ring and the back of my hand. It makes me melt a little, both his easy acceptance of something that seems impossible just because I say it's true *and* his easy acceptance of something that even I am having a hard time accepting. Me as the gargoyle queen.

I mean, it's one thing to be queen when I have no subjects. It's another thing altogether to rule thousands of gargoyles all over the world. A big part of me wants to run as far and as fast as I can from the responsibility.

It's so strange to me the way Cyrus is willing to do anything for more power when all I want to do is give up the power that I've got. I'm eighteen years old and until seven months ago didn't know this world existed. How on earth can I be expected to rule in it?

The Crown on my palm itches a little, reminding me that giving up power or anything else isn't an option for me. Not when Cyrus is hell-bent on destroying anyone and everyone who doesn't bow to him.

"Where *is* the Gargoyle Court?" Rafael asks.

"Ireland," Dawud and I say at exactly the same moment.

I turn to them with lifted brows, and they shrug a little. "Or at least, that's what the stories handed down in my pack always say, though not exactly where in Ireland."

"Your pack has stories about gargoyles?" I ask.

"*Everyone* has stories about gargoyles," Eden tells me. "We just didn't know any of them were true until you."

"So you think we should go to Ireland?" Byron asks, watching me closely.

"I think it's our best option at this point. The Gargoyle Court is in Cork, in a massive castle on a cliff overlooking the ocean. Isolated and well-protected. It will give us a place to get some rest and work through our next steps." I pause and blow out a long breath before saying the part of the plan I hate. "And it gives us a chance to rally the Gargoyle Army. Or at least the part of it that's at the Court. There weren't that many, but adding a few dozen people to our ranks who can do what I can do... It can't be a bad thing, right?"

"Not a bad thing at all," Macy says, grinning. "Do you think they can all grow as big as you did at the end of the Ludares battle or the Unkillable Beast did on the island?"

"That would be sweet," Liam says. "You could just stomp the Vampire Court to dust."

"And my asshole father with it," Jaxon says in a disgusted voice.

"Sounds good to me," Dawud adds. "As long as we get my brother out first, I say obliterate the whole damn place."

"I don't know if other gargoyles can do that," I say. "I mean, if I can, they should be able to, right?"

I turn to Hudson for reassurance, but he's just watching me with a contemplative look on his face.

"What's wrong?" I ask softly as our friends continue to talk about how cool it would be if the gargoyles could just crush the Vampire Court like giants dancing at a rave.

"Nothing's wrong," he answers. "I just don't think the growing thing you did at Ludares was a gargoyle power."

Shock ripples through me. "What do you mean? The Unkillable Beast— Alistair—was also huge."

"He was huge because he'd been using stone to repair himself for centuries.

Your power is totally different. Don't forget I lived inside your mind for, well, a very long time." He winks at me. "I became very *intimate* with what makes you tick."

Normally, a comment like that would make me blush, pull me out of my own head, but honestly, this time, the effort falls flat. My mind is swirling with thoughts of what Alistair said about my grandmother...and her penchant for biting. What if I am part monster? Something horrific and scary and huge? Unease slithers along my spine, but I tell myself it's no big deal. If Hudson was worried about it, he would have said something long ago. My mate is nothing if not proactive, even when I don't want him to be.

"So what do you think it is?" I finally get the nerve to ask.

At the same time, Eden says, "I don't know about the rest of you, but I'm ready to get out of this field."

"More than ready," Dawud says as they sift their fingers through the grass. Did they drop something? They must find whatever it was, because they quickly stuff something into their pocket, then look at Macy. "Are you going to do your thing?" They wave an arm in a swirly motion.

"I can't." Macy sighs. "I've never been to Cork."

Dawud looks surprised. "Witches can't open portals to places they've never been?"

Macy looks just as surprised. "Um, no. We have magic, but we're not *gods*. What do they teach you in that wolf pack of yours anyway?"

"Apparently not enough." They look around. "So how are we going to get there, then?"

"They really don't teach you much, do they?" Eden teases as she pulls up Google Maps on her phone and holds it out for the rest of us to see. "It looks like our best bet is a straight shot northwest from here. We'll hit the Atlantic eventually, but we can keep low."

"Keep low?" Dawud asks, even as their eyes go wide.

"Only one way to get there from here," Flint says with a grin that almost reaches his eyes. "We fly, baby."

The air around him shimmers, and seconds later, he's in his dragon form—complete with a dragon foot and claw prosthetic.

"Holy shit, it worked!" Byron exclaims, bending down to get a look at Flint's magic foot.

Thank God. I don't know what Viola did or why she helped us, but I will forever be grateful that she did.

As the others are oohing and aahing over Flint's new prosthetic, I turn back to Hudson. "What were you going to say? About my powers?"

He goes to answer but at the last second shakes his head. "It's not a big deal," he says, then smirks. "No pun intended."

"It feels like a *big* deal," I shoot back, adding air quotes around "big," and there's a part of me that wants to press him for an answer. But honestly, I've got enough on my plate right now worrying about what I'm going to say to the gargoyles at the Gargoyle Court. Worrying about some nebulous other power that I might possibly have—if Hudson is even right—is going to have to wait. For tonight, at least, I'm totally resurrecting my Shit I Don't Need to Deal With Today file and shoving this question inside.

"Uh, you want us to fly?" Dawud's eyes are huge as they take several steps away from Flint. "Like, on your back?"

"It's not bad at all," Macy says as Byron gives her a huge boost onto Flint's back. She holds a hand out to Dawud. "Come on. Byron and I will help you up."

Dawud still looks skeptical.

"It's pretty much your only option at this point, so just do it and don't think about it," Liam tells them. "Unless you can run on water."

Dawud scowls at him, but in the end, they let Byron lift them up. Macy grabs their hand and pulls them the last little way onto Flint, and Dawud settles in with a grateful look. At least until Flint moves beneath them. Then they let loose with a shout so loud, it rings through the countryside.

It only stops because they slap a hand over their mouth in horror while the rest of us laugh.

Flint's dragon snorts his own laughter out, and then—because he's Flint—he does a little dance to freak Dawud out even more. Flint's totally hoping they'll scream again, but apparently their jaw is locked shut, because this time, Dawud doesn't make a sound. They do close their eyes and take several deep breaths, but that seems fair. I remember doing the same thing when Flint invited me to fly with him the very first time.

"You going to fly?" Hudson asks me, holding my hand even as he steps toward Eden, who is just completing her shift.

"Damn straight," I tell him with a grin. "But don't worry. I'll catch you if you fall."

I expect him to laugh, but instead his eyes are completely serious when he answers, "Ditto."

He turns away before I can ask him what he means, querying Eden for her permission to climb on. Her dragon nods, and he jumps lightly onto her back, followed quickly by Rafael and Liam, both of whom look as freaked out as Dawud. Of the Order, only Byron seems comfortable being on a dragon's back.

It makes me feel a little bad for them and for the stupid unwritten rules Katmere had against the different paranormals mingling. Hudson, Jaxon, Macy, Flint, Eden, Mekhi, Xavier, Gwen, Luca—they've absolutely been the best part of this whole world for me, even better than finding out I'm a gargoyle. I can't imagine what my life would be like if we'd followed those ridiculous norms and stuck to our own groups.

Because it makes me sad to think about it, I blow Hudson a kiss. Then I look at Jaxon—who's planning on doing his telekinesis thing—and say, "Last one to Ireland has to dance like a chicken."

"So that's how it is, huh?" he asks.

"That's how it is," I say as I shift.

The second I've got my wings, I shoot straight into the air and take off, leaving a surprised Jaxon, Eden, and Flint to eat my dust.

And I try really, really hard not to worry the entire flight about what reception we'll get once our motley group of paranormals arrives at the Gargoyle Court.

29

Passed with
Flying Dragons

Despite the way the flight started, it ends up being a very different ride than usual. No flips, no loop the loops, no sprints between Eden and Flint or Jaxon and me. There is only quiet contemplation as we fly over Europe and then the English Channel and into the Celtic Sea.

As we approach a distant island, I can feel the Court as clearly as my own heartbeat. It's like there's a string running between us that's slowly getting rolled up, pulling me closer with each crank of the wheel.

"We're almost there," I shout to the others right before I move to drop lower and lower.

I'm coasting right above the Celtic Sea now, the sunrise just barely painting the water a beautiful orange as the sun winks above the horizon and reminds me of early-morning beach runs in San Diego. For the first time, I wonder if my parents chose to run to California because it was on the water, too. The Pacific, not the Atlantic, but still the ocean. Still close to the water that is such an integral part of my powers.

A quick glance at my friends tells me that exhaustion is setting in for all of them. Flint is lagging a little behind, his wings spread out at his sides as he tries to coast on the wind currents as much as possible. Eden is still flapping her wings, but each rise and fall seems to be taking longer and longer. Even Hudson is slumping a little, like sheer will is the only thing holding him upright.

Ahead, I can see the rocky cliffs of Cork in the distance. Despite my own exhaustion, excitement thrums in my blood—a kind of primal drive that pushes me faster and faster until finally I can see it on the horizon.

The fancy iron fence that surrounds the Gargoyle Court and the stone castle that lies right inside the fence.

Nerves join the excitement as I wonder how they'll receive my friends and me. Will Chastain follow my directions or will he choose to remain loyal to Alistair even after the gargoyle king very clearly passed the baton to me? Will the other gargoyles accept me, or will they ignore me? And what will I do if they choose not to listen to me? How will I fix it? More importantly, can it even be fixed?

The questions chase themselves around in my head, getting harder and more daunting the closer I get to the Gargoyle Court. Until suddenly, I'm right on top of it—or what should be it.

I land slowly, wondering if I've gotten it wrong. Wondering if the beacon that guided me here is defective. Wondering if, somehow, I really had imagined the hours I spent here with Alistair.

Because this place where I'm standing is nothing like the place I visited yesterday. The fancy iron fence is the same, but that's it.

The courtyard I walked through? Gone.

The castle where I watched other gargoyles train? Nothing but piles of rock and random vines.

The other gargoyles themselves? Gone, as if they had never been.

This Gargoyle Court—*my* Gargoyle Court? A dream that just became my nightmare.

30

Talk About a Fixer-Upper

As soon as Eden hits the ground, Hudson is by my side.

He doesn't say anything at first, and neither do I. Instead, we just stand there gazing at the destruction.

There is no courtyard left.

No foyer and grand hall.

No wide, round towers that reach from the ground up to the sky.

There's nothing left except a bunch of rubble and even more broken dreams. Which seems about right as I can feel my own ideas, my own hopes, shattering on the buckled ground at my feet.

"I've got to say, I'm not big on their aesthetic." The words are sarcastic, but Hudson's tone is soft—as is the look he gives me as he gently bumps his shoulder against my own.

"A little too *end of the world* for you?" I ask as I lean into him.

He rolls his eyes. "A little too *walls are so last century*."

"I do like a good wall," I tell him, and somehow I'm smiling when two minutes ago it felt like I'd never smile again.

"And here I thought four walls was the way to go." He pulls my back against his chest, his arms reaching around to hold me tight against him, and rests his chin on the top of my head.

"You always were an overachiever."

He feels good, really good, even in the face of all this destruction. So I lean against him and take a moment to breathe. Just breathe.

"You okay?" he asks after a few seconds.

"Not when you ask like that," I shoot back.

"Like what?"

"Like you expect me to break any second now. Or like I'm already broken." I pull away. "I didn't hallucinate an entire Gargoyle Court. It was here. It was right here."

"I have absolutely no doubt that it was," Hudson reassures me in a way that convinces me he really does believe me.

Still, I turn back to the rubble, wondering if there was a way Cyrus could have done this. Could he have beaten me here and torn the whole place down just to make sure we didn't have a safe haven of any sort? But if so, what happened to the gargoyles I saw training here yesterday? Are they buried under the rocks, trapped and waiting for me to find them?

The thought spurs me to action, has me moving through the dilapidated, rusted-out fence and into the area that was once a glorious courtyard overlooking the ocean. But it only takes a few seconds for logic to kick in—as well as my apparently less-than-keen observation skills.

This place didn't collapse recently. It's been like this for decades, maybe even centuries. Whole areas of rock have been overgrown with weeds and vines. The iron fence is rusted to hell and back. And scattered willy-nilly throughout the ruins are the bones of animals who came to investigate and ended up getting trapped in the debris.

No, this isn't Cyrus's fault. Or at least, it's not Cyrus's fault anytime in the last century. Before that, it's anyone's guess.

"I don't understand," I whisper as our other friends gather around. "It wasn't a dream. It wasn't."

I run my thumb over the emerald in my ring. It's as hard—and as real—as ever. "I didn't make this place up. I saw it so clearly." I walk over to the left of the courtyard, to a pile of large stones covered in ivy. "This was a tower—one of four. It had stained glass windows and squared-off battlements, and it was right here. *Right here.*"

"No one is doubting you, Grace," Macy says.

"*I'm* doubting me," I shoot back. "How could I not be?"

"No offense, but I'm doubting you, too," Dawud says with a shrug. "I mean, this seems more than a little"—they mime like I've been smoking something—"to me."

It feels like that's the worst thing they could have said when I'm already doubting myself, and I can feel my friends getting ready to lay into them for being so insensitive. But at the same time, it's also the *best* thing they could have said, because it makes me laugh, even in the face of whatever all this is.

"I don't know what's going on with me," I tell Dawud and the rest of my friends. "It seemed so real when Alistair brought me here."

"It probably was real," Jaxon answers. His smile is a little soft when he tells me, "'There are more things in heaven and hell, Horatio, than are dreamt of in your philosophy.'"

"You mean heaven and earth, don't you?" I say, and now I'm grinning right back at him, because how can I not? Those were practically the first words he ever said to me—a warning and a promise, though I didn't know it at the time.

"After the last few days?" he asks, brow raised. "I definitely mean heaven and hell. I'm pretty sure neither Shakespeare nor Hamlet ever lived through a few weeks like we've had."

"You have a point there." I make a face at him, relief a wild thing within me despite the mess we're in.

A lot of truly horrible things have happened, but the fact that Jaxon is doing so well right now makes me happier than I can ever express. No one would know from looking at him that he died less than forty-eight hours ago.

He looks good, really good. Plus, for the first time in a long time, it feels good to be around him again. The uncomfortable tension between us has pretty much disappeared, and in its place is something else—something that feels like respect and appreciation and love.

Something that feels like more than friendship and less than romance.

Something that feels an awful lot like family.

He's right that a lot of terrible things have happened, but the fact that Jaxon and I have ended up here, where we should have been all along, makes everything else feel not so bad. Add in the fact that Hudson and I finally have our shit sorted, too, at least I think we do, and I can't help but be cautiously optimistic that things are going to be okay. Even if the rest of our lives—and our world—are in shambles.

"So what do we do now?" Eden asks. She's sitting on top of a large pile of stones, and she looks beat, like she can barely keep her eyes open.

"I think we need to find a hotel," I say. "Someplace out of the way where Cyrus and his followers won't think to look for us. We need to sleep for a while, and then we might actually have a fighting chance. Or at least be able to convince ourselves that we do."

"Already on it," Hudson says, thumbs flying over his phone screen. "I found a house not that far from here through an app. I've rented several cottages for the next month just in case we need a base of operations for longer, and because they had no one on the property last night, the owner has agreed to let us check in now for a small fee."

"An app? You mean like Airbnb?" I ask, astonished.

"Something like that," he answers with a grin.

"I thought we had to book in advance and be, like, twenty-five or something to rent one of those places."

"I'm two hundred years old and rich as fuck, Grace." His tone is droll as he pulls a pair of sunglasses out of his jacket pocket and slides them on just as rays from the early-morning sun hit the edges of the courtyard. "Occasionally, it has its perks."

It might be the most Hudson Vega thing he's ever said—I mean, besides comparing Jaxon to the Goodyear Blimp—and I can't help cracking up. "You're ridiculous. You know that, right?"

His answering smirk says it all. "I've texted all of you but Dawud the address—sorry, I don't know your number—and I'll meet you there. But I've got to go."

"Wait, why?" I grab hold of his arm as he moves to turn away, and his smirk grows more pronounced.

And then I get it, even before I register the way his eyes linger on the hollow of my throat. He drank from me in prison only forty-eight hours ago. I'm not sure how long drinking from a human makes a vampire hypersensitive to the sun, but clearly two days is not enough.

"Go!" I tell him, dropping his hand and giving him a little shove toward the fence.

"That's what I'm trying to do," he replies with a look that has me feeling all kinds of things I should be too exhausted to feel.

"I'll take that as my cue as well," Jaxon says and fades away. Which, not going to lie, surprises me more than a little.

Especially when I turn to make a comment to Flint and find him looking anywhere and everywhere but at me, the Order already fading after Jaxon. I open my mouth to say something to Flint—just to see how he'll respond—but before I can, Eden holds up her phone.

"I've mapped it out. You ready to go?"

"I was ready ten minutes ago," Dawud answers, and they grin even as the air around them begins to sparkle.

Seconds later, we take to the sky, and while I've lost my chance to ask Flint what's going on, I haven't forgotten the look on his face as Jaxon faded away. Intense, angry, terrified.

I could be wrong, but something tells me the next few days are going to be more interesting than even I'd imagined.

31

This Little
Lighthouse of Mine

It turns out Hudson didn't just rent us a house. He rented us a freaking compound—complete with an actual, working lighthouse.

"A lighthouse!"

Hudson grins. "Yes."

"You rented us a lighthouse!"

"And the two houses right down the road that go with it," he points out as he rests his shoulders—and one Dior Explorer–clad foot—against the wall.

He looks good like this—really good—but I'm not about to tell him that. Partly because his ego is big enough already and partly because, "You rented us a *lighthouse*."

"I did." He lifts one too-sexy brow. "Are you going to keep saying that?"

"Probably. And I'll probably be all heart-eyed while I do."

"Okay." Several seconds pass before he asks, "Any particular reason why?"

"Because you rented us a lighthouse!" I throw my arms out and twirl around in circles, letting myself forget, for a little while, why we even need to rent a place to stay. "It's like, the coolest thing ever!"

"I'm glad you like it."

"It's a lighthouse. On the ocean. Just for you and me. What's not to love?"

He doesn't answer, but when I catch sight of him as I'm spinning, I realize he doesn't need to. His face says everything, and that only makes me twirl faster.

I stumble to a stop because I've actually made myself dizzy with all the turning in circles. Of course, Hudson takes the opening, reaching out and snagging my hand before pulling me against him.

"Are you planning on taking advantage of me just because I'm dizzy?" I tease, slapping a playful hand against his chest.

"I was actually planning on steadying you because you were dizzy, but if you insist..."

He sweeps me into his arms as fast as a heartbeat and fades up the never-ending circle of stairs until he gets to the bedroom, where he tosses me on the very comfortable-looking bed.

It's thrilling and amusing at the same time, and I laugh as I land with a soft bounce. I hold out my arms to him, expecting him to come lay with me. Instead, Hudson drops my backpack on the end of the bed, then sits next to me and strokes my entirely too messy curls out of my eyes.

"You're so beautiful," he murmurs, his fingers lingering on the curve of my cheek.

"You're beautiful," I tell him back, turning my head so I can kiss his palm.

"Well, yes," he agrees with an oh-so-serious tilt of his head. "That's true. But the two aren't mutually exclusive."

"Oh my God." I grab a pillow and smack him with it. "You're unbelievable, you know that?"

"I believe you've mentioned it a time or three hundred," he answers right back before snagging the pillow from my unsuspecting hands. I brace for him to softly attack me back with it, but he tosses it on the floor before finally stretching out on the bed next to me.

"Are you hungry?" he asks.

"I am, but not enough to leave this bed to order food." I reach for my bag. "I think there's a couple more Pop-Tarts in here anyway."

He rolls his eyes. "One can't live on Pop-Tarts alone, Grace."

"Maybe not, but I'm totally willing to give it a try." I open the crinkly silver package and break off a piece of the cherry-flavored pastry before shoving it in my mouth.

Hudson shakes his head, but his eyes are indulgent as he watches me.

"How about you?" I ask after I take a few more bites. "Are you hungry?"

I meant the words innocuously enough, but the second they leave my mouth, they take on a life of their own. Hudson's eyes gleam, my stomach flips, and suddenly the whole room feels lit up with a tension that has my heart beating way too fast.

"What do you think?" he asks after several charged seconds drag by.

"I think you're starving," I tell him, just before I lift my chin in invitation. "I know I am."

"Have another cherry Pop-Tart, then." But his eyes are fire as they race over me, lingering on my lips...and my throat.

I tilt my head a little more and stroke my fingers over the sensitive skin at the base of my neck. "That's not the kind of hunger I'm talking about."

Hudson makes a sound deep in his chest—part pleasure, part pain—and releases a long, shuddering breath that has my hands shaking and my stomach clenching in anticipation, even before he lowers his mouth to my neck.

"Grace." My name is a little more than a whisper, a little less than a prayer, as he presses gentle kisses along my collarbone and the hollow of my throat. His lips are warm and soft, and they feel so good—*he* feels so good—that I place my hand against the quilt to make sure I'm not floating away.

Except Hudson's got me like he always does, his hands sliding down to hold my hips and press me even more firmly against him.

My fingers clutch convulsively at the brown silk of his hair as he kisses his way back up my neck. Pleasure slides through me, makes it impossible not to let loose the whimper welling inside me.

The sound of Hudson's answering groan—a little dark, a little desperate, and all dangerous—takes the intensity up a notch or twelve. My fingers tighten in his hair; my body arches against his as I gasp out his name.

I'm desperate for him to stop playing.

Desperate for him to do what my body is screaming for.

Desperate for him to do what my every cell, my every molecule, is *begging* for.

Hudson knows—of course he knows. His dark little snicker is proof that he's holding back on purpose, *torturing* me on purpose. Maybe I should be annoyed by his restraint, by the way he stokes the need seething inside me until it grows into something wicked and wild and wanton. Until it grows into something that I barely recognize.

And maybe I would be if it was someone—anyone—else. But this is Hudson. This is my mate. And the way he's trembling against me is proof that he is just as overwhelmed, just as lost in how new and precious this all is as I am and doesn't want to rush a single moment. Which is enough, more than enough, for now.

At least until he presses a long, lingering kiss on the delicate skin behind my ear.

Just like that, my whole body goes on red alert. My restraint melts away, as does my pride.

"Please," I beg, arching my neck until it nearly hurts in an effort to give him all the access. "Hudson, *please*."

"Please what?" he growls in a voice so raspy, I almost don't recognize it.

I want to answer him—I try to answer him—but my voice is gone, drowned in the wild cacophony of sensations rushing through me.

And when he finally lowers his mouth to his favorite spot, the pulse point at the side of my throat, my entire soul cries out for him.

He kisses me once, twice, and just like that, my blood is gasoline, the tip of his fang as it coasts along my skin the match that sets me ablaze. That ignites me, even before he groans and finally—*finally*—strikes.

His hands tighten on my hips as his fangs sink deep, and for one brief moment, I feel the sharp pain of it all, the sudden, violent piercing through skin and tissue, blood and vein. But the pain fades as quickly as it came, leaving nothing but pleasure and heat in its wake. Heat that brushes over my skin, swims through my blood, sizzles along my nerve endings. Heat that swamps me, overwhelms me, makes me burn and burn and burn.

I'm shaking now, electricity zinging through my body, lighting me up like the aurora borealis that dances across the night sky in Alaska.

And as Hudson slides deeper, his fangs sinking into me—through me—I can't help thinking that folklore has it all wrong. The stories say vampire bites are something to fear, but there is nothing scary about Hudson's bite, unless you count the way it makes me feel.

The way it makes me need.

The way Hudson makes me crave him, until nothing and no one else exists but us.

Until there is no Cyrus.

No war.

No death.

Until there is nothing but Hudson and the current arcing between us.

He groans low in his throat, his fingers digging into my hips even as I arch and tremble against him. Even as I plead with him to take more of me. More and more and more, until there is no me and no him. There is only us, drowning in each other. Incandescent with pleasure.

I shiver with each second that passes, and I lean farther into Hudson, letting him take all of me—right up until he pulls away with a growl.

I whimper, try to hold on to him, to keep him deep inside me. But he is having none of it.

He lifts his head, cursing as he puts a few inches of distance between us.

It isn't much, isn't anything, really, but I feel it in my gut as I try to hang on to him. As I try to pull him back to my throat, back to my vein.

But Hudson resists, his bright blue eyes staring down at me with a concern that pours ice water over the flames deep inside me.

"I'm fine," I tell him, anticipating the question he's going to ask. "You didn't take much."

"I took too much," he shoots back in the proper British accent that turns me on at least as often as it annoys me. "You're shaking."

I roll my eyes even as I lean into him, taking my turn at pressing kisses along the strong, lean column of his throat. "I'm pretty sure my shakiness has nothing to do with blood loss."

"Oh yeah?" He lifts a brow. "And what does it have to do with, then?"

"Kiss me and I'll show you," I whisper against his skin.

"Show me, and I'll kiss *you*," he counters.

"I was hoping you'd say that." I scrape my teeth along his cut-glass jaw, and it's his turn to melt into me.

"I love you," he whispers into my hair, and the words are a jolt to my system. A good jolt, but a jolt nonetheless.

Someday, maybe, they'll be familiar. Comfortable. A warm blanket to wrap around my heart and soul. But today, they're fireworks. An explosion deep inside me that rocks me to my very core.

"I love you more," I whisper back, kissing my way down Hudson's throat. I nuzzle his collarbone even as my fingers dance along the buttons of his shirt. He needs a shower and so do I, but for now, the raw heat of him feels good.

Being so close to him only makes the urgency more intense.

I tear at his shirt and mine, my fingers tangling in the fabric in my desperation to feel him against me. I need to hold him, to touch him, to know that no matter what happens next, *this* will always be here.

Hudson will always be here.

But before I can find a way to tell him that, Hudson breaks away from me—chest heaving, eyes gleaming, a tiny drop of my blood glistening on his bottom lip. His usually perfectly coiffed hair is disheveled, and he looks sexy as hell. I want nothing more than to run my hands through the silky waves again, to pull him up and over me and let the heat take us away from this mess for a little while.

But he's holding my hands in his, and it's obvious he's got something to say by the way he closes his eyes and takes one long, shuddering breath.

"What's wrong?" I ask.

He shakes his head. "I just love you, that's all."

"I love you, too."

"And I'm sorry—"

"For loving me?" I ask, a sudden chill chasing away all the heat inside me.

"No!" His eyes—his beautiful blue-sky eyes—fly open. "I could never be sorry for that. I'll love you for the rest of my life."

"You mean eternity?" I say with a laugh. "I can get behind that."

"That's what I wanted to talk to you about, actually."

"Eternity?" I tease, doing my best to ignore the warning bells going off in my head. Because this is Hudson, and he would never do anything to hurt me.

He swallows, his jaw working furiously. "I need you to do something for me."

"Anything." The response comes from deep inside me.

This time when he closes his eyes, he dips his chin so that his hair falls forward. I push it back up so I can see his eyes when he opens them, focusing on the way the soft, cool strands feel wrapped around my fingers instead of worrying about whatever it is he's about to tell me. I mean, it doesn't take a genius to figure out that whatever it is, I'm not going to like it.

He lifts my hand, and this time he's the one who kisses my palm. He's the one who holds on tight for one second, two. Then he opens his eyes, and there's a resolve there that was missing a few moments ago. My stomach shimmies a little, and not in a good way, even before he places my other hand, with the Crown tattoo, over his chest.

"I want you to use this on me."

"What do you mean?" I ask, confused.

"I want you to use the Crown to take away my powers."

32

I Just Want
to Power Down

I burst out laughing. I can't help it. The idea is just so absurd that there's nothing else I can do.

"Yeah, right," I finally say, flipping onto my side on the bed next to him. "I thought you were actually going to say something serious."

"I *am* being serious." He rolls onto his side, propping himself up on an elbow. "I really meant what I said. I need you to—"

"Of course you don't mean it," I deny, trying to ignore the sick feeling that's growing in the pit of my stomach at just the idea of what he's saying. "There's no way you could actually *want* me to take your power—and no way I would ever do it, even if you asked me to."

"You just told me you'd do anything for me," he answers quietly.

"And I would," I tell him. "Anything that's the least bit reasonable, I would do for you in a heartbeat. I would die for you, Hudson. But this?" I shake my head. "This isn't okay. You can't just ask me to—"

He lifts a brow. "Make it so I can't carelessly hurt anyone ever again?"

"You've never carelessly hurt anyone in your life." I take a deep breath, then blow it out slowly as horror churns in my belly. "Besides, this isn't about stopping you from hurting other people. This is about asking me to hurt *you*. Surely you can see that's what you're doing."

"I'm asking you to *help* me, Grace. You're the only one in the whole world who can." The torment in his voice has tears burning behind my eyes.

But I can't do what he wants. I can't. Even if I can figure out a way to find the missing Gargoyle Army and make the Crown work before we face Cyrus—and there's no guarantee of that—I can't just use it on my mate. I can't just strip him of one of the things that makes him who he is, even if that's what he thinks he wants.

I take a deep breath, then blow it out slowly in an effort to stave off the panic burning in my chest. "Hudson, I don't think this is what you really want."

"Even though I'm telling you that it's exactly what I want?" he demands with the confidence that's as much a part of him as his blue eyes and dark hair.

That's as much a part of him as his powers.

"It's been a terrible few days. None of us is in a good headspace. We were in prison a few days ago, then the battle, then Katmere. How can you even think of making a decision like this when we haven't had a chance to process everything that's happened?"

"It's because I *have* processed what happened that I'm asking you to do this." He shoves a frustrated hand through his hair. "Can you imagine how it feels to know that Luca is dead because I didn't use my powers before he was killed? Or that my baby brother needed a dragon heart to survive because I was too afraid to use my abilities?" His voice breaks. "Or that I'm really afraid of what will happen if I *do* use my gift?"

He shoves off the bed and starts pacing the room even as he's careful not to go near the sunlight pouring in through the window. "You have no idea what a burden this power is, made worse because, when it comes to your safety, I can't be trusted to think before I act."

"They were there to kill us, Hudson!" It's my turn to be frustrated, my turn to tug at my hair. "It's not like you just annihilated a bunch of innocent wolves. If they'd had a shot at ripping out our throats, they would have taken it."

"And if there was another wolf like Dawud in that pack? Someone who couldn't run as fast as them or who wasn't as brave as they are? What if I killed them, too?"

"You don't know that there was anyone else like Dawud—"

"And you don't know that there wasn't!" he snarls. "Besides, now we'll never know. That's my whole point."

"So your answer is to give up your powers forever? Even though you might have done the right thing? Even though those wolves might have killed every single one of us?" I shake my head. "That doesn't make sense. We're in the middle of a battle for the whole world, a battle that will determine how paranormals and humans will live for centuries—and even *if* we'll live. You're the most powerful weapon we've got, and you want me to just drain you of your powers because you might make a mistake?"

"There's no might about it. I did make a mistake. In fact, I've made several." He blows out a long breath, kind of shakes his head. "And I didn't mean for you to take them this second. I meant after we fight Cyrus. But I'm not asking this because I want you to save the world. I'm asking this because I want you to save *me*."

The hurt in his voice is unmistakable, and it breaks my heart. And it also tells me more clearly than any words that I've handled this wrong. But can anyone really blame me? Of all the things in all the world that I ever thought Hudson might ask of me, this wasn't even on the radar.

Then again, maybe it should have been. I've always known that Hudson has a very uneasy relationship with his powers—first, because of the way Cyrus used him when he was a child, and then because of what he did with them when he first got to Katmere. Add in everything that's happened lately, and is there any wonder that he's freaking out? Any wonder he thinks this is his only option?

But it's not. It can't be. Hudson's power is an integral part of him—as intrinsic to who he is as the sarcastic shield he maintains to keep others at bay and the powerful kindness that he tries so hard to keep others from seeing.

I'm frustrated, scared, and more than a little upset. How can he ask me to be the one to hurt him like this? I want nothing more than to pull the covers over my head and pretend this conversation never happened. But even though we're at a stalemate, I can't just leave things like this. Not when Hudson is so obviously suffering.

I don't know what to do to fix any of this, but sitting here arguing with him is only going to make things worse. So I climb off the bed with a sigh and cross to where he's standing. Or should I say leaning, considering he's doing that sexy-as-hell *shoulder against the wall* thing, arms crossed over his chest. He usually only does this particular pose when he's trying to act like he doesn't give a fuck about what's going on, and the fact that he feels the need to use it now, with me, makes me feel like the world's shittiest mate.

"Hey," I say when we're once again face-to-face. "Can we talk about this some more?"

He lifts a brow. "It's hard to talk when someone has already made up their mind."

"Yeah, well, I could say the same about you." It's the wrong thing to say, and I know it the second the words leave my mouth. Shit. "I didn't mean—"

"Do you know what it's like to be me, Grace? Do you know what it's like to spend your childhood locked away so you could become the strongest weapon possible? What it's like to have to work, every second, to make sure you don't hurt someone or take their will away from them?"

Sadness wells up inside me. I hate that he's in pain, hate even more that he thinks the only way to stop that agony is to have me violate him, *hurt him*, in this most terrible way. "Oh, Hudson. I can't even imagine—"

"No, you can't. That's the point. And you don't even know half of how my powers work—what they cost me." He throws his arms up in frustration and turns to walk away. But at the last second, he turns back to me and—very quietly—says, "Every time I use them, a little bit of the light fades inside me, Grace. I'm afraid one of these days, I may not make it back to you. I may not make it back to *me*."

"Then don't use them!" I beg him. If he doesn't use his powers, then everything will be okay. He won't have to suffer, and I won't have to be the person who takes away a part of him that makes him who he is.

But Hudson just shakes his head and turns to stare at the ocean out the window. "You forgive me for Luca dying, but one day, someone will die who you won't be able to forgive me for not saving. And I'll lose anyway, Grace."

"I would never blame you for not killing someone to save us," I plead, grabbing his shirt and turning him to face me fully, to see the conviction on my face.

"What if it were Macy who dies next, and I was right there? All I had to do was disintegrate two wolves to save her. What then?"

I want to say he's wrong. That I would understand, but for a second, I open my mouth to say of course he would kill two wolves to save Macy—and that's when I realize he's right. We all assume it's Hudson's choice when to use his gifts to save us, but is it really? I know that I will always love him. I will always be on his side and support his choices. But if I'm being honest, there's a part of me that would be shattered that he didn't do everything he could to save the last family I have left, the girl who would do anything to save the rest of us.

And he can see it in my eyes, too, because he whispers on a ragged breath, "Grace, I am begging you. Please. Don't leave me like this. I don't know how much longer I can take it without losing myself forever, without losing you."

And just like that, my heart breaks wide open. Because I would do anything for Hudson—absolutely anything. Except this. As much pain as I know his gifts cause him, deep down I know something he hasn't considered. While using his powers might one day break him in a way he can't recover from, there's no guarantee. And with his mate by his side, I have a chance of pulling him back, of helping him always find himself again. But if I were to take his powers and someone tried to harm *me*—and succeeded because he didn't have his abilities—well, that's a pain his soul would never survive, no matter who was left to pick up the pieces. I know this as surely as I take my next breath—because I would feel exactly the same way if our roles were reversed and something happened to him.

Being a mate means having each other's backs. Always. And I would wear the Crown for an eternity if it meant saving my mate's life.

Either way, now isn't the time to convince Hudson I'm right. We're exhausted to our bones. But I can tell he's waiting on me to agree to end his pain, just as I am certain for the first time since I've known him, I'm going to disappoint him.

And I don't have a clue where we're supposed to go from here.

33

Sometimes the Coffee Breaks You

He must read my refusal on my face because his shoulders slump for a second, maybe two.

Then he straightens up, and he's got his inscrutable face on, the one he shows the world. Even his eyes—which are always soft for me these days—look blank.

"Hudson—"

"It's okay," he says, and his smile as he tucks my hair behind my ear is one of the saddest things I've ever seen. "Why don't we try to get a little sleep?"

I want to argue with him, want to stay up until we solve this problem. But the truth is, I am so tired that my head feels fuzzy, and trying to deal with this feels like the end of the world. Maybe some sleep is exactly what we both need before we try to come at this problem again.

God knows, being a little more clearheaded definitely won't hurt anything.

"Okay." I get up to head to the bathroom to take a shower, but I'm afraid I could fall asleep standing under the water. In the end, I strip down to my bra and panties and climb into bed. Hudson joins me seconds later, and I'm asleep before he even manages to pull the blanket over us.

I sleep like a stone—pun totally intended—for four hours and only wake up because Hudson is sitting on the end of the bed with a cup of delivery coffee in his hand.

The cowardly side of me wants to keep my focus on the coffee—anything is better than seeing the defeated look that was in his eyes when we went to bed—but he deserves better than that. Our relationship deserves better than that.

So I slowly, carefully lift my gaze to his and shiver in relief when I realize the eyes staring back at me are as soft and indulgent as usual. Still, I can't help but ask, "Are you okay?" Because I'm not sure that I am.

"I'm chuffed. Amazing what even a few hours' sleep will do for a bloke."

Now I'm really concerned, because usually Hudson only sounds this British when he's pissed as hell and swearing up a storm. Which means what exactly? He's pretending to be okay but actually isn't? Or he's accepted my decision and is trying to live with it?

Either one is a punch to my gut—the last thing I ever want to do is hurt him—as is the fact that I don't know what to do, what to say, to make things better for him.

In the end, he makes things better by holding the cup of coffee just out of my reach. "You've got fifteen seconds to wake up and take this," he teases, "or it's going straight down the drain."

"You wouldn't dare!" I say, taking the lifeline he's offered me. Offered us.

"You don't think so?" He starts to stand up, but I grab on to him and pull him back down, then reach for the cup with grabby hands.

"Give me, give me, give me," I tell him.

He offers it over with a grin. "I tried four different places, and apparently Ireland is not big on Dr Pepper. Or Pop-Tarts." He hands me a white paper sack. "There's a fruit salad in there, along with some yogurt, a muffin, and a sandwich from the bakery down the road."

"What bakery?" I ask, looking out the window at the cliffs and raging ocean, which go on for as far as the eye can see. The only structures in sight are the two houses that are part of this property, where the others are staying. "And what road?"

He shrugs. "Okay, maybe it's a little farther than down the road. But I tip well, so it all evens out in the end."

"Of course it does." I roll my eyes as I put my surprisingly delicious takeout coffee on the nightstand and reach for the bag. My stomach is so excited at the prospect of real food that it's practically dancing—which is when I realize it's been a while since I've eaten something other than Pop-Tarts. Maybe Hudson is right. A girl can't live on Pop-Tarts alone, no matter how much she wants to.

"What about Macy and the others?" I ask as I fork up a grape.

"I ordered food for them, too," he answers as he takes a long swallow from the water bottle on the dresser.

"You're the best," I tell him with a grin, finally beginning to really relax. *Things are okay between us*, I tell myself. *Hudson is okay. Maybe all we really did need was some sleep.*

He tilts his head in that way he has that means, *Obviously.* "I try."

We talk about nothing special while I eat—Ireland, our friends, Cyrus—but the minute I finish the last bite of sandwich, Hudson takes my hand and says,

"We need to talk."

And shit. There goes my optimism. And my ability to breathe. Because, a few hours' sleep or not, I haven't changed my mind about his powers. "I'm sorry, Hudson. I'm so sorry—"

"Don't worry," he says, holding up a hand to stop me. "It's not about that."

"Then what?" I ask warily. "Because no good conversation ever begins with those words."

"Maybe not," he answers with a rueful look. "But let's just say there are degrees of bad, and this one isn't all that."

"Okay." I pull in one last bracing sip of coffee as panic brushes its wings against the inside of my stomach, turning it hollow and jumpy and making me regret all the food I just ate. "So what kind of bad is this?"

"Not bad at all, if you take the long view."

"Fantastic. I mean, who doesn't love to play the long game?" I give a heartfelt sigh even as I brace myself for whatever he is going to say. "Okay, then. What's up?"

He starts to talk, then breaks off with a nervous laugh. "Why don't we both just relax for a second?"

I lift a brow. "Pretty sure the ship has sailed on that one."

"Yeah." He sighs. "You're right."

And then he doesn't say anything else for what feels like forever.

I'm super antsy now, anxiety crawling around my insides, turning them to mush. I try to tell myself that whatever it is Hudson has to say isn't that big of a deal, but Hudson isn't known for making a big deal out of nothing—last night being a prime example. So whatever it is, it's important, and these days, important almost always translates to bad.

"I've been thinking about the Gargoyle Court," he finally says, right before I'm about to jump out of my skin.

It's not the turn I expected the conversation to take, and I blink at him for a few seconds, then start with, "What about it?" Before he can say anything, I continue. "I know everyone thinks I'm delusional, but I swear—"

"None of us think you're delusional," he soothes. "Which is why I've spent the last several hours going over what you saw. And trying to come up with an answer."

"Did you find one?" I ask, even though I already know. Hudson wouldn't be trying to be so delicate with me if he hadn't thought of something. And if that something wasn't likely to upset me.

"Maybe." He narrows his eyes in contemplation. "Do you remember that night in the laundry room? When you danced with me?"

"You mean when you told me to shut up and dance?" I ask with a soft grin, because of course I remember.

"I believe the music did that." He flashes me a wicked smile.

"And who controlled the music?"

He shrugs. "Not my fault I have good taste and impeccable timing."

"Not to mention a totally manageable ego," I shoot back with a roll of my eyes.

"Being humble is highly overrated." His grin fades. "Anyway, that's when you saw all the strings for the first time, right?"

"It is, yeah," I agree. I can't figure out where he's going with this, but I know it's somewhere important. I can see it in his eyes, hear it in his voice.

"It's the first time I saw your bond with Jaxon up close and personal." He grimaces. "That was fun."

"I bet." I squeeze his hand. "What are you getting at here, Hudson? Because I need to tell you, this piece-by-piece thing you've got going on is really freaking me out."

"Sorry. I'm just trying to lay the groundwork." He leans over and gently kisses me. "And there's nothing to be freaked out about anyway. I promise."

"Okay." I don't believe him, but I figure now isn't the time to get into that. Not if I have any hope of him getting to the point sometime soon.

"There was also a green string. Do you remember it?"

"Remember it? I see it every time I go to touch any of my strings. Which I do all the time, considering the platinum string is how I become a gargoyle."

"Yeah." He clears his throat. "So do you know what that green string connects you to?"

And just that easily, the butterflies in my stomach become giant man-eating moths. "I think the better question is, do *you* know what the connection is?"

His gaze is steady on mine as he answers, "Maybe."

34

(Green) String Theory

"'Maybe' isn't actually an answer," I say, watching him closely for anything that might give away what he's thinking.

"It is when I don't know for sure if I'm right." He pauses. "I'd planned to talk to you about it when we first got back to Katmere, but honestly, there just hasn't been time, and I wasn't even sure I was right. But your memories of going to the Gargoyle Court... Like I said, I'm not for sure that I'm right..."

"Yeah, well, you don't know if you're wrong, either, so just spit it out before I totally lose my shit here. Who does my green string connect me to?"

"Do you ever remember touching it?" he asks. "Maybe brushing against it?"

I'm about to say I don't think so, but when I look inside myself at the strings, I can't help noticing just how close the green string is to my platinum one. And considering how often I reach for that string—and the situations I'm in when I do—anything is possible.

"I don't know. I mean, maybe I have. Why?"

"Can you really try to think about it?" he asks. "Did you touch it that time in the library when we were having a fight and you turned to stone?"

"I don't think so..." I begin, but the look on his face says this is important—really important—so I close my eyes and try to picture it in my head.

"I was so mad at you that day. You were being a total jerk, and I just reached in and grabbed the platinum string and—" I break off as I see my hand wrap around my gargoyle string and, as I do, my knuckles just barely graze the green string.

"Is that why you freaked out?" I ask. "Because you knew I was touching that string?"

"I freaked out because you were turning to stone—real stone, like you did those four months we were trapped together."

"Are you saying it was the same?" I ask incredulously.

"I'm saying it seemed the same to me, both times."

"But that doesn't make any sense." I shake my head even as I try to wrap my brain around what he's saying. "I didn't even know the strings existed when I first turned to stone, so how could I have touched the green string way back then?"

"Instinct?" he suggests. "Accident? If it happened, does it really matter how?"

"I don't even know why it matters that it might have happened," I tell him.

"Because you want to know how you got to the Gargoyle Court. And I'm pretty sure the green string is the answer."

"But I didn't touch the green string before we went to the Gargoyle Court."

"Are you sure about that?" Hudson asks.

"Of course I'm sure. He brushed against me and—" I break off as I realize that Hudson might be right. I was rushing for my platinum string when it happened, and I wasn't being overly careful about it. It's totally possible that my fingers brushed against the green string.

"I don't understand," I say after a second. "I've never been to the Gargoyle Court. I never even imagined that it might still exist. How could I be the one who took us there just by brushing against my green string?"

"I don't know, but I'm almost positive you did."

"All my strings connect me to someone. You, my friends, my gargoyle. So why does this string have the power to—" I break off, searching for the best way to describe what the green string does and realizing I don't even know.

"Freeze time?" Hudson fills in the blank.

My stomach—and everything else inside me—plummets to the floor. "Is that what it does?" I whisper. "Freezes time?"

"It's what you do. It's what you did with us for those four months. And it's what you did—or I should say the opposite of what you did—when we came back and, well, time was different."

"What does being able to freeze and unfreeze—" I ask, but Hudson quickly interrupts me.

"Grace, who else do we know who can freeze and unfreeze time?"

"Who else—" I break off as horror swamps me. "I don't want to talk about this anymore."

"I think we *have* to talk about it," Hudson says grimly. "Because she's the only other person in the world I know of who can do what you do."

"Which means what exactly?" I ask, even though the sick feeling in my stomach warns me that I already know.

"I'm not sure. But I think we'd better find out." He clenches his jaw before adding, "The Bloodletter might be the only person who can help us find the Gargoyle Army, Grace."

35

Buckle Up, Buttercup

"I knew you were going to say that," I groan, rolling over to bury my face in the nearest pillow. I don't want to see that woman again. I just don't.

Damn it. Damn it. Damn it. I barely resist the urge to scream my head off into the pillow—the only thing stopping me is the fact that I can feel Hudson's eyes on me, and I know he's already concerned. The last thing I need is to lose it completely in front of him.

But come on. That woman is heinous. *Heinous.* I know she's helped me—for a price—every time I've asked something of her, but does help unraveling her mess negate the fact that she's the one who caused it to begin with? Does it negate the fact that she's the one who set all this in motion when she manipulated a mating bond between Jaxon and me?

My parents' deaths, Xavier's and Luca's deaths, Flint's leg, *Jaxon's soul*... All these things are because the Bloodletter meddled in my life.

It's that thought that has me turning over, that thought that has me reaching for Hudson's hand and pulling it to my chest where I can cradle it as I look into his eyes. He's grinning down at me indulgently, but the corners of that million-dollar smile of his are wilted and just a little forced-looking. His cheekbones seem a little more prominent than usual, and his gorgeous eyes look storm-tossed, like a cyclone is whirling inside his head, just out of sight.

"You okay?" I ask, even though I know he is anything but.

The grin kicks up a notch. "Of course."

"You don't look okay." I reach my free hand up to stroke his cheek.

He gives me a mock-affronted look. "Wow. So the bloom is off the rose already, huh?"

I roll my eyes. "You know what I mean."

"Do I?" Carefully, he moves the remnants of my lunch off the bed. And then he tackles me, rolling me over and over until we're balanced on the opposite edge of the bed. He's on top of me, his ridiculous face only inches from mine.

"Still think I look bad?" he asks, his fingers dancing over my ribs as he tickles me.

I'm too busy laughing my head off to answer.

"Is that a no?" he asks as he tickles harder and faster.

"Stop!" I gasp, laughing so hard, I'm practically crying. "Please stop!"

His fingers slow. "Does that mean you're done insulting me?"

"I don't know," I say, grabbing both his hands in mine. "Does that mean you're done throwing a wobbly?"

"Throwing a wobbly?" His brows shoot up. "*Someone's* been practicing their Britishisms. Although technically, I was *not* throwing a tantrum, I'll have you know."

Oh yeah, I got that word wrong. Dammit. I'd been reading up on British slang and wanted to impress him. "Yeah, well, someone is mated to a Brit, and she figures she should probably be able to understand him the next time he *throws a wobbly* and busts out the slang."

His eyes take on a wicked gleam. "I think you understand me just fine."

"I do," I agree. "Which is why I'm worried about you, Hudson."

"Nothing to be worried about," he answers, and for a second I think he's going to tickle me again. In the end, though, he just grins down at me with a soft look in his eyes.

I know I should push, know I should make him talk about what's bothering him. But when he's looking at me like this, and we have a few moments to just be, without all the shit we have to deal with crashing in on us, I don't want to push. I don't want to do anything but hold Hudson close to my heart—and the rest of me—for as long as I can.

So I do, wrapping my arms and legs around his body and burrowing as tightly against him as I can possibly get. "I love you," I whisper against the cool skin of his throat. I can feel his heart beating too fast, can feel the ragged up and down of his chest as he struggles against demons he doesn't want to share.

"I love you, too," he whispers back and just holds me, too.

Eventually, though, reality intrudes in the guise of a string of text messages hitting both our phones at the same time. The others are awake and ready to plan.

Hudson rolls away to grab his phone, and I pull a pillow and yank it over my face. Maybe if I play ostrich, I can get away with not being part of this discussion. And subsequently not doing what I know needs to be done.

"You know the longer you hide under there, the more decisions will be made without you, right?" he asks, amusement threading its way through his accent.

"You act like that's a bad thing," I shoot back—and end up with a mouth full of pillowcase for my trouble.

Hudson laughs as he pulls the pillow off my face.

"Hey, give that back." I make a grab for the pillow, but he holds it out of reach. "You're really not going to be reasonable about this, are you?"

His smirk grows bigger. "Because I'm the one being unreasonable here."

"Fine." I flop back onto the bed and stare at the white tile ceiling. "We can go see the Bloodletter."

"And you'll keep an open mind when you talk to her?"

"Are you serious?" I demand incredulously. "You're the one who is constantly fighting with her, so why are you lecturing me about keeping an open mind?"

"I'm allowed to fight with her—she hates me. But she has a major soft spot for you. Which means if we want to get anything out of her, you need to play nice with the old bird."

"What does it say about me that a homicidal old woman with a major agenda has a soft spot for me?" I wonder.

Hudson grins and finally drops the pillow next to me on the bed. "That you're so amazing, even a psychopath has to love you?"

"Now you're just kissing up." And then, just so he doesn't think he's gotten away with anything, I pick the pillow up and throw it at him.

He catches it with a wink—big surprise—then asks, "Is it working?"

"What do you think?" I climb out of bed, snagging my backpack on the way to the bathroom. Maybe I'll feel better about this whole thing after I get dressed.

With that thought in mind, I brush my teeth, turn the shower on, and try really, really hard to ignore the fact that Hudson has Linkin Park's "One Step Closer" playing softly in the other room. I know he thinks I can't hear it with the shower running, but it's one of those songs that's impossible to ignore—especially considering what he asked me before we passed out.

Is it just a random selection from a playlist? Or did Hudson subconsciously choose this song because it mirrors how he's feeling? Just how close he *is* to breaking?

It's a fucked-up thought in the middle of a fucked-up situation, and I spend half an hour stewing about the whole mess while I shower and get dressed. It's a little after ten a.m. now, which means it's the middle of the night in Alaska— maybe not the best time to drop in on the Bloodletter, but since sunrise is still another three hours away, it's pretty much the perfect time for Hudson to be there, considering he can't be in the sunlight right now. Which means I have almost no time to prepare for this. I just have to do it.

Still, before we go in there begging for answers—which pisses me off just to think about—I figure I should at least try to make sure Hudson is right. So after I pull on my hoodie, I lean against the bathroom vanity and close my eyes. Then I take a deep breath and let myself look—really *look*—at all the strings deep inside me. Which, oddly enough, doesn't mean actually looking with my eyes.

I mean, it's just easier to describe how I *see* my strings as *looking* at something, but I'm not using my eyes to see them. I think of them and then can see them in my mind, the same way I can see my childhood teddy bear, Rascal, or my mother's smile when I choose. And so I *look* inside for my strings, and they're all there, just like always.

The bright blue mating bond string with Hudson. The now-all-black string that connects me to Jaxon. My platinum gargoyle string. The hot-pink one for Macy. The super-thin turquoise one that is my mom and the russet-brown one that is my dad—I shudder a little as I realize just how precarious those bonds have gotten. It makes sense, I guess, considering they've been gone for months now. But it still hurts more than I want to admit to see them disappearing a little bit at a time.

I go through all the strings one by one, saving the green one for last because I don't want to deal with it. And, not going to lie, because I'm a little scared of it, too. Especially since it's glowing brighter than any other string except my mating bond with Hudson. I don't know what that means, and I'm not sure I want to know. The last thing I want or need to find out is that I'm also mated to some vengeful old woman who lives in a cave.

It's a little too paranormal Mother Goose for me, thank you very much.

Still, I'm learning that hiding from my problems doesn't make them go away. So I take a deep breath and, without letting myself think any more about it, I grab the green string intentionally for the first time in my life.

And I am not prepared in the slightest for what happens next. I thought maybe I would turn to stone, maybe the clock on my phone would slow down. Hell, maybe I would even turn into a twenty-foot-tall gargoyle.

Any of those things would have been better than this, this *anarchy*.

36

You Bring Out the TNT in Me

Electricity zaps through my body so fast that it steals my breath. And then I feel it, coiling deep inside me, like a cobra waiting to strike. More and more power, twisting, turning, filling every cell in my body until there's nowhere left for it to go. The tattoo on my arm that can store magic fills instantly, and still, there's even more power coursing through my veins, screaming at me to let it out. Let it do what it was meant to do: destroy everything in its path.

And I've never been more afraid in my life. Of this thing inside me, this burning need to set the world on fire and just watch it burn, burn, burn.

I instantly let go of the string, but the power coiling all my muscles tight is still shrieking to be set free, and I know I only have seconds before I can't control it anymore. My gaze bounces around the bathroom for an exit, but as soon as I realize the only way out is the bathroom door, I hear Hudson in the other room tell someone, "Come on in. Grace is just getting out of the shower, but—"

Acting purely on instinct, I dive into the bathtub and curl into myself…just as my body explodes, or what I think is my body exploding. There is a deafening, thunderous clap as all the electricity inside me is released in an instant. The shock wave shakes the walls, the mirror shatters, and the ceiling caves in around me, exploding plaster causing a dense fog of dust to make it impossible to see anything.

Hudson throws open the door as I take in shallow breaths, my ears ringing and my vision blurring, a panic attack seizing my body. What did I just do? And how?

I didn't hold the string for more than a couple of seconds, and it almost swallowed me whole, turned me into someone I barely recognized—a monster who wanted to devour the world.

I pull my knees up under my chin as I rock back and forth in the bathtub, tears streaming down my cheeks. For a minute, I worry my tears will scare

Hudson, but I must have accidentally turned on the shower when I hopped into the bathtub because water is spraying against one side of my face, washing away my tears.

"It's okay, Grace. I've got you," Hudson whispers in my hair, but I can't figure out how, when I'm in the bathtub and he's by the door...

The ground is moving up and down, and I blink. "Did I— Did I break the Earth?" My voice is thin and shaky, but Hudson must have heard me, because he chuckles, although it sounds more like nervous laughter than that I actually said something funny.

"No, babe, you didn't break the Earth. But I'm pretty sure I'm never getting my deposit back. In fact, I might now need to own a lighthouse."

Something feels soft beneath my legs before I realize Hudson must have carried me from the bathroom back to bed. His hands roam over my wet clothes, checking for injuries, but I'm too shocked to do more than pull into myself in silence. It's almost impossible to get a lungful of air into my chest, and I'm feeling faint from the shallow breaths, my hands shaking as I wrap them around my knees and wrap myself into a ball.

"Is she okay?" Macy asks from the doorway, then gasps. "What happened?"

"Can you tell me what two plus two is, Grace?" Hudson asks.

Why is he giving me a math test when I can barely breathe? Oh my God, I must have hit my head, and he's worried I have a concussion. My teeth are chattering so painfully, it feels like they're going to shatter at any moment, but I manage to say, "Fa-four."

"That's right, babe. What about four plus four?"

I take another quick breath, then another, and stutter, "Ay-eight."

"And eight plus eight?"

I take a deeper breath this time and open my eyes to show him I'm okay. He must be frantic if he's this concerned about a head injury. After another slow breath, I manage to say, "Six-teen."

Hudson lets out a long sigh, slides his body onto the bed beside me, then scoops me onto his lap. I curl into his warmth, my teeth already chattering less as he wraps his arms around me.

"Take one more deep breath, Grace. That's right. You're going to be okay." His hands stroke up and down my arms, chasing away the icy wake left by touching that damn green string.

I glance at my cousin, who waves her wand toward the bathroom before walking over to stand beside the bed now, shifting from foot to foot, unsure what to do, how to help. I reach out and grab her hand. "I'm fa-fine."

Jaxon and Mekhi are in the doorway an instant later, their gazes both locked on the bathroom I'd just been in, mouths hanging open, and I turn to see what they're looking at. And freeze.

The entire bathroom wall separating the bedroom from the bathroom is gone. As is the wall on the other side of the tub, giving the room a lovely wide view of the ocean beyond. The sink is lying on the ground, cracked into two porcelain chunks beside broken pipes, and I vaguely realize Macy must have been waving her wand to stop the water that's coating the room from continuing to spray. The bathtub survived the explosion, but not much else. Part of the ceiling lay across the edges of the tub, where my legs were. I shiver as I realize that a couple of inches higher and it would have come crashing down directly on my head instead.

"What the fuck happened here?" Jaxon asks, his head swinging to Hudson and me. "Are you okay, Grace?"

"I'm fa-fine," I repeat a little steadier, but that's all I can manage to get out.

Hudson raises one eyebrow and says, "I'm pretty sure Grace decided to grab her green string—and shaved a hundred years off my life."

37

More Like
Tickety Boo-Boo

"The green string is—" I pause, sort through my vocabulary for how to describe it, and realize there really is no perfect word. Eventually, I settle on the best answer I can. "Dangerous."

Hudson grins down at me. "Well, that sounds exciting."

"Sure, okay." I shake my head. My mate is seriously deluded if he thinks *that* was fun. I'm still weak when I turn back to my cousin, but one look at her makes me shove my own problems to the side. Because my sweet cousin looks like she's a woman on a mission. And not just any mission—one where she plans to take no prisoners.

She looks fierce as hell, her hair done up in shades of red, orange, and yellow, making her head look like she's caught fire. Thick eyeliner edges the lids of her eyes, and her clothes are solid black like coal.

"Your hair looks amazing," I say, and it's true.

All she says is, "It felt like time for a change."

"Well, I love it," I tell her, reaching out to touch the vividly colored strands. "You look incredible."

"Fake it till you make it, right?" she says with an unhappy twist of her lips, and my chest squeezes tight.

"Something like that," I agree as I motion for her to sit on the side of the bed. "What's up?"

She rolls her eyes. "I wanted to complain about my mom, but that can wait." She gestures to the missing wall, then waves her wand at me, instantly drying my clothes before tucking the wand back into her fanny pack. "Felt like a little minor redecorating this morning?"

I start to brush it off, but the look she gives me warns me not to do that. I sigh deeply—I really don't like thinking about what this means—and say, "Hudson thinks my green string ties me to the Bloodletter in some way."

"The Bloodletter?" Macy's eyes go wide, and her voice squeaks a little as she asks, "Like, *lives in a cave and is the most dangerous paranormal on the planet* Bloodletter?"

"Is there another one?" Hudson asks drily.

"God, I hope not." She mock shudders. "So how does that make you feel?"

My gaze flicks to Jaxon's back as he and Mekhi are lifting the fallen ceiling and dealing with the destruction in the bathroom. He acts like he's not listening to every word we're saying, but he hesitates at Macy's question, and I know he's waiting to hear my response. What I find more curious is that he doesn't seem at all surprised to hear I'm somehow linked to the Bloodletter. I make a mental note to ask him about it later, then turn back to Macy.

"How do you think it makes me feel? Like I want to puke. She's awful, and I swear to God, if I find out I'm mated to her, too, I'm hanging up my wings, my crown, and everything else I can think of."

Hudson laughs. "Mating bonds don't work that way. You can't have multiple mates without the other mate interested—"

"Yeah, I've heard that before," I interrupt with a snort. "And look where that got me."

"Mated to me is where that got you, thank you very much." He tries to sound properly indignant, but he's laughing too hard.

"So what do you want to do?" Macy asks after a second.

"What do I *want* to do?" I counter. "Or what do I think we *should* do?"

She laughs. "One of these days, those two things are going to be the same."

"Yeah, well, today is definitely not that day."

"That's what I figured." She pauses, twirling one fire-red lock of hair around her finger as she looks anywhere but at me. "Do you think she knows anything about my mother?"

"Honestly? I think she knows something about everything. I definitely think you should ask her when we go."

"So we're going?" Hudson asks.

"Once again, the difference between 'want' and 'should.' Of course we're going. Do I want to? Not even a little bit. But I have questions and so does Macy, and we both deserve answers."

"I know you're right. But the truth is, I don't even know what I'm supposed to ask." Macy throws up her hands as she looks back and forth between Hudson and me.

"How about, 'Why did my mother abandon me to run off with the vampire king?'" Hudson suggests. "Or, 'Why hasn't she contacted me in nearly a decade?' Or, my personal favorite, 'Why would a witch work for the most evil fucking vampire in existence?'"

"All good questions," Macy agrees on a shaky breath. "The only problem? I don't know if I can handle finding out the answers."

"Oh, Mace." I squeeze her hand.

She squeezes mine back for a second before pulling away. "And not just that, why wouldn't my father tell me? He let me think she just left us and that he had no idea where she was."

"Maybe he doesn't—" I say, but she cuts me off before I can add anything else.

"I don't believe that. You know how many times he speaks to Cyrus in a year? Or how many times he's been to the Vampire Court over the last eight years?" She shakes her head. "There's no way he didn't know. And that means he deliberately didn't tell me. Worse, he flat-out lied to me when I asked."

She's right. I know she's right, just like I have a pretty good idea of what she's feeling. Because every time I find out my mom and dad lied to me about something else, it makes me feel the same way. Betrayed. Hurt. Angry. Gullible.

Like, how didn't I know? How didn't I see all the tiny inconsistencies there must have been? Nobody keeps this many lies hidden—lies that have to do with everything they are and everything they believe—without making some mistakes. How did I not see through it all?

The fact that Macy is probably asking herself that same question—and feeling that same pain—makes me furious with Uncle Finn. Why would he keep this from her? And was he ever going to tell her? Or was he going to let her live her life thinking her mother had just vanished off the face of the earth?

"We really do have to visit the Bloodletter," I say, the words sticking in my throat. Because if I had my way, I'd never see that bitch again. "If we're going to rescue the kids and see your parents again, we need more answers. And Hudson and I think she might be able to tell us where the Gargoyle Army is hiding."

"Well, an army at our backs would be helpful," Macy agrees with a sigh. "When?"

I want to put it off, but when my gaze meets Hudson's electric-blue one, I know that's not going to be an option. Even before he quirks a brow and says, "There's no time like the present."

38

Divide and
Get Conquered

"I knew you were going to say that." Macy sighs again. "I can open a portal to Alaska, but not one into the Bloodletter's actual cave, since I've never been there, so make sure you bring your jacket."

She's talking to me, not Hudson, obviously. My hoodie is the warmest thing I packed, and I'm already wearing that. I get up and look through my backpack, though, to see if there's anything else I can layer and register the fact that I've only got one more set of clean clothes left, which means I'll have to do laundry as soon as we get back to the lighthouse. We all will, considering the others don't even have that.

Jaxon and Mekhi went to gather the gang, so I've got a few more minutes to enhance my wardrobe for the trip ahead.

"Can I just say that needing to worry about having clean underwear and stopping the apocalypse at the same time really freaking sucks?" I grumble as I pull my sweatshirt off over my head to layer on another T-shirt under it.

"True story," Macy agrees.

"I'll go shopping when it gets dark," Hudson says, closing his phone after an interesting call with the homeowner.

From what I could overhear, he is now the proud owner of a historic lighthouse in Ireland. Which, I have to admit, only makes me cringe a little that it's because I blew up a bathroom. I mean, when this is all over, I totally plan to come back here and show my mate how much I *really* love lighthouses.

"The former owner is going to send a contractor over to put some plastic over our new...window." Hudson winks at me and adds, "I'll see if I can pick up a few things for everyone when I go later."

"You don't have to do that—" I start, but Macy gives me a *shut up right now* look before batting her lashes and flashing him a super-sweet smile.

"You're the best, Hudson."

"So Grace keeps telling me," he agrees with a sly grin directed at me.

I roll my eyes. "As if." But when he holds out a hand to me, I take it. Because he's Hudson and he's mine, ridiculous requests—and ridiculous ego—aside.

"Usually, I like doing portals outside because there's more room, but since that's out of the question with neighbors so near," Macy says, "I can probably get one going downstairs."

"Considering what you did to get us to the Witch Court, I'm pretty sure you could open a portal anywhere," Hudson tells her.

"Right?" I shake my head, still astonished at the way she held the portal open even after she'd come through it. "That was completely badass. I mean, I didn't even know that was possible."

"That's because very few witches can do it," Hudson tells me before turning to my cousin. "The Witch Court should be kissing your arse instead of kicking you out."

"Yeah, well, the Vampire Court should do the same for you," she answers. "Cyrus is...I can't think of a strong-enough word."

"A psychopath," Hudson says flatly.

"Agreed," she says, and we all turn to head down the stairs.

Jaxon must have told everyone to get over here fast, because the whole gang is crowded into the narrow downstairs living room. Mekhi is lounging on the brown leather sofa, his legs propped up on the coffee table. Byron is sitting beside him, while the rest of the Order is hanging out on the barstools at the kitchen countertop. Dawud is taking up the only chair while Flint and Eden are leaning against the far wall. And Jaxon is just standing in the middle of the room like he owns it.

There isn't three square feet without a body in it, and I wonder if Macy plans to open a portal in the closet.

"We're going to the Bloodletter's," I announce. "Not everyone needs to go, though, if they don't want to. I know I don't want to."

"Seriously?" Dawud asks, eyes wide. "You're just going to drop in on her?" They sound like it's the most bizarre thing they've ever heard. Then again, maybe it is. The woman is practically feral, after all.

"I'm in!" Mekhi's booted feet hit the floor. "I've always wanted to meet her."

"Me too," Liam agrees.

"No," Jaxon says, "I need the Order, except for Mekhi, to go to the Vampire Court."

The room falls silent as every last one of us gapes at him.

"It's the only solution," he says. "We need information. Where Cyrus is keeping the kids, are they in danger right this minute, or do we have more time to strategize, anything useful."

Hudson clears his throat. "So you're leading your friends to their deaths, then? I didn't know you had it in you, Jaxon."

That earns him a glare. "Luca's parents were loyal to Cyrus—there's no reason to assume the Order won't be welcome as well. And if they seem suspicious, tell them you're all tired of being on the losing side of the fight." He waves a hand in my direction.

"Gee, thanks," I grumble.

Liam shakes his head. "I don't think anyone's going to buy that. I think we should all stick together. You might need our help with the Bloodletter."

"*Make* them buy it," Jaxon says. "We're only going to get so far without someone on the inside. It'll be safer if it's the whole group of you. Besides, I was raised by the Bloodletter. We'll be fine. You're needed to spy on Court for us."

Liam looks like he's going to object again, but Dawud's hand shoots up. "I'll go. No one knows I'm here, and Cyrus trusts my family."

I arch a brow. That last little bit is a lot to unpack, but I'll save my questions for when we're not so pressed for time. "Eden and Flint are coming with us."

Flint rubs his hands together. "Well, *this* ought to be fun."

"Is there anything we need to do to prepare?" Eden asks, looking a little shaken.

"Just make sure you keep your hands in your pockets," I mutter as I grab my shoes from their spot near the door and bend down to put them on. "She bites."

Jaxon shoots me a reproving look. "Only when she's hungry."

"Or provoked," Hudson volunteers.

"Yeah, well, you would know," Jaxon tells him.

He shrugs. "It's not my fault she doesn't appreciate my sense of humor."

"Because so many others do," Flint accuses.

I know he's lost his boyfriend and his leg to this fight—not to mention his brother. I know his mother sacrificed her dragon heart to save Jaxon, which might very well cost him his legacy, as well. I know he's got a right to be furious. But that doesn't mean he has a right to take it out on Hudson, who's fighting right alongside him, whenever he wants.

I don't call him out on it, though, not in front of everyone. But I'm definitely going to find a time to talk to him about it again later.

Macy turns to Jaxon. "Where is her cave? I don't need exact coordinates, but a general idea would be good so I know what part of Alaska I've visited that's closest to her."

"Aim for Copper Center, if you've been," Jaxon answers. "I'll take it from there."

"As it turns out, I have been to Copper Center itself more than once," Macy answers with a grin. "Which should make this a lot easier than I was afraid of. But first, let me open a portal near the Vampire Court for the others."

She lifts her arms and starts to spin the portal open. Behind us, the Order and Dawud get their final instructions from Jaxon, Mekhi offering some advice about where they might be holding the kids. Flint watches with a tight-lipped expression. Across the room, Hudson and Eden laugh about something I wish I could hear. Maybe it'd calm me down.

Because at the moment, I can't help the fear swirling in my stomach that I'm not going to like what the Bloodletter has to tell me about my green string and the shitstorm I just made of my bathroom.

39

It Sucks to Not Suck You Anymore

After a quick trip through Macy's rainbow portal, Jaxon, Flint, Mekhi, Eden, Macy, Hudson, and I find ourselves right in the middle of Copper Center, Alaska—at one in the morning. Or at least, I'm assuming it's right in the middle of the town, as we're surrounded by buildings, which I've found doesn't happen very often in this state.

"Nice job, Macy," Jaxon says, giving her an encouraging little pat on the shoulder. It's so unlike him that she turns to stare at him with her mouth open—as do I. I'm just beginning to wonder if he was body snatched in the portal when he follows it up with, "Let's get going."

The fact that he fades straight north without even thinking to ask the rest of our opinions reassures me, though. He's the same old Jaxon, even if he's looking more approachable than I've ever seen him.

Hudson rolls his eyes at me, and I just laugh. At least until he scoops me up in his arms and fades after Jaxon across a wide-open field.

"I was going to fly," I say, even as I settle myself more comfortably against him.

"I figured. But if you flew, I wouldn't get to do this," he answers, leaning forward so that his lips skate across my cheek. "Or this," he continues, right before he kisses me quickly.

"You make a solid point," I agree. I'm out of breath, and so is he, though I'm pretty sure it has nothing to do with how fast he's running. To test the theory, I kiss him again, then can't help laughing when he stumbles over a rock for pretty much the first time *ever*.

"Bloody hell!" he mutters even as he catches himself—and me. "You're dangerous, woman."

"Glad you finally figured that out," I tease as we race over the ground. It's dark, obviously, but the moon is bright enough that I can see the flowers and the creek beds with water rushing down them.

I've never been here when the whole area wasn't covered with snow, and I'm surprised my hoodie is enough defense from freezing my butt off.

After about thirty minutes, Hudson stops fading and comes to an abrupt stop next to Jaxon.

"Is this it?" Mekhi catches up and asks, wide-eyed and a little excited.

"This is it," Jaxon answers as he walks carefully through the rocky ground toward the cave entrance, still partially camouflaged.

We all decide now is a good time to take a quick break before we enter the vampire's lair. You never know with her if you'll need all your strength for a fight or not.

"Hey, can I talk to you for a minute?" I ask Jaxon, motioning with my head to join me off to the side of the cave entrance. Macy and the dragons are milling around, grabbing a water or snack after the journey here, psyching themselves up to confront a woman who regularly hangs people upside down in her house over a bucket.

"Sure, what's up?" He follows me around a tree and smiles down at me, and there's something about him in this moment—something warmer than I'm used to—that just kind of opens him up.

He's still got the whole bossy attitude—I don't think anything will change that—but he looks less isolated, more *happy*, I guess is the word I'm looking for. Which makes me hesitate on whether or not we should have this discussion. I decided the other day that he deserves to know the truth about the Bloodletter, about what she did with our mating bond, but the last thing I want to do is hurt him any more than he's already been hurt.

But when he lifts his brows, I can't think of anything else to say to take its place. Plus, I don't have the right to keep this information from him. I thought I did, justified why there was no point giving him the truth if it would only cause him pain, but I hate when other people keep stuff from me. I can't just turn around and do the same to him.

Which is why I nod toward an area a little farther away from the rest of the group and their super-hearing abilities and begin to walk that way. Jaxon follows me, but when I glance back at the group, I notice Hudson is watching us. He doesn't look jealous, and to be honest, he doesn't even look curious. He just looks resigned, and I realize a little late that I probably should have given him a heads-up that I planned to tell Jaxon everything. I'm not even sure why I didn't. Maybe I thought he'd try to talk me out of it.

"Grace?" Jaxon asks when I continue to stare behind me. "Are you okay?"

"Yeah, of course." I yank my attention back to him. I am the one who started this, after all. "I wanted to talk to you for a couple of minutes. About the—" Nerves get the better of me and my voice breaks, so I clear my throat and try again. "About the Bloodletter. There's something you should know."

Understanding dawns on his face, and he reaches for my hand, squeezes it tightly. "You don't have to say it."

"Yes, I do. I don't want to not tell you something—"

"She already told me," he interrupts. "The last time I was here. It's okay, Grace."

Of all the things I expected Jaxon freaking Vega to say to me in this situation, *It's okay, Grace* didn't even rank in the top one hundred thousand. For a second, I think my head might explode as the anxiety that had been coiling in my stomach launches upward, lodges in the back of my throat.

It takes me a little bit to actually form words again, but eventually I manage. "Wait a minute. She told you what she did? *With the mating bond?*"

"She did," he answers. "I know it sucks—"

"You know it sucks?" I squawk loudly enough that one of the bald eagles flying above us will probably mistake it for a mating cry. "That's all you have to say about what she did to us? That it *sucks*?"

His smile falters, and for a brief moment, that same sad look that breaks my heart is back in his eyes. "I don't know what else to say, Grace. I hate that you got hurt, hate everything you've had to go through because of one misguided decision—"

"Misguided?" I wonder if I should be looking around for cameras right about now. Because surely, surely I'm being punked. There is no other explanation for Jaxon taking this so calmly. "How can you be so understanding? How can you just forgive her for nearly destroying our lives like that? You almost lost your soul, Jaxon. You almost..." I break off, unable to even talk about what almost happened just a few days ago.

"She gave me you," he answers simply. "Whatever else happened, whatever else will happen in the future, she gave me the gift of being loved by you. Of loving you. Do you know what that means for someone like me? I didn't feel anything my whole life, and then you came into it and now I can feel...everything."

Tears bloom in his obsidian eyes. He blinks them away as quickly as they came, but it doesn't matter. Because I saw them, and they break my heart wide open all over again.

"Oh, Jaxon—"

"It really is okay, Grace." He reaches forward and boings one of my curls like he used to. "Being able to love you means maybe I'll be able to love someone else someday, maybe even the mate who was actually meant for me. Before you, I never could have imagined such a thing. And now..." He shrugs. "Now it doesn't sound so bad."

My heart pangs at his words. Not because I still love him like that—Hudson is my everything—but because I *still* love him. He's my family, and I want nothing more than for him to be happy—not just someday, but right now.

"You're the best. You know that, right?" I ask.

He shrugs. "Maybe."

I roll my eyes and bump him with my shoulder, but he just laughs and asks, "What do you call a boomerang that won't come back?"

"A boomewon't?" I ask without much hope.

"A what?" He shakes his head in mock disgust. "That was really bad. Like, really, really bad."

"Oh yeah? So what's the answer, genius?"

"A stick, obviously."

It's my turn to laugh, because, "That's so bad, it's good."

He looks extra proud of himself. "Exactly."

We turn to walk back toward the cave, and my eyes immediately go to Hudson. He's not watching us anymore. In fact, he's not looking at anyone. Instead, he's leaning up against a tree off to the side, scrolling through his phone like he's on the most fascinating feed ever.

He looks normal, so normal that I'm sure the others don't even notice. But I know him well enough to see the way his index finger is tapping on the back of the phone case like it does when he feels uncomfortable. I can see the tight jaw and braced shoulders, like he's prepared for a blow—and to make sure it looks like it rolls right off his back.

The pain at seeing him like that is way worse than a pang to the heart. It's a punch to the stomach, an ache that travels all the way through me.

Maybe that's why I turn to Jaxon and ask, "Hey, can you do me a favor?"

"Of course. Anything." His brows shoot up.

"Lay off Hudson a little. He—"

"It's not that easy, Grace."

"I know it's not. But think about the conversation we just had. You forgave the Bloodletter so easily, and she nearly destroyed you. She nearly killed your soul."

"Yeah, but he let Luca—"

"Do you think it's easy for him?" I ask, annoyance turning my voice sharp.

He crosses his arms over his chest. "It doesn't look hard."

"To kill people?" I ask, incredulous. "You don't think it weighs on him? You don't think it hurts him every time he uses his power like that? He may not let you see it, but he's struggling. Struggling with the fact that he didn't step in before Luca died. Struggling even more that he *did* step in and kill all those wolves indiscriminately."

I shake my head, realizing for the first time that I'm disappointed in Jaxon. Disappointed in Flint and Mekhi and Macy, too. Hudson is hurting to the point of begging me to take away his powers, and they can't see beyond their own emotions.

"It's a terrible power to have, Jaxon. The decision over who lives and who dies with a snap of your fingers—less than that, really. With a thought. One quick thought. In that one tiny moment, someone's brother will never come home, someone's child, someone's mother. And you know as well as I do, most of the people who follow Cyrus aren't evil like him. They just want to step out of the shadows." My voice catches as tears clog my throat. "And Hudson killed them all in the blink of an eye to save us at Katmere. If you can't see what that cost him, what it continues to cost him, then you're the worst brother ever, and he deserves better."

The muscle in Jaxon's jaw clenches, but he doesn't say anything, doesn't uncross his arms. But he is listening, I can tell, so I press my advantage. "The Bloodletter had a detailed plan that took away our choice in a mate, a plan that nearly cost you your soul. And you forgive her like it's nothing. But your brother doesn't want to use his power to kill people, doesn't want to be anything like your father, and *he's* the asshole?"

Jaxon doesn't respond, but he does nod before we turn and continue walking back to the others. And when we do, he looks at Hudson and asks, "Want to give me a hand with the rest of these wards?"

It's not much, but it's a start. And I will take it.

40

My, What Big Fangs You Have

Nothing looks familiar to me, but it's dark, and the obligatory layers of snow are long gone, so I'm not surprised. Then again, I had a terrible time finding the cave even when it was light out.

Jaxon obviously doesn't have the same problem, since he walks unerringly toward a tiny opening in the rocks, unraveling safeguards as he goes. Hudson takes the opposite side, removing safeguards there as well. They're both superfast at it, and within a couple of minutes, we're walking down the narrow ice chute that leads us deeper into the cave.

It's dark, so I pull out my phone to light the way to keep from slipping on the ice. Macy does the same thing, and we exchange commiserating looks as we pick our way down the slick tunnel.

A quick glance at Flint shows that his new prosthetic is holding up well, despite how slippery the ground is. I can't help noticing, though, that I'm not the only one checking. Jaxon—who has dropped back to the rear—is walking right behind Flint, his eyes locked on the dragon and poised to catch him at the first sign of a problem.

Flint, on the other hand, isn't paying attention to any of us—and he's not paying attention to the ice, either. He's locked inside his head, his jaw working and gaze far away.

"This place is wicked," Eden says, and when my flashlight glances off her, I can see she's looking around, eyes wide with awe.

"You have no idea how much," I tell her.

"What do you mean—" Eden breaks off as we round a corner. And what I mean becomes exceptionally obvious.

Because right in front of us, to the left, is my least favorite part of the Bloodletter's Cave—I mean, except for her.

It's the draining station.

And it's being put to full use—what looks to be an entire group of hikers hanging from the chains embedded in the ceiling. Their throats are cut open, and they are draining into buckets, which is a sight I've sadly gotten used to over my past couple of visits.

What is different this time, however, is that the Bloodletter is standing next to them, wiping blood from her lips with a fine linen napkin. Blood, I'm pretty sure, that is still warm.

She *just* killed these people—all six of them. And judging from the lack of defensive wounds I can see on them, even in a group, they never stood a chance.

And I get it. Or at least I tell myself I do. This is part of this world. Humans are the food supply for vampires. And while some, like my friends, drink a mixture of animal blood and blood from a more-than-willing human whom they *don't* kill (hello, Hudson), others are a little more old-fashioned. Like the Bloodletter. And Cyrus. And who knows how many others.

It's terrible to think about, though. And even more terrible to see—which is why I make a point of not looking too closely. At the bodies currently draining or the drops of blood on the Bloodletter's chin.

Macy stumbles when she gets her first look at the hikers. She screams a little as she falls, and I honestly don't know if it's the fall or the dead hikers that have her so freaked out. Probably both.

Eden darts forward and catches Macy. "Did she just—" she starts to ask, then snaps her mouth shut when the Bloodletter turns to look at her with swirling green eyes.

"My dear Jaxon, you've brought an entire tour group," the Bloodletter says in a saccharin-sweet voice that cuts like a scalpel. "And with no warning. To what do I owe the *honor*?"

Jaxon bows his head, and not for the first time, I'm struck by how much deference he shows this woman. How much respect and kindness and fear she engenders in him.

After everything that's happened—everything that I've learned about her— it's almost more than I can bear.

Maybe that's why I step forward and tell her, "Coming here was my idea."

Of course, Hudson chooses that exact moment to follow with, "Solitude is highly overrated. But we don't have to tell you that, since you know so much about it." The fact that he's leaning against an icy wall, playing Sudoku on his phone while he says it like the game is a million times more fascinating than standing in front of the most badass vampire in existence, only makes it more of a *fuck you* to her.

And every single person here knows it.

Jaxon makes a choking sound deep in his throat, and I'm pretty sure the noise coming from Macy is a whimper. Flint and Eden don't make a sound, but they don't have to. The looks on their faces say it all, like they're just waiting for her to smite him.

I, on the other hand, half expect her to freeze him like she did last time, but she makes no move toward him. She does, however, shoot him a look as cold and sharp as the icicles hanging from the ceiling of this tunnel. "And yet, here you are. Which I can only assume means my aid isn't overrated, even if I myself am."

"I don't know about that," he responds with a shrug. "Even a broken clock is right twice a day."

Now Macy isn't the only one whimpering. Flint lets go of his mad long enough to look at Hudson like he's lost his mind…and also to glance around the ice chute for an escape hatch. I don't blame him. If Hudson keeps antagonizing her, we're definitely going to need one. Or two.

Which is why I step between them. I love Hudson, but if the Bloodletter loses her temper and turns him into a cockroach because of his attitude, I'm going to have to seriously reconsider our mating bond.

"I'm the one who needs advice," I say, resting a gentle hand on Hudson's arm to keep him from saying anything else. He and the Bloodletter took an instant dislike to each other when they first met—mostly because at the time, she was trying to convince me that he was a stone-cold killer with no remorse. Add in the fact that she created a fake mating bond between Jaxon and me, and she is pretty much his least favorite person on the planet. Which is saying something, considering Cyrus exists.

Not that I blame him. I feel exactly the same way about her. But I also don't want to have to come back here again, so I'd rather just suck it up and get the information we need. If she's somehow tied me to her the way she tied Jaxon and me together, I want to know about it. And then I want to figure out how to make it disappear.

At first, the Bloodletter doesn't even bother to look at me. Instead, she stays laser focused on Hudson—eyes narrowed, teeth bared, fists clenched. While he, on the other hand, barely deigns to glance her way. I've known him for months, and I have never seen him this interested in his phone. Or Sudoku.

I rush on, in the hopes she stops looking at my mate as if she'd like to see him hanging over a bucket. "I'm able to see connections to everyone who has an emotional tie to me in my head, including to my gargoyle. I see colored strings, for lack of a better word. And one of those strings...I think one of those strings ties me to you. And it's powerful."

The Bloodletter takes her time turning to look at me, but when she does, her expression is considerably softer.

"Come." She holds a hand out to me. "I find the cold tires me lately. Let's go into my parlor where it's warm."

And then, without pausing to see if any of us is bothering to follow her, she turns and toddles back down the icy walkway, looking for all the world like she's aged a hundred years in the months since we've seen her last.

41

Don't You Mean
Darth Madar?

"Jaxon, can you please get me a blanket?" she asks, her voice wavering just a little as she sinks down on the white velvet sofa.

The sitting room has changed again, I notice, as Jaxon pulls a blanket out of the chest by his feet. The walls are lavender now, the same color as the armchairs positioned across from us. Both the couch and chairs have pillows with violets and greenery on them, and the fireplace at the end of the room casts a rosy glow on all of us.

"She has a fire?" Macy whispers to me as Jaxon lays the blanket over the Bloodletter's lap. "In an ice cave?"

"How does she keep the ice from melting?" Eden asks.

"It's an illusion," I answer. "Just like the rest of the room." And her frailty? I wonder as she takes a minute to arrange herself. Is that an illusion, too? And if it is, what is the most powerful vampire in the world going for by pretending to be weak?

"Would anyone like some tea?" the Bloodletter asks, waving her hand, and a teapot and cups suddenly appear on the coffee table.

"Is there really tea?" Macy asks in an aside. "Or is that an illusion, too?"

I shrug, shake my head. Despite the fact that there is some bizarre green string connecting us, I am about as far from an expert on the Bloodletter as anyone can get.

When no one answers, my cousin says, "Thank you. I'd like some tea," into the silence. The look she shoots me says that there's only one way to find out.

A savage amusement lights the Bloodletter's eyes when she turns to her. "By all means, dear."

Macy leans over, tipping the teapot and pouring the warm amber liquid into a cup. She grabs a pair of little tongs and drops two sugar cubes into the hot liquid as well. Though that leads to another question—

"Where does she get the sugar cubes if she prefers her food...bloody?" Eden wonders softly.

Yeah. That question.

Macy's hand shakes as she leans over the cup, blowing softly to cool the tea before she takes a sip. I mean, she said she wanted a cup. She can't back out of it now just because we're all suddenly unsure where the sugar—or tea, for that matter—comes from. The pleasantly surprised look on her face, though, says it's actually good—which is another question for another day. Because when the Bloodletter pins me with her very direct, very intimidating gaze, I realize that our time is up.

Even before she says, "Grace, dear. Why don't you come sit on the couch with me? We can talk about this question of yours."

I don't want to sit on the couch. In fact, I don't want to go anywhere near her. But the look in her eyes says she won't take no for an answer. And since we—since *I*—need her help, it's the same old story, different day. Play by her rules or get out.

Which is why I make my way toward her, under Hudson's and the rest of my friends' careful gazes. I don't, however, sit on the couch. Instead, I choose to sink into one of the pretty lavender armchairs. Being accommodating is one thing, but being a pushover is another.

And I am more than sick of being a pushover when it comes to this woman, who has caused the people I care about so much pain. This woman whose machinations set so many horrible things in motion.

The Bloodletter raises her brows at my choice of seat, and when that doesn't get me to change my mind, she stares me down for several seconds as my friends shift uncomfortably. I stare back, refusing to be intimidated by her for one second more. Is she capable of killing me? Absolutely. Do I believe she'll do it right here, right now, in front of her precious Jaxon? I don't think so. Not when she's going through so much trouble to put on a show for him.

"Why don't you come sit on the sofa, Grace?" she finally says in a voice made of steel. "Lately, my hearing isn't what it used to be."

"I'm comfortable here, thank you," I tell her, deliberately raising the volume of my voice so the poor old thing can hear me. I barely resist an eye roll at the thought.

Her eyes narrow, and I wait for her next parry. Which—it turns out—is to snap her fingers and freeze everyone else in the room. As soon as they're frozen, her face somehow changes from the soft vulnerability she's been projecting since we got here into the hard, violent woman I know and definitely don't love. The woman who is more than capable of taking down an entire hunting party without batting an eyelash.

"What game are you playing, Grace?" she snaps out in a voice that brooks no more disobedience.

But I'm over catering to her. If she wants to rip out my throat, then I guess she's going to have to try to do just that. Because I'm not rolling over for her. Not this time. Not ever again.

"I'm pretty sure that's the question I should be asking you," I snap back.

"I'm not the one who came to find *you*," she replies, and she's not wrong. Which grates just a bit too much for my liking.

I narrow my gaze on her. "No, but you're the one who keeps making it necessary for me to come to you." Then, taking a deep breath in an effort to keep my worry at bay, I brush my hand over the green string deep inside me as well as the strings of my friends and mate. That's how I unfroze Hudson when we were here last time, and maybe it will work—

A glance over my shoulder shows that it has. My friends are all unfrozen, and none of them look like they're any wiser for it. Except maybe Hudson, who is watching both of us with careful, considering eyes.

The Bloodletter has her hand lifted, like she's ready to freeze my friends yet again. And I lean forward, say through clenched teeth, "Stop. Stop trying to play God with my friends and me."

She pauses at my words, her lips twisting into something that looks a lot like an amused smirk. "You're asking for more than you know, Grace."

"Oh yeah? And why is that?" Because, seriously, how egotistical does a person have to be to have a comeback like that?

"It's kind of hard for me not to play God," she finally says. "Considering who I am."

"The oldest vampire in existence?" I make sure that my tone says it's no big deal.

"The God of Chaos," she answers, her green eyes doing that strange swirly thing that makes everything inside me feel queasy. "And that green string you keep brushing against? It *does* connect us—because you're my granddaughter."

42

I Don't Think
There's a Chromosome
for This

Her words hang in the air like a grenade with the pin just pulled. And like a grenade, there's only a few seconds of stillness before the bomb explodes and all hell breaks loose.

Shock ricochets through the room.

Macy gasps.

Mekhi rocks back on his feet.

Eden murmurs, "Holy shit!"

Even Flint's normal thundercloud expression dissolves in an astonished, "What did she say?"

Only Hudson and Jaxon don't respond to her words, and as my blood runs cold, I turn around to look for them—to see if they believe her. To see if *I* should believe her.

Hudson hasn't moved from where he's leaning against the wall, but there's a tension in him that wasn't there before. A kind of watchfulness that tells me, appearances aside, he's paying very close attention to this conversation and that maybe—just maybe—she isn't saying anything that he didn't expect to hear. Which makes me wonder what else he's been piecing together in that too-sharp brain of his and why he hasn't seen fit to share any of it with me.

When our gazes meet, he smiles just a little. There's encouragement in that smile, encouragement and support and a belief in me that grounds me, that makes me believe that I can do anything—even if that means taking on the Bloodletter on her own turf.

Jaxon, on the other hand, looks as shocked as I feel—not to mention angry as hell when he marches forward to stand behind me.

"What are you talking about?" he demands. "You're a vampire—"

"I choose to be a vampire," she answers. "Just like my sister chooses to be human. And Grace is a gargoyle. That doesn't mean there isn't something else there."

"You could choose to be something else?" I can't stop the question from tumbling out of my lips. It's such a contrary thought to how I feel, that being a gargoyle is a part of who I am on a cellular level. Would I choose to be a different creature if I could?

The Bloodletter raises one regal brow. "Of course. I created paranormal creatures from the source of my power, so they are all a piece of me, and I them. All my creatures are beautiful and perfect. Well, except"—she glances over at Flint—"the dragons. I still cannot believe I gave you so much power and strength, and you prefer to let a little bauble or gold bring you to your knees. Such an ultimately weak creature."

Flint growls, leaping forward and landing before Jaxon. "You bi—"

But Flint breaks off when she sends him slamming against the nearest wall. Jaxon rushes to Flint's side, but he shrugs off Jaxon's help, pushing himself to his feet on his own. Not willing to leave the insult against his people alone, he goes to lunge for the Bloodletter—who looks nothing if not amused—but Mekhi and Eden are right there, blocking his path to her.

"What's wrong with you?" Flint yells, anger radiating from every pore. "Who the fuck does she think she is?"

"Someone who can do and say whatever she wants," she answers calmly.

A god, she seems to be implying.

"Yeah, well, god or not, you're still an asshole," he snarls.

This time, she doesn't bother throwing him into a wall. Instead, she snaps her fingers, and Flint ends up hanging upside down, inches from the ceiling.

"Someone ought to teach you to keep a civil tongue," she snarls back.

His only answer is to flip her off while upside down. Which only pisses her off more. She lifts a hand to smite him—or whatever the hell it is gods do—but Jaxon moves in front of Flint.

"Don't do it," he warns, and for a second it looks like she's going to smite him, too. But in the end, she just shakes her head and drops her hand with a sigh.

Flint falls along with it, so quickly that he has no chance to shift, no chance to right himself. I shriek and start to race for him, but Jaxon is already there to catch him, his black boots braced on the slippery ice.

Flint lands against him with an "oompf," and for a second, it feels like time stops. But then Flint is growling, "Get the fuck off me," as he shoves at Jaxon's chest.

Jaxon lets go the second he's got Flint's feet safely on the ground, but he keeps a steadying hand on the dragon's elbow—at least until Flint shrugs him off.

Silence reigns across the cave as we all come to grips with the fact that the Bloodletter is even more powerful than we thought. That—despite her little fragile act from earlier—she is most likely more than capable of kicking any and all of our asses.

It's a hard pill to swallow, considering what she just told us.

But now that the shock has worn off from her initial declaration—or at least dulled it a little—I want to argue with her, to tell her it's impossible we're related.

Then she turns to me, and I see something new in her swirling green eyes.

Something that looks a whole lot like vulnerability.

Or at least it feels that way, especially when I think about the fact that she called me her granddaughter.

My head pounds. My stomach rolls and pitches. My knees shake.

The God of Chaos. She's the *God of Chaos*? I didn't even know that was a thing. I didn't know any of this was a thing.

I mean, yes, the Crone told us a story about how the God of Chaos created paranormal creatures, but I thought that's what it was—a story. And I know this world is filled with a myriad of creatures and experiences I never imagined were real before I stepped inside Katmere Academy, but *actual gods*? Of chaos and who only knows what else? That's a far cry from figuring out my boyfriend is a vampire.

And she thinks she's my grandmother?

Like tumblers in a lock clicking into place, Alistair's comment that his mate might bite me if I insult her makes so much sense now. The gargoyle king is mated to the Bloodletter. Which is not the weirdest thing I've discovered today, sadly.

But then my stomach turns to stone as a horrifying thought occurs to me. I promised the Unkillable Beast I'd give his mate the Crown.

43

Mommy
Not So Dearest

"**Y**ou may call me Grand-mère," she continues. "Although your power is that of a daughter, not a granddaughter."

"I don't know what that means," I tell her and bite my lip. There's a part of me—a huge part, if I'm being honest—that hopes she's being metaphorical.

She looks like she's about to say more but then glances toward the others and tells them, "Sit." As she does, extra chairs pop up around the room.

Though there is now a seat right next to him, Hudson makes his way over to me and sits in the other lavender chair while Eden and Mekhi finally take a load off, too. Flint and Jaxon don't move to sit.

The Bloodletter smiles thinly as she turns back to me, one eyebrow arching as she ignores my comment and asks, "What really brings you here, Grace?"

"I told you. The green string."

She steeples her hands in front of her chin and looks at me over them. "But you've been aware of that *string* for months. What suddenly made you decide to come to me about it today?"

"Hudson realized that when I touched it, I could do some of the same things you can do. Add in the fact that Alistair told me to come—"

"You've seen him?" The Bloodletter's gaze narrows as she leans forward and grips my hand so hard, it hurts. "Is he all right? Where is he?"

I pull away slightly, but she's shaking beneath that psychopath exterior, and my heart softens just a tiny bit.

"Yes, I saw him, but he's gone now," I say, thinking about that last encounter in the hallway. "He said he had to go find his mate. As for how he is…" I trail off, not sure how to describe him when "all right" seems like a stretch.

"He's confused." Hudson steps in, keeps me from floundering any more. "He was chained in a cave for a thousand years and attacked regularly by people who wanted to kill him. I feel like that would make anyone a little off."

"It's the voices," I tell her. "He hears gargoyles' voices talking all at once inside his mind, begging him to come back, to save them. He can't quiet them, and he can't think over them. There are too many."

"Too many?" Flint speaks up for the first time. "How many gargoyles are there?"

"Thousands," the Bloodletter and I answer at the same time.

"Thousands and thousands," she continues when I fall silent. "And Alistair has been trapped with them for more than a millennium. He could filter them when he was in command. But being trapped in that cave…" She looks around her own cave. "I can see why he had a more difficult time blocking them as they became more desperate. There are so very many of them."

Another spurt of sympathy leaks through for her. I try to tamp it down, which shouldn't be hard when I remember all the terrible things she's done. But then I think about the fact that the Unkillable Beast is her mate and wonder if being trapped for a thousand years without Hudson would erode my humanity as well.

Which makes me consider what I would do to free Hudson if he were trapped for a thousand years. I don't like to think that I would put anyone else's life or happiness in jeopardy to save his, but I can't say that for sure. There isn't much I wouldn't do to keep him healthy and whole. Including fight with him about taking his powers when I really believe it's something he'll regret later.

"I don't get it," Macy says. "I thought Grace was the only gargoyle born in a thousand years. When she turned to stone at Katmere, it was a huge deal. Experts came from all over to see her because—"

"Because they believe her to be an impossibility," the Bloodletter finishes for her. "And she would be had she not come from a long line of gargoyles. Her mother was one, as was her mother, and her mother before her."

My throat tightens as betrayal sucks the oxygen from the room. I knew my mom had to be a gargoyle when Alistair told me I was his progeny, but hearing the Bloodletter say it, realizing my mother never told me something so essential about myself, is heartbreaking. Hudson must sense my distress, because he reaches over and pulls my hand into his lap, his strong fingers lacing with mine and squeezing.

"My mother knew she was a gargoyle?" I choke the question past the tightness in my throat on a ragged whisper. "And she never told me?"

The Bloodletter's eyes widen as she takes in my reaction. "She didn't know what she was any more than you knew."

I blink back the tears in my eyes, trying to sort through the information the Bloodletter has shared so far. I am beyond frustrated at her methods of only telling us what she thinks we need to know. "Why can't you ever just tell us everything?" I shake my head. "You know, we could have killed your *mate* when you sent us for the heartstone without telling us who he really was!"

The Bloodletter smirks. "No, you couldn't have. He's called the Unkillable Beast for a reason." When it's clear from my raised brows that I still don't understand, she shrugs. "He's mated to a god, Grace."

I shoot Hudson a quick glance and swallow. Then I ask her, "Does that mean Hudson is immortal, truly immortal, like me, because he's my mate?"

But she shakes her head. "I was born a god. I will always be a god, even if my power has been reduced to that of a demigod due to my sister poisoning me." She leans back against the sofa cushions. "You are the descendant of a god and a gargoyle, therefore you will never be more than a demigod. Well, unless you were to Transcend, but that's a conversation for a different day."

My shoulders sag. For a moment, I allowed myself to imagine a world where I wasn't afraid something, or someone, would one day take my mate from me. That I'd never lose the person I love most in the world like I lost my parents.

I grit my teeth. "Regardless, don't you think everything would be easier if you just laid it all on the table? Told us everything for once?"

"Yeah, and maybe we wouldn't have to watch more of our friends die," Flint snaps, and I flinch. From his pain but also a little bit from fear at how the Bloodletter will react. It wasn't that long ago she had him hung from the ceiling like fresh meat at a farmer's market.

But she doesn't even glance his way, her gaze continuing to hold mine.

"I am going to do something I do not normally offer anyone, Grace," the Bloodletter eventually says. "I am going to give you a choice. I can tell you how to find the Gargoyle Army—the real reason you came to see me today"—Macy gasps, but the Bloodletter doesn't miss a beat—"but it will require telling you everything about where you came from and who you really are. And I cannot promise you will like what you hear. Or...I can tell you how to run from Cyrus forever. Hide your friends, too. Both options will stop Cyrus, for now, but choosing to run won't save those kids. Nor will it prevent him from continuing down his search for ultimate power, but you can have a full life. Away from death and destruction. As far away from pain as a person can hope to be. The choice is yours, Grace."

And there it is, my weakness laid bare before everyone. Because I want so badly to take the out she's giving me, and I can tell she knows it, too. I don't want to learn anything about my green string or how we're related, how my parents might have lied to me my entire life in ways I can't even fathom, or how I might be a pawn in a giant game of chess being played among gods, expected to live and die at another's whim, expose how little control I actually have in my life. I just want to go back to Hudson's lighthouse and be with the boy I love and forget there's a big, scary world out there.

My heart is pounding against my ribs so hard, it's a wonder they don't crack, and I wipe my damp palm along my jeans. I'm sure my other hand is just as sweaty, but Hudson doesn't seem interested in ever letting it go. Letting *me* go.

I turn toward my mate and bite my lip. I know what I *should* do. But the Bloodletter gave me a choice. The blue pill or the red one, to quote one of my favorite movies, and I want to take the blue pill so, so badly, my hands are shaking with the effort not to run. My lungs tighten.

Then my gaze connects with Hudson's, and the breath stills in my chest.

In a blink, his oceanic eyes take in everything I'm trying so hard to hide. He knows. He knows I'm struggling with a panic attack, that I'm always struggling with them. He knows I want to take her offer and hide from Cyrus, that I'd do anything to avoid the feeling that I can't breathe, that I can't control my own body. And he knows if we do, it'll likely mean we end up living in some cave at the ass end of Alaska, wards on the walls to keep Cyrus from getting in just like the Bloodletter has. Or worse, we go on the run, and he'll have to use his gifts, chip away at his soul week after week, to keep us safe. But he doesn't mind. He's got me.

His eyes crinkle just a little at the corners, speaking without words that if this is what I want to do, if this is what I *need* to do, he's with me a thousand percent. This isn't a question of me giving up on myself, like with the giant fight, and needing my mate to give me a kick in the ass to dig deeper and keep going, to believe in myself as much as he does. No, this is Hudson supporting whatever decision I need to make for my mental health—and just like that, I take a deep breath, fill my lungs with the oxygen I didn't know I was denying myself, and my shoulders relax.

As if there was any doubt, he mouths, *I love you.* And I melt. I just melt.

I mouth back, *I know,* and he squeezes my hand, one corner of his mouth tipping up in a half smile.

My gaze flicks to Jaxon, standing next to a fat red chair, his jaw set, his eyebrows raised as if to ask, *Why aren't you demanding she tell you everything?* And Flint, slightly in front of him with his fists on his hips, weight on the balls of his feet, ready to take on the Bloodletter again with his bare hands. Macy's hair that's like living flames, her eyes begging me to find out what happened to her mother at any cost. Even Mekhi and Eden have already assumed that of course I will want to hear how to defeat Cyrus, how to rescue the kids. They're both leaning forward, arms on their knees, eyes trained on the Bloodletter, ready to listen to whatever story she wants to tell us.

In fact, the only two people who've guessed I want to run away are Hudson and the Bloodletter. My gaze shifts to her swirling green eyes, and she has one eyebrow raised as she stares me down. She gave me a choice, but it's just as obvious she already knows which option I'll choose, and she's tired of me wasting her time.

And she's right.

No matter how badly I want to run away right now, I won't. I may have a panic attack while she's talking, I may even need a good cry afterward, but that doesn't mean I won't do everything I can to save my people, save this world from Cyrus, prevent others from suffering.

"Well, child? Which is it to be?" the Bloodletter asks.

I take another deep breath, tilt my chin as I hold her gaze steady. "I'd like to know exactly how to kick Cyrus's butt back to whatever rock he crawled out from under. Tell me everything."

It's only slightly unsettling that the Bloodletter and my mate respond at exactly the same time with, "That's my girl."

44

"Like all stories, it's best if we start at the beginning." She looks from one of us to another as she takes in our group. "In the beginning, two gods gave birth to twins, two daughters. One was the God of Chaos and the other the God of Order—"

"Wait," I interrupt. "We've heard this story. What were their names?" My mind searches back to the story the Crone told us before Hudson and I went to prison, but I can't recall their exact names.

The Bloodletter arches a brow. "You've heard the story of Cassia and Adria? Perhaps as a bedtime story?"

I shake my head. "No, a witch called the Crone told us recently. We had heard she built the prison Hudson and I were being sent to, and we went to her asking for a way out."

Her brows slash down. "You went to my sister for help? And she *gave* it?"

"The Crone is the God of Order?" Macy squeaks. "But—she implied the God of Order was basically a bitch."

"Adria is cunning, my dear," the Bloodletter says to Macy. "If she told you the story, then she had a purpose. And I sincerely doubt it was to benefit me—or you. She positively hates all paranormal creatures, hence why she built the prison to keep them locked away."

Okay, that actually makes more sense. I glance at Hudson, and he shrugs. I can't believe we never made that connection. Then something occurs to me. "But the Crone is a witch. How can she hate paranormals if she *is* one?"

The Bloodletter laughs without humor. "Adria is no witch. She's a god, same as I am. I'm sure it tickles her to no end that paranormals are coming to *her* for help, believing she is one of them."

"But she did help us," I insist. "Without her flowers, Hudson and I would still be in prison."

"And she did this for free, did she?" the Bloodletter asks.

"Well, not entirely, of course. Nothing in this world is free. Especially nothing of value." I paraphrase the Crone's words. "I was required to owe her a favor, at a time of her choosing, in return."

The Bloodletter leans forward, her green eyes piercing straight through me. "Listen to me carefully, Grace. You cannot do this favor for her, no matter what it is. Adria has wanted only one thing since we were children, to see the death of every paranormal creature, and she would sleep with the devil himself to achieve this goal. And did."

My pulse trips at her words, but I think back on my conditions to the favor she can ask. "I insisted on caveats before I would agree. She cannot ask me to do anything that will harm anyone, either directly or indirectly." Surely this is enough to ensure my favor cannot be used against anyone.

The Bloodletter shakes her head, pity turning down the corners of her mouth. "There is always a loophole in magic, my dear. Always." She smooths the blanket Jaxon brought her on her lap. "But perhaps I should finish my story first."

I nod, eager now to hear how the Bloodletter will tell the tale of these two gods versus the Crone. Hudson voices the same thought but with considerably less diplomacy. "By all means. A catfight between two sisters in which the fate of all paranormals hangs in the balance feels like something the rest of us should definitely know more about."

The Bloodletter sighs. "You really are a cheeky bastard, aren't you?" She turns to me. "Are you sure this is the mate you want? I could smite him for you, if you like, free you up to find another."

Hudson stiffens next to me, but there's no fire behind the Bloodletter's words. In fact, if I'm not mistaken, there's a fair bit of approval in my choice glowing in her eyes. "He's fine for now, thanks," I reply with a wink at him.

Which makes Hudson roll his eyes and mutter under his breath, "Definitely related."

The Bloodletter continues. "I'm sure my sister told you that the God of Order was so angered by my creation, she poisoned the Cup of Life, which took my godhood and trapped me on earth as a demigod. Which of course trapped her as well, as what happens to one must happen to the other." We all nod. "Angered even more that she was now stuck here in a world of paranormals, watching her humans die before her very eyes, she set upon her agenda of wiping all paranormals from the face of the earth. She built prisons for your kind, prisons with unbreakable curses where no one is ever set free. She trained hunters and equipped them with all they'd need to kill each species." She turns to Flint. "And the hunters were successful. So successful, they helped humans hunt dragons to near extinction, if I remember correctly, which is why I helped create the Dragon Boneyard so you could at least honor your dead."

Flint's eyes widen as his eyebrows shoot up. "*You* created our sacred Boneyard? I thought the witches did that through a pact. At least, that's what we're taught in school."

The Bloodletter shakes her head. "I have done a great many things to protect your kind, which is why it bothers me to no end that you worship a pile of gold instead." Her gaze slides to Jaxon, and a softness settles in her features. "But I suppose I will get over it soon enough now that I have a dragon in the family."

Dragon in the family? She must be referring to Jaxon's dragon heart, although I wouldn't necessarily call him a dragon.

She turns back to me and continues. "It was a dark time, living among you, watching my sister and her hunters chase you down, force you into the shadows. And so we waged war against the humans. If they wouldn't let you into the light, we would drag them into the shadows with us. I taught vampires how to grow stronger"—she holds Hudson's gaze—"and how to develop gifts. I took charge of our armies...and I showed no mercy."

With a wave of her hand, we're suddenly surrounded by hundreds and hundreds of creatures and humans charging at each other on a massive field. Fierce battle cries, metal slashing against metal, and the screams of the dying, even the pitiful sobs of the wounded crushed under the heavy bodies of the dead toppling onto them all mix in a terrifying symphony of war that chills my blood. And in the center of the melee is a much younger Bloodletter, outfitted in black from head to toe, two vicious triple-bladed and double-sided knives clenched in her hands as she slices through her enemies like butter. Dozens of humans charge her with their swords raised, and she fades, ducks, flips, twists—and with each graceful dodge, her elegant knives arc through the air with deadly precision and slice into muscle and tendon. One by one, they fall. Piles and piles of bodies lay at her feet. And her face and clothes are drenched in their blood.

"*Bloodletter,*" I whisper.

"Yes, I was given that horrible name for my relentless hunger for the blood of humans." She waves her hand, and the horrid scene disappears. "But not everyone could stomach the killing, the bloodshed, and our own factions began to disintegrate, to side with the humans. We ended up losing the First Great War two thousand years ago, and we tried to go home and regroup, find some semblance of a life in those of us left. But my sister saw her dream within sight now, and she refused to allow you any peace from her hunters. With our kind nearly extinct, I knew I had to do something. So I trapped myself in here, sacrificed myself—which meant I trapped my sister, too. It was the only way to stop her, or at least slow her down."

The Bloodletter pauses, and the emptiness in her eyes is replaced by something else, something almost *proud*. "And then I knew I had to give you a gift that would help you survive. A gift so precious, even I didn't know the full extent of what I had done at first." She pauses again. "With as much of my godhood as I could draw, I created the magic of mating bonds. I thought if you were at least mated, you would have a better chance of survival, a better chance to see a hunter coming at you if you were not alone."

I gasp. "Is that how you knew how to create a fake mating bond between Jaxon and me?"

Everyone except Hudson and Jaxon gasps at that statement, and my stomach sinks. I blurted out Jaxon's private business without thinking, something I had no idea if he wished to remain a secret or not, and I feel awful. I twist in my seat to catch his gaze and mouth, *I'm sorry*. He tosses me a half smile, and I know he forgives me, but I want to say more or at least offer him a hug in apology. And I would, if Flint wasn't staring at Jaxon like he's never seen him before—and Jaxon turns to stare right back. And now all I want to do is face forward again and not be a fly on the wall for whatever is going on between those two.

"Of course, dear," the Bloodletter confirms. "But let's not get ahead of ourselves just yet." Her gaze turns to the fire, her eyes swirling as if caught in the flames. "Magic has a funny way of finding its place in the universe, seeking its purpose. And once unleashed, it takes on a life of its own."

An eerie quiet settles in the room, the crackling fire with its random hisses and pops the only sound, as no one wants to interrupt the Bloodletter again. It's as though we can sense that what she's about to tell us next is going to change everything.

"And my plan worked. Paranormals were again learning to thrive, just starting to step back into the light, which only escalated my sister's anger toward your kind. And her vengeance knows no bounds." The Bloodletter's gaze snaps to mine, and a chill skates along my spine.

"So our parent created gargoyles, and that was the beginning of the end."

45

You Can Pick Your Friends but You Can't Pick Your Poison

I blink. "But I thought gargoyles were created to bring balance? I thought we were good?"

"You were. Or at least, that was the hope of your king as he went from faction to faction, securing peace treaties and alliances. The last faction he sought out, the one he felt would be the hardest to convince, was of course the Vampire Court."

Hudson sneers, "Yeah, I can't see dear old Dad ever agreeing to stay at home and knit a sweater when he could be slaughtering someone."

The Bloodletter holds Hudson's gaze. "Yes, well, I suppose that's true. But that's not who the gargoyle king sought out. Your father was not the ruler then. I was."

My eyebrows nearly reach my hairline. "*You* were the vampire queen?"

"I was," she says. "Until the gargoyle king and I shook hands upon first meeting."

Understanding blooms in my chest. "You were mated."

The Bloodletter's entire demeanor shifts. Gone is the ruthless vampire with bodies hanging in the corner. Instead, a smile turns up the ends of her mouth. "Imagine my surprise to discover I had a mate, that my own magic would find me again. Or that I would ever feel like a schoolgirl with a crush, giddy and in love."

The Bloodletter sighs. "It seems only yesterday that Alistair and I were dancing through the marble halls of the Gargoyle Court. There was such laughter there then. Such joy and power and grace."

She pauses at the word "grace" and smiles at me. Then, with a wave of her hand, the cave around us transforms into a giant banquet room, filled with women in brightly colored gowns and men in richly shaded tunics.

The room itself is pristine, made almost entirely of white stone—white marble floor, white alabaster columns with gargoyle faces carved into the smooth surface, and white stone walls covered in nature tapestries spun in shades of cream and white with gold thread. My favorite is a white waterfall strewn with golden flowers as it spills down a rocky mountain.

Running most of the length of the room—right down the center—is a huge banquet table loaded with the most delicious-looking dishes. Roasted chickens. Grilled fish. Platters of baked breads and cheese. Huge plates of fruit—peaches, grapes, apples, pomegranates, figs, and some others that I've never seen before.

People crowd around the table, eating and drinking and laughing. At the end of the hall is a small area where musicians play and people dance. Right in the center of the floor is the Bloodletter, dressed in an elaborate crimson gown that trails along the floor behind her like a river of velvet. Rubies drip from her ears, throat, and the tiara on her head as she laughs up at Alistair, who is twirling her around the small dance floor. He's dressed in a white tunic embroidered with gold thread, and on his head is a crown that looks exactly like the one currently tattooed on my hand.

"The Court is beautiful," Macy breathes as we all watch the party unfold in front of our fascinated eyes.

"This was our mating ceremony," the Bloodletter says, and there's something in her voice—something in her eyes—that has me watching her instead of the scene playing out in front of me. "It was an incredible day. Everyone came to celebrate with us, and they stayed for three days. It was the first time I'd ever seen so many gargoyles up close—the first time anyone outside the Gargoyle Court had, I think.

"Including your father." She turns to Jaxon and Hudson. "He began plotting their demise that night. We just didn't know it yet."

She closes her fist, and the scene disappears. As it turns to darkness, a violent thunderstorm fills the room. Lightning cracks, thunder booms, rain pounds until we're all soaked to the skin. But it passes as quickly as it came on, and soon the fire is blazing in the hearth again, drying us just as quickly. And the Bloodletter is standing in the center of the room dressed in the same red dress she celebrated her mating in as snowflakes gently float down from the ceiling.

"I believe it was during our mating ceremony that Cyrus initially became jealous. He was my first lieutenant, and he was committed to the idea of paranormals one day ruling the human world. A fanatic, even, which of course was of value to me when I was also focused on war. But from the minute I was mated to the gargoyle king, I had a different agenda entirely. I wanted what Alistair wanted, peace. And Cyrus felt betrayed.

"He convinced the Circle that I was no longer loyal to the Vampire Court, that my allegiances were now aligned with the Gargoyle Court, and he was not entirely wrong. So I stepped aside, named him my successor, and moved to the Gargoyle Court. By now, I was pregnant with our first child, and I wanted to spend every moment of every day with my darling mate."

I could understand that. I squeeze Hudson's hand. I never want to be apart from my mate, either.

She continues. "But being Cyrus, he couldn't rest until he'd figured out how to break the treaty and continue to kill humans. And that meant he'd have to destroy the Gargoyle Army first."

The wind picks up with her words, blowing the snow into flurries all around us. *Just another illusion*, I tell myself. Her breeze whips through my hair, slaps it against my cheeks hard enough to hurt. I glance over at Hudson with a kind of *what the fuck* expression, but as I do, I realize that the wind is so powerful that it's managed to mess with even his indestructible hairstyle, so that pieces of hair block his eyes as they whip against his cheeks.

It's the first time I've ever seen him like this other than when he gets out of the shower before bed, but our relationship is so new that even those times are rare. It makes him look younger somehow, more vulnerable, and for the first time, I wonder if his Brit Boy pompadour is a deliberate choice. If it's his armor the same way Flint's grin used to be his. The way Jaxon's *always has to be in charge* personality hides his vulnerabilities.

It's a strange thought to be having right now, but it shakes me nonetheless. I mean, I know Hudson has vulnerabilities. Everyone does. But even at his softest with me, he seems so powerful. So in control. So strong.

Shoving my curls out of my eyes—and mouth—I raise my voice over the vicious howl of the wind and ask, "What did Cyrus do to destroy the Gargoyle Army?"

Maybe it's the wrong question to ask—I actually don't know what the right questions are—but this seems like a better bet when it comes to finding out as much information as possible as quickly as possible.

"He poisoned them."

"Poisoned them?" It's the last thing I expect to hear, and it sounds more than a little far-fetched to me. "But there were thousands of them. How could he possibly have poisoned them all?"

"Magic, of course," she answers, the wind dying back down. "Back then, Cyrus had the ability to control energy. He could move currents in any direction, currents of energy or even magic. My sister, also wanting the gargoyles gone so she could finish wiping out all paranormals, betrayed me one final time. She told Cyrus that gargoyles could communicate telepathically—which means there is a magical thread connecting them all—and she gave him the poison she had used against me in the Cup of Life. A god-killer poison. They didn't stand a chance."

She pauses, her eyes glassy with unshed tears, and my stomach twists. Whatever she's about to say is going to be awful, worse than awful, if it can make *her* cry.

"Adria bound Cyrus's gift to the poison, allowing him to drink it without being harmed himself. He then bit a gargoyle too young to defend himself properly, and Cyrus used his vampiric ability to push the poison along that magical thread—"

"And poisoned the entire Army at once," I finish for her as horror slithers through me.

"Every single gargoyle, even the children," she repeats, her eyes filled with a mixture of swirling power and unfathomable despair.

"And that's why there are no gargoyles left?" Macy asks as she gets up and joins me next to the Bloodletter, her hand reaching for my free one and squeezing. "Because Cyrus killed them all?"

"He didn't kill them," the Bloodletter tells us. "Oh, he tried—but he didn't consider one thing."

As I take in the firm set of the Bloodletter's jaw, the piercing gaze that captures my own, I know exactly what Cyrus overlooked. "He underestimated *you*."

She smiles back at me, a smile of pure rage. "He forgot I am not merely a vampire. I am the God of Chaos."

46

The Thanksgiving Guest List Just Got Chaotic

"But I thought he *did* destroy them," Eden chimes in for the first time. "That's why Grace's existence was so unexpected. Because she is the only gargoyle to be born in a thousand years."

"That doesn't mean the ones who existed before her are dead," the Bloodletter says.

"We saw the Court," Jaxon objects. "There's no one there. It's completely destroyed."

"Gone doesn't mean dead." The Bloodletter locks eyes with Hudson. "You should know that better than anyone."

"Cyrus's gift isn't his eternal bite?" Hudson asks, one eyebrow raised.

The Bloodletter rolls her eyes. "Eternal bite. Your father always was dramatic. No, that's not his gift at all. That bite is the poison still in his body."

Something about this story is bothering me. "How did Cyrus manage to poison the gargoyles, or even channel the poison, considering magic doesn't work on them?"

"Channeling energy is something gargoyles were meant to do. You're natural conduits. Cyrus simply used that gift against you. And as I said, the poison is meant to kill a god, so it's no stretch to use it to kill a mere gargoyle." She's staring at something over my shoulder now, lost in thought.

Flint breaks his glowering silence. "But his bite didn't kill Grace. She's just fine."

The Bloodletter's gaze whips back to mine. "You've been bitten by the vampire king? When?" There's an urgency in her voice that I've never heard before.

"A couple of months ago." My hand goes instinctively to the small scar on my neck that I usually try really hard not to think about. "After I became gargoyle queen."

Her eyes begin to glow the same bright emerald green as the string that binds us together.

"Then he must know who you are now, must have tasted your magic."

Not gonna lie, I cringe at the visual of Cyrus "tasting" me. Seriously gross.

"Is that why—" I was about to ask if that's why he wanted to send Hudson to prison, hoping I'd join him and get me off the chessboard, but I break off as she fades to me in a blink, reaches out, and pulls me to my feet. It's not the first time she has touched me since I met her, but it is the first time I can literally feel the power inside her.

It's right under the surface—roiling, seething, looking for an outlet. I can feel it reaching for my own power, feel it winding itself around me as it tries to find an opening—

I slam a mental wall down between us so fast and hard that it has the Bloodletter stumbling back.

"I hoped your godhood hadn't grown enough yet for him to sense it," she whispers after a moment. "But unfortunately, it has. Time is of the essence now. He will stop at nothing to get his hands on you, Grace. Nothing. You're both the key to his destruction—and to his most fervent desire for more power."

As though she hasn't freaked me out enough, she leans closer and says, "*Only the Gargoyle Army can save you now. If you can be saved at all.*"

47

Try to Seed
It My Way

"**W**here *is* the Gargoyle Army?" I ask on a tremulous breath, choosing to ignore her ominous threat about Cyrus entirely. I mean, no kidding he wants to get his hands on me for some reason I'm not going to like. Katmere is dust because of that. Instead, I focus on the other part of her warning—the part that implies the Army *can* be saved. I'm almost too afraid of the answer. I want to believe they're alive, that there are others like me out there, that Cyrus didn't kill an entire species, but it seems unlikely that the Bloodletter was able to keep them hidden for a thousand years.

"Why, I froze them in time, of course," she replies, and I've got to admit, I wasn't expecting that answer.

I turn toward Hudson, my breath coming fast as another thought occurs to me. And it must also occur to Hudson, because his eyes widen and he says, "Alistair took you to the frozen Gargoyle Court."

A smile overtakes my face. "They're alive, Hudson. They're really alive."

And suddenly, everything seems possible.

If the Gargoyle Army is alive, my friends and I just need to find a loophole to save them. And if we can save them, we can get the kids back. We can defeat Cyrus once and for all. And maybe Hudson and I won't have to hide in a cave at the ass end of Alaska, for the rest of our lives.

"Can you unfreeze them now?" I ask, eager to show everyone the amazing Court, how hard the gargoyles train for battle.

But the Bloodletter shakes her head. "Not until we can cure them. I gave Alistair's lieutenant a God Stone, which prevents the poison from working further as long as they remain frozen in time. Remove the God Stone, and the poison will still kill them in the frozen Court, only more slowly. But unfreeze them entirely, and they'll have mere hours to live unless they turn to solid stone and remain that way forever."

Sadness crashes into me, churning my stomach, and I reach out for Hudson to help keep me on my feet, but he's already ten steps ahead of me, his arms snaking around my waist, looping in front of me and pulling my back snug against his chest.

"It's okay," he soothes in my ear. "We'll find a way to save them."

I close my eyes and let his warmth, his strength, seep into my shaking body. I need to focus, to think. There's always a loophole in magic. That's what the Bloodletter said earlier. We just need to find it.

The Bloodletter adds, "There might be a way to save them without an antidote. Though I'm not sure it will work, since Grace's magic is still growing."

Hudson rolls his eyes. "Because that's how all good ideas begin, by pointing out how shitty they are."

Everyone ignores his sarcasm.

I know I do. He's rattled, furious. The idea of him putting himself at risk makes me feel exactly the same way. But I can't just leave the Gargoyle Army trapped in time forever.

Hudson growls low in his chest. "I have a suggestion. Can't we just kill the wanker? Isn't it his ability pushing the poison through their bodies?"

"I like the kill-Cyrus plan," Jaxon admits. "If we have a chance to take the asshole out, I think we should do it."

"Not until you free the Gargoyle Army," the Bloodletter hisses. "I froze the Army to save them, which trapped his power to channel energy with them, but it's still tied to him...which means he is as immortal as the frozen Army. Have you never wondered why no one has killed him yet? Why I haven't killed him myself instead of hiding out in a damn ice cave?"

I glance around the harsh, cold room and agree. No one would ever willingly live here, especially not without their mate.

"What's your really bad idea?" I ask, even as I brace for the pushback from Hudson. Normally, he's the first one to tell me I can do anything I need to, but when it comes to his father, he tends to get a little more overprotective of all of us. Not that I blame him. Cyrus is a monster, no doubt. But that's just one more reason why I have to save the Gargoyle Army. As brave and powerful as I think my friends are, we're no match for the vampire king on our own.

By now, the rest of the Order and Dawud must be at the Vampire Court. What if they discover Cyrus really is draining the kids of their magic? What if he's already killed some of them? If we have any hope of stopping Cyrus, we're going to need an army. Not to mention, yeah, we just need to free them because they're my people.

I glance down at the ring Alistair gave me. He named me his successor for no other reason than I'm his granddaughter. Shame burns my cheeks as I realize I haven't earned the right to be their queen. I'm not even sure I can, but I can at least start with trying to free them.

"A bad idea is better than leaving my people frozen in time one day more," I say.

"Grace." Hudson turns me to look at him, and for the first time maybe ever, I see fear in his deep blue eyes. Not for himself but for me. And I get it. But we don't have a choice.

"I'll be fine," I assure him, then face the Bloodletter again. "Okay. What do I have to do?"

The Bloodletter snaps her fingers, and all of the furniture, the fireplace, everything disappears. Somehow, without those trappings of home, I'm reminded how lonely and isolated the Bloodletter has lived for a thousand years. The icy cave is cold. Sterile. Soulless. And my sympathy for the ancient vampire inches up another millimeter. Not enough to warrant a Christmas card, of course, but a little higher than before.

"Follow me." She walks to the center of the room, and I can't help the shiver that races down my spine. "You mentioned you've seen a *string* that reminds you of me, yes?"

I nod. "A bright green string."

"Your demigod string." And when the Bloodletter says it like that, it's both an answer and a threat. "When my baby was born, Cyrus came for her. I knew I had to protect her, so I built this prison in the ice to stop him." She motions to the icy walls around us. "But he had already trapped your grandfather and poisoned the other gargoyles, and I knew I couldn't afford to believe I might not also be defeated. So I took steps to protect her from the king."

She motions with her hands for everyone else to step back against the walls, to give us room to do, well, whatever she has planned for us to do. Hudson hesitates, keeps a tight hold on my hand.

"Together," he says when I look at him questioningly. "You may have to do this, but that doesn't mean you have to do it alone. I'm going to be right here holding on to you the whole time. And if things get bad, you just keep holding on right back. Deal?"

My heart melts, because no matter what happens—no matter how many problems or rabid vampire kings try to come between us—Hudson is my mate.

And that is everything.

"Deal," I tell him, squeezing his hand one more time before turning back to the god who got us into this mess. "What happened to your child?"

"I hid her. From Cyrus. From the world. From even myself," she replies. Her eyes grow sad as she makes a series of complicated movements with her hands, sometimes slashing harsh lines, other times curving through the air in giant dips and twists. After she finishes one rather beautiful series of gestures, a glowing symbol appears in front of her, and everyone gasps. She turns slightly and makes similar but different movements.

Another symbol appears, the glowing light dancing off the walls of the ice cave like tiny flickering white flames. There's something about this symbol, two V's on their side, that looks familiar, but I can't quite place it.

She turns and begins another symbol as she continues her story. "I took my baby's godhood as well as her gargoyle—her *strings*—and I pressed them into a small frozen seed, bound it to my magic, and hid her power deep inside where even she couldn't find it, to be passed down from mother to daughter, for generations if necessary. Like magic calls to like magic, so I knew one day she would return to me. She might be my daughter, or my granddaughter, or my great-great-granddaughter, but one day, my magic would come back to me, the same as the mating bond magic found me."

"Dayum." Hudson draws the word out. "Does that mean your daughters never knew who they really were or what they were capable of? Their entire lives?"

I know I spent most of my life not knowing I was a gargoyle, but now I can't imagine not having that part of myself anymore. Maybe if I'd never known, I wouldn't know to miss it, but I can't help feeling sad for my mother and grandmother and the other women in my maternal line, so many generations of women never realizing how much power they really had hidden inside them.

"Not until my magic found me," she agrees. "It's the only way I could be sure Cyrus would never find my daughter before she was ready. When your mother and the coven came to me, asking for my help in creating a gargoyle, I recognized her immediately. I agreed to help, but I didn't gift them with a gargoyle like they thought. Your parents were already pregnant with you the old-fashioned way, and being gargoyle was in her lineage. But I released the magic…and for the first time in a thousand years, Grace, it was free to grow. In you." Her eyes narrow for a second on me. "And by the looks of it, it's still got a lot of growing to do."

She shakes her head, goes back to waving her hands in the air. "I always knew my daughter would be the key to freeing everyone. The Army. Alistair.

Everyone. Only another gargoyle would be able to hear Alistair and free him. Only another gargoyle who was also a demigod could ever travel to the frozen Court. I can freeze the Court, but a gargoyle could also travel there. And only a demigod who is also connected to the gargoyle magic thread might be able to use her magic to save them all."

While she's been talking, I can't help but notice there are more than a dozen symbols floating in the air now, almost forming a complete circle around the three of us, our friends still pressed against the ice walls outside the circle.

"How can my demigod string save the Army?" I ask, and a part of me really hopes it doesn't include actually touching the string. The last time I tried to hold my green string, well, Hudson became the proud owner of a slightly damaged lighthouse.

"Well, if we had an antidote, it would be easier." The Bloodletter makes one last swoosh through the air, and the remaining symbol flares to life and completes the circle. Then she pivots to me, her eyes lit with diabolical pleasure, and says, "But we might be able to use your demigod strength to drive the poison out."

She pinches the forefinger and thumb of her hands together, then draws them apart, and a thin, glowing string appears stretched between her hands. "Imagine you have a string connecting you and the Army." She ties a knot in the middle of the string. "And on the other end of this string is Cyrus, using his ability to control magical currents to send a poison from inside his body down this string." As she says this, the end of the string in her right hand begins to glow red, the crimson light moving along the string, around and around through the knot, and all the way to the other end of the string.

"If you were to use your natural gargoyle ability to channel magic, you might be able to use your demigod strength to push the poison in the other direction." The crimson glow begins to recede, traveling back across the string, around the knot, and to the hand where it originated. "If you're strong enough, you just might be able to push the poison out of every gargoyle—and shove it back down Cyrus's throat."

48

All the Strings Attached

The Bloodletter continues. "With Cyrus's ability no longer linked to the frozen Army, he will lose his immortality. And finally, finally I can leave this cave and teach that man what happens when you piss off a god for a thousand years."

Hudson bristles. "But when she touches the string connecting every gargoyle to her, won't the poison just follow the thread back to Grace, still being pushed by Cyrus's ability?"

The Bloodletter shakes her head. "It already has."

What? I pat my hands against my stomach and arms, testing to see if I feel ill, which I know makes no sense. But hey, someone just told me I was infected with a magical poison. I'm patting *something* to make sure I'm okay.

Hudson must be thinking the same thing because he runs his hands up and down my arms as well, pulls me close.

"I feel fine," I assure her.

"Obviously," she says, as though that was the silliest thing she's heard all year. "I was poisoned before you were born, and you are my progeny. Therefore, you inherited some of my immunity. Hence why Cyrus's bite didn't kill you, either."

Okay, well, that only makes sense *after* she says it. I stand by that.

"Now, if your mate can take his hands off you for at least five minutes, come here and let's get started." She motions to a space in the center of the circle.

"No chance," Hudson replies, picking up my hand again and walking with me to the center. "Where she goes, I go."

I expect the Bloodletter to make an obnoxious comment, but she surprises us both with, "Yes, I remember those early days," and her gaze focuses on something over my shoulder for a minute before she shakes her head.

I glance at our friends outside the magical circle, but something seems off about them. Jaxon is standing beside Mekhi and Flint, but his hand is half raised as if about to point at something. Eden is beside Macy, and they're leaning close, like they're talking quietly, but neither is speaking.

I'm about to ask the Bloodletter what's going on when she says, "Everything and everyone outside this circle is frozen in time. I won't be able to keep this up for long, though, so we best hurry."

Hudson's eyebrows shoot up, and he blurts out, "*Everyone* outside the circle is frozen? Like the whole world?"

"It's more that time is frozen than anyone is actually frozen. We can't risk Grace accidentally unfreezing the Army. Therefore, I've given her room to work here in the space between moments." She arches one brow at me. "But that moment is shrinking every second we waste. Now, come here."

I hustle to the middle of the circle, and she gives me some basic instructions on what to do next, but in the end, it apparently all boils down to, "See what feels right."

I want to laugh, because what feels right is packing up my friends and getting as far away from here as fast as we possibly can. But since that isn't an option—why is that never an option?—I grit my jaw and dive in. I close my eyes and run through her instructions in my head.

I'm supposed to find the connection to all gargoyles inside me with one hand and reach for my green string with the other—then hold on like hell and push. She mentions it should be easy to find the right direction to push the poison, as it'll be stronger in only one direction and that's closest to where it originated—Cyrus.

I know what Alistair feels like when he talks inside my head, but I have no idea how to try to form that connection with any other gargoyle—especially since Alistair was the one who formed it with me. Still, I take a deep breath, close my eyes, and open myself to whatever is out there as I try desperately to see what thousands of other gargoyles might look like.

Thousands of points of light.

That's the answer that comes through the darkness and the fear buried deep in the pit of my stomach. Against the blackness of my closed eyes, thousands of pinpricks of light start to appear. Like stars over the ocean in the middle of the night, the dots of light go on as far as I can see—and as far as my consciousness can reach.

The sheer magnitude of the numbers is daunting, and there's a part of me that doesn't even want to try. There are too many stars—too many souls—I have to try to reach. There's no way I can get them all.

But then, that's what Cyrus is counting on. It's what he always counts on in these untenable situations. That I'll get scared and give up before I ever try. But I've never done that before, and I'm not going to do it now, no matter how Sisyphean the task in front of me seems.

So, not knowing what else to do, I reach out and try to scoop a handful of stars out of the sky.

It doesn't work—big surprise.

Still, I try again and again, but each time I reach for them, they get farther away, like they have no desire to be touched by me. Or worse, like they have no desire to be saved.

The thought freaks me out more than a little. After all, I'm going on faith here, believing what the Bloodletter tells me even though she's been less than forthcoming—less than honest—before. Is she lying again? Trying to get me to do something I shouldn't because it serves her agenda?

The idea pulls me out of the zone, or whatever it is, and the stars begin to fade. At first, I let them—what makes me think I can do this anyway?

But then the voice inside me—no, not *the voice*, Alistair—says, *Hold, Grace. Hold, hold, hold.*

I don't know what I'm supposed to hold, considering the stars keep slipping through my fingers like so much dust, but he is so insistent—*Hold, Grace, hold—* that I can't just give up. And I definitely can't walk away. Not if I ever want to face him, or myself, again.

So I do the only thing I can. I hold even more tightly to Hudson and lean forward in my mind and scoop a giant armful of stars toward me with both hands.

This time it works...sort of. The stars don't retreat from me like they had been, but as they slip from my fingers and tumble across the inky blackness, they grow bigger, longer. They thin out until they don't look like stars at all. Instead, they appear as thousands and thousands of gossamer strings of light, stretched out in front of me. And with a deep breath, I reach out and wrap one of my arms around the entire curtain of light.

But suddenly the thin strings are vibrating in my grasp. Softly at first and then harder and harder, until electric shocks sizzle their way up my arm and it feels like my shoulder is going to be wrenched from the socket.

It seems like more proof that they don't want me to touch them—don't want me to help them—so I start to let the threads go. But the second I ease back, Alistair's voice comes through loud and clear in my head. *Grace, you must hold on.*

He sounds like the gargoyle king now, not like the Unkillable Beast, and I listen to him instinctively. I hug the strings tighter to my chest, and I hold on to every single one of them despite the electric shocks pumping through my body.

The pain is intense, nearly overwhelming, and I know I won't be able to hold them forever—or even much longer. So I take a deep breath, try to breathe through the agony, and use my other hand to reach for the green string that connects me to the Bloodletter. The green string that felt earlier like it connects me to the universe itself.

Hudson cries out when I drop his hand, but I don't have the energy to reassure him right now. Not when it's taking every ounce of energy I have to hold on to the strings of light, every ounce of willpower I have not to drop them and end the agony.

My knuckles brush against the green string, and everything inside me trembles. The pain doesn't go away, and time doesn't seem to stop the way it typically does when I brush against the string. I can hear Hudson calling my name, feel him reaching for me through the maelstrom of sensations tearing through me, but it sounds as though he is across a vast, empty field in my mind, and I cannot focus on him.

I push the need to answer him down, push him away—just for now—and focus on the green string that is right at my fingertips. There's a part of me that worries about holding it, a part of me that worries I might accidentally unfreeze the Army, like the Bloodletter suggested I might, and what if her circle doesn't prevent it?

But as I look more closely at the shimmering gargoyle strings, I realize I don't need to worry about unfreezing the poisoned Army. I recognize the Bloodletter's magic immediately. It's wrapped around every string, and it is immense. I don't think I could ever punch through that amount of power. Ever.

It's this thought that has me doing more than just brushing against my green string this time, more than just lightly clasping it in my hand. If I'm going to do this, I have to commit. Have to just do it.

And so I wrap my hand around my demigod string and hold it as tightly as I can—even as all hell breaks loose.

Lightning flashes, and a loud cracking sound fills the room above me. The wind from earlier returns like a hurricane, slamming into me so hard that I nearly topple over. Hudson saves me—I can feel his hands on my waist even through the storm and the wind and the green and silver strings—holding me in place as the world rages around me.

There's another flash of lightning, another loud crack. And for a second,

Remy's face flashes before my eyes.

He's grinning at me in a *what kind of mess have you gotten yourself into now* kind of way, and he looks so real that I can't help thinking he's actually here in front of me.

"Remy!" I call out, try to reach for him, but he disappears with a wink at the same moment the slender silver strings are ripped from my hand.

I make a grab for them, but they're already too far away, the wind blowing them out, out, out into the darkness around me.

"Grace!" Hudson yells from outside the inner world I'm standing in, and instinctively I turn toward him.

"Hudson?" I gasp as the wind continues to knock me around.

"Grace! There you are!" He grabs on to me, pulls me into his chest. "I was afraid we'd lost—"

He breaks off as yet another crack sounds above us.

"Let go!" he shouts to be heard above the noise.

"Let go?" I repeat. "Of what?"

"The green string." Hudson's voice blends with Alistair's until they are both echoing inside me.

"Let go of the green string," they both say again.

So I do, more than a little surprised that I haven't done so already. And that's when hell really breaks loose.

49

Bravely Going Where No Icicle Has Gone Before

The Bloodletter, Hudson, and I are still inside the circle created by the symbols, and while the wind is fierce, it seems to not exist outside the circle. But then an ominous crack echoes through the room.

"What the bloody hell was that?" Hudson growls.

I'm about to tell him I don't have a clue when half the ceiling collapses right before my horrified eyes, the first falling rock destroying one of the floating runes, and our circle winks out instantly.

The wind I've been wrestling with ever since I tried to grab the gargoyle strings tears through the place, sending everyone spinning.

Macy goes flying and Mekhi reaches for her, but they both end up getting tossed and don't stop until they crash hard into the wall where there's usually a fireplace.

Flint's legs get knocked out from under him, and he ends up flat on his butt.

Jaxon's using his telekinesis to try to stop Eden from slamming into another wall, his own feet barely still under him.

Sharp icicles and heavy rocks rain down on our heads, and I'm convinced we're all going to die. That my lack of control has somehow brought about a cave-in of such epic proportions that even a bunch of paranormals can't survive it.

The thought has guilt and terror spiraling through me, has my knees going weak and panic crawling just under my skin. I do my best to fight it back—now is pretty much the worst possible time for a panic attack—but it's not easy. Especially since I know I'm the one who caused it—me and my damn green string. I swear, I'm never touching it again if I can help it.

"It's going to be okay," Hudson whispers against my cheek as the world falls in around us. "This isn't your fault."

"It's totally my fault," I tell him even as I let myself sag against his hard chest and absorb his strength into my weak knees and too-tight throat.

"It's not," he insists. "No one knows how to ride a bike the very first time they get on one."

Part of me wants to tell him he's wrong, that wielding the green string is no different than any of the other strings I have deep inside me. But we both know that's not true. This green string—this demigod string—is different than anything I've ever touched before. Different than anything I've ever felt before.

It's that understanding that finally calms my frazzled nerves and freaked-out heart, and it's that understanding that lets me trust my knees to support me as I take a series of long, slow breaths. As I do, the tempest around me starts to calm, too. The ceiling stops cracking, ice stops falling, and flying debris settles back onto the ground.

As the dust—or in this case ice chips—settles, Hudson finally backs away from me. He must have disintegrated all the ice rocks that he saw raining down, as there are no large boulders around us, just an endless number of snowflakes floating gently to the ground. I step out from behind him to find the Bloodletter's cave in shambles. And Flint surrounded by several really large, really wicked-looking icicles behind Hudson.

"Oh my God!" I shout, running toward him. "I'm so sorry. Are you all right?"

"I have to say, Grace, you've got good aim. Thank God." He grabs hold of two of the largest icicles sticking in the ground around him and crushes them like it's nothing, then does the same to the remaining ones. "Any closer and I'd have had an icicle through some things that icicles should never, ever go through."

He says the last to make me laugh, but I'm too busy looking at the last ice dagger that missed his upper leg by mere inches. It makes me sick to realize how easily one of these could have impaled him, and it would have been my fault. My fault for not being able to control the power that comes with the green string and my fault for trying to when I knew I wasn't ready.

My thoughts must be all over my face, though, because Flint gently bumps his shoulder against mine. "Hey, it's okay," he tells me. "I'm tougher than I look—part and parcel of that whole dragon thing."

"Still, you could have—"

"But I didn't." He grins at me. "Besides, haven't you heard? Dragons are practically indestructible."

"'Practically' being the key word here," I say.

"Don't worry about it, Grace. I'm all good." I know I still look doubtful, because he crosses his heart and says, "I swear."

"To whom?" I shoot back. "The God of Chaos?"

He laughs. "Well, she knows I'd prefer to worship a tennis bracelet."

I nearly choke on my laugh as my gaze bounces around the cave to see if the Bloodletter heard his comment.

"What do we do now?" Macy asks as Mekhi helps her up. Her eyes are wide, and her flame-colored hair is so tousled from the storm that it looks like literal flames sticking out from her head.

"Run?" I suggest, only half facetiously. I can't see the Bloodletter being okay with the disaster I just made of her cave.

Surprisingly, though, she walks closer and says, "Some things you can't run from, Grace. Your power is one of those things."

Then she waves a hand, and her sitting room is back the way it was—and in perfect condition.

"That's it?" Eden glances around. "A little wave of your hand and everything is fine again?"

"That's it," the Bloodletter agrees as she surveys the room with satisfaction. "Though I do think 'fine' is a bit of an understatement, don't you?"

"And here I was thinking it was a bit of an overstatement." The words, said in a very pissy male voice I don't recognize at all, ring through the cave. "Then again, you and I rarely see eye to eye on anything, do we, Cassia?"

50

Life's a Beach,
or Is It Just a B*tch?

I shoot a quick glance at Hudson and Jaxon and mouth, *Cassia?* They both look as mystified as I feel—Jaxon shaking his head and Hudson giving a careless little shrug—before we all turn to face the owner of the voice that is still echoing through the Bloodletter's Cave.

As I do, I get my third shock in as many minutes. Because the voice belongs to a tall, ripped, *old* guy wearing bright teal board shorts, navy-blue snorkel fins, and a pair of sunglasses with bright blue lenses. He's also got full-on Einstein hair—silver, long, pushed back from his face in an *I don't give a shit* style—pierced ears, pierced *nipples*, and a tattoo sleeve of a staircase over water leading to an ornate, crumbling clock.

Oh, and if that isn't enough, he also looks *pissed as hell.*

"Don't blame me, Jikan," the Bloodletter—*Cassia?*—says in a bored voice. "It's hard to take you seriously when you insist on showing off your pierced nipples everywhere you go."

"I was at the *beach*," he answers, holding up the swimming mask and snorkel he's carrying as evidence. You know, in case we missed the board shorts and fins. "In *Hawaii*. For the first time in *five hundred years.*"

"Well, don't let us keep you." She rolls her eyes. "I'm sure you have something simply riveting to do, like counting the grains of sand on the North Shore."

His eyes narrow. "I was snorkeling. There was coral. And beautiful fish. And a *dolphin*."

"In that case, I can see why you're upset." The Bloodletter gives him the most mocking smile I have ever seen. "You don't see that every day in the middle of the Sahara."

"No, I don't," he grinds out. "Which is pretty much my point."

"You should go on vacation more often, then," she tells him in an unflappable voice. "It would probably put you in a better mood."

"Yes, well, we can't all lounge around all day in our own personal ice caves thinking up ways to screw the universe, now can we? Some of us have actual work to do." He sneers at her as he walks closer. "Thanks to others of us."

"No one asked for your help." The Bloodletter starts toward him, and I'm reminded of two gunfighters in the Old West getting ready for a showdown. If they suddenly decided to pull out pistols and take aim at each other, I don't think I'd be the least bit surprised.

"You may not have asked for it," he says, looking around the newly immaculate room with a frown. "But you clearly need it."

And with that, he reaches into the pocket of his electric-teal board shorts. I brace myself for him to pull out a weapon of some kind, and from the way Hudson steps in front of me, I know he's thinking the same thing. Instead, Jikan pulls out an old-fashioned gold pocket watch. Like, an honest-to-god pocket watch with a chain and an ornate flip cover and everything.

"Oh, I get it," Flint says. "'Jikan' in Japanese means 'time.' Cool."

"Enough talk." Jikan holds up his watch. "Here's an idea: why don't we kill two questions with one stone?"

"I think you mean bird," Flint suggests.

He turns to him with brows raised over the rims of his sunglasses. "Excuse me?"

"The saying," he explains, and I've got to hand it to him, he doesn't shrink an inch despite being the focus of Jikan's very intimidating scowl. "It's kill two birds with one stone, not two questions."

"Of course it's a dragon who thinks we should kill two birds. That's your answer to everything. Although I don't know what you've got against the poor creatures. They're quite majestic, if you think about it."

Flint's eyes grow wide. "I wasn't— I'm not saying we should kill—"

"Stop talking. It's giving me a headache." Jikan shifts his gaze back to me. "Are you quite finished?"

Finished? I haven't even gotten started. "Why are you being so rude to everyone—"

"*Why* do you ask so many questions, little stone girl?" he counters. "For a piece of rock, you sure are inquisitive."

"A piece of rock?" Jaxon repeats, sounding outraged on my behalf. "What the hell—"

"Shut it, goth boy. Nobody wants to listen to you, and no one has time for one of your temper tantrums anyway."

I'm not sure if Jaxon chokes on his outrage or his own saliva, but either way, the sound he makes is a cross between a dying rhino and a hippo in heat. "Excuse me? What did you just say?"

Jikan narrows his eyes. "First of all, no. Second—"

"No what?" Jaxon demands.

"No, I won't excuse you. Obviously. And second, I never repeat myself." He shakes his head as he looks down at his pocket watch, muttering a veiled threat. "It really is ridiculous how fragile vampires are."

At this point, I'm pretty sure that if vampires could have a stroke, Jaxon would be having one right now. Hudson, on the other hand, looks half amused, half fascinated by Jikan's very obvious attitude problems. Then again, he could just be admiring his game. With Hudson, you never quite know what's going through his head.

"Who is this guy?" Jaxon demands.

"I don't know, but he just might be my new personal hero," Hudson says. *"Goth boy."*

Jaxon turns to him with a *what the fuck* expression, but before he can say anything, Jikan continues. "Is question time done now, boys and girls? Because, riveting as your ignorance is, I have a luau to be at in an hour, and poi is my favorite. So let's get this show on the road, shall we?"

"What show is that, exactly?" I ask.

He lowers his sunglasses just enough that I can see his blazing mahogany eyes over the top. "The show where I fix what you and Cassia fucked up. I don't know why you feel the need to keep sticking your messy fingers in my elegant cake, Cassia, but I wish you would stop."

"Pie," Flint corrects him.

"3.14159 and so on until the end of, well, me," he answers distractedly. "Why?"

"No, I mean it's putting your fingers in my pie—"

Jikan looks totally affronted. "I can assure you, young dragon, that I have no desire to put my fingers in your teenaged pie or anywhere else."

Now Flint is the one who's choking. "It's an expression—"

"That's what they all say." He clears his throat. "Now, on to the business at hand. Fixing Grace's latest disaster."

"Latest?" I ask, choosing to ignore the fact that the word comes out sounding like a squawk. "Exactly how many disasters have there been?"

"You mean besides that giant one at the end of November?" he asks archly.

"What happened in November—" I break off as I figure out exactly what he's referring to. "Wait a minute. Who are you?"

"The God of Time." Hudson manages to sound bored. "And I'm guessing he's pissed because *Cassia* over there—"

"You may *not* call me that," the Bloodletter grinds out.

Hudson doesn't acknowledge the interruption. Instead, he continues smoothly. "Just paused time for you, and then it blew up."

"It's a blow job, all right," Jikan says, shaking his head. "Lucky for you, I'm around to fix it. Cracks in time this big can let all kinds of nasty things through."

There's so much to unpack in that statement that I almost don't know where to start. Deciding to leave the blow-job comment alone—Mekhi is already laughing enough for the whole group of us—I focus on the important part of what he said. Namely, the crack in time. That I somehow must have caused.

Fan-freaking-tastic.

As my stomach twists itself into a giant knot, I tell myself to breathe. Just breathe. Because Jikan says he can fix whatever I broke, and I'm just going to have to believe him or I will lose it completely. I will never forgive myself if I accidentally unfroze the Gargoyle Army and they die.

Of course, if I'm going to believe him, it would help to know if he is who Hudson thinks he is. I hope so. I really, really hope so, because I'm not sure who else to trust to fix whatever mess the Bloodletter and I have made.

It's funny how last year I would have laughed at the idea of a god of time, and now I'm praying that he not only exists but that he's here in front of me right now. Of course, back then I thought vampires and werewolves only existed in fiction...

"Are you really the God of Time?" Macy beats me to the question, though, speaking up for the first time since Jikan appeared.

He sighs. "I prefer to be called the Historian, but yes, that is my official title."

Flint laughs. "You make it sound like a job."

"Which part of 'I'm on my first vacation in five hundred years' did you not understand?" he asks, once again holding up his scuba mask. "If working round the sundial since the beginning of time isn't job enough for you, I'm not sure what is.

"Speaking of which..." Jikan drops the scuba mask on the Bloodletter's coffee table and gestures toward the couch. "Sit down, will you, and stay out of my way. This can be delicate work."

"What exactly are you going to do?" I ask, glancing around the room in an effort to figure out what he's talking about. Everything looks normal to me, but it's obviously not if the God of Time—excuse me, the *Historian*—decided to interrupt scuba diving to show up in an Alaskan cave.

For a minute, it looks like he's about to make a snarky comeback, but in the end, he just sighs and beckons us toward him.

Jaxon holds a hand out to stop the rest of us and walks forward first, which seems both brave and foolhardy at the same time. But he's barely taken two steps before the Historian rolls his eyes and says, "Not you. Her."

There's a part of me that hopes he's talking about the Bloodletter. But even before he lowers his glasses again and focuses those laser-brown eyes on mine, I know he's referring to me. I am the one who can apparently add "breaking time" to her repertoire of tricks, after all.

I reluctantly move forward and am not surprised at all to find Hudson right behind me.

"I just said—"

"I know what you said," Hudson answers mildly. "But you want her, you get me, too. We're kind of a package deal."

This time the Historian rips off his glasses and uses every ounce of ferocity he has—which is a lot—to stare Hudson down. Hudson, of course, stares right back for what feels like forever. And then out of the blue asks, "Do you smell toast?"

"Toast?" the Historian responds incredulously.

My mate gives his patented shrug. "I can't decide if you're having a stroke or just in a trance, so I figured I should check."

Surprise registers in the Historian's eyes, followed quickly by annoyance. And then he snaps his fingers.

And Hudson disappears.

51

A Stitch in Time
Saves My A$$

S hock holds me—holds all of us—immobile. And then the Bloodletter says, "Why didn't I think of that?"

"What did you do?" I demand. "Where'd he go?"

"Where the fuck is my brother?" Jaxon charges toward the Historian. "What did you do to him?"

"Nothing compared to what you did to him," the Historian answers mildly. "Or are we all just supposed to forget about that?"

"You're a real asshole, you know that?" Jaxon growls.

The Historian's only response is to lift his hand, his thumb braced against his middle finger like he's about to snap again.

Jaxon freezes, jaw working and hands clenched into fists.

"Stop!" I tell them—not just Jaxon and the Historian but our friends, too, all of whom are moving closer. Considering I wouldn't put it past any of them to bum-rush the Historian, I place myself directly in front of him. And ask, "Can you please bring him back?"

He tilts his head to the side like he's considering it for a second, then answers, "I don't know. I kind of like it without him."

He's playing with me, like a cat with a mouse, and it pisses me off. Then again, everything about this trip is pissing me off. But I bite the inside of my cheek as I say as nicely as I can while it still comes across as a command, "Let him go, please."

He lifts a brow. "You don't actually think I'm going to take orders from a baby demigod like you, do you?"

"I guess that depends."

"On what?"

I square my shoulders and shove the fear and panic down deep inside myself. After sending a quick prayer into the universe that I'm doing the right thing, I answer, "On whether or not you actually want to make it to that luau."

And then I take a deep breath and grab on to my green string as tightly as I can.

A loud cracking sound tears through the room.

"Oh shit," Flint mutters from behind me.

"Grace, stop!" Macy urges from behind me as well. "Don't."

But I hold on, my gaze locked with the Historian's, and pray he can't tell that holding my green string is freaking me out, filling my body with an energy I know all too well I have no idea how to control. This power scares the absolute hell out of me. As another ominous crack echoes around the room, the corners of my mouth start to turn up, and I realize this power doesn't frighten me because of the destruction it causes—but because I like it. Which is altogether even scarier as fuck, if I'm being honest.

Thankfully, his eyes narrow on my growing smile, and then he snaps, and just like that, Hudson blinks back into existence.

"Oh my God." I let go of the string in an instant. As I do, the cavern quiets, and I've never been so grateful for a luau in my life.

Hudson wraps an arm around me, and unlike the times when he was frozen and didn't have any immediate clue that it had happened, this time he seems to know exactly what the Historian did. Strangely, he doesn't seem upset by it at all. Instead, he's wearing a huge grin on his face.

"Where—" I start to ask, but he cuts me off with a shake of his head and a quick press of his lips to my forehead.

Then, holding my hand, he turns to the Historian. "That was pretty cool, mate. Thanks for the ride."

"It wasn't supposed to be—" Jikan breaks off with a shake of his head. "Never mind. Let's just get to work before your girlfriend opens a wormhole."

"Can I do that?" I ask, horrified.

"Can she do that?" Hudson asks at the same time, only he looks intrigued. Which gets my back up in all kinds of ways. I don't know what it is about this God of Time, but Hudson is way too interested in what he can do instead of worrying about what he can do *to us*.

"Just a little time-related humor," the Historian tells us. Which isn't an answer. "And no, she most definitely can't."

"So what did I break?" I ask to change the subject, moving closer to him despite the non-Alistair voice in the back of my head screaming at me to get as far away from him as I can manage. "And how are you going to fix it?"

Jikan is walking around the room now, staring up at the ceiling, which is once again in perfect condition—or, at least, in as perfect condition as the inside of an ice cave can be—and I decide he isn't going to answer me. But after coming back to the same corner four separate times, he calls me over.

This time I go alone, shooting Hudson a warning look when he tries to come with me. I'm not up for another dick-measuring contest right now.

"Do you see that?" the Historian asks, pointing up at the very top of the cave.

I squint, but all I see are ice and rock. "No."

His sigh is disappointed. "Well, maybe next time." He pauses to glare at me. "Not that I'm expecting there to be a next time." Then he pulls his pocket watch back out.

"Wait!" I exclaim, searching the ceiling even harder. "What am I supposed to see?" I need him to tell me so that if anything like this ever happens again, I'll know if I caused any permanent damage to the future or the present day.

"You either see it or you don't," he tells me with a shrug. "And if you don't, there's no way to teach you to see it."

With that, he flips the cover on his pocket watch and holds the whole thing up. He's taller than I am—again, not hard—so I can't see the face of the watch. I can't see anything, really, except a strange blue light that seems to emanate from the face of the pocket watch. It forms a circle around him and then a circle around us, growing bigger and bigger with each minute that he holds it open.

And then, when the circle is wide enough—when it encompasses all of us and the entire room—the Historian reaches in and grabs what looks to be a handful of light. And then he hurls it straight at the ceiling, at the spot he pointed out to me earlier.

I brace myself, expecting some kind of explosion or something—it feels like something is always exploding these days—but the only thing that happens is the blue light coats that entire portion of the ceiling before spreading farther and farther across the cave.

"That's it?" Macy whispers. "That's how you fix a crack in time? With some light?"

"It's a little more complicated than that," the Historian answers.

He snaps his fingers, and the largest pair of knitting needles I've ever seen appears in his hand. He snaps again, and Julia Michaels and Niall Horan's "What a Time" starts echoing through the entire ice cave.

Hudson is on one side of me now and Macy is on the other. I look between both of them to see if they know what's happening—the Historian definitely doesn't seem like the pop-music type—but they both look as bewildered as I do. Especially when the chorus repeats itself in the middle of the song and the Historian starts bopping his head and singing along with his eyes closed—all while knitting the air in front of him at a superfast speed.

"Is everyone else seeing this?" Flint hisses out of the corner of his mouth. "Or has the Tylenol I've been taking made me delusional?"

"Tylenol doesn't make you delusional." Eden snorts.

"So this is real, then?" Flint looks gobsmacked.

"It's something," Mekhi says.

The Historian chooses that moment to open his eyes and finds us all staring at him. "What?" he asks as the song repeats the chorus in an endless loop. "It's a bop."

To prove it, he closes his eyes again and returns to moving his head back and forth in rhythm to the currently never-ending chorus. And while I like the song a lot—One Direction forever, baby—after hearing the chorus what feels like 311 times in a row, even Macy and I are ready to call uncle.

The Historian, however, is happily bopping along as he knits and knits and knits. There's no yarn or anything else attached to the knitting needles, but he just keeps moving the tips of them back and forth in rhythm to the music until finally—right in the middle of the 312th repetition of the chorus, he just stops.

The music stops, too—thank God—as he holds up the knitting needles and proclaims, "Voilà!"

At first, I think he's completely forgotten us, considering he's been knitting nothing for more than five minutes as if we're not even there, but then I see them: tiny, gossamer-thin threads floating through the light all around him. "What are those?" I ask, reaching forward so I can feel one against my fingertips.

But a quick rap of his knitting needles on my knuckles has me yanking my hand back. "Those are the strands of time," he says, "untouched by baby-demigod hands." He shoots me a look. "And they need to stay that way."

"What strands?" Eden asks, leaning forward to get a better look. "I don't see anything."

"I don't, either," Macy agrees.

"They're right there," I tell them, pointing to several strands near us even as I take pains not to touch them. My knuckles still hurt from the first smack.

But my friends look baffled. Even Hudson shakes his head and says, "It looks like there's nothing there to us, Grace."

"But there is something there." I rub my eyes, then take another look just to be sure the Historian isn't putting me on. He's not. The gossamer strands are right in front of us.

"Watch this," the Historian says, spinning the knitting needles between his fingers like drumsticks.

"Always the show-off," the Bloodletter tells him with a roll of her eyes.

He snorts. "Like you're one to talk."

And then he thrusts forward with a knitting needle, hooks one of the long panels of threads on the tip, and brings it up to whirl it around his head. He spins the panel around and around and around and then just lets it go.

The second he does, the threads fly everywhere. Around the room, up to the ceiling, against the walls, and—terrifyingly—straight into my friends and me. I expect them to wrap around us, maybe even to bind us, but in the end, what happens is so much more bizarre. The threads pass straight through us.

I feel them under my skin, slicing through muscle and blood, veins and bones. It doesn't hurt, but it does feel incredibly strange, like a million dragonflies zinging through every part of me. But when I turn to Hudson to see if he's okay, to see if the threads are hurting him, he's just standing there like he doesn't have a clue what's happening.

Macy looks the same. So do Jaxon and Flint and the others. None of them has a clue that the Historian just pushed these things, whatever they are, straight through our skin.

Seconds later, the strange zinging stops inside me. Frantic, I look around, trying to figure out what happened, and realize the strings have passed right through us. I can see them behind Macy and Hudson now—thin and delicate as ever as they continue to sweep around the room, going through whatever is in their path.

"I'm impressed," the Historian says to me. "I didn't know if you'd be able to see them. But apparently, you're the real deal."

"What does that mean?" I ask. "And why can't the others see the strings?"

"What strings?" Flint asks, and he's back to sounding pissed—which is to say, normal these days.

The Historian just rolls his eyes at him. "It's a god thing," he tells me, like that explains it.

Before I can ask him any more questions, he gives his knitting needles one more big drumstick spin. They disappear mid-flip, because of course they do. Forget surf bum and crotchety old man. I'm beginning to think the Historian is a frustrated rock star.

"Now what?" I ask, because I still haven't seen anything happen in that top right corner of the cave he was looking at earlier.

"Now?" He raises both brows. "We wait."

"Wait?" Jaxon asks. "For what?"

The Historian grins, and somehow it's even scarier-looking than his frown. "You'll see."

52

Big Bang Me

I don't know what his "you'll see" means, but it doesn't sound good. Especially when he follows it up with, "In the meantime, Grace, we need to have a talk."

"A talk?" I ask, nerves churning in my already jumpy stomach. "About what?"

"Your newfound power. You can't just go around using it will-o'-the-wasp whenever you feel like—"

"Will of the wasp?" I ask, feeling like I missed something. "What do wasps have to do with anything?"

"I think he means will-o'-the-wisp," Hudson answers softly.

"Okay, but that still doesn't make sense." I shake my head. "I'm not the one who froze time for the whole world." I point at the Bloodletter. "She did."

"Well, it's just good, sound advice, isn't it?" he asks archly. "But also, you're the one who tore through her magic like a kid in a candy store and ripped a hole in time."

"I don't want that to happen again, either. Not even sure how it *did* happen," I tell him, wringing my hands.

"Because you don't know the basics of controlling your power, obviously," Jikan accuses.

"Stop harassing the child, Jikan," the Bloodletter admonishes, then turns to me and says, "He just doesn't want to admit that we can control time, what with him lording it over everyone that he is the *God of Time*." She says that last bit like he'd made up the title and she's humoring him.

"You do *not* control time, Cassia." Jikan bristles, and they go into another Wild West staring contest—that the Bloodletter apparently wins, as his shoulders finally lower and he admits, "Chaos controls the arrow of time. Nothing more."

"Wait. I can travel in time?" I ask, the first inkling of excitement about possibly being a demigod curling in my stomach. I'd love to go back in time and meet Kafka. Ask him why the fuck it had to be a cockroach. I had nightmares for weeks.

Jikan straightens his spine, standing to his full height before declaring, "Only the God of Time can surf *those* waves."

It's such an absurd statement that I can't help but giggle a little.

"We can control the *flow* of time, Grace," the Bloodletter explains.

Jikan nods. "Time flows from order to entropy, and in that sense, as a demigod of chaos, you can start and stop it, to some degree, but nothing more. If you were smart, though, you would never do either, because I won't be so nice the next time I have to show up to fix one of your mistakes."

He was nice this time?

"But if 'all she can do' is start or stop time," Hudson says, adding air quotes and tossing me a wink, "which I happen to think sounds pretty impressive, then how did she rip a hole in it?"

Jikan turns to the Bloodletter, and they have some kind of silent conversation with their eyes, because after a bit, he sighs heavily. Then he says, "She just did. And it's like I said earlier. When you make cracks in time, you leave openings for all kinds of unsavory things."

"Unsavory how?" I ask as a chill works its way down my spine. "What kind of bad magic are we talking about?"

"It's not all bad," he tells me. "It's just problematic—for me, for Cassia, and eventually for you, too." He glances around the Bloodletter's sitting room, shaking his head. "Now, I have a wave with my name on it. But first"—he nails me with a hard gaze—"a warning. Time is not to be messed with, least of all by a baby demigod. Do it again, and I will halt my truce with your grandmother and unfreeze your kin."

I gasp. Hell, we all gasp. Everyone except Hudson, who just narrows his eyes on the Historian. He's basically threatening to kill my entire species if I don't play nice, which is just rude as fuck. "I can't make that promise! I don't even know how I did what I did that brought you here today!"

Hudson moves to wrap an arm around my shoulders, but I'm beyond needing comfort. I'm pissed.

I put my hands on my hips and lift my chin. "If you don't want me messing with your precious strands of time, then help me save my people. Because if you don't, if you're willing to watch thousands of people die just to prove a point, I will spend every day of my life fucking with time. You will be knitting your fingers to the bone fixing the shit I plan on breaking."

I draw in several quick breaths, my hands shaking that I just played chicken with a god and pretty sure I'm now about to be smited. Or smote. Smitten? Either way, honestly, enough is enough.

"Grace—" The Bloodletter tries to calm me down, but I'm way too worked up for that.

"No!" I tell her. "I'm serious. For once, why don't you precious gods try leading with the truth? For once, why don't you try telling us what we need to know instead of making us bumble around in the dark until someone dies? I don't mind doing what has to be done, but I am damn sick of watching the people I love die or get injured because we never have the full story. So if you ever want to see a dolphin again, tell us how to save my people!"

I pause to take several more deep breaths, and Hudson adds, "She's right." Then he wades in even further, because he's Hudson and he always, always has my back. "You can get pissed off and snap us to another plane of existence, but it doesn't negate the fact that Grace is right. The Bloodletter says she just needs to use her green string, but you see what happens when Grace touches it. Mayhem."

"Well, that's because she's just a baby demigod of chaos. Stop touching your string until you mature." Jikan says this like it's obvious.

"I. Am. Not. A. Baby." In fact, what I am is seething right now.

But Jikan rolls his eyes. "I wasn't calling *you* a baby. But you are a baby demigod, although I'm not sure how." He turns to the Bloodletter. "Did you do this? Stop her godhood from growing?"

His question turns my anger to ice, and I slowly turn to face her. "Did you do something else to me?"

The Bloodletter shakes her head. "It wasn't me, child. I released your magic the day your mother came to me with you in her womb. Someone else stopped the seed of your magic from growing until recently. It's there, but it's wild, and young, and hungry. It is pure chaos, with no direction, no focus, and no control." She shakes her head in disappointment. "It will grow if you give it time, but unfortunately, it's clear you're not strong enough yet to remove the poison from the Army with it."

The fight drains out of me as quickly as it came. I was so busy being afraid of what would happen if I touched my green string, I didn't even consider *nothing*.

But Hudson is having none of it. "You consider what Grace just did to this cave weak? Hell, Jikan here says she tore a hole in time itself. And you think she needs to be stronger?"

"This isn't even a fraction of what Grace will be capable of one day," the

Bloodletter replies, pride evident in her voice. "But she must first learn to walk before she can run."

"Well, there's one way—" Jikan begins, but the Bloodletter interrupts. "No."

Again, some kind of silent conversation goes on between the Historian and the Bloodletter, ending with the Bloodletter giving one hard shake of her head and the Historian shrugging. Which makes me angry again, and I bite out at the Bloodletter, "You won't let him tell me how to save my people? Your *mate's* people?"

"You can't, Grace. Not this way. You don't have enough power yet." She actually sounds like it might matter to her what happens to me, but I don't care. There are thousands of gargoyles frozen in time, gargoyles who will never age, never have children, never truly live, unless someone saves them. I may not think I'm ready to be the queen of this Army, but I'm all they've got, and I'll be damned if I don't go down trying.

"Thanks for underestimating me, *Grand-mère*." I draw the words out with a smirk, echoing how Cyrus did the same to her all those years ago.

And I must have struck a chord, because she holds my gaze for a beat, shame in her brilliant green eyes, then she turns to Jikan and says, "Tell her."

He folds his arms across his chest. "There *is* something that can defeat this god-killer weapon, an antidote to all poisons called the Tears of Eleos." He shakes his head. "But Cassia is right. The only one I know of during this time is impossible to reach."

"What does it do?" Eden asks. "How do we use it?"

"And where do we find it?" Flint follows up.

"It restores life when you drink it," the Historian answers. "If you want it to save your Army, merely let it coat your gargoyle strings. As for where you find it...St. Augustine, Florida, of course."

"Florida?" I ask incredulously. "The key to defeating the most powerful poison on earth is in *Florida*?"

"Where did you expect it to be?" he answers. "Mount Olympus?"

When he puts it like that, Florida seems as good a place as any.

He stands up and surveys the cave's ceiling with satisfaction. "Everything is fixed, and my luau doesn't start for another ten minutes. Perfect timing. As always."

"Wait, that's it?" Macy asks in disbelief. "That's all you're going to tell us? That we need to go to St. Augustine, Florida?"

"Well, that, and to be careful. What you need is not meant for human or baby—er—*young* demigod hands. It is guarded by a powerful, ancient creature that knows no nature except death, for what better way to protect life than with its antithesis? It cannot be reasoned with—it cannot be defeated."

"Sounds easy," Hudson says facetiously.

"If it were easy, everyone would be doing it," the Historian tells him—and of course, that sounds about right. "Now, if you'll excuse me, I have a pig to carve."

Before I can think of anything to say to that, he reaches into the opening he's created in the middle of the air and plucks one of the gossamer-thin threads.

And just like that, everything goes black.

53

Shoppe Till You Drop

"**W**here are we?" Macy asks when the darkness disappears as suddenly as it came on to reveal we've all been *moved* to a different place.

"I don't know," Eden answers, glancing around at the row of small buildings and cobblestone road. "But it's pretty cool."

"What's cool about a bunch of old buildings?" Flint sneers. But he's looking around like the rest of us, taking it all in.

Thankfully, it's still dark—or mostly dark—the sun just a hint on the horizon. That means Hudson is okay being out here, at least for a little while, which is a good thing because I still have no idea where we are. Except to know that Flint is right—we are surrounded by a bunch of old buildings.

The sky is still painted the dark purple of predawn escapades, but the area around us is lit up by quirky gas-lamp light posts. We're in a narrow cobblestone walkway between old buildings with wooden balconies strung with lights. Each floor of each building has a sign hanging in front of it, and that's when I figure out that we're in an old-time market.

On either side of us, there's a chocolate shop, an antique shop, a milliner's, and a rare bookstore that I can't help drooling over, and a little farther up the cobblestones are a restaurant, a cute old-time pub, and a toy shop. All the shops are dark right now, since it's so early, but in another time when the lives of hundreds of Katmere students and my entire species aren't hanging in the balance, I would love to come back and walk this whole marketplace.

For now, though, I'd settle for figuring out where we are.

When I say as much to my friends, Macy answers, pointing to a nearby sign. "We're in St. Augustine, Florida."

"Is that what he did to you?" I ask Hudson as we find a map at the end of the walkway. "Just snap you to a different place like this?"

"Different place, different time. It was impressive, actually."

"That's why you weren't mad when you got back." I shake my head. "You looked impressed, but I couldn't figure out why if he snapped you out of existence."

"Not out of existence. Just to a tiny island somewhere as the sun was getting ready to come up." When my eyes go big, he laughs. "Yeah, the threat was implicit but very much there."

"So now that we know we're in St. Augustine," Macy says, pointing to the top of the map that reads ST. AUGUSTINE HISTORIC OLD CITY SHOPPES, "what are we supposed to do next?"

"Figure out where the 'old and powerful magic' shop is?" Flint suggests, tongue in cheek.

"Not to mention the fact that it's going to be light soon," I add, glancing at the sky. "Hudson needs to be out of here before the sun comes up."

"What Hudson needs is to stop drinking your blood so we can actually get shit done," Eden mutters.

I duck my head as my cheeks flame. I mean, she's probably right, but getting called out on it in front of everyone is super embarrassing. The fact that only vampires who feed on human blood can't go into sunlight for a couple of days turns out to be the world's most inconvenient hickey. Forget turtlenecks, Hudson needs a full hazmat suit...and I need a very deep hole to hide in.

Hudson wraps an arm around my waist and pulls me close. "What we need," he says in his most proper British accent, "is to stop getting jerked around by gods for their own amusement."

"Yeah, but since that's not going to happen anytime soon, I'm with Eden," Jaxon answers. "Lay off your own personal bloodmobile. At least for a little while."

"Of course you would say that," Flint taunts. "No ulterior motives in there for you, huh, Jax?"

If possible, my cheeks get even redder. All I want to do is figure out what we're supposed to find here in St. Augustine—and do it before the sun comes up and fries my mate to hell and back. And honestly, after that, I want to have a sit-down with Flint and give him a big hug—and then tell him he has got to let this anger directed at everyone go. Every time he lashes out, I'm reminded how much pain he's truly in, and I'm afraid he's going to do something reckless one day that will get him killed.

"Seriously?" Mekhi says. "Our classmates are in the hands of a madman, and you guys are going to stand here fighting about stupid shit? Can we please focus on the goal for more than three seconds at a time?"

"What is the goal again?" Macy asks. "I mean, besides getting everyone from Katmere back. What is the goal here? Because I didn't see anyone asking how to find my mother back in that cave."

Her words punch my stomach like a heavyweight champ, and I gasp. She's right, too. I promised Macy if we went, I'd ask the Bloodletter about her mother, and I didn't keep my word. Shame heats my cheeks that we spent that entire trip asking about me and how to save my people.

"If we find a cure for the Army, then they will help us free everyone," Hudson answers. "We cannot defeat my father alone—especially not now that we've learned as long as the Army is frozen, he's immortal, too."

I hold up my hand for a visual aid. "This Crown thing only works with the Army, and we know it scares the shit out of Cyrus, so..."

"Then let's figure out how to find these Tears of Eleos and save everyone, including Macy's parents," Jaxon jumps in, sending me an apologetic look. "It's probably some magical sapphire pendant or something."

"Worn around the neck of a mindless killing machine," Mekhi adds with a grin, like facing down a bejeweled beast sounds fun.

"By all means, then, let's find its hidey-hole and jump right in," Flint says, a half grin flashing across his face and reminding me for just a second of my old friend.

"Well, I don't think Jikan would have gone through the trouble of sending us all this way only to make us have to travel farther," Hudson muses, staring at the storefront Jikan dropped us right in front of.

"And that means what exactly?" Eden asks. Then she turns to see what Hudson is staring at and says, "You can't be serious."

When I see what he's looking at, too, I have to admit, I'm with Eden on this.

"A taffy shop?" I ask. "The place that holds the magic of one of the most powerful, ancient gods in the world...is a saltwater taffy shop?"

54

Not So
Laffy Taffy

I can't help thinking Hudson might be right, though, as I scoot out from behind Jaxon to get a better look at the taffy shop. The glass-paned windows are covered in posters of various illustrations of monsters, with a wooden sign above the window proudly proclaiming the name of the shop: MONSTER TAFFY. "Whoever owns it believes in truth in advertising."

"Or making taffy out of creatures," Mekhi deadpans.

"I'm just saying, if there's a dragon-size taffy vat in there, I am out," Flint agrees.

"To be fair, if there's a dragon-size anything in there, we should probably all be out," Macy shoots back. "I know this crowd isn't big on it, but survival of the smart-enough-to-run-like-hell is a real thing."

"Are we going in or what?" Jaxon asks, striding toward the pink-cotton-candy-colored door.

I squeeze Hudson's hand and move to stand with Jaxon, only to find Hudson hell-bent on doing the same exact thing.

Jaxon looks at us in surprise, but Hudson shrugs. "Somebody's got to be brave enough to be the distraction so the survival of the run-like-hell crew can actually happen."

Everyone chuckles at this, even Flint, just like Hudson meant them to, and the tension of a moment ago begins to roll off our shoulders. Just one more reason why I love this guy so much.

In the end, I'm the one who pushes open the door. And I'm the first to step into what feels a whole lot like a Brothers Grimm fairy tale.

The four walls of the store are a giant mural of a starry black sky looking down on dozens of leafless white trees. I know it's impossible for a tree to look like it's in pain, impossible for a tree to *be* in pain, especially a painted one, but something about these trees screams agony to me. They are bent and twisted and gnarled, their very existence a testament to the darkest side of those fairy tales.

And the tree theme doesn't stop there. Life-size statues of trees—all twisted and warped and sad-looking—are scattered around the store. Hanging from their branches are clear plastic globes filled with every color of taffy imaginable.

I don't think it's my imagination running wild when I say that they look like poisoned apples—so much so that I can't help but look around for a magic mirror on the wall. Turns out, I don't have far to look. There's a very large, very ornate mirror on the wall at the back of the store, and right in front of it is a matching golden chalice with diamonds on it sitting on a stone pedestal next to the checkout station. A checkout station that is currently being manned by one of the most spectacular women I have ever seen.

She's tall—several inches taller than Hudson, in fact—with pale skin, bright violet eyes, and straight black hair that nearly touches the floor. Her curvy figure is poured into black pants and a matching vest, and her thigh-high boots are black leather circled with silver chains and charms. She wears half a dozen chains around her neck and twice as many rings on her fingers—all of which have some kind of magical symbol on them. Her nails are long and pointy and the same dark-red shade as her lips.

In other words, she's pretty much the sexiest wicked witch to ever walk the earth. It's a look that is definitely not lost on my friends—or my mate—considering Jaxon, Hudson, Macy, and Eden are staring at her like she's a fantasy come to life while Mekhi and Flint look absolutely terrified.

I'm somewhere in the middle—scared but intrigued—so that when I feel an inexorable pull toward the front counter, I don't even bother to fight it. I mean, we *are* here to talk to her...

But I've only taken a few steps before Macy reaches out and grabs my elbow. "Don't," she orders in the sharpest voice I've ever heard from her.

"What's wrong?" I ask, trying to figure out what she's so worked up about.

"You need to wait until she invites you to speak to her."

My brows shoot up. "Is that some kind of witch etiquette I don't know?"

"She's not a witch," Macy whispers.

"You're right, she's not," Eden agrees. "She's not human—I can smell the magic on her—but I can't figure out what kind of paranormal she is."

"Then how do you know I can't approach her first?" I ask. "This *is* a shop."

"Common sense?" Hudson queries softly. "It doesn't take a genius to figure out she's more than capable of eating the whole lot of us for her daily tea and still have room for dinner. I have a strong sense why this shop is named 'Monster Taffy.'"

Hmm. Maybe he wasn't as entranced by her as I had originally thought.

Macy clears her throat impatiently, and I turn my attention back to her. "Because the sign says so?"

She points to a black sign labeled RULES hanging right next to the mirror on the front wall. And as it turns out, rule number one really is, "Wait to Be Asked Before Approaching the Counter. No Exceptions."

"Okay, then. I guess we're waiting even though we're the only ones in here."

I step back to join the others on the black *X* near the front door, where we wait. And wait. And wait.

Precious minutes pass, minutes when dawn begins to break across the sky with its streaks of orange and red and yellow. A part of me is freaking out— Hudson can't be out in daylight until my blood is fully gone from his system. The only hope is that when we're finished, Macy can portal us out of here.

Several more minutes go by as we wait for her to look up from the crossword puzzle she's doing. But after her initial glance at us when we first walked in, she hasn't looked up once.

What the hell? I mouth to Macy as Hudson shifts restlessly beside me.

My cousin shrugs, but she doesn't look like she's in any hurry to disturb her. Neither does anyone else, except maybe Flint and Jaxon, who just look impatient. But I'm too scared to send either of them up there to ask, because let's be honest, they're both more the *demand answers* not *ask questions* sort—which will get them eaten, most likely.

I guess that means it's up to me. Fan-freaking-tastic.

After a few seconds of looking at her really hard and willing her to look up doesn't work, I finally bite the bullet and clear my throat.

She doesn't so much as blink.

I clear my throat again, a little bit louder this time.

Still nothing.

"Grace—" Macy starts, but I cut her off. Enough really is enough.

"Excuse me—"

"Scram." She says the word with absolutely no inflection.

"I'm sorry?"

The woman doesn't bother to look up from her crossword when she answers, "Not yet, but you will be. Now go."

"But we need—"

I break off as her hand shoots out and slaps against the Rules poster. One dark-red nail points directly at rule number two: "We reserve the right to refuse service to anyone for any reason." The fact that she does this while filling in an answer on her crossword at the exact same time makes the move extra impressive. Or maybe it's just that she's done it so many times before that it's muscle memory by now.

Either way, I'm not going anywhere until I at least get to talk to someone. I clear my throat one more time. "I'm really sorry, but—"

"You already said that." And then she yawns and doesn't even bother to cover her mouth.

It's a move I know well, and I glare at Hudson, who tries to pretend he has no idea what I'm upset about. But the tiny little grin playing around the edges of his mouth says everything.

Apparently, there's a handbook out there somewhere titled *How to Be a Paranormal Asshole*, and both she and my mate have read it. Then again, underneath it all, Hudson is a really amazing person. Maybe she is, too.

The thought bolsters me—along with months of confronting Hudson at his most assholish—and I decide to just go for it. Besides, I've already been threatened once today, by a god who thought smiting me was a reasonable option. After that, any other threat seems like not that big of a deal.

After taking a deep breath and pasting on my sweetest, most nonthreatening smile, I walk across the stained black concrete floor and don't stop until I'm right in front of the register. I try not to let it bother me that she stares at me with unblinking violet eyes the entire time.

"Are there rocks in your ears, gargoyle?" she demands after trying—and failing—to stare me down. "Or do you have a death wish?"

"Neither," I answer. "I'm just desperate."

"Desperation has no place here," she answers. "It will only get you killed."

"It's a taffy shop. I don't think the candy cares if I'm desperate or not." God knows some of those trees look pretty desperate to me.

"All right, then." She holds her arms out wide. "What kind of taffy would you like?"

"Um, taffy?" It's not the question I was expecting.

She lifts a brow. "This is a taffy shop. And since I assume the vamps and dragons back there aren't planning on eating any, then yes. What kind. Of taffy. Would. You. Like?"

Wondering if this is some kind of test, I look back at the trees and the plastic balls of colored treats hanging from their branches. "Can I have one of each kind, please?"

"Amateur," she answers with a snort.

Then she reaches into the basket behind her and pulls out a large plastic globe filled with what looks to be every color taffy the store offers. She drops it on the counter between us and says, "That will be thirty-five twenty-six, please."

"Oh, right." I fumble for the front pocket of my backpack where I always keep my wallet, but Hudson is already there.

He drops a hundred dollar bill on the counter. "Keep the change."

She laughs. "No shit."

Then she scoops the money, her pen, and her book of crossword puzzles and heads for the door at the back of the shop. "Have a nice day," she calls over her shoulders with a laugh that chills my blood.

55

"**T**hat went well," Macy comments from her spot by the door.

"I didn't see anybody else stepping up, so..." I trail off as I pick up the globe of saltwater taffy and spin it between my hands. "What are we supposed to do now? Try every piece until something happens?"

"What exactly do you think is going to happen?" Flint demands. "You'll magically be filled with knowledge about ancient gods and their ancient magical weapons?"

"Hey, be nice," Macy scolds him. Apparently, I'm not the only one who has noticed his less-than-sterling attitude lately.

"That *was* nice," he replies.

Not going to lie, his response sets my teeth on edge. And maybe if we weren't in the middle of something this important, I would call him on it. But right now, we have bigger things to worry about than Flint's foul mood, and the last thing I want is to be derailed now that I've finally got the taffy in my hands.

A glance at Hudson shows him watching me, trying to gauge what I'm thinking and feeling. He must figure it out, though, because he doesn't say anything. Instead, he simply glances from me to Flint and back again. I have no doubt there was a warning look in his eyes when he glanced at Flint, but I appreciate the fact that he's letting me handle it my way. The last thing any of us needs right now is a fight between the two of them.

Eden must agree, because she jumps in before Flint has a chance to say anything else obnoxious. "You can throw that candy away. It won't do anything."

"How do you know that?" Mekhi asks. "We haven't even tried one."

"Because she wouldn't have given it up so freely if it had any value," Macy answers matter-of-factly.

"Great." I look down at the candy with distaste. "So what am I supposed to do with all of this now?"

"Just leave it on the counter," Jaxon tells me.

"What's plan B? Or are we on plan G now?" Eden asks, glancing at her phone and placing one black boot on the edge of a low shelf. "It's almost seven a.m."

"I know," I tell her. "Believe me, I know. But we need this antidote to free the Gargoyle Army—"

"Screw the Gargoyle Army," Flint shoots back. "I'm sorry, but they've been trapped in stone for a thousand years. A couple more days won't hurt."

"No, but going after Cyrus without backup will." I shake my head. "I know this sucks. I know you want to get to the Vampire Court. We all do. But we've fought Cyrus before, and it hasn't exactly gone well. We need backup to have any chance."

"If we can sneak in there and free the kids and the Katmere instructors without him figuring it out, we'll have a shit ton of backup to help us get out of the Court. The Witch Court agreed to help us if we freed the kids," Macy argues. "We just need to get in undetected. Who cares how much noise we make getting out?"

"And if we get caught?" Jaxon asks. "Who's going to rescue them then? Rescue *us*?"

Macy makes a noise deep in her throat. "You can't keep making that argument no matter what we say."

"Sure we can," Hudson says. He's leaning a shoulder against one of the eerie black walls, but the intensity in his eyes belies the casualness of the pose. "You've never lived with Cyrus. You've never actually seen him in action. You've certainly never gone up against him. So we can absolutely keep making the argument that if we try it on our own, we're going to get our asses kicked. Been there."

"Done that," Jaxon chimes in.

"Got our asses handed to us," Hudson finishes.

"Yeah, well, you lived to tell the story," Macy says. "That's enough—"

"*Some* of us lived," Flint grinds out. "The part you keep forgetting is that some of us didn't. And I'm ready to show Cyrus some goddamn payback."

Macy nods. "And you're also forgetting my *mother* is in there." Her voice wobbles. "She will help us—"

"You mean the mother who abandoned you years ago and has been hiding out with Cyrus ever since?" Jaxon's words are harsh, but he's not wrong. As much as I want to help find my aunt, everything in me is urging me that we need to save the Army if we have any chance.

"There's no need to attack her," Eden snaps at Jaxon but then turns to Macy and says more softly, "I'm sorry, Macy. He may have said it in a dickish way, but he's right. We don't really know which side your mom stands on or why. And I, for one, am tired of attending funerals. We need help."

"I can't believe you—" Macy starts.

"Enough." Jaxon puts an end to the argument with a slash of his hand, every bit the vampire prince I first met. "We're here now, and we're going to see this through."

"Fine." Macy looks pissed as she crosses her arms and leans back on her heels. "Tell me how you're going to do that, and I'll stop arguing about heading straight to the Vampire Court."

"I'm just going to ask her," I say. "I mean, seriously, what's the worst she can do?"

"Eat your beating heart out of your still-warm body," Mekhi suggests.

"Disembowel you and feast on your entrails," Flint adds.

"Decapitate you and use your head as an ornament for one of these hideous trees," Macy finishes.

When we all turn to stare at her in surprise—torture isn't usually my sunny cousin's modus operandi—she just shrugs. "Oh, come on. You've seen that woman. Do any of you really believe she isn't capable of all those things and worse?"

I have to admit, it's a fair point. But standing around here bickering isn't going to get us anywhere, and Eden's right about one thing. Time is ticking by. The longer we leave all the Katmere students and teachers at the Vampire Court, the more likely it is that something terrible is going to happen to them.

So instead of hanging back and trying to reach a consensus, I put my money where my mouth is. I duck behind the counter and knock on the door the woman disappeared through a few minutes ago. Hudson is behind me in a heartbeat, followed by Jaxon and Macy nearly as quickly. But the truth is, I didn't expect any less. We may fight, but I've got to believe in the end we've got each other's backs.

Several seconds pass and no one comes to the door, so I knock again, a little harder and more insistent this time.

Still no answer.

"Screw it," I mutter and reach for the door handle. One way or the other, I'm getting answers.

I expect the door to be locked, but it isn't. The knob turns smoothly under my hands, and the door swings wide.

I don't know what I'm expecting to see when I open the door—a storage room or a human sacrifice altar are just a few of the things that flit through my head. The woman who sold me the taffy seems capable of either—and anything in between.

What we find, though, is something so far beyond what I could ever have imagined. The taffy shop opens up into a short hall with a couple of doors on either side, the length of which leads to a giant round arena in the vein of the Colosseum from ancient Rome. The ground is made up of grass and dirt, and while there's no one on the field yet, the stacked stands are packed with paranormals of all kinds.

It makes no sense—we saw this area from the outside when we were looking for the taffy shop, and there was nothing here but more stores. How on earth could there be a giant coliseum that none of us saw?

"Is it a Ludares field?" I ask.

"I don't think so," Hudson answers. "It's not the right shape. Ludares fields are rectangular, and that's a circle."

"So what happens here—"

"I'm impressed, gargoyle." The woman is back, only this time she's dressed in a form-fitting sports jersey that has the name *Tess* on the front in huge block letters, along with *3,695* written in much smaller numbers. The same black harness belt completes the look. "I didn't think you had it in you to open the door."

"It was unlocked," I tell her. "I mean, it wasn't hard to get in here."

"Actually, that's where you're wrong." She makes a clicking noise in the corner of her mouth. "For someone who isn't immune to magic, it's very hard to turn that door. Pretty damn impossible, actually."

She steps back and sweeps an arm out to encompass the field. "So what do you think?"

"I don't know what I'm looking at," I answer.

"You're looking at what you came here to find," she says. "Obviously."

"Actually, I think there's been some mistake. We're looking for—"

"What everyone is looking for when they come to St. Augustine, Florida. The Fountain of Youth. This field is how you get to try to earn it."

56

Trial by Misfire

"Wait a minute." Jaxon steps in, looking as bamboozled as I feel. "You're telling us the Tears of Eleos that Jikan told us about is really the Fountain of Youth?"

Tess raises one brow. "Or the reverse is true."

But Jaxon doesn't miss a beat. "And we need to play a game to get this... thing?"

She laughs and tosses her long black hair behind her. "More like you need to prepare to suffer like you've never suffered before. But sure, you can call it a game to win the elixir if it makes you feel better."

"I don't understand," I say.

Now it's her turn to look confused. "You mean Jikan really didn't tell you anything about the Impossible Trials? That's amusing."

Well, this sounds promising. I mean, we already defeated an Unkillable Beast and beat an Unbreakable Curse. What's an Impossible Trials for our group? Hopefully not impossible. "No, he didn't," I say to Tess. "But I'm guessing by the name of the Trials, you're implying that to seek the Tears could result in death at any moment? Cute." But it's not cute at all.

Neither is it cute that a god chose to leave out important details when sending us on another quest. I really need to get a T-shirt that says: *I prefer to work in the dark*. You know, to match the tattoo on my forehead.

I roll my eyes and glance at my friends, hoping they have a clue, but I'm actually a little shocked to see their faces looking just as surprised as mine probably does.

I turn back to the taffy maker and say, "All he said was that there is some powerful antidote in St. Augustine, Florida, that would help us deal with a god-killer poison."

It sounds convoluted when I say it out loud to someone who isn't in my group, but the look on her face says the Historian was right on, even if he was a total jerk about giving us the details.

"He mentioned it's protected by an ancient creature, so we're here to slay a monster, take the elixir, and save an army." Which sounds even more convoluted than my previous statement, if I'm being honest, but I lift my chin anyway.

She just kind of shakes her head. "And I was actually starting to like you."

"The fact that we don't know anything more about the Trials changes that how exactly?" Flint asks.

"Well, it increases your chance of death from ninety-nine-point-nine percent to a definite one hundred, so..." She sighs. "Yeah, definitely no point getting attached."

"That's some interesting math you've got going on there," Eden comments.

"Math based on experience is the most accurate kind," Tess counters. "And I've had a lot of experience watching people compete and suffer."

"Why do paranormals love to watch their kind die in stupid contests?" I mutter. I'm just so over this. From Ludares to fighting the giants to get out of prison, it's all getting a little ridiculous. And bloodthirsty.

"Oh, this arena and stands haven't always been here, gargoyle." She answers what I thought had been a rhetorical question. "People have been searching for the Tears—the Fountain of Youth—in this place for more than a millennium. Eventually humans started expanding into the area, so we hid it even more. Turns out, it's a huge moneymaker watching the most foolish of our kind try to win as well."

"You mean die," Flint bites out. "You like watching people die."

She glares at the dragon. "I never say what I don't mean. Everyone who comes to watch is rooting for someone to succeed, to win in the face of overwhelming odds. It's all I've *ever* wanted."

"Well, then, you won't mind humoring us," Hudson says. "What exactly are the Impossible Trials, and why is the probability of death so high?"

Tess looks like she's thinking about whether or not she wants to answer, but in the end, she shrugs and says, "The Trials are how you get to the Fountain of Youth, of course. They're a series of tests that makes the seeker prove that they have the skill, the power, and the heart to break the curse and release its ancient magic."

I shiver at the word "curse," and my gaze meets Hudson's. He twines his hand in mine and squeezes, then leans into me and whispers, "We beat unbreakable curses for breakfast." And I flash him a quick smile.

"With a ninety-nine-percent death toll, I'm going to assume the Trials are dangerous," Macy comments.

"One hundred percent death toll," Tess corrects. "I said you had a ninety-nine-point-nine-percent *chance* of dying. And honestly, that's just me being optimistic because I'm convinced someday someone will actually succeed."

"One hundred percent death toll?" I ask as fear settles in the pit of my stomach. "You mean *no one* has ever survived the Trials before?"

"Of course not. Why else would we still have the Tears here? It's a one-and-done kind of elixir. If someone actually won, I would finally get to hang up my taffy-making instruments."

I don't know what to say to that, and it's pretty obvious that the others don't, either. Silence reigns, but just when it looks like Tess is about to bid us farewell, Hudson asks, "So if we decide we want to compete in the Trials, what is it we need to do exactly?"

Tess's response is immediate. "You shouldn't compete."

"Yeah, I think we've figured that much out," Hudson tells her. "But what if we have to compete?"

"Well, if you have to, then you have to, I suppose." Again, she starts to turn away.

"No, what he means is, how does it work?" I ask. "Do we sign up? Do we all get to compete together? When would the competition begin? How do we know if we win or lose one of the tests?"

"Well, the competition begins whenever you choose to challenge it. Anytime, day or night. You know you've won if you're still alive at the end, and you know you lost if you're dead," Tess answers. The fact that she does so with a straight face and every semblance of being serious makes me even more concerned *and* confused.

"As for the other questions, no more than twelve can compete at once. You walking onto that field is sign-up enough, and—" She glances at her watch. "The competition can begin as soon as you're ready."

This time when she starts to walk away, we let her go. Not because I've given up on the idea of competing for the cure for my people but because we need to at least discuss what we're going to do. I feel like everyone needs to be completely on board before we risk our lives for what sounds like a nearly impossible chance at survival.

But surprisingly, Tess only gets a few steps away before she turns back to me. "Find another way, Grace."

I startle that she knows my name. "I don't think there is another way. That's the problem."

"When one path leads you to certain death, there's always another way," she tells me. "Your power is strong, but it's new, and it's changing, and that is a detriment to you. Right now, you lack the confidence to wield it, and that will get you—and your friends—killed."

"My friends have power, too. They've had it longer and can control theirs better." I don't know why I'm arguing with her, except I'm looking for a reason to stay here. Looking for a reason to actually go through with a plan that is looking more and more foolhardy by the second.

"You're right. There's a fair bit of talent in all of them. But their power doesn't compare to what I sense is growing in you, and you are the one who is uncertain."

"That—"

"Come back some other time, Grace. You're not ready for this." She taps the number on her shirt. "3,695 people have competed. None has survived. Let's not make it 3,701."

A sudden lump appears in my throat, and I have to cough several times before I can actually speak around it. "What if we choose to compete anyway?"

"Everyone thinks they're going to win, kid," she replies. "Otherwise, we'd never get out of bed."

This time when she leaves, none of us even tries to stop her.

57

Dead If We Do, Dead If We Don't

"So are you ready to head to the Vampire Court?" Macy asks, more than a little sarcasm in her voice.

"We haven't made a decision yet," Jaxon growls.

"Oh, really? Because I'm definitely okay with not being the 3,696th person to die," Macy fires back. "And you should be, too."

"She's got a point," Mekhi says. "It feels pretty shitty to just throw our lives away on Trials we're not sure we even need to complete to free the kids and stop Cyrus." He turns to me before I can jump in and adds, "Yes, we all want to free the Army. I was all for this plan if we had a shot at freeing them, but it sounds like the only thing we have a shot at here is getting dead."

Which brings up another point. Why *did* Jikan send us here? He knows I'm in no shape to control my power or compete. But I can't help shaking the feeling he had a reason. Of course, like every god I've ever met, he just didn't bother to give me the big picture.

"But—" I start to say, before Macy interrupts me.

"No, Grace." She grabs my hand. "My mother is in the Vampire Court, and I refuse to believe she's there willingly, that she left me willingly." Her eyes well with tears. "I have stood by you and your decision to free the Army, but now is not the time. We need to focus on those in danger *today*. The kids. My dad. My mom."

And oh God, my heart cracks open and my eyes fill with instant tears. How did I forget about Uncle Finn—that Macy stands to lose *both* her parents if we don't rescue them? I know *exactly* how it feels to lose both your parents at once, and I cannot allow that to happen to my bubbly and innocent cousin. She deserves all the pink dreams and rainbows this world has to offer.

Which is why I am even more certain freeing the Army is our only chance at saving them. "If your mom has been there for years, we have to believe she's in no immediate danger, Macy. And Cyrus is stealing 'young' magic—so Uncle Finn is most likely alive to keep the children calm."

"You don't know that!" Macy cries out.

"No, I don't know it for sure, but it makes the most sense." I squeeze her hands.

"I agree," Hudson says as he holds Macy's gaze. "Your parents are okay, Macy. We will get them out."

I take a deep breath and shrug the tears wetting my cheeks off on my shoulder.

"Let's head back to the lighthouse and make a plan," I suggest. "Maybe if we get the Order to come back with us, Tess will say we have better odds at winning."

Jaxon starts to say something, but his phone beeps with a very specific text alert, and he holds up a hand as he pulls his phone out. "It's Byron," he says, and then he's scrolling through a series of messages as they come in.

"What's going on?" Eden asks, and for the first time since I met her, there is real fear in her voice. "Is everybody okay?"

It's what we're all wondering, and we wait in agony for Jaxon to finish reading the texts.

"They know where the kids are," he says after the longest minute on record.

"That's good, right?" Eden asks.

"Yeah," he answers, but he sounds completely distracted.

"What's wrong?" I ask, reaching out to put a hand on his arm for support. "What aren't you telling us?"

He glances from me to Hudson and Macy, then back again. "He's not just holding them hostage. Marise wasn't lying. He's—" He shakes his head, and this time he's the one who has to clear his throat. "He's stealing their magic. Draining them completely. Anyone whose parents aren't loyal to the cause."

The entire group of us recoils in horror.

"Can he—can he do that without—" I break off, not wanting to say it out loud any more than Jaxon did.

"It's possible to do it without killing them," Macy says, her words thick with grief. "It's not easy, though. He'd have to..." Her voice cracks.

"He'd have to torture them." Hudson says the words that none of us wants to say. His tone is flat, but his eyes are alive with so many emotions that I can't begin to untangle them all. "He'd have to break them."

Macy cries out, and her knees must buckle because she starts to go down. Eden catches her and holds her up with a hand on her elbow. She bows her head, takes a deep, shuddering breath, then says, "We have to go. *We have to go.*"

"I know," Jaxon agrees. "Just give me a few minutes to figure out—"

"They don't have a few minutes!" Macy rages, breaking away from Eden. "If you won't go, I will. I'll—"

"Die before you ever find your mother," Hudson tells her.

I shoot him a *what the hell* look, but he just gives me a *you know I'm right* look right back. Then he turns to Jaxon. "You said the Order knew where Cyrus was holding them."

"They do. They're in the dungeons. Near the…" Jaxon trails off, his eyes locked with Hudson's.

Whatever he's not saying hits Hudson like a body blow. He doesn't flinch, but I'm watching him closely and can see the impact of it roll over him. His eyes go flat, his breath stutters, and his hands clench into fists.

"Near where?" Macy asks, her voice shaking. "Just tell me where I'm building a portal, and I'll get us there."

"The Crypts," Hudson answers. "It's where he does all this kind of work."

"He's done this before?" Flint speaks up for the first time, and for once, he doesn't sound angry. He sounds terrified.

"He's tried." Hudson shoves a hand through his hair, and I wonder if he even knows he's trembling a little. "It never worked before, but maybe he's figured something out that we don't know."

"But why?" Flint asks. "Why would he steal magic from children? And not just from other types of paranormals, but from vampires as well?"

"I don't know. The Bloodletter said his real power is trapped with the Gargoyle Army. Maybe he's trying to replace it or needs more to free it. Whatever the reason, rest assured the only thing people in power ever want is more power," Hudson continues. "And I can only guess what he'll do when he gets enough of it."

"What does that mean?" I ask, afraid I already know the answer.

"To wage a war against humans that he can finally win," Hudson tells me. "What he's been working toward my entire life."

I turn to Hudson and Jaxon. "Can you get us into the Vampire Court without Cyrus knowing about it?"

"No," Hudson answers immediately.

"Well, then, we're screwed," Eden interrupts. "Because we can't go in there guns blazing. At least not without the Witch or Dragon Court at our backs."

"And we know both Courts can't or won't help," Flint adds. "So we're on our own on that front. But I still say we go."

"And to hell with what comes next?" Jaxon asks, and it's clear we're at an impasse.

Flint, Macy, and Mekhi face the rest of us, and I've never felt more certain that no matter what we do—we're doomed if we do it divided like this.

"Why don't we head back to Ireland, get some food and rest, and figure out our next move with clearer heads?" I suggest, trying to breathe some calm into the situation. "Rushing into anything is only going to get us all killed. And besides, we really need to wait until dark anyway to make a move, right?"

"Kids are being *tortured*, Grace," Macy accuses, and gone is my sweet, always smiling cousin who would follow me anywhere. In her place is a desert of disappointment stretching between us that I'm not sure how to walk across and reach her again. But I know I have to try.

I squeeze her arm. "And we *will* save them. And your family. I'm just suggesting we take a moment and figure out our next move instead of rushing to our deaths. We will end up saving no one if we don't."

I plead with her with my eyes, and eventually, her shoulders relax and she gives me a quick nod. "I'll build a portal to the lighthouse."

As she pulls out her wand and begins the necessary steps to open a portal, I can't help but notice she never agreed with me.

58

The Walk of
Hell Yeah I Did

"Hi there, sleepyhead," Hudson murmurs, and my eyes flutter open as he sinks down on the bed beside me.

It takes me a second to remember where we are. The lighthouse. "What time is it?" I ask, rubbing the sleep from my eyes.

"You crashed as soon as we got back. It's a little after six in the evening."

I shoot straight up. "You shouldn't have let me sleep that long!"

He smiles, smooths a curl off my forehead and behind my ear. "Hey, I learned a long time ago never to get between you and a bed when you're sleepy. You had a lot of revelations to process. Your body knows what it needs. Besides, like you said, we can't make a move until night, and we only slept four hours before heading to the Bloodletter's Cave."

Have we really slept so little? It's odd how I'm getting used to this frantic exhaustion, this thickness in my blood, as though my body has already accepted what my mind has not. That this is the new normal and there is nothing I can do about it.

And if I'm feeling this way, I can only imagine how the others are handling the stress and sleep deprivation. Maybe that's why we can't find a way through this mess we're in. We're too locked in personal survival mode to connect the way we usually do. No wonder everything feels like it's crumbling beneath our feet. We're on the edge of the abyss and there's nothing left to keep us from falling in. "I'm worried, Hudson. We're never going to defeat Cyrus if we don't work together."

He nods. "Everyone agreed to meet back here at seven to strategize, so don't stress, okay?"

For the first time since leaving the Witch Court, the knot in my stomach starts to ease, and I lean back against the pillows again. I sigh and close my eyes, praying that Macy is willing to hear me out now. That Flint can see beyond his anger and need for revenge. That Jaxon can convince the Order to help us win the Trials.

"You can sleep more if you need to, babe. You've got at least another hour before everyone gets here," Hudson says, and my eyelids flutter open again, my gaze connecting with his warm blue eyes, a half smile lifting up one corner of his mouth.

He's got an arm braced on the mattress, caging me in, and I just lay here and take in the view. His blue dress shirt is unbuttoned and hanging open, displaying washboard abs above a pair of low-slung jeans. His hair is wet and lying across his forehead in careless waves, and he smells strongly of the amber and sandalwood shower gel I love.

"No, I'm awake now," I tell him, burrowing my face against his outer thigh even as my hand wanders up to stroke his warm, flat stomach.

"Oh yeah?" he says, and there is a decidedly interested note in his voice that wasn't there before. His accent is thicker than normal as he asks, "And what should I do about that?"

"Get between me and a bed?" I deadpan, then feel my cheeks warm. I roll out of bed before he can notice.

"Hey!" He catches my hand. "Where are you going?"

I give him the closest thing to a sexy look that I have in my repertoire, enjoying the way his breath hitches in his throat as I do. "To brush my teeth," I answer, right before I dart into the bathroom and slam the door, thrilled we've settled in a different bedroom than the one missing a wall into the en suite since my green-string debacle the day before.

I come back out five minutes later—teeth brushed and face freshly scrubbed— to find Hudson stretched out on his side of the bed looking hotter than anyone should ever have the right to look.

For the first time, like, ever, he hasn't bothered to fix his hair into its normal pompadour, so it's laying soft and tousled against his forehead, curling slightly on the ends as it dries. He hasn't shaved yet, so he's got a little bit of stubble on his jaw that I am suddenly dying to kiss, his jeans-clad legs are crossed at the ankles, his feet bare, and he's got one arm bent behind his head, further opening his dress shirt and giving me a view that has my mouth watering and my fingers itching to touch.

The tiniest tips of his fangs peek out over his full bottom lip while his eyes—burning a dark, hot blue—track my every movement as I walk back toward the bed.

It doesn't take a genius to figure out he knows exactly why I was in such a rush to brush my teeth, and I hesitate, wondering what I should do next.

Normally, I'd crawl back under the sheets and let Hudson take the lead, but there's something vulnerable about him lying there, waiting, watching, letting me decide where this moment leads that makes me want to seize control for just a little while.

So instead of climbing in on my side of the bed, I walk around to his, conscious as I do of his eyes following me the whole way, like the predator he is. Too bad for him that I'm not the least bit interested in being prey right now.

I take my time getting to him, enjoying the promise of what's to come. Enjoying even more the fact that for once, he's the one shifting in anticipation, the one holding his breath as he waits to see what I do next.

I finally stop right next to him, my gaze locked on his. When I make no move to join him, though, he pulls his hand from behind his head to reach for me, but I evade him easily.

That has him quirking a brow, his skin flushing and eyelids growing heavy. But he makes no move to touch me again.

As a reward, I lean over, smiling to myself as he lifts his lips for a kiss. But that's not where I want to taste him, and I move just a little lower, so that I can press warm, open-mouthed kisses against the pulse thrumming in his neck, taking a quick bite in exactly the same spot he loves to drink from me before nibbling my way down the center of his body.

"Grace." His voice is gravel, his hands twisting in the bedsheets before I ever get past the very top of his eight-pack.

"Hudson," I mimic as power thrums along my nerve endings, and I slowly, slowly, slowly kiss my way back up to his collarbone, his jaw, his perfect, perfect lips.

He groans the moment our mouths meet, and I take instant advantage, nipping at his bottom lip before delving inside his mouth, licking, tasting, devouring the heat between us. He's like sweet summer rain against my tongue, and I let myself get lost in the moment. Lost in him.

At least until he starts to roll onto his side and pull me into him. Then I dart back, giving my head a quick shake as we draw in ragged breaths.

"Oh, it's going to be like that, huh?" he asks with a wicked smile.

"Not *like* that," I tell him. "That."

And then—because I can't wait any longer, either—I climb onto the bed, onto him. My knees settle on either side of his hips, and I rock against him, my hands stroking all that glorious, glorious skin of his even as I lean down and take his mouth with mine again.

He groans, deeper and hotter this time, and his hands move to cup my hips and ass.

"Not yet," I tell him, prying his stroking fingers away from my body even though there's a part of me that wants nothing more than to let him do whatever he wants to me.

But this is my time to explore Hudson, my time to find out about all the things he likes. So I twine his fingers in mine and lean forward until I can press his hands into the mattress next to his head, pushing my weight down to hold him immobile as I hungrily take his mouth with mine.

Fire and electricity and need roar through me as I kiss and touch and explore all the sweet and sexy parts of my mate. Of Hudson. My Hudson.

And he lets me, leaving himself completely at my mercy even as his breathing grows harsh, as his eyes go dark and tormented.

Even as sweat coats his chest and his body arches and trembles against mine.

Even as he starts to fall apart, begging me with his mouth, with the low growls in the back of his throat, with the relentless hunger in the slide of his tongue against mine to take whatever I need.

Which is why I give him two more quick kisses before pulling back just enough to gaze into his storm-swept eyes. And what I see there squeezes my chest like a vise.

Hudson looks stripped bare. Open and vulnerable in a way that makes my breath catch.

Because this is Hudson, wicked, wild, wonderful Hudson, but in all the time we've been together—all the time we've laughed and fought and loved—he's never once looked fragile.

But today he does. Today he looks like one wrong move from me, and he'll shatter like porcelain.

It scares me even as it makes me want to wrap myself around him and tell him it's going to be okay. That I'll never hurt him. That I'll always, always catch him if he falls. But I can tell he's too far gone to hear me.

So in the end, I do the only thing I can. I cede my newfound control and offer all that I am—all that I have inside me—to him, telling him with my body instead of my words that I know exactly what he needs right now to feel safe again.

I release his hands and set him free.

He takes over in a flash, his fingers tangling in my shirt for one wild moment before he rips it in half and tosses it over his shoulder, shrugs off his own clothes. And then he's everywhere. His mouth, his hands, his body—over me, beneath me, beside me, inside me. Every part of him touching, holding, taking every part of me until I'm drowning in sensation. Drowning in him.

And nothing has ever felt so good.

Maybe that's why I arch against this boy I love more than my own life, why I slide my hands around his neck and cup the back of his head, why I tilt my head to the side and wait for him to take what I'm offering.

Because who knows when—or if—we'll ever have this chance again.

My desperation must communicate itself to him because he rolls me over and sinks deep. Ecstasy tears through me even before he scrapes his teeth over the upper curve of my breast. He lingers there for long seconds—teasing me, tasting me—before slipping through my skin and into my vein like he belongs there. Like he was made to be there always.

Satisfaction roars through me. Once, twice, then again and again as Hudson moves against me.

It swamps me, pulls me under, turns me inside out and upside down, until it's impossible to know where he ends and I begin.

Until he is all that I know and all that I need.

Until there's nothing left but love and heat and the agony of always wanting more.

We explode like the sun, burn like a supernova, and as he takes me over one more time, all I can think is that the physicists are right.

We really are made of stardust.

Which is why, when Hudson eventually pulls me against his side, tucks the cool sheets around our bodies as our breathing slows again, I can't help the fear that starts to twist in my stomach that this was it, our last perfect moment before all hell breaks loose.

So when the bedroom door suddenly bangs open and Jaxon fades to the end of the bed, a part of me isn't even surprised.

"We have an emergency," Jaxon bites out. "They're gone!"

59

The Old Bait-and-Ditch

Having your ex barge in after you've had possibly the best sex the world has ever known—with his *brother*—is just wrong. I yank the sheets tighter under my chin and wait for the hole I'm praying for to swallow me.

"Dude," Hudson drawls, and Jaxon turns around so fast, it's almost comical.

"Umm, yeah, like I said, they're gone," Jaxon repeats.

Hudson slides his arm out from under my head and throws his legs over the side of the bed. He leans down to grab his discarded clothes, shoving one leg in, then the other before standing up and replying, "Who is gone?"

I glance at my clothes scattered around the room. My jeans are in a pile beside the bed, and my T-shirt is—my gaze darts from the floor to the dresser to the fan?—apparently hanging from the fan. Well, what's left of my shirt. Honestly, it looks more like a rag now, the two sides rent in pieces from Hudson's enthusiasm earlier. I shoot him a raised brow, and he shrugs as he zips his jeans but leaves the top button undone.

And I know Jaxon is standing there. I know he's trying to tell us something important. I know we have life-and-death situations we need to be thinking about. But still—my mate in his low-slung jeans, the tapering of hair just above the open button, those washboard abs, the baby-blue dress shirt he pulls on but leaves unbuttoned so my eyes can gobble up the rest of him—until my heated gaze collides with his smirk. I should be embarrassed he knows the exact effect he has on me, but I lick my lips, and his breathing suddenly matches my own ragged breaths. And just like that, the match that's always poised between us is lit again.

My heart is pounding against my chest, my blood singing in my veins. For Hudson. Always for Hudson. And if his breathing is any indication, his heart is beating just as fast for me.

My mind dances with ideas of shoving Jaxon out of the room and having my wicked way with my mate again, but I keep forgetting I'm dealing with vampires. And they have exceptional hearing.

"For fuck's sake, you two. You sound like you're about to have a heart attack." Jaxon shakes his head and walks toward the door. "I'll give you sixty seconds to get dressed and meet me downstairs. Shit has gone sideways." And with that, he fades out of the room, the door snicking closed a second later with a hushed click.

Hudson runs a shaky hand through his hair that's dried tousled across his forehead, his shield gone. "For fook's sake, woman. You're gonna be the death of me." I love it when he's so overwhelmed, his accent thickens. Even better, his tone is filled with wonder. I feel ten feet tall and can't help smirking at him for once. Which he catches and fades to me in a blink, caging me between his arms as he leans forward and kisses me quick and hard.

"There is no way I'm gonna let my brother think sixty seconds is enough time for"—he gestures at the bed—"us. So get up and get dressed." And then he plants another quick kiss on my lips before disappearing down the stairs.

I chuckle under my breath, hop out of bed, and quickly grab clean clothes, then stare at my wild curls in the mirror. There's no time for a shower, and brushing them will just make matters worse, so I grab a hair tie and pull the mass into a quick ponytail. Satisfied this is as good as it's going to get in sixty seconds, I head downstairs to find out what was so urgent, it had Jaxon barging into our bedroom. I can't even imagine who he was referring to who's gone now.

As I round the bottom stair, I hear Hudson grumble, "The fucking wankers."

"What?" I ask, joining him across from Jaxon and Eden. "What's happened?"

"Macy, Flint, and Mekhi portaled to the Vampire Court while you were... 'showering.'" Eden adds air quotes around the last word, and I blush. But then her words actually sink in...

And I'm so shocked, my eyebrows nearly hit my hairline. "Macy is gone?"

"I tried to stop her," Eden says. "But she was certain that no matter what, you would want to save the Army before saving her parents. She wasn't mad about it. Said she totally understood...and that you'd understand she couldn't risk losing both her parents."

My stomach sinks. "I can't believe Macy really thinks I would miss an opportunity to save Uncle Finn and Aunt Rowena. They are the only family I have left!" I throw my arms out wide. "But just because you want to save someone doesn't mean you *can* save them. At least alone. We need help. We need the Army."

Eden's eyes narrow on me. "Can you honestly tell me you only want to save the Army to have backup to save the kids? Or do you just want to save them because you're their queen?"

I start to protest, but Eden holds up a hand to stop me.

"As the gargoyle queen, you have every right to put your people first, Grace," she continues. "And maybe that's not what you're doing. But I can see why Macy would feel differently. Can't you?"

"If you believe that, then why didn't you go with them?" Jaxon asks.

Eden shrugs. "Just because I question your true motives in trying to save the Army doesn't mean I don't agree we need *someone* to have our backs. The Dragon Court is in disarray, the Witch Court refuses to help, the Wolf and Vampire Courts are in alliance with Cyrus, there's no real rebellion except the eleven of us, honestly. And now we've learned there are apparently even gods who have no interest in helping us. I agree with you. Our best chance was the Army."

"Was?" I ask her.

But Hudson answers, "We won't survive the Trials with just the four of us, Grace."

And I know he's right. It was seriously iffy we had a chance with the whole gang. Now? There's only one thing we can do now.

"We have to follow them. No matter what we were going to agree to do next, I knew it had to be together," I say, and by the looks on everyone's faces, they agree.

A part of me is so mad at our friends for deserting us, for not talking this through, but the truth is, I don't know if they could have convinced me not to save the Army first. I also don't know if Eden's right, if I only want to save them because I feel responsible for their lives, or if I truly believe we need them to defeat Cyrus. But I am honest enough to admit I was convinced I was right.

I twist the ring on my finger, the weight almost too much to bear, but I know no matter what my reasons, I can't focus on my people right now. I have to save my other family.

I blow out a long breath. "So does anyone have any ideas for how to break into the Vampire Court and not die a horrible death?"

Hudson nods. "The one part of the Court Cyrus never visits, the one part he has no idea about, is the servants' quarters. And my lair is right above the south side of those quarters."

"If we get caught, you'll be handing the keys to your *lair* to Cyrus," Jaxon warns.

The brothers exchange a long, devastating look that I don't understand. Then Hudson shrugs, shoving his hands deep in his pockets. "If it's the only way to get in, the only way to keep our friends and Dawud's brother and everyone else alive? I'll risk it." He swallows, jaw clenched and throat working. Then he says faintly, "And to hell with what comes next.

"Of course," Hudson continues sheepishly, "we'll need to wait until dark to travel. I'm assuming our only ride is Eden, and I don't think she'd like a crispy vampire on her back."

"What makes you think I want *any* guy on my back?" Eden fires back and nudges him with her shoulder, a half smile playing across her face.

Hudson snort laughs. "Fair enough."

I don't hear Eden's next comment as an idea tickles the back of my mind. I turn to Hudson. "Do you think you could sketch the layout of the Vampire Court for me? If the kids are near the Crypts, and we have to enter through the servants' quarters, I'd love to know how far we'll have to travel—or more importantly, how many guards we might need to avoid."

Hudson raises a brow. "You have an idea?"

"Yeah." I nod. "But it feels like a really bad one."

Jaxon chuckles. "Well, we know how much Hudson loves those," he says, referring to Hudson's comment earlier at the Bloodletter wanting to try her bad idea.

"Hey, if it ends up with an ice spike near a certain dragon's nether regions, I'm not opposed this time," Hudson teases.

Jaxon stiffens and changes the subject. "So what's this bad idea, Grace?"

"Well," I say, "I could freeze guards by brushing against my green string—*not* holding it—and allow us to sneak right past." I mean, I think I could. Well, in theory. I swallow hard as I admit nothing "in theory" seems to be going as expected.

Eden's eyes widen with respect. "Hell, girl, this sounds like a fantastic idea! What's not to love about it?"

"You mean other than accidentally bringing the Vampire Court down on our heads?" I toss back, wringing my hands. "Also, Jikan said he'd unfreeze the Army if I ever played with time again."

We're all silent as we consider this possibility, but eventually Hudson says, "I don't think we have to worry about him if you freeze a couple of guards, Grace. You've frozen and unfrozen us before, albeit unintentionally, and so has the Bloodletter, and he's never said a peep. As long as you don't grab your demigod string and tear a hole in time, I think we're safe."

I nod. That's exactly what I was thinking, though that doesn't mean it doesn't still frighten me to consider. But then I think of my cousin, desperate to save her parents. Flint in pain over the loss of Luca and his leg. Mekhi, who's had my back since the first day I arrived at Katmere, likely sick and tired of his Court's role in his friends' deaths, too. And I know it's the right decision. I let my friends down not showing them how important their needs were to me, as important as my own, and I have no intention of letting them down again.

If Cyrus gets his hands on them, I have no doubt he will torture them first and steal their power for their part in the massacre on the island. Which is something I am willing to risk almost anything to prevent.

"So how about that sketch?" I ask.

Eden pulls a notebook out of her backpack and hands it to Hudson with a pen, and we all settle down at the kitchen table to familiarize ourselves with the layout of the Vampire Court.

I glance around at my other three friends, dread knotting my stomach. Because of choices I made, our group is shattered, and I have no idea how to put it back together again. More, I'm desperately afraid that by breaking apart, we are giving Cyrus exactly what he wants. And if that's the case, I don't have a clue how we're supposed to get out of this alive.

60

Kicked to the
Curb Appeal

After sunset, Eden flies us from Ireland to England and glides in as close to the Vampire Court as we dare go, which is a nearby hotel. We hop off in an alley, Eden shifts, and Hudson directs us down the street and around a corner. After a couple of blocks, his long strides pick up speed, and I know we must be getting close to his lair.

"Now that we're almost there, are you going to tell us how we'll get from your lair to inside the Vampire Court?" I ask.

"We're using an age-old method," Hudson says as we take a sharp left turn into a new alley.

"Oh God," Eden says. "Tell me we aren't going to have to go through any of London's sanitation tunnels."

Hudson looks affronted. "What kind of mate do you think I am?" he demands. "I'd never make Grace wade through human waste."

"Wow, thanks," Eden teases him.

Jaxon joins in. "At least we know where the rest of us stand."

There's a lull in the conversation as they wait for Hudson to deny it, but he just looks at them out of deliberately bland eyes. I know he's teasing, but I can tell they aren't so sure. Which apparently works for him, as he never straightens anyone out.

We turn around another corner into an even darker, narrower alley, then walk down it about halfway until we get to a dark, narrow house. It sits back only a few feet from the sidewalk, a rusted wrought-iron gate leading up three short stairs to a dingy gray door.

There are wrought-iron bars over boarded-up windows, too, and the paint is chipped and peeling in several places.

"*This* is your lair?" Eden asks, looking at the place with distaste. "Even the sanitation tunnels look better than this place."

"Don't judge a book by the paper it's written on," Hudson tells her.

"I...have no idea what that means," Eden answers, looking confused.

"It means—" Hudson rolls his eyes. "Never mind what it means. Just get me that plant, will you, Grace?"

He points to the saddest, sickest-looking fern I've ever seen. The thing is withered almost beyond recognition. Even its once-white pot is pathetic-looking, chipped and cracked and stained brown in various spots.

"What is this poor plant going to do for us?" I query as I pick it up.

"What did I just say about books and paper?" he answers, reaching into the pot and pulling out a key. "Watch your step—a couple of the boards are rotten out here," he tosses over his shoulder as he bounds up the stairs and onto the crumbling, decrepit porch.

"Only a couple?" Jaxon comments as he sidesteps a cracked board.

Hudson is too busy unlocking the four padlocks on the front door to answer. He pulls off the last padlock, throws the door open, and walks inside.

We pile in after him, eyes wide as he flips on a light, and we take in a living room that somehow looks even worse than the outside of the house.

I wait for him to tell us he's joking, but instead he just heads toward a bookcase at the back of the room. It's my first clue that this place might actually belong to him—the thing is packed to the brim with old books—but it's still hard to imagine him choosing to live here, like this.

The others must feel the same way, as neither of them has moved since he flipped on the lights. They're both just standing in the center of the room, taking in the awfulness.

There's a lot to take in.

To begin with, the furniture is so worn that I'm pretty sure the only things holding it together are the stains. The carpet is torn in several places and stained in several others. The truly horrible yellow velvet wallpaper is faded and peeling, and the curtains look like an entire pack of wildcats climbed them in a fury.

As I move to get a better look at the wallpaper, I can't help thinking that story I read junior year by Charlotte Perkins Gilman suddenly makes a lot more sense. If I was locked in here with this stuff for any length of time, I'm pretty sure I'd go mad, too.

"This is your house?" Jaxon asks. I kind of feel the need for clarification myself.

"It is," Hudson answers with no hesitation. Seconds later, there's a loud screeching sound as he uses one hand to push the loaded bookcase several feet closer to us.

"Why?" The look on Eden's face is half horrified and half fascinated, which I totally get. This is so not Hudson in any way.

But he just shrugs. "You'll see."

I wander toward my mate, curious about what he's doing. Even more curious about his reasoning for this house, because if I've learned anything about Armani Boy in the last few months, it's that he is fastidious to a fault. Every hair in place, every wrinkle annihilated. Even if I ignore that, his room at school couldn't be more opposite this.

Hudson likes his creature comforts and has never made any bones about it.

"What are you doing back here?" I ask as I narrowly avoid tripping on a very large tear in the puke-green carpet.

He dips his head toward the wall and answers, "Watch and learn."

And just like that, things start to make sense. Because behind the bookcase is a giant reinforced steel door, protected by a security code and handprint analysis.

He grins wickedly at me and enters a code before pressing his hand to the analysis plate. Seconds later, the door swings open and reveals a gleaming wooden staircase going down.

"Shall we?" he asks.

"We shall," I answer. This is his plan, after all. And besides, I'm beyond curious about what's in there.

The three of us follow him down the stairs into a huge, open basement—and then stop and just stare. Like his room at school, there are giant bookcases everywhere overflowing with books. Thousands upon thousands upon thousands, lining half the room from its floor to its very tall ceiling. But that's not what has us stopped in our tracks.

We couldn't be more shocked if the space had been decorated in pink sparkly walls and random beanbags.

"This—this looks like—" I don't have any words.

Thankfully, Eden isn't as verbally challenged. "Dude, it looks like Restoration Hardware shot their catalog in here. Their entire catalog."

Yes. That.

The whole room is at least half the size of a football field, the walls not covered by bookshelves painted a pearl white, with lamps and sconces and chandeliers bathing the entire space in soft light. And everywhere the eyes can look is a tasteful mix of rustic and modern pieces, almost exclusively in white, tan, or black. The loftlike space is divided into eight distinct "sections" based on the strategic placement of rugs and furniture, but each space echoes the same aesthetic.

The first area on our right is clearly where Hudson spends his time listening to music. Two black metal bookshelves filled with albums tower over a scattering of big, comfy-looking tan chairs and ottomans, a massive white shag rug that I'm dying to sink my toes into, a media cabinet filled with sound equipment.

As though none of us wants to miss a single thing, we start to walk through the lair, taking in every detail.

Farther down is obviously his exercise space—more axes, of course, but also several bows and quivers of different types as well as various targets hanging on the walls. Beside this area are two overstuffed white sectionals with ecru pillows on them, facing a massive TV mounted on the wall with a half dozen gaming controllers scattered about the space along with an expensive-looking VR headset. A couple of rustic wooden end tables with lamps and coffee tables holding a smattering of magazines finish the area.

All the way at the other end of the room is a giant brass bed, but unlike his bed at school, this one is done up all in white. White sheets, white blankets, white pillows, white comforter. On either side of the bed are heavy, antique nightstands holding elaborately carved silver lamps.

But for once, it's not the bed I'm looking at. Because the area to the left of the bed boasts an accent wall in a shade of black I'd recognize anywhere. A couch and bookshelves complete the cozy reading area that has my heart racing.

"This is the room I painted when you were still in my head," I whisper.

"It is," he agrees, his voice so quiet, I have to strain to hear it.

"That's why you were so insistent about the color of the walls."

"Armani black," he answers with a roll of his eyes. "I did agonize over getting the color perfect the first time myself."

But there's something in the mocking, self-derisive tone that tells me I've hit a hot button. That there's a lot more emotional volatility to this subject than I would expect.

It's a thought that's underscored by the fact that he doesn't stick around for more conversation. Instead, he walks over to another reinforced steel door, this one with even more security than the previous.

I'm too busy turning around, glancing again at the white bed, white walls, white couches, lamps, and chandeliers, to follow him. Everything about the space screams light and joy—and it's so familiar, it makes my chest ache. The details elude me, but I know in my bones I've been here before. Loved here before. And let it slip through my fingers like water.

Hudson notices my preoccupation and comes up behind me, resting his hands on my shoulders as he leans in and asks, "You okay?"

His breath tickles my ear, and I let myself sink into him for just a few precious seconds. "This is where we were. This is—" My voice breaks.

"This was our home, yes. For a while, at least."

I sigh, blinking away the tears that I don't have time for right now and that I don't want to shed in front of Hudson. It's ridiculous to get this upset when we're mated now anyway.

Or it's ridiculous if I don't let myself think about what it must have been like to be Hudson when we first got back to Katmere. What it must have been like to be him when my mating bond with Jaxon showed up again. If I do let myself think about that, if I do let myself dwell on how much it must have hurt him, it breaks me deep inside in a way I'm not sure I'll ever completely recover from.

A way I don't have any right to expect him to ever fully recover from.

I think back to the look on his face in bed earlier, the desperation in his gaze that he was mere glass in my hands, and my chest squeezes tight. How hard must it be for him, for someone we all forget too often was raised without an ounce of love in his life, to open up and trust again, when the first time he did...I just forgot about him like he never mattered at all?

"Hey," he tells me, like he can read my thoughts. "I'd do it all over again to end up here with you."

"I don't know why," I whisper. "After what I did to you—"

"You didn't do anything to me," he answers, sliding his hand up to the back of my head and pulling me in so that my face is buried against his chest. "Fate's a fickle bitch, and so is *Cassia*." He says her name in such a mocking tone, I know that poking at her with it is going to provide him with entirely too much entertainment in the years to come. "But that has nothing to do with you, Grace. You've never done anything but love me—even when you didn't remember."

"That's not true," I choke out, doing my best to will away the lump of tears stuck in my throat.

"It's my truth," he answers. "And it's what I'll always choose to remember about you. About us."

A sob escapes my throat, and I muffle it against his shirt while he strokes a hand through my curls. Other sobs are right there, just waiting to get out, but I shove them back down. Now is not the time, not when our friends—including Jaxon—are in the room with us. And not when our other friends are counting on us to break into the Vampire Court and help them save those kids and their family from whatever horrors Cyrus has in store for them.

"Grace." He sighs, holding me tight for one second, two.

"It's okay," I tell him, drying my eyes against his immaculate shirt—which I'm sure he's going to love later. "I'm okay."

He grins down at me. "You're more than okay."

I wipe my face one more time, as surreptitiously as I can. Then duck out from behind Hudson to find Jaxon and Eden studiously engaged in something other than looking at us. Which I appreciate even if it does make me feel incredibly self-conscious.

Figuring the best way to get through it is just to get back to business, I ask, "So how do we get to the Vampire Court from here?"

Hudson doesn't answer. But he does walk back over to the super-scary security door at the other end of the room, and after he lets it scan his handprint and his eyeball and enters a security code, the door swings open.

"Who's going first?"

"Into the dark and creepy tunnel?" Eden jokes. "Obviously—"

Jaxon goes first—big surprise—followed by Eden, while Hudson and I pull up the rear after he grabs a small bag out of a chest near the door.

Hudson explains that the tunnel we're in leads from his lair directly into the servants' quarters, which we learned from his drawing leads into the dungeons. As we walk along the narrow shaft, I have to admit it's nowhere near as scary as I expected it to be. To be honest, it's not even as scary as the tunnels I used to take to art class back at Katmere.

It's just a regular tunnel with wooden beams above our heads and rocks lining the walls. The floor is made of pavers and sand, and there isn't a stray vampire fang or even a spider to be found. I'm not sure how it's possible that there isn't even one cobweb, considering we're in a centuries-old tunnel, but I'm definitely not complaining.

I am curious, though. About the tunnel and, more, about how Cyrus is okay with having an entrance like this into his Court—or whether he doesn't know about it.

We turn a corner to the right, and Hudson comments, "We're almost there. Just another hundred meters or so."

"And it's just going to be okay?" I ask. "Cyrus isn't going to have the entrance guarded?" For a man who usually takes care of every detail—to our detriment—it seems odd that he would be so laissez-faire with security. Very, very odd.

"I've actually got the same question," Jaxon says. "If he's keeping them in the dungeon, won't he have major security on every entrance?"

"I'm sure he does. But he doesn't know this entrance exists, so..."

"How does he not know?" Jaxon looks skeptical. "I don't know him the way you do, but it seems like he would know everything about his Court—even the parts he almost never enters."

"I'm sure he does. But this is my tunnel. I built it over the course of a hundred years, one centimeter at a time, and he has never found it."

Well, that explains the neatness. No cobweb would dare darken the heights of a tunnel built for Hudson Vega's exclusive use.

"Are you sure?" Eden asks. "You haven't been here in a while, and I'd really hate to walk straight into a trap."

"At some point, I'm sure we'll run into a trap or ten," Hudson tells her. "But not from this tunnel."

I can tell the others still aren't as certain as he is, but there's a power in Hudson's surety that calms my own nerves. Besides, if I know nothing else, I know that there's no way Hudson would ever lead me into an ambush.

Besides, it's not like there's another way into this place. At least not for us.

About fifty yards up, we run into yet another reinforced steel door with its own security system. It has biometrics just like the other doors, and like the other doors, it appears it can only be operated exclusively by Hudson.

After he's scanned what feels like twelve different parts of his body, a loud click echoes through the tunnel. Seconds later, the door slides open. And just that easily, we are face-to-face with two very large, very armed members of Cyrus's exclusive Vampire Guard.

61

Why So Crypt-ic?

"**F**uck," Jaxon mutters, pushing to the front of the group. Already I can feel a fine tremor in the ground beneath our feet. "I told you—"

"And I told you," Hudson answers, shouldering him aside, "I've got this. How are you, Darius?"

He holds his hand out to shake the other vampire's, and as their palms connect, I can't help but see the flash of a gold coin changing hands.

"I'm good, Your Highness. How are you?"

"We've been better," Hudson responds even as he moves to shake the second guard's hand. Once again, I see gold flash between them. "Nice to see you, Vincenzo."

He ducks his head so that his longish black hair falls into his face. "You as well, Your Highness. But I've got to tell you, you picked a terrible time to visit."

"So I've heard." Hudson leans in, and this time when he speaks, his voice is barely audible even to me, who is standing only a couple of feet away. "Where is he keeping them?"

Relief flashes across the bigger guard's face—Darius, I think Hudson called him. "They're in a couple of places. Most of them are in the sublevel waiting for—" He breaks off with a shake of his head. For the first time, I notice there's sweat on his brow.

"The others are in the wells," Vincenzo tells him.

"The wells?" Hudson asks incredulously. "Why would he—"

"He puts them there when he's done with them. They're isolated, so no one can hear them scream."

Chills slide down my spine like claws. So Cyrus tortures them, ruins them, then abandons them to scream where no one can hear them? "That's the worst thing I've ever heard."

Jaxon and Hudson exchange a quick look, and there's something in their eyes that has me holding my breath as everything inside me turns to ice. I'm not about to ask for an explanation now in front of everyone, but I'm definitely going to be asking for one later. Because if it's anywhere near as bad as what I'm thinking...

My fists clench. I've never really wanted to hurt anyone in my life, but I am done with Cyrus. I am done with him starting shit that gets people I care about hurt or killed, and I am so fucking done with him doing shit to hurt Hudson and Jaxon. The people I love deserve more than to spend their lives being terrorized by him. One way or another, it's going to end this time, and I'm going to be the one to end it—even if it destroys me.

Hell, I've got a baby demigod string, and I might be afraid to use it, but kicking Cyrus's ass could be just the motivation I need to try again.

"At least they're alive," Hudson says, then asks, "who's guarding them?"

"The dungeons near the crypt were built by the Blacksmith." Darius shrugs. "Without magic or abilities, they're not going anywhere, so it's just a couple of guards on that level, one near the wells."

"Where's everyone else?" Jaxon demands.

"Guarding the entrances to make sure you can't slip in." Vincenzo grins. "I myself am supposed to be on the sublevel entrance with about fifteen other guards."

"And I'm supposed to be on the main level," Darius adds. "But I had a family emergency right around the time your texts came through."

"I appreciate that." Hudson's smile is grim but determined. "Are the stairwells clear?"

"The last I saw, they were, yeah. We did a quick recon while we were waiting for you. The biggest concentration of guards is on the top level, near the king."

"Dear old Dad always was one to cover his own ass first," Hudson says as we start to walk down the hallway with the guards, eyes peeled for any movement or activity. "Is my mother with him?"

"The queen is visiting her sister," Vincenzo answers. "It is my understanding that the screams...upset her digestion."

"Well, we definitely wouldn't want that to happen," Jaxon says with disgust.

Hudson pauses. "And what about the others? Have you seen them yet?"

Vincenzo darts a glance at Darius before telling Hudson, "I'm sorry, Your Highness. They put up a fight but were captured before we could get to them."

I gasp, knowing immediately they're referring to Flint, Macy, and Mekhi. "Are they—" I can barely get the question out. "Are they in the wells?"

My stomach clenches, acid crawling up my throat as I imagine my cousin, my friends, lying in the bottom of a well, powerless and screaming in pain. I feel a little faint and place a hand on Hudson's arm. He reaches up with his other hand and places it over mine.

"No, they're still in the dungeons, Miss..."

"Ah, yes," Hudson says, "forgive my manners. Let me introduce you to my mate, Grace—the gargoyle queen."

The two guards snap their boots together and immediately bow deep as they murmur, "Your Highness."

But as soon as they straighten, Darius glances down the hall and back, then whispers, "You should not have come, Your Highness." He's looking directly at me, and an icy chill prickles my neck. "If you are captured, I fear all hope will be lost. He has plans—"

Vincenzo interrupts and addresses Hudson. "We've said too much. We have families of our own to worry about, Your Highness. But be warned, things are very different since you were last here. Cyrus has made powerful allies. Now, let us continue." And with that, Vincenzo begins walking down the hallway again, the rest of us following.

I have so many questions, I don't even know where to begin, but a quick glance from Hudson tells me now is not the time to ask. Instead, I focus on where we're going, keeping a sharp eye for any other guards I might have to freeze quickly.

There are twists and turns every few dozen feet, and I half expect someone to jump out at us from some hidden doorway or wall niche. The others must feel the same, because no one says a word until we end up passing through giant stone archways into a massive chamber.

The light is pretty dim down here, and I'm so busy looking for threats from the Vampire Guard that it takes me a couple of minutes to realize where we are. And, more importantly, what's around us. Namely dozens of concrete tombs, most with elaborate carvings and jewels embedded in the sides and tops.

"Is this what I think it is?" Eden whispers right about the time I figure out where we are.

"It's the royal mausoleum," Jaxon tells her. "It's where members of the royal families are put when we die. And when it's time for our Descent."

"Descent?" Eden asks. "What does that mean?"

Jaxon hesitates. "All vampires are born with speed and strength and several other advantages. But the royal family—and only the royal family—develops an extra power over the first part of their lives."

"Power or powers," Hudson elaborates. "Depending on…" He trails off and suddenly becomes very interested in the tomb we're standing closest to.

"Depending on what?" I ask. Before he can answer, I turn to Jaxon. "This is why you have telekinesis. And why you"—I turn back to Hudson—"can vaporize things with just a thought?"

"Don't forget about the persuasion stuff," Eden says.

"Believe me, I'm not," I answer. "How did that happen anyway? That Jaxon got one gift and Hudson got two?"

For the first time ever, Hudson doesn't answer me. Instead, he turns and starts walking toward the end of the mausoleum as fast as he can go without actually fading.

Jaxon stares after him for a second before turning back to me with a sigh. By now, every instinct I have is on high alert. There's something more to this story than "royal vampires magically get a power."

Something dark.

And something Hudson doesn't want to talk about.

Of course, that only makes me more determined to figure it out. If something has my mate this upset, I pretty much figure I need to know what it is.

When he turns and realizes I have no plans to follow him until he elaborates, he runs a hand through his thick hair, leaving a few sections standing up at odds, but he sighs and walks back over to me.

"It's not that big a deal, Grace," Hudson finally says. "From the time we're children, we're fed blood mixed with a special elixir, half sleeping potion and half something else entirely—which we now know is from the Bloodletter. Then we're locked inside our tomb down here for somewhere between fifty and a hundred years—"

"Wait a minute." Eden looks between them, wide-eyed. "You're locked in a concrete tomb for a hundred years?"

"Pretty much. It's where the whole vampires-in-coffins folklore comes from," Jaxon answers, but he doesn't sound pleased.

"That makes a weird kind of sense," I say, too horrified at the idea of Hudson or Jaxon locked in a concrete coffin for a hundred years to dwell. "But I don't get it. They just put you under for a hundred years and you never wake up?"

"No, they wake you up once a month," Hudson explains. "They bring you out for a day or two, check you over to see if your power is evolving, then dose you again and put you back in the tombs."

"No," Jaxon says in a voice filled with horror. "That's not how it works. They put you under for a year and then wake you up for a week."

"And that's better how?" Eden asks.

"It's better because the more you use the elixir, the faster it loses efficacy." Jaxon looks stricken as he stares at Hudson. "That's why the time varies so widely between vampires. Some go under for fifty. Others go under for a hundred years. It stops once the sleeping potion stops working.

"Or at least it's supposed to," he adds as he studies Hudson's face.

Hudson shrugs. "It's not a big deal."

"It's a huge fucking deal if they woke you up twelve times a year," Jaxon counters. "The effects would have worn off sometime between year four and year ten."

Hudson doesn't say anything, and somehow that's a million times worse. My heart beats way too fast as I wait for his answer, while my empty stomach threatens to crawl right up my throat. If what Jaxon is saying is true...

"Hudson?" I finally ask when I can trust my voice—and my stomach—to behave. "Is that true? Did the sleeping potion wear off before they let you out permanently?"

"It's fine," he tries to reassure me. "I've always had a vivid imagination and kept myself occupied."

"It's not fine," Jaxon snaps. "Everyone knows they kept you under for one hundred and twenty years. That's—" He breaks off with a shake of his head, like he can't bear to say the words.

But he doesn't have to. I can do the math well enough on my own, and it's more horrifying than I originally thought.

Hudson was forced to spend more than one hundred years locked in a dark concrete box—and he was awake for every second of it.

I wrap my arms around my waist as an even worse thought occurs to me. Possibly the only thing worse than being locked in a tomb for a hundred years—they woke him up once a month, showed him the light he was missing, the world he was denied, and then they put him right back in that cold and dark hell.

My stomach goes from crawling up my throat to full-on somersaulting as I realize the extent to which Cyrus has tortured him, and it takes every ounce of concentration I can muster to keep from having a panic attack right here in the middle of Hudson and Jaxon's sacred family burial place.

And that's before Hudson shrugs and says, "It's hard to complain when I got two kick-ass powers out of the deal."

Yeah, I can't help thinking as we move toward the door on the other side of the tomb. *Two kick-ass powers he can't wait to get rid of.* The thought has my already bruised and battered heart threatening to crack wide open. I think back to his lair, filled with the two things he was denied for a *hundred years*—space and light—and I raise a shaky hand and cover my mouth before I cry out.

"Hey." Hudson pulls me into his arms, his warmth chasing away the chill in my veins. "Good people have shite lives all around the world, Grace. At least I have you."

I hug him back, this boy who refuses to let anyone break him, and I am in awe of his strength.

"We need to go now, Your Highness," Darius urges, and we turn to follow him again, but he stops dead a few feet from the exit, his hands coming up to cup his throat.

"Darius?" Vincenzo rushes forward. "What hap—"

He breaks off as a knife flies straight into the center of his chest. He has one second to issue a surprised, "Oh," before death claims him, and he falls face forward onto the ground.

62

Knife to
Meet You

"I t's a shame, really," a sly female voice comments from the shadows. "I expected them to put up more of a fight. Then again, I guess it's true what they say. You really do get what you pay for." Her crisp British accent bites off every syllable.

I whirl around, searching the shadows as I try to figure out who is in here with us. Hudson and the others do the same thing, but it doesn't look like any of them has been able to spot her, either. Which is concerning, considering the other three can see in the dark.

"Who's in here with us?" Eden demands, her weight shifting to the balls of her feet in her Doc Martens.

I shiver. There's something extra creepy about being hunted by someone you can't see. Especially when that person has just killed two other people right in front of you—people who just happened to be members of one of the most elite vampire guards in the world.

Not wanting to wait until something else happens, I reach inside myself and grab my platinum string. If I'm going to fight some disembodied voice in the dark, I'm going to do it as a gargoyle.

Except nothing happens, even when I give the string an extra-tight squeeze.

I try again, but still nothing happens. Before I can try a third time, the voice comes back—this time from a different corner of the room.

"Did you really think a couple of gold coins were going to keep you safe, Hudson?" She makes a *tsk-tsk* sound. "Honestly, you should know better than that by now." A knife goes flying by me, so close that I can feel the air it displaces brush against my cheek.

"What the fuck?" Hudson growls.

Seconds later, another knife comes at us. This one just barely grazes the outside of Eden's biceps.

She gasps, but that's the only sound she makes as she clamps a hand down on the cut, and the rest of us fan out, trying to figure out what's happening. The knives are all coming from the same direction, so we hone in on that corner of the room, move closer.

Hudson must figure out that I can't shift, because he gets right in front of me, blocking me from any other weapons with the sheer width of his shoulders.

At the same time, Jaxon and Eden charge the shadows, only to come up empty-handed.

"If you know so much, why don't you come out here and explain it to us?" Jaxon calls as he turns around, looking for whoever is doing this.

"Oh, I intend to." And just like that, she's there in front of us, jumping down from the top of one of the coffins near the back of the mausoleum. We all watch, wide-eyed, as she saunters toward the light.

"Who are you?" Hudson demands, moving a little bit to the left to make sure he's between the girl and everyone else even as Jaxon starts to do the same thing.

"Still asking questions," she mocks as she finally steps into the light, and I get my first good look at her.

It shocks me, shocks all of us, because this *girl* is the last person anyone would expect that voice—and those knife-throwing skills—to belong to.

To begin with, she's probably younger than me—or at least, she looks a little younger. Sixteen, maybe seventeen if you push it, with ruby-red hair she wears twisted into a bun at the nape of her slender, elegant neck. Her eyes are wide and dark, a sharp contrast to her alabaster skin, and as she steps farther into the light, the look in them is even more sly than her voice.

She's tall—close to six feet if I were to take a guess—but too thin, like it's been way too long since her last meal. She's dressed entirely in black, which only accentuates her pale skin and long, slender limbs.

Tight long-sleeve black shirt cinched with a black harness-type belt.

Tight black leather pants.

Low-heeled black boots.

Even the thin leather cord she has triple wrapped around her right wrist is black.

As for the five hundred knives she has strapped all over her person? They don't scream "overkill" *at all*—more like just the right amount of kill, or at least I'm sure that's what she tells herself. How else can she terrorize a group of people anytime she wants?

And while five hundred might be a slight exaggeration, I'm pretty sure two hundred isn't. Maybe even two-fifty. It's clear she had this outfit custom-made and kept telling the seamstress, "More knives, more knives."

Still, I try to look past the knives—which is even harder than it sounds—to get a good look at the girl underneath. Because, despite all the weapons, she looks just a little fragile. Like a ballerina who has taken one too many falls.

But somehow that only makes her more beautiful. At least until she opens her mouth and goes back to being scary as fuck.

"Then again, you always were the idealistic one, weren't you, Hudson?" she mocks.

The fact that she knows him, or thinks she does, is really strange, considering he doesn't seem to have any idea who she is. And when she continues—"The poor little lost boy who never understood the three most basic fundamentals"—ice slides along the inside of my veins.

Because there are only a couple people in the world who know Hudson well enough to see how lost he is under the facade, and this stranger definitely shouldn't be one of them. I mean, yeah, it could just be a good guess, but something about the way she's looking at him tells me it's more than just speculation.

"And what exactly are these fundamentals you're so impressed with?" Hudson asks.

He sounds bored, like he's barely paying attention, but a quick glance at his face shows that he's watching every single move she makes. And that he, too, is wondering if she's taking shots in the dark or if she knows something she shouldn't.

"Isn't it obvious?" She holds up a hand so she can tick the points off on her fingers. "One, greed always wins. Two, loyalty doesn't exist."

She pauses for a second to let the words sink in, but Hudson only lifts a brow. "Did you forget the third one, or can't you count that high?"

The snide, mocking voice he uses startles me, gives me pause. I haven't heard it in months—not since he stopped trying to hide his feelings from me—and it has me looking at this girl more closely. I have no idea who she is, but she's got Hudson's back way up and all of his defense mechanisms firmly in place.

A quick glance at Jaxon tells me he notices it, too—and that he's as baffled as I am. Even before the girl says, "I can count just fine. Maybe you've got me confused with baby brother over there?"

Jaxon goes from looking confused to looking insulted—I mean, who can blame him—but before he can object, she continues. "The third is the most obvious and the first thing our shite father taught me. Blood is only thicker than water when it's running down the drain."

63

Dungeons and Daggers

The girl smiles sharply, her fangs glinting even in the dim light of the mausoleum as we gasp as one. Hudson and Jaxon have a sister? A quick glance at them says clearly, not that they knew.

Then, before any of us can react, she waves a careless hand and orders, "Seize them."

Moments later, what looks to be an entire battalion of the Vampire Guard floods the room.

The guards come toward us, and we move so that we're in a circle, our backs together. Again, I reach for my platinum string, and again, I come up empty.

"What's happening?" Eden asks, and she sounds more panicked than I've ever heard her. "I can't find my dragon."

"I can't find my telekinesis, either," Jaxon mutters, ducking just in time to avoid a giant fist flying toward him.

"They must have some kind of spell that blocks our magic, like they did in the Aethereum," Hudson says as he dodges a couple of ham-handed fists, then delivers a kick to the solar plexus that has one guard stumbling backward.

But when he glances over to check on me, he ends up with a fist straight to the nose. Blood flies out, and the girl—whoever she is—laughs from the doorway. "I'd say sorry about the pain you're all about to feel, but the pain's my favorite part. Have fun," she tells the guards, and I swear I can hear her laughing all the way down the hallway.

I start to fight, too, kicking one guard who tries to grab me and slamming my head back into the chin of another. But there are dozens of them and only four of us. Even with our powers, we'd be outgunned. Without them, the fight is over before it's even begun.

Once they've got us in unbreakable chains, they drag us down to a huge room with thick bars I'm guessing are made of the same material as our cuffs. Inside,

I can see Katmere students—some still in their distinctive purple hoodies—and several instructors I recognize as well.

I might be happier to see them if we weren't also about to be stuck in the dungeon with them. The guards open the door with a clang and shove us inside without bothering to take the cuffs off.

"Turn around," a guard orders gruffly once we're all locked in the cell. Only then, when our backs are to them and there's no chance for us to escape, do they remove the chains from around our wrists.

Eden's come off first, and the second she's free, she's across the room, laughing and crying as she wraps her arms around another girl, a dragon a year younger than us. I'm near the end—between Jaxon and Hudson—and as I wait my turn, I can't help looking from student to student. Wondering who we'll find here. Wondering more, who has already been taken to the wells.

I find Macy's ex, Cam, and Amka, the librarian who's been so kind to me. I see the wolf girl who sat next to me in art for most of second semester and several of the dragons who were in my Physics of Flight class. But no matter how hard I look, I don't see my uncle Finn anywhere.

I hope that just means he's in the back—it's a big cell, but there are a lot of people in it, and it's pretty crowded—not that Cyrus has already taken a shot at torturing him.

"What do we do now?" Jaxon asks, though Hudson isn't paying attention. He's already turned around, studying the faces of the guards as if looking for something—or someone. But I don't focus on that, because I've just seen exactly the faces I need to see most.

Another set of guards has approached the cells with more prisoners, and they undo their chains and shove them in with us one by one. Flint. Mekhi. Dawud. Rafael. Byron. Liam. And Macy.

Dawud races over to a boy who looks remarkably similar—Amir—while my cousin rushes toward me, wraps her arms around my waist, and cries out, "You came for us."

"Of course we did. We're family." I squeeze her back, and we just hold each other for a minute, Macy obviously glad to see me and me so, so relieved she's not at the bottom of a well.

Eventually, we pull apart, and Macy says, tears on the tips of her lashes, "I'm sorry we snuck off."

I shake my head. "No, I understand. I'm sorry I wasn't listening to you."

She swipes at the tears that have tumbled down her cheeks and sniffs. "I had to find my parents."

"Shhh," I soothe, squeezing her again. "It's okay."

Someone coughs to our left, and we separate again.

"Foster's in the back, Mace," Cam says, and for the first time since I've known him, he doesn't sound like a jerk. "He's in rough shape, but he's okay."

"Daddy!" Macy shouts as she starts running for the back of the dungeon. "Daddy, where—"

"Macy?" Uncle Finn bursts through one of the crowds of students and grabs Macy in a hug. "Thank God you're all right. I thought—" His voice breaks.

"I thought the same about you," she says, hugging him tightly.

"What about Grace? Is she—"

"I'm right here, Uncle Finn." I move to give him a brief hug, too, but the second I brush against his right shoulder, he winces.

"Where does it hurt?" Macy asks, but the truth is, the better question might be where it doesn't. It's obvious he put up a hell of a fight when they came to take Katmere, which doesn't actually surprise me at all. Uncle Finn has always been super protective of his students.

His face is battered, his eyes blackened, and the left side of his jaw is swollen to nearly twice its usual size. His clothes are torn and bloodied, and the knuckles on both his hands are shredded. Plus, now that the adrenaline of seeing Macy is wearing off, he's walking with a pretty pronounced limp.

"It doesn't," he tells her, dropping a kiss on the top of her head. "Now that I know you're alive, the rest of this is nothing to worry about."

I admire his fighting spirit, but he's listing to the side pretty badly at this point, so I have a hard time believing him.

"Don't worry, Daddy. We'll get you out of here," Macy tells him.

I exchange a look with Hudson, who has come up beside me. I'm all for getting out of here, but I'm not so big on making promises we can't keep. And right now, we're powerless and locked up in a dungeon. Escaping seems like a pipe dream when right now all I want is for the people I love to survive.

That, in and of itself, seems improbable. If Cyrus really kidnapped all these people because he wants to drain their power, it seems that his first choice at this point would be his sons. After all, they are the most powerful paranormals in the room—some of the most powerful paranormals in the world—and he's gone to great pains to make them that way. Why wouldn't he try to drain them first? Or maybe the better question is, why hasn't he tried to drain them before?

"You doing all right?" Hudson asks me, his blue eyes searching mine.

I give him an *are you kidding me?* look.

Before I can say anything, though, Macy says, "Mom's here, Dad. We went to the Witch Court, and they told me she's been here all along. Once we get out of here, we need to find her. We need to—"

"Macy." Uncle Finn holds up a hand to stop her. "I already know where your mother is."

"What do you mean, you know? How is that possible?"

My uncle doesn't answer. He just studies Macy's face, his hands shaking. Eventually, he rasps, "I was only trying to protect you."

Macy pulls back. "What do you mean? Protect me from what?" For the first time since I've known her, her face is filled with suspicion and, worse, with betrayal.

"I didn't want you to find out this way," he tells her, and I can see the words hit her like a body blow. Not that I blame her. In my opinion, those are pretty much the nine worst words in the English language, because whatever comes after them is always, always, *always* bad.

"Find out what?" she asks and narrows her eyes, rests her clenched hands on her hips. "What didn't you tell me, Dad?"

Uncle Finn takes her hand, then limps around another group of students.

I turn to Hudson. "I need—"

"Go," he says. "I want to talk to Jaxon about the evil-as-fuck sister we never knew we had. Come find us when you're done."

I nod, then take off after Macy and Uncle Finn.

They weave around two more groups of kids before they get to the back corner of the dungeon. And there, crumpled on the ground in the shadows, is a woman who barely resembles my aunt Rowena.

Her naturally blond hair is the same color I remember—the same color as Macy's underneath all the hair dye—and the small, heart-shaped birthmark on her cheek is still there as well. But that's all the resemblance I can find between my laughing, vibrant aunt and the poor, broken woman currently huddled under Uncle Finn's favorite checked blazer.

Her skin is sallow, her hazel eyes sunken and ringed with dark circles. Her clothes—which have obviously seen better days—hang on her gaunt frame like a shroud.

Macy cries out when she sees her and drops to her knees. "Mom, oh my God, Mom." Tears stream down her face as she wraps herself around her mother.

A low, keening cry comes from my aunt as she strokes Macy's hair. Tears leak from her own eyes as she struggles to hug her daughter. "My baby, my baby," she repeats in a voice that is cracked and haunted.

"What happened to you?" Macy whispers.

Her mom doesn't answer—she's so broken, I'm not sure she can formulate an answer to what is obviously a very complex question—and Macy doesn't push. Instead, she just sits there and lets her mother touch her cheeks and her hair over and over again. "So pretty," my aunt whispers. "So pretty."

Eventually, Aunt Rowena falls asleep, and Macy wipes the tears from her face. Then, after she gently unwraps her mom's arms from around her and the woman doesn't stir, Macy gets to her feet. And turns on her father with a fury I've never seen from my happy, gentle cousin.

"What did you do?" she demands as she advances on Uncle Finn.

"I had nothing to do with this, Macy." He holds his hands up beseechingly. "I couldn't control anything about her punishment, and I couldn't free her no matter how hard I tried or how many avenues I explored. And I've tried. Believe me, I've tried for a decade."

"You've known for ten years that she was locked in this place?" Macy demands. "And you never told me?"

Her voice is loud enough that it's attracting other students' attention—which gets our friends' attention. They make their way over to us as Macy continues to try to get answers from Uncle Finn.

"What good would it do to tell you she was in here?" he asks. "It would only hurt you."

"Because thinking my mother chose to abandon me didn't hurt?" she shoots back. "Thinking that she was out there somewhere just living her life and not wanting me didn't hurt? What kind of father would do something like that?"

Her words hit Uncle Finn like fists, and I can see him flinching a little more with each one. It worries me, because he's obviously injured and already devastated at the state he's found his wife in. Having Macy turn on him, too, must be unbearable.

What he did was wrong—really, really wrong—but he's not in a good place at the moment, and berating him will only make it worse.

It's that thought that has me stepping forward and resting a hand on my cousin's shoulder. "Macy, maybe we should—"

She whirls on me. "Don't *Macy* me! He lied to me for a decade. He left my mother in this hellhole for Cyrus to torture for ten years. And now he's making excuses!"

"I'm not," he tells her. "You have every right to be angry with me—"

"You don't have any right to tell me what *rights* I have," she snarls at him. "You don't even have the right to talk to me."

She looks down at her mother, who is curled up in a ball as if trying to ward off the pain even in her sleep. "How could you do this?" she asks again. "How could you—" Her voice breaks, and Mekhi reaches for her and pulls her in for a hug. She buries her head on his shoulder but wipes her hands over her face before whispering to her father, "Tell me everything."

64

Father Doesn't
Know Best

"There's not a lot more to tell," my uncle says.

Macy looks down at her sleeping, shivering mother and answers, "Oh, I think there is."

He sighs. "She didn't want you to know. Neither of us did. We wanted to keep you away from the front lines."

"Know what exactly?" she asks snarkily, pulling away from Mekhi to face Uncle Finn again as Hudson rejoins us. "That Cyrus has been keeping her locked up in a cage for a decade? Torturing her for a decade?"

"Much as I would like to lay all the blame on Cyrus for the state your mother is in, it's a lot more complicated than that."

"What's complicated about it? The man is a monster who has spent his life perfecting the art of hurting people." She gestures to her mother. "Look at her."

"Yes, but he's not the one torturing your mother." Uncle Finn's gaze meets mine. "The Crone is."

"The *Crone*?" The words come out of my mouth before I even know I'm going to say them. Heat sweeps through me, followed by guilt that threatens to steal my breath.

I'm the one who put us in that house. *I'm* the one who wanted to go to the Crone. *I* took Macy there, into the home of the woman who—all this time... That bitch. That heinous fucking *bitch*. We were there. Macy was *right there*, in her house, and she never said a damn word to any of us.

Hudson puts a supportive hand on my lower back, as if he knows that I'm beating myself up over what I did. He doesn't say a word, but I know he's trying to tell me that it's not my fault. That I couldn't have known.

But that's not true. I might not have known what the Crone was doing to Macy's mother, but Hudson warned me against going there. I didn't listen to him and now... Now I owe a favor to the woman who has tortured my aunt for years. I would say it doesn't get much worse than that, but in this world, things can always get worse.

"But why?" Macy asks. "Why would the Crone want to hurt Mom? She's spent her whole life helping people. She's never done anything to anyone, so why—"

"The Crone did her a favor once," Uncle Finn answers. "And in return, your mother had to do a favor for the Crone."

"And?" Macy asks.

"And she failed."

"So that gives the Crone the right to torture her for the rest of her life?" Macy demands. "That's total BS. Grace owes the Crone a favor, too. Does that mean, if something goes wrong, she'll just get to torture Grace for eternity? Of course n—" She breaks off, her eyes going wide as she swings around to look at me.

But that's okay, because I'm pretty sure my eyes have gone just as wide. I know Hudson has practically turned to stone behind me.

"At no point did anyone mention eternal torture as the price of failing to complete a favor," Flint says to no one in particular. "I'm pretty sure we would have remembered that."

"Grace owes the Crone a favor?" Uncle Finn sounds horrified.

"Let's not worry about that right now," I answer, because there is only so much my freaked-out brain can take before I go into a full-blown panic attack. And right now, I am pretty close to the limit. "What favor does Aunt Rowena owe the Crone? And if we complete it, can we free her from this dungeon?"

"Not to put too fine a point on it," Eden interjects, "but right now, we're in no position to free anyone from this dungeon or anyplace else."

My uncle ignores her in favor of answering my question. "Cyrus doesn't have her in this dungeon because she failed the favor. He has her in here because she's been convicted of spying on the Vampire Court. Normally that crime carries with it a sentence of death. But she is the cousin of the witch queen. Killing her would be a bad political move."

"So why didn't the queen do something?" Macy asks. "If Cyrus didn't kill Mom because he feared retaliation from the Witch Court, why didn't Imogen parlay that into a pardon for Mom?"

"She did do something," Uncle Finn explains. "She got him to commute her sentence from death to life in prison."

Macy's laugh is harsh and painful to hear. "And she thinks that's fair?"

Uncle Finn's gaze bounces from Macy's to mine. "Things are more complicated than that, honey."

I swallow, my gaze going to Aunt Rowena's sleeping body. Or what used to be my aunt. The person huddled on the floor, too weak to even wake with people shouting nearby, her bones poking up beneath the blanket in harsh angles, is only a shell of the woman I used to know. A ghost who forgot to die somewhere along the way.

My knees almost give out beneath me as a vise squeezes my chest so tight, I can only breathe in short gasps. Hudson's arm snakes around my waist, supporting me, but I barely notice. It's taking every ounce of energy I have not to give in to the urge to vomit the bile burning its way up my throat as the voice in my head just keeps repeating that I owe the Crone a favor, too.

Macy doesn't notice, though. She's too busy yelling at Uncle Finn.

"You should have told me. I'm not a child." Then she looks him straight in the eye and says, "You've had ten years to free my mother. It's my turn now, and I won't fail."

Uncle Finn looks stricken, but he doesn't defend himself. In fact, he doesn't say anything at all. No one does, until a mocking clap rings through the dungeon. Followed by an all-too-familiar voice saying, "And here I thought I was going to need an insulin shot to get through the cute little family reunion. Looks like a ball gag would have been a better choice."

65

You Say Potato,
I Say Murdering Thief

The crowd around us titters nervously, and I turn, expecting the worst. Sure enough, the redhead from earlier is directly behind us, leaning against one of the dungeon's heavy stone columns on the other side of the bars as she cleans her nails with the tip of a metallic black switchblade. Because apparently a nail file isn't badass enough.

"Who the fuck is she?" Flint asks with a frown.

"Trouble," Eden answers, and she's definitely not wrong. It's written all over the other girl's fuck-you attitude.

I am ready to throw a name or three at this one if someone else doesn't. Beelzebub, for one. Or maybe just go for straight-up Lucifer? She does kind of look like a Lucifer.

"Her name is Isadora Vega," Uncle Finn says.

"Oh, hell no," Mekhi mutters. "Tell me she's not another Vega kid."

Hudson gives him a mild look. "I'd be offended if I didn't happen to agree with you so completely."

"Wait, does that mean she's got an extra power, too?" Eden asks, and I have to admit, I've been wondering the same thing since she casually announced she was my mate's sister.

"I don't know," Isadora answers with a wicked, crimson-colored grin. "Why don't you come a little closer and see if you can figure it out?"

"I'd rather jump into a tank of flesh-eating piranhas," Flint mutters under his breath.

She laughs, then makes that little *tsk-tsk* sound again. "As if I'd share with piranhas. Dragons are my favorite afternoon snack. I think it's the wings."

"What do you want, Isadora?" My uncle sounds firmer—and also more exhausted—than I have ever heard him.

"Same thing I always want, *Finn*. But since world domination is a few months off, I guess I'll just have to settle for you." She quirks a finger and beckons him over.

"She isn't really your sister, is she?" I hiss at Hudson. "I mean, you'd know if Cyrus had another kid, wouldn't you?"

"I think so," he answers, but there's a look in his eyes that says it just might be possible.

And I get it. I mean, I don't know if he sees it, but there's something about that razor-edged wit that seems really familiar, especially combined with that negligent shoulder lean against the column. And that's not even mentioning the whole *do what I want to do because I want to* attitude that is pure Jaxon.

"I'm not going anywhere with you," Uncle Finn tells her coldly.

"Does that mean you're going to put up a fight?" Her eyes go wide, and she claps her hands together. "Pretty please?"

"Don't play with your food, daughter." Cyrus's voice rings through the dungeon. "It's such an unattractive habit."

Isadora doesn't answer him. Instead, she just tosses her knife super high in the air. It spins end over end for what feels like forever but is probably only a few seconds, then she catches it and has it sheathed again before I can even blink.

Cyrus is right behind her now, and he doesn't look impressed as he surveys my friends and me. Then again, the feeling is entirely mutual.

He might be decked out in the hottest Tom Ford suit on the market, gray checked with a lavender tie, every tooth in his socially acceptable grin polished to a blinding white and every hair on his handsome head combed to perfection, but to me he still looks like the monster he is. It's in his cobalt-blue eyes, in the way he holds his body, in the twisted little sneer that makes an appearance the second he thinks he can get away with it.

He waves at a guard to open the cell door about ten feet to the left of us, other students milling on that side of the dungeon.

"Come with me," he orders the group of us, then turns and walks away like he just expects us to follow him, no questions asked. Which is so not going to happen.

"And if we don't?" Jaxon asks, eyes narrowed and hands loose by his sides, like he's spoiling for a fight.

Cyrus pauses several feet away with a long-suffering sigh. And when he glances over his shoulder, the look on his face asks, *Do you really want to challenge me on this?*

Since the answer is pretty much, *Hell yes, we always want to challenge you,* none of us moves so much as a muscle.

Cyrus sighs again—and it's even more put-upon this time. Then, quick as the snake he is, he reaches out and grabs the closest person to him, a freshman witch with a hot-pink pixie cut a lot like the one Macy used to wear.

Before I can register what he's going to do, he yanks the girl toward him, and then he strikes, his fangs slamming straight through the skin at the base of her neck and into her carotid artery.

"Stop!" Hudson yells, launching himself at his father, but two guards step between them and block him.

It's already too late anyway, and we all know it. She's dead before Hudson can get to her, dead before she even hits the floor. It's one of the most horrifying things I've ever witnessed, and it shakes me to my bones.

"Have somebody clean this mess up," Cyrus tells the guards, waving a careless hand at the girl now crumpled on the floor as he pulls a red silk handkerchief from his suit pocket and dabs at the drops of blood in the corners of his mouth.

I look away, my stomach churning, and end up locking eyes with Isadora. I don't know what I expect to see in hers—avarice, glee, maybe even hunger—but instead there's a deliberate blankness there, like someone who has been forced to watch this a million times and who knows she'll have to watch it a million more. Whether or not that's a problem for her, I can't tell.

Cyrus delicately sidesteps the puddle of blood pooling on the dungeon floor as two guards come to clear away the girl. "I'm still hungry, so I am more than happy to do this a few more times," he tells Hudson, who is staring at him with narrowed eyes. "Or you and your friends can come with me."

"Are we going to end up an appetizer?" Flint snarks.

But Cyrus just lifts a brow. "Would you prefer to be the main course?"

Flint looks like he wants to say more, but in the end must think better of it, because he just shrugs. And falls into line with the rest of us as we follow Cyrus to the front of the dungeon and upstairs, where I'm afraid the real torture takes place.

66

This Is What it Really Means to Go Medieval

I don't think I had an actual idea in mind of where the guards were taking us, but this seems about right, I decide as I walk into the tower. Because yeah, it looks like pretty much every torture tower I've seen in a movie or TV show—which isn't worrisome at all.

Especially not the arm and leg shackles embedded in the curved wall every five feet or so. Or the giant industrial work shelves filled with items that can only be described as torture devices. I'm especially repelled by one that looks like a giant bear trap with huge, triangular metal teeth that are guaranteed to amputate an arm or a leg or whatever else happens to get forced into it.

Yeah, not worrisome at all, at least not if you're training to be a psychopath. Then again, Cyrus's picture should be the dictionary definition of the word, so it's not like I'm exactly surprised.

And judging from the looks on the others' faces, they aren't surprised, either. Worried, nervous, and in Macy's case absolutely terrified, yes. Surprised, no.

I'm trying not to show it, but I'm completely freaking out, too. Not just by the giant trap and other torture instruments over there, but because there's a sick feeling in my stomach right now telling me that this is it. That there's no way Cyrus is going to let us get away without draining our powers. Not when he's finally got us at his mercy.

Not that "mercy" is a word he's familiar with. No, he's going to enjoy every second of what he does to us here—the worse the better. Not for the first time since we ended up at this damn Court, I can't help wondering which will be better—death or ending up in that damn well?

The fact that I'm pretty sure the answer is death only freaks me out more.

I think about fighting, and from the looks on my friends' faces, so do they. But without their powers, there isn't much they can do—not when Cyrus considers us such a threat that he's got four guards on each one of us.

Jaxon lashes out with his foot anyway, tripping the guard currently trying to buckle his left arm into a shackle. He ends up getting a club to the face for his trouble, and I can't help crying out at the sound of his nose breaking under the wood.

Hudson stiffens beside me, but when I glance at him, he looks bored—as if being shoved into a torture chamber is an everyday occurrence for him. But his eyes are watchful as they slowly, carefully take in every inch of the room. *Is he looking for an escape?* I wonder. *Or trying to figure out how to get his hands on a weapon?*

More guards are lined up shoulder to shoulder in front of the weapons now, so that seems impossible. Then again, we've been in impossible situations before, and somehow we're still here.

I hold on to that thought as two guards grab me and shove me against the wall, while another one locks the shackles around my wrists first and then my ankles.

I can't help looking at Hudson again as the cuffs squeeze closed. As I do, I think about all the time we've lost—and the future we should have to make up for that time. And fuck it, chained or not, I'm not going down without a fight. I owe it to Hudson—and to the others—to fight as hard as I can. I don't know what fighting looks like right now, but I'm going to have to figure it out pretty quick. Otherwise—

"You know, Grace," Cyrus says as he strides through the doorway in his immaculate suit. Even in this horrible place, he looks like he's on his way to a fancy dinner date instead of planning to torture eleven kids. Then again, for him, it might very well be the same thing.

"I've really got to hand it to you," he continues as he stops only a few inches from my face. "You really go out of your way to make things easy for me. If I wasn't on an accelerated timetable, I'd be a little distraught at not getting more of a chance to use my skills."

He sounds amused and smarmy and somehow also conciliatory enough to raise my back. Because if there is anything I hate more than some man pointing out my mistakes, it's when that man gloats like an egomaniac while doing it. The fact that he might be right—and that I already feel guilty as hell for not keeping my friends out of this mess—only makes me feel worse.

And that's before he continues. "I was prepared to lose legions to capture you after Ludares, when I bit you and realized you were Cassia's long-lost offspring." He shakes his head. "But you practically volunteered to go to prison with my feckless son and made it so easy for me."

His words turn the anger and anxiety inside me into a slow-simmering rage, but I don't respond. He's needling me, trying to get under my skin, and I refuse to give him the satisfaction.

When I don't answer, he makes a production of taking off his jacket and draping it over one of the few chairs in the room. Then he undoes his cuff links— amethyst and silver—and drops them in the pocket of his perfectly tailored trousers before he begins to roll up his sleeves.

"I admit, it never occurred to me that you would actually be able to fight your way through—and out of—the Aethereum when Adria shorted you a flower. It was quite an accomplishment, and I figured you'd take your second chance and run as far as you could, but instead you came right to me again, didn't you? And gave me a shot not just at you but at all your friends."

He shakes his head as if mystified, but I'm not naive enough to believe that. This is a perfectly written, perfectly delivered speech, meant to undermine my confidence in myself. Of course, the fact that I know that doesn't stop it from working. Especially when it's hard to argue with his logic.

I did play right into his hands multiple times. I did ignore all the warning signs and put my friends in danger over and over again, even when I didn't mean to or was just trying to save them. Not for the first time, I think about the favor I owe the Crone—it's hard not to when Cyrus calls her Adria like they're best friends or something and he knows all about our visit to her.

Does that knowledge mean he's been working with her all along? Just the idea makes me want to kick myself—especially when I think about the Crone being able to call her favor in whenever she wants. Or, I wonder with burgeoning horror, whenever Cyrus wants? Did I somehow unwittingly tie myself to the vampire king when I was trying to do the exact opposite?

Cyrus pauses for effect—or more likely to see if I'm going to explode and yell my head off at him. But there's no way I'm going to break and give him that kind of satisfaction. Not when he's already taken so much from me.

Instead, I keep my head down and my jaw locked as his words wash over me like acid. *Don't look up*, I tell myself over and over again. *Don't look at him. Don't look. Don't, don't, don't.*

After a few seconds that seem to stretch for an eternity, Cyrus sighs heavily. "And now there's this latest predicament you've gotten everyone in. I was certain I was going to have to send out search parties and drag you kicking and screaming back to my Court. Yet here you are. You didn't even bother to try to broker some kind of treaty when you got here. No, not you, Grace. You just walked right into my dungeon like you couldn't stay away."

He tuts, shakes his head. "For a thousand years, I've been planning what I would do when I finally found one of Cassia's descendants. I marshaled legions of soldiers just to capture you, to get what I've been denied all these years." He gives another condescending chuckle, another shake of his head. "But at no point did I ever think one of Cassia's line would be so silly, so absolutely absurd, as to hand me everything I've ever wanted on a silver platter. So thank you, really. You've given me more than I ever could have asked for."

Even knowing what Cyrus is doing, even knowing that he's trying to undermine whatever confidence I have left, I still feel like the world's biggest loser. Because he's right. Nothing he's saying is a lie. Everything happened just like he said it did.

From my very first day in this world, I've felt like someone was playing chess with me. And yet I've never developed a strategy, never tried to change the game in my favor. Instead, I've only ever thought one move ahead, even when it was with only the best intentions—and now I'm here, in this torture chamber. And so are all my friends.

I haven't just taken myself down with my mistakes, my lack of foresight, I've taken everyone I've loved down, too. How can I ever make it up to them? And how can any of us ever come back from the mistakes I've made?

Cyrus walks over to the shelves with all the scary-looking stuff on them. He stands there for a moment, as if contemplating what vile weapon he wants to use on us. Eventually he picks up two long metal rods with wickedly sharp points, and my stomach drops through the floor.

I don't know what those things are for, but everything inside me warns that it's not good. That this is it. I've rushed in every opportunity I could, and now everyone is going to suffer because of me.

I just wish I knew how to stop it.

67

Liar, Liar,
Chest on Fire

Cyrus turns back to face us, those metal rods clutched in his hands. As he does, his eyes meet Hudson's, and for a second, I see delight there. Unmitigated joy at the idea of finally—finally—being able to pay Hudson back for what he did to him on that Ludares field.

He even raises a brow as he walks straight toward my mate, as if daring him to beg for his life. Hudson would never do such a thing, but I would. If I wasn't shackled, I'd throw myself in front of him right now and make Cyrus kill me instead in an effort to give Hudson a few more precious moments to figure out how to stop him.

But I am shackled, and there is nothing for me to do but watch as Cyrus stops right in front of Hudson.

Please, I beg the universe. Please don't let him hurt Hudson. Don't let him hurt any of them. They don't deserve to be drained of their powers—they don't deserve to die—because of mistakes I've made. Please, please, please.

"With whom should I start?" Cyrus asks, and his gaze is still locked on Hudson's.

"With me," I answer, keeping my voice steady despite the terror rising like a wave inside me. Please, please, please, let him leave them alone. "You just gave that whole pretty speech about how hard you were prepared to work to catch me. If I'm really that special, why don't you start with me?"

"What is that saying humans like to use? Maybe I'm 'saving the best for last.'"

"We both know I'm not the best," I tell him. "I'm just the one you've decided is most useful to you."

"Aren't you the clever one?" His cool smile shows more than a flash of fang.

"I try," I answer, determined to keep him talking as long as I can. My friends—my mate—are super smart and super resourceful, which means the longer I can keep Cyrus's attention on me, the more time I give them to figure out a way out of this. "Why is that, by the way? What do I have that makes you need me so badly?"

He tilts his head, like he's thinking about the question—or, more precisely, thinking about whether or not he wants to answer it. Since I can't afford for him to lose interest in our discussion, I throw out the first thing I can think of.

"If it's the Crown, having it won't do you any good. It takes the Gargoyle Army to activate it, and you know they're gone."

"Are they now?" He twirls the metal rods in his hand, like he's actually thinking about what I said. But the calculating gleam in his eye says otherwise when he continues. "'Gone' doesn't mean 'dead,' now does it, Grace?"

My blood freezes in my veins as he repeats what the Bloodletter told me almost word for word. How could he quote her like that, in those exact words, unless...someone told him about our visit?

But who?

Please, no. It can't be. It just can't be.

But a quick look at Hudson tells me he's thinking the exact same thing I am, which makes me feel even worse, when I didn't think that was possible. Still, I do a running list in my head of everyone who was in the cave with us when the Bloodletter was talking about the Army.

Hudson, Jaxon, Eden, Macy, Flint, Mekhi, and me. I can't believe it was any of them—I would, and have, trusted each of them with my life, and they have never let me down. Even now, divided as we are, I don't believe any of them would sell me out. Not my mate, not my ex-mate, not my cousin, not three of my best friends. None of them would do it.

So who else could it be? The only other people we've told about the conversation are Dawud, Liam, Rafael, and Byron. But that doesn't make any sense, either. Dawud is desperate to save their brother any way they can. Liam, Rafael, and Byron are loyal to Jaxon and have been forever. There's no way one of them would have betrayed us.

Or is there?

Just the idea makes me want to throw up. We've been through so much together—good and bad—how could any of them have done such a thing?

They couldn't, I tell myself. This is just Cyrus trying to get into our heads. Trying to tear us apart because we're too strong when we're together.

I'm not going to fall for his tricks. Not this time.

But even as I stare him down, there's a tiny, niggling doubt in the back of my head that wasn't there before. The thought of a betrayal I never before would have imagined.

I try to hide it, try to keep my face and eyes as blank as Hudson does at times like this. But I must have some tell that he doesn't have, because the glee returns to Cyrus's face. Like he knows he's got me on the rails, and he couldn't be happier.

"I can practically see the wheels turning in your head from here, Grace." He smirks at me. "You're figuring it out. I'm glad—it means you're finally learning."

He pivots away from Hudson then—and from me—and starts following the curve of the wall until he stops right in front of Liam. Ice slices through my veins even as my stomach churns.

"Fuck, no," Jaxon mutters from his spot beside Hudson. "That's bullshit."

"I haven't said anything yet," his father tells him. "But then, I don't really have to, do I? You've already figured out that Liam here has been only too happy to keep me apprised of your movements."

"That's not true!" Liam yells. "I never—"

Cyrus cuts him off mid-sentence by plunging the metal rods deep into Liam's chest.

Macy screams.

Jaxon rattles his restraints as he tries to break free.

And the rest of us stare, speechless, as Liam freezes mid-argument.

At first, I think he's dead, but I can see the tears leaking from the corners of his eyes. And, after a long, silent moment, I can hear the death rattle in his chest as he tries to suck air into his punctured lungs, the rods paralyzing his body.

"What's happening?" I whisper to Hudson, but he doesn't answer. He just watches the scene unfold with a blank face and narrowed eyes.

And just that easily, panic is a crashing wave inside me, squeezing my chest, pulling me under.

Determined not to give in to it—not here and definitely not now—I look away from Liam's gray face and trembling form. I still refuse to believe he had been betraying us all this time, even if a tiny voice in the back of my head is whispering that it would explain how Cyrus knew exactly when we were going to the island to free the Beast. And, oh God, if what he said was true about working with the Crone...then he knew we'd go see her in the first place.

Just as that thought takes form, another one, even more frightening, has me fighting back the fear slamming into my chest. If Liam told Cyrus we were going to ask the Crone for a way to break out of the Aethereum, then did he always plan to force me to owe her a favor? What does he ultimately want from me, if not the God Stone? Have I risked a lifetime of pain and suffering just to hand him the final winning move on a platter?

A vision of my aunt's magically tortured and gaunt body springs to mind, but I shove it down. Shove down the fear and the second-guessing and even the devastating sense of betrayal by Liam. This is exactly what Cyrus wants. To keep us frightened and acting on that fear, leading us straight to whatever evil plan he's hatched.

My gaze bounces around the room, looking for anything to focus on other than my friends chained up and poor Liam's body. Anything but the torture implements in the corner and the evil bastard peacocking in the middle of the room.

That's when I catch sight of Isadora for the first time. She's leaning against the back wall, cleaning her nails with a knife like what's going on is completely normal.

She doesn't glance up once, not even when Jaxon snarls, "I'll kill you with my bare hands, you fucking bastard."

For the first time since he walked into the room, Cyrus looks shocked. "Why?"

"What do you mean, why?" Byron growls. "You just impaled our friend."

"He was a coward," Cyrus answers, still looking mystified. "And worse, he was a traitor. He sold out his friends for a seat at the table. He's no one you should mourn—and no one I would actually allow at my table once his usefulness is gone. He didn't have loyalty, and loyalty is everything." He glances slyly at Hudson. "Don't you think so, son?"

Hudson doesn't answer. In fact, like Isadora, who is running her fingers lightly along the sharp edge of her blade now, he doesn't so much as glance at his father.

At least not until Cyrus turns to his daughter and asks, "Isadora, if you wouldn't mind?"

It looks like her shoulders stiffen for a second, though the truth is it happens so fast that it might have just been my imagination. It only takes her a moment to rub her knife against the leg of her pants and then slide it back into its sheath before she walks over to her father.

"Of course, Daddy." She says it like a little girl would, all sweet and ingratiating, and it grosses me out.

Then again, nearly everything about these two grosses me out. And that's before Isadora reaches for the two metal rods sticking out of Liam's chest like a tuning fork. As her hands close around them, she takes a deep breath, then squeezes them together.

Liam lets out a silent scream as the rods start to glow red-hot. Isadora's head falls back, and her entire body goes stiff as her hands start to turn red now, too. They're glowing, her veins lighting up from within, shining more and more brightly until I start to wonder if she's going to burst into flames like a phoenix.

But then she moves so that she can hold both metal rods—squeezed together—with one hand. With her other hand, she reaches for Cyrus, glowing palm up.

He doesn't hesitate before grabbing it, and just like that, I know what she's doing. And I know what's going to happen next.

Though everything inside me urges me to look away, I can't. It's too horrible.

Because Isadora is Cyrus's secret weapon for stealing magic and right now, she's taking every single drop that Liam has.

68

There Really Are Some Things You Can't Get Online

L iam knows what's happening—I can see it in his eyes, in his face, in the silent scream he can't release.

He's not making a sound, but he doesn't have to. Tears are flowing unchecked down his cheeks, and his eyes are alive with so much fear, it paralyzes me. Paralyzes all of us, if the stillness and the silence of my friends are any indication.

I can see the power leaving his body, bit by bit. But it's not that I see the magic flowing from him drop by drop, it's that I can see what its absence is leaving behind.

It's like Isadora is taking his very soul along with his power, and I have never seen anything more horrifying in my life.

"She's a Soul Siphon," Mekhi whispers in shock, and I can tell immediately he must be right. Liam shrinks in front of our eyes, his muscles and flesh atrophying more with each second that passes. But it's more than just losing mass. It's like *he* is disappearing as well. His skin turns a sickly shade of yellow, and his eyes sink deep into his skull as though he is nothing but skin and bones.

He sags forward, so weak that even the restraints can't hold him upright. Isadora shifts, starts to move back now, but Cyrus stops her with a snarl.

"Finish him," he demands.

"Gladly," she answers, but she doesn't sound nearly as enthusiastic—or as ingratiating—as she did earlier.

Seconds later, Liam stops crying, his eyes closing on a ragged sigh that chills my blood. He's dead. Oh my God, he's dead and Isadora killed him without so much as a second thought.

I pray that I'm wrong, pray that he's just passed out from the pain. But then Isadora drops her father's hand and yanks the rods from Liam's chest, and I know I'm not wrong. The Order has just lost another member.

Macy is crying now, too, soft and sad, like the world is ending. And I get it. I really do, because who knows which one of us Cyrus and his cold-as-fuck daughter are going to go for next.

I watch in horror as Liam's shrunken wrists slide right out of the cuffs, and his lifeless body crumples to the ground at Isadora's feet with a sickening *thud*. She barely even seems to notice him, though, as she walks back to the tool shelf and drops the rods into a glass jar that has a clear liquid in it. A moment later, the liquid takes on a reddish cast as Liam's blood washes off the rods and swirls round and round.

There's a part of me that still can't believe this is happening, that still can't believe Liam is dead. Sixty seconds ago, he was alive and protesting Cyrus's accusations. Now he's dead on the floor, a husk of the person he once was.

My stomach pitches and rolls as flashes of what just happened click through my mind over and over again. It may have only taken Isadora a minute to drain and then kill Liam, but I have no doubt the images of her attack will stay with me forever.

I expect Jaxon to lose his shit now, but he surprises me by not saying a word. Then again, no one does. The whole room is eerily quiet in the aftermath of Liam's death, and I know it's because all my friends are as horrified—as devastated—as I am.

Cyrus, on the other hand, is looking even more pleased with himself as he rolls his shoulders and shakes his arms back and forth, like he's just had a really hard workout.

"Yes, that will do for now, Isadora," he says as he continues to shake out his arms, and I realize what is happening. He's in the middle of absorbing all the power—all the magic—that he just stole from Liam. The bastard.

After he's done his post-murder stretches, he walks back toward me, a questioning look on his face, almost as if he's checking to make sure he has my attention.

Which he absolutely, positively does. Watching Liam die like that has done one thing for me. It's convinced me that I will do anything, absolutely anything, not to have that happen to anyone else I love.

"What do you want?" I ask in a voice rusty with unshed tears.

"The God Stone," he answers. "And you're the only one who can get it for me."

"And why is that exactly?" I ask, determined not to back down even though I'm so nauseous, I feel like I'm going to throw up any second.

"Because the God Stone is at the frozen Gargoyle Court, and you're the only one who can access it, of course. Liam couldn't wait to tell me, so don't bother denying it."

"If it is where you say it is, what exactly makes you think I'll get it for you?" I demand.

He just smiles, like I've said something funny. Though his words are anything but. "Because if you don't, I'll make sure that you have a front-row seat as every single person you love dies the same way Liam did. And next time, I won't show any mercy."

69

The One Where
Everyone Might Die

Cyrus's words explode through me like a bomb.

I'm still reeling from Liam's death, and now he's telling me he'll kill all my friends the same way? Even his own sons?

I can't imagine the amount of evil that would take. Then again, I don't have to imagine it when the vampire king himself is standing right in front of me. Not to mention his vile, vicious daughter.

"Why bother to threaten?" Hudson asks, and it's the first thing he's said since he whispered my name all those minutes ago. "Why not just start taking us out? I volunteer to go first."

"He doesn't mean that!" I screech as I give Hudson a *what the fuck* look. "What are you doing?" I hiss at him.

It was bad enough watching Liam die like that—maybe he was a traitor, maybe he wasn't, but he was still a person. He didn't deserve to die at all, but if he was going to, he should have at least died with some fucking dignity.

The idea of watching my mate—the boy I love more than my own life—die like that? No way. No fucking way.

Bile churns in my stomach, starts crawling up my throat at just the thought of Hudson ending up like Liam.

Or Jaxon, for that matter. Or Macy or Flint or Eden or any of my friends. I won't let it happen. I can't.

But Hudson obviously has other ideas as he shrugs and says, "I'd rather die any way that bastard wants than be the reason you did something to hurt your people, Grace."

"Isn't that sweet?" Cyrus sneers. "Young love is so touching. Too bad Grace has other plans. Don't you, Grace?"

He's right. I do have other plans, no matter how hard it is for me to give him that satisfaction. But he's put me in an impossible situation, given me a terrible, horrible, awful choice to make.

But I will make the choice—and it will be to save Hudson. That will always be my choice, no matter how awful the situation is. No matter how diabolical Cyrus can be. It might not be the right decision for the gargoyle queen to make, but it is the right decision for Hudson's mate to make. Right now, with the sound of Liam's gasps still echoing in the air around me, it is the only decision I *can* make.

And if that means I'm not a good queen—or that I'm not worthy to be queen— well then, so be it. It's not anything I haven't thought myself a million times.

Still, distress crawls in my belly, and my shoulders sag. I'm terrified of being queen, but it's terrible to know I've failed at it before I even got the chance to try.

"No, Grace." Hudson's voice is hoarse, the look on his face saying he knows I've made my decision. "You can't do this. We're not worth destroying what's left of your people. Nothing is."

"Speak for yourself, vampire," Flint says out of the blue, but there's no bite to his words. "I mean, I agree with you. But speak for your own damn self."

"Fair point," Hudson answers with a rough chuckle that makes me want to scream. It's like they're talking about what time to take tea—not when to die in one of the most painful ways imaginable.

"How touching," Cyrus says before giving the most obnoxious slow clap I have ever seen—or heard—in my life. "But I don't think we need to go full Greek tragedy just yet, do we, Grace?"

I'm pretty sure I can't say anything to Cyrus that doesn't begin and end with what a total bastard he is, so I don't answer. Not that that stops him—I'm beginning to think nothing can.

"Find the God Stone and bring it to me," he tells me. "And you have my word that I will let you, your friends, and all the Katmere Academy students and faculty go free."

"How do I know you're telling the truth?" I shoot back. "Your word hasn't exactly proven to be worth much in the past."

He inclines his head in acknowledgment before adding, "Because once I have the Stone, I'll no longer have any need of them—or the rest of your friends."

"That's a pretty powerful order for a little Stone, isn't it? Are you even sure it's worth all that?" Macy comments, but it's obvious she doesn't expect an answer. Cyrus may be an arrogant ass, but he's not the mustache-twirling, Scooby-villain type who will reveal his evil plan the second anyone asks.

Still, he shocks all of us by giving a surprisingly full belly laugh before replying, "Your ignorance is truly impressive."

It's rude as hell—which sounds about right for him—but it's not much of an answer. Then again, we weren't actually expecting one.

Isadora doesn't seem to know that, though, because she rolls her eyes and answers, "It's called the *God* Stone."

As her words sink in, my heart stutters in my chest. I try to think back to our last conversation with the Bloodletter, because it suddenly seems very apropos. She'd mentioned that there was a way to become a god. It just never occurred to me that the way was with the same Stone currently keeping the Gargoyle Army frozen in time and alive.

"You think you can become a god," I whisper as horror sweeps through me.

"Bravo, dear girl." Cyrus claps again, but this one sounds more sincere, and more theatrical, than the last one. "But we've wasted enough time for today. You need to get to the Gargoyle Court and retrieve the Stone. And just in case you decide to drag your feet once you get there, I'll add a little incentive. For every day that passes without you returning the Stone to me, I will kill another student. Maybe I'll start with the rest of my son's precious Order…"

His gaze meets Macy's wide one. "Or maybe I'll start with your own dear uncle Finn."

Macy doesn't give him the satisfaction of pleading with him not to hurt her father, but she can't hide the new influx of tears in her eyes—or the fact that her entire body is shaking.

I hate how smug he is, hate even more that he's backed me into a corner I can't escape from.

My mind races for another option—there has to be another way, even if I haven't thought of it yet. There just has to be.

"But I don't even know how to get to the Gargoyle Court. I've only been there once before, and that was by accident. What if I can't find it?"

"I'm not one to give advice, but I will say that I have plenty of motivation chained to this wall right now." Cyrus shrugs before waving his hand in a gesture that encompasses all my friends. "You're a resourceful girl, Grace. I suggest you find some of that can-do attitude that's usually so annoying."

Oh, hell no. He thinks I'm going to take off for the Gargoyle Court and leave my friends—and my mate—chained to a wall, at his total and complete mercy? No way. No freaking way.

"I can't do that," I tell him as the very beginning of a plan starts to come to me. "General Chastain is guarding the Stone. I've met him, and if there's one thing I know, it's that I can't defeat him alone. I need my friends with me if I have any hope of getting the God Stone, let alone bringing it back here to you."

I hold my breath as Cyrus studies me with narrowed eyes. More than just sparks of a plan are coming to me now and, if I play this right, I just might be able to save everyone—my friends, the Katmere Academy students, and the entire Gargoyle Army. But it all depends on whether or not Cyrus decides to call my bluff right here, right now.

"You said yourself just a few minutes ago that I'm a silly girl," I continue. "You can't actually expect me to defeat the most powerful gargoyle general in existence all alone? Which means either my friends go with me, or you might as well start killing us now because I can't do it by myself. I just can't."

Silence stretches between us, taut as a circus high-wire, and I start to think I've gone too far. But one of Cyrus's biggest weaknesses is his belief that he's stronger and smarter than anyone else in the room, and as he slowly nods, I realize that that weakness has chosen this moment to rear its ugly head again.

Which is perfectly fine with me. Cyrus has spent his whole life underestimating the women in my family. Now it's time to show him just what we can do. I am the demigod of chaos, after all. And I have a plan.

70

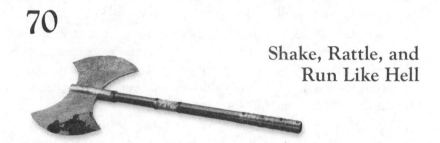

Shake, Rattle, and Run Like Hell

I t's that thought that straightens my backbone and has me staring Cyrus down despite the fact that I'm still shackled to the wall. He has to go through all this in the hopes of one day becoming a god. I already am one…or at least, I'm a demigod. He's a vampire with delusions of his own importance.

I can't wait for the chance to show him just how unimportant he really is—which I will get started on right after he agrees to let my friends come with me.

He has to agree. He has to. It really is the only way for my plan to work.

He quirks a brow as our staring contest continues, which nearly makes me laugh. If he thinks an intimidating smirk is going to back me down, he obviously doesn't know his sons at all. I've been going head-to-head with similar looks from Jaxon and Hudson from pretty much the day I got to Katmere Academy, and I win more than I lose.

Apparently, practice makes perfect, because Cyrus gives it a few more seconds, then concedes with a bored wave of his hand. "Fine, whatever. You can take my useless sons and a few of the others. But what *remains* of the Order stays here. For every day you keep me waiting, I'll feed one of them to the wolves." He smirks. "They'll enjoy snacking on their bones, don't you think?"

What I think is that he really is a monster—and it has nothing to do with his fangs and aversion to sunlight. No, this man is a monster because every thought in his head, every single thing he does, is for himself. He doesn't care who he hurts, who he uses, even who he *destroys* as long as he gets what he wants. He'll go out of his way to hurt someone just to prove a point.

It's disgusting, and I'm determined to make it stop. Maybe not today, but soon. Very, very soon.

"Also," he says slyly out of the corner of his mouth, "you'll take Isadora with you."

He has to be kidding. Not the demon child herself.

I manage to control my face enough that my abhorrence doesn't show—but the others have no chill. Jaxon growls, Macy whimpers, and Flint mutters, "Well, fuck."

Only Hudson and Eden manage to keep their distress under wraps. That doesn't mean I can't still feel it, but at least they don't wave the white flag like the others do.

Cyrus loves it, though. He chuckles like the evil bastard he is.

Isadora, however, doesn't seem nearly as amused. Her poker face is as good as Hudson's, but she's spent the last few minutes scratching what I'm sure is some kind of demonic hell carving into the table in the corner without pause. But the constant scrape, scrape, scrape of her knife against the wood surface stutters for just the barest of seconds at his words.

Her discomfiture doesn't last long, but it's enough to let me know that she wasn't expecting Cyrus to send her with us. Maybe that knowledge should worry me. She is a force to be reckoned with, after all. One who has a terrifying penchant for blades of all sizes.

But to be honest, it encourages me. If Isadora didn't have a clue this would happen, it means that Cyrus is the one going off plan. He's the one acting on impulse. And if, for once, he's not five steps ahead, that means I've got the chance to gain a little ground—especially now that I can see the board clearly for pretty much the first time ever.

Not that any of that means I actually want to hang out with Isadora at the Gargoyle Court—or anywhere else, for that matter. The girl is scary as fuck, and every minute we spend with her feels like it lowers all of our chances of actually being able to keep our fingers and toes...and anything else we might be attached to.

I'm not about to share those misgivings with Cyrus. I'm keeping any advantage I can get, no matter how small. Which is why I affect the most careless shrug I can muster. "Works for me. The more the merrier, I always say."

"You never say that," Macy hisses under her breath.

"Maybe not, but I think it a lot," I tell her before turning back to Cyrus. "I am going to need one more thing, however."

Now both his brows go up. "You certainly have a lot of demands for someone currently chained to a wall."

"What can I say? I'm high-maintenance." This time I toss my hair like a champ, channeling the inner diva I definitely don't have. "But that is a nice segue into what I wanted to talk about."

I shake my wrist, rattling the chains attached to it. "You're going to have to uncuff me. I can't use my abilities with these magic-canceling cuffs on, and there's no way I'll be able to take us to the frozen Court otherwise. Plus, being chained to this wall has been *unbearable*."

I'm laying it on thick—maybe too thick—but Cyrus eats it up. Big shock. He's so willing to believe that I'm just a silly, weak little girl that he'll take any opportunity to prove to himself that he's right.

Normally, misogyny on this level would offend the hell out of me, but right now? I'll take any advantage I can get. Some of the most powerful women in the world got that way because a man—or several men—underestimated them. I'm more than willing to let Cyrus make the same mistake.

It must work, because he gives a little half nod toward one of the guards, who then rushes forward to unlock my restraints. Thank God. I feel like a bird who can finally spread her wings the minute I sense my gargoyle again.

Of course, a quick glance at Hudson and Jaxon—both of whom give me tiny little shakes of their heads—warns me not to spread my wings too far. Not that I'd planned on using my powers now anyway. Not when my entire plan is built on the premise that Cyrus underestimates me.

Besides, for my plan to work, I need to get that damn God Stone for this bastard and pray that I'm not *over*estimating my powers and those of my friends when we work together. Because while Cyrus is playing with his Stone and planning his ascension to godhood, I know exactly how we're going to move our chess piece next. It's time for the queen to take control of this board—and I have a plan he won't see coming.

We will give him his damn Stone, but then we are going after the Tears of Eleos. And we are going to win those damn Trials.

Once we do that, we'll free my army and use the Crown to make sure Cyrus never hurts *anyone* ever again.

Easy frickin peasy.

I stick my hand out to Cyrus to seal the deal. He looks at it for long seconds, like it's suddenly become a rattlesnake ready to strike. But in the end, his palm slides against mine in a shake.

As he clasps my hand in his, I reiterate the terms before he can. "So the deal is, I bring you the God Stone and you let everyone from Katmere Academy go free, including the teachers and Uncle Finn. You won't harm any of them—or anyone else—and when we leave, we get to take everyone with us, including my aunt Rowena. Do we have an agreement?"

Cyrus answers, "I assure you that I will not keep anyone prisoner if you bring me the Stone in the next twenty-four hours. But for every day you make me wait, I will kill a prisoner, starting with Jaxon's precious Order. Deal?"

I swallow hard, trying to push down the fear churning in my stomach. I have to trust myself to get this done—it's the only way out of this mess that I can see. More, it's the only way to defeat Cyrus once and for all, which I absolutely want to do.

"Deal," I say, and I'm proud of the fact my voice doesn't waver at all.

As soon as I agree, electricity zings between us, electrifying my arm and stealing my breath as a small tattoo of a bloody dagger burns itself into existence on my forearm.

It's one of the most beautiful—and one of the most evil—things I have ever seen.

"What the fuck have you done?" Jaxon whispers.

"What I had to do," I answer, reluctant to glance at Hudson.

But he squeezes our mating bond string, and I meet his gaze, his eyes crinkling just a little at the corners as warmth pours down the bond and into me. Of course he's got my back—I never should have doubted it for a second. And as my gaze bounces around from Macy to Mekhi to Jaxon to Dawud and Eden and Flint, I realize that no matter what has happened between us, they all do. Just like I have theirs, no matter what happens next.

But as the burning in the tattoo finally subsides, I can't help but wonder if Sartre had it right after all. If you're forced to make a deal with the devil, doesn't it mean you've already lost?

71

The Frozen Court Never Bothered Me Anyway

I look at my friends, still chained to the wall around me, then turn to Cyrus. "I don't think I can take them with me if they're also chained up. Can you unlock their chains as well?"

"No," Cyrus says, and it's clear it's not up for discussion.

I try anyway. "But—"

"I don't care if they go with you—you do," Cyrus reminds me. "So figure it out or don't. Makes no difference to me."

I bite my lip, running through my mind what I did, even accidentally, to take Alistair and myself to the Gargoyle Court the last time. I wasn't thinking of the Gargoyle Court. I didn't even know it existed. Could Alistair have been thinking of it? Is that how it works?

I don't know where Hudson and I went during our time together, but I know we spent at least some time in his lair. Did we end up there because he'd been thinking of it when we'd accidentally touched, too?

"Ticktock, Grace," Cyrus says, looking down at his watch. "Poor Rafael there only has twenty-three hours and forty-five minutes and counting."

"I think I know what to do," I say and do my best to ignore Cyrus's taunt. Instead, I turn to Isadora and motion to the space in front of Flint, Dawud, and Macy on either side of him. "I need you to stand right there." I secure my backpack on my back—my supplies are sure as hell coming with me where we are going.

Isadora glances at the spot I'm pointing, then to Flint, clearly considering if I might be trying something.

I sigh loudly. "Look, I have to be touching everyone to take them with me. Since Cyrus refuses to unshackle them, I'm going to need you to stand in front of Flint, Dawud, and Macy so they can touch *you*. I'll stand in front of Hudson, Jaxon, and Eden. Then you and I can hold hands, and that should bring everyone. I think."

"Do it," Cyrus says, and Isadora shoves the knife she'd been using to carve the furniture back into its sheath and saunters over like she hasn't a care in the world.

She stops in exactly the spot I'd motioned to but looks over her shoulder at Flint, Dawud, and Macy and murmurs, "Touch me with anything more than one fingertip and that'll be the only finger I allow you to keep."

As threats go, that was a pretty good one, so I'm not surprised at all when my three friends gingerly place one solitary finger on Isadora's shoulders.

I stand next to her and toss over my shoulder to the rest of the gang, "Okay, everyone else grab on to me now."

I instantly recognize Hudson's warm hand gliding along my elbow. Jaxon's heavier hand lands on my shoulder and squeezes. Eden reaches for my other shoulder.

Turning to Isadora, I raise one brow. "Might I grab your hand now without a finger threat? Or do you want to find out exactly who'd win in a vampire-versus-gargoyle showdown?" It's not a question. It's a challenge, and when she answers with a raised eyebrow of her own, I know she understands. I'm only going to take so much of her threats before I start issuing a few of my own. And since I'm not currently magic-bound by cuffs, I have every intention of following through if necessary.

"Honey, I'm something altogether new, so you might want to tread carefully," she says.

I toss back, "Ditto," before reaching down to grab her hand.

"Okay," I explain, "I need everyone to picture the Gargoyle Court in your mind. That's where you want to go. Not the decrepit, ruined Court but the Court in all its grandeur. Close your eyes and imagine what it looked like a thousand years ago. Imagine you're there right now."

I pause and remember the beauty of the Court as I first saw it with Alistair, how desperately I'd wished I could paint it and what that artwork would look like, trying to re-create the images for my friends now.

"You can hear the Celtic Sea pounding against the cliffs just beyond an ornate metal gate," I say. "And just beyond that are seventy-five-foot-tall walls surrounding a massive castle, larger than any castle you've ever seen, with four towers rising into the brilliant blue sky like sentries. You're standing in the grand foyer of the castle, surrounded by pristine white marble floors and alabaster sculptures, and beyond two giant open doors is the training field, where you can see hundreds of gargoyles practicing hand-to-hand combat, laughing when someone lands a great offensive strike, swords clanging as they connect with metal shields, giant wings flapping as several gargoyles take to the skies for aerial combat training. The whole place is alive with activity. Can you see it? Hold it in your mind..."

I take a deep breath and reach for my green string. Slowly, slowly, *slowly*, my fingers brush past my demigod string as I grab ahold of my platinum string. And turn to stone.

When I open my eyes again, we're standing in the center of the Gargoyle Court. But it's not the ruined Court my friends and I saw at the beginning of this very long day. No, this is the Gargoyle Court frozen in its heyday. Marble floors, elaborate tapestries on the walls, thick white candles burning in gold candelabras and chandeliers around the Great Hall, where we are currently standing.

It worked!

There is one glaring difference between the last time I was here and this time, though. We're the only people around. It *is* nighttime here at the moment, I can tell, so maybe everyone is in bed.

"*This* is the Gargoyle Court?" Macy asks, sounding delighted as she looks around. "It's so different than what I expected!"

"What did you expect?" I ask as we walk deeper into the room, and my friends fan out to look at the statues and tapestries.

"I don't know," she answers, and it's obvious she's really thinking about it. "I guess I expected the architecture to be darker, more gothic. And to have a bunch of gargoyle statues everywhere."

"You know, right, that the gargoyle statues would probably be real people?" I ask, brows raised.

"I know, I know. I just—" She breaks off with a half smile, which is probably the most any of us can muster since what happened to Liam. "This place is really cool, that's all."

"So what plan has that big brain of yours cooked up, Grace?" Hudson asks, and suddenly everyone who'd been taking in the Court decor turns as one to hear my answer—including Isadora.

"Well," I start, biting my lip. "We get the God Stone and give it to Cyrus and everyone goes free." My gaze darts to Isadora, and the others take the hint.

"Obviously. Duh," Eden says. "Solid plan."

"I thought it was a strong one." I wink at her.

"He means, how do you plan to *get* the Stone, Grace." Isadora draws out each word.

I don't bother to tell her that that is definitely *not* what he meant. Instead, I say, "When I came before, I was here for at least half an hour, but when I returned to Katmere, only five minutes had passed. I think for every day in our time that passes, six days pass here in the frozen Court. That gives us a little less than six days to find the Stone and figure out how we're going to take it—hopefully without being noticed. I'd really rather not fight our way out, especially against my own people."

"Wait—" Eden counts on her fingers. "Does that mean everyone has been trapped here for six thousand years?"

My mouth opens on a gasp at the thought, but Dawud speaks up. "No, I don't think that's how it would work here. Just like if you're in a car, the ground is rushing past but nothing inside the car with you is moving. When the car itself stops moving, though, and you step outside, you will be in a different location."

"Which means what exactly?" Flint asks.

"We're in a time bubble." Dawud shuffles their feet, and I can tell they're struggling to find the words to explain it to a bunch of people who did *not* pay attention in their science classes like Dawud did. "But not the same bubble as those frozen originally. A bubble in a bubble of time. For those originally frozen, time actually isn't moving at all inside their bubble. As I understand from when Mekhi was catching us up on what happened in the Bloodletter's cave—"

And just like that, they stop talking. Everyone is looking anywhere but at one another, in fact. Liam was in that meeting. If Cyrus is to be believed, he listened avidly to Mekhi's words—and then told Cyrus everything.

"I refuse to believe Liam was a traitor," Jaxon says quietly, his gaze seeking out each of ours one by one. "But even if he were, he was still my friend."

And that really says it all, doesn't it?

"Liam isn't just the worst thing he's ever done. None of us are," I say with conviction and watch as we all wrestle with our memories of Liam.

"Oh, for fuck's sake." Isadora throws her hands wide. "People do shit things and sometimes shit things happen to them. Deal with it."

Jaxon's shoulders stiffen, but Hudson coughs and changes the subject like he's helming the *Titanic*. "Well, regardless of how time is passing for the gargoyles, let's assume Grace's math is correct. That means we have five days to get the God Stone." He leans against a wall and crosses his arms over his chest. "We might have to fight our way out, Grace, but I agree. Let's first try to steal the Stone. Which means we need a reason to visit so they take us in, lower their guard, and we can search for it."

I smile at him, knowing exactly where his mind is going. "Alistair already introduced me as their queen. Obviously, I want to visit my subjects, see how they are faring in this frozen Court, yes?"

"That explains *your* presence, but I think an entourage of vampires and dragons, plus a witch and a wolf, might raise a few eyebrows," Jaxon says.

We all toss out ideas to explain their presence—and every suggestion is shot down in turn. Everything from posing as ambassadors to a group of traveling circus performers, although no one really believed Flint was serious about that one.

"What did you notice were interests they had when you first visited, Grace? Anything stand out? Anything they were talking about they might need help with?" Hudson asks.

I shake my head. "I really wasn't here very long. Sorry." I walk over to a large, ornate chair and plop down into the seat. "All I know for certain about the Gargoyle Army is they take their training very seriously."

"Well, that's it, then, isn't it?" Hudson says. When no one seems to understand what he means, he elaborates. "You've brought us to help them train."

"The Army trains all the time already, Hudson," I try to explain, but he shakes his head.

"But do they train how to defeat a vampire—against a real vampire?"

"That is brilli—" I start to say, but Jaxon holds a hand up to stop me.

"Someone is coming," he says, his head cocked to the side as he listens to something in the distance.

It doesn't take long for me to hear the heavy boots approaching, too. Just before the doors to the room are flung open and Chastain walks in, flanked by some seriously badass-looking guards. Carrying even more badass swords.

72

Take It with a Block of Salt

"What the hell?" Flint growls, straightening up to his very intimidating full height. He stumbles a little on his new prosthetic, but he rights himself quickly enough that I don't think anyone else notices.

Under normal circumstances, Jaxon might have. But right now, he's too busy pushing to the front of the group to put himself between the sword-wielding guards and the rest of us to pay attention to an unsteady leg.

Except Hudson puts a hand out to stop him before he gets past the two of us. "Grace's Court, Grace's call," he says quietly, and I'd be lying if I said that it didn't feel good—especially when Jaxon freezes mid-motion.

Most of the time I feel like a total imposter at this whole gargoyle-queen stuff, so the fact that my mate always remembers—and acknowledges it—makes me feel better. More, it makes it feel real, and that matters more than I can say. As does the fact that he stays by my side to back me up, weight balanced on the balls of his feet and hands loose at his sides so that he can respond faster.

Taking a deep breath, I step in front of the whole group—blocking them with my body—and issue the command, "Stop!" with as much authority as I can muster.

It must be enough, though, because the gargoyles do exactly that. Even Chastain.

"What are you doing here?" he demands in a voice that says I'm far from welcome. Added to that, he neither calls me Grace nor Queen nor Your Majesty, an omission that is especially noticeable considering his less-than-welcoming tone.

It's definitely not the tone, or the attitude, someone should take with their queen, but I don't run a dictatorship here. People are allowed to be themselves around me—God knows I'll never rule by fear like Cyrus or stand on intense ceremony like the witches.

Besides, I'm not actually his queen. At least not here in the eleventh century, which is where we are—and where he has been stuck for a thousand years. Maybe the attitude has to do with him considering me an imposter or a usurper or any of the other not-good words that end in -er.

Besides, we did drop in late at night with no warning. It's not exactly the earmark of a *let's be friends* visit. Especially during this time period.

"I'm sorry to just drop in like this," I say in as placating a voice as I can manage without also sounding submissive. "Alistair told us we will need the Army if we stand any chance of defeating the vampire king."

Behind me, I can feel my friends shift at the lie, and I pray they don't say anything to give me—or it—away. I hate lying and I'm absolutely terrible at it, so any backup they can give me right now would be greatly appreciated.

"And you believe that time is coming?" Chastain asks. He sounds skeptical but willing to believe, and I notice he looks wearier than he did when I first met him with Alistair. They must have been training late tonight.

"I do," I say. "And I know you've been preparing our soldiers for that time. In fact, I was so impressed by your training that I witnessed, I thought perhaps you might want to train against someone other than yourselves."

Chastain's eyebrows shoot up as he takes in each of my friends, measuring our worth and dismissing each in turn. "I don't believe a *vampire* has anything to teach us."

"I could teach you manners, for a start," Hudson says. "And deference to your queen. Two things off the top of my head you're sorely lacking."

Chastain clenches his jaw, but I rush in before he can respond. "War is coming, Chastain. You've waited for a thousand years, and I can tell you with certainty that Cyrus's final move is only *days* away." My voice rings with sincerity. "In fact, we only have five days to help teach you what we can. What kind of leader doesn't avail himself of every tool in his arsenal, every chance to study his enemy up close, before taking his troops into war?"

"That's impossible," Chastain says. "Cyrus does not have what he needs."

Which means Chastain knows what Cyrus needs and exactly where to find it. The God Stone.

Isadora must sense how close we are to discovering the Stone's location because she stops tossing one of her knives up in the air long enough to look Chastain dead in the eye and say, "While time has been a prison for you, Cyrus has used his to find a way to get everything he's ever wanted. You've already lost; you just can't see it."

"How dare you—" Chastain starts, but suddenly I'm just over it. Over all of it.

Yes, we're lying to him and here to steal the God Stone, but I have a plan. I am thinking two steps ahead for once, and I *will* be freeing my army. And when I do, they're going to need every advantage they can get if we hope to defeat Cyrus.

"Enough!" I say with finality. "I am the gargoyle queen, and I insist that you train my army and prepare for war, Chastain. And the best way to do that is to show them exactly how to defeat each of the four factions: witches, wolves, dragons, and vampires. My friends are volunteering to offer their insights, and you *will* avail yourself of their knowledge. Even one *hour* fighting any one of my friends could save your lives."

My hands are shaking so badly that I clasp them behind my back, widening my stance into what I hope resembles some sort of military pose—although if I'm being honest, I've really only ever seen them done on TV. I have no idea if he will even listen to what I'm asking. Hell, if I thought he'd really take orders from me, I'd just order him to give me the God Stone. Duh. But still, I hold his gaze and hope he sees the reason in my demand.

Eventually, Chastain nods. "As you wish, Your Majesty." Before I can celebrate my victory, though, a sly look narrows his eyes and he asks, "And will you be training as well?"

Fuck. I already know he thinks I'm weak and not a fit ruler, but if I agree to train, he's going to see exactly how weak I really am. I glance over at Hudson, but he's grinning like he thinks I'm going to hand them their asses on the field. I roll my eyes at him. My poor mate is lovesick, clearly.

Regardless, I know I don't have a choice. Not if I want Chastain to let down his guard and trust me enough to tell me where the God Stone is hidden. I swallow the giant lump in my throat and raise my chin. "I am looking forward to it."

73

Death by Taffeta

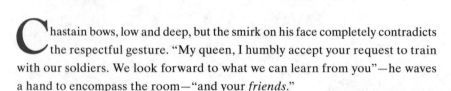

Chastain bows, low and deep, but the smirk on his face completely contradicts the respectful gesture. "My queen, I humbly accept your request to train with our soldiers. We look forward to what we can learn from you"—he waves a hand to encompass the room—"and your *friends*."

Then, rising again, he announces, "Training begins at five a.m. sharp. I suggest you get some rest. You'll need it." Then he beckons us to follow him into the hall, presumably to take us to vacant sleeping quarters.

Instead, we enter an anteroom filled with beautiful sculptures. I stop at one of a woman in a flowing gown, her head leaning against the shoulder of a tall, thin man in dress attire. It's such a sweet pose that I elbow Hudson so he doesn't miss it, a soft smile peeking from the corners of his mouth as we stare at the exquisitely detailed piece of artwork.

But then I realize that the stone is moving, eyelids fluttering open, shoulders squaring as both shift from stone to human form.

"Is that what it looks like when I shift?" I ask Hudson as the woman's horns slowly retract back into her head, leaving bumps in her long brown hair right where they used to be.

Surreptitiously, I slide a hand over my own hair, just wanting to make sure it's lying flat—or as flat as eight million curls can lie after a day in a damp, humid dungeon without hair products.

Hudson just laughs and takes my hand off my head, lacing his fingers through mine instead. "You look beautiful when you shift," he tells me with the wicked grin I love so much. "And your horns are *almost* my favorite part."

Deciding I can wait for a more private time to ask him what his actual favorite part is, I turn back to Chastain just as he says, "It is my honor to introduce you to your serving staff, Your Majesty."

I'm listening closely, so I hear the tiny bit of mocking in his tone as he addresses me. I don't call him on it, though, as the staff in front of me bow and curtsy as one. Right now, meeting them is more important than dealing with Chastain's surly attitude.

"I'm Grace," I tell them, stepping forward to extend a hand to the woman, who is dressed in a simple white linen shift. "And this is my mate, Hudson."

Hudson looks startled for a second—like he didn't expect me to include him—so I shoot him a look that says, *We're in this together*. He got me into this whole *sitting on the Circle/being gargoyle queen* mess to begin with. No way am I letting him just fly under the radar now.

"It is a pleasure to meet you," she tells us with a strong Irish accent. "I am Siobhan."

"And I am her mate, Colin," says the dark-haired man standing next to her—also in an Irish accent.

I smile as I turn and introduce each of my friends to them.

"Siobhan and Colin will show you to the guest rooms," Chastain says dismissively after all the introductions have been performed. He sounds more than a little annoyed that it has taken so long, but I don't care. If these are my subjects, I want to learn more about them. I owe it to them—and to myself.

"Until tomorrow," he says with an insouciant bow of his head before he turns and walks away.

"I can bring you some food before you sleep," Siobhan says. "You will need it if you are joining training."

Her eyes dart from Hudson to Jaxon, then to Isadora, who has been completely silent since her one jab at Chastain. "I'm sorry, but we don't have any b-blood—" She stumbles over the last word.

"Sure you do," Isadora comments. "O positive, if I'm not mistaken."

"I'm sorry?" Siobhan says faintly.

"I'm not," Isadora answers as her fangs elongate and her eyes light up. "It's my favorite—"

"Stop it!" I tell her firmly, stepping between her and Siobhan, turning to the other woman. "Please forgive my *bestie*," I say, and the vampire growls low. I ignore her. "She's the fun one in our group. Always making jokes." Now her growls turn to gurgles as she almost chokes on her affront, but I have to hand it to her, she doesn't correct me.

Siobhan smiles. "Oh yes, I love jokes," she says and then adds, "but there's plenty of time for joking tomorrow. Now you need rest. Our commander takes training very seriously." She pauses before adding, "Of course, we would all be lost without him." Then, without another word, she turns and leads us down a narrow hallway and up a flight of stairs and down another, wider hallway.

Finally, she stops in front of a door. "This room is the most beautiful shades of blue and purple. It is my favorite room in the entire castle, fit for a queen, milady."

She's clearly speaking to me, but Isadora inserts herself between myself and Siobhan.

"Wonderful. I'll take it," Isadora says, and she grabs the knobs on both doors and pushes them open with a flourish, presumably to show me what I'll be missing, but stops dead in her tracks. The room is definitely decorated in gorgeous shades of blue and purple—taffeta.

A giant four-poster bed dominates the space, layers upon layers of taffeta cascading from the ceiling to create a romantic cocoon of fabric. The windows are equally covered in layers of draped taffeta, as are a small dressing table and ornate chair. So, so, so much taffeta.

"Hey, Isadora, the eighties called, and they want their prom dress back," Eden jokes, and everyone laughs. "I think it's perfect for a vampire *princess*."

Flint cackles as he peers over my head to get a better look at the room and says, "That almost makes this trip worth it."

"Is there something wrong with the room?" Siobhan asks, blinking at each of us.

"It's beautiful, Siobhan," I tell her and squeeze her hand, careful to make sure she doesn't think we're making fun of her tastes. "She loves it. Don't you, Isadora?"

To her credit, Isadora turns to face us and says, "Why, yes, it's amazing. So many different ways to hide a body in here." And with that, she slams both doors closed in our faces. Which only makes us laugh harder.

Siobhan leads us to the next door, and I glance down at my phone, then hold it up so everyone can see the time. "It's nearly eleven. Which means we've got six hours before we start training tomorrow." *And other things*, I try to convey with my eyes, though I don't want to say it out loud in front of Siobhan.

The others grumble—I don't think any of them is sold on the training part of this plan, but I still can't think of any other cover that would explain why we're here. Besides, Chastain may be a jerk, but Alistair swore he was one hell of a general. And I know he's one hell of a fighter—I saw that with my own eyes. A little refresher course in Cyrus's dirty tricks from a guy like that isn't a bad idea at all, considering where this all is going to end up.

Siobhan shows Hudson and me to our room last, and by the time we get inside, I feel nearly as exhausted as the others. The last thing I see as Siobhan closes the door—while assuring us that she'll be sending food up momentarily—is Dawud back out in the hallway, sliding a loose rock out of the wall and slipping it into their pocket.

74

Chamber
Absolutely Nots

"**S**o, real question," I ask as Hudson and I sink down onto the bed without even bothering to check out the room. I'm so exhausted right now that the room just having a bed is good enough for me. "Do we think Dawud is a kleptomaniac, or are they building a rocket to space made out of everyday items?"

Hudson laughs but doesn't bother to open his eyes. "I'm pretty sure the truth falls somewhere in the middle."

"I don't know. They're smart. I can totally see them building a rocket."

"With rocks?" Hudson lifts a skeptical brow.

"They've got more than stones in their backpack, and I know you know it. I would bet you noticed their little habit before I did."

Hudson doesn't answer, and I glance over to see if he's fallen asleep. He hasn't, but he seems really, really close. Poor baby.

I get up to grab the blanket that's draped over the chair. Despite being springtime, it's a little cold in here, and since I don't want to disturb him by pulling the covers down, this seems like the next best thing.

But I've barely taken a step before Hudson's hand snakes out and he pulls me back down—this time on top of him.

"Stay," he murmurs, wrapping his arms around my waist as he snuggles his face into my neck.

It feels good—he feels good—so I do, letting myself relax for the first time in what seems like weeks.

Feeling his heartbeat against mine.

Feeling his chest rise and fall beneath mine.

There's a part of me that's afraid it's only happening because he's almost asleep and his defenses are lowered, and that scares me. Makes me hold on to him tighter. He's my mate, and I know there's nothing in the universe that can change that. It's not like Jaxon, where some messed-up spell can just take it all away from me—from us. Hudson is mine. He was born to be mine, and I was born to be his.

And yet, sometimes it feels so nebulous—so fragile, like everything we have is going to slip right through my fingers if I don't hold on tightly enough. If I don't fight hard enough. And what happened with Liam less than an hour ago only brings that home.

A sense of dread pools in my stomach at the memory of Liam's death. We've lost so much that I keep waiting to lose one more thing. Keep waiting for the other shoe, boot, dragon hoard to drop and crush Hudson or me or both of us to smithereens.

I'm not going to let that happen. Not this time. I've already lost more than enough. I won't lose him, too.

"Hey," he whispers, rolling over so that I'm beneath him, and I realize for the first time that I'm crying. "Are you all right?"

I don't know what to say, don't know how to tell him that I'm scared. That I love him so much that I'm terrified this world—this harsh, dangerous, beautiful world—won't let me keep him.

So I don't say that. I don't say anything. Instead, I just shake my head. And this time, I'm the one who buries my face against him. I'm the one who wraps my hands around his waist.

I'm the one who holds on as tightly as I possibly can.

As I do, I swear to myself that I won't let him go. Not this time. Not ever again.

But Hudson isn't buying it—at all. Instead, he pulls back so he can get a better look at me. "Grace?" he whispers, even as he cups my face in his hands and rubs his thumbs over my wet cheeks. "What can I do?"

I shake my head again, do my best to stifle the sob rising up inside me. Just when I'm afraid I'm going to lose the battle, the door to our room flies open, and Macy bounces in.

"How lucky are you right now that I love you?" she asks, not even fazed by the fact that Hudson is on top of me on the bed. We're fully clothed, true, but still.

Hudson doesn't seem as pleased. "What do you want?" he grouses.

"To save your asses." She snickers. "Literally."

"I don't even know what that means," I tell her, totally bemused as I watch her walk over to the closed door that I assume leads to our bathroom.

She cackles in response.

"Are you high?" Hudson asks as he rolls off me.

"No," she answers with a roll of her eyes. "And you're going to be really glad I'm not in about five seconds."

"Why is that?" I ask as Hudson and I make our way over to the bathroom.

Macy laughs again—albeit a little less excitedly this time. Instead, she just waves a hand at the bathroom in a *Come on down, you're the next contestant on* The Price is Right kind of way.

"What?" I ask again, moving past her to see what the big deal is and— Oh. Oh. *Oh.* "Is that a…"

"Chamber pot?" she asks in a singsong voice. "Why yes, Grace. Yes, it is."

"I don't. I mean, I can't. I mean—"

"Yeah," my cousin says with a satisfied nod. "Exactly."

Even Hudson looks horrified, and he's been alive for two hundred years. Underground in some kind of weird vampire on-again, off-again coma for a lot of them, it turns out, but still alive. And if even he's freaked out, then this really is as bad as I think it is. Maybe even worse—though, to be honest, I'm not sure how that could be possible right now.

"Tell me you're here to fix this. Tell me the reason we're lucky to be loved by you is that you are here to fix this," I say, not even bothering to hide the pleading note from my voice.

"Oh, I am," she agrees. "And because you are my cousin and best friend, you get second dibs at my magic."

"Second?" I ask.

She gives me a look. "If you think I didn't already fix my room, then you've got an inflated sense of your value to me."

"Fair enough," I say with a laugh. "Fix it, please."

"I will. Yours and the others'—except Isadora's," she says with a wicked little grin.

"Sounds fair to me," Hudson says as he peers into the bathroom, looking for all the world like a little boy who has just lost his favorite toy. "Is it pushing my luck to ask for a shower, too?"

"If it is, you're taking baths for the next five days," I tell him. "Because a functioning toilet is totally the top priority here."

"I know, babe. I'm definitely not here to interfere with that."

"I think I can manage a shower, too," Macy says with a laugh. "Just don't expect four jets and a rain setting, okay?"

"At this point, I'll settle for a spigot and a drain," Hudson says drily.

"Right?" I agree. I mean, how did it never occur to me that when the Gargoyle

Court got frozen in time a thousand years ago, everything got frozen in time...
including its plumbing issues—or should I say lack of plumbing issues?

I know we didn't have a choice about whether or not to do this—at least not
if we wanted to get out of that damn dungeon—but I swear I would have thought
more about staying here if I'd known about this.

Then again, it's not like Cyrus had showers installed in the dungeon, either...
but he did have toilets, and that is a huge step above chamber pots.

More like chamber nots, thank you very much.

Macy waves a hand, and the "chamber not" disappears—to be replaced by
a toilet. It's just a regular, plain old white toilet, but I'm not going to lie. I've
never been so happy to see one in my life.

Another wave of Macy's hand and a small shower cube appears in the corner
of the dressing room. It's not fancy, but I'm with Hudson on this. I'm good with
a faucet and a drain.

"They work?" I ask, stepping forward to turn on the shower, just to be sure.

"They do," Macy tells me.

"What are they connected to?" Hudson asks. "I mean, there's no sewer
system here, so—"

"Actually, I did a little magical snooping while I was trying to figure this out,
and there is," Macy corrects him. "It's a lot more rudimentary than the ones
we're used to, but the gargoyles are smart. They modeled their drainage system
after ancient Egypt, so they hooked into one of the rivers—I'm not sure which
one—and laid bricks like pipes to flush everything out to sea. I just used magic
to redirect things a little, and voilà. Indoor plumbing."

"I love you the most," I tell Macy.

She grins. "As you should."

She winks at Hudson, who says, "Right now, I'm totally okay with her
loving you most."

"That's because you love your shower most," I say with a laugh.

He shrugs, but the look on his face says very clearly that I'm not wrong.

"Go enjoy your shower." Macy nudges him toward the bathroom. "I'm going
to go save Eden before I start in on the others."

"You are a goddess," I tell her as I walk her toward the door.

She laughs. "I think you've got us confused, but just this once, I'll take the
compliment. Now go grab that shower before Hudson beats you to it."

The sound of a creaky shower turning on floods the room before she's even
done talking. "Too late," I tell her.

"Well, look at it this way. At least you don't have to worry about running out of hot water."

"Because of magic?" I ask hopefully.

"Because there is none," she answers. "Even magic will only get you so far."

"Well, that's not very—" I break off as Hudson's shocked yelp fills the room.

Now it's my turn to laugh. "That almost makes me not having any hot water worth it. Almost."

"I do what I can," Macy says with a wink before slipping out the door.

Two minutes later, I'm in a dressing gown Siobhan left out for me, snuggled under blankets, and drifting off to sleep before Hudson even climbs in bed.

Everything in me is urging me to get as much rest as possible—before Chastain uses me as an example of everything not to do in battle during training tomorrow.

75

Eat, Drink, and Be Wary

Siobhan knocks on my door at four in the morning with a loaded tray of food. I try to tell her that it's just me—that Hudson is a vampire and doesn't eat—but she just shakes her head and tells me to eat up. I'll need all the calories.

Considering the tray has enough food on it to fuel an Olympic swimmer through the most grueling workout of their life, I'm a little concerned about what's in store for me today. For us.

After putting the tray on the table near the window, I crawl back into bed with Hudson. I know I need to get up, but there's something about the feel of his arms around me—his heart beating against mine—that makes it easier to face whatever's coming next.

I sink into him, and he wraps an arm around my waist to pull me close. He nuzzles his face into my hair, breathes me in, and for a minute, everything is okay. For a minute, it's just him and me and our future stretched out between us.

Tears spring to my eyes at the thought, but I bat them away before they can roll down my cheeks and make Hudson ask a bunch of questions I don't want to answer. But here, in his arms, in the moments before dawn breaks across the sky, it's hard not to remember. Hard not to think about those four months I forgot for so long. Those four months that changed…everything.

I just hope what's happening now—between us and around us—doesn't change everything again. Especially not for the worse.

The thought makes me antsy, makes it hard for me to lay here with Hudson and dream about everything being okay on the other side of this. Not when everything is so uncertain right now.

So I do the only thing I can think of to do right now. I roll over and kiss Hudson, then start to climb out of bed.

His hand snakes out and holds on to mine. "We still have, like, fifty minutes before we need to be down there."

"I know. I just want to get an early start." I reach back and stroke a hand through his sleep-tousled hair.

"I'll get up with—"

"It's all right," I tell him. "Stay in bed. I could use a little time to think anyway."

"You okay?" Those sleepy eyes go watchful.

"Yeah," I answer, though I'm a little too in my feelings right now for that to be true. But what am I supposed to do? Whine about him feeling too far away when the weight of the whole world rests on our shoulders? Tell him how scared I am that we're all going to die?

He knows what I'm feeling because he's feeling it, too. Isolated. Frustrated. A little desperate. Determined to put an end to Cyrus's terror once and for all.

There's no need to talk about it right now. No need to do anything but work our butts off to make sure we're still standing when we get to the other side of this nightmare.

"I'm going to take a walk, clear my head," I tell him as I press another kiss to his mouth. "No need for you to miss out on sleep."

For a second, I think he's going to argue with me, but everything I'm feeling must be written on my face, because he just says, "Okay." Right before he sits up and pulls me in for a kiss that reminds me of all the things we have and all the reasons we need to fight.

I spend a couple of minutes brushing my teeth and winding my hair up into the tightest bun I can manage—which isn't very, but a girl's got to take what she can get. Siobhan brought Hudson and me some training clothes with the breakfast tray, and I slip mine on. Gray leggings, gray shirt, gray tunic. Not exactly exciting sartorial choices, but a uniform is a uniform, even if it's a thousand years old.

When I'm dressed—I choose my Chucks over the handmade leather shoes Siobhan brought—I grab the food tray and head into the hallway. I've still got about forty minutes before training starts, and I plan to find a nice place on the battlements to have breakfast.

But I've only gone a couple of steps before I run into Flint in the hallway. He's dressed in the same clothes I am—definitely a training uniform—and he's a few steps ahead, so he hasn't seen me yet. I start to call out to him, but I stop at the last minute. Because as I watch him walk down the hallway, it becomes so obvious that he's struggling.

Struggling to walk.

Struggling to breathe.

Struggling to be.

It makes me want to take back every annoyed thought I've had about him over the last few days. Because of course he's angry. Of course he's miserable. Of course he's in pain.

Dragons have incredible healing capabilities, but it's only been a few days since he lost his leg. A couple of days since he had to learn to walk with a prosthetic. When he's around us, he makes it look easy. But walking behind him, watching him rub his leg and play with the places where the prosthetic attaches, I realize it isn't. Not by a long shot.

Plus, there's Luca. I'm so freaked out by the fear of something happening to Hudson—or to our relationship—that I couldn't even stay in bed because my head was turning it over and over. The worst already happened to Flint, and instead of getting a few days, weeks, months to process that loss, he got about four hours, and then it was right back into the breach.

Yeah, he's been an asshole. But he deserves time. I've been an asshole—and a lousy friend—for thinking, for one second, that he didn't have the right to be as angry and as big of a jerk as he wants to be.

And so I follow behind him as quietly as I can, waiting for an opportunity to make myself known that won't embarrass him or make him feel weak. It finally comes when he gets to the end of the hallway and leans against the wall to take a rest.

I stop, too, giving him a couple of minutes to get his breath. Then make a point of walking as loudly and as fast as I can.

He turns to look at me as I rush down the second half of the hallway, acting like I've only just come out of my room. I hope he'll talk to me, but if he doesn't, I'm prepared to just flash him a smile and hurry on by.

But under all the anger, he's still the same guy who offered me a piggyback ride up the stairs because of my altitude sickness my first day at Katmere. And when he sees me rushing with the heavy tray, he calls, "Hey, Grace. You need some help with that?"

His push away from the wall is a little stiff, but when he walks toward me, the limp is gone. So are the downcast head and eyes. And I hate it. I hate every second of the fact that he feels the need to hide from me—to pretend with me—when all I want to do is be his friend and help him any way that he'll let me. And I hate every second of the division between us that makes it feel necessary.

Which is why I do the exact opposite of what I want to do—which is not ask him for anything when I know he's hurting—and say instead, "Actually, yeah. This tray is a lot heavier than I thought. Could you help me carry it?"

"Of course." He slips it from my hands like it's nothing, though his eyes widen when he sees the amount of food on it. "Planning on eating the food supplies for a small nation, are you?"

"Apparently Siobhan thinks that's exactly what I should do," I answer with a laugh. "But I'd love to share if you're up for it."

He seems to think about it for a second, his amber eyes clouding over as he shoves a hand through his afro. But in the end, he flashes me the million-dollar smile I haven't seen in way too long and says, "Yeah, sure. Where you headed?"

I change my mind on the fly—the last thing he needs to be doing with his leg right now is climbing all the way to the battlements. "There are a couple of benches in the courtyard. I thought I'd head out there and watch the sunrise as I eat."

"Good idea," he tells me as we walk toward the front of the castle. "Then you'll be early for training and that Chastain jerk can't say a word."

"That might have been a little of the method behind my madness," I tell him as we walk by the Great Hall and out the front door. "Just once it would be nice if Chastain looked at me like I wasn't a total waste of space."

"I thought that was how trainers were supposed to look at you. Isn't that what your teachers did when you were young? Tear you down, make you feel like shit, and then build you back up again?"

"My *teachers*? Um, no."

When I look at him, horrified, he shrugs. "Maybe it's a dragon thing."

"Maybe," I agree, faintly horrified by the description.

We're outside now, and I steer us toward the benches I remember from my first visit with Alistair. We sit so we're both staring out at the sea, the tray of food between us.

And it's not awkward at all...except when we both try to talk at the same time. And when we both reach for the same apple. And when we both shut up at the same time and look everywhere but at each other.

God. This is worse than my first date. Way worse, considering the tension between us is real tension from two people on different sides of an impossible divide and not just nerves and fear of embarrassment.

We end up just sitting there for a while, the only sound the roar of the ocean as it hits the shore. Eventually, I grab a piece of thick bread and eat it with some butter and a couple thin pieces of meat that remind me of bacon. The silence makes me so anxious that I can barely swallow, but I force the food down. Something tells me that an hour into training, I'll be dying for the calories.

When the tension gets so thick between us that we could scoop it with an ice-cream spoon, I take a deep breath and say, "Flint—"

"Don't," he answers before I can say anything else.

It's the last thing I expect him to say, especially considering I barely know what I'm going to say, so how can he? "But I—"

"Just don't," he interrupts again. "Please. I can't go there right now—at least not if you want me to be any use at training today."

It's not what I want him to say—none of this is what I wanted when I finagled him into this bizarre little picnic—but I can't argue with him when he puts it like that. So instead of trying to push my very scattered agenda, I pick up the tray between us and put it on the ground. Then I scoot over and wrap my arms around Flint in the biggest, tightest hug I can manage.

At first, I think he's going to pull away, and I brace myself for just that.

But he doesn't.

He doesn't hug me back, though, and he doesn't even relax into the hug. For a long time, he just kind of sits there, head up, back ramrod straight, eyes focused on the faraway horizon.

The voice in the back of my head is urging me to let go as it shouts at me that this is a huge mistake. But I make a point of never being the first one to let go of a hug—you never know when the other person really needs the comfort—and so I don't let go this time, either. I just sit there, holding Flint, telling myself that he'd pull away if he didn't want the hug.

Time passes, seconds into minutes, and still Flint doesn't move. And just when I'm about to give up, just when I'm about to decide that my philosophy has failed me, he turns and hugs me back. He pulls me toward him and squeezes so tightly that for a moment, I think he might actually break a bone or three.

But I still don't let go—a couple of broken ribs are a small price to pay for this one not-so-perfect moment. Because it's real and it matters—we matter.

And it gives me something I haven't had in days.

Hope.

Hope that we might find our way back to each other, not just Flint and me, but all of us.

Hope that, somehow, everything is going to work out exactly as it should.

And most of all, hope that when we finally make it through this twisted, terrible, seemingly never-ending nightmare, we'll all still be standing, shoulder to shoulder, on the other side.

It's a lot to hope for when Flint and I can't even say two real sentences to each other. But right here, right now—as the sun breaks over the Celtic Sea and my ribs ache from the strength of Flint's love and loss, rage and despair—it feels like more than a hope.

It feels like a promise.

76

Why You Wanna Give Me the Runaround?

An hour and a half later, the feeling of promise is gone, and all that's left in its place is pain.

I mean, seriously, how many laps around a castle is one person supposed to be able to run?

"Pick it up, Grace," Chastain says in a smug voice that makes me want to throw something at him—like another gargoyle or one of Isadora's really big, really shiny knives.

Currently, he's hovering several feet above me in full gargoyle form—*the better to criticize you, my dear*, I think to myself in my best *big, bad wolf who not only ate the grandmother but the whole extended family, too* tone.

"At this rate, you're going to be out here for an hour after everyone else," he shouts down at me. "But I guess you're okay with that?"

When the people who are lapping me are dragons, vampires, a werewolf, a witch, and a bunch of gargoyles who have literally had nothing else to do for a thousand years but run? Yeah, I'm pretty okay with that.

I start to say as much to Chastain, but before I can get the words out, he makes a tutting sound and flies away—probably to find some new way to torture me, since doing so seems to have given the man a new lease on life.

I swear, he looks ten years younger than he did when Alistair and I first showed up here. It's like every time he yells at me, he loses a month. Which means if we stay here the full five days I'm planning on, the man should be in diapers, sucking on a pacifier, by the time we leave.

"You've got this, Grace!" Macy says as she catches up to me—and by "catches up," I mean "laps me." "You're almost there."

I make a face at her as she runs by, but she just laughs…and speeds up.

About thirty seconds later, Jaxon laps me for what I'm pretty sure is the eighth time, but I don't think that counts, as they've been fading at least as much as they've been running normally. And no one who isn't a vampire or a fighter jet can keep up with that. Isadora, of course, faded the whole way and is now back inside the castle entryway with Hudson, who was allowed to skip the running, since he still cannot be in sunlight. Jaxon no longer has the same concern, and I can't wait to ask him what's up with that later.

Dawud shifted and probably set a new course record. The lucky duck. I tried to shift and fly the course, but Chastain took great delight in pointing out the exercise was running. I was within my right to shift if I wanted, but then I'd be lugging my concrete ass around this field, which I think we can all agree wasn't going to happen.

Maybe it's my competitive spirit, maybe it's the fact that I can see Chastain heading back this way and I don't want to get yelled at again. But whatever it is, I somehow find a burst of speed inside me. I catch up to Jaxon, who grins at me and then falls in beside me.

He could fade and leave me in the dust at any time, but he doesn't. Instead, he stays with me, the both of us gradually going faster and faster until we've caught up with Macy and actually passed her. My lungs and legs are burning, but I keep at it for the remaining three laps—and so does Jaxon, even though he finished his required laps a while ago. He stays with me the whole time, and when I finally finish, he sticks around and collapses on the ground with me.

It's cool out—only about sixty degrees or so—but I'm drenched with sweat anyway. Then again, I don't think I've ever run that fast in my life. Or that far.

At home, I'd be heading to my room for a shower and a change of clothes, but we're only an hour into training here. Plus, a quick glance inside the open doors of the castle shows Hudson standing next to a truly impressive array of medieval weapons that I'm pretty sure I'm about to have to learn how to use.

"You ready to head back?" Jaxon asks.

I look over at Hudson, who is currently studying a long pole with an open circle attached to the top of it like it's the most fascinating thing he's ever seen. It doesn't seem that interesting to me—until he picks it up and turns it sideways, and I realize the circle has eight large spikes attached to its inside edge, and they are all pointing straight into the center of the circle, like it's just waiting to capture some poor person and tear their flesh off their bones.

Actually, it still doesn't seem that interesting to me. Horrifying, yes. Traumatizing, absolutely. Interesting? Not so much.

And can I just ask, what the hell is it with weapons creators from the beginning of time that makes them always want to craft something that will cause the most pain and damage possible? I mean, being able to defend yourself is one thing. Sticking three-inch sticks into someone around the diameter of their waist is something else entirely.

"Not even close," I finally answer Jaxon when I'm able to tear my eyes off whatever the hell that weapon is.

"Thanks," I tell him, brushing the dirt and foliage off my butt. "I'm not sure I would have made those last couple of laps without you."

"You would have made them." Jaxon grins at me. "You might have had to crawl over the field to do it, but you would have finished."

I laugh because he's right. Running aimlessly for no apparent purpose is totally not my thing, but quitting is less my thing—especially in front of a bunch of gargoyles I'm supposed to lead.

"Hey, you okay?" Jaxon asks, his dark eyes running over me as if looking for some running-related injury.

I force a smile I'm far from feeling. "I'm fabulous."

"Oh yeah?" He gives me a doubtful look, but I just roll my eyes and pretend there's not a pretty big part deep inside me that's freaking out about this whole situation. He glances over to where Isadora is showing Hudson a particularly brutal-looking weapon with long spikes, then back to me. "She's too far to hear. What's the real plan, Grace?"

I blink at him. Afraid if I say it out loud, it's going to sound even more ludicrous than it's currently sounding in my head. Just then, Macy cruises over to us and plops down.

"Grace filling you in on the grand plan?" she asks.

"She's about to," Jaxon says pointedly, and I know my time is up.

I start to open my mouth and tell them everything when two giant dragon shadows race along my legs. A pop of magic later, Flint and Eden walk over and sit down next to us.

"So, plan time?" Eden asks, and I chuckle that we all know one another so well. In fact, for just this moment, it almost feels like it used to. And suddenly, I'm not afraid to share my plan with them. They'll have my back.

I glance over at Hudson, and he sends me a quick smile before leading Isadora by the shoulder deeper into the armory to look at more scary ways to kill. He's keeping her distracted for us, and I tell myself he deserves a pint of blood tonight. Especially as he waves at Dawud, when Isadora isn't looking, then us, and the wolf heads our way.

As they join us, I take a deep breath and then explain everything.

"If we don't give Cyrus the God Stone, he will kill everyone. Slowly and torturously. We all agree, yes?" I ask, and everyone nods. "There is no loophole there. No way to get out of that one simple equation: give him the Stone or die, because the dungeons cancel all our strengths." I take another deep breath and then just blurt it out. "So we're going to give him the God Stone. And while he's preoccupied making himself all-powerful, we're going to compete in the Trials, *and we are going to win them*. We are going to take the Tears and heal the Army, which makes Cyrus vulnerable again, and then I am going to take this Crown"—I hold my hand with the tattoo on it for everyone to see—"I am going to take this Crown that so many suffered for us to retrieve, and I am going to make their deaths mean something. I will take my army, and we will face Cyrus together, we will get him against the ropes, and we will use the Crown to take away everything the God Stone gave him. And then we will make him pay for everyone he's ever hurt. We will end it."

I'm breathing fast now, my heart racing as I rushed through the plan, afraid at any point someone would stop me and tell me it's futile. But instead, everyone just sits in silence, absorbing what I've said, processing our chances, most likely.

Flint coughs. "Um, so just a quick take on this—what makes you think we can suddenly win the Trials? That Tess lady seemed pretty adamant we were gonna lose, and lose big."

There's no heat in his words, and my chest tightens as I realize he's got my back again, even if to follow me into certain death. And that's why I know we're going to win.

"Exactly, Flint. We already know what it's like to lose—and lose big, too. Which Cyrus thinks makes us weak," I say and shake my head. "But losing doesn't make you weak. Every time you have to pick yourself back up again, you grow stronger. Every time you have to find the courage to try again, to hope again, to trust again"—I glance at everyone, knowing we're all thinking of Liam, before I continue—"every time we get back up again, we grow stronger. And we *are* stronger. We can do this. Together. I just know it."

"Soooo." Eden draws out the word. "You're saying we're a bunch of big losers and that means we're gonna win?"

"Well, I think I said it more eloquently," I joke. "But yes, essentially."

"Cool," Eden says.

"Plus," I add, "it goes without saying that if we don't do this, Cyrus will turn himself into a god to start—and finish—the bloodiest war this world has ever seen. Starting with everyone who opposed him."

"Soooo." Eden draws the word out again. "Your pitch is we're all gonna die a bloody death anyway, but let's take our losing streak and parlay that into a blitz play for the Fountain of Youth?"

Okay, that time it definitely sounded worse than how I said it.

"I'm in," Jaxon says. Nothing else. But he glances at Flint, holds his gaze for a beat until Flint nods.

"I'm in, too," Flint says.

"Oh, I'm definitely in any plan that might involve that blowhard getting what he's got coming," Eden says.

"Me too," Macy adds with a wicked grin.

We all turn as one to Dawud now.

They hold up their hands. "Hey, I haven't been a part of this losing streak that's supposedly making everyone stronger, so that's a wash for me," they start. "But that being said, I hate bullies. And Cyrus is an overgrown bully. So count me in."

Everyone cheers and ruffles Dawud's hair.

"You had me worried for a second there, kid," Flint teases.

"Worried about what?" Isadora asks, and we all jerk like we've been struck by a live wire. How long had she been standing there?

"Dawud was just saying they thought they were developing a crush on you, Isadora," Flint teases, and the tips of both Dawud's *and* Isadora's ears turn flame red. "But then I assured them it was just indigestion."

Isadora rolls her eyes. "You're all childish," she mutters and walks away.

Dawud turns to Flint and hisses, "Not. Cool. She could have killed me and barbecued my leg over an open flame."

Which has all of us cracking up laughing.

By the time we've gotten control of ourselves again, we've gotten up and meandered back over to the castle, where Hudson joins us and just says, "So we're going to give Cyrus the God Stone, go crush the Trials, and then cram the Crown down that pompous ass's mouth, right?"

My eyebrows shoot up. "How did you know that was my plan?"

"It was the only smart move." He pulls me into his arms. "And my mate is wicked smart."

Flint makes gagging noises, but Hudson ignores him and leans down for a quick kiss, which I definitely return.

"Playtime is over, children!" Chastain barks from our left, and we all groan. "Everyone except Hudson grab a weapon and head to the practice field." He nods toward my mate and tosses over his shoulder at the gargoyle soldiers behind him, "That one's apparently a lover, not a fighter."

Everyone snickers as my gaze narrows on Chastain's, and I bite out, "You better *hope* you never see my lover fight, Chastain. You wouldn't last five minutes."

Because yeah, the blood-shaming-slash-sex-shaming has just got to stop. I am so over it. Which is why I turn to my mate, fist his shirt in my hand, and pull him down for a scorching kiss in front of everyone. Several gargoyles cheer or whistle as the kiss goes on. Even Macy shouts out "you go, girl," but I only vaguely hear them as everything except the feel of Hudson fades into the distance.

This boy is my everything, and he deserves for the world to see I am so damn proud to be lucky enough to be his mate. With one final brush of my lips against his, I lean back and smooth the nonexistent wrinkles from my tunic before turning on my heel and walking toward the practice field. But not before I catch the blinding grin splitting Hudson's face. Or the grit of Chastain's jaw at being shown up.

I know for certain I will be paying for that move later, but it was totally worth it.

77

It's a Double-Edged Broadsword

Chastain is standing in the training area now, watching me. Because of course he is. Determined not to get on his bad side any more than I already have, I hustle toward him. And then pull up short when he slams a broadsword into my hand.

Or at least I think it's a broadsword. I'm not exactly up on my medieval weaponry, but the thing in my hand seems like that's what it should be called. It's got a decorative hilt inlaid with beautiful semiprecious stones and a thick double-edged blade that is pretty close to three feet long and looks dangerous as hell.

The thing also weighs about eight million pounds. Okay, more like five or six, but the idea of swinging it—let alone lifting it over my head—definitely gives me pause. So I guess if this isn't a broadsword, I think it should be. And also, I never want to actually hold one if it's bigger than this.

Still, I'm not going to ask Chastain to tell me more about the weapon—or express my doubts that I can actually fight with it. I've told him we're here to help train the Gargoyle Army. I need to act like I know how to do that.

I swear, one of these days there's going to be some situation in this world where I don't feel like I have to fake it till I make it. But today is very definitely not that situation.

I rest the heavy sword on my shoulder and wander over to a shaded area where Hudson is seated, his legs stretched out in front of him, a copy of *Medea* in his hands. I should have known he would have already found the library in this place—and a tragedy to read.

"That's a good look for you," Hudson says, the heat from our kiss earlier still burning in his gaze. "Very sexy."

I roll my eyes. "What is it about a woman with a weapon that turns guys on?"

"Many, many things," he answers with a wicked glint in his eyes. "Some of which I would be more than happy to show you when we're done training."

"I'll keep that in mind," I answer with an amused shake of my head. I start to step back, to head over to the training circles and try to figure out what I'm supposed to do with this thing, when Hudson puts a hand on my elbow.

"Hey." The laughter fades from his eyes, and he leans closer so that I can hear him when he lowers his voice to little more than a whisper. "You belong here."

The words hit me harder than I expect them to—probably because they go to the heart of the feelings I've been having all day—and I rear back. "What does that mean?" I ask, pulling my elbow from his light grip.

"I just thought you might need to hear it." He leans down now, so that his lips are almost brushing my ear when he continues. "I know it doesn't feel like it right now, but you don't need to be the strongest or fastest or most badass to be a great ruler, Grace. You just have to care about their happiness more than your own."

I stare at the ground, shuffling my feet, shame twisting in my stomach. "Like how I would sacrifice them all to save you?"

"You wouldn't," he says, and he sounds so certain, I lift my gaze to meet his.

"How do you know that?" I whisper.

He shrugs, leaning back and pulling open his book again before answering. "Because you would never be as selfish as I would."

I know he didn't mean his words to be a knife to my chest, but my heart stutters nonetheless. Does he really believe I wouldn't sacrifice the *world* to save him? "I would," I whisper, and he looks back up at me, nothing but love and tenderness in his gaze.

"No, you wouldn't, Grace. And it's one of the reasons I love you so damn much." He smiles. "You're so impossibly strong. You will always sacrifice your own happiness for others, and *that* is what is going to make you an amazing ruler." He waves a hand toward the practice field. "Now, get out there and show them what you can do."

I follow his directions and walk toward the field because I can't be late, not with Chastain riding me as hard as he has been. But that doesn't mean I'm done with this conversation, because I'm not. Not by a long shot.

How can Hudson think for even one second that I wouldn't sacrifice anything—sacrifice everything—to save him? He's my mate and my best friend wrapped up into one, and I can't imagine a day without him, let alone a lifetime. I would give up the crown in a second to save him, would give up my *life* to save him, and he thinks I would just let him die?

No, this conversation isn't over. I need to know what I've done to make him believe such a thing. And what I can do to make him understand just how much I love and need him.

Once I get to the training area, Chastain orders a younger gargoyle to take the field opposite me, jeering that he should take it easy on their queen. The mockery makes all the gargoyles who have gathered to watch laugh, and I know I should care. I should care that he refuses to give me an ounce of respect. Should care that he seems as dismissive of me as he is of Cyrus.

But I don't.

All I can think about is the realization that Hudson was right. Ruling has nothing to do with how strong or how fast you are.

Ruling is ultimately about loss.

Because no matter what happens, no matter what choices I make, in the end someone will always lose. And worse, the choice of who suffers the most loss will be mine to bear.

78

Catwalk This Way

"**A**gain!" Chastain tells me, and though his tone is even, I can feel the annoyance rolling off him in waves. "Sword up, both hands on the hilt, now swing."

My shoulders are aching from the weight of pulling the broadsword over my head again and again and again. We've been at it for more than two hours now, and I think I'm finally getting the movements down—lift, swing, twist, parry, try not to get knocked off my feet. Don't rinse. Repeat.

Speaking of not rinsing…sweat drips down my back, but I lift the broadsword one more time as another gargoyle—a tall, beautiful woman with brown skin and an array of earrings in her ears named Moira—swings her sword around to connect with mine. I force myself not to flinch as the swords connect, and I hold my parry long enough for my arms to stop vibrating.

She whirls backward, her sword coming in low this time, and instinct has me snapping my wings and jumping up high enough to miss the swing entirely. As I come down, I bring my sword around and stop it just at the back of her neck.

"Woo-hoo!" Macy yells from where she's taken a break to watch. "Go get 'em, Grace!"

I shake my head, a little embarrassed by her enthusiasm but also more than a little pleased that someone noticed and thought I did well, considering Chastain looks like he just swallowed the most bitter lemon of all time. Then again, that's what he's looked like all morning—at least when his gaze lands on any of my friends or me…with one glaring exception.

He loves Isadora.

He doesn't laugh and joke around with her the way he does with so many of the members of the Gargoyle Army, but I'm pretty sure that's because Isadora doesn't know how to joke. But he's constantly praising her form, her knife skills (which are admittedly impressive), her speed.

And I get it. She is totally a badass with all her knives, but is she really so good that she deserves about fifty compliments an hour? Especially considering she's on Cyrus's side? I know you're supposed to keep your enemies close, but surely crawling up their ass is a little too close for anyone, even Chastain. *He doesn't know she's with Cyrus*, a small voice in the back of my head whispers, but I kick my inner sense of fair play to the curb. My shoulders fucking ache.

"Foster, get over here," Chastain calls to me, and I'm so surprised, I nearly drop the broadsword. But since that will more than likely get me yelled at some more, I hang on by my fingertips even as I walk toward him.

"What do you need?" I ask when I finally get to him. Which, admittedly, is not how most of the Army speaks to him. But I keep thinking of Nuri and how she handles herself. I know I'm nowhere near as badass as the dragon queen is, but I'm trying to cultivate the persona of a queen, instead of just the eighteen-year-old girl Chastain sees.

At first, Chastain doesn't answer. Instead, he looks at me like he can't believe I'm not bowing and scraping. Part of me can't believe it, either. But my friends and I are working our butts off taking turns to train the Gargoyle Army. I know it was originally a ruse to explain our presence, but as we started sparring with the soldiers, learning their names and friendships, it's slowly turning into so much more.

Somehow, in all my plans to kick Cyrus's ass, I forgot about something. I've spent all this time thinking about how I can use the Gargoyle Army to help me activate the Crown and beat him, that I forgot to think about them as something other than an army. I forgot to think about them as people.

It was one thing when I didn't know them, when I hadn't fought with them or eaten dinner with them or talked to them. They were just nameless, faceless entities—chess pieces for me to maneuver—and it didn't matter to me if we lost some in the fight as long as we stopped Cyrus.

But now, with each person I meet—each person I am responsible for leading—I'm overwhelmed with questions, with worry. Will Trent survive the war? Will Moira? Will any of them?

I glance around at the hundreds of soldiers on the field, sparring or talking or getting a drink of water, and I can't fight the blade of Hudson's earlier words as they skate along my skin.

"I want you to move the air." Chastain's words pull me from my thoughts.

I blink up at him. "Move the air?" I ask, unsure of what he's asking me to do. "With what?"

"With your power," he answers me, looking so shocked that I have to ask that he forgets to be annoyed.

"I'm sorry," I say after several seconds of the two of us staring at each other in bewilderment. "I don't know what that means."

He looks at me like he thinks I'm joking. Then lifts a hand and *moves the freaking air*. It hits me like a punch right in the center of my sternum.

The punch takes my breath away and nearly knocks me over, but I use every ounce of energy I have left to keep myself grounded. No way am I giving him the satisfaction of knocking me over. Not today.

I'm also not giving him the satisfaction of hearing me say how cool what he just did is. Not after the way he's treated me since I got here.

Chastain gives me an arch look when I manage to keep my feet firmly planted on the rock floor. But all he says is, "Move the air."

Like it's that easy.

Then again, maybe it is. I think about the water I pulled together during the Ludares tournament and the earth I used to heal when Cyrus bit me. Hudson helped me learn how to light a candle, and a lot of people helped me learn to fly. But no one taught me how to manipulate water or earth. I just figured it out once I realized it was possible. Now that I know this is possible, I can figure it out, too.

Or at least I hope I can.

I want to ask Chastain to show me what he did in slow motion this time, but the truth is, he didn't do much of anything. He just punched out lightly with his hand, and I felt the air hit me like a body blow.

With that thought in mind, I take a deep breath. Try to focus my mind and the energy in my body. And then I punch out with my hand, hard and fast.

Nothing happens, except Chastain starts to look smug again—which pisses me off, considering I'm trying to do something I didn't even know was possible two minutes ago. In the end, I do my best to ignore him and the obnoxious look on his face, though it's even harder than it sounds.

I take a couple more deep breaths and try to find the energy in the element. It's harder than it was with water, but it's there. I can feel it right there, just beyond my grasp.

This time, I close my eyes when I reach for it, visualize the air brushing against my skin. Moving through my open fingers. Gathering on my palm as I curl my fingers around it.

And this time when I punch out, I feel the air move. Feel the explosion of molecules around my fist. Watch as the breeze I created blows against Chastain's hair and collar.

I did it. I really did it. It was nowhere near as powerful as what Chastain did, but it was something. And considering it was only my second attempt, I will definitely take it.

"Do it again," Chastain tells me.

So I do—three more times to be exact, and each one is more powerful than the last. None of them is close to the punch to the sternum that hit me, but as the air blows Chastain's hair straight up, I'm beginning to think that maybe I can get there.

I wait for him to say again *again*, but he doesn't. Instead, he turns toward Isadora—who is currently throwing knives at a moving target, surprise, surprise— and beckons her over to us. Which is just fantastic, considering I'm pretty sure I'm about to replace that moving target.

Chastain validates the idea when he takes several steps away from me. Then we both watch as Isadora catwalks over to me like the Gargoyle Court is one giant runway, and she's the main attraction.

"Who do you need me to kill?" she asks when she finally stops in front of him.

"No one right now," he answers like her question is the most normal thing in the world. "But that could change at any moment."

"Let me know when it does." She turns to catwalk back from whence she came—which is more than okay with me—but Chastain steps in front of her.

She gives him a look that says she's fine making him her next target if he doesn't move, but he doesn't flinch. Just motions for her to turn around and says, "I think it's time to raise the stakes of today's training for our visitors here."

My screaming muscles don't agree, but it's not like I have a choice.

He guides the two of us to an area I'd noticed earlier on the practice field that was worn down in the shape of a large circle. As we enter the space, I can't help but feel we're entering a fight ring of some sort, and I wonder if any of my other friends have noticed I'm being led to my possible execution.

Which of course they have as I quickly spot Jaxon and the rest of my friends circle up on my right just as Hudson fades to a nearby tree and leans against it like he hasn't a care in the world. Which I see right through because hello, he must have been listening to everything on the field to realize I'd just been told to spar with the she-devil herself, and so he risked fading past sunlight to get closer. I shoot him a quick look that says, *Thanks for the confidence*, and laugh when he shrugs back with a smile because I totally read that as, *Hey, I'm just here to help carry away the body.* My body probably, but no need splitting hairs.

"Bailigh!" Chastain barks out once he reaches the center of the circle, and every single gargoyle on the field immediately stops what they're doing to hustle over, fanning out around the edges.

"It's time to choose the Watch Guard!" he says, and everyone cheers. This doesn't sound so awful. I'm an excellent lookout. I'm not sure what I'd have to watch for, but okay, I can do this. I'm starting to feel more confident until Chastain looks me dead in the eyes, a smirk turning up one corner of his mouth like he knows something I don't and he can't wait to see my reaction when he tells me.

"The rules are simple, Grace. I name someone as the Watch Guard every day, and they enter this ring." He gestures to the more-than-thirty-foot-wide circle we're currently standing in. "Anyone can challenge my choice by entering the ring and facing off with you. They will have four minutes to best the Watch Guard. Whoever is winning when the four minutes are up is declared the new Watch Guard."

"What happens then?" Macy asks.

"Another challenger may enter the ring."

"No, I mean, what happens if no one else wants to challenge the last Watch Guard?"

"Glorious honor," Chastain says, like that says it all.

The woman I met when I'd first visited the frozen Court with Chastain steps forward, her braids swinging as she pivots to face Macy. "The Watch Guard is our most revered position in the Army. Every person here places their faith in the Watch Guard every night, knowing we can sleep easy, we can regain our strength to fight another day, because of their sacrifice. To give that gift to your brethren is truly an honor beyond measure."

I don't know why, but I get the sense this Watch Guard thing is akin to being named Employee of the Month on steroids. Maybe it's how Chastain has been able to keep so many people training for a thousand years, day in and day out, with no clear sense of when this purgatory would end and they would enter the real battle. Which, okay, great idea, but I am okay not getting my picture hung on the wall in the break room today.

"To be named Watch Guard is to be worthy of ruling our people, of leading an army." Chastain holds my gaze, point made. Then turns to his army and says with a flourish, "Which is why today I am naming our queen Watch Guard."

The crowd cheers, and I know they're thinking he's bestowing a great honor upon me. But that's not what he's doing at all. Chastain wants to prove to everyone exactly how unworthy I am to be their queen. And as if that weren't the absolute worst, he turns to Isadora and says, "Now, Izzy, I'm hoping that you would do me the honor of being our queen's first challenger."

Izzy? I mouth to Macy, but she just shrugs. I glance at Isadora, expecting her to be contemplating which knife to use to remove Chastain's tongue for the nickname, but she's acting like she didn't hear the shortened moniker at all. Which tells me everything I need to know. She loves it. What is it with these Vegas that they think the best way to hide their emotions is to act like they're bored?

And that's when it dawns on me. Isadora must have daddy issues as bad as Hudson and Jaxon—big enough to drive a semi through—and thus Chastain's approval secretly means the world to her. I sigh. Which means she's going to try twice as hard to kick my ass for him.

"It would be my pleasure," she tells him, her stance immediately shifting to the balls of her feet.

I don't even have time to consider how best to defend myself when Chastain shouts, "Go."

I never even get the chance to grab my platinum string before *Izzy* strikes.

79

Finders, Keepers, Losers, Creepers

"**W**ell, that wasn't humiliating *at all*," I say to no one in particular, adjusting the ice bag so it fully covers what feels like a third horn growing in the middle of my forehead.

The mattress dips next to me, and Flint says, "Hey, it was a sucker shot. Don't worry about it."

"But can you imagine the precision involved in her throw that she perfectly timed the butt of her knife to hit Grace in the head and not the blade?" Dawud says, the awe in their voice impossible to miss.

"Right?" Eden agrees enthusiastically. "That shit was impressive as hell."

I groan. "And embarrassing. Don't forget that part." I lift one eyelid to look into Flint's face. "That has to be a new record for fastest Watch Guard defeat. I wouldn't be surprised if there was a leaderboard—or loser board—with my name on it somewhere."

"Aww, it wasn't that bad." Jaxon sits down on my other side, smiling at me softly.

"He's right," Macy agrees with a smirk. "All anyone is going to be talking about tonight is how your boyfriend started smoking as he rushed to your side on the field. We would have had a crispy-fried vampire on our hands if Jaxon and Flint hadn't yanked him back into the shade once he'd seen you were going to live."

I groan louder. Great. That's exactly what I need. Not only can I not last five seconds in the ring, but my boyfriend had to rush to check on me, I got knocked out so bad. I sincerely hope my bed turns into a giant hole right now and swallows me up.

"Please tell me *someone* beat her for Watch Guard," I beg, praying to everything holy that I won't have to spend all of dinner listening to her go on and on about her *glorious honor*—and yes, I'm totally hearing Loki's voice in my head now.

"Oh, Artelya made her eat dirt." Macy grins at me, explaining that's the name of the soldier who had explained more about the Watch Guard earlier. "I recorded the fight on my phone, if you wanna see the video."

And that is why I love my cousin.

"Gimme, gimme," I say, and Flint shuffles aside so Macy can climb on the bed next to me. I inch into a sitting position against the pillows, careful to keep the ice pack on my forehead, and watch what has to be the best four-minute video of my life. Artelya didn't knock Izzy out, but she clearly bested her, ending with a seriously badass move where she grabbed the vampire mid-fade, lifted her up in the air with a flick of her wings, and then slammed her down into the dirt with a resounding *thud*.

"That's gonna leave a mark," I say, and Macy and I giggle. "Let's watch it again."

"We need to talk about this Watch Guard thing," Jaxon says. "We'd planned to take turns spending our evenings searching for the God Stone, but if there's a guard posted every night, we're going to need to work out how not to raise their suspicions."

Which is how we end up telling Siobhan we're all too sore to attend dinner tonight and spend the time instead figuring out a strategy for finding the God Stone. We finally decide to divide the Court into quadrants, two of us taking a turn every night to search their quadrant and telling anyone who asks that they're creating a survey of the Court for the queen, who wants to rebuild it in our time—it being left in ruins for too long. Everyone agrees that's the easiest reason to justify us snooping into every corner of the castle and grounds. Dawud and Flint offer to take the first shift tonight.

Still, we don't know exactly what we're looking for, but Hudson feels fairly strongly it will be giving off some serious power, so we should be able to sense it if we get near enough. Jaxon agrees. Macy bets everyone five dollars it will be hidden as an eyeball in an animal statue or painting, clearly having seen one too many cheesy action flicks. We all take the bet.

Izzy doesn't disturb us once while we plot, probably gloating with the other gargoyles about how handily she defeated their queen, sucking up Chastain's praise. And I know, I sound bitter and jealous, which I probably am. I mean, I'm already struggling with this responsibility, I don't need some rabid vampire parading around for everyone to see exactly what I already know.

I didn't earn my title of queen. I gave it to myself when I thought I was the last gargoyle alive—when it didn't mean nearly as much.

I twist the ring on my finger absently. And even this, I didn't earn. Alistair gave it to me for no other reason than nepotism.

That doesn't mean I want her to rub my nose in it. Nor does it mean I'm stepping aside.

I *am* their queen, even if only by birthright, and I will not let them down. Nor can we afford to lose command of the Army. We need them for my plan to work, otherwise we can't risk giving Cyrus the God Stone no matter how many of the people I love he threatens to kill.

So I will train and I will learn and I will convince them that I deserve this honor. Well, as soon as my head stops feeling like it's going to split apart like a freshly sliced apple.

Everyone finally files out of our room, and I call the shower first. If it was a little bigger than a postage stamp, or I was a little less sore, I'd invite Hudson to join me. See if maybe that doesn't thaw him out a little. It didn't escape my attention that he spent most of the strategy session on the other side of the room playing Sudoku on his phone. He was upset about something, and I'm guessing it was the second ten years I'd likely shaved off his life this week when I hit the ground in the ring like a sack of potatoes.

I take as quick a shower as possible, not wanting to leave him stewing with his thoughts too long, and am again grateful I shoved some travel-size toiletries in my bag before we left Katmere what feels like a lifetime ago. I'm trying to stretch the small bottles of shampoo and conditioner I brought with me as far as I can get them. The Gargoyle Court has really good-smelling soaps—I know Hudson is using them to wash his hair and so are a lot of the others—but they don't have the same curly mess on their heads that I do. If I don't want to look like a poodle that's been through one of those high-powered dryers at the car wash, I need to stay the course as long as I can.

When I come out, Hudson is asleep. With his eyes closed and a stray curl from his normal pompadour winding over his forehead, he looks a lot younger—a lot more defenseless—than he does during the day.

It makes me ache to see him like this, stretched out on our bed like it's the most natural thing in the world, and I can't resist the pull of him. I crawl into bed beside him and cuddle up close.

Even in his sleep, he reaches out for me, draws me in.

He feels good—really, really good—and I'm so tired that I don't even fight it when I start to drift off to sleep with him.

I have no idea how long we sleep, but I don't wake up on my own and neither does Hudson. In fact, we don't wake up at all until a loud moaning sound starts coming through the still-dark windows.

"Do you hear that?" I ask, shaking Hudson awake.

"Hear what?" he grouses, but I know he's paying attention because he goes still about one second after I ask, his head cocked to the side like he's trying to figure out what's going on.

Before either of us can identify who or what is making the noise, there's a loud pounding on the door. Followed by Dawud yelling for us to open up.

80

Whisper Sweet Not-So-Nothings

"What's wrong?" I exclaim as I throw open the doors.

"Go to your window." Their voice is urgent and so is the look on their face as Macy and Flint pile into our room. In the hallway, Eden is pounding on doors, yelling for Jaxon to "come quick!"

"What's happening?" I look to Hudson, who is already standing at the window with the curtains pulled back.

"It looks like we're under attack," he answers, sounding a little bewildered and a lot cold, as the sound of a bell clanging echoes throughout the castle. An alarm.

"We're frozen in time," I say, making my way to the window. "Driving a car while inside it, remember? How can anything be attacking us if we're in a moving car?" I have to raise my voice to be heard over the shouts coming from below—as well as the strange *clackity* sound filling the air.

"I have no idea," Macy comments. "Unless some of their enemies were somehow frozen in time with the Gargoyle Court all those years ago."

"Still, shouldn't the Gargoyle Army have killed them by now?" I demand. "A thousand years is a long time to keep attacking a place and not be defeated."

The clanging bell is getting closer and closer to us, and we can hear now someone is shouting, "North wall! North wall!" in between bell clangs.

We all exchange a quick look before the others rush out of my room to get dressed. Hudson already has his training uniform on and is pulling on his shoes as I reach for my sweatshirt. He waits patiently while I throw on the rest of my clothes and pull my hair into a scrunchie.

"Who do you think it is?" I ask, my heart pounding in my chest.

Hudson holds my gaze. "I don't know, but I'm starting to sense it has something to do with their sacred Watch Guard."

And the vise around my chest squeezes the breath from my lungs. No, no, no. I cannot afford to have a panic attack right now. Not when my people need me.

As I pull small puffs of air into my lungs, I pray to everyone I can name to please make this stop, but the attack only gets worse. It's not just that there's someone out there who probably wants to kill us that's twisting my stomach in fear—it's that I won't be strong enough to fight alongside my kin like they should expect I can.

"Hey." Hudson fades to me, kneeling down in front of the chair he was sitting in to put on his shoes, and grabs my face gently. "This is a bad one, isn't it?"

There's no judgment in his voice. No frustration that I'm slowing us down from getting out there and helping with the fight. His fathomless blue eyes are filled with love.

"Can you tell me what two plus two is?" he asks, and I blink.

Does he think I hit my head again, like in the lighthouse? "Not a con-con-concussion," I stutter. My veins feel like they're filling with ice, and my teeth start chattering, my whole body trembling. But the harder I fight the panic attack, the more my body quakes.

Hudson reaches up and smooths a loose curl from my forehead and pushes it behind my ear. "I know, babe. But tell me anyway, will you? What's two plus two?"

I don't have the energy to argue, and he doesn't look like he's going to back down, so I push the word out. "Fa-four."

He smiles. "Good. And four plus four?"

"E-eight."

"Eight plus eight?"

What in the world does simple addition matter when my army is about to fight someone so terrible, they created a Watch Guard to stay vigilant against them? But I can't say any of that right now, what with my teeth chattering, so instead I grit my jaw and say, "S-six-sixteen."

"You're doing great, Grace," Hudson says. "Can you tell me what's sixteen plus sixteen?"

I blink, then answer, "Thir-thirty-two-two."

"And thirty-two plus thirty-two?"

By the time we reach 256, the trembling has stopped and I can finally draw a deep breath into my starved lungs. As I feel the panic attack ease, I sigh and lay my head across Hudson's shoulder. He pulls me closer and kisses the side of my neck.

"There you go, Grace," he soothes. "All better now."

And he's right. That was one of the worst panic attacks I've had in months, and it passed in just a couple of minutes. I'm not even shaking as badly as I usually do.

I lean back and hold his gaze. "Why were you testing my math skills just then?"

The tops of his cheeks turn an interesting shade of pink, and he shrugs. "You're my mate, and I want to always be there for you, so I researched ways to help ease panic attacks. Apparently, some researchers have found that math engages a totally different part of your brain than the part that causes panic attacks. So, you know, doing simple math can get you to focus on something other than the attack, and hopefully it eases it."

I swallow the giant lump forming in my throat. "You researched how to help me with my panic attacks?"

"Yeah." He shrugs like it's no big deal, but it means the world to me.

"I love you," I say, and I've never meant anything more.

"I know," he responds with a half smile. "Now, let's go see if your people need some help. Hey, maybe we can just toss Izzy at whoever is about to attack the castle. That should at least give you another fun video to play on repeat."

He winks and I laugh, just like he wanted. The last of my tremors fade as I give him a quick but thorough kiss—a promise of how I want to show my love for him later. As I lean back, there is a definite hunger burning in his gaze.

"Right, then," he says, his accent thicker than usual. "Let's go kick some arse so we can finish that kiss."

He's just so adorable, flustered and turned on, that I lean forward to give him another quick kiss.

"For fuck's sake—" Jaxon shouts from the doorway and I spring back guiltily. "Do you two *ever* stop? In case you can't hear the maniacal bell clanging, the castle is under attack!"

Hudson rolls his eyes as he helps me up and tosses at Jaxon, "Hey, brother, don't be hating on me just because you can walk in the sunlight today."

I smother a laugh with my hand as Jaxon's face turns an interesting shade of red. He mutters, "Asshole," then fades away, and I can't keep the laugh in anymore.

"That was mean," I chide Hudson.

He starts to reply, but a sudden scream from the battlement outside our window stops him cold. And then everything happens at once.

Hudson scoops me up and fades us to the others standing on the stone wall.

Gargoyles are flying above us, shooting flaming arrows at the attackers, who have managed to scale this section of the wall, and I get my first look at the *creatures* that are attacking the castle.

And then I scream.

81

Welcome to the Danger Bones

"**A**re they skeletons?" Macy whispers in horror.

I don't know. I don't know *what* to call these *creatures*, but "skeleton" doesn't seem right. The shape of their bones is all wrong, for one. Some legs are bent at an impossible angle, feet positioned backward, skulls twisted at odd positions, ribs missing. And that's not even mentioning how some of the bones are splintered so badly, it almost looks like fur.

The bones are in the general shape of a human, if you overlook the odd angles and twists, and they're clearly trying to walk upright, but that's about the only human thing I can see about this inhuman army mindlessly trying to get inside the castle.

As they race up the sides of the walls, their bones *thwack-thwack-thwack* against one another as they use the skeleton bodies beneath them as steps for the next wave to climb higher. Their nails *clickety-clack* against the walls—and the sound is enough to give me nightmares for years. But then one of the gargoyles shooting flaming arrows into the bone stairway must hit their target, because one of the skeletons lets out a howling screech, like wind whistling between two bones, high-pitched and terrifying.

The screaming eventually dies down until another flaming arrow hits its target, and then another skeleton releases an agonized screech that sends shivers down my spine.

Suddenly, there's a sickening crunch as the bones of the bodies on the bottom crack and splinter under the weight of the ones above them—and I swallow the lump forming in the back of my throat. I know exactly how these skeletons became so grossly disfigured, and it's everything in me not to vomit the bile churning in my stomach.

I don't even have to ask how many times these creatures have tried to scale these walls that almost every skeleton looks so broken, they only barely still give the hint of being human. Chastain already told me. They choose a new Watch Guard *every day*.

As the thwacking of bones gets closer, more gargoyles take to the skies with flaming arrows. I want to join them in the fight, but they move with such uniformity, it's clear they've practiced this over and over, how to fly in a tight squadron without their giant stone wings crashing into one another. I worry I will just get in their way, possibly be the reason they don't succeed in stopping this attack wave and a skeleton breaches the castle.

The thought is no sooner in my head before a bony hand reaches over the side of a wall no more than thirty feet away from me. Moira is the closest gargoyle to the creature, and she shifts immediately into her stone form, her shield raised, and swings her sword down on the stone hand gripping the top of the wall, its severed finger bones falling like pebbles to the stone ground.

Next, she takes the butt of her sword and cracks it against the skull of the creature, but fast as lightning, it turns its head and sinks its teeth into her fleshy wrist. She cries out and drops her sword, focusing on frantically pounding the skull into the side of the wall, all the while screaming, "Get it off! Get it off! Get it off!"

No one rushes to help her, though. In fact, the other gargoyles widen the area around her and the hideous skeleton creature. I glance around to locate Chastain, but he's at the far end of this section of wall directing his fliers to focus arrows near the bottom of the wall. He hasn't seen that Moira is under attack yet.

"We have to help her!" I shout and rush to her side, but Hudson yanks me back.

"Don't!" he snaps.

"We have to help her!" I shout again and fight against him, clawing his arms to get free, but he doesn't loosen his hold.

"We can't," he whispers, and I don't understand. Hudson has never run from a fight in his life.

"There's still time!" I plead. "We can save her!"

"No, we can't." He doesn't say anything else, and my eyes widen as I finally see what he'd seen with his better night vision.

The flesh on her wrist is disintegrating. Decaying within seconds, becoming flakes that the wind picks up and carries away like dust.

And it's not just where the skeleton is still biting her. The infection is moving up her arm rapidly, and if the crazed look in her eyes is any indication, she knows it. She knows she's dying, and there's nothing anyone can do to save her.

Well, no gargoyle.

I turn to face Hudson, tears streaming down my cheeks, and I don't even have to ask. His shoulders sag, and I know he's already guessed what I'm going to ask him to do. No, what I would beg him to do.

These aren't people—they're just skeletons. They're already dead. He won't be killing a living person; he'll just be ending the suffering of these mindless creatures. I tell myself anything I can to justify asking this of Hudson, but as Moira's screams rise, I know I don't have a choice.

"I'm sorry," I whisper, and salty tears run over my lips and coat my tongue.

"I already told you, Grace," he says, wiping away some of my tears with his thumb. "Don't ever apologize to me for wanting to save your people."

I shake my head frantically, desperate to explain that this isn't the same thing. I'm not choosing my people over my mate. I would never do that. But these skeletons are already dead. Surely it's no different than disintegrating a stadium!

I don't say any of that, though, because Hudson reaches out a hand into the air and closes his eyes, and I can tell he's focusing on separating the bone creatures from everything else, and I don't want to distract him.

His hand starts to shake and then his whole arm, but still he holds it up, reaching out to find every last skeleton with his mind. And then, just as someone shouts that another creature has reached the top of the wall, Hudson closes his fist.

And every skeleton turns to dust instantly.

The Gargoyle Army stops shouting and shooting arrows, the thwacking of bones and *clackety-clack* against the wall is gone, too. The only sound is a soft breeze carrying the dust of the Skeleton Army out to sea.

I rush over to Moira, the skull no longer biting her wrist, and hope we killed the creature in time to save her. Two other gargoyles reach her first and immediately start channeling earth magic to stop the infection.

"Is she going to be okay?" I ask, my voice raw and shaky.

"I think so," a gargoyle answers. "Though I don't know how."

Chastain lands next to me, tucking his wings away instantly as he shifts back to his human form. "What have you done?" he asks.

And I turn to wave Hudson over, so Chastain can thank him properly, but what I see has my heart stopping cold.

My proud and strong mate is on the ground, his arms wrapped around his knees, tears streaming down his face as he just keeps repeating, "They were gargoyles. They were gargoyles. They were gargoyles."

82

Not Your
Beck-and-Call Boy

Hudson is upstairs asleep.

And I want answers.

It took over an hour to get him to calm down enough to sleep. He kept babbling about the skeletons being gargoyles, which makes absolutely no sense.

The last thing he said to me before his eyelids finally closed was that they'd be back.

Which makes even less sense. He disintegrated them all. I saw it with my own eyes. But if Hudson said it, it's likely true.

So I begged Macy and Eden to stay with him while I went in search of Chastain.

I find him after only ten minutes of searching in the library, staring at the shitty stained glass windows.

"I need answers," I snap, hands on my hips.

Chastain slowly turns to face me, but the look in his eyes has me shuffling backward.

He looks murderous.

"*You* need answers?" he sneers. "I lost two of my best soldiers tonight, and your mate could have stopped all of this immediately."

My heart skips at the loss. Two? They must have been on the other side of the battlement than I was on.

But that's no excuse for his attitude right now.

"Don't you dare blame Hudson for having no idea a goddamn bone army was going to attack the castle tonight! What *were* those creatures?" I demand. Chastain has no right to be righteous when he didn't bother to prepare us at all for what was to come.

"We're in a frozen Court, Grace." He waves his hand. "Time doesn't exist here for us. We don't age...and we don't die."

His words are like a gunshot ricocheting in my chest. "So they *were* gargoyles, like Hudson said," I whisper. Oh my God. What did I ask him to do?

"Yes," he says, and all the fight seems to leave him as his shoulders sag. "The first person who died at Court did so from a training accident. We buried him, said our goodbyes, and expected that to be it. But a few days later, the first skeleton attacked."

His eyes look more haunted than I've ever seen them.

"We didn't know what the creature was, but it took an entire battalion of us fighting it to take it down. We lost three good men and women that night." He sighs. "And by the next night, that first skeleton came back—with three more."

He rubs a hand across his eyes. "Ever since, they come back. Every night. And every night, their numbers have grown with our fallen brothers and sisters from the previous battle."

I choke on a sob, then whisper, "But why? Why do they keep coming back?"

Chastain turns and holds my gaze, his own fathomless with despair. "This is their home, Grace. They're trying to come home."

As I think back to the sheer number of skeletons piling on top of one another to be able to scale a seventy-five-foot wall, I gasp. "In total, how many have you lost?"

"More than five thousand," he says on a ragged breath. "And because they can't die, nothing can die here, no matter how many we beat back at night, they re-form the next day and attack again the following night. We've been losing more and more soldiers to the Skeleton Army the last few years, their numbers now far greater than ours, and I'd started to lose hope that we'd not all end up becoming those mindless creatures."

"Oh my God, I can't even imagine," I say, swiping at the few tears gathering in my eyes.

"It's going to be okay, Grace," he says, a smile tilting up the corners of his mouth. "Everything is going to be okay now that you're here."

I want to believe so badly that he's actually talking about me, maybe even accepting me as his queen. But he's not. I know exactly who he thinks is here to save them.

"He can't," I say and shake my head. "He can't do it again."

"What do you mean?" Chastain asks. "Does he need more time to recover? Even sparing us the fight a few nights a week will give us all hope, give us a fighting chance at survival."

And I want to give that to Chastain more than I've ever wanted anything.

But I can't. I don't know exactly why, Hudson's never really explained to me how his gift works before, but I know now it's far more complicated than any of us thinks. And it costs him far more than anyone should have to pay.

Because if he were just disintegrating bones, Hudson would have no way of knowing they were really gargoyles.

"He can't," I repeat. "We'll have to find another way."

"Grace, there is no other way," Chastain says. "Our numbers are barely four thousand now. Three in the frozen Court and another thousand around the world waiting for a signal it is time to fight."

"But I thought you were frozen in time to prevent the poison from spreading. How could there be any gargoyle not dead from the poison outside this space?" I ask.

"Do you know so little about what you are?" He manages to make the question sound like a condemnation. "When a gargoyle is in solid form, we are in stasis. Our blood does not flow, and thus the poison cannot harm us until we shift from that form. There are gargoyles all around the world, stone sentries waiting patiently for the call to service, for an antidote so they can bring Cyrus to justice for his crimes."

I think about the gargoyles I've seen in pictures resting at the tops of buildings and wonder if those are carvings or my kin in stasis.

"That's why Hudson must help us survive the Skeleton Army," Chastain says. "We owe it to gargoyles everywhere who have not given up hope that the Army would come for them one day."

I shake my head and say, "This is not his fight. The cost is too high to ask of anyone, and I will not ask him to do this again." And with that, I turn to leave.

But Chastain's voice chases me from behind. "You would choose your mate over your people?"

I don't even hesitate as I turn and say, "Every time."

83

A Mate with Destiny

Hudson didn't stir when I climbed in bed with him this morning, nor when I pulled his trembling body against mine. And he was gone by the time I woke up.

But I'm not surprised when I see him in the same shady chair he reclined in yesterday, *Medea* spread open on his lap.

Flint and Dawud reported at breakfast that they'd not discovered the God Stone in their quadrant last night. And no God Stone means another day of training—another night of skeleton monsters—until we can search for the Stone again.

I walk over to Hudson and sit down next to him. "Morning," I murmur.

He glances up from the page he was reading. "Good morning, Grace," he says and offers a smile that never reaches his eyes.

"How did you know the skeletons were gargoyles?" I blurt out the question that's been burning a hole in my thoughts all morning.

I meant to wait until we were alone, but I realize now that I have to know the weight of my sins. I won't be able to focus on anything until I can figure out exactly what harm I've caused my mate—and how I can fix it.

He shrugs and says, "Just a guess." But he won't meet my gaze.

"Hudson," I say and lean close enough to cover his hand with my own. "You've never lied to me before. Please don't start now."

He jerks, and I know I've scored a direct hit. And I wait. And wait.

Eventually, his shoulders sag and he sighs. "To destroy a stadium, I just find the edges where the air meets wood or concrete, and I separate the molecules. But a person, or creature, it's a lot of moving parts. It's hard to find all their edges—unless I slip into their mind and feel what they feel." He runs a hand through his hair, chuckles without an ounce of humor. "I've never really tried to explain it before. But it's like, you always know where your hand is without sometimes being able to see it, right? So I do the same thing. I slip into their minds and find their sense of self, their knowledge of where *they* are…and then I tear them apart."

I gasp. Oh God, it's so much worse than I ever could have imagined. "You're with them when they die, aren't you?" And then I hold my breath as I wait for the boy I love to confirm I asked him to die five thousand deaths last night.

He whispers, "Yes," and I can't stop the tears tracking down my cheeks.

"Fuck," Flint says, and I look up to see the entire gang standing about ten feet behind Hudson. And from the shock on everyone's faces, they heard everything Hudson said.

And in a flash, a wide smile splits Hudson's face. "Hey, it's no big deal. Those creatures this morning weren't thinking much anyway." When no one seems to have anything to add to that, Hudson whispers, "I did them a favor."

"Chastain told me that no one can die in this space. Time is frozen, and death requires time to pass," I explain. "Those creatures were gargoyles who can't die, so I think you're right and you gave them at least some measure of peace, no matter how brief, Hudson."

I squeeze his hand again, but he pulls back to close his book and sit up.

"I see Chastain is ready for another day of training," Hudson says, effectively closing the topic. For now. I have every intention of talking to him later, telling him exactly how sorry I am and how I will never ask this of him again. We all make choices and have our own fates. It's not up to Hudson to fix so many wrongs, especially when none is of his making.

And I plan on making that clear to everyone at dinner tonight—right after I spend the day getting my ass handed to me in training again.

As I walk away, I turn to give Hudson a quick smile over my shoulder, but he's not looking in my direction. He's staring at the section of wall where Moira had been standing, a look of unbearable pain skating across his features that makes me stumble. But then he blinks and it's gone, replaced by a coldness that chills me to my bones.

Hudson has always used a mask of indifference to keep his emotions hidden, but this is different. Even when he's leaning against a wall and playing Sudoku, I can still see *him* in the lazy scroll of his fingers, in the humor lurking in his hooded eyes. But this—this isn't Hudson.

This is someone in so much pain, the only way to deal with it is to convince himself he can't feel anything at all.

And I get it. I do. When my parents died, I would have done anything to make myself stop feeling that pain. But the thing is, without that pain, it's nearly impossible to heal. Because the only way past it is through it.

The trick is figuring out how to heal when the broken thing is you—or worse, your mate.

84

The Slingshot Heard Round the World

We've been warming up on the training field for about two hours, and by "warming up" I mean Chastain has made us run until my lungs are burning and my legs are pure jelly, when he turns to the Army and shouts, "Bailigh!"

Everyone immediately stops what they were doing and lines up around the same circle where we fought to become Watch Guard yesterday.

"Isn't this early to be fighting for Watch Guard?" I whisper to Macy, but she just shrugs.

"After seeing those creatures last night, I vote it's never too early to find tonight's Watch Guard," she whispers back.

As Chastain steps into the circle, I half hope he names me the first Watch Guard. At least when Izzy knocks me out again, I can spend the rest of the day in bed with Hudson, holding my mate and helping him work through what happened last night.

"My brethren, we lost two of our bravest in last night's battle." The Army, as one, strikes their swords against their shields in agreement, and Chastain continues. "We would have lost more if not for our queen and her guests." Swords clang against metal again. "And so I have considered their offer to train with us, show us if we are ready to meet our enemies on the battlefield, and I have accepted." *Clang.* "Today, we will show gargoyles are made of more than just stone." *Clang.* "We are the righteous protectors of the weak." *Clang.* "When others run, we stand and fight." *Clang.* "And we do not stop until our enemies have met our mettle." *Clang.* "On the tips of our swords."

The Army bangs their swords against their shields over and over in deafening applause, until Chastain raises his hands and they quiet again to hear what final statement he'll share next.

"My brethren." He turns in a circle, arms still raised and making eye contact with as many gargoyles as he can. "It's time we show our queen what a gargoyle can *really* do in battle!"

As the crowd erupts in another cacophony of swords banging against shields, I have to hand it to Chastain. He's managed to rally the troops while getting another dig in on my right to lead the Gargoyle Army. Wonderful.

He turns back to my group of friends and says, "Who do we want to see eat our dirt first? Shall we show the dragons who really commands the air?" *Clang.* "Or maybe teach the vampires what is true strength?" *Clang. Clang.* "Or how weak the witches are without their magic?" *Clang. Clang. Clang. Clang.* "But I know, perhaps we should show how a wolf's teeth are no match for our mighty stone!"

As the crowd erupts into more swords banging on shields, I can't help but lean in close to Macy and whisper, "Cyrus's grandstanding has nothing on this guy."

God save us all from blowhard men. Like, really.

I must not be the only one who is over this posturing, because Dawud steps into the ring, their gangly young body looking even smaller when standing next to Chastain's thick one covered in armor. I can't help the gasp that escapes my lips, but Dawud just tosses me a grin and says, "I've got this, Grace."

It's such a Hudson thing to say that I can't repress the smile that curves my mouth. My mate must have a fan in the young wolf, and my gaze darts over to the shaded area to see if he caught the exchange, but Hudson isn't there anymore. I glance around the various other shaded areas scattered around the training space, but I don't see him anywhere.

"Did Hudson leave?" I ask Jaxon.

He leans forward and whispers in my ear, "He went to search for the God Stone."

I nod, the tightness in my chest easing.

If he's hunting for the Stone, then we're one step closer to getting out of this frozen nightmare. One step closer to winning the Trials and ending the gargoyles' suffering, too.

"We may not have as many secrets as the dragons, but we do have a few," Dawud says.

"What's there to know about the wolves?" One of the other gargoyles I haven't met yet snickers. "Avoid the teeth and claws and carry a little bit of silver. They'll be running scared with their tails between their legs in no time. They're just a bunch of stupid dogs, after all."

I'm so horrified by the blatant contempt and prejudice in that statement that

I start to step forward and call them on it. I mean, most of the werewolves I've met have been pretty terrible people, but Xavier was one of the best.

Before I can say anything, though, Dawud clears their throat a couple of times and answers, "It's a little more complicated than that."

"Is it now?" asks a gargoyle named Rodrigo. Or at least I think that's his name—we were introduced on the first day of training, but I was so exhausted by the end that I can't be sure my memory is correct. "Do you want to give us a little demonstration?"

"I was going more for an intellectual discussion," Dawud answers with a tired sigh. "But of course. We can have a demonstration if you'd like."

"Oh, I'd like." Rodrigo snickers. "Just give me a minute."

We all watch as he walks over to a female gargoyle—Bridget, I think her name was—who hands him what looks like a silver ring.

He takes it with a laugh, then slides it onto his finger, all of which I watch with disbelief.

"Wait a minute." I step into the center of the ring. "You can't just use a weapon like that on Dawud—"

"It's fine, Grace," Dawud tells me.

"No, it's not." Jaxon steps forward. "Getting us to tell you stuff you can use in battle or participating in a little friendly training is one thing. But it's sure as hell not okay to use something that you know is going to hurt someone—possibly kill them—"

"It's fine," Dawud says again, and this time their tone is a little more adamant. "If this is what he wants to do, this is what we'll do."

I'm totally pissed now. I know Rodrigo is picking on Dawud because he thinks they're the weak link in our group. That just because they're skinny and a little nerdy, they're easy pickings. And maybe they are—fighting hasn't exactly been their strong suit that I've ever seen—but that doesn't mean someone gets to hurt them deliberately.

Not in my Court and not to someone who is just trying to help out.

"Dawud, no—" I start, but they cut me off.

"Yes, Grace." The look they give me this time says very clearly that they don't want my help and that I should butt out.

Doing so goes against everything I think is right and just, but it's not like they left me a lot of choice here. Which is why I sigh heavily, but I don't make any more objections, even when Rodrigo—with the silver ring still on his finger—starts to circle Dawud, who is standing loosely with their hands by their sides.

Dawud turns with Rodrigo, making sure to never leave their back exposed to the gargoyle. But it only takes a minute or two of circling each other before Rodrigo makes his move, lunging straight into the circle and trying to grab Dawud.

Dawud jumps to the side, partially shifting as they do, so that when they lash out with their hand against Rodrigo's shoulder, their sharp claws slice through Rodrigo's clothes.

"What the—" the gargoyle growls as he whirls around.

But Dawud simply watches him with the same calm and curious expression they normally wear. "Tip number one. Wolves can partially shift."

"Oh yeah?" Rodrigo taunts. "Let's see how well those claws do against stone." He shifts into his full gargoyle form.

"Not well," Dawud agrees, then ducks as Rodrigo swings one giant stone fist at their head.

Rodrigo roars in outrage at the miss and whirls around to come after Dawud again. This time when he swings, Dawud drops down and knocks Rodrigo's feet out from under him, shockingly fast.

I watch Rodrigo fall face-first into the stone ground and, for a moment, can't believe my eyes. I would say this is a Dawud none of us has ever seen before, but that's not exactly true. They're not full-on fighting with Rodrigo. Instead, they're using their head, being strategic, using Rodrigo's own strength against him.

Rodrigo rolls over with a roar and jumps to his feet. Now there is murder on his face, and I start to get nervous. Really nervous. Dawud is good at mind games—great at them, apparently—but they're no match for a pissed-off Rodrigo once the gargoyle gets his hands on them.

"Tip number two," Dawud explains just loud enough to be heard above Rodrigo's grunts. "If they can, wolves always go for the feet. Always."

"Why is that?" Artelya calls from the crowd. She and the other gargoyles have gotten a lot more interested in what Dawud has to say in the last two minutes.

They shrug. "It's a lot easier to hold on to the jugular when your opponent is on the ground."

They say it so matter-of-factly that my hand goes to my own throat. No wonder vampires and wolves are teaming up. They have more in common than I thought.

A quick glance at the others shows that Macy, Flint, and Eden are all having the same reaction I am—a little impressed and a little nervous now that we're finally getting to see what's under Dawud's calm and slightly shy exterior. Jaxon and Izzy, however, just look impressed and not surprised at all. Is that because they know the wolves better than we do? Or because they've already figured out Dawud in a way we haven't?

I make a note to ask Jaxon about it later, but then Rodrigo goes racing toward Dawud, loaded for bear, and I brace myself for the worst. But Dawud goes low and trips him again. This time, though, Rodrigo seems prepared for it, and as he falls, he whirls and punches out with the massive fist that has the silver ring on it.

He hits Dawud straight in the jaw, and their head flies back. We all gasp, not because of the punch—though it was a hard one—but because of the ring.

"What the hell?" Jaxon demands of Chastain even as Macy and Mekhi rush forward to see if Dawud is okay. "I thought we were training, not trying to kill people?"

Chastain doesn't say anything, but even he is watching Dawud with concern. Right now, their head is down, hand covering the spot where the punch landed, but already I can see blood leaking onto the ground.

I am about to call enough and move from the outer rim of the designated training circle to Dawud's side when they raise their head. Their face is bruised and swelling a little bit from the punch, and the corner of their mouth is bloody, but other than that, they look remarkably fine.

"Tip number three," they say in the same calm, steady voice they always have. "Silver doesn't do shit to wolves."

And that's when I realize they let Rodrigo hit them—just to make the point they wanted to make.

Rodrigo must realize it, too, because he's practically frothing at the mouth to get to Dawud. It makes me nervous—with that much enmity, someone is going to get hurt. And while Dawud may have a few tricks up their sleeve, I'm pretty sure Rodrigo can crush them if he ever manages to get his massive gargoyle arms around them.

Thankfully, Chastain steps in before Rodrigo can go for round four. Rodrigo snarls at the interruption, but the general holds up a hand that quiets him instantly.

"You've shown us three defensive tips, which we appreciate very much." His lips twist a little as he glances at Rodrigo. "Some of us more than others, obviously. But what about offensive tips? What would you do if you found yourself fighting off a gargoyle?"

"What would I do?" Dawud asks, wiping the blood away from the corner of their mouth with a linen rag someone offered them.

They think about it for a second, then reach into their pocket and pull out the stone I saw them take from the hallway our first night here. They glance around the giant training area like they're looking for something—or someone. They must find it, because they reach back into their pocket and say, "I would do this."

85

Who Needs Chemistry When You've Got Physics?

A quick glance at my friends' faces says they're feeling the exact same things I am—anger at Chastain, fear for Dawud, indecision about whether to step in or let whatever's about to happen play out.

In fact, the only one from our group who doesn't seem to be freaking out is Dawud. They are as cool and calm as they usually are, even as they reach into their pocket and pull out a slingshot.

It's small, pocket-size, and when Chastain sees it, he gives an exasperated shake of his head. Rodrigo isn't nearly as restrained. The huge gargoyle starts laughing his ass off. He even goes so far as to bend over and slap his knee like Dawud's slingshot is the funniest thing he's ever seen.

"Am I supposed to be afraid of a little twig?" he taunts, walking over to where Chastain is standing near the edge of the circle, and they share a look as if to say, *Can you believe this kid?*

Annoyance twists in my belly, and now I want to storm the field even more— just to punch the giant jerk in his giant nose. But Dawud remains unbothered as they slowly, carefully put the rock in the slingshot, and for the first time I'm wondering if their seemingly random scavenging actually has a point.

"That's it?" Rodrigo asks when he sees the rock. "That's all you've got?"

"It's enough," Dawud replies noncommittally.

Then they study the distance between themselves and Rodrigo and walk in a half circle until they're the full thirty-foot distance of the arena away from him. It feels like the entire training field leans forward now, trying to see what's going to happen. Logic says nothing good for Dawud, but they seem so completely unruffled that it gives me pause.

At least until they point the slingshot about eighteen inches to the right of Rodrigo.

The gargoyles all around me start to laugh and jeer. A bunch of catcalling and insults ensue, and if I were Dawud, I'm pretty sure I would slink off the field. But they just take their time turning a little more to the left now, lining up the slingshot with I don't know what.

"Are you going to do something?" Rodrigo demands. "Or should I just go ahead and stomp you into the ground now?"

Fear twists in my belly as I take in Dawud's thinner frame, Rodrigo's chest and arms thick with muscles from many lifetimes of training. I'm with Chastain—what do they plan to do with that tiny rock and slingshot to bring this giant stone warrior down? Especially aiming at something to the right of their target?

But I don't have to wonder for long because, so fast I can barely see them, Dawud launches themselves straight up into the air, at least six impressive feet, twisting as they go. The slingshot twists with them, and they line up their shot in a flash, pull the rubber band back taut, and then fire the rock—straight at Rodrigo's kneecap.

There's a crack when the rock connects, so loud and ominous that I can hear it standing all these feet away. It doesn't sound good, and now I'm leaning forward even more to see what—

Rodrigo's leg gives out instantly, and he crumples with a bellow of pain, catching his weight on his arms at the last minute so his kneecap doesn't crash into the hard ground beneath him. He's in an awkward position now, his weight balanced on his arms and one good knee while the injured one is hovering an inch off the ground.

"I'm going to fucking kill you!" he snarls at Dawud, who still doesn't look the least bit upset. That in and of itself astounds me, considering they just took out someone's knee in a training exercise. I mean, yeah, gargoyles heal fast, but still. They took out Rodrigo's knee.

I wait for Dawud to bow to Chastain now that they've shown the general what they can do. Instead, they launch themselves into the air again, and this time they drop the slingshot on the ground where they were standing.

As they jump, they shift into wolf form and land several feet away. Before I can so much as blink, they're heading for Rodrigo at the fastest damn run I've ever seen. I'm terrified they're going to forget the rules completely and go for the jugular, which isn't what this is supposed to be about.

I wring my hands, a scream clawing at the back of my throat even as I mutter a quick prayer that they won't murder a gargoyle right here, in the middle of the training circle. But four feet before they reach Rodrigo, Dawud's wolf leaps into the air and twists just as they shift back to their human form, their fist arcing through the air and slamming straight into Rodrigo's jaw with maximum force.

For a moment, nothing happens except I swear I can see cartoon birds circling Rodrigo's head. But then, with no warning whatsoever, the gargoyle slumps forward and lands face-first in the dirt. He's out cold, and I can't say that I'm the least bit sorry about it.

Chastain runs over the field to Dawud, shock that they won clearly evident on his face. "How did you do that?" he demands.

"Tip number four," Dawud answers with a shrug. "Mass times acceleration equals force—meaning even the smallest things can pack a massive punch if they're moving fast enough. Physics is a thing."

"But why did you twist in the air before every attack?" Artelya asks, clearly fascinated by this lesson, and Dawud preens under her attention.

"Twisting like that, in midair, creates torque...and torque increases acceleration." They say it like it's the most obvious thing in the world, and maybe it is, because Artelya nods.

"Ahh, yes, I always find when I bring my sword down from a jump spin, my opponent staggers back even farther. I just never heard it explained like this before," she says.

Dawud is oblivious to the tightening of Chastain's jaw as they grin back at Artelya. "I was the runt of my litter, but I was never the omega."

"I'd love to hear more," she says, and they start to walk away.

I just faintly catch Dawud telling her they dream of being alpha of their own pack one day, a pack that prizes brains over brawn, when they stop and toss over their shoulder one last bit of advice at Chastain and the other gargoyles still hovering around the training circle. "Oh, and tip number five, wolves can jump really high in human form."

And then they turn and walk away, but not before catching my eye and winking, actually winking.

I can't help but grin back. Because only Dawud would use physics to win a brawl.

86

Rock, Fang, Scissors

Several gargoyles rush to Rodrigo's side and rest a palm on the earth and another on his back as they channel healing magic into his prone body. I know as well as the next gargoyle that using earth magic to heal is slow, and we all wait patiently as they tend to their fallen comrade.

Above their heads, a row of dark storm clouds rolls in, blocking out the sun and turning the air around us an eerie gunmetal gray that I really hope isn't an omen of bad things to come.

Rodrigo starts to rustle, pulling my attention back to the training field. Chastain walks over and commands, "Don't heal him completely. His knee should ache a bit today to remind him never to underestimate an opponent again."

Harsh, but I have to admit, I like it. I really hate bullies.

Chastain turns to Flint and Eden now. "Do the dragons want to take a shot at besting my warriors next?"

"I think we're going to pass," Flint says.

Chastain looks unimpressed, but he doesn't say anything more.

I lean toward Flint and say quietly, "You know, I wouldn't let them do anything to hurt the dragons."

"No offense, Grace, but I don't think you'd be able to stop them."

The response grates on my nerves a little bit—maybe because deep down I know he's right. Still, "I have the Crown. I control the Army."

Flint looks doubtful. "That may be so, but I wouldn't trust that Chastain guy as far as I can throw him. I'm not convinced teaching him how to defeat us isn't exactly what he wants."

Nice to know I'm not the only one put off by Chastain's attitude, but I don't think he would betray us. He's got as much to gain from taking Cyrus out as we do. Still, I don't want to fight with Flint anymore, so I just tease him back. "To be fair, you can throw him pretty far, as you are such a badass dragon."

"True comment." He grins, pretends to do a little muscle flex. "In fact—" He breaks off mid-sentence, his grin turning to a scowl in the blink of an eye.

I glance behind me to see what got him so pissed off so quickly. But all I see is Jaxon striding into the center of the training circle like he owns it.

I turn back around to ask what's up, but Flint is already striding away, his fists clenched by his sides.

I watch him go with a weight pressing down on my chest. Everything is so messed up right now, and I can't figure out how to fix it, no matter how hard I try. I know things have gone really sideways, know that there's nothing I can do to make up for everything that Flint has lost. But right now, the threat is bigger than ever, and we need to be coming together, not falling apart.

"Hey." Hudson's hand comes down on my shoulder, and when I turn to look up at him, his eyes are warmer than they've been in a while. Seeing that doesn't make the ache deep inside me go away, but it does make it a little bit better, which is more than I expected. "Thought I'd take advantage of the sudden shade and see how you were doing."

"You just missed Dawud take down a gargoyle twice their size," Macy tells him with glee. "It was amazing."

I lean back against him with a sigh and soak in the solid strength of him as Macy walks him through Dawud's epic battle. I let his warmth burrow inside me, let it chase away just a little bit of the fear that's been growing ever since we watched Katmere fall.

Ever since I realized that nothing is solid in this new world of shifting alliances and broken promises. More, nothing is safe. I don't know how to fight that, and I sure as hell don't know how to win against it.

Inside the training circle, Jaxon goes flying and ends up skidding across the stone, face-first.

Hudson winces. "That's going to hurt."

"Should we stop this?" I ask as Jaxon leaps up and launches himself at one of the five gargoyles currently in the circle with him.

The gargoyle goes to grab him out of the air, but Jaxon is already on the ground, knocking the gargoyle's legs out from under him and landing on top of him. He grabs his head in a lock, and though he doesn't break his neck, the implication is there.

One opponent down, four to go. He turns to take on two more, but instead of acknowledging the fact that he's supposed to be out, the gargoyle he just pinned rears up and grabs on to Jaxon, who isn't expecting the attack. Seconds later, Jaxon goes flying across the room again—this time crashing into a wall so hard that the chandelier shakes.

"I can't watch this anymore," Hudson says, and at first I think he's going to follow Flint out.

Instead, he fades to where Jaxon is shaking his head to clear it. I watch as he offers him a hand and says something that makes Jaxon roll his eyes and laugh at the same time.

As they move back into the circle, Jaxon waves an arm in a *be my guest* kind of way. "By all means, have at it, big brother," he mocks. "Show me how it's really done."

"Yeah, well, don't get too excited," Hudson shoots back. "I'm not sure you can handle how it's really done."

Jaxon's eyes narrow. "Don't push your luck."

"See, that's where we differ." Hudson grins. "For you, it's luck. For me, it's just pure skill."

For a second, I think Jaxon's going to say to hell with the gargoyles and go after Hudson himself. But he just laughs and holds his hand up in a backward peace sign that I'm pretty sure means he's flipping him off, Brit-style, before heading to the sidelines.

I glance over at Isadora, who is sitting alone on one of the stone benches off to the side. She's been there, looking bored, since training started, and at first I assumed it was because she wasn't about to help the Army learn how to defeat her father. But she perks up a little as Hudson positions himself on the opposite side of now seven badass-looking gargoyles.

"The first thing you need to know about fighting vampires," he says, jumping back to avoid a powerful sword swing to the stomach, "is that we're faster than you, and we have better reflexes."

To prove it, he lashes out with a hand and sends a gargoyle flying before he even had a clue Hudson was going to attack. "You can't keep up with us in a one-on-one fight." He turns around and kicks another gargoyle in the stomach so hard that he lands on his butt, several feet away.

"Or even a two-on-one fight." Hudson smirks. "But that just means you shouldn't be fighting to win right off the bat. You should be fighting to fatigue."

He bends over and sends an attacking gargoyle rolling right over his back, then grabs on to an arm and leg and spins around before tossing him like a discus right at the gargoyle he'd kicked in the stomach a few moments ago. The poor guy had just gotten to his feet after the blow, and now he's on the ground again, buried under the biggest gargoyle on the field.

"What do you mean?" Chastain asks, circling the action. He's watching every movement of Hudson's with interest, and it makes me uneasy as Flint's words come back to me. Is he really trying to learn how to defeat Cyrus's army, or is he looking for a weakness in my mate specifically?

The fact that I don't know the answer is something I'm going to have to deal with sooner rather than later. I mean, the whole point is to win the Trials to cure them of the poison so they can help us defeat Cyrus and use the Crown. I always just assumed the Army would want that—to punish the vampire who poisoned them and trapped them here for a millennium. But what if I'm wrong? What if all they want to do is be freed, to finally start living again, really living?

Maybe Chastain dreams of one day finding a mate and retiring to a little village in Ireland. I try to imagine this powerful general troubled with nothing more than tending a little vegetable garden and defending his home from the occasional thunderstorm.

"Stop dropping your shoulder, Thomas!" Chastain barks out as Hudson tosses another gargoyle across the training area to land with a painful *thud*.

I shake my head. Chastain was born to lead. And if the tension in his jaw every time Hudson beats an attacker back is any indication, Chastain cannot tolerate seeing anyone in his army suffer. Of course he'll want to stop Cyrus from ever harming them again.

"You aren't going to be able to outrun the vampires. You aren't going to be able to out-attack them, either. Our reflexes are too fast. So your best bet is to exhaust Cyrus's army." As if to prove his point, he ducks at the last second and avoids an attack from behind, then whips around and delivers a one-two-three-punch combination to a gargoyle who had barely started to move into position.

"And how do you suggest we do that?" Chastain asks.

"Make them fade. Over and over again. Our ability to fade isn't limitless—it takes a lot of energy and eventually, it will wear us down. You've got wings. Use them. Make them fade after you, make them jump to try to get you. Eventually, you'll tire them out and that's when you strike."

He whirls around with preternatural speed and, with one powerful sweep of his arm, sends three gargoyles slamming to the ground.

The fight begins in earnest then, eight gargoyles piling onto Hudson in one coordinated move. He manages to get out from under them, then races across the training circle. They chase him—on foot and by air—but just when it looks like they've got him cornered, Jaxon jumps into the melee.

He's doing his telekinetic thing and hovering several feet off the ground, which means he can grab on to the flying gargoyles, one at a time, and send them soaring toward Hudson. Who snatches them out of the sky and slams them down.

I know this is my army, and I should be outraged on their behalf, but the truth is, my mate and his brother are putting on way too good of a show. For two guys who have spent most of the time they've been around each other at odds, they make a really good team.

I glance over at Isadora again, who is leaning forward now, elbows braced on her knees as she watches the battle with an interest I've never seen from her before. She even winces when one of the gargoyles gets a good lick in on Jaxon.

"You don't have to stay on the other side, you know." Even as I say the words, I wonder if I'm making a mistake. But there's something in her eyes—something lurking under all the ice and mockery—that makes me think there's more there. Like maybe she's actually a lot like Hudson.

"I don't know what you're talking about." The ice is back double-fold.

"I'm just saying, there's another way to live besides under Cyrus's thumb. Hudson found it, and so can you."

"Aren't you cute?" she responds acidly.

"I'm just saying—"

"I know what you're saying," she snarls. "And who the hell are you to think you know what I want?"

"I don't," I answer. "I just know that it feels better to have someone in your corner than it does to be alone."

Isadora doesn't answer, but for a second—just a second—she looks vulnerable.

I decide to push my advantage, even knowing it's probably stupid. "You've got two really incredible brothers. I'm the first to admit that they're prickly as all hell, but they're both really good guys who would do anything for the people they love."

"For you, don't you mean?" she snarls, and any hint of vulnerability has once again been buried beneath a mound of attitude.

"For me, yeah. Absolutely. But also for Macy and Mekhi and Flint and Eden and others. Once they accept you as one of theirs, they never go back." I pause and look up at the dark clouds still rolling in and blocking out the sun. I wonder briefly if it's an omen of what's headed our way or maybe the hope that all this pain will soon be washed away. Either way, change is coming. I turn back to Isadora and take one more risk. "You're already family to them. That love and protection will be there if you want it."

Isadora bites her lower lip and glances back at the training circle, where Jaxon and Hudson have just finished destroying their opposition. They're standing in the center of the circle, hands on their hips and grinning at each other, while eight gargoyles lay groaning around them.

My heart melts a little at the sight, but it seems to have the opposite effect on Isadora, who turns away with a deliberate roll of her eyes. "All this sweetness might work for you, but if I've learned anything from Cyrus, it's that nothing's free. And frankly, I'd rather stick with the payment plan I've already got set up."

87

Knife First, Think Later

I expect her to walk away, but instead she stops on the other side of the circle and watches as another round of soldiers challenges Hudson and Jaxon. There are ten this time, and judging from the insignias on their tunics, they are members of some sort of elite guard. And they look like they want to tear them apart.

My stomach clenches, and I'm not going to lie—I freak out just a little bit. Not because I don't have faith in Hudson and Jaxon but because these are ten of the best fighters in the whole Gargoyle Army. Not to mention the fact that they're only using their vampire skills to spar—no special powers involved.

It's a lot to ask of anyone.

It turns out I worried for nothing, though, because the two of them make pretty quick work of these guards, too. The tall female guard with the tight blond topknot gives Jaxon the most trouble, but even she ends up on her butt after about ten minutes.

Hudson reaches down to help her up as Jaxon walks over to talk to one of the other guards.

But as Hudson turns to join him outside the training circle, Isadora calls out, "Looks to me like what you need is a real challenge."

Her gaze darts to Chastain, who calls out, "Izzy. Show us something we haven't seen yet."

"Oh, I assure you, you've never seen this before," she says. "That is, if Hudson isn't too tired, of course."

Hudson lifts a brow and turns back to look at his sister, who's watching him with her booted foot propped on a bench and a knife in her hand. "By all means. Let's show them what a real fight looks like, shall we?"

"By all means," she mimics as she moves out from behind the bench and swaggers toward him. "Though to be honest, I'm not sure how much of a fight it'll actually be."

Hudson's eyes narrow at the challenge, and while everyone else around the circle hoots and hollers, I know him well enough to see how divided he is. He doesn't want to fight his sister, but he also doesn't want to rebuff the first interest she's shown in him.

"Only one way to find out," he finally answers. "But you'd have to stop talking for that to happen."

This time, it's Isadora's eyes that narrow. She starts to respond—thinks better of it because of his last comment—and settles for catwalking her ass to the center of the training circle.

And can I just say... Vampires? It's impossible not to love them, but they sure do have a strange way of showing they love you back. Mostly they do it by not killing you, which is better than the alternative. But it sure does look funny from the outside.

"Let me know when you want to start, *sis*," Hudson comments as they square off across the circle.

"I thought we already had," Isadora answers and lets a knife fly.

It's a shock—to Hudson as well as the audience—and I gasp as it slices right through the outside of Hudson's left biceps.

It doesn't seem to faze him, though. He just lifts a brow and asks, "So that's how it's going to be, hmm?"

"That's how it's always been," she answers, fading across the circle and snatching a broadsword right out of the hands of a gargoyle guard. The second her fingers close around the hilt, she's swinging it at Hudson's back.

So apparently the no-killing thing is more of a choice than an actual requirement, which is so not a reassuring thought.

"Hudson!" I scream, my heart in my throat.

But he's moving before I even get the first sound out of my mouth, dropping to the ground and sweeping her feet out from under her so fast that Isadora actually hangs in midair for a second before the rest of her body catches on to the fact that there's nothing left to support her.

She hits the ground hard but is up nearly as quickly. And now she looks pissed as hell—which, can I just say, seems a little ridiculous, considering how she started this sparring-turned-death-match.

This time, when she brings the sword around, she's aiming to slice him clean in half—and if Hudson moved just a millisecond slower, she might actually have succeeded. As it is, she slices the tip across his belly, leaving a hole in his shirt and a thin line of blood on his torso.

"Hey, Hudson!" Eden shouts, and Hudson turns just in time to snatch the sword the dragon sends flying at him right out of thin air.

He brings the sword around as he completes the spin, and the sound of steel against steel rings through the entryway. If possible, Isadora looks even angrier—though I'm not sure who she's more pissed at. Hudson for meeting her blow or Eden for tossing him the sword to do it.

Although that question is answered when she releases a primal scream the next time she brings her sword down, aiming straight for Hudson's head—or, to be more specific, aiming at decapitating Hudson's head.

So, definitely angrier at Hudson, then, especially when he responds by bringing his sword up to meet hers with enough strength that he sends hers spinning through the air. Eden leaps forward and catches it, and for a second, I think she's going to toss it back to Isadora. But the look of abject loathing in the vampire's eyes must change Eden's mind, because she keeps a firm grip on it.

Isadora turns back to Hudson with a sneer. "How does it feel to know you're so pathetic, your friends have to cheat to help you win?"

"Pretty good," he answers, "considering it means I've got friends."

She whips a knife out of the belt at her waist and sends it flying at him. He fades a few inches to the left, and the knife whizzes past and would have embedded itself into a watching gargoyle if he hasn't shifted at the last minute. Thankfully, the blade bounces off his stone body and falls to the ground.

But Hudson already turned to see where the knife would land, probably to see if he was going to have to fade in front of any onlookers in its path—and that's all the opening Isadora needed. In a blink, she's fading to him, grabbing his arm without coming out of her fade, and using that momentum to toss him across the entire field. My breath lodges in the back of my throat as he skids to a halt like a rag doll just inside the giant open doors leading to the Great Hall.

He's already on his feet again by the time she fades across the field to the Great Hall to get to him, with the rest of us racing across the field to see what happens next. But Isadora jumps up right before she reaches Hudson, then parkours off the center of the nearby wall so that she's flying toward the huge iron chandelier hanging fifty feet above the grand ballroom floor.

Once she reaches it, she grabs on to the bottom edge of it and hangs there spinning for a second or two. I have just enough time to wonder what she could possibly be doing before she brings her foot up to rest on the side bar of the chandelier, nearly turning upside down in the process. Then, using her foot for leverage, she rips the entire bottom bar off the chandelier.

The crowd gasps as the bar comes free and she starts to fall, but Isadora barely seems to notice. Instead, she rotates in midair so that she lands on her feet, the heavy iron bar pulled back over her head.

I've never seen anything like it, and apparently neither has Hudson, because his eyes widen just a little at the sight of her. Even I have to admit she looks powerful as fuck—something I might admire if she wasn't currently trying to kill my mate.

But she is, so I'm a lot more worried and a lot less impressed than I would otherwise be. Especially when she roars—yes, roars—as she brings the iron bar down straight at the top of Hudson's head.

He meets it with his sword, but she just twirls and swings again. This one connects with his shoulder, and she taunts, "Maybe you'd be less distracted if you actually let our father train you properly."

This time he's the one swinging the sword, and she barely manages to get the iron bar down in time to keep him from slicing her leg clean off. "Yes, well, maybe if you'd spent less time kissing our father's ass, you might have actually learned to think for yourself."

Her only response is a hiss and another swing of the iron bar. She aims low this time, and he jumps right over it.

She swings again, and he parries it with his sword.

"You think I had a choice?" she demands. "After you fucked off, I had no choice."

He swings this time, and she does a backward somersault right over the blade.

"There's always a choice," Hudson shoots back. "You just weren't brave enough to make it."

"I did what I had to do," Isadora snarls as she runs up the nearest wall again. This time she comes down right away, slamming the iron bar onto his sword as hard as she can.

He stumbles just a little and comes back with a hard swing of his sword. It happens so fast, she barely gets the pipe up in time, and she ends up falling to her knees under the strength of the blow.

"You're doing what you want to do," he snarls right back at her. "And to hell with who gets hurt."

Just as he brings the sword down again, she rolls away and jumps to her feet. Then the two of them go at it for real. No more talking, no more showmanship, just powerful blow after powerful blow as the battle rages on and on and on.

They're both breathing hard now, and they're both tiring—the weapons aren't swinging quite as fast and the answering parries aren't quite as strong. Neither is willing to give up, but neither is able to best the other, either. I've just decided that I'm going to have to get in the middle of it and break it up before someone actually ends up dead when Hudson finally sees a break in her form.

Lashing out, he yells, "Enough!" and lands a powerful kick to her solar plexus.

Izzy goes flying. She soars close to fifteen feet before crashing into the ground at the edge of the training circle. As she hits the harsh, unforgiving rocks, her grip on the iron pipe relaxes and it lands several feet away.

88

Nothing Says I Love
You Like a Dagger
to the Heart

The crowd gasps, and even Hudson looks concerned, dropping his sword as he rushes toward her.

But he's only taken a couple of steps before Isadora is back on her feet and this time, she is incandescent with fury. "You think you know me?" she screams at him.

Seconds later, a dagger goes flying right by his cheek, and everyone on that side of the room scatters to avoid getting hit by it and whatever else she decides to throw.

"You don't know the first thing about me!" Another dagger soars straight at him, and this time he has to dive to the side to avoid getting hit.

"Do you think this is the life I chose for myself?" she demands.

Two more daggers are leveled straight at his heart, and *my* heart stops until he jumps a good six feet off the ground to avoid them.

"Do you think I wanted to be Cyrus's bastard?"

Another dagger goes flying. This one is long and wicked-looking, and Hudson doesn't move quite fast enough to avoid getting clipped in the shoulder. Blood seeps through the torn sleeve of his tunic.

"One more weapon for him to use against his mate?"

This time she sends a black dagger straight for his eye. The whole crowd lets out horrified "oooohs," and I hold my breath until Hudson ducks out of the way.

My palms are damp by now, my heart beating way too fast. Panic is a wild bird within me, its wings fluttering against my ribs as I try to figure out what to do. I want to step in, but instinct tells me that Hudson won't thank me for it. That whatever this is, it's between his sister and him.

Knowing that doesn't make it any easier for me to stay on the sidelines. And it sure as hell doesn't make it easier for me to watch everything that's happening.

"You can say I had a choice, but that wasn't true for me."

She throws a dagger straight at his heart, but Hudson sidesteps it.

"I was given one choice. One," she says through gritted teeth.

This time the dagger that goes soaring at Hudson is short, with a large ruby embedded in its hilt. He dodges it at the last second.

"Be of value."

Another dagger, another dodge.

"Or be of no value at all."

Another dagger, another dodge.

"Be a dutiful daughter."

Two more daggers rapid-fire.

Hudson gives up trying to dodge them now; they're coming too fast and he's finally winded, so he just disintegrates them before they can touch him.

But that only seems to infuriate Isadora more, something I didn't think was possible until she lets loose with a volley of daggers unlike anything I have ever seen before. One after another after another after another. Faster and faster and faster.

Hudson disintegrates them all, which only has her throwing even faster.

"Or get locked in a crypt."

Six more daggers, one for every word.

The fact that he's stopping all of them should make her rethink what she's doing. But her rage only makes her throw faster, until the words and knives are flying at the exact same rate.

"After—"

Another dagger.

"A."

Another dagger.

"Thousand."

Two more daggers, one for each syllable.

"Years."

Another dagger.

"I would."

Another dagger.

"Do *anything*."

Another dagger.

"Would murder."

Another dagger.

"Anyone."

Another dagger.

"Not to go back."

A volley of daggers, one after another, so fast and so many that Hudson barely has time to disintegrate them before they reach him now.

"I am *never* going back."

Another dagger, aiming straight for his throat.

Hudson waves his hand and disintegrates it, but the look on his face says it doesn't matter if the knife hit or not. Her words cut just as deeply as any knife could. Maybe even more deeply.

"Isadora, I—"

"Don't you dare talk to me," she hisses. And then, like something out of a horror movie, she sends one last dagger flying straight for his heart, but when he waves his hand to disintegrate it—the dagger re-forms as though it continued to travel and is now only an inch from his chest, too close and too fast to fade out of its path.

"Hudson, move!" I scream. "Go!"

My warning comes too late. The dagger embeds itself in his shoulder.

But in true, fucked-up vampire fashion, Hudson barely seems to notice that he has a knife sticking out of his body. Instead, he's focused entirely on Isadora—and what she just made possible.

"How?" he asks, his blue eyes laser focused on hers.

"I already told you that I am something altogether different," she answers, her chin raised defiantly. "It's not my fault that you chose not to believe me."

And just like that, she turns on her heels and walks away.

As one, the crowd parts to let her go.

89

Out with the Old,
In with the Clue

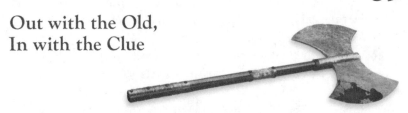

The second Isadora leaves the circle, I'm running for Hudson.

"Are you okay?" I ask, probing at his shoulder around the dagger. "What can I do?"

"I'm fine," he answers, but he's still watching his sister walk away.

"Um, no offense, but you have a dagger in your shoulder," I tell him. "That's not exactly fine in any world—even this one."

"That was an impressive fight," Chastain says from behind me. "On both your parts."

"Do we have a clinic?" I demand.

"A clinic?" He looks confused, and for the millionth time I remember that we're frozen in the middle of the freaking eleventh century.

"A place where we can go and he can rest while I help heal him."

"Gargoyles don't normally need clinics." Chastain eyes me disdainfully. "And neither should your vampire for something as minor as this."

"Minor?" I turn back to Hudson, wondering if maybe I imagined Isadora re-forming the dagger and driving it into my mate's body. But nope, the dagger is definitely still there. And so is the blood all around the area. "He's bleeding! And impaled!"

"Not for long," Hudson says, then reaches up and pulls the dagger from his shoulder without so much as a flinch.

"Let me see." I get closer, start probing the wound as I prepare to gather energy to heal it, then watch—wide-eyed—as the wound starts healing over in front of me.

"Just like that?" I ask, even though I'm literally watching the torn skin close.

Hudson grins at me. "Just like that."

I shake my head, blow out a long breath. Because of course I know that vampires heal quickly, especially if it's a flesh wound. It's just that I don't tend to see that many flesh wounds—especially on my mate. Every vampire I've actually seen injured has been mortally injured and incapable of healing themselves.

Which, now that I think about it, is totally the point. Vampires heal themselves quickly and quietly when they can. And if they can't, it's because they're too far gone to do it.

Within seconds, Hudson's shoulder is fully healed except for a nasty bruise. As are the various cuts from the other daggers Cyrus's little sociopath threw at him.

"What the hell was that?" Eden asks as she comes up behind Hudson, looking as bewildered as I feel.

Flint joins us. "That girl has some issues."

"That girl is a *warrior*," Chastain snaps.

"Excuse me?" I ask as indignation replaces the last of the fear inside me. "You think her throwing daggers at my unarmed mate makes her a warrior?"

"I think her heart makes her a warrior," he answers, surveying the daggers embedded in the walls and tapestries behind us, as well as scattered across the stone floor. "Look at all these daggers she threw at him. That's a lot of commitment."

"It's a lot of something," Flint mutters under his breath.

"It was a temper tantrum," I tell him, totally not understanding what Isadora did that he finds so impressive. "She had a reckless, dangerous temper tantrum, and you think that makes her a warrior."

"I think she committed to a path and was willing to die for it. That's what warriors do."

That's the most ridiculous, shortsighted thing I have ever heard. And considering Cyrus Vega has tried to gaslight me several times these last several months, that is saying something.

But come on. It is absurd to put someone on a pedestal because she *loses her shit* in a spectacular fashion. I mean, yeah, none of us could take our eyes off what was happening. But that's because it was a train wreck, not because it was worthy of admiration.

And I get it. What Isadora said was horrible. What happened to her at Cyrus's hands was horrible. Nobody doubts that. Nobody denies it. But that doesn't give her the right to take all her rage and pain out on Hudson, who has never done a damn thing to her. He didn't know she existed before a couple of days ago, and she's been firmly on his father's side the whole time.

So what exactly does she want from him? And what exactly does Chastain see in her meltdown that makes him so impressed by her?

I tell myself it doesn't matter, tell myself to just focus on Hudson and keep my mouth shut. But the truth is, it does matter. I've been here busting my ass to impress him, and I haven't tried to kill anyone once. Surely that should earn me a point or three.

I mean, not to quote a long-dead comedian, but what does a queen have to do to get a little respect around here?

But even as I ask myself the question, I realize that we're never going to see eye to eye on this. Not just on whether or not Isadora is a "warrior" but on the whole *how to rule* thing. And maybe it's time I stop trying.

Maybe it's time I stop trying to appease him.

Maybe it's time I stop trying to fit into some mold that I've never even seen.

Maybe it's time I stop trying to be the queen he thinks I should be and be the queen I want to be.

God knows, it's not like I can do worse in his mind than I already am.

Which is why I finally stop trying to earn his respect and simply say what I'm thinking. "In my mind, a great warrior is someone willing to die for what they believe in, die for the people they love, the people they've sworn to protect. Isadora wouldn't die protecting anyone but herself." I shake my head. "But hey, I guess we just have very different definitions of what's worth fighting for."

I wait for Chastain to say something else, but he has nothing else to say—at least not to me. Big shock. Instead, he walks over to the wooden windowsill where some of Isadora's daggers are still embedded. He stands there looking at them, then reaches up and pulls one out of the wall.

As he does, the large orange stone embedded in his ring glints in the light.

And everything inside me freezes. Because after all these days of looking, I have finally found the God Stone. And it was in plain sight all along.

I don't know how I know it's the God Stone, but I do. It's like it's calling me home. A feeling of being wrapped in my mother's arms fills my senses, tugs at my memories of my mother's loving embrace, nearly pulling my knees from under me. I stagger to the side, one hand jutting out to grab on to a table as wave after wave of power rolls through me.

I glance at Hudson, eyes wide, and realize he's figured it out, too. Maybe he feels the same call I do. Or maybe he's just smart enough to realize that of course Chastain would never feel anyone was strong enough to guard the Stone but himself.

Before I can think better of it, I comment, "Your ring is really beautiful.

It's such an incredible amber—I don't think I've ever seen a gemstone quite that color before."

Hudson gives me a *could you be more obvious?* look, but Chastain is still facing the window, so—thankfully—he doesn't see it. He does glance at his ring, however, and when he turns around to face me again, there's a fierce satisfaction in his eyes.

"This ring is worn by the person who has proven themselves to be the most powerful in the Gargoyle Army. At one point or another, nearly everyone in this Court has challenged me for it. Only one has ever won it." He smiles at Artelya, who is standing straight and proud just a few feet away.

"Only for a day," she answers, but that doesn't soften the pride in her eyes or the strength in her shoulders. "I only had it for a day before you challenged me—and won it back."

He inclines his head. "The time will come when the student is better than the teacher. But that time is not today, even if the teacher grows tired."

He looks toward the hallway Isadora took in her grand exit. And muses, "Maybe the bean ghaiscíoch ceann dearg is finally the one who will prove herself worthy."

I don't need to know Irish to know he just said something about Isadora being a warrior again, and I'd be lying if I said it didn't get my back up.

"But not the gargoyle queen?" The question is out of my mouth before I can stop it.

Chastain simply answers, "Carrying this responsibility is only for the bravest of hearts."

Wow. Because that didn't hurt at all, despite the pep talk I just gave myself.

"How do you know I'll never wear that ring?" I ask as an idea comes to me. "What if I want to challenge you?"

I know it's a long shot—he didn't get to be leader of the Gargoyle Army because he doesn't know what he's doing—but still, it's something. And now that he's given me the road map on the rightful way to claim the ring, it seems impossible not to try for it.

"You will never challenge me," he says, like it's a given. Or an absolute, which pisses me off, because I am a lot of things, but I am *not* a coward.

Which is why I pull my shoulders back, stick my chin up, and say, "I *am* challenging you."

"No, you're not," he tells me, leaning forward so I can't miss a single word he's about to say. "Because I only accept worthy challenges."

As Chastain turns and walks away, Hudson takes my hand and murmurs,

"He has no idea who you are or what you can do. That's on him, Grace. Not on you."

He's right. Chastain doesn't know, because he refuses to try. But he's going to before I leave this place. Because one way or another, I'm going to get that ring off his finger.

90

There's Cliffhangers and then There's Cliff Hangers

Two days later, we still don't have the ring.

We've all gathered on the cliffs overlooking the sea to discuss exactly how we're going to get it, but I am only vaguely paying attention.

I can't take my eyes off my mate, who is sitting just outside our circle of friends, one knee drawn up while he lazily traces circles in the grass. Gone is his usual pompadour, waves of rich brown hair falling in haphazard waves across his forehead. His jaw is dark with stubble, and his clothes appear looser across his broad shoulders.

He's refused to feed off me, no matter how often I beg.

I wish I could believe he wasn't feeding out of some gallant need to make sure I keep up my strength for training. But I know that's not it at all.

It's because we've spent two more days in this godforsaken Court.

It's because every night when the alarm bells sounded, my mate walked up to the battlements like he was being led to the gallows. And without anyone asking, he raised his hand, latched his mind onto five thousand gargoyles in mindless agony—and then killed them.

Each time, his reaction grew worse, with last night taking both Jaxon and Flint holding him down while he thrashed and screamed for more than an hour before he finally passed out.

We've all begged Hudson not to do it again. Hell, it even looked like Chastain couldn't stomach it anymore when Hudson had fallen to the ground, tears coursing unchecked down his cheeks while he let out a keening scream as though his very soul were being split in two.

Which is why I know exactly why he hasn't fed from me. He can't bring himself to feel anything, even joy.

I'm terrified one more night, one more sacrifice, and I'll lose him forever to the darkness.

And I will not let that happen.

So I called an emergency meeting on the cliffs today, and I'm not leaving until we have a plan to take the Stone. Today.

"We could chop his hand off," Hudson suggests, and a quick glance around shows me the others are having a hard time figuring out if he's being serious or not.

"No," Isadora says from where she's sitting cross-legged on top of a large rock, the ocean at her back. "He would never let his guard slip enough to allow that to happen."

"I tried 'accidentally' setting his hand on fire at lunch today, figuring he'd have to take the ring off to clean his wounds," Flint tells us with a sigh. "But he just changed to stone and made me run an extra ten laps for my 'carelessness.'" He puts air quotes around the last word.

"The man has the personality of a feral hog," Eden mutters.

"My father will gut you like a feral hog if you don't get that Stone," Isadora remarks casually.

Because who doesn't make casual remarks like that about others? I swear, the girl is a menace—and not just because she keeps trying to kill my mate. Although that's beginning to get on my nerves, too.

"Chastain's not that bad," Macy defends. "He's just a guy in charge of a really terrible situation."

"We've been in charge of some really terrible situations," I counter, because much as I adore my cousin, sometimes her hot-pink-colored glasses are a little much. Then again, she isn't the one he enjoys tormenting on an hourly basis. "Doesn't mean we act like jerks about it."

"Yeah, but our bad situations only last a few days," she tells me. "I mean, one way or the other, we figure it out. His has lasted a thousand years."

She has a good point. Being frozen in time for a thousand years would definitely make me grumpy. I like to think I wouldn't take it out on the girl trying to help me—who also happens to be my queen—but different strokes for different folks, as my dad used to say.

"Look," Isadora says, and it's the most invested I've heard her sound since that day in the crypt when she ordered us captured. "I don't care how we get the ring, but we are running out of time, and I am *not* going back without it."

"I should have just taken it when he turned to stone," Flint says. "But the fire attracted a lot of attention, and too many people were watching, so—"

"That doesn't make any sense," Jaxon interjects. "The ring must turn to stone when he does. I see it happen with Grace all the time."

"Yeah, well, maybe Grace is special or maybe Chastain is. But I saw it with my own eyes—the ring didn't turn to stone. It was right there. That's why I thought about grabbing it. Because it was very noticeable against his stone hand."

"It's got to be because of what it is," I say. "Gargoyles are immune to all but the most ancient magic. Maybe the God Stone is immune to *all* magic—even the ability to shift."

"Well, then, let's do it again," Jaxon suggests. "Flint can shoot fire at him, the rest of you can create an even bigger distraction than the fire, and Hudson or I can fade to him and take the ring. We can be there and back in less than a second, and Chastain can't shift that fast."

"Good plan," Flint deadpans. "Except I'm pretty sure Chastain isn't letting me within a hundred yards of him right now. He knows something is up."

They all continue to toss more ideas back and forth, but I have the kernel of my own idea forming. The kind that's so bad, it might work.

"Chastain isn't the only person who can make himself turn to stone," I say, and everyone grows silent. Even Isadora.

Hudson turns to face me, and I'm not even a little surprised he's already guessed what I plan to do. "Do you think you can do it?"

I bite my lip. "I'll have to get close, and there's only one way I can think to do that…"

His gaze holds mine for a beat, and then his eyebrows shoot up as he figures out what I'm trying not to say in front of Isadora. It's bad enough she insists on being involved in every discussion to secure the God Stone, but that doesn't mean I have any intention of giving away my ultimate plans after that.

Instead, I watch as Hudson turns to stare off into the distant sea, all the angles playing out in his quick mind. He's thinking through each advantage—and flaw—of my plan, exactly like I need him to. "And what if you piss off a certain God of Time?"

I swallow. "My people will survive anything he does," I say cryptically, not wanting to say more in front of Isadora. "I think he has a soft spot for the Bloodletter, so I think he will for me, too. At least I hope so."

When our eyes meet again, he simply says, "Grace Foster, you are a total badass."

Pandemonium breaks out as everyone starts asking what I plan to do, but neither Hudson nor I reply. Hudson because he wants me to take all the credit—I know him. But I don't want any credit for being willing to risk the lives of every gargoyle in existence.

I only hope the Army will one day forgive me.

91

Below the Age of Descent

Hudson and I decide to go back to our room to pack while everyone else heads to lunch. I casually mentioned I might want a brief nap, and Hudson being Hudson, he wanted to make sure I take it. But we've got about two hours before the afternoon training sessions, and I want to use that time to try to reach my mate, because something isn't right.

As I try to figure out a way to get him to talk to me, he walks around the room, grabbing up an extra T-shirt and shoving it into his knapsack.

I can tell by his sharp movements, by the way he's avoiding eye contact and the set of his jaw, that he both wants to be near me and he doesn't. He's got some sort of internal battle going on, and I'm afraid I know what it is.

Hudson is my mate. He needs to be near me, *wants* to be near me, just as much as I crave having him next to me. But at the same time, he knows he can't hide from me and is currently dreading the fact that I'm going to try to make him open up. He's afraid that I'll crash through his walls before the mortar he's so carefully laid has set, leaving him vulnerable against the Skeleton Army tonight.

So I don't do that.

After all, there's more than one way to get on the other side of a wall. Even one as high and strong as Hudson is currently building.

Stooping down to pick up a tank top of my own, I don't even glance at him as I ask, "Do you think Izzy really is a thousand years old?"

Hudson stops moving completely, and when I glance at him out of the corner of my eye, it's to find him standing stock-still, his hand paused in midair in the act of reaching for a pair of drying socks.

Good. I've surprised him.

It only lasts a second before he grabs the socks, but it's enough to let me know I'm on the right track. "She's got no reason to lie," he answers after a moment.

"Still, do vampires really age that slowly?" I plop down on the edge of the bed and pretend to be absorbed in folding my shirt. "Will you still look this young in a thousand years, too?" It's not something I've ever considered, but then I've never had to before. Now, all I can think about is him looking nineteen forever. "Oh God, what if I'm a wrinkled mess in a hundred years and you still look good enough to eat?" I groan, and I don't even have to fake my alarm. It's a terrible, terrible thought.

Hudson shoots me an *are you serious right now* look. "First off, if you ever do get wrinkles, they'll be as beautiful to me as your curls." He shakes his head and sits down on the bed next to me. "Secondly, born vampires are just as susceptible to the signs of aging as any species, albeit on a much slower basis."

It's a good answer, and I should probably be swooning a little. But I'm too distracted by the heat from his thigh. He's sitting so close to me, and yet we're not touching—another sign that he's worried I'm going to try to get through his defenses. I want to touch him so badly, but I'm playing the long game here. So instead of giving in to the itch in my fingers to reach for him, I instead scooch my butt backward until I can lay my head on my pillow.

"So then how could she be a thousand years old and still look sixteen?" I ask.

Hudson rubs a hand over the stubble on his jaw before answering, "At a guess, I would say our shite father kept her locked in a bloody crypt for most of her life."

I gasp, horrified at the very idea of some poor child being locked in a crypt for what must have felt like eternity—even if that child is Isadora. "But—but you said the elixir stops working over time, right?"

He scoots up the bed until he's laying down next to me. I start to think I'm making progress until he crosses his arms over his chest, being careful to keep at least a foot between us even now.

"There are stories of vampires being kept under for hundreds of years, actually." His voice is thoughtful, his eyes far away. "It's true the elixir stops working the more often you use it, but if he didn't awaken her at all, I guess in theory she would have just stayed in stasis. We don't age in stasis."

It still sounds horrible, but then that's the point, isn't it? My poor mate has been tortured pretty much his entire life. "What was the whole process called again?" I coax him to continue. "Descending?"

"Descent," he corrects. "When we turn five, there's a huge celebration. That's when we reach the Age of Descent. I still remember the festival my father threw for me. At the time, I couldn't imagine there being a bigger celebration anywhere, ever."

His breathing is even now, steady. I have a million questions, but I don't ask them. I know there is a story here, and I think Hudson wants to tell me. I just have to be patient, let him find his own way to it.

"Father had the cooks slaughter fifty pigs for the festival and make about a thousand different pies. The castle was filled with so many people that it was overflowing, and they were all dressed in their finest gowns and waistcoats. I climbed to the tallest tower at one point, just to count the number of carriages that arrived." He chuckles. "Of course, what I was really counting were the number of presents I would receive that day, as every guest brought one."

I smile, trying to imagine Hudson as a small child—innocent and maybe even happy. "Did you wear your hair in a pompadour even back then?" I tease.

He snort laughs. "Hardly. I know it's shocking, but I was *difficult* in my early years."

"*So* shocking," I agree.

He reaches up and tugs thoughtlessly at a few of the locks resting on his forehead. I don't even think he realizes what he's doing. "My hair was always a bit long and wild back then."

"Seriously?" I flip onto my side and rest my head on my hand as I grin at him. "If you've been keeping a portrait from me of you looking like a young Jason Momoa, I will never forgive you."

He's smiling when he rolls to face me. "Is this when you ask me to get into some kinky role-playing? I warn you, I'd make a terrible Aquaman."

Thinking of his long, lean body in Aquaman's wet suit makes me want to disagree. "Later. Definitely later," I tease. "So you were five when? Like the 1800s?"

I know both he and Jaxon have mentioned being hundreds of years old at times, but I've never thought of either of them as more than eighteen or nineteen. At least not until I start to do the math in my head... "Oh my God, am I, like, your seven thousandth girlfriend?"

"More like my eight thousandth," he deadpans, then rolls his eyes when I squawk. "Seriously, woman, that would be a new girlfriend every ten days. Who's got time for that?"

"Oh, I'm pretty sure you'd make time," I answer archly.

But he just shakes his head, then reaches out to run a finger down my cheek. The feel of his skin against mine sends little shivers of excitement along my spine, partly because I love the way he feels and partly because he breached the self-imposed distance he's been keeping between us. "Besides," he adds, "you're forgetting I spent most of my life in stasis. Although I will admit, I do feel the passage of all that time."

"What does that mean?" I ask, because something tells me I need to know.

But then he drops his hand, turning to his side to stare at the ceiling, and I want to kick myself for pushing him too far.

Silence has turned the air still and cold around us before he finally answers, "How do you mark time passing in your life? You remember the first day this came out or this movie was big or people wore this style of clothing, right?" I nod. "Well, it's the same for me. I may have only experienced those times for a day every month, but I remember riding in a carriage to travel to the market. I remember seeing my first car and my first computer. I remember all sorts of inventions and trends."

He says it so casually, like living through all that was nothing. Or worse, like waking up every month to realize everyone else continued living their lives while his was stuck is a totally normal thing. Like it's okay he was just the boy shoved back in a dark box until it was time to show him the next thing he would miss out on.

My heart cracks wide open at the thought, the pain of what he must have suffered squeezing the breath from my lungs. I want to reach out and scoop him up in my arms, want to hold him close and promise that nothing bad is ever going to happen to him again.

But I can't promise that, especially not right now. And he wouldn't let me anyway, considering I can't even touch him at the moment. If I push too hard, I know he'll stop talking.

So I change the subject instead. "I'm still trying to figure Isadora out—or should I say *Izzy*? She seems to love it when Chastain calls her that."

"You noticed that, too, eh?" he asks.

"It's hard to miss how she literally preens under his attention," I say, but there's no judgment. If I were raised by Cyrus, I can only imagine the daddy issues I'd have. "So you think Cyrus just kept her in stasis all that time?"

Hudson rolls onto his back again. "No." He pauses. "She said he kept waking her, but also—"

"Yes?" I ask and hold my breath. There's something Hudson doesn't want to tell me, but I'm willing to wait patiently until he does—even if it kills me. After a minute, he lets out a long sigh.

"She has two abilities," he says, as though that explains it all. "Two very strong abilities. She's a Soul Siphon *and* she can rematerialize anything I disintegrate."

"What does her having two abilities have to do with Cyrus waking her?" I ask.

Softly, so softly I'm not sure I hear the words, he whispers, "Because that's what he did to me."

92

Tomb of Doom

I can't move. I can't think. I'm not even sure I take a breath. I knew from the discussion in the crypt room that Cyrus woke Hudson more often than Jaxon, but I didn't know the reason was to give him more abilities. It seems like a shit thing to do to your kid, but Cyrus isn't exactly a loving parent. Still, something doesn't quite add up...

"If the elixir stops working after a while, then how could waking you more frequently give you more abilities?" I ask.

"Not all of the elixir stops working," he says. "Just the sleeping-potion half."

That's right. I remember him saying that earlier, but only now does it start to make a horrible, horrible kind of sense. "And it's the other half of the elixir that gives you your abilities?"

"Yeah." His voice is clipped again, which tells me that no matter how awful I think his early life was, it was actually so much worse.

I want to hug him so badly, but if I do, I'll never get to the bottom of what's going on. It will be a Band-Aid instead of a cure, and that's the last thing I want right now. So I swallow back my outrage and my pain and ask, "If Izzy has two abilities, then she was given more elixir than Jaxon. At some point, the sleeping-potion part stopped working, but she's one thousand years old..."

My mind is racing, trying to figure out exactly what this means. "And she hasn't aged more than sixteen years, so that means she was in stasis for most of that time..."

I trail off, horror washing over me that the most awful, most horrible, most terrible thing in the world that was done to Hudson—was done to Izzy even longer. No wonder she's so fucked-up.

That doesn't mean I'm close to forgiving her for murdering Liam or siphoning the magic from any of the other students, but, well, I guess I'm gaining a little sympathy for the devil.

I don't say anything for a while, and neither does he. Instead, we lay there, listening to each other breathe, processing what all of this could mean.

"Do you think Izzy could have more than *two* abilities?" I finally ask. "I mean, if more elixir equals more abilities, and she was kept in Descent for a thousand years..."

"Probably. It certainly explains her ability to siphon souls," he answers.

"How?" I ask, not sure how being in stasis longer has anything to do with an ability to steal souls. But then Hudson swallows hard, and I know whatever it is, whatever the connection he sees—I'm not going to like it.

"I started to go mad in there." He whispers the words like they're his greatest shame, and it breaks my heart all over again.

"Who wouldn't?" I whisper back, afraid to break this tenuous moment. "The fact that you managed to make it out and still be so strong and kind and brilliant is the shocker, Hudson, not the fact that you nearly lost your mind."

He shakes his head like he doesn't—or can't—believe me. "It wasn't like that."

"It was exactly like that," I counter and try to get the picture of Hudson trapped under a thousand pounds of stone out of my head. It doesn't work.

The picture of my mate suffering in the dark will be with me every day—every second—until I die.

He shrugs. "Either way...I did it myself."

"Did what?"

"Gave myself a second power." He clears his throat, blows out a long breath. "I didn't mean to. I wasn't trying to be more powerful. I was just—"

His voice breaks, so he clears his throat again. Shoves a hand through his hair. Looks straight up at the ceiling without blinking.

"I just wanted to not be there anymore. I wanted to be anything or anywhere but trapped in that tomb where every hour felt like an eternity." He gives a little half-hearted laugh. "So I did it. One day, I just disintegrated myself. Being dust, being nothing, was so much better than being an animal in my father's cage."

Oh my God. Tears bloom in my eyes, but I push them back down. Now isn't the time for them, even though I'm weeping all the way to my soul. "You just..."

"Disappeared," he tells me, snapping his fingers. Instantly, the book on the bedside table turns to dust. "For a few minutes, then for a few hours, and eventually for a few days. I just ceased to exist. It was the most peace I'd ever known. Somehow, though, I would always end up coming back together again. The first time I came back, I cried for hours."

I clench my teeth and my fists, press my lips together as tightly as I can. And still a sob breaks through the rigid control I'm keeping on myself. But how can

I not sob? Little boy Hudson *cried* because he couldn't stay dust.

Hudson pulls back, alarmed. "Grace, it's o—"

"Don't you dare tell me it's okay," I whisper, and now the tears are coming fast and furious. "Torturing a child is not okay. Leaving you to go insane is not okay. Making you wish for death—" My voice breaks. "It's not okay. It will never be okay. It will never be—"

I break off as a million different thoughts run through my head, all of them centered on destroying Cyrus, just obliterating him off the face of the earth. Except death is too good for him. Everything is too good for him except, maybe, being trapped in the dark for a thousand years.

He did this to his son—his *son*—because he wanted him to be a weapon. No, not just his son. He did it to his *daughter*, too, and for much, much longer. For the first time, I understand why Delilah sent Jaxon to the Bloodletter.

"Please don't cry." Hudson looks panicked, flipping onto his side again to face me. "I didn't tell you this to hurt you—"

"Hurt me? You're not hurting me, Hudson," I say. "You're giving me the resolve I need to do *anything* to make that bastard pay."

He looks blank for a second, like he can't wrap his head around what I'm saying. Like he's so disassociated from what happened to him that he can't understand why someone who loves him would be enraged on his behalf. Then again, maybe no one ever has been before.

"I don't want you to cry about something that happened a long time ago—"

"Thirteen years," I say, swiping at the tears on my cheeks with my forearm.

"What?"

"It stopped happening thirteen years ago, right? You were buried, off and on, from the time you were five until thirteen years ago. Which is in my freaking lifetime, so don't pull that whole *it happened a long time ago* bullshit on me."

He looks shocked, but then he laughs for the first time since the Skeleton Army came, and the weight resting on my shoulders lessens just the tiniest bit, enough for me to gain control of my tears at least. "There's my Grace, kicking my ass even when she's crying for me."

"Nice." I roll my eyes, then focus on what he hasn't told me yet. "So you went from disintegrating yourself to disintegrating other things?"

"Yes. And I found when I disintegrated other things, it wasn't like when I did it to myself. They stayed gone."

"Like the tomb? Please tell me you disintegrated that damn tomb so you weren't trapped in it anymore."

"I bloody well tried." He grins, and this time it almost reaches his eyes. "The fooking thing wouldn't disintegrate. Anything else, I could destroy. But not that. I still don't know why."

"Because your father is a fucking monster who probably had a spell put on it once he realized what you could do," I say. "The jackass."

"Where were you two hundred years ago?" he teases.

"Believe me, I'm asking myself the very same question," I shoot back, only I'm not kidding. How the hell could Delilah have let her husband do this to her son? How could anyone in the Court let him do such a horrible thing to a child? It boggles the mind.

He laughs, but when I don't laugh with him, his face turns serious. "You know I'm okay, right?"

"Um, first of all, you're better than okay," I tell him. "Secondly, you turned out better than anyone has the right to expect. And thirdly, neither of those things makes me want to destroy your father any less."

He raises a brow. "To be fair, you've wanted to destroy him for a while."

"Yeah, well, that's nothing compared to how I feel about the wanker now." Just the idea of seeing him, of handing him the God Stone so he can keep working on his disgusting, morally bankrupt plan, makes me see all the shades of red.

"Do you ever wonder what your life would be like if you hadn't ended up in the middle of this mess?" Hudson asks out of the blue.

"What do you mean?"

"If your parents hadn't been murdered. If you'd gotten to graduate high school in San Diego. If you were heading off to college in August instead of trying to figure out how to free your people so you can ascend the gargoyle throne. You know, all the normal stuff you left behind when you got to Katmere Academy."

"I don't, actually," I answer, getting up so I can walk into the bathroom and splash some water on my tearstained face.

"Seriously?" he asks from where he's now leaning against the bathroom doorframe. "You never wonder?"

"I don't let myself think about it." I grab the length of linen that functions as a towel and dry my face.

"Because it hurts?" he asks, watching me closely.

Part of me wants to tell him to leave it alone, that I obviously don't want to talk about this. But considering what I just put him through, it only seems fair that I answer a few of his questions as well.

"Because I'm angry, and I'm trying really hard not to be."

"At me?" he asks.

"Why would I be angry at you?" I can't keep the shock out of my voice.

He shrugs. "Because if Lia hadn't brought me back—"

What? Does he seriously think I'd imagine the world a better place without Hudson Vega in it? Which makes me consider something else. "Were you ever really dead?"

He looks surprised by the question, but already I can see the truth in his eyes.

"You weren't, were you?" I ask. "You just disintegrated yourself."

"It was that or kill Jaxon, and there's no way I was going to do that. He's my baby brother. My happiest childhood memories are when he was allowed to play with me the one day of the month I was awoken. Well, until he reached his own Age of Descent."

I let that image soak in before asking, "So where did you go for that time? What did you do?"

"Honestly, it was just like those moments in the tomb. It was peaceful. No pain. No worries. Just nothing for that brief moment in time."

"Brief?" I ask. "You were dead for a *year*."

"It didn't feel like it. But time passes differently in different dimensions." When I look confused, he glances outside. "Like here. The first time you came to the frozen Court, you said it felt like you were here for thirty minutes, but back at Katmere it was only a few minutes. We've been here for three days now, but it's probably not three days back at the Vampire Court. So who knows how long it was for me? I just know it didn't feel long."

His voice is relaxed when he talks about the different nature of time, but there's something deep in his eyes that makes me think there's more to the story than he's willing to say.

And that's when something shocking pops into my head, so shocking, in fact, that at first I can't even get my mind around it. But now that it's there, I have to know. I have to ask.

"Hudson." He looks at me with raised brows and I try to swallow, but in the space from one breath to the next, my mouth has become the Sahara. "Those four months, when we were frozen together...was it really four months? Or was it longer?"

For what feels like forever, he doesn't answer. He just holds my gaze, and suddenly I can see thousands of days—of experiences—in his eyes. Oh my God.

"Hudson—"

"It doesn't matter," he answers and turns and walks away—taking a huge piece of my heart with him.

93

Drink Me, Baby,
One More Time

"**I**'m okay," he tells me when I follow after him, even though I know he's not.

"You're not," I challenge, turning him around so I can see his face. "You're worn out and hungry." I tilt my head so he has a clear path to my vein. "You need to feed."

His response is instantaneous—a growl, low and deep in the back of his throat—and I brace myself for the feel of his fangs sinking through my skin. And wait. And wait. And wait.

"What's wrong?" I finally ask. "Why won't you feed from me?"

"I can't," he says, his voice low and rough like the words were torn from his body.

In a blink, he's on the other side of the room, as far from me as he can get, hands shoved deep in his pockets.

"You can't what?" I demand. "Feed from your mate?"

I get that he's trying to wall up his emotions, that he thinks he needs to do that to survive what might be asked of him again tonight, but I also know he's going to need his strength for the coming battle. I'm not willing to let him put his safety at risk because he's too damn stubborn to feed.

"You *need* to feed, Hudson," I repeat, pushing him.

"I know what I need," he snaps back. "And it's not that. It's not you."

His words hit like a match to gasoline, and I go up in flames. Anger rips through me, has me all but leaping across the room to get in his face. "What exactly does that mean?" I demand. "You don't need me?"

"You know what I mean, Grace." He shoves a weary hand through his hair, like my little fit is taking too much of his energy. Which somehow just pisses me off more. Partly because this isn't Hudson—not my Hudson, the guy who has been my partner, my mate, for longer even than I was willing to admit. And partly because I can see right through him.

He's hurting, and he wants me to leave him alone. Because I won't, he's lashing out—to protect himself and, in some skewed, fucked-up way, to protect me.

But he's not protecting either of us by refusing to feed, by refusing to let me get close to him. He's just breaking us apart, and I am not okay with that. We've fought too long and too hard to be together. There's no way I'm going to let him shatter us to pieces just because he's too much of a guy to tell me what's hurting him.

Fuck that.

"You don't need me?" I repeat again. Only this time, I don't get in his face. Instead, I back away just enough that he can see me—see all of me. And then I slip my shirt over my head.

"What are you doing?" he asks hoarsely.

"What does it look like I'm doing?" I rest my hand on my collarbone, trail a lazy finger back and forth across my pulse point. "I'm getting comfortable."

"Getting—" He breaks off, his jaw working furiously. But his eyes—those beautiful, depthless eyes of his—are locked on my throat. Exactly where I want them.

"Stop it, Grace."

"Stop what?" I ask, brows arched. And yes, I'm provoking him. But he deserves it. He doesn't get to abuse himself and expect me to sit by and watch it. That's not going to happen, not now. Not ever. And he sure as hell doesn't get to snap and snarl at me while he's doing it.

To prove it to him, and to myself, I tilt my head back a little, exposing my jugular to him even as I continue to stroke my fingers up and down my throat.

"Damn it—" He lets out a frustrated growl, but his eyes never leave my throat. "You don't know what you're asking."

"I know exactly what I'm asking," I growl back, stalking closer to him. "I know exactly what I want."

He backs away, eyes wide, and that's when I know I've got him. Because little ol' me has big, bad Hudson Vega on the run.

I'd be lying if I said I didn't like it.

"Please, Grace. I don't want to hurt you."

I reach up and pull my hair down, letting the curls tumble over my shoulders and down my back. The scent of them—of me—fills the air between us.

Hudson's throat works even as his fangs descend, the sexy tips of them scraping against his lower lip.

My heartbeat kicks up, and I know he can hear it. More, I know he can see it in the pulse point throbbing beneath my finger. He's so close to breaking that I can feel it, feel him. So I walk closer, closer, closer, forcing him to back up until he's pinned between the wall and me.

Then I pull my hair out of the way, tilt my head to the side, and wait for him to snap.

It takes a second, maybe two. And then he's on me, his hands tangling in my hair as he pulls me against him.

His mouth slams down on mine, taking, devouring, destroying me in one slide of his fangs against my lip, one quick slide of his tongue against my own.

Then he's yanking my head back with a growl, baring my throat to his starving eyes.

"Do it," I tell him, my body erupting with want, with need, with a craving that I know will never go away. "Do it, do it, do it."

He snarls then, a sound so low and vicious that it should chill my blood. Instead it only makes me hotter and I reach up, sliding my hands into his hair. "Do it," I whisper one more time.

For one second, he looks at me with eyes that are as hot and angry and hurting as I am. And then he strikes like lightning.

I gasp as his fangs strike home, slicing through skin to the vein beneath.

For one moment there is pain, red-hot and sizzling, but the moment Hudson starts to drink, it vanishes like so much mist. In its place is a riot of sensation so powerful that it all but tears me apart.

Ecstasy, aching, joy, fury, fever, ice. And need. So much need that I nearly drown in it as it crashes over me, around me, through me.

Need for my mate.

Need for Hudson.

Need for all the power and love that rages between us even in the difficult times.

Hudson groans then, sinks deeper, and another wave of sensation rolls over me.

This one doesn't just break around me. It pulls me under, deeper and deeper and deeper until everything that I am, everything that I'll ever want, is tied up with Hudson. My Hudson.

I reach for him then, my hands clutching at his shirt, my body arching into his. I can still taste his anger, can still feel the rigid strength of it in the body pressed so tightly to mine.

But I don't fight it. Instead, I give in to it—and in to him.

I give myself to Hudson, to his darkness and his light. To the pain that lives inside him and the emotions shredding him from the inside out. I surrender to it all and as I start to sink, I pray that it's enough to bring him back to me. That it's enough to bring him back to us.

Searching for a State of Grace

Darkness is welling up around me when Hudson finally pulls away.

"Are you all right?" he demands, his eyes hot with anger and the bloodlust that hasn't yet subsided.

"Of course I am." I reach for him again, but he backs away from me. The rejection cuts like a blade, wounding me and stoking a whole new anger at the same time.

"I shouldn't have taken so much. I'm sorry. I didn't mean to hurt you."

"Why do you always do that?" I demand. "Why do you always assume that you've hurt me? You think I won't tell you if you do? What does that say about your trust in me?"

"It's not you I don't trust, Grace."

"Don't I know it," I snarl. "But you need to stop being so afraid that you're going to hurt me."

His gaze turns cold, a mental wall slamming down—to keep me out or him in, I'm not sure even he knows. "You don't know what I need, Grace."

I throw my arms wide. "Maybe that's because you won't tell me!" I place my hands on my hips, narrow my eyes on him as I reach for my tank top and put it on. "Did you ever think if you stop trying to block out the pain you're in, maybe if you share it, we can get through it? Together?"

He laughs, but there's no humor in it. "*We* aren't getting through this. I told you what using my gift does to me. I begged you to take it away, but you refused. So, no, there's no getting through this, and there's definitely no getting around it."

"Getting around what?" I demand, my anger ramping up all over again. "You say shit like that, but then you never explain. Either tell me or don't, but stop acting like I'm an idiot because I don't know what you won't tell me."

"I'm trying to protect you—" he starts, but I cut him off with a glare.

"When have I ever asked you to protect me? I'm your mate, which means we're partners. And partners share things, even the bad things. So spill it, will you?"

He doesn't spill it, at least not at first. Instead, he stands there, eyes locked with mine, and breathes. Just breathes. It's such an un-Hudson-like thing to do that it throws me, until I figure out that he's as close to a panic attack as I have ever seen him.

Before I can recover from that realization, he takes one more deep breath, then slays me with his next words. "Every time I disintegrate someone, they take a piece of my *soul* with them."

It's the last thing I expect to hear, and yet it isn't totally unexpected. Not when his comment about Izzy becoming a Soul Siphon circles my mind, aligning with the information he just gave me. Oh my God. Their biggest gifts—the ones that only come from unrelenting torture—come from breaking their own souls.

Hudson knows how to reach inside people to disintegrate them because it's second nature for him, to seek out his own soul and disintegrate it. And what about Izzy? Did she lose her soul in that crypt after a millennium? Did she have to instinctively learn to steal others' souls to try to find her own? It's a horrible thought, but then everything about this is horrible.

Still, tragic as it all is, it convinces me that not pushing Hudson earlier was the wrong tactic for me to take. After what he's been through, he's never going to bring that wall down voluntarily. It is going to take a sledgehammer to do it. Which means it's not coming down without a fight. I don't want to hurt him, but I can't leave him like this. Not when it means he'll just keep hurting himself.

"No one is stealing your soul, Hudson. You're *letting* them take it."

His eyebrows nearly hit his hairline before slashing down in fury. "You fooking think I want to feel like this? You fooking think I wouldn't give *anything* to not lose you again?"

"What makes you think you're going to lose me?" I ask as everything becomes a little clearer.

"How could I not?" he shoots back. "Look at me. Look at what I am. Look at what I've done."

"I'm looking at you. And I understand you feel—" I start to say, but Hudson is in my face in a blink.

"No. You don't get to tell me what I feel." His voice is deadly quiet. "*How* I feel." His breaths are coming fast now. "You have no idea how much pain I'm in. You can't take the death of your parents and think you have an *ounce* of understanding. Multiply that times five thousand and you still wouldn't get close."

"Just because my suffering isn't from the worst horror possible doesn't mean it feels any less than yours, Hudson," I snap back. "Suffering isn't a competition."

"You know what your problem is, Grace?" he sneers. "You think I'm just some broken bird you're going to nurse back to health, don't you? You think you'll just hold me and rock me and love me and every broken piece of me will eventually heal. But what if I'm too broken? Did you ever think of that? Because eventually, they're going to take so much of my soul that there won't be enough left to fix."

His words hit me like an anvil, but I don't let him see it. I can't. Instead, I arch one eyebrow at him and force myself to push at another brick in his wall. "That is such bullshit."

He staggers back like I struck him. "What did you say?"

I get in his face, poking his chest with my finger to emphasize each word. "I said. That. Is. Such. Bullshit." I hold his gaze. "You will never be too broken for me to love you."

"How could you possibly know that?" he snaps.

"Because," I say, moving closer, stepping right up against him, "you forget I can see our mating-bond string. My soul"—I tap a finger against my chest, then move it to tap his—"attached to your soul. And it is as strong as ever, Hudson."

"You don't know that. You can't know that." He shakes his head, and there's such desperation in his eyes that it breaks my heart all over again. He wants to believe, but it hurts too much. I understand that better than most. But I believe in him, and I believe in us. It's time that he believes, too.

"I wish you could see it," I whisper. "It's the most beautiful blue I've ever seen—as deep and dark and rich as your eyes. And it glows, Hudson. It glows with health, with power, with the strength of everything we are and everything we can be. You just have to trust it. You just have to trust me."

And there it is, the first brick falling. I see it in his eyes, feel it in the way his body yearns for mine.

I squeeze our mating-bond string to show him that I'm right, that it's not just there, it's stronger than ever. "And yes, I *can* tell what you're feeling. And it's not the fear of losing your soul."

Another brick crumbles to the ground.

"It's guilt." I reach up and cup his cheek. "You *give* them a piece of your soul so you don't feel guilty for killing them."

Two more bricks tumble down.

"You want to be destroyed because you think you deserve it."

Another brick falls.

"Because you have the most kind and loving soul I have ever seen." I reach up and cup his other cheek. "And if you didn't, you wouldn't be torturing yourself for their deaths."

A whole chunk of wall hits the ground with a massive *crash*.

"But you need to give yourself some grace, Hudson. This is war, and there will always be casualties." Tears well in my eyes as I hold his turbulent blue gaze. "Don't let *us* become one of those casualties."

95

Some Like It
Hot—Really Hot

Hudson makes a sound deep in his throat. "Don't," he whispers. "Don't do this to me."

"All I'm doing is loving you," I whisper right back. And this time when I reach for him, he doesn't back away.

But he doesn't hold me back, either. He's too hurt, too broken.

"I love you, Hudson," I whisper again, pressing soft, sweet kisses into his palm, his fingers, the back of his hand.

He makes another tortured sound that breaks me a little, too. To heal us both, I stand on tiptoes and press my mouth to his. Softly. Sweetly. Like we're two regular people who have regular lives and all the time in the world.

It takes a moment, but eventually his lips start moving against mine. Heat stirs inside me, but not the usual kind. Not the sizzle that turns my blood to fire and my mind into a red haze.

No, this heat is softer, kinder, gentler, and it feels good after everything we've just been through. Like it's coating the broken places inside me too and smoothing away the jagged edges.

"Grace." When he says my name this time, it is a little more than a whisper and a little less than a prayer, as he finally yields and wraps his arms around me.

I lean into him, pressing kisses along his collarbone and reveling in the warm amber scent of him. The luxurious taste of him.

He groans deep in his throat, and it's his turn to kiss me.

Relief sweeps through me at the brush of his lips on mine—so warm, so sweet, so familiar. This is Hudson, my Hudson, and having him with me, really with me, for the first time in far too long feels more profound than I could have imagined. And when he licks his way across my lips and I open for him, it's like coming home.

I gasp and wind myself around him, desperate to get as close to him as I can. Desperate to feel all of him in all the ways I possibly can.

I slide my hands along his back, tugging his shirt up so that I can feel the warmth of his skin beneath my palms. He shivers a little as I dance my fingertips up his spine, but that just makes this moment sweeter. Because he's not hiding from me any longer. He's in this with me and that's all that matters. The rest will take care of itself.

"I love you," I whisper against his lips, and he sighs, his whole body trembling against mine.

He deepens our kiss, our tongues sliding together, and just like that, my body is an inferno, the tip of his fang as it coasts along my skin the match that sets me ablaze.

Hudson shifts then, sliding my tank top off before moving us toward the bed in a spin that has my heart jumping just a little. He strips off his own shirt next, then lowers me down to the mattress and stretches out on top of me.

"I love you," I tell him as our eyes meet once more.

He smiles then. It's just a small smile, a little upturn of his lips, but it's real and honest and it feels so good to witness it. Because while I can still see the pain lingering in the depths of his eyes, I can see the love now, too. And the joy.

The same joy takes flight inside me as I roll him over and straddle his hips.

He lifts a brow at me, that little smile turning into the wicked grin I know so well.

It makes our fight worth it—makes everything worth it—because here, in this moment, his wall is nothing but rubble at our feet.

It's that thought that has me sliding a hand down his chest.

That thought that has me pressing kisses to his neck, his shoulders, his chest.

And that thought that has me feeling for the first time in what seems like an eternity that everything is going to be all right. Even before Hudson rolls me back over and shows me that, right here, right now, he feels exactly the same way.

96

Talk About a Dead Ringer

W e're a couple of minutes late by the time we get to the training field, Hudson hanging under a tree in the shade since he'd finally fed, and I hang out near one of the benches and pretend I don't feel Chastain's watchful—and disdainful—gaze on me the whole time. Instead, I take a deep breath and focus on getting my head right. This needs to work, which means I need to not mess it up.

Which is why I don't give myself any more time to get in my head. The second the other gargoyles make it back to the circle—along with the rest of my friends—I walk up to Chastain, who is standing in the center of it.

"I challenge you for the ring," I tell him quietly but firmly. My plan doesn't require besting Chastain and winning the ring. I'm not that delusional. But I *do* need him to accept the challenge.

He doesn't even bother to look up at me—big surprise. Just twists his mouth into a smirk that somehow makes him seem like an even bigger asshole than usual. And answers, "I already told you how I feel about challenges from the likes of you."

The disdain in his voice is meant to hurt me, but all it does is piss me off. "Yes, well, I haven't had a chance to tell you how I feel about disrespect from the likes of you," I snap back.

Chastain doesn't say anything, but his eyes jerk up and go wide for a moment before narrowing to slits. I keep my gaze focused on him, but I can feel everyone around us leaning in, ears perked and bodies poised for whatever comes next.

"It's time you get to see just what someone *worthy*"—I inject even more contempt into the word than he used yesterday—"is capable of."

I wait for him to refuse, prepare to force him into the challenge if I have to, but before either of us can do anything, Artelya grabs a sword and shield and steps into the training circle. "I am ready for the challenge."

I ignore her, because she is not the one I want to fight. The one I *have* to fight for our plan to work.

"I thank you, Artelya," Chastain says with more formality and respect than he has ever shown me. "But if our *queen* is ready to prove her worthiness to us, then by all means. Let her prove it to me." He says the last with a dismissive wave of his hand that takes my annoyance into hyperdrive.

Who does this guy think he is? I've never done anything to him. I've shown up every day for training and given it my all. I've tried to never run away from any challenge that he presented me with, so what is his deal…? I mean, unless he knows I'm here to take the ring, he has no reason to dislike me.

I don't say anything, though, because Chastain already has his broadsword ready with rage in his eyes. I can tell this is going to hurt like hell, but I don't care. I'm finally getting my chance to fight him, and no matter what happens, I'm getting in some licks.

I start to turn to get a sword, but experience in this Court has taught me never to turn your back on your enemy. So I glance around, trying to figure out what to do, considering I can't walk backward all the way to the wall where the weapons are hanging.

In the end, I don't have to worry about it, because Hudson grabs a sword and fades it out to me.

"Thanks," I whisper, but he's already gone—a trail of smoke in his wake—and making me chuckle. Such a show-off. Then I turn and raise my sword—just in time to block a powerful overhead blow from Chastain. The ass.

I pull my sword back, prepare to attack, and he comes at me again. And this time, the blow nearly brings me to my knees.

97

Way Too Close
a Shave and
a Haircut

Somehow, I manage to stand upright, which I count as a win, considering I just got hammered with a freaking broadsword—which is not anything I thought I would ever say in my lifetime. I swear, if nothing else, we need to unfreeze the Gargoyle Court and get out of this era where everything was settled with a damn sword before my arms actually fall off.

Whirling away on legs that suddenly feel like gelatin, I manage to get my sword around and slam it against the backs of his knees. He stumbles but doesn't fall, and then he's coming at me with his sword raised to deliver a powerful blow.

I duck and spin in the other direction, and the blow meant to take my head off swings right by. Normally, I'd jump back, move away from his sword, and make him come to me. But I'm not trying to best this man at a sword fight— one, because that's pretty much impossible considering he's been training and fighting with a sword for more than a thousand years and I've been using one for...five days. And two, I don't need to fight him. I just need to get close enough to actually touch him.

Originally, I thought it would make more sense to just walk up behind him and brush my hand against his arm or something, but he's always on guard when I'm around, so I didn't think he would let me that close anyway. And also, I need to freeze him in a situation where the other gargoyles won't want to respond to help him before I can get the ring. No one would dare interfere in a challenge fight—or hopefully not before I take what I need.

But Chastain is a cagey opponent, and he swings around, cutting up with the sword and, as I dive out of the way, he ends up taking off about two inches of my hair on the right side—which was so not part of the plan. It's also better than if he took a lot more, but I'm too mad to think about that.

He's playing with me. I know it, he knows it, and honestly, so does everyone in the audience. This man has spent his entire life training with a sword. I'm no match for him. He could have ended this already if he wanted. He just prefers to humiliate me a bit at a time.

He swings again, and I'm pretty sure he's angling for more hair, and that is so not going to happen. So I drop to the ground and roll, which has all the gargoyles watching laughing as they think I'm giving up.

But I'm nowhere close to giving up, because it's as I roll by him, forcing him to turn around instead of jump out of the way, that I reach out a hand and brush it against his leg—at the same time I brush against the edge of the green string deep inside me.

It's a long shot, I know—trying to freeze someone who is already frozen in time—and I keep rolling, just in case it doesn't work. But when I've moved past him and then jumped to my feet, I realize it *did* work. He is solid stone, one leg braced in front of the other, sword on the upswing, face tight in concentration. The ring distinctly *not* stone on his hand.

My heart is pounding in my chest as I realize it worked, that we can take the ring and get out of the Court. I dash toward Chastain, but Eden shouts to my left, and I whirl around.

My stomach sinks as I underestimated what the other gargoyles would do if I froze their leader. They're all rushing toward me—and I have to say, a thousand soldiers bum-rushing the field to get to you is heart-poundingly frightening.

As quickly as I can, I brush against the green string and touch Chastain at the same time.

He finishes his swing as he unfreezes, but then he realizes I'm no longer where I was standing, and the sword sings through the air nowhere near me. He spins around, eyes wide and wild, searching me out.

He demands, "How did you do that?"

A quick glance to the left shows me the other gargoyles are retreating back out of the circle, so I refocus on Chastain. "I told you I had other gifts. You never asked what they were."

"I'm asking now. You can freeze people?"

"I can do a lot of things," I hedge, even as I glance around the room, looking for—

"Then let's fight," he snarls. "And see who can win this challenge."

I can tell he's furious that I got the best of him, furious that some girl he doesn't respect could stop a fight with him in the blink of an eye. But when he lifts his sword in the air and charges at me, I freak out a little bit.

Because I thought this would be over by now. I was sure that if I froze him,

I'd have plenty of time to take the ring—

Chastain swings and I duck, stumbling away. I think about diving around to the opposite side from where he's swinging—if I freeze him again, maybe the Army won't rush the field again because they see he's fine.

This time, when he begins a complicated flip-spin maneuver, I don't even try to dodge him. I turn to solid stone, absorb the massive sword strike, and then shift again, reaching out to grab his wrist and brush against my demigod string.

He freezes, I reach for his hand, and the entire Army pounds across the field toward me again.

Even if I get the ring, I'm not going to make it out of this fight circle alive, I realize.

I quickly dash to the side of him as I brush against my green string again, unfreezing him instantly.

"How come every time I freeze you, the entire Army charges into the circle?" I ask, taunting him. Maybe if I attack his pride, he'll command them to stop reacting. "Are they so afraid their general will be defeated by a girl?"

"The Gargoyle Army is sworn to protect those defenseless, my *queen*," he says, circling me with his sword raised again. "When you take the coward's way, when you freeze me, the entire Army is honor bound to protect me. To call them off would be to change the very essence of what we stand for."

His words cut deeper than any sword.

I want to scream at him that this is war, that not everything is black-and-white—that I am *not* without honor. But I know it will do no good. Chastain already made up his mind about me, made it up within minutes of being introduced, in fact. I'd been weighed and found desperately wanting.

And I'll be honest, I'm just so over it.

He's left me no option but to hope I can throw a Hail Mary and not anger a god.

I send up a silent prayer that Jikan won't notice what I'm about to do. He didn't seem to mind that I froze us in the Vampire Court to come here. Surely freezing a few more people for a minute—maybe less if I can get to the ring fast enough—won't show up on his radar. I mean, really, he's probably surfing anyway, right?

So I drop low and roll again—as far away from him as I can.

And as I do, I reach deep inside my mind for all the shimmering strings I can find. They are thin and silver and though I've not touched them since the Bloodletter's cave, I wrap my arm around them all and pull them against my chest as tightly as I can—just as I brush against my green string.

Moments later, every gargoyle on the training field freezes.

Now all I have to do is grab the ring from Chastain's hand and unfreeze them as we leave the Court. I dash to Chastain, shouting over my shoulder at my friends, "Get ready! We're going to have to leave fast, as soon as I get the ring!"

I reach Chastain's side in a blink, my hand already reaching for his finger, when a loud thunderclap jerks me around.

And just like that, the God of Time appears.

And he does not look happy.

98

Time and Tide Wait for No Man... Or Do They?

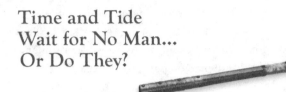

The vacation in Hawaii must be over, because the board shorts and flippers are long gone.

Instead, Jikan is dressed to the nine hundreds in a fully decked-out tuxedo—and not just any tuxedo. No, this suit is one only the God of Time could pull off, even though I don't have a clue how he's doing it.

Made of rich maroon velvet overlaid with a gold brocade pattern, it *should* scream Las Vegas and a Night of a Thousand Showgirls. But it doesn't. Somehow it looks like a million bucks, maybe more, and Jikan looks even better.

Maybe it's how well the suit is cut and tailored.

Maybe it's the perfect accessories in the form of gold globe cuff links, a Patek Philippe watch, and fancy black dress loafers made of crocodile leather with gold ornamentation.

Or maybe it's the fact that it doesn't matter how outrageous the clothes are, they work for the God of Time because he's even more outrageous. From the tips of his silver hair to the tips of his ornamental loafers, the man oozes style and power and—at the moment—anger. So much anger that he can barely get his words out.

"What did you do?" he demands after surveying the field—and the situation—with frigid eyes. "What. Did. You. *Do?*"

Even though I knew this was possible—that Jikan would be very angry—nerves still jangle in the pit of my stomach. "I was—"

"That wasn't a question," he snaps.

I swallow hard before trying again. "I just want to explain—"

He holds a hand up and brings his fingers and thumb together in the universal *shut your trap* gesture. "You need to be very, very quiet right now, or you will not like what I do to you."

He steps away from me and starts pacing around the training circle with slow, deliberate steps, looking at each of the frozen gargoyles in turn.

"I thought I was very explicit during our last conversation," he continues as he circles Chastain, who is frozen with his sword raised.

"You were," I tell him, trying to strike the right balance of remorse and frustration. I might actually have been able to manage it, too, if the nerves weren't throwing me off. Facing him when I accidentally caused a problem was one thing. Facing him now that I've done it on purpose...it's harder than I thought it would be.

"Apparently not," he answers, surveying the field again. "Considering you couldn't follow the simplest of instructions." He bites the words off, so that each syllable sounds, and feels, like a gunshot even as he walks farther onto the field.

This time, he pauses at Artelya, who is frozen in perfect guard formation. He walks all the way around her, studying her closely, though I don't know what he's looking for.

Suddenly, his dark gaze jerks back to mine. "I warned you not to do this."

"I know." I force the words past my dry throat. "But I had no choice. If you'll just let me get Chastain's ring, I will put everything back the way it was and leave immediately. I promise."

"You promised you'd stop messing with time, and look how well that turned out," he thunders. "No, you were warned, and you did what you wanted to do anyway. So egotistical, thinking you know what's best. And for that, the consequences are yours to bear. I am no longer honoring my truce with your grandmother. The Gargoyle Court will be unfrozen in time."

"Please! No!" I cry out, not the least ashamed of the begging. I knew it was possible that he might react this way, but the reality of it, the realization that the Gargoyle Army—my family and some of my friends—might go from waking up and communing over breakfast tomorrow to frozen in stasis, possibly for an eternity, has tears welling up in my eyes and spilling down my cheeks. "It's not their fault. I'm trying to save my people. I swear I'm trying to save everyone. I just need the ring." I sob. "I just need the ring."

My mind is racing as I struggle for what to say that will make him not follow through on his threat and unfreeze the Army. Chastain told me there are gargoyles alive outside the frozen Court in their solid stone form, impervious to the poison in their systems. But still, they won't be *alive* anymore, not really. And I did this to them without a second thought.

"Punish *me*. Please. Not them. Just give the ring to my friends, leave the Gargoyle Court frozen, and you can do anything you want to me," I plead.

Hudson growls, but I have no choice. Jikan is right. I did this. I need to make it right. I need to explain.

"I just needed a moment of time on my side. Just one moment. No more. I was going to unfreeze them, Jikan. I swear."

"But time is not your business," he snarls at me. "Is it?"

"I—"

"Are you the God of Time?" he asks. "No, you're not. I'm the God of Time. You know how I know that?" He pulls the pocket watch he was carrying in the Bloodletter's cave out of his pocket. "Because I'm the one holding this. And this belongs to the God of Time. It's the universal timekeeper—and when I say universal, I mean *universal*—and the official recorder of time from the very beginning.

"I've maintained time beyond this frozen Court because Cassia begged me. And for that woman to beg anyone for anything—it is a sight to behold. But this?" he all but roars as he gestures to everyone frozen around us. "Freezing people in time who are *already* frozen in time? Do you know what happens when you do that? Any guesses?" he demands.

"I—"

"You *tear* time."

"I'm sorry," I tell him. "I didn't know—"

"Of course you didn't know. You don't know anything about any of this and yet you continue to muck about in it like it's your personal playground. That stops here, tonight."

My entire body goes on red alert, because he's either going to smite me right here—and judging from the way he's looking at me, that's a distinct possibility—or he's going to do what I brought him here to do. What I so desperately need him to do.

"You will learn your place, *little demigod*." He says the last like it's the biggest insult he can come up with. "Just remember, you brought this on yourself."

His gaze floats around the frozen Court, at the frozen gargoyles scattered around the training field, and then back at me one last time. "But I am not heartless. I will move your *where* to the new *when* so you can say your goodbyes."

I have absolutely no idea what he means, but I sincerely hope by "say your goodbyes," no one is going to die today. By smiting or poison.

He holds the pocket watch up and winds it back three times. Then snaps his fingers and disappears.

99

The Softer
Side of Stone

As soon as Jikan's gone, I spin around and realize it worked. The Gargoyle Court is a disaster. It looks just like it did when my friends and I landed here after Katmere fell. Broken down, destroyed, nothing but ruins overgrown with weeds that look even sadder in the glow of moonlight. My friends and I are all here in one piece, and we even have our backpacks again. Plus this time, the gargoyles are here, too, and they are no longer frozen.

Chastain stands in the center of the training circle, sword still raised. But then he wraps his arm around his waist as he spins, taking in the crumbling castle, the pain in his stomach, and suddenly he's in the back of my head, yelling, *Fortify!*

All around me, gargoyles turn to stone just as I hoped they would, and that's when it hits me that the command I heard in my head was meant for all the gargoyles. Just like when Alistair used to speak to me—only this time, it covers all the gargoyles.

I turn back to Chastain, expecting him to have turned to stone, too. But he's still alive, though he's clutching his stomach like he's in agony.

"You have to turn to stone," I tell him. "It's the only thing that will save you now."

The first kernel of understanding dawns in his eyes. "You did this?" he whispers, falling to his knees as the poison runs unchecked through his body. "What have you done?"

I drop to the ground beside him.

"Be careful, Grace!" Hudson shouts out, but I ignore him.

"Everyone, please stand back," I beg, my voice shaking. "Let me do this."

I look into Chastain's grimacing face. "You have to turn to stone. It's the only way to save yourself. The only way to save the Army."

He looks around at all the gargoyles locked in stone. "The Army is safe for now."

"But you aren't! You'll die if you don't turn."

"And the Army will die if I do," he tells me. "If I turn to stone, the ring is vulnerable. Anyone can take it. And so I will stand guard for as long as I can."

"And if you don't? You'll die."

"Then that's the way it's going to have to be. It is my duty to protect this ring, and I will do so with my dying breath. I would rather be dead and lose the ring than lose it because I was a coward and saved myself first."

Panic riots through me, turning my lungs to concrete and my stomach to lava. Chastain has to turn to stone. He has to—

I gasp, tears blooming in my eyes as I realize this stubborn man is going to make me take it from his dead hand. The ultimate proof of my cowardice.

"I know you have never liked me, Chastain. You have always found me unworthy," I tell him. "But I need you to trust me. I did this for a reason, one I can't explain right now." My gaze darts to Izzy, and I'm shocked to see what look like tears in her eyes.

"Trust *you*?" he demands. "Someone who would kill her own people to take a powerful ring for herself?"

His words hit as hard as he means them to, but I force myself to ignore that and focus on what's really important here. "I didn't do it for myself!" I cry out, tears running down my cheeks. "And I didn't do it to kill the Army. But you need to trust me. Turn to stone and give me the ring. I promise I will protect my people."

"Protect them?" He waves a hand, coughing. "Look at them. They're stone— and they'll be stone forever now. The *only* way we could survive the poison outside of stasis is within the frozen Court."

"But they weren't alive there, either. Not really. Not the way they want to be—not the way they should be. And eventually, they would have all joined the Skeleton Army, and we both know it. This way, those souls are finally set free, the Skeleton Army is released from their timeless agony. And the surviving gargoyles will one day live again without poison. I just need the ring." I'm breathing fast now as I rush through my plea.

"And you think I should just give it to you?" he spits out. "Only a coward would expect such a thing—but then, I've always known you were a coward. You failed to prove yourself in training, failed to earn the ring when you challenged me, and now you're willing to kill thousands of people—*your* people—just to get a ring that doesn't belong to you. Can you imagine anything more cowardly than that?"

"And you're so closed-minded and set in your ways that you refuse to see what's right in front of you. For God's sake, listen to me before it's too late—"

"You're not worthy of my ear and worse, you're not worthy of being a gargoyle. You're certainly not worthy of being the gargoyle queen. So no, I won't listen to you. And I would rather give this ring to the vampires than let you have it."

His words wound me, but they make me angry, too. Because he's refusing to even give me a chance. Just like everyone else in this whole damn world.

From the minute I showed up at Katmere Academy, I have had to prove myself.

Prove to the students at Katmere that I was worthy enough to live when so many people wanted me dead.

Prove to Cyrus and the rest of the faction leaders that I was powerful enough to hold a spot on the Circle—and claim a position that should have been mine by birthright.

Prove to Jaxon that I'm strong enough and that he doesn't have to coddle me.

Prove to Nuri that I'm worthy of trust and that I can be counted on to help save her people.

Hell, I even had to prove to *myself* that I was strong enough, tough enough, to be a worthy mate for the most powerful vampire alive.

But no more. I am done proving myself to everyone. Yes, I've made mistakes. Yes, I'll make more mistakes. But I've gotten a hell of a lot of things right, too. And I am done apologizing for being late to the party. I *am* the gargoyle queen, and I *will* save my people.

One way or the other, Chastain is going to give the ring to me, whether it's from his cold dead body or not.

Which is why I lean forward and look him straight in his pained, proud eyes. "Then you're going to get your wish," I tell him. "If I don't give the ring to Cyrus, he is going to kill hundreds of kids, not to mention all the teachers and staff, from Katmere Academy. I can't let that happen—more, I won't. I wasn't there when they were taken, but I will damn well be there to make sure they get freed."

He narrows his eyes, as though trying to figure out if I'm lying or not, but I ignore him.

"The Gargoyle Army will not die without the ring, Chastain. You will not live, I know, not truly. But you will not die, either," I try to explain. "But those kids... They will be *tortured* if I don't give Cyrus the ring. And so yes, I chose the lesser of two evils. Allow the Gargoyle Army to continue to not-really-live in the frozen Court or save those kids, and I chose the kids. But that doesn't mean

I have given up on my people. I *will* find a way to cure the Army and I *will* free you. And I don't really care if you believe me or not. Do you want to know why? Because I am your goddamn queen, and you *will* do as I command. Now, *fortify!*"

Chastain coughs, then closes his eyes as pain racks his body. It's hard to watch, knowing that I caused it. Knowing also that he can stop it but he's just too stubborn to do so. "All you had to do from the beginning was tell me the truth. A gargoyle's purpose is to protect those who cannot protect themselves, and children are the most precious of those. I would have given you the ring the first day, even if it meant the death of the Army. A gargoyle will always sacrifice their life to save the defenseless, Grace."

Shame swamps me at his words, because I always looked at him as an obstacle, something to get around. It never occurred to me that he might actually be an ally, that he might be willing to help me save everyone. It makes me feel like a bad person that I didn't even consider it—and more, it makes me feel like a bad gargoyle.

I knew gargoyles were created to protect; I just didn't realize how much of who they are and what they believe is wrapped up in that one mission.

But I'm not the only one to blame here.

"Well, next time, give a lady a chance, will ya?"

He nods, then extends his fingers to make removing the ring easier. And says, "It has been my honor to lead our people, to protect them, for a millennium. And now it is yours."

I take a deep breath, start to tell him that I won't let him down. But it's too late. He's already turned to stone.

100

No Time
Like the
Not-So-Present

Tears burn the back of my throat. It catches me by surprise, considering Chastain and I have done nothing but have issues since the first time we met. Besides the last few moments before he turned to stone, he's never even been nice to me.

Yet, as I kneel here looking up at him, all I can feel is sadness. It was always my plan to take his ring, and I knew it would make the poison start to work again in the frozen Court, but time would be on my side. It would take years to harm them, and I only needed a day to win the Trials and save them. And if I don't win—I am certain one of the first things Cyrus will do once he becomes a god is smite the Army once and for all. They really were fucked any way you looked at it, whether they knew it or not.

And yet, seeing Chastain turned to stone, seeing all of them turned to stone, brings a heaviness to my heart that I wasn't expecting.

Because it's on me to make sure they don't stay this way. On me to make sure I didn't take away the only shot at life they had, no matter how brief. It wasn't the right kind of life, but it was something. And now we're here, at a place where *frozen in time* suddenly doesn't sound so bad.

Turning to stone is natural for a gargoyle. Being trapped that way for eternity...not so much. And if we fail at the Trials, that's exactly what will happen. And worse, I will have sent all my friends to their deaths, too.

Panic wells up in me at the thought. My heart starts to beat too fast, my hands are shaking, and I forget how to breathe. I force my lungs to remember and draw in one slow, shaky breath. I hold it, then blow it back out just as slowly. In, out. In, out. In, out.

And then I start to do addition in my head. Four plus four is eight...

By 256, the roaring in my ears goes away, as does the rapid-fire pounding of my heart. The panic recedes—but it doesn't go away completely, and I'm not sure it will until I find a way to free the Army—but at least I can think past it now.

And as I do, I reach forward with trembling hands and slide the God Stone from Chastain's finger.

The moment I touch it, a feeling of power like nothing I've ever felt before comes over me. When Alistair first passed me the Crown, I felt nothing. A minor burning and itch in my palm, that's all. But that warmth, that electrical charge, is *nothing* compared to what it feels like to touch this ring. Nothing compared to the overwhelming heat and intensity and feeling that comes just from holding it. It's like holding the sun in the palm of my hand.

I turn it over, stare deep into the vibrant orange heart of the Stone. And wonder how on earth I'm going to turn this over to Cyrus. The man is obsessed with power—having it, wielding it, taking it. How can I possibly hand something like this over to him? Something that's guaranteed to give him more power than he ever dreamed?

I can't.

But I have to.

It's a slippery slope, even believing he's going to keep his end of the bargain. Because what happens if I give him this Stone and he doesn't release everyone from Katmere? What if there's a loophole in our magical agreement I didn't foresee? How are we going to be able to stop him?

Will we even have a chance to?

I don't know. There's no easy answer...except for one.

If we don't bring the Stone back, if we double-cross Cyrus, he will kill every single person he took from Katmere Academy. Or worse, he will torture them, suck their magic dry, and then leave them to die, tormented and alone.

When I think about Uncle Finn and Aunt Rowena, when I think about Gwen and Dawud's brother, Amir, and all the kids I went to class with, I know that there really is only one answer.

Is it problematic? Yes. Is it dangerous? Absolutely. Is it guaranteed to work? Not even close. But it is the only way I can live with myself, the only way I can look myself in the mirror.

We have to give the ring to Cyrus. What happens then is anyone's guess, but there's no way I can leave my friends and family and classmates to die the kind of death he has planned for them. Not if there's a chance I can stop it.

All of which is just one more reason we cannot fail at the Trials. We have to win, we have to get the pendant or fountain or whatever it is, and we have to free the Gargoyle Army and take down Cyrus. It's the only way to stop him and protect everyone we need to protect.

There is no other option.

"Do we just leave them like this?" Macy asks in a small voice. She's standing beside Artelya, who looks as majestic in stone as she does in real life. Chin up, eyes clear, body ready to fight.

"I think we have to," I answer. There's nowhere else to put them, no castle left to lock them inside to keep them safe. Just the ruins of the Gargoyle Court scattered at their feet.

"It doesn't seem right," Flint says, and for once he doesn't sound angry. Just sad.

"None of this is right," Jaxon replies. "It hasn't been for a long time."

Flint looks at him, long and slow, and for the first time in days, something besides rage passes between them.

I don't know what it is, but it feels fitting that whatever is happening here, surrounded by these people who are braver than I ever could have imagined, is more than the anger and blame and fear that came before.

The only way to get out of this mess is to trust one another. It's the only thing Cyrus doesn't have. He rules by fear, by force, and so he'll never understand what it means to actually be united with anyone or anything but his own ambition.

But we do. It may not look like it right now, with everyone splintered all over the place, but that stops here. Enough is enough.

My gaze meets Hudson's oceanic one across the training field, and there's something in his eyes that's been missing for days, too. Resolve. Determination. Hope.

Hope that we'll get to the other side of this.

Hope that we'll actually be able to pull it off.

Hope that, when we do, life will be better than it has been in a while. And so will we.

I smile at him just to see the way his eyes light up and his lips curl in an answering grin. We've got a long way to go to make this right—for the world and for us—but maybe, just maybe, we'll be able to do it as a real team instead of a fractured one just trying to hold on through the mess and the pain.

Maybe, just maybe, we'll all be okay at the end of this.

"So." Eden clears her throat as her gaze lands on Izzy. "What happens now? Do you unfreeze us, too, and magically send us back to the Vampire Court? I mean, aren't we still frozen statues there?"

That is a very good question. As I glance around at the ruined Court, which is in our timeline, I realize what Jikan meant by changing our *where* in the *when*. I don't know how he did it, but he must have moved our frozen selves from Cyrus's dungeon to here. As he would say, he *is* the God of Time. I'm pretty sure there isn't much he can't do.

"Unfortunately, we're no longer in the Vampire Court. Jikan moved us." I sigh.

Eden nods. "So we're flying back?" she asks. "If so, can I ask that you turn Isadora into a statue for the trip? I think she'd make a good hood ornament."

"Oh, I think we can find a faster way back to the Court than that." The disembodied voice—as thick and rich as a New Orleans praline—comes out of nowhere. "Though I do love a good hood ornament."

I screech in excitement as the air around us starts to spark and shimmer. Because I would know that voice anywhere. "Remy!" I shout as my favorite cell mate and warlock appears right in the center of what's left of the training circle, a huge grin on his handsome face.

Seconds later, Calder shimmers into existence right beside him. "While I'm all for riding a dragon or two," she says, batting her big brown eyes at Flint, "I do like a little more privacy when I do it. Besides," she says with a careless shrug that has Eden all but standing at attention, "I just got my hair done, and wind shear is terrible for my Brazilian blowout."

101

Bewitched and Bedazzled

"What are you doing here?" I demand. I grab Remy in a hard hug, my arms barely reaching around his massive frame as I stare up at his shaggy dark hair and forest-green eyes. It feels like I haven't seen him in a year, even though I know it's only been a week, if that.

He hugs me just as tightly, then pulls back with a wink. "I told you you'd see me again, *cher*."

Hudson rolls his eyes, then moves in beside me, which would make me laugh if I hadn't just forced my entire army to turn to stone. He does hold his hand out to Remy, though. "Good to see you, though I'm not sure why you're here."

I step on Hudson's foot and hiss, "Rude," at him under my breath.

But Remy just laughs. "Nice to see some things haven't changed."

"Though some things have, huh?" He turns to Flint with a grimace. "Sorry about your man. And your leg."

Flint just kind of stares at him, like he doesn't know what to say to that. And maybe he doesn't. No one at the Gargoyle Court mentioned his leg at all, and most of us go out of our way not to talk about it, either. Eventually he just says, "Thanks," and ducks his head.

"I like your new leg," Calder says as she envelops him in a jasmine-and-vanilla-scented hug. "Plus, we can bedazzle it before our date."

"Date?" Flint asks.

"Bedazzle?" Eden echoes, looking like it is taking every ounce of strength she has not to crack up.

"I bought a hot-glue gun and a bucket full of semiprecious stones as soon as Remy saw what happened," Calder elaborates, clapping her hands several times in the little-girl way that she has. "I can't wait!"

"By all means, then," Jaxon interjects sardonically. "Let the bedazzling begin."

"It's going to be so beautiful. Not as beautiful as me, but…" She shrugs, as if to say, *What is?* Which is a good point, since the manticore just might be the most beautiful person I have ever seen. And that's saying something, considering who I'm mated to.

"Why don't you tell him about the date you have planned?" Remy urges in the most innocent voice I've ever heard from the warlock—which only has me bracing myself for Flint's explosion.

"I got us front-row tickets for the new BTS tour when it comes to New York. We're going to have the best time! I even got us matching 'Butter' shirts."

"Are they bedazzled?" Eden asks in an aside that has Macy laughing.

Calder hears her, though. "Of course not. That would take away from Flint's leg."

"We definitely wouldn't want that," Jaxon manages to say with a straight face.

The sarcasm must hit Calder this time, because she turns to Jaxon with narrowed eyes. That quickly grow wide when she catches sight of him. "Well, hello there," she says as she twists a lock of her hair around her finger. "How are you?"

She's laying on all the sex appeal now—all of it—and Jaxon looks both a little dazed and a little uncomfortable.

Dawud, on the other hand, looks like they're one small step away from howling at the moon. Eden and Macy look just as enamored as the first time they met her, too. Then again, it's hard to blame them. She is a force to be reckoned with.

"In a hurry, actually," Jaxon answers Calder, looking at me like he wants me to get things moving.

"I bet," Flint says under his breath.

Jaxon's newly tanned face turns red and, for a second, I think he's finally had enough of Flint's digs. But in the end, he just grinds his teeth and stares off into the distance. Of course, Flint is doing the exact same thing—in the opposite direction—which isn't ridiculous *at all*.

I turn back to Remy, who's watching all the fireworks going on with the smirk of a man on the other side of the drama…one who just happens to be able to see the future.

I make a face at him, but he just winks at me—which makes Hudson roll his eyes so hard, I'd be surprised if it didn't hurt.

"You never answered my question," I tell him as Flint and Jaxon continue to snipe at each other behind us. "Why did you come?"

"You're going to need me for what comes next. And Calder insisted on joining, too," he tells me with a nod toward Calder.

"And you just came?" I ask, astonished—but also not—that he would. "You know it's going to be dangerous, right?"

"So that means what? I should just leave you guys to do it alone?" he asks with a quick lift of his brows. "That's not how friendship works. I'm pretty sure a cute little brunette said something like that to me once."

"Yeah, well, that cute little brunette's mate is going to rearrange more than your timeline if you don't knock it off," Hudson comments mildly.

Remy tries for a wounded look, but there's a wicked glint in his eye that says he's enjoying matching wits with Hudson. Of course, the amusement in Hudson's eyes basically says the feeling is mutual. Which makes me shake my head—if I live to be a thousand, I will never understand the whole friendly posturing thing so many men seem to enjoy.

Izzy makes a disgusted sound. "Do you need whipped cream and a cherry to go with all that sweetness, or are you done now?"

Remy glances over at her, then does a quick double take as everything about him goes still.

I shoot Hudson a baffled look, but he just shrugs as the two of them continue to stare at each other for several seconds.

Eventually Izzy snarls and looks away, but Remy continues to watch her through narrowed eyes. Which only pisses her off so much that she pulls out a dagger and starts cleaning her nails with it, like doing it with a razor-sharp blade is the most natural thing in the world.

"What do you think is going to happen when we give Cyrus the Stone?" Flint asks the group. "It must be bad if Remy felt the need to come help."

"I haven't seen it yet," he answers. "I just had a feeling that I needed to be here, so here I am."

Izzy snorts and shakes her head before switching the dagger to her other hand.

"I assume it means Cyrus is going to double-cross us, don't you think?" I say, looking between Jaxon and Hudson. Next to Izzy—who definitely isn't feeling any team spirit at the moment—the two of them know their father best.

"I think it's a safe bet to always assume our father is going to double-cross you," Jaxon comments.

"Now there's an understatement." Hudson's laugh is unamused.

"I've figured he would all along," I comment. "Which is why I think I've got the basics of a plan."

"Let's hear it," Macy tells me.

"I think I should plan on trying to freeze him and then—" I start, completely forgetting Izzy is on the devil's side.

"Is that your answer to everything?" Sarcasm drips from Izzy's voice straight onto me. "Freeze it? What happens when someone doesn't freeze?"

"It hasn't happened yet," Macy reminds her.

"Yeah, well, shit happens when you least need it to."

"And sometimes people make shit happen." Remy's eyes narrow. "You planning on making something happen?"

"I guess that depends if you keep asking stupid questions," she shoots back with a scowl.

He doesn't answer, just holds her gaze until she turns around with a huff.

"What are we going to do if she is a problem?" Jaxon asks softly. "She's too dangerous to have on Cyrus's side if he's going to screw us over."

"Don't worry about it," Remy answers after a second. "I can handle her."

"I'd like to see you try," Izzy snarls.

There's a wicked edge to Remy's grin as he answers, "Well, why don't you come on over here then, *cher*? We'll see what we can do about that."

Her only answer is a dagger flying by his cheek with only millimeters to spare.

102

On a Ring and a Prayer

R emy doesn't even flinch. Instead, he just waves a hand and spins the dagger around mid-flight, then sends it soaring toward Calder, who snatches it out of the air. "Oooh, pretty," she says before sliding it into her giant designer handbag. "Thank you."

"That's mine," Izzy says, fading to her and reaching for her bag.

Calder shifts in an instant, a deep growl coming from her throat and curved, catlike talons springing from her fingers. Isadora rears back in surprise even before Calder takes a swing at her.

Seconds later, the talons are gone, and Calder is back to being her normal, smiley self. "Next time, don't throw your stuff away if you want to keep it," she tells Izzy, who looks between Calder and Remy like she's not sure who she wants to maim more.

Remy just tosses her a wink. Then turns to me and nods at the ring I've slipped onto my finger. "Is that the God Stone?"

"It is." I hold it out for him to see.

"I thought it'd be bigger."

"Yeah, that's what she said," Eden comments.

Remy snickers. "Nice."

He lifts my hand up to examine the ring, but his eyes dart toward Izzy. At first, I think it's because he's—rightfully—worried that her next dagger won't miss. But there's something else going on there, and about the fourth time it happens, something clicks in my brain.

"Well, that's interesting," I tell him after I recover from the surprise.

"Not as interesting as this mess you've gotten yourself into," he answers.

"Did you really just use the worst segue ever to change the subject?" I ask in return.

"Wow. Judgy much?"

"You have no idea," Jaxon says.

"Hey!" I glare at him. "Where did that come from?"

"Just calling it like I see it," he teases.

"Well then, maybe you need glasses."

Hudson's snickering at this point, and so are Macy and Eden. Even Flint has a smile ghosting around the corners of his lips, and it makes me so happy, I rack my brain for a zinger to hit Jaxon with. If playful banter is what Flint needs to feel like himself, even for a few seconds, then I am more than willing to give it to him.

Izzy, apparently, isn't nearly as concerned as I am, though. Because she cuts right through the banter with a snarled, "Exciting as this reunion is, my father is waiting on his ring—unless, that is, you want to delay and see what happens then. I wouldn't if I were you."

"That's what portals are for," Remy tells her. "We can be at the Vampire Court in less than a minute, *cher*."

"No, we can't," she talks over him, and it's fascinating to listen to her proper British accent tangling with his slow, sexy Cajun drawl. "There will be no portals. We're flying."

He lifts a brow. "I thought you were worried about speed."

"Speed *and* accuracy are what I'm going for," she tells him.

"Oh yeah?" Both brows go up this time, and a wicked grin crosses his face. "I'll remember that."

She rolls her eyes, makes a disgusted sound deep in her throat. "I mean, there's no way I'm going to trust you to open a portal to the Vampire Court. I don't know you. You could have me wandering the desert tonight instead of sleeping in my very comfortable bed, and I am not okay with that."

"Charming though the image of you living the Bedouin life is," he answers, "I'll make sure the portal goes where we need it to go. As for your obvious trust issues...you should probably work on that. Not everyone wants to kill you or screw you, you know."

He ends with a wicked little twist of his lips that says he dares her to keep pushing at him. And at first, I think Izzy's head might explode. Like, actually explode.

Usually, she lets you know she's mad by narrowing her eyes or firming up her lips, but right now her face is red, her eyes are narrowed to slits, and I'm pretty sure smoke is coming out of her ears. The girl is furious, and I fear for Remy's life.

Hudson must feel the same way, because even as I ease forward a little to put myself in front of Remy, he moves to put himself in front of me. Now at least she has to go through both of us to get to him...

I'm not saying she still won't do that, but at least we have a shot in hell of slowing her down before murder and mayhem occur.

In the end, though, she settles for crossing her arms over her chest and sending him a superior look. "There will be no portal."

"And you think you can stop me, *cher*?" he challenges.

"Dude, she's a Soul Siphon," Flint says, then under his breath, "I would not fuck with that if I were you."

Remy laughs. He actually full-on laughs. And says, "Good luck with stealing *my* magic, if you must."

He turns away, dismissing her, and swirls his hand in the air, one quick loop, and then a portal starts to form instantly. Izzy fades to him before I can blink, and I gasp as she puts a hand in the air and then squeezes it into a fist, just like Hudson did to destroy the Skeleton Army—presumably yanking Remy's soul out of his body.

But Remy just chuckles. "Well, this is going to be fun."

Izzy gapes at him—we all do—but Remy is too busy giving her an *is that all you can do* look to say anything to the rest of us.

"That's amazing!" Macy exclaims. "It usually takes me several minutes to get a portal started. You just swirled your hand and boom! Portal."

She's half starry-eyed and half shocked, and I get it. I spent the first couple of days in prison with Remy feeling the exact same way, like I just can't believe he's real.

"How did you—? How c-can you—?" Izzy stutters, and I must admit, it's kind of nice to see her at a loss for words for once.

"I ate breakfast three hundred yards from four thousand inmates who were trained to kill me, so don't think for one second that you can come down here, wave a *fist*, and make me nervous." His voice is more serious than I've ever heard it, his eyes faraway, and I suddenly remember how helpless I felt in that cell with him. How helpless we both felt. No wonder he's so not playing around now with Izzy's threat.

"Wait..." Flint says. "Isn't that a quote from *A Few Good Men*?"

Remy's serious expression immediately dissolves into one of pure joy. "You've seen it? Isn't that movie great?"

Calder rolls her eyes. "Now you've done it. He *loves* that flick."

"That movie is fantastic!" Flint grins. "Aaron Sorkin. Best dialogue ever."

"You want me on that wall; you *need* me on that wall." Remy does a fair imitation of Jack Nicholson and fist-bumps Flint. "We are seriously gonna have a movie night, you and me, as soon as we fix this little Cyrus mess. You in?"

"Totally," Flint says, and I can't miss how Jaxon is staring at the big, goofy grin on our friend's face, the smile we haven't seen since Luca's death.

"Who is Aaron Sorkin?" Izzy asks and, as one, we all turn to stare at her like she's grown a second head. "Whatever. I'll kill him, too, if he gets in my way."

And we all bust out laughing. Everyone except Remy, who is staring at her with a thoughtful expression and Calder, who has stopped tossing her hair long enough to study her like she's a science experiment.

As the laughter dies down, though, Calder declares, "I like you. We shall now become best friends."

Which sets us all off laughing again. Even Remy chuckles this time.

Eventually the laughter dies down, and Remy turns to Izzy. "Don't be upset, *cher*. You're welcome to join our movie night."

"Hey," Flint starts. "If you're bringing a plus-one, then so am I."

Remy shrugs. "Like I always say, the more the merrier."

"I hope that's not a bad prison joke," Hudson says, and Flint groans.

"Dude. Just no," Flint says, but he's grinning. And again, Jaxon can't take his eyes off him. We are definitely going to talk about this later, but first—

"Just curious, but why are you immune to Izzy's power?" I ask Remy.

Remy holds Izzy's gaze, and I can tell she wants to look away, act like she doesn't care, but she is also dying to know. Probably so she can stop whatever's getting in the way and suck his soul for good, what with her being bloodthirsty as fuck and all.

After a beat, he winks at her and says, "She's got power, I'll give her that. But I already had my magic stolen from me once. It'll take more than a mere demigod to ever take it from me again."

"Demigod?" Jaxon repeats as the rest of us rear back in surprise. His eyes go to his sister, like he expects there to be a blinking light-up sign on her forehead with an arrow pointing down. "How is that possible?"

Izzy just shrugs before she whips another knife out of her belt and starts cleaning her nails again.

It's a defensive move, pure and simple, and even while I'm trying to come to grips with what Remy said, Dawud speaks up for the first time. "Wait. Isadora is a demigod?"

"You didn't know?" Remorse flashes in Remy's eyes, and he turns to her.

"I'm sorry. I won't say any more. It's your secret to tell."

"What does that even mean?" Jaxon demands, looking between the two of them. "Who is your—"

"None of your damn business!" Izzy fumes. "So back off before you no longer have a tongue."

I nearly burst out laughing at the look on his face. Izzy is awful, but there's a part of me that admires her, too. I mean, I have all the trouble with boundaries, but she just lays hers out there with barbed wire and land mines. I've got to respect that about her.

"Anything else we need to do before we get this show on the road?" Remy asks me. His eyes are watchful, like he already knows, and can I just say there's something comforting and also really annoying about having a friend who knows what you're going to do before you do it.

"Yeah," I say softly.

I slide the ring off my finger, then walk over to Izzy and—under the shocked gazes of my friends—hold it out to her.

But they aren't the only ones who are shocked. "What are you doing?" she asks, all but recoiling from the God Stone. "Why would you give that to me?"

She looks so horrified, I almost laugh, but in the end, I manage to hold in my amusement. "You know this ring is powerful enough to free you from Cyrus, right?"

"Don't," she bites out sharply.

"Why would you tell her that?" Flint demands, and he sounds furious. Then again, he almost always sounds furious these days—unless he's making movie dates with Remy, of course.

"Because she deserves to know that I won't judge her for giving Cyrus the ring," I answer, my eyes steady on Izzy's dark blue ones.

"What makes you think I care what you think?" she snarls as she slides the ring on her finger, a shudder running through her. "You don't know me."

"Because you'll give that ring to your father to free the kids from Katmere—and you'll regret it, you'll wonder *what-if*, and you'll blame yourself."

Her laugh is ice-cold. "You are delusional if you think I give a shit about freeing those kids."

"Oh, I know you don't care about them. But you won't use it to free yourself, either," I say. And I know I'm pushing things, know I'm about to run smack-dab into one of those barbed-wire boundaries of hers, but I don't care. I think she needs to hear this. And I think everyone else does, too.

Especially Remy, if what I suspect is true. But he barely looks like he's listening.

Still, all I can do is try, so I continue. "You'll give the ring to your father because he's gaslit and punished you for not proving your worth for, I'd imagine, your entire life. Hope is not something you're ready to deal with yet."

For a second, just a second, fear flashes into Izzy's eyes. But it disappears as quickly as it came, with rage taking its place. "You don't know anything about me."

"Maybe not," I agree. "But here's the thing—if I give it to him, he'll consider he just made me bow to his whims. It's meaningless. But if you bring it back, you will gain his respect and maybe, just maybe, realize you never needed it to begin with. You are a force, Izzy, and if Remy is right, far more powerful than Cyrus is without that ring. You can choose something else for yourself if you want."

Her hands shake, and I'm pretty sure she's about to reach for a knife to shut me up forever, but I have to finish. If what Hudson shared with me about her is true, she deserves to know someone understands.

"But I want you to know I understand why you won't leave, why you'll give that monster the ring and stay. It's not your fault. Anyone in your shoes would." I sigh and glance at Hudson and Jaxon before turning back to her. "But I think you will be ready to leave someday. And when that day comes, I just want you to know that I'll be here to help you. And so will your brothers."

Jaxon squawks a little at that, but Calder and Macy both hush him.

"Why are you doing this to me?" Izzy demands, and there's a shakiness to her voice I've never heard before.

"Because someone needs to acknowledge you're just as trapped in Cyrus's web as we are," I answer. Then—knowing I've pushed enough—I step back and link my arm through Remy's. "Now, you ready to meet the biggest narcissist ever born?"

He laughs. "Who knew there was someone out there who could actually give Calder some competition?"

But Calder just rolls her eyes and fluffs her hair. "Jealousy is so unbecoming."

"So is vanity," Izzy snarls at her.

"Not when it's a table," Calder singsongs back. Then she pauses, her eyes going wide. "I could use a new vanity table. One with lights. Remy!"

"I'll get you one as soon as we're done here, okay?" he promises with a laugh.

"More than okay. Perfect!" She cracks her knuckles. "Now, where's this vampire who needs his nuts ripped off? I've got a great roaster at home that

I've been wanting to try out."

Everyone cracks up, because how can we not when Calder's on her game?

As we walk toward the portal Remy has held open all this time with absolutely no effort, I realize Dawud has finally snapped out of whatever trance they went into the moment Calder showed up.

The quiet, studious wolf has basically turned into a star-eyed emoji, and it is a sight to see.

"Ready?" Hudson asks, coming up on my non-Remy side.

"As I'll ever be," I reply, taking his hand.

"All right, then." Remy grins. "Let's blow this Popsicle stand."

And just like that, the three of us step into the portal first.

103

A Very
Untasty Freeze

And I thought Macy's portals were nice.

But if hers are the BMWs of portals, Remy's are the Maseratis. Fast, sleek, and absolutely gorgeous, with its riotous colors spinning all around us, his portal drops us straight into the Vampire Court. There is no falling, no stretching, no pain or pressure. Just a couple of quick steps and we are exactly where we need to be—although I would have preferred *outside* the dungeon cell and not in it.

The students are all still there, as far as I can tell, and I breathe a sigh of relief that Cyrus has kept up his side of the bargain and not harmed them yet. Mekhi, Rafael, and Byron instantly rush forward and pull Jaxon into a group hug.

"Man, it's good to see you," Mekhi says, patting Jaxon on the back.

"Gimme a sec, and I'll get us a portal out of here in no time," Remy says.

"How are you using magic inside these cells?" Izzy asks, and for the first time, there's just a wee bit of awe in her voice.

He turns to her and winks. "I guess I've got secrets, too, *cher.*"

Footsteps suddenly pound down the stairs into the dungeon, and I miss her response as Cyrus appears at our cell door.

"Did you get it?" Cyrus asks, and there's no chill in his voice. No control. Just pure, unadulterated greed.

"Would I be here if we didn't?" Izzy asks him.

"Show it to me!" he demands, a rabid intensity in every syllable as he motions for a guard to open the cell door for her.

Izzy saunters out and holds up the ring with its powerful orange stone, and he cackles—actually cackles—before grabbing the ring out of her hand and staring at it like Sméagol from Lord of the Rings. I swear, at this point it wouldn't surprise me if he called it his precious and started petting it like Sméagol, too. My stomach twists at the sight of him holding the one object that can make him an even more powerful enemy, but I grit my teeth and tell myself again there was no other choice.

"When your statues disappeared, I wasn't the least bit concerned," he tells us without ever looking up from the ring, "I knew you would return with what I sought, Isadora." His eyes still stare at the ring with so much lust, he doesn't see how her shoulders square just the tiniest bit, how her chin lifts under his praise. When he waves his hand and adds, "Of course you would. You know what would happen to you if you didn't," no one is surprised the compliment was anything but.

No one except Izzy, who hides the sagging in her shoulders by leaning against the nearby wall and whipping out a dagger to clean her nails. "I aim to please, Father."

With the doors open, we quickly file out, Jaxon, Hudson, Macy, Eden, and Dawud as well as Remy and Calder. But when the rest of the Order goes to follow suit, Cyrus waves a hand, and the guards slam the door shut.

"Aren't you forgetting something?" Hudson asks, brows raised.

Cyrus doesn't answer, which is scary in a whole different way. I've seen Cyrus in several moods over the last few months—angry, snide, determined, boastful, frustrated—but I've never seen him like this.

Never seen him so totally obsessed over anyone or anything—even me, and he really, really hates me.

When close to thirty seconds pass and we still don't get an answer, I jump in. "You forgot the kids and faculty. You promised to free them, and we're not leaving here without them."

That snaps his head up, his eyes narrowing in on my face. "This is my Court," he tells me in a voice that brooks no argument. "And this is my house. You'll leave when I tell you that you can go, and you'll forget about what I tell you to forget about. And right now, I'm telling you to forget the kids and get the hell out. Before I change my mind about letting you go."

"But we have a contract," I say and point to the tattoo on my forearm.

"Yes, you didn't fulfill your side of the agreement," Cyrus says. "Izzy brought me the ring, not you."

My stomach sinks as my gaze bounces around my friends' faces, and I make a mental note to ask Hudson later to explain every level of magical contract possible. For now, I just want to smack my head. How could I have not seen this loophole?

"Well, we have a problem, then, *Dad*." Hudson steps forward. "Because we aren't leaving here without them."

Annoyance flashes across Cyrus's face. "Well, then, you can go back in the dungeon cell with them. It's your choice." He raises a hand, and the vampire guards against the back wall start moving toward us.

He's called Hudson's bluff, which means we're out of time and options. I'm going to have to get close enough to touch him and hope the others can figure out how to use what I do to their advantage. The thought makes my skin crawl, but it's not like Cyrus is leaving me with a lot of options here.

I glance at Hudson and Remy, and it's obvious they both know what I'm thinking. Hudson nods, and Remy gives a *go ahead* raise of his eyebrows.

"Isn't there something you're forgetting?" I ask, shuffling closer to him with each word.

"My dear Grace," he says, though his tone reveals there is nothing dear about me. "You've already given me everything I need." He slides the ring onto his finger, and I can tell the moment he feels the power of the God Stone. His whole body trembles, and his face lights with an unholy delight. But he's also distracted.

It's what I've been waiting for—an opening to touch him. I glance at Hudson, make sure he's ready to take out the guards, then lay my hand on Cyrus just as Hudson grabs the guard closest to him. I reach deep inside myself and brush the back of my hand across my green string.

Just like that, Cyrus freezes. But I realize with dawning horror that I must have also brushed against my platinum string—those two strings really are too close together for comfort—and managed to freeze the two of us together.

104

Of War
and Wankers

I swear, this green string should come with an instruction manual, because the absolute last thing I would ever want is to be frozen in time together with Cyrus. Like, who the hell wants to be anywhere with that man, let alone trapped in his mind? I'm going to need to douse myself in Lysol about a million times when I escape from here just to get rid of the slimy feeling.

To be honest, I'm surprised he's not screaming at me to get the hell out of his head as he strides down the black marble hallway in high fashion from what I guess was about twelve hundred years ago. Black leggings with some kind of patterned gray knee sock pulled over them, a long black tunic with silver embroidery on the sleeves and around the hem, a black leather belt and shoes, and a silver cloak fastened over his left shoulder.

Every inch of his clothing—and the boots on his feet—is perfect, but then I would expect nothing less from Cyrus. Even in the middle of battle, I've never seen him look anything but sartorially perfect.

I have absolutely no idea where he's going—though I can tell it's in the Vampire Court—but he's in a hurry to get there, walking so fast, I have to all but run to keep up. Eventually, we reach a heavy wooden door at the very end of the hall, and Cyrus throws it open and strides in.

It's a large space, and it looks like an office or a conference room, but as he gets closer to the table in the center of the area, I realize it's a war room. There is a giant circular table dominating the middle, a map inlaid in its surface and groups of different-colored markers scattered about it, and an older man sitting at the table, assessing it, with a small group of servants standing at attention behind him.

As I step closer, I realize that he has the number of each type of paranormal listed per region, along with their weaknesses and the best way to either turn them or eliminate them. Because apparently Cyrus's quest for world domination is nothing new.

Once the door to the war room is closed behind him, Cyrus takes off his cloak and drops it over the nearest sofa. Then, rolling up his sleeves, he approaches the table in the center of the room.

From where I'm standing, almost hidden by a large tapestry and sculpture, it looks like a very detailed *Risk* game...which isn't concerning at all. I mean, it's not like a thousand years is a long time to work out all the flaws in your plans for world domination.

"Have you made any progress?" Cyrus asks the other man as he takes up a spot on the opposite side of the table.

"Actually, I think I have. If you look over here—" He breaks off mid-word as he glances up at Cyrus. "Still seeing that witch, are you?" His voice is filled with innuendo.

"How could you possibly know that?" Cyrus snaps.

"You have a little—" I realize what he's pointing at: a smudge of red lip paint at the edge of Cyrus's collar.

"Yes, well, it's the last time I need to bother with her. I got what I wanted. She's becoming a nuisance anyway."

"Don't they all, Your Majesty?" The older vampire's smile is as cold and malicious as anything I've ever seen from Cyrus.

"You're telling me," Cyrus says before turning to snarl at one of the servants in the room. "Have my valet lay out my blue tunic. And make sure he lays out a new doublet with it. The queen and I will be dining formally this evening."

Then he turns back to the map and says, "I've been thinking, Miles. If we concentrate our forces over here, we can eliminate the resistance stronghold once and for all."

I almost move forward to get a better look at where he's pointing, but I'm starting to think maybe he can't see me. Maybe I brought us to a memory of his and not a place, and he can't see me because I'm not part of the memory?

Miles looks surprised. "Isn't that your wife's village? How is she going to react to that?"

"I can handle the queen," Cyrus snaps.

"Can you?" Miles asks, and that's when I clue in on just how important he is. I can't imagine Cyrus tolerating being questioned by anyone he employs. "Because you know how she is if you upset her."

Cyrus turns and pours a goblet of blood from the decanter on the leather-topped furniture that runs the side length of the room. "Delilah will be fine."

"That rabid dog of a woman has never been fine a day in her life." Miles snorts. "I never could figure out why you would marry her and mingle your pure bloodline with hers."

"Even rabid dogs have their uses," Cyrus replies before taking a long sip of blood.

"You know she drained a whole group of villagers dry in that little town of hers? Right before her father sold her to you. She went on a rampage and killed an entire group of men in one night." He shakes his head. "Talk about a woman who doesn't know her place."

"Know about it?" Cyrus's smile is colder than I've ever seen from him—and that's saying something. "That's what attracted me to her in the first place."

Now Miles simply looks confused as he, too, turns to pour himself some blood. "But aren't you worried that she'll turn on you that way? She can't be controlled."

"Of course she can. And do you really think I'm going to fear a woman? Or anyone else, for that matter?" He leans over and shifts a couple of pieces on the map before turning back to Miles. "You know, don't you, my friend, that dogs are bred for different things?"

"Of course. Some are hunters, some are companions—"

"And some exist only to be vicious," Cyrus finishes for him. "No one wants one of those dogs in the house—they cause too many problems with the children and the servants. But if you are worried about being attacked—worried about defending yourself—there's nothing you want more than a vicious dog in your garden. Am I right?"

My stomach churns at the cruelty of his words. What is wrong with this man, to liken his wife to a rabid dog? I'm no fan of Delilah's—what she did to Jaxon, what she has let Cyrus do to Hudson and Izzy—marks her as a truly heinous person in my books.

But the way Cyrus is talking about her? No one deserves for their husband to say this about them, not even a thousand years ago when women were certainly treated differently. It's dehumanizing. And disrespectful. And just awful in every way. She's a vicious dog he keeps in his garden?

For a second, I think I might actually throw up.

But if I do, I could miss something important. Something I need to know about Cyrus or Delilah or how to fix this and free everyone from Katmere once and for all.

So I swallow down the bile creeping up my throat and focus instead on trying to remember anything and everything I can from this conversation. Because as he was staring at the God Stone, Cyrus must have been thinking about this moment if he brought us here as I brushed against my demigod string. It's important to him, to using the God Stone, and that makes it very important to me, too.

"Of course," Miles agrees with a nod.

"Thank you." Cyrus lifts his goblet to his mouth, and this time he doesn't lower it until he's drained it dry. When he finally pulls the cup away from his mouth, his lips are stained an unbecoming red that makes him look almost as unhinged as he is accusing Delilah of being.

At least until he picks up a cloth from the sideboard and wipes his mouth. He takes his time, as if getting his thoughts in order. Or steeling himself for some battle to come.

Eventually, though, he turns back around and pins Miles with a look that is so blatantly innocent that it is clearly anything but. "Can we also agree that I cannot rule my people if I am seen as vicious or uncontrollable or...rabid? They've already been under the rule of someone with that demeanor and feared her so much, they sided with the humans. I cannot hope to lead our kind into the light if they fear me. I must appear calm, reasonable, strong at all costs. I am the respected leader, and Delilah—my ruthless, rabid queen—is the dog who does what needs to be done *while I hold her rope.*"

105

Good. There's evil, and then there's just disgusting. This is disgusting, so much so that I feel dirty even hearing it. And that's before Miles asks, "And if she were to one day slip that rope, my old friend?"

Cyrus laughs, but there is no humor in the sound. "Do you think me so weak now? That I can't even control my own monster?"

"It's not about controlling her." Miles leans over the table and moves some of the blue wooden markers to a different section of the map entirely. "It's that even the strongest man can occasionally take his eye off the prize."

"I am not any man," Cyrus answers as he studies the map with narrowed eyes. It takes a minute or two, but then he reaches for the blue markers and moves them back to where they started. Then he picks up several of the purple ones and puts them in their place. "I think we'll be better able to maintain control in the north if we use the wolves instead of the witches on the north ridge.

"Besides, soon all of this won't matter. I finally have what I need to put the humans in their place and to bring our people into the light once and for all. The witch is in love with me, and now she is with child."

"So true love conquers all?" Miles looks skeptical.

"Love is a farce. Power is everything—and she has plenty of power, though she foolishly thinks to throw hers away so she can be with me."

"I see." Miles's face lights up with an unholy glee. "And you, of course, have plans to be there to catch it when she does?"

"Something like that." Cyrus drums his fingers on the table as he continues to study every facet of the map. "She's a demigod who is holding the winning hand—the ticket to becoming a god. And she thinks to give all that up for me."

"And this helps you how?" Miles shakes his head. "Wouldn't it be better if you had a goddess on your side?"

"That's why you're my trusted adviser, old friend, while I am the king. You always think too small." He picks up a piece that looks an awful lot like a crown and moves it to a different place on the map—a place that looks like it's part of Ireland or Scotland based on my admittedly sketchy knowledge of geography, but I'm not close enough to tell for sure. "Because if there is a way for her to become a god..."

"Then there's a way for you to as well."

"Exactly." Cyrus points a manicured finger at him. "And I only need one more thing to accomplish my goals—which I will have in May, only eight months from now."

Miles thinks for a minute about what Cyrus said, then nods. "It's a sound plan, except the humans in Rome are getting restless. How do you plan on keeping their hunting parties under control for that many months?"

Cyrus pushes a few of the purple pieces into Italy. "Let the witches befuddle anyone who is anxious about the recent deaths. We keep them around for a reason."

"We do indeed." Miles steps back from the table and reaches for his own coat, which is laying over one of the bloodred chairs in front of the bookcases. "I do have one last question, Your Majesty, if I may be so bold."

"I didn't think you could be anything but bold," Cyrus counters. "It is why I chose you to be my adviser."

"An honor I am more than happy to fulfill," Miles says. "But what do you plan on doing if Delilah gets wind of these plans—or if she finds out about the witch? She won't be happy."

"You're right, she won't. But, you know, sometimes there is no other recourse except to put down a rabid dog."

"And you can do that, if you have to?"

"Do it?" Cyrus lifts a brow. "I would relish it. In fact—"

He continues speaking, but I don't hear any more because suddenly a voice from the shadows says, "Well, look what we have here. Are you having fun spying on me, Grace?"

My heart leaps to my chest, starts beating extra fast. Because I know that voice, it features in several of my current nightmares.

It means Cyrus—the real Cyrus and not the memory—has found me.

Shit, shit, shit.

I don't think it's been enough time. Has it been enough time?

How long was Cyrus talking to Miles anyway? Twenty minutes? Thirty? More? And that's in the frozen world. What about the real world?

What's the ratio again? Six times the amount of time passes in the frozen world than the real world? Or is it three times the time passes in the frozen world than the real world? I can't remember now.

Why can't I remember?

"Are you going to answer me, Grace?" Cyrus's voice is low and sibilant, every syllable a warning and every sound a threat that has panic beating in my ears, fear racing through my blood.

What do I do? What do I do?

"I didn't mean to spy," I tell him. "I just saw you. That's all."

Think, Grace. Think. How long has it been?

At least thirty minutes, I decide. It was a long conversation, plus there was walking and drinking and plotting and drinking... Yeah, thirty minutes sounds about right. So that translates into how many minutes in the real world?

"I'm very careful, Grace," Cyrus whispers, and my name is an actual hiss on his tongue. "People don't just see me unless they're looking very, very carefully. Do you know what we do to spies in the Vampire Court?"

An image of Macy's mother, the way I saw her last, pops into my head. Poor Aunt Rowena, curled up in a ball on the floor of the dungeon. Bruised, emaciated, mentally strung out from years upon years of torture. Just the thought stokes my fear up another notch, even as it has anger burning in my belly.

And that threat—combined with the feel of something sharp and knifelike poking me in the stomach—tells me I'm out of time. I brush against the green string and bring us right back to the real world.

The only problem? In the time I was gone, the real world has turned completely upside down.

106

Out of the Fire, Into the Jail Cell

There's a lot of shouting and screaming as Cyrus and I unfreeze in the dungeon. We're still on the outside of the cell, right in front of the iron door, but everyone else has moved—and not in a good way.

Izzy is only a few feet away, and she's standing over Jaxon and Hudson, who are gray and half conscious on the ground at her feet. She's got a hand on each of them, and I watch in horror as she does her best to drain them of every ounce of power they have.

I start to rush to them, but the truth is the entire dungeon is in chaos, and everywhere I look, one of my friends needs help. Remy and Calder are fighting what looks like an entire squadron of vampire guards, while Macy and Dawud—in human form—are taking on a group of prison guards.

The vampire queen herself, who I'd thought wasn't even currently at Court, is in the center of the melee, kicking ass and tossing the Order and Flint around like they're rag dolls—or rags—and Eden is locked in a death struggle with a vampire I don't recognize. I decide she looks like she's in the most trouble, so I turn toward her, but before I can take more than a step, Delilah sends Mekhi soaring around the iron bars at the front of the dungeon.

He hits with a sickening *thud* and then slides face-first onto the ground. I scream as his head hits the stone and take off running toward him, but Cyrus is right there in front of me. He yanks me up and holds me, dangling, about three feet off the ground.

He tangles his hands in my hair, shoving my head over to the side so that my neck is fully exposed. Then he lets out the loudest, most booming shout I've ever heard from him—or anyone—as he yells, "Stop. Now."

His voice is so loud that it ricochets off the stone walls and floor and ceiling, filling the entire dungeon with the sound of his rage. Everyone in the room at least glances our way, and then my friends freeze as they realize the same thing that I'm just beginning to understand. My very vulnerable neck is completely exposed to his fangs.

The knowledge sends a wave of horror rushing through me as I remember what happened the last time he bit me. And I'm not the only one. In those quick couple of seconds, I see the terror on Hudson's and Jaxon's faces, too.

It can't happen again. It just can't. I start to try to turn to stone—he can't bite me then—but I've forgotten I'm in a prison cell built by the Blacksmith Vander Bracka. Just like the Aetherum, my gargoyle is gone. None of us has any of our abilities—well, except my demigod string, which appears to be immune to whatever is canceling our magic. I don't even have time to wonder if that's why I wasn't dragged into the nightmares in prison, because the cell Vander built doesn't affect my green string, before I admit the king's fangs also most definitely still work and are poised to strike at any moment.

Everyone stops fighting as they realize they've been beaten—again.

"Toss them in the cell with the others," Cyrus snarls as he opens his hand and lets me fall as if I'm little more than a speck of dust to him. Which I am.

I hit the ground hard, nearly fall to my knees.

"Get them in the cell," Cyrus snarls. "How they could even put up a fight against all of you, I don't know. But it will not happen again."

We're not fighting anymore, but the guards grab on to us anyway and roughly shove us into the cell. I'm racking my brain, trying to figure out what to do to get us out of this mess, even before the gate clangs shut behind us.

"Been here, done this before, huh, Grace?" Remy asks as he finds a place against the wall. He leans into it and then slides down until he's sitting on the floor, the cell obviously preventing him from creating a portal.

"Isn't that the truth?" I ask, thinking of the week we all spent locked in a prison cell together. "If I never—" I break off as Cyrus barks orders at Delilah.

"Keep an eye on them while I have a meeting with my guards. And for God's sake, don't screw this up, too." Then he turns to Isadora and says, "Get upstairs to my office. Before I talk to them, *you* have some explaining to do."

I start to turn away, but it's hard to miss the way Delilah's beautiful face hardens. I'm not sure if it's because Cyrus ordered her around or if it's because he left her down here in the dungeon while he took Isadora—clearly his illegitimate child from an affair he had while married to Delilah—and all his guards upstairs.

I'm betting it's a little bit of both, because both are a hard pill to swallow for anyone, let alone the vampire queen. And it's because I think it is a little bit of both that I take my life in my hands as soon as Cyrus is gone. And ask Delilah,

"Do you actually like it when your husband orders you around like that in front of people? I'm just asking because it makes him look like a tool and you look like a total doormat."

Then I sit back and wait for the explosion.

It doesn't take long.

107

Hailing All
the Marys

"Have you actually lost your mind?" Jaxon shouts as Delilah whirls on me with a snarl. "She's going to eviscerate you."

"It's a valid question," Calder tells him, examining her glittery nail polish for any chips after the fight. "Doormats have a sucky life with everyone wiping their feet on them. Who wants to be one of those?"

Hudson tries to ease in front of me—which tells me just how pissed he thinks Delilah is, considering he usually stands back to see if I need his support before jumping in—but I won't let him. This is a Hail Mary of a plan, but it's the only one I've got right now, and I'm going to do my best to make sure it works. I didn't risk everything to give Cyrus the God Stone so we could make our next move, only to lose to some magical loophole in a bad contract.

"You know nothing of my relationship with my mate," she snarls as she takes several steps closer to the bars. "And for someone who has made as big a mess of her mated relationships as you have, you've got no room to cast aspersions on us."

She's not wrong there, but still. Now's not the time to dwell on the past—not when the future of so many people depends on us getting the hell out of here.

"More than you might think, actually," I tell her. "But then a rabid dog doesn't think much, does she?"

"What did you just say to her?" Jaxon asks, horrified.

"What did you just say to me?" she echoes, eyes narrowed and teeth bared. But there's something in her face—in her expression—that tells me this isn't the first time she's heard that description in reference to herself. Which is exactly what I was hoping, as it lends legitimacy to everything I'm about to tell her.

If I'm lucky, I can drive a wedge between her and Cyrus deep enough that she decides to stop whatever he has planned for us.

"When I was frozen, I was locked in a memory with Cyrus. It was more than a thousand years ago—since he'd just knocked up some witch, with Isadora,

I'm guessing—and he was telling a man named Miles that you were his attack dog. That he held your rope but was more than capable of putting you down if he had to."

There was a lot more to that conversation—other stuff he said that was equally bad about her—but that's enough to set her off, I think.

Sure enough, Delilah is at the bars in a blink, every single thing about her seething in rage. Seething with the need for destruction—which makes me think I was right. I've definitely hit a sore spot, just as I intended.

But considering I'm the one she currently looks like she wants to kill—in fact, if those bars weren't between us, I'm pretty sure I'd be dead right now—I need to press a little harder. I mean, yes, killing the messenger is one thing. But the other is killing the son of a bitch who did the really bad stuff to begin with... or at least stabbing him in the back.

"You don't know what you're talking about," she screeches.

"Oh, I'm pretty sure we both know that's not true," I answer.

And then, ignoring the way Hudson and Jaxon are so tense that I'm afraid they might break in half, I take a deep breath and put what I hope is the final nail in Cyrus's coffin. "Before you met Cyrus, you went on a rampage in your village, killing many men and draining them dry. Your father had to cover it up before hysteria took over all the humans in the neighboring villages, but word got out among the vampires."

She's watching me closely now, her eyes tracking every move I make. I don't know if it's because she is imagining doing the same to me as those villagers or if it's because she's beginning to believe me. Either way, there's nothing to do at this point but finish it. So I do and pray I've made the right decision, pray that I haven't just condemned Hudson to having to try to keep his mother from killing his mate.

"Did you know that's why Cyrus wanted to marry you? He contacted your father right after that incident, didn't he?" Delilah doesn't say anything, and she doesn't move away from the bars. But her shoulders sag just the barest millimeter, and I know she believes me.

I press my advantage, feeling terrible that I'm deliberately hurting anyone, but too many lives depend on this. "Aren't you tired of being his lapdog, trotted out to kill shit whenever he needs you, being at his beck and call? He thinks you're his property, and he can use you however he wants. Don't you want to make that stop? Don't you want to be free?"

108

Hell Hath No Fury Like a Vampire Scorned

"You have no idea what I want," Delilah spits back at me, but she's gone pasty white, the only color in her face the two red spots burning on her cheekbones. "You think it was easy being a woman a thousand years ago? You think it's easy bowing your back for a man? Back then there was no choice—even for vampires. The name of the game was to find the strongest man you could to protect you and your children."

She tosses her head, holds it up high now. "I did that. I made it through what was done to me in that village, and I found a way out—on the arm of a man who would protect me. Maybe it's not because he loves me, maybe it's just because I belong to him and no one messes with what belongs to Cyrus Vega, but the end result is the same. I *survived*."

I hate, hate, hate that a kernel of sympathy is welling up inside me for Delilah. This is the woman who scarred Jaxon—after giving him up to be raised by someone else.

The woman who allowed Hudson to be tortured for nearly two centuries so that her husband could have another powerful weapon.

The woman who let her husband turn his illegitimate daughter into a servant who cleans up whatever messes he tells her to.

All so that Delilah could survive. All so that she could have the life of a queen.

I remind myself of that—and of the way Jaxon looked when I first got to Katmere, always ducking his head and brushing his hair forward to hide the scar she gave him—and tamp down the sympathy. Then I push forward with the plan, determined to draw enough blood to move her to action.

"But are you really living?" I ask after a second. "What do you have to mark all these years you've spent doing whatever Cyrus wanted you to? A crown that you get to wear because he lets you? Children who have nearly been destroyed by the man you love—children you've nearly destroyed yourself?"

"I've never hurt them—"

"Oh, I beg to differ on that," I snap back. I know I should control this, know that I have to lead her where I want her to go. But it's really hard to do that when she just stood there and said she never hurt Hudson or Jaxon.

What a crock of shit.

"You physically scarred one son permanently—something that's really hard to do to a vampire. You sent him away when he was little more than a child to be raised by someone else. The other son, you let Cyrus abuse and torment and use until he had no choice but to build a shell around himself and his emotions so thick and hard that he nearly got lost in there. Nearly died in there just because he was so desperate to escape being used."

Delilah blinks at that—that's all, just a blink, but it's enough to make me think that I'm getting through to her. Or at least that I'm hitting a nerve, which is something. Hudson told me he really thinks she has a heart in there somewhere, and maybe he's right. Maybe she really isn't as stone-cold dead inside as Cyrus is.

If that's the case, then I've got the advantage now, and I have to press it one last time. I mean, who knows how much longer Cyrus and Isadora are going to be gone? Because the one thing I do know is that the second one of them shows their face down here again, my plan goes up in smoke.

And if a Hail Mary plan gets set on fire, I'm pretty sure this entire place will go up in flames—with all of us in it.

I refuse to let that happen.

"But Hudson still defends you," I tell her. "He says you were trying to protect him, though Jaxon pretty much thinks the opposite. But just in case Hudson is right, just in case there's a mother with an actual heart buried in there somewhere—a woman who's tired of watching her children be sacrificed on the altar of her mate's ambition—then do something about it."

She blinks again, her eyes shifting from me to Hudson and Jaxon, who are now standing on either side of me.

"Let us go," I tell her, meeting those ruthless black eyes of hers with my own. "Let us go and I promise you, I'll find a way to give you the one thing you want most in this world."

"And how is it you would presume to think you know what I want, little girl?" Delilah scoffs. "Do you think it's love? Do you think I want to sit around watching movies with my boys, maybe doing arts and crafts with them? Baking up some nice blood cookies?"

She steps back from the bars now, straightening up so that she looks every inch the queen in her bloodred Prada suit and five-inch heels. "I am the vampire queen, and I'm not going to be tied down to the two of them just to get rid of their father."

Jaxon stiffens beside me, and Hudson shows no reaction at all—which is how I know she hurt them both with that last comment. Part of me wants nothing more than to slap the shit out of her for what she's done to these two guys I love in very different ways. She's managed to nearly destroy my mate and my best friend, and she deserves to pay for it.

But that's for later. Right now...right now I just have to keep my eye on the prize a little bit longer, and maybe there will actually be a later.

"I don't think being tied to them is what you want at all. But I do think, if I were married to someone who made me give up my kids and forced me to do his bidding for a thousand years, I know what I would want—and I'm pretty sure it's the same thing you want. Revenge."

Delilah's eyes widen at that, and I know I've got her. She wants revenge as much as she wants her next breath—maybe more—and I don't even blame her. "I can give you that—and not some petty little revenge, either. True vengeance against the man who has cheated on you, mocked you, used you, and kept you—and your children—on a rope for far too long."

Jaxon makes a small choking sound beside me, and Hudson shoots me a *take it down a notch* look, but they're not women, so they don't get it. I'm big-game fishing, and I've got her on the line. I just need to reel her in.

"True vengeance against the mate who has done his best to destroy you and everything you've ever cared about, I will give it to you. All you have to do is help us now."

It's the last card I have to play, the last move I can make unless she actually lets us out of here, and I hold my breath as I wait to see if it worked.

All around me, I can sense my friends doing the same thing. Jaxon and Hudson are at my sides, but the others are pretending to be doing something—anything—else but listening. But they, too, are only a few feet away and I can feel them, poised, waiting for whatever happens next.

She wants to take the deal—I can feel the rage and hate rolling off her in waves. But Delilah hasn't stayed alive as long as she has by being foolish. And she knows as well as anyone what the price is for going against Cyrus...and just how many guards are down here listening to us talk right now, just waiting for the chance to advance their own careers by running to him with news of what is happening.

Which is why sarcasm drips off every word when she asks, "You don't actually expect me to think a little girl like you is going to be the one to bring Cyrus down and give me my revenge? Because you're right. I do want him to pay—for much more than just taking my children from me. But look at you, locked up in a dungeon with a bunch of kids."

She looks from me to her sons and then beyond to everyone else. "You're in no position to make such an offer, and I won't risk the repercussions of going against my mate on the whim of a girl who thinks she's got more power than she has."

It's my turn to narrow my eyes, my turn to stand up straight like the queen I am determined to become. And then I look right at her and answer, "I think we're both tired of being underestimated, don't you?"

My words must hit home because Delilah flinches. She actually flinches, and it tells me everything I need to know.

"I'm so confident I can deliver your revenge, I'm willing to sign on the dotted line."

Hudson gasps and Jaxon barks, "No!"

And I get it, I do. But there's only so many ways this is going to end. Either we spend eternity in this dungeon or get drained by Izzy and die a blessedly quick death. Or we get out and compete in the Trials, and again either die a hopefully quick death or have the one thing that will allow me to deliver on my promise to her. So yeah, it's either death, in which case the magical contract will be moot, or success, and I can fulfill the deal.

Delilah looks shocked for a second, but then her eyes light up with an unholy glee, like she is finally beginning to believe that I mean what I say.

Jaxon, in the meantime, mutters a whole lot of curse words. "Are you fucking kidding me? You can't bind yourself to her. She's a heartless monster. Look what happened when you made a deal with Cyrus—"

"Grace has this, Jaxon," Hudson interrupts, looking straight at me as he says it. "I don't know how you've got it, I don't know what you think you're going to be able to do to make this happen, but if you think you've got it, then you've got it."

Jaxon throws his hands up, shakes his head. "I swear, you're as ridiculous as she is."

But I barely hear him. I'm too busy thinking about how much I love Hudson, and how that's never going to change. We've had our issues lately, but that doesn't mean he doesn't believe in me. He's never doubted me, not once, and there's no way I'm going to let him down now.

So I raise my brow as I turn back to Delilah and ask, "So are you ready for a little payback or not?"

For long seconds, Delilah doesn't answer. She just looks at me like she's trying to see straight into my mind. Eventually, though, she heaves a dramatic sigh and says, "I'm finally beginning to figure out what my sons see in you, gargoyle girl." Then, quick as a cobra, she reaches through the bars and grabs my hand.

"I will free you from the Vampire Court today," she says. "And you will grant me the revenge I seek against my mate."

"If you free us from the Vampire Court today—*everyone* from Katmere, students and faculty, plus Rowena, alive and healthy, and safely allow us to travel to the Witch Court"—thank you, Cyrus, for teaching me to look for loopholes— "then I promise to return and grant you the revenge you seek against your mate."

I start to leave it at that, but I have no idea what her idea of revenge is except to know that it is bad and dark—probably darker than I want to go. So at the end, I tack on, "That does not result in Cyrus's death."

Delilah's laugh is low and filled with humor—and honesty. "Oh, dear child, you have no worries on that front. The last thing I want is for that man to escape my wrath with anything as easy and painless as death."

I try to swallow, but my mouth is a desert with no moisture in sight. *Please, please, please,* I silently plead to the universe. *Don't ever let me get into a position where I have to cross this woman…over anything. She is not someone who will take it lying down.*

"Are we in agreement?" I ask after a second.

"We are," she answers, and suddenly the heat on my arm where she's grabbed me gets kicked up a notch. I can tell Delilah feels it, too, because she gasps as it gets really hot.

Despite that, she doesn't let go—this is too important for a few minor burns to chase either one of us away. Seconds later, my skin begins to cool and she loosens her hold on me. I glance down at the new tattoo on the inside of my wrist. It's tiny, so I have to look closely to figure out what it is—it turns out it's an elaborate lock, and Delilah's tattoo is a fancy key.

Looks like we really are tied together by this thing, whether I like it or not.

"So what happens now?" I ask.

"Now?" She moves so fast, I swear she vanishes and returns between one blink and another. Five seconds, tops, and she's standing in front of our cell again and licking the blood from her fingers before the five guards' bodies even hit the ground next to their hearts. Then she waves a hand and, just like that, the cell doors unlock and swing open. "Now, you leave."

109

It's In the
Demigod DNA

"How did you do that?" Jaxon asks suspiciously.

Delilah rolls her eyes on a sigh. "Where do you think you got all your power from, Jaxon? Your father?" She laughs without humor. "Why everyone insists on believing that man's hype about himself, I will never know. He is just a vampire, after all."

It's a good point, one that gets me thinking about all kinds of things I don't have time to contemplate right now. Especially when the vampire queen throws up her hands and says, "Well? Are we going or what?"

"Just like that?" I ask doubtfully. It seems too easy, like maybe she's letting us go just so we can be caught by Cyrus and his guards again.

"That was the arrangement," she answers impatiently. "Though if you want to back out—"

"We're not backing out," Macy says quickly. "Come on, let's get everybody out of here before Cyrus and Isadora come back."

Delilah turns to lead everyone out, then pauses, turns back to me. "Cyrus needs to use the God Stone at Katmere at midnight—it's the super blood moon lunar eclipse, the only one this year."

"Katmere?" I ask, my heart hurting at the memory of all that rubble. "Katmere's gone."

Delilah arches a brow at me. "There's an altar just down the path to the west of Katmere, past a giant tree. That's all I know, but I would suggest doing whatever you plan on doing before he gets there."

I mentally calculate the time zones between here, Florida, and Alaska, and the time it'll likely take us to complete the Trials, and I'm not gonna lie. It's going to be close. But then, I try to remind myself, it won't matter if he's a god or not if the Army is freed and the Crown working.

I hold the woman's gaze. "Thank you, Delilah."

I can tell she's uncomfortable accepting my appreciation, especially when she sneers back, "I look forward to you delivering my revenge, is all."

I shake my head, then turn back to my friends and urge them to hurry.

Jaxon and the Order take the lead with the vampires, following right behind Delilah as she starts down the long, dark hallway that runs in front of the cells. Eden and Flint shepherd out the dragons right behind them—one in front and one pulling up the rear with the stragglers, with some of the teachers jumping in to help—while Dawud and Calder do the same with the wolves.

"Hudson and Remy can get the witches," I tell Macy as we make our way to the back of the dungeon. "You and I will get your parents."

"Thanks." She flashes me a grateful smile as I bend over to help Uncle Finn to his feet.

"You doing okay?" I ask him.

"Doing great now," he answers, though the words come out tight and a little breathless.

Despite the obvious pain, he turns to my aunt and reaches out a hand to her. "Come on, Rowena. Thanks to our daughter and our niece, it's finally time to get you out of here."

Rowena lets out a disbelieving little cry and allows Macy and Uncle Finn to help her up and get her moving. It's slow going, though, and she winces with nearly every step.

"Would it help if I carried you?" Hudson asks from his spot at the back of the group of witches. "I don't want to take a chance on you hurting yourself worse."

At first, it looks like Uncle Finn is going to object—it's obvious he wants to be the one to carry his wife to safety—but he is in terrible shape himself.

My uncle must realize it, too, because he nods and says, "Thank you, Hudson," before turning to Aunt Rowena. "This is Grace's mate, Rowena. His name is Hudson. He won't hurt you, but he can help us get you out of here if you let him."

For a second, it looks like my aunt is going to say no—and to be honest, I wouldn't blame her. She's been trapped in here for years as Cyrus's, and surely plenty of the vampire guards', punching bag. If she doesn't want to let a strange vampire carry her, I would totally get it. And would find a way to carry her myself.

But Aunt Rowena is coherent enough to understand what's at stake here, so though she glances nervously at Hudson, she nods and only flinches a little when he bends to scoop her up.

"I'll do my best not to jostle or hurt you," he tells her as we race toward the front of the cell. "But please, tell me if I do."

She nods again, but she still doesn't speak. In fact, she doesn't make a sound until we get to the iron gates at the front of the prison cell. But once Hudson tries to walk through them, she screams like she's being murdered.

He freezes instantly, his gaze shooting to mine in a plea for help it would be impossible not to recognize.

"What's wrong, Mom?" Macy asks, racing to her side. "What hurts?"

Macy looks at Hudson, but he just shakes his head. "I didn't shift position at all. I don't know what's wrong."

"I don't think I can go," my aunt says after a second, her voice cracking with the reflection of everything she's suffered.

"Why not?" Macy asks, and there are tears trembling in her beautiful blue eyes. "Mom? It's safe. Cyrus won't hurt you, but we've got to go now."

"It's not that. Cyrus is the one keeping me in the dungeon, but—" She breaks off and sinks back against Hudson's chest, like the effort of talking is just too much for her. Which it might be, considering everything she's been through—plus whatever just happened to her that made her scream like she was being set on fire.

"What is it, Mom?" Macy pleads. "Tell us what you need, and we'll do it. I swear."

"I owe a favor to the Crone," Aunt Rowena finally answers. "I don't think I can leave here until I repay it."

"What's the favor?" I ask. "We'll do it for you."

It's a brazen promise, I know, but time is ticking away. The longer we stay here, the greater the chance is that Cyrus finds us. And I have no other cards up my sleeves, nothing else I can play to get us another chance out of this place.

Aunt Rowena looks at Uncle Finn, and he nods. "They're not children anymore, Ro. Our daughter and her friends—" His voice breaks, and he clears his throat before trying to speak again. "They've done truly awe-inspiring things."

My aunt must believe him—or she simply has no more fight in her—because she nods. Then whispers, "I have to bring her daughter to her."

"Her daughter?" Hudson blurts out, shocked. "The Crone has a daughter in the Vampire Court?"

And suddenly, everything clicks. Everything.

Cyrus wasn't having an affair with a witch. He was having an affair with the Crone. And the Crone's daughter would be a demigod like me. A demigod like *Izzy*.

"Izzy is her daughter," I tell them. "And, apparently, my cousin."

Hudson's eyes go wide, and I can tell he's suddenly putting together the puzzle pieces we've got in the same way that I have.

"Why do you look so upset?" Uncle Finn says. "At least now that we know who she is, we can come up with a plan to get her to come with us."

Macy laughs, but not in a good way. "Spoken like a man who's never tried to get Isadora Vega to do something she doesn't want to do."

Which is about the truest thing I've heard in a long time. Because not only do we have to convince Izzy to come with us—we need to do it before she screams to her father that we're in the middle of an escape.

110

The Nearest Existential Crisis May Be Behind You

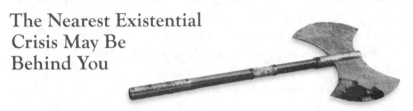

"**W**e need the others," Macy says as the implications of my realization start to come home to us. "There's no way we can kidnap Isadora alone."

"Kidnap?" Uncle Finn repeats, sounding alarmed.

"I don't think there's any other way we're getting her out of here," I tell him, then turn to Macy. "And you're right. You stay with your mom, and Hudson and I will run and get the others."

"Actually, I have something else I need to do," Hudson says as he gently places Macy's mom back on the cold dungeon floor.

"Where's that?" I ask.

Hudson shoots me an *I'll tell you in a minute* look, then turns to Uncle Finn and says, "The students need you to come with them. And I need to talk to you first."

Uncle Finn looks like he wants to protest, and I get it. His wife and daughter are sitting on the floor of a dungeon that one of them currently cannot leave. It's a big ask to expect him to just walk away from that. But on the other hand, he's the headmaster of Katmere, and we're leaving here with hundreds of Katmere students.

It's his duty to help get them to safety, and he knows it.

Which is why he nods and then bends down and kisses and hugs Aunt Rowena and Macy. As he says goodbye to her mother, Macy looks up at me with tears in her eyes and determination on her face.

"It's going to be all right," I tell Uncle Finn after he's said a choked goodbye to Macy and Aunt Ro. "Aunt Rowena will be right behind you, and I promise we'll keep Macy safe."

"I know." He pulls me in for a hug and then kisses the top of my head. "But I need you to keep yourself safe, too, Grace. I need my favorite niece to come back with Macy, okay?"

I hug him tighter. "I'm your only niece, Uncle Finn."

"Doesn't mean you're not my favorite." He pulls back and looks me straight in the eye. "Plus, it's just more reason to keep yourself safe. I need a niece."

"Okay," I say with a laugh. "Good argument."

As we start walking again, he turns to Hudson. "What did you want to talk to me about?"

"I have to go to the wells and get the others," Hudson says quietly, and my heart drops to my toes.

Gwen and all the others who've been hurt by Cyrus. Who've been drained. I almost forgot about them, would have forgotten about them, if Hudson hadn't remembered. The knowledge devastates me, has me wanting to cry because what's the point of doing all this if I just forget about the people who need me most? The people we're fighting so hard to save?

The shame I'm feeling must be on my face, because Hudson takes my hand and says very quietly, "You would have remembered."

"I don't think so. I was so wrapped up in everything else that I—"

"You would have remembered," he tells me, more firmly this time. "So don't beat yourself up about it. I'm taking care of it."

"So what are you going to do?" my uncle asks.

"When we get past the crypts, I'm going to break off and go down to the wells and get whoever's—" He breaks off because I know he doesn't want to say the words. He's going to get whoever is still alive.

My heart breaks when I think of Gwen, kind, brilliant, talented Gwen, maybe dying down there.

Hudson clears his throat, then continues. "From what I understand, the plan is for the witch instructors from Katmere to make portals to the Witch Court once Jaxon and the others get them out of range of the dampening effect of the dungeon. I was going to have you supervise that and, depending on how fast it goes, hold a portal open for whomever I'm bringing up from the wells. I'm sure a couple members of the Order will stay and help you get them across."

"In the meantime," I pick up where he left off, "the rest of us will be figuring out a way to get Izzy to the Crone. As soon as we've got her, Macy will make a portal there. Then comes the actual hard part. We've got to go back to St. Augustine, Florida, and pass the—"

"Impossible Trials?" Uncle Finn says incredulously. "You're going for the Tears of Eleos?"

"We have to try," I answer. "There's no other way to free the Gargoyle Army. We have to do it because I promised I would—they don't deserve to be frozen like that forever—and because we need the Army if we're going to have any chance of defeating Cyrus once and for all."

My uncle looks a little dazed when I finish laying out the plan for him, but he looks impressed, too. "Are you sure about this, Grace?" His gaze shifts between Hudson and me. "You know it's a long shot, right? Nobody's ever completed the Trials. And if you compete for it and lose—" It's his turn to stop talking in the middle of a sentence.

"We know, Uncle Finn. But there is no other way to get what we need. So we're going to do it, and we're going to win." I say it with way more confidence than I'm feeling, but at this point, what else is there to do? "Which means I have one more favor to ask of you."

"Anything," he tells me.

"When you get to the Witch Court, I need you to get them on board with helping us. They wouldn't before, but that was because they were afraid of what Cyrus would do to their children. But we made an agreement that if we freed the children, they would help us."

"I'll make sure they do," he answers. "What do you need from them?"

Before I can answer, Remy comes racing back down the hall toward us. "There you are! We were beginning to wonder what was going on," he tells us.

"Sorry, we got held up." I don't bother to tell him why—there's no time for that right now—so I turn back to my uncle. "I need witches in cities all over the world, wherever there are big concentrations of gargoyle statues atop buildings. Paris, Chicago, Quito, Beijing. We're going to need them everywhere."

I name off the places I've learned about since I started researching gargoyles all those months ago. "Once we use the Tears of Eleos tomorrow to cure them, we're going to need portals for them to get through."

"Portals to where?" he asks me.

"Katmere."

He gives me a strange look, and believe me, I get it. Of all the places in the world for this showdown to end up, the pile of dust and bricks that used to be Katmere Academy would not have made my list of the top one hundred places I imagined it would be. But Katmere is where Delilah says Cyrus will be at midnight to use the God Stone, so that is where we will be...along with—I hope—the Gargoyle Army.

"Just trust me, Uncle Finn. Katmere. Tomorrow."

"You know I trust you, Grace." He turns to my mate. "And you, Hudson."

"Well, that's not too bright of you," Hudson responds.

But Uncle Finn just laughs. "I think it's pretty right on." He starts to turn away, to follow Remy back down the hall, but stops at the last minute. "I'm sorry, but I can't go without asking one more time. The Impossible Trials? You're sure, Grace?"

"She'll complete them," Remy tells him.

My uncle gives him a *who the hell are you* look, but Hudson and I are too busy exchanging wide-eyed looks to introduce them. The problem with Remy being able to tell the future is, when he says something, you never know if he's saying it the way everyone else is, with more hope than conviction, or if he's saying it because he *knows* I'll reach the end. And the second question is, why did he say *she*? Was it because my uncle was talking to me specifically? Or because no one else completes it?

That thought is too awful to think about—especially if I'm actually going to take my friends back to that taffy shop—and it's not what I need to be focusing on right now anyway. At this exact moment, the only thing that matters is finding Izzy and getting out of here before Cyrus realizes we're missing. Hopefully, he'll be too busy chewing out his troops for the next while for anyone to notice we're gone. Honestly, Sméagol has his prize, so I expect him to see no need to sully himself with the dungeons now, but that doesn't mean we have time to dawdle.

Then again, when do we ever? If nothing else comes from defeating Cyrus once and for all, the idea that I'll be able to take a nap every once in a while—or maybe even get a full night's sleep—appeals to me the most.

I'm tired, and I feel like I've been tired for a really long time. It's not a good feeling, considering it's only been a couple of months since I turned eighteen. And it's an even worse feeling considering what I still have to do before I get to take one of those naps.

We stop for a couple of minutes to fill Remy in on the plan, then go our separate ways—Remy back to round up the others and deliver Uncle Finn and Hudson to the wells, and me back to Macy and Aunt Ro.

111

I Hate to
Kidnap and Run

I make it back to Macy and Aunt Rowena only a few minutes before Remy shows up again with the others—and every single one of them looks like I feel. Like we should be doing something right the hell now.

We even know what to do. The only problem is, we have no idea *how* to do it. The Vampire Court is huge—how on earth do we find Izzy before someone finds us? Or worse, finds out the dungeon is completely empty?

"I don't even know where her rooms would be," Jaxon says as he paces back and forth urgently. "I mean, I guess we could start at my father's office, but considering how many guards he's got, that seems like a bad idea."

"Unless you're an adrenaline junkie, yeah," Mekhi answers.

"So where do we non–adrenaline junkies start?" Dawud asks.

"I would have thought you'd start by leaving." Delilah's bold, rich voice booms through the cell. She's standing at the entrance, watching us incredulously. "Didn't I just get you out of here? Why are you back in the cage?"

"Because Rowena can't leave," I say, gesturing to my aunt, who is lying on the floor, looking sicker by the minute.

"So ten of you need to stay with her?" If possible, she sounds even more incredulous. "You know what? Never mind." She puts up a hand and starts to walk away. "I fulfilled my part of the bargain. I take no responsibility if you refuse to leave. Good luck fulfilling your end of our agreement from here."

She starts to walk up the stairs toward the main levels of the Vampire Court when the answer we've been searching for hits me.

"Wait." I push past Hudson and Calder and run through the cell gate to catch her. "Please."

She sighs in obvious irritation, but she stops. She does not, however, turn around. "What?" she bites out.

"You've more than met your end of the bargain, and you don't owe me anything more—"

"So why exactly are you still talking to me?" is her clipped reply.

"Because I'm hoping you'll help us anyway. Because we have no one else to ask."

Another sigh. "And?"

"If we're going to defeat Cyrus, we'll need to have Izzy on our side. We need to find her."

"It's not like it's hard. It seems like that bitch is always underfoot," Delilah replies acidly.

And can I just say, ouch? I mean, I can see why Delilah has issues with her—she is a regular reminder of Cyrus's infidelity. And she is a royal pain in the ass. But it's not her fault Cyrus cheated on Delilah, though I can't help wondering if she's been treated that way for the entirety of the time she spends out of her crypt.

If so, is there any wonder why she's...personality challenged?

Not that I'm about to say that to Delilah when I still need her help. Instead, I go with, "I'm sure it does. But since we can't go up there and look for her, I was wondering if you might help me..." I pause, trying to think of a description that doesn't sound like I'm planning on kidnapping the vampire king's daughter.

"Lure her downstairs to you?" Delilah asks drily.

"Something like that, yeah."

"If it gets Cyrus's bastard out of my house once and for all, I *would be happy to*," she tells me. "What exactly would you like me to do?"

"Give her a reason to immediately come to the dungeon—one that doesn't tip her off that we're free and waiting for her."

Delilah gives me a *no shit* look, then walks up the stairs, stiletto heels clicking with each step. I watch her go, wondering how Cyrus sleeps at night. If I'd screwed the vampire queen over anywhere near as completely as he did, I'd sleep with one eye open for fear of a well-placed Christian Louboutin straight through the heart.

Of course, he's probably too arrogant to believe his dog would turn around and bite him back. Pretty sure he's about to learn that lesson the hard way.

"Do you think she'll really do it?" Macy asks when I finally move to head back into the cell.

"I do," I answer. "But I could just be hoping really hard."

Hudson walks up behind me and, in a low voice, asks, "What is the plan, if you don't mind my asking? Just so we can get ready."

"Funny you should ask," I tell him, doing my best impression of eye batting.

I figure if you're about to ask your mate and your friends to carry close to two thousand pounds of solid stone, you should at least make a show of it. "It involves you getting to show off all those incredible muscles you guys are always bragging about."

"Oh really?" He lifts a brow, and since he hasn't fixed his pompadour in days, his hair is falling into his eyes and he looks entirely too adorable for words. If the others weren't here right now...

Apparently, some of my interest shows on my face because Hudson's gaze goes from warm to smoldering in the space of a heartbeat. Despite everything going on and where we currently are, my breath catches in my throat. For a moment, we're the only two people in the room.

"Muscles?" Calder says with such glee that our moment is broken, and I glance over to see her licking her lips even as she twirls a lock of hair around her finger. "I love me some men with strong muscles."

And when she bats her eyes, I get to see how it's really done. Because suddenly, Dawud is standing about an inch and a half taller, and they can't wait to ask what we need moved.

Which makes Eden and Macy snicker and roll their eyes at each other—at least until we hear Delilah speaking loudly enough that her words echo down the stone staircase. "I don't know what the little stone bitch wants to tell you, Isadora. I just know that she is insisting it's important."

It's the only warning we're going to get, and we spring into action.

112

You Can Never
Go Home Again

Macy and her mom stay in the cell for obvious reasons, but the magical contract should let them join us in the portal as soon as we have Izzy with us. The rest of the group races through the cell doors and scatters. Eden, Flint, and Dawud race to the left of the stairs—out of sight in case we need someone to take Izzy by surprise.

Jaxon and Mekhi do the same on the right, while Hudson, Remy, and Calder stand a few feet from the stairs to provide the distraction. They are the first people she's going to see when she comes down the stairs, and it's going to be very obvious, very quickly, that something is very wrong.

I position myself just behind the stairs. It's the best spot in the whole area to ambush someone, and that is exactly what I plan to do. With the different powers we have, we could tear this place to the ground—but that is the last thing I want to do. Which means—as long as we don't want to alert Cyrus to what's going on here—taking Izzy by surprise is the best way to fight her right now. Plus, after everything that's happened, I'll take any advantage I can get.

"You couldn't just find out what she wanted, Delilah, instead of letting her drag me into this musty old hellhole again? You know I hate—"

She breaks off mid-sentence when she sees exactly what we want her to—Hudson, Remy, and Calder standing right in front of the staircase, looking like they'd be more than happy to eat her for breakfast.

She has a dagger in both hands before I can take another breath, but that doesn't matter. Because I don't give her even a second to throw them before I reach out and freeze her.

Our bodies turn to stone in an instant. It's a feeling I'm ready for but one that has Izzy completely disoriented.

She reaches out, tries to grab on to the stone wall of the dungeon, but it's gone. In its place is the olive-green accent wall in the living room of the home

I grew up in.

I blink when I see it, shocked that we've ended up here—I definitely wasn't thinking about it when I froze us. In fact, I figured we'd end up in whatever place had come to Izzy's mind, not mine. For about the billion-trillionth time, I wonder how this power really works. I can simply freeze someone, stop that arrow of time from moving forward like Jikan mentioned. I can do that if I just brush against my demigod string. I think I've figured that one out.

But if I touch my green string *and* my platinum string, well, that's where things get foggy. I can freeze people and take them to a different time that's on a different plane, like the frozen Court, *or* to a memory, like Cyrus and his war room. So where exactly did I really take Hudson for those four-maybe-more months we were trapped together? And why can't I remember any of it?

I shake my head. I don't have time to get lost in those thoughts right now. Not when I've got a very pissed-off vampire in my childhood home.

I glance around because I can't help myself—it's been eight months since I've been in this room—and nearly cry out when I realize that I've taken us back to the day my parents died.

Fuck. Just…fuck. My knees almost buckle, but I keep them locked because I'm not alone. I'm with Izzy, and if there is one thing I've learned about Cyrus's daughter, it's that showing weakness in front of her is a really terrible idea.

I still don't know why this is where we landed, and I regret it for a lot of reasons. But there's no way I'm going to show her that.

Except…I whirl around and realize Izzy already knows. She's watching me with a sneer on her face and contempt in her eyes.

"Did you really think you could outsmart me?" she demands as we circle each other behind the oversize gray sofa I used to stretch out on and do my homework every day after school. "I've been preparing for this moment since the day we met.

"While you were making a fool of yourself in that training circle, trying to impress the general, I was watching and learning how this gift of yours works. And by the way—some free advice, even though I know you didn't ask for it. You're the queen, you numpty. *He's* supposed to impress *you*."

"I don't—" I break off as my mother opens the fridge in the kitchen, where she is trying to make dinner.

She's wearing her favorite red sweater and a new skirt she and I bought during a shopping trip the weekend before she died. That's how I know what day it is—and how I know what's coming. It's the only time she ever wore it.

She looks beautiful and vibrant and alive, and for a second I miss her so much, it almost brings me to my knees. It's been eight months since she died. Eight months since she wrapped me in a vanilla-and-chai-scented hug and told me that she loves me. Eight months since she obliterated me at Scrabble. And I've never missed her more.

The pain that finally quieted down to a dull ache with occasional sharp pangs is back in full force as I watch her pull out a bunch of vegetables to make a salad. On the stove, the teakettle is going to make the cup of health tea she always insisted I drink with dinner, and something in the oven smells delicious. Chicken enchiladas, if I remember correctly.

She always made the best enchiladas.

Another wave of sadness rolls over me as I remember all the times I helped her make the sauce through the years. How many times I helped her roll up the tortillas. Tears burn behind my eyes as she starts to chop up cucumbers for the salad, and that's when I realize something is different about this vision. More, something is off.

I never smell things in the memories I visit when I'm frozen, and I never feel so intimately connected to them. Yes, this is a really awful day in my life, but still. This doesn't feel like a regular memory.

Which means—

"I wondered if you'd figure it out," Isadora sneers. "It definitely took you long enough."

113

Memory Lane
Is a Road in Hell

"What are you doing?" I demand as I start putting things together. "How are you controlling what's going on in my memory? I'm the one who froze us. I'm the one who—"

"Should be in charge?" Isadora laughs harshly. "Grace, you don't have the guts to be in charge. You want to be the *nice* girl, you want to play by the rules, but in case you haven't figured it out yet, nice girls don't get anything in this world except destroyed."

She's baiting me, and I know it. But that doesn't mean there isn't truth to her words. It's hard to do the right thing when you're fighting people who don't care about what's right. Who don't care about anything but getting what they want. But if I don't, if I just give up and do the same things they do—Cyrus, Lia, Isadora, Delilah—then what exactly am I fighting to save anyway?

Telling myself that helps, and it lets me focus on what's really important. "You didn't answer my question."

"You're right. I didn't." She narrows her eyes at me. "You don't really think you're the only one around who's special, do you? Just because you can freeze time and spy on people who have no control over it? I may not be able to freeze time and just yank someone out of the world for a while, but I can do this."

She snaps her fingers, and just like that, my father is in the kitchen with my mom, and they are furious with each other. I notice right away as I walk in the front door from school, and guilt and pain start to claw at my stomach. I know what's coming, and I don't want to go there right now. To be honest, I don't want to go there ever again. But I don't have a choice.

Whatever Izzy is doing, however she's manipulating this, I'm not just watching a memory; I'm *living* it. I *am* that younger version of myself. And like a puppet on a string, I'm compelled to do everything exactly as it occurred in my memory.

"We can't do this!" my mom shouts at my dad, which is a rare enough occurrence that I put my backpack down on the couch and sneak over so I can get a better vantage point for what's going on in the kitchen. My parents aren't perfect—they fight just like everybody else's—but it's usually more discussion than argument, more talking than yelling.

So if my mom is this worked up, whatever it is they're fighting about has got to be bad.

"I don't think we have a choice, Aria," my dad tells her. "Grace has to learn—"

"She will. She can. We can teach her."

"I don't think so." He paces back and forth in front of the island, another sign of his agitation. "What she has to learn is bigger than us."

"So what, Cillian? We just throw her to the wolves?" My mom looks like she's about to cry, and it twists my stomach into knots, has fear skating down my spine and sadness knocking around inside me like a bowling ball that's gone in the gutter. I can feel it shattering a different part of me with each crash.

"That's not what I meant and you know it." My father sighs. "But we can't keep her here forever. Eventually it will stop being a protection and start being a curse. She's seventeen. We were younger than she is when our parents sent us to school."

"Yeah, but next year is soon enough." Tears coat her voice. "She's planning on going away to college anyway—"

"Next year is too late. You read the email. You know things are getting bad. You know it's only a matter of time before—" He breaks off, takes a deep breath. "She needs to be able to protect herself."

"Why?" my mother demands. "We've protected her this far. And the tea—the tea keeps her safe, Cillian. We can hold everything off for just a while longer."

I gasp. I don't remember anything about the tea my mother fed me nightly having to do with their fighting.

"Can we, though?"

"We have. All these years—"

"Because no one has come looking. That doesn't mean that won't change." He sighs. "You know we're almost out of that tea that keeps her gargoyle hidden, and my sister is gone now, so we can't get more."

My knees almost give out under me. Oh my God. The reason Aunt Rowena owes the Crone a favor—it's all my fault. She went to get a tea to hide my abilities for my parents. To keep me safe. A sob escapes my throat, and I shove my fist in my mouth, try to push down the pain starting to engulf me. The guilt stealing my very breath.

Macy thinks her mother abandoned her because of me. It's my fault.

My mother stands up from the kitchen table where she's been sitting, her hands wrapped around a cup of tea. "I know! But that doesn't mean anyone will come for sure."

"Yes, it does!" It's my dad's turn to yell. "We've always known we couldn't keep her here forever. Finn says things are coming to a head. If that's true—"

My breath catches in my throat, and my lungs start to feel like they're going to explode. Because I had forgotten they'd mentioned Uncle Finn, didn't realize he or possibly Katmere had anything to do with this fight. I'd originally assumed they didn't know about my gargoyle, but clearly they did. What if that's why they were fighting the day they wrecked? A whimper escapes my throat. What if they wrecked *because* they were fighting about what to do with me?

Guilt swamps me, has tears burning behind my eyes even as it nearly drives me to my knees. I did this. I made this happen. They were trying to protect me when they died, and I only made things worse. Because—

"If that's true, what is Grace going to be able to do about it?" my mom demands.

"More than we think." My dad crosses to her then, takes her hands in his. "Do you actually believe I want this any more than you do? But this is what she was born for. She was born—"

"To be our daughter!" my mom snaps.

"Yes." My dad nods. "But that's not all she is. Going away will help her. If you stop and think, you'll know I'm right."

My mother sighs, looks defeated. "I know." She drops her head on his chest. "I just don't want her to go—"

"Go where?" I demand, barging into the kitchen filled with righteous indignation. "It's my senior year!"

"Grace." My mom looks stricken. "We wanted to make some decisions before we talked to you—"

"Decisions? What decisions do you have to make? I'm not going anywhere until I graduate."

They exchange a long look, and anger spreads through me. "You can't do that! You can't just send me away because you think...what? I don't even know. And where would I go, anyway?"

"Your uncle is headmaster at a school—"

"Uncle Finn? I haven't seen him in years. And he lives in Alaska." I laugh incredulously. "There's no way you're actually sending me to Alaska. No way!"

"It's not that simple, Grace," my mom says.

"Yeah, well, I think it is. And I'm not going. You can't make me."

"We're not arguing about this right now, Grace," my dad tells me. "You have homework to finish, and we have some thinking to do. In fact—"

He breaks off as Heather honks her horn from the end of the driveway—her way of telling me I forgot something in her car.

"I'm not going," I tell him as I march toward the front door. "You can talk all you want. No way are you shipping me off to Alaska. No freaking way!"

I head for the front door, more furious than I can ever remember being.

"Why don't you take a little time to calm down," my mom says. "We'll talk about it over dinner, and maybe you'll change your mind once you hear what we have to tell you—"

"I'm not coming to dinner. I'm going to Heather's," I shoot back. "I mean, I wouldn't want to burden you with my presence when you so obviously don't want me."

I slam the door behind me, then march down the front walk to Heather's car. Except the car disappears, and then I'm standing in the morgue, listening to some assistant coroner tell me he's sorry but I'm the only one who can identify the bodies. Before I can even understand what he's saying, he leads me into a very cold room where a sheet covers a still form in the center of the area.

"No! No, no, no, no, no." The word becomes my mantra, my prayer, as the room closes in on me. As it loses air.

My legs go out from under me, and I hit the ground as the coroner starts to pull down the sheet. And there she is. My mother. My beautiful, vibrant mother.

Pain and panic explode within me, and it's all I can do to breathe through it. There's a tiny part of my brain telling me to think, to figure this out, but it's impossible when blame and remorse and terror are rolling around inside me. When all I can do or think or feel is focused on my mother's dead body...and on the fact that there's another body lying there, under another sheet.

"It's her," I manage to choke out, my nose burning with the antiseptic smell of the lab.

The coroner nods and moves on to the second sheet, and it takes every ounce of strength I have not to scream. Because my father is under that sheet and—

Suddenly, he sits up, the sheet dropping away from his bloody, broken face. And he reaches for me. "You did this, Grace," he says despite his broken, misshapen jaw. "You did this to us—"

The pain is overwhelming. Devastating. Crushing, so crushing that I struggle to find a way to breathe. To just be.

And that's when it hits me, just how close this is to what Hudson and Flint had to live through in the prison just a few days ago. Which means this isn't real. It's artificial. And if I'm not doing it—

"You bitch!" I whirl on Isadora. "This is your fault. You're doing this to me."

I can't believe it took me so long to figure it out—the Crone designed that heinous prison, so of course her daughter would have a similar ability.

"You're right, I am," she shoots back with a smile as sharp as a scalpel. "And I'm going to keep doing it until you do the one thing that will make it stop."

114

Choose
Your Delusions

I zzy shrugs. "I may not be able to freeze time like you can, but I discovered at the Gargoyle Court that I can do something even better. I can create illusions that make you feel time is frozen, like you're stuck in the worst moment of your life, and you can't get out of it, no matter what you do."

"Only you would think that's a good thing," I snarl.

She just grins and snaps. Seconds later, I get to watch myself walk back in the door from school as my mother pulls vegetables out of the fridge.

Not again. Please, not again. I'm not naive enough to ask her to stop, though. The last thing Izzy needs is more ammunition against me.

But she doesn't need me to beg to know that her latest weapon is effective. How can she think anything else when it's all I can do to watch as my parents get into the same fight about sending me away. Except this one is even more detailed, with my dad insisting that he knows what's best for me and my mother fighting him tooth and nail, even as she brews me a cup of that stupid tea.

And after we get to the end, after my father sits up in the morgue and tells me that it's all my fault that they're there, it starts back at the beginning yet again. Each iteration is more detailed, each iteration makes me remember a little more about what life in my house was like before my parents died.

Things were obviously in motion, the machinations of the Bloodletter and Cyrus and the Crone—and God only knows who else—though I was blissfully unaware of it all. Or at least I think they were coming to a head. I can't be sure if everything that's being said is a memory, or if it's just another illusion created by Izzy to hurt me.

Or should I say another incredibly efficient illusion, because the girl knows just where to shove the knife to cause the maximum damage, no pun intended. Every time the scene starts over, I die a little more inside, even though I struggle so hard not to let her know.

I mean, Aunt Rowena has been suffering for years because of me, tortured in Cyrus's hellish prison and unable to escape because of a favor she owed for me. And now that we finally have a chance to help her pay back that favor and free her forever, the least I can do is live through one of the worst days of my life a few more times.

The fact that it hurts more each time doesn't matter. Neither does the fact that panic is a wild animal within me—trapped and vicious and determined to destroy anything it comes in contact with. My breathing is harsh, my heartbeat is out of control, and my whole body is shaking so hard that my teeth are chattering.

Still, I hold it together until Izzy starts the memory over a sixth time. And this time, instead of being dressed in her favorite sweater and new skirt, my mother is covered in blood. The side of her face is ripped open, her hair is matted to her head, and her chest—there's a gaping wound in the center of it, through which I can actually see her heart struggling to beat.

"Why won't you just agree, Grace?" she asks, looking straight at me as she pours hot water into a cup. "Why would you do this to me? Why would you hurt me like this—"

"Stop." The word escapes on a whimper, and even though I know this isn't true—even though I know Izzy is manipulating everything, I can't watch it again. Not like this, with my beautiful, kind, happy-go-lucky mother shredded to pieces.

"Please stop," I whisper, tears pouring down my face as I try to control the panic racing through me. It doesn't work, and my uneasy stomach threatens to revolt completely.

"You don't have to do this," I tell her when I can speak without worrying about puking. "You don't have to be as cruel as your father."

"You think this is cruel?" Izzy looks at me with surprise. "I'm just trying to help you break free of the guilt, Grace. Why torture yourself with something you had no control over? Something you can't change?"

She sounds genuinely curious, which horrifies me nearly as much as what she's doing to me. So much so that I can't help but answer, "They're my parents. And they're dead."

"So what?" She shrugs. "My mother's dead, and it's the best thing that ever happened to me. Look at you, crying on the floor like a baby over two people who were always supposed to die before you. At least when she died early, my mom left me without any mommy issues."

Shock races through me. Isadora thinks her mother is dead? How is that possible? We all know now who her mom is—and that she's alive and rotten as all hell. How can Isadora not know?

The answer comes as easily as the question. Fucking Cyrus, who would rather lie to his only daughter about her mother than deal with anything the truth might bring.

"That's not—" I start to tell her the truth—no one should think their parents are dead when they aren't—but then I realize she will never believe me until she sees the truth with her own two eyes. And if she is doing this to me now, I can't imagine what she'll think up if she believes I'm lying about her mother.

Better to keep quiet now and live to show her the truth.

Unfortunately, that decision means watching as the memory repeats again and again on a loop, each time getting more enhanced and further away from the truth. It's horrible to see my parents like that, walking around in their kitchen with the injuries they sustained in the car accident on full display. More than once, I almost cave and unfreeze us just to get away from it, but in the end, I don't. Instead, I tell myself I can take it just a few more minutes if it means getting Aunt Rowena to safety. Just a few more minutes if it means we never have to go back to the damn Vampire Court again.

But somewhere in the middle of reliving all the pain and emotional devastation of that last evening with my parents, something else happens, too. I realize that Izzy was right—no matter what I've been telling myself, their deaths are not my fault.

The girl at the kitchen screaming at them that she won't move to some school in Alaska is just that. A girl. She's an angry child lashing out at her parents because she knows they'll love her anyway. And they do, despite her sounding a little like a spoiled brat.

But it's more than that, too. Because even in the middle of that screaming argument, they never tell her—they never tell *me*—the truth. They never give me a chance to understand the crisis, and they never give me a chance to make a real choice, about Alaska or my life.

And that's not fair. It wasn't fair of me not to hear them out about Katmere, but it wasn't fair of them not to tell me about anything else—including the fact that they begged the Bloodletter to help create me and then ended up hiding me from everyone, including myself, my entire life.

Misguided? Yes.

Done out of love? Yes.

Okay? Not even close.

But I guess that's the thing about the past. You can't change it. You can't fix it. You can only understand it. And if you're lucky, make sure you don't make those mistakes again.

"Look at you," Izzy mocks, and I realize the panic has receded and so has the pain.

I mean, it still hurts to think of this day—I have no doubt it will always hurt to think about the day my parents died—but it's back to being the dull pain I'm used to these days. It's chronic, but most days it's also bearable.

"I guess you're not as heartbroken by your parents' deaths as you want everyone to think."

"That's the thing, isn't it?" I reply as the truth continues to soak deep inside me. "When you focus on the bad things that happen, you only let yourself feel the pain. But when you remember the good that comes with the bad, you get a chance to remember the joy instead. And joy heals in a way guilt never will.

"My parents loved me," I continue. "And I loved them. I'm choosing to focus on that, to remember that."

"Isn't that so enlightened of you?" Izzy snarls.

"I'm sorry that you never knew a parent's love—" I start to say, thinking to show her that there is another way, but I stop as I realize that was *not* the way to ever begin a sentence with Izzy. She is positively murderous, and I know I've pushed too far. Fear skitters down my spine as she bares her fangs, and I know I need to get the hell out of here fast if I hope to keep my jugular *inside* my body.

Surely, enough time has passed for the guys to get us somewhere safe. And if it hasn't, well, I'll find a way to deal with the very pissed-off Izzy there, in the real world where I'm certain I can get the hell out of her way.

So I unfreeze us.

115

Epic Girl Battle: Wings vs. Fangs

Izzy comes out of stone swinging and screaming.

We're outside the Crone's gingerbread house, the dark sky bathed in moonlight so we can clearly see when Izzy's fist connects with Hudson's jaw, snapping his head back on his neck. Then she's whirling around and kicking out at Remy, catching him high and hard enough on his upper thigh to have him swearing under his breath.

"Knock it off!" Remy growls at her when he recovers, but she just hisses and bares her fangs at him—while kicking out again.

This time, her foot doesn't connect, though. Instead, he dodges, whirling around her so fast, she doesn't even know where to look, let alone where to kick. And when she tries to turn with him, he grabs her arms from behind and pulls them back, wrapping his hands around her wrists to restrain her.

In response, she absolutely, positively, totally, and completely loses her shit. Screaming, snarling, swearing, she tries desperately to buck him off while the rest of us look on wide-eyed.

Hudson gives me a *should I help him* look, and I realize for the first time that I'm not the only one who picked up on the undercurrents earlier when Remy first showed up at the unfrozen Gargoyle Court.

I don't know what to tell him—I've been wondering the same thing—so I just shrug. But that's before Izzy manages to get a hand free and slashes out to rake her razor-sharp fingernails down Remy's right cheek.

"Oh, hell no," Calder growls, leaping into the fray.

Wresting Izzy from Remy's grip, Calder tangles her hand in the vampire's topknot and then spins her around by her hair. "Enough?" she asks as Izzy screeches in pain. "Or do you want more?"

"Calder! Stop!" Remy shouts, trying to get in between the two of them.

But Izzy doesn't appreciate the help. Instead, she lashes out even as she wrestles with Calder, and this time, her foot catches Remy high enough that every guy in the room winces.

"What the hell?" he roars as he all but doubles over.

"I don't need your help, you fucking wanker!" she yells at him as she reaches behind her and grabs up a couple of handfuls of Calder's gorgeous hair.

I can't help shooting a quick look at Hudson at her word choice, and he gives me a sheepish grin that clearly says, *Like brother, like sister.*

At this point, Remy is practically on the floor, while Izzy and Calder are literally trying to murder each other—all without letting go of the other's hair. Isadora's long red hair has fallen out of its topknot, which just gives Calder more to lock her claws into. Which means the two of them are now scratching and snarling and spinning in circles, all while holding on to the hair of their enemy.

And every guy in the place—including Remy from his place on the floor—is watching in total and complete fascination. Even Flint seems spellbound by the absolute *girl fight* going on in front of him.

And no. Just no.

A quick look at Eden tells me she's got the same attitude about this whole thing as I do, so together we shove our way past the gaping, gawking guys and wade into the fray.

I grab on to Isadora and nearly get a fang to the wrist for my trouble. Eden has Calder, and though it seems hard to imagine, I'm pretty sure I'm getting the better end of the deal, considering Calder nearly takes her head off.

"Enough!" I say, but they barely acknowledge I exist, so I say it a second time, louder. Still nothing. Except this time, I get a set of claws to the neck as Calder makes a lunge for Isadora and gets me instead.

"What the hell, Eden?" I demand.

"Sorry." She sounds as testy as I do, but then she did just take a hot-pink-sequined elbow to the eye.

I'm considering freezing Izzy again, just to get her to chill out for a second, but then we'll be right back here in two minutes, so it won't do us any good. Instead, I try to grab her hands and end up getting punched in the shoulder so hard, my arm goes numb for a few seconds.

"Hudson!" I shoot him a *what the hell* look. "Are you going to help me or what?"

Hudson seems utterly terrified. "Um." He glances at the other guys, all of whom take two giant steps away from him as every single one of them refuses to meet my eyes.

"Seriously?" I demand as Calder breaks free of Eden and leaps at Izzy. "You're not going to help at all?"

All the guys—including Hudson—shake their heads, and I end up with a manticore claw to the cheek as I try to help Eden get Calder under some kind of control again. "Damn it!" I yell, and that's it. I've had enough.

I shift and then—holding Isadora as tightly as I can—I fly straight up toward the sky, at least ten feet off the ground.

Calder lets out a shriek as she jumps and tries to grab on to her prize, but I'm pissed off now, and I kick her in the face hard enough with my stone foot to have her grabbing her cheek and settling onto the ground to sulk.

Izzy crows in triumph and starts to trash talk, so I open my arms with no warning and let her crash back to earth—giving her an extra shove on the way down so that she lands on her butt instead of her feet.

And then I come back to the ground, making sure to land between them. "Enough!" I say again, and though they both hiss at me, neither makes a move to go after the other, so I'm calling it a success.

Once I make sure they've chilled out, I whirl on Hudson, who looks appropriately embarrassed now that the fight is over—as he should. "What the hell were you doing?" I demand of him—and the rest of them.

"Are you kidding me?" Mekhi answers. "No man who values any part of his body would get in the middle of that!"

"Women can be vicious," Flint agrees. "I already lost one leg this month, thank you very much. I was *not* risking a second one."

"You're all freaking cowards." I glare at my mate. "Especially you."

He nods right along with the rest of them, and I give him a look that promises this isn't over.

Then turn back to Izzy just in time to hear her demand, "Where am I? You know it's illegal to kidnap people, right?"

"This from the girl who captured everyone in this room at knifepoint and threw us in a dungeon against our will," I shoot right back. "With hundreds of kids who had also been kidnapped and were in the process of being tortured? I'm pretty sure the guilt won't keep me up tonight."

"I always knew you weren't as goody-goody as you let on," she sneers.

"Seriously?" I ask, my eyebrows shooting toward my hairline. "That's what you got out of what I had to say?"

"To be fair," she answers, "you're so boring, I try not to listen to too much that comes out of your mouth."

My gaze narrows as I contemplate saying *to hell with peace* and punching her in the mouth myself. But Remy must figure out how close to the edge I am, because this time he steps between us *before* the violence starts.

"Give us five minutes," he tells her. "I promise you won't regret it."

"I already regret it," she snarls. But when their eyes meet, she throws up a hand and says, "Whatever. Do what you want—you will anyway."

She's right on that front. I'm not leaving here—none of us is leaving here—until the Crone sees Izzy and Aunt Rowena is free. But it's more than that. There's a part of me that thinks seeing that her mother isn't dead, that her mother has been trapped on this island her entire life, will allow Izzy to let some of her anger issues go. She's still got Cyrus the Evil Bastard daddy issues, but knowing your mom isn't really dead—I glance at Macy—or didn't abandon you... That's got to help, right?

With that thought in mind, I walk toward the door of the Crone's perfect gingerbread house. The wind is high tonight, and it whips the ocean into a frenzy all around the island, and I tell myself it's not a bad omen. But then, why wouldn't it be? It's not like I've got a lot of faith in anything going particularly well right now, considering everything that's gotten us to this point.

Still, I'm on borrowed time and I don't have any to waste. Which is why I take a deep breath, knock, and then pray for the best...or at least, not the worst.

116

The Difference
Is Knife and Day

It takes a moment for someone to come to the door, and when they do, I'm prepared to fast-talk my way past the Crone's creepy manservant security people. But she either figured out something big was happening, or they have the day off, because when the door swings open, the Crone is the one standing there.

She's dressed in a long, flowing dress, just like before. And just like before, she looks like Mother Earth. This time, her brown hair that's really every color in the universe is twisted up in a topknot, not unlike the one Isadora usually wears.

"Grace." She looks surprised to see me, but she does seem curious. "I didn't expect to see you so soon."

"I know." I think about trying to break the news to her slowly, but the truth is we don't have time for that. Izzy can only be counted on not to try to murder someone for one minute, maybe two. And besides, we have a lot of other places we need to be right now.

And so I just say it—there's no sugarcoating this anyway. "We're here to satisfy Rowena's favor, at long last. But know that you may only have a few minutes with her—we're not going to force her to stay here any longer than that."

For a moment, the Crone's expression doesn't change. It remains mildly quizzical and just a little sly. But as my words sink in—as she turns and sees first my aunt Rowena and then Izzy herself—her face seems to collapse.

Disbelief comes first, followed by shock, followed by something that looks a lot like joy and pain and sorrow and relief all mixed up together. Then come the tears, silently pouring down the Crone's face as she walks slowly, haltingly toward her daughter.

Izzy, in the meantime, just looks confused. And furious. And maybe—just maybe—a little bit worried under everything else. Which makes me wonder if she might know what this is about after all.

The Crone finally makes it to Izzy, but she's still crying as she reaches out to cup her daughter's cheek. Right before her palm connects, though, Isadora loses her shit yet again.

She backs away from the Crone, already reaching for her knives as she screams, "That's it. You have thirty seconds to get me the fuck out of here."

When none of us responds, she whirls on me. "I'm fucking serious, Grace. I want to go back to London. Now."

Her hand is on the hilt of a dagger, and my heart is in my throat as I instinctively start to reach for my green and platinum strings. I'm standing between the God of Order and her long-lost, murderous daughter—and all I can think of is how they're my family. The family I didn't know I had. The Crone is my aunt, even if my grandmother says she can't be trusted. Izzy is my cousin, and *everyone* says *she* can't be trusted. But all I want right now is for everyone to calm the fuck down and for Izzy to stop throwing her knives long enough to just listen.

But it's clear she's having none of that when her hand darts into a hidden pocket and pulls out a blade. I gasp—afraid of where she might throw it—but it suddenly turns into a daisy. She snarls in frustration and reaches for another one, but it turns into a pale-pink rose.

This time she lets out a full-blown scream, fangs and all, that sends a chill skating down my spine and has me inching even closer to touching my green and platinum strings. "Do it again," she yells at Remy, "and I'll kill you."

She doesn't even have to reach for a knife this time before they all turn to flowers. Dahlias, peonies, lilies, roses, daisies, pouring out of her clothes and onto the ground under Remy's watchful gaze. His signature grin is gone, and in its place is an intensity that's impossible to miss.

"Take me home," she growls at me. "Take me home or I swear I'll—"

And I can only guess how scared she must be feeling right now, all the emotions and questions swirling inside her head.

I bite my lip and consider what to do next. We've done what we've come here to do, satisfied Aunt Rowena's contract. We could leave now, do as Izzy wants and get her as far from here as possible. But is that really what she wants? What she needs? The others don't know her backstory yet, but I do, and I can't be another person who doesn't at least try to help. Yes, in the end she might be the evil killing machine Cyrus raised her to be, but I have to hope, like Hudson, she just needs someone to believe she's worth fighting for. That she wants a different life for herself.

"Would you just shut up and listen to someone else talk for a second?" I demand, more exasperated than I can ever remember being. "I swear to God, Isadora, one of these days you're going to stop leading with your knives and actually let someone have a damn conversation with you."

"Or they'll take too long and I'll cut out their tongue," she retorts.

"You planning on using a peony for that?" Hudson asks from where he's leaning against one of the front poles on the wide wraparound porch. "Or will a daisy do?"

"You—" She starts after him, metaphorical claws out this time, but I plant myself firmly in her way. Hudson isn't the only one in this relationship with protective instincts, after all.

"You mother isn't dead, Izzy," I say while I actually have her attention. "Cyrus lied to you. This woman—the Crone—is your mother."

Isadora was poised to shout over me again—more, she was poised to attack me. But as my words sink in, she backs off. She stops fighting and just looks from me to the Crone and back again. Long seconds pass, and I'm guessing she's trying to absorb what I've just told her. And I get it.

Macy is still trying to deal with the fact that her mom was trapped all this time, that she didn't leave her. I can't imagine what it would feel like to think your mom was dead and to find out that she isn't.

Finally, just when I'm about to try to say something else to her, Izzy turns to the Crone and asks, "Is it true?"

The Crone nods. "Yes. I'm your mother." She starts to cry again. "I'm sorry. I'm so sorry, Isadora."

But Isadora doesn't care. She starts backing away from the Crone like she's afraid the woman is going to set her on fire. "I need to go." She pins me with a glare. "You need to let me go."

"Wait," the Crone says, holding an ineffectual hand out to her daughter. "Please, let me—"

"What?" Isadora asks caustically. "Explain? What's there to explain except that you gave me to *Cyrus* to raise?"

"That's not true. He told me you were dead, that my sister had killed her own child—which would kill you, too—and I believed him because..." She shakes her head. "Because I was gullible and sad, and I wanted someone to blame for the fact that you weren't in my arms."

Izzy lifts her chin. "Nice story, but if you really believed I was dead, why would you send some witch into the Vampire Court to look for me?"

"Because when Rowena showed up here, looking for a special tea to hide a gargoyle's powers, I knew that must mean Alistair and my sister's daughter survived. That this child had to be some kind of grandchild of theirs. And if that was the case, if my sister had a child who had lived, then so did mine."

She pauses for a moment, her eyes unfocused as tears still tremble on her cheeks. Eventually, though, she continues. "What happens to one, happens to both applies to every aspect of our lives. Every aspect of Chaos and Order. And so I gave her the tea. And claimed a favor in return—to find you, as I knew that if I showed up at the Vampire Court, it would only put you in danger. That was the last thing I wanted to do."

"Am I supposed to be impressed by that?" Izzy yawns. "Because I'm not."

I wait for the Crone to take offense—I learned last time I was here that it's not hard to offend her—but she just looks even sadder, if possible.

I can feel myself weakening toward her, but then I remember one very important fact—my people are dying because she helped Cyrus poison them.

"You know the Bloodletter never kidnapped your daughter, don't you?" The words come out more harshly than I intend, but once they're out there, I have no desire to take them back.

The Crone doesn't reply—of course she doesn't. There's no defense against the truth.

"Cyrus is the one who stole your daughter. He needs her to help him become a god, and I can't stop him without the Gargoyle Army."

She still doesn't say anything—not one word about what she did or why she did it—but I don't expect her to. It's not like she's big on personal responsibility or anything.

Still, she hasn't shut me down and that's something. So I press the only tiny advantage I have, saying, "And I can't get the Army to help me until I unfreeze them—which I can't do until I have an antidote to the poison. The poison *you* gave him."

I wait for her to offer to help, but she doesn't. She just watches me with eyes older than the world we're living in.

"Please," I ask her when her silence continues. "Give us the antidote. I can't let the last of my people die. I just can't."

"I didn't mean to do it," she whispers, and for a second it looks like she might actually mean it. She sinks down onto the porch steps, looking small and fragile against their wide planks. "I trusted him. I believed him when he said she'd killed my daughter rather than let Cyrus have a demigod's power to rule. And I wanted to make her pay."

Her gaze looks off into the distance but then turns to Aunt Rowena, who is still leaning against Flint, or more likely, still being held up by the strong dragon. "I'm sorry. I know what it's like to live for so many years without your daughter, and I never meant to visit that curse upon you."

Both Aunt Rowena's and Macy's eyes fill with tears, but they don't say anything. They just look away, and it's not like I can blame them. What the Crone did to them was truly despicable.

The Crone turns to me. And says, "You are so much like your grandmother."

Wow. Okay. Definitely not what I was expecting her to say. I'm not even sure it's a compliment, given the Bloodletter has kept her trapped on this island for a millennium.

But then she smiles and continues. "I can see you're coming into your godhood finally, but you still have quite a ways to go." She waves at Izzy. "The flowers were a nice touch, though."

My eyebrows shoot up. "That wasn't me." I point to my left. "That was Remy."

"Um, *cher*," Remy drawls. "Hate to break it to you, but I'd rather have let her stab me in the heart than risk pissing her off more with that trick and getting another kick to the gonads." As though they remember that pain from earlier, the guys in the group all shudder.

"But—how?" I ask. Sure, I'd been reaching for my green string at the time, but I hadn't touched it.

The Crone looks at me archly. "Did Cassia not tell you that chaos magic gave birth to Mother Nature? You are a part of that magic, just as she is, of course."

"Mother Nature?" I repeat incredulously, because come on. I mean, *come on*. I look to Hudson to see what he thinks of all this, but he seems as baffled as I am.

"We need to go," Jaxon says, stepping forward. "Are you going to give Grace the antidote to what's poisoning her army or not? My father is making his move tomorrow, and I'd like to beat that bastard back before he becomes a god."

"Hear, hear," Hudson agrees.

"She won't," Remy says, his eyes swirling eerily.

"Can't or won't?" I ask her.

"Does it matter?" she replies, and the fragile woman who was sitting on the stairs is replaced instantly by a woman of steel. Her chin goes up as she rises to her full height and says, "I do not have an antidote, but if I did, I would not give it to you. I want Cyrus to become a false god. It's the only way I can be assured of my ultimate vengeance for taking my daughter from me, and he will feel the wrath of a true god when I am done."

Well…that's just the dumbest thing I've ever heard. "Do you know how many powerful women want revenge against Cyrus? Hell, Delilah alone would help you remove his balls with a rusty spoon *today*." I shake my head. "If everyone who hates this asshole were to just team up, we could bring down the—"

The Crone sneers, "I would never work with *her*. I don't need *anyone* to seek my final revenge. I am the God of Order, and I will make that *vampire* regret betraying me for as long as the sun burns in the sky."

Her voice grew with each word she spoke, and now her hair is flying around her face, the different-colored strands catching the moonlight and creating thousands of prisms of light, so bright that the entire island is suddenly bathed in its glow. Her eyes burn a brilliant eerie blue and, as she raises her hands by her sides, every plant and tree on the small island begins to shrivel and decay, bark and leaves turning to ash and floating away in seconds, every rock melting back into the sand, until all that is left is a pristine white beach that stretches for over a mile unblemished.

After that little display, she lowers her hands, and her eyes go back to their normal blue, her hair falling against her shoulders as though the breeze that kicked it up a minute ago were nothing more than a phantom.

Izzy's eyes are wide as she stares at her mother and what she's just done with a mere thought. Remy is watching Izzy intently, and Calder is watching him. Everyone else seems floored as well.

Almost everyone. Hudson is completely unimpressed, shrugs, and says, "Brilliant. Well, you enjoy your island shade"—which makes Flint snicker because yeah, she just turned every tree on the island to ash—"but Grace and I have an army to save and an asshole to bring to his knees." He turns to Remy and motions in front of him. "If you wouldn't mind, Remy?"

A wide grin splits Remy's face. "Of course." And then he waves his hand, making two distinct ovals in the air—and two portals open in a flash.

"Which one takes me to the Vampire Court?" Izzy demands.

"The one on the right." He lifts a brow. "In a hurry?"

She doesn't bother to answer, just flips him—and the rest of us—off as she walks toward the portal.

We're in a hurry, too—a really big hurry. And still it bothers me to let Izzy go like this, especially not when I felt so connected to everything and everyone just a few minutes ago. And I've never seen anyone more alienated from everyone than Izzy in my whole life—except maybe the other two Vega siblings.

Maybe that's why I step in front of the portal right before she goes through, even though experience has taught me she won't appreciate it.

"Get out of my way," she snarls.

"It doesn't have to be like this," I answer. "You don't have to go back to him and whatever bullshit he expects of you."

"You don't know anything about my life," she snaps, trying to shove past me, but I hold my ground.

Sometimes it doesn't hurt to be able to shift into a thousand-pound statue at will—and it definitely doesn't hurt to be able to partially shift, so that it becomes pretty apparent very quickly that no one is moving me unless I want them to.

"You're right, I don't. But you don't have anything there but a father in name only. Here, you have a family if you want us. Two brothers, a mother, a…c-cousin." I stumble a little over the last bit, but that doesn't make it any less true.

"And we're not the only ones," I continue as I look from Macy to Flint to Remy to Dawud to Mekhi to Calder to Eden. "Family isn't always about blood. God knows, Cyrus has done a shit ton of damage to all of you. Don't you think it's time the Vegas take back their power? Claim a new family?"

Hudson steps forward, and I think he's going to say something customarily sardonic. But instead—for the first time in a while—he pulls off the Band-Aid and lets us see what's underneath. Including the soft, broken bits that hurt so much.

"You don't need to let him take another piece of you," he tells his sister. "In fact, you don't need to give him anything at all."

"No one takes anything from me I don't want them to have," she tells him.

"No one knows better than I do exactly how much of you he'll take," he continues as though she hadn't spoken. "But all you have to do is not go through that portal. Stay here with your mother or"—he gestures to the other portal, though he doesn't tell her where it's going—"come with us. The choice is yours."

For a moment, I think she's going to do it. I think she's going to say, *To hell with Cyrus and the epic level of shit he puts us all through.*

But in the end, it doesn't happen. Instead, she just sneers at Hudson and says, "You think you're so smart; you really think you're going to win, don't you?" She levels a glare on me next. "Whatever you've been planning that you never wanted me to hear back in the frozen Court, just know this. He's already won. You just weren't paying attention enough to see it."

With that bone-chilling statement, she turns back to Hudson and Jaxon and tosses out, "Thanks, but I think I'll stick with the winning team."

And then she walks through the portal.

117

Hair Today, Gone Tomorrow

"**A**aaaand that's your cue to leave," Remy says and motions to the other portal as he steps in front of the one back to the Vampire Court. "I'll be right behind you." And steps through.

Jaxon and Hudson move to follow him, but it snaps shut in their faces.

"Should we be concerned?" Jaxon asks.

Hudson lifts a brow. "For Remy or Isadora?"

The rest of us laugh, because he makes a good point. I mean, I'm a big believer that Remy can handle just about anything, but Izzy's a lot, even with flowers for knives.

"She's going to be so mad," Macy says as we migrate, all together, toward the portal that leads to the Witch Court.

"You act like we'll be able to tell the difference," Flint growls with a roll of his eyes. "No offense, but that girl is always mad."

"And by 'mad,' he means 'rabid,'" Dawud adds, then holds their hands up in a *hey, don't shoot the messenger type* apology when Jaxon whirls on them.

"Dude, it's true," Mekhi says. "We were at Court a few days before you arrived, and I swear all she did was threaten to murder people. And actually murder people, now that I think about it."

"Wait a minute." Jaxon pauses right before he was going to enter the portal. "You knew about my sister and didn't tell me."

"Knew about Isadora, yeah," Byron says. "Knew she was Cyrus's little pet, absolutely. Knew she was your sister? Not a clue. It's not like you guys look alike."

"So how did Cyrus explain her?" Hudson asks. "Just another vampire servant?"

"I don't know that he did, honestly," Rafael tells him. "Everyone at Court just knew her when we got there."

"We just assumed she was one of his new pets—you know how he picks up a couple of the most vicious every year to try them out, see if he wants to go through the trouble of letting them train to be guards."

The answer seems to mollify Hudson, though Jaxon still looks pissed. Of course, Jaxon wasn't raised at Court, so he doesn't know how things go. Not the way Hudson does.

As we start filing through Remy's portal—and no, it hasn't escaped my notice that his magic is so strong that he can literally hold the portal open when he isn't even here—I try to catch Hudson's eye. I want to get his take on what Izzy might have meant with her parting shot.

But Hudson is staring intently at Jaxon and Flint as they argue over which of them should go through the portal next.

"I don't need someone walking behind me like I'm going to topple over any second," Flint growls.

"And I don't trust the Crone not to shoot a parting lightning bolt at us. So I'll go through when everyone else goes through," Jaxon tells him, as though that decides it.

Flint's eyes narrow as he crosses his arms, and I'm afraid we're in for pistols at dawn if I can't find a way to move these two along.

Especially when Flint shoves his shoulders back and lifts his chin in the universal posture for pissed-off, which then has Jaxon mimicking the pose while indignation rolls off him in waves.

I rack my brain, still trying to figure out how to fix this, when Calder purrs, "How about I stay behind with you two sexy things? Rampant testosterone does wonders for my skin-care routine."

I can't tell if she's serious or not, but she gets them moving so fast, they stumble over each other as they try to get through the portal at the same time.

"Was it something I said?" Calder calls after them, right before she gives a truly spectacular hair toss and winks at Eden, who is laughing too hard to catch her breath.

With that problem solved, the rest of us file through the portal straight into the heart of the Witch Court—the Great Hall. I swear, one of these days, Remy is going to tell me his secret, considering he's never been here, but for now I'm just going to be grateful that the king and queen are nowhere to be found. But Uncle Finn is, which I'm sure is why Remy chose this spot to begin with.

Uncle Finn is holding a cup of coffee and pacing back and forth in front of the portal when we walk through en masse. He lets out a little shout when he sees Aunt Rowena in Hudson's arms and rushes over to take her.

"You freed her," he says, looking among the group of us. "You really freed her."

"We told you we would," Jaxon says. He sounds a little cocky, but I know him well enough to see the sentimental glint in his eyes. He's nearly as happy as I am that we managed to rescue Aunt Rowena.

"Yes, you did," Uncle Finn says, and there's a sentimental look on his face, too, as he studies all of us. "I know it's been a terrible couple of weeks since graduation, but can I just say how incredibly proud I am of each and every one of you? And how proud I am to have gotten to be your headmaster. The men and women you've become…" He shakes his head, even ends up trying to mask a sniffle or two. "I couldn't have asked for anything more for any of you. You are truly phenomenal."

"You're right, they are." Aunt Rowena rests her head on his chest as she, too, looks each of us in the eye. She stops when she gets to me, her smile wide in her too-thin face, and she reaches out and squeezes my arm. "Thank you, Grace. For everything."

"I think I'm the one who needs to be thanking you," I tell her, and I channel some earth magic through her hand. It's not much, but I can see a little color return to her cheeks, and she smiles her thanks. Which only makes my chest tighten painfully as guilt swirls in my stomach. She wouldn't be so ill if she hadn't helped my parents hide my gargoyle.

"No you don't, dear," she dismisses, then looks at Uncle Finn. "Do you have rooms lined up for everyone? I'm sure they would like a shower and something to eat."

I'm pretty sure five of our stomachs growl at the exact second she mentions food, and Uncle Finn laughs. "I think we can get that taken care of." He looks at the vampires. "For all of you. How does that sound?"

I nod. The Witch Court wasn't exactly welcoming last time we visited, but we just returned all of their children. That should buy us at least some chicken nuggets and a soft bed.

"Sounds great," Mekhi says, and we start to follow him into the over-the-top hallway that leads to the guest rooms.

As Mekhi and Jaxon head to their rooms, I listen quietly as they debate the merits of O-positive versus -negative blood. Eden, Rafael, and Dawud challenge one another to a paper football game while they wait on their meal. Flint teases Byron that his new magical prosthetic can actually make him run faster than Byron can fade—a good-natured taunt to which Byron laughs and tells him they're fighting words. Next to them, Macy tries to toss M&M's into Calder's mouth, but her aim is so bad that Calder ends up throwing them back at her until both of them are laughing hysterically.

It's a good moment, a good slice-of-life in the middle of all this destruction, and as I watch them, I can't help wondering who will be missing the next time we get together. Please God, don't let anyone be missing.

These are my friends sitting here—my family—laughing and teasing and loving one another. I can't lose them. I can't lose any of them.

Yet I'm asking them to do the impossible, to do something Tess flat-out said no one has ever been able to do before. And they all said yes.

My stomach pitches at the thought—and at the realization that they are going to compete in the Trials tomorrow because I asked them to. Because they trust and love me as much as I trust and love them. And because they believed me when I told them we could win.

But what if we can't?

What if I'm wrong?

What if I'm leading all of us into certain death because I'm too proud to admit that Cyrus has won and that it's all my fault? Am I so desperate to save my people and fix my mistake that I've convinced myself, convinced my friends, that we are strong enough to win?

And what happens if we aren't?

118

Hugs and Curses

Most of the guest rooms are taken by the kids from Katmere as they wait on their parents to pick them up, so Uncle Finn has all of us double up. And because he's my uncle Finn, that means I'm doubling up with Macy and not Hudson, which kind of ruins my plans to corner him for a talk.

But it is nice to hang with my cousin again, even though I can't help but notice that realizing her parents have lied her entire life has changed her. Since I first got to Katmere, my cousin's bubbly innocence has been infectious. My lighthouse in troubled waters, always guiding me safely back to shore.

But as I watch her snap open drawers and rustle through her backpack, I can't help but notice that some of her light has dimmed. For the first time since I met her, she looks like an F. Scott Fitzgerald quote I was obsessed with my junior year. "The gates were closed, the sun was down, and there was no beauty left but the gray beauty of steel that withstands all time. Even the grief he could have borne was left behind in the country of youth."

I keep getting caught up in how much I have lost. How much Hudson and Jaxon and Flint have lost, and I forget about Macy. Happy, irrepressible Macy, whose bubble this damn war has finally burst.

It breaks my heart.

When her mom knocks on our door, I offer to take a shower first so they can spend a few minutes alone. Aunt Rowena doesn't seem to want to let Macy out of her sight right now, and the feeling definitely seems to be mutual. I'm really glad she took some time to visit with the healers in the Court, though. She's already looking vastly better than how we discovered her in the dungeons. Macy and her mom have a lot to discuss now that she's feeling able to talk. Which is why I decide to sneak over to Hudson and Jaxon's room as soon as I've packed whatever I can for the Trials.

When I come out of the bathroom thirty minutes later, after the most glorious shower in existence—I'm grateful to Macy for what she did in my room at the frozen Court, but it does not stand up against actual modern plumbing—I find Macy's mom sitting on the bed with a large leather case next to her.

Macy's on the other side of the bed with a beautiful velvet box and a red pouch.

"What are you up to?" I ask as I move closer for a better look.

"Packing some runes I think might help with the Trials," she answers. I glance down and watch as they arrange on the quilt a wide array of stones with symbols etched into their smooth surfaces.

My heart tightens painfully as I remember a bag of similar runes that my father left for me. Uncle Finn put them in the safe in his office to give to me later, but now they're likely buried under the weight of the rubble that used to be Katmere, and I'll never see them again.

"What is that?" I ask, pointing to one rune in particular, curious because the lines running through it are really beautiful.

"Malachite," Aunt Rowena answers with a smile. "It's one of my favorites."

"It helps empower its owner," Macy says, "and helps manifest change, so I thought it would be a good one for the Trials."

"Tiger's-eye would be another good one," my aunt suggests, pointing to a brown stone with gold lines running through it.

"That one's for protection." I remember from the stone I'd given Jaxon when his soul had been dying. We'd never talked about it, but I always hoped he kept that stone with him even after Nuri had given him her heart.

"Exactly, Grace." My aunt grins. "And personal power, which you girls can never have too much of."

Macy and I nod our enthusiastic agreement.

We spend a few more minutes picking out stones before Macy's mom opens the top of the case she has on her side of the bed. Macy peers over to see what's in there, then squeals with delight.

"Mom! Are those—"

"Viola's potions?" Aunt Rowena finishes. "Why, yes they are, my darling daughter."

"And she said we could have them?" Macy looks skeptical.

"She said I should let you pick three you think you might need, and then I should pick out one for you as well."

"So four?" Macy's eyes go huge. "She never lets anyone take that many."

"I think she's just very excited to have me back," my aunt tells her. "And also anxious to help protect you from…"

The smile Aunt Rowena's been wearing all night falters, but she shores it up after only a couple of seconds.

Macy goes around the bed to hug her anyway. "It's going to be okay, Mom. I promise."

"I know," Aunt Rowena answers, but she doesn't sound as confident as she's trying to. Not that any of us blame her. I can't help thinking that I was obviously suffering from some kind of delusion when I told myself we would win this thing and free the Gargoyle Army, like it was just any other task we had to do. Because the closer we get to this Impossible Trials thing, the more I want to turn tail and run.

I'm not going to, but I want to. And more specifically, I want to tell my friends to. I'm the gargoyle queen. It's my duty to go into those Trials and do everything I can to win the Tears of Eleos so I can free the Army—even if they believe I betrayed them. But that doesn't mean the people I care about need to do it with me. Honestly, I'd be happy if they left me to do it on my own if it means that they are safe.

"So what potions should I take?" Macy asks extra brightly, trying—I'm sure—to break up any of the residual worry that is filling the room.

Aunt Rowena looks like she wants to say more, but in the end, she just sighs. And says, "Well, if you're going to fight an unknown adversary, the one potion no witch should be without is…" She looks through the box, pulling out the different-colored potions and then putting them back before finally finding a chartreuse-colored one and holding it up. "This one."

"What does it do?" Macy asks, taking the potion with gentle hands.

"What you most need it to," Aunt Rowena answers, resting her hand on top of Macy's and squeezing.

"Oh, Mom." Tears bloom in Macy's eyes, and I think she's going to turn away. But then she turns to her mom and buries her face against her shoulder as she hugs her as though they could make up for every hug they'd ever missed in this one embrace.

"I'm so sorry," I whisper, because the need to apologize has been eating at me since I saw my aunt on the floor of that dungeon. "None of this would have happened if you hadn't needed to get the tea for me—"

119

Nothing Is Set in Stone, Even a Gargoyle

"Don't apologize," Aunt Rowena says. "We all played our part to get to where we are now. I was there when your mom and dad and our coven went to the Bloodletter to ask for help in creating a gargoyle. While we thought we had failed, we were all thrilled when your parents discovered—years later—that it had worked. In you. I'm your aunt, and I was your mother's best friend. It was my honor to help protect you."

Her words cause tears to burn in the backs of my own eyes, and I start to turn away. Maybe I should be angry she helped my parents hide such a fundamental part of who I am from me my entire life. But I can't be. Looking at my aunt now, her shoulders still stooped from years of magical torture, of trying to do what she and my parents thought was best for me, trying to keep me hidden from Cyrus as long as they could... She's suffered enough.

When Aunt Rowena holds an arm out and says, "Come here, Grace," I rush into her arms.

As she wraps one arm around me and one around Macy, it takes everything inside me not to break down. Because there is something really wonderful about being held in a mother's arms again after so long. I don't think I realized how much I needed it—or how much I missed it—until Aunt Rowena's hug made me feel safe in a way I haven't felt in a long, long time.

When I pull away, Aunt Rowena smiles at me and runs a soft hand down my cheek before doing the same to Macy. "What strong, powerful, beautiful young ladies you've both grown into while I was away," she says softly. "I'm so proud of you."

"Don't you start crying, Mom," Macy tells her. "Or I'm going to end up bawling my eyes out, and we don't have time for that."

"Fair enough," Aunt Rowena says before turning to me. "I need to talk to Grace anyway."

"That doesn't sound ominous at all," I tell her with a grin.

"I figure ominous happened a long time ago," she answers. "This is just filling in the blanks with stuff Finn was likely too cautious to tell you." She shakes her head. "I swear, that man wants nothing more than to protect every single one of you from everything."

Since that sounds like Uncle Finn—I've been having to pry information out of him piece by piece since I got to Katmere—I don't bother to defend him. Instead, I ask, "So what hasn't he told me?"

"Well, I'm guessing you didn't know that I asked the Crone for the tea that kept your gargoyle hidden before now, right?" I nod. "You need to understand that magic is not meant to be put into a box for very long. We'd always intended you would attend Katmere, begin your training there, protected by Finn and others, giving you the support and protection to explore what it means to be the first gargoyle in a thousand years. I think with my disappearance, though, everyone became more cautious and decided to keep you hidden longer."

I let out a breath. That my parents hadn't meant to keep something so fundamental about me hidden my whole life—which I have to admit I considered was possible—is a weight I didn't know I'd been carrying.

"But now that I learned from the Crone today that you are the granddaughter of the God of Chaos, well... That changes things, Grace." She stares intently into my eyes.

"The tea would have also kept that part of your nature locked away. And chaos magic is...ancient. Powerful. And most assuredly angry that it's not been set free. One day, it will be stronger than your gargoyle and human sides, and that might be scary for you."

Her words make my stomach clench. I'm used to my gargoyle—I like my gargoyle—but this demigod thing? I'm not nearly as okay with that. Maybe it's because I nearly killed everyone with the green string in the Bloodletter's cave; maybe it's because neither the Crone nor the Bloodletter is the type of person I want to be. Or maybe it's just that I'm scared.

Scared of the power. Scared of the responsibility. Scared of once again becoming something else. Something different. Something I don't think I'll ever understand.

"What should I do?" I force myself to ask even though I don't want to know the answer, and I know Hudson would be very proud of me right now.

"That kind of ancient magic, passed down from mother to daughter, won't be held back forever—and that's a good thing. Don't hold it back, Grace. Accept it. Embrace it. Learn to wield it the way it's meant to be wielded."

The churning in my stomach gets worse, kicking up the anxiety I'm trying so hard to keep in check. I take a deep breath, do my best to ignore the nerves skittering along my spine.

It's just a conversation, I tell myself as Aunt Rowena continues to talk. Just a conversation. Nothing is written in stone. Not even me, gargoyle or not.

"I don't know if I can do that," I tell her honestly. "It's hard to control, and I don't want to mess anything up. And I definitely don't want to hurt anyone."

"Surrendering to the power inside you can be very scary, sweetie, but it's only then that we truly see all that we are capable of becoming. And you, my dear niece, are capable of so much more than you know. Embrace all of your magic, and let it embrace you back," she tells me. "Besides, sometimes causing a little mayhem is exactly what you need to do."

"I don't—" I break off as panic tightens my throat, makes it hard to breathe.

"It's okay," Aunt Rowena tells me as she reaches out to pat my hand. "I didn't mean to upset you."

"You didn't," I answer, though that's not exactly true. But it's not her fault I can't control my abilities, and it's definitely not her fault I can't come to grips with all the different facets of myself.

She doesn't look like she believes me, but she doesn't say anything else. She takes my hand and admires the tattoo that winds all the way up to my elbow. I start to tell her about it—about what it can do and why I have it—but she must already know.

Because instead of asking about it, she puts her hand on top of it and closes her eyes. Seconds later, I feel a gentle warmth running along my skin and when I look down, my tattoo is glowing again. Not the way it does when I channel magic from someone, but something is definitely going on.

My aunt must see the question in my eyes, but she just grins. "A little magical boost never hurt anyone," she tells me and squeezes my hand. "You'll know when you need it."

And just like that, I'm blinking back tears again. My aunt is so much like Macy—so generous, so kind, so smart when it comes to understanding what makes people tick—that it makes me feel even worse that she spent all those years locked in Cyrus's dungeon. All those years locked away from the family who loves her and the world she works so hard even now to make a better place.

"Thank you," I whisper when I can get the words past the tears clogging my throat. "For everything you've done for me."

"Oh, Grace." She wraps both arms around me now and pulls me in for a long hug. "I can't wait to see every part of you come to life. Human. Gargoyle. Demigod. And of course, a witch."

"A what?" I ask, confusion in my voice.

"A witch. Don't forget what your father was." She nods to the runes I haven't put back in my bag yet. "There's magic in your blood."

"I don't think that's true. I can't do magic, not the way Macy can. Not the way you and Uncle Finn can. I can only do what my gargoyle can do—"

"You lit a candle once, remember?" Macy says.

"Yeah, but I didn't actually do that. Hudson did. I just kind of channeled what he gave me—"

"Hudson's a vampire, silly." Macy's smile takes over her whole face. "He might have given you a power boost, but he can't make fire. That candle—that magic? That was all you."

And just like that, the tears I've tried so hard to hold at bay spill over. Because it's nice to think I have something of my dad in me, something besides my smile and curly hair that comes from him.

Something that I can hold on to, even if I haven't been able to do any other spells since then.

I ask my aunt about why I haven't been able to, but she just shrugs. "I don't know, Grace. My best guess would be your gargoyle nullifies the magic inside you, since it is immune to it."

"Yeah, but it doesn't nullify the demigod magic." More's the pity.

"Mom said demigod magic is ancient." Macy claps her hands. "And the Crone said the first time we visited her that gargoyles are not immune to ancient magic! And that means—"

She breaks off as a knock sounds at the door.

120

The Rune
Where It Happened

"Come in," Macy calls.

"You made it!" I say with a grin as Remy sticks his head in the door.

"I did." He pretends to stagger a little. "Though that Isadora is a bit of a wild woman, isn't she, *cher*?"

"That's one way to put it." I shake my head. "I mean, I would have gone with psychopath, but whatever."

"Nah, she's not that bad. She does keep me on my toes, though."

"And she will for many years to come, huh?" I shoot him a sly grin, but he just shrugs.

"That remains to be seen." He nods toward the bed where Macy and Aunt Rowena continue to sort through runes, picking just the right ones to bring. "I brought you something as well."

With a flourish, he pulls an ornate box from behind his back, similar to the one on the bed but much more familiar. My breath catches. I couldn't have been more surprised if Remy had pulled an ostrich from behind his back.

"How did you—? When—?" I reach out with shaky hands and take the offered box, pull it close to my chest.

Remy shrugs. "I know you meant to get them out of your uncle's safe—you know, before everything went to shit. Besides, you're going to need them."

"How did you know about them?" I ask, because I have to ask. I know Remy is an insanely powerful warlock, and if what my aunt told me about magic not liking being kept in a box is true, I can only imagine how much more powerful he will become as he sets his free. But this, knowing about my father's gift to me and that I lost it...

He stops, and for a second, I think he's actually going to answer the question. But this is Remy, after all, and in the end, he just gives me an enigmatic grin. "Jaxon told me to tell you we leave in an hour. He wants us to meet in the Great

Hall." He rolls his eyes—whether at the room's name or Jaxon's high-handedness, I'm not sure.

"Okay, then," Macy says with a grin. "Let's go kick some Impossible Trials ass."

"Say that five times fast," I tell her.

"Right? The name alone is enough to—" She reaches out to pat Remy on the arm but breaks off as his eyes start to do that weird swirling thing they do right before he says something terrible.

But this time when it stops, Remy doesn't say anything. He just turns to go, without so much as one of his signature smiles.

"Hey!" I call after him. "What did you see? Are we going to get the Tears? Will everyone be okay?"

And then I hold my breath, because I'm not sure I want to know the answer to that question. Not now, when we don't have a choice but to move forward.

For a second, I don't think he's going to answer. But finally, he blows out a long breath and says, "The future is constantly changing, Grace. Just because I see it ending one way doesn't mean that's how it will actually end." He takes a deep inhale, then admits, "And just telling you something bad might happen could actually cause it to happen."

"How is that even possible?" Macy asks.

He shrugs. "Maybe I see you getting hit by a bus today, so I tell you not to walk on J Street at eight p.m. You don't. Instead, you don't go into work at all that day—and you accidentally leave the stove on and burn your home down with your family in it."

Okay, harsh. But not the same thing here, like, at all. "I think we can all agree we'd rather have any future than dying horrifically in the arena for the amusement of others, Remy."

He looks like he's weighing his next words very, very carefully.

Eventually, he takes a deep breath and says, "A leader isn't great because they're always right. A great leader instead makes room for others to be right."

I blink up at him.

"You can be a great leader, Grace," he says, and something in the softness of his voice makes my chest squeeze tight.

"Thank you, Remy," I whisper, a little overwhelmed by his belief in me.

He squeezes me quick before stepping back, then nods toward the bed. "We'll definitely have a better shot with those runes."

Just before he walks out the door, he pauses and tosses over his shoulder, "By the way, I gave your boyfriend a gift that just keeps giving. You can thank me later."

And with a wink, he walks out.

121

Die on the Dotted Line

Macy's portal lets us off about ten feet from the taffy shop in St. Augustine, and Monster Taffy looks even more ominous in the middle of the night than it was at dawn. We all agreed there was no time to waste in getting to the Trials—the lunar eclipse blood moon is only a few hours away, after all—so we're hoping Tess meant it when she said the Trials could begin anytime, "day or night."

I glance over at Hudson, standing on the sidewalk, and grin. Remy's "gift that just keeps giving" turned out to be a ring that allows Hudson to feed from his mate and yet still walk in the sunlight, and I have to admit, knowing we are only racing against a lunar eclipse's clock and not the sun's feels great. I am so here for no one knowing the details of our sex life ever again.

But right now, as we stare at the front of Monster Taffy, I'm beginning to feel like one of those characters in horror movies everyone makes fun of—the ones who move into the creepy-as-fuck house they know is haunted and then invite the first guy they see with the hockey mask and the bloody knife in for tea.

Or it could just be that I know what's waiting for us inside, and that's what's creeping me out. God knows, I want to be anywhere but here doing anything but what we're about to do.

But since that's not an option, I squeeze Hudson's hand. There's no one else I'd want by my side right now. And not just because of his power.

"You okay?" he asks, those ridiculous blue eyes of his watchful as they search my face.

"If you define 'okay' as 'convinced this is the worst idea we've ever had,' then sure. I'm okay," I answer.

"I still think the worst idea you ever had was mating up with Jaxon," he teases. "But this could run a close second."

"Yeah, because being Jaxon's mate and entering a contest that has literally killed every person who has ever entered it are totally the same thing." I roll my eyes at him.

He makes a *who knows* face. "To be fair, mating with Jaxon and entering a contest that kills every person who enters it might actually be the same thing. Maybe you're the lucky one who actually makes it out of both."

"You guys know I'm standing right here, right?" Jaxon deadpans and everyone laughs, breaking the tension exactly the way Hudson planned.

"Hey, guys, I finally guessed what Hudson promised me with my promise ring." I toss a big smile over my shoulder to the rest of the gang as they follow Hudson and me to the front door of the taffy shop.

When Hudson only raises one brow in question, I continue. "He promised to go to karaoke with me anytime I ask."

He snort-laughs as I place my hand on the shop doorknob but don't turn it yet. Instead, I turn and tease him just a little bit more. "We're totally going to do a duet of 'Story of My Life'!"

And now everyone is cracking up at the idea of Hudson pretending to be Harry Styles to make me happy.

"What if you have terrible pitch?" he asks.

"You'd love me anyway," I reply, and his smile overtakes his whole face.

"I would," he says. "Doesn't mean I'd karaoke with you, though."

"Hey!" I poke him, laughing.

But Remy says, "I'll sing with you, *cher*," and Hudson tosses him a death glare—which makes us all break out into more laughter.

Holding my mate's hand, looking into the faces of all my friends as we share this one perfect happy moment, I feel blessed. Flint, Jaxon, Mekhi, Macy, Eden, Byron, Dawud, Remy, Calder, and Rafael. My family.

I cross my fingers that it isn't locked, then pull at the door to the taffy shop. Thankfully, it opens, and as we walk through, I pray I can keep them all safe.

Hudson leans down and whispers in my ear, "We all make our own choices."

And he's right. I know he's right. A defeatist attitude never helped anyone do anything. But as I look at all the weird, foreboding, *fairy tale from hell* trees in this place, it makes it hard to remember that when all I want is to leave here and spend more time just hanging with my friends.

Sure, we really can't afford to waste any time while Cyrus is probably leading an army to Katmere as we speak, but the heart wants what the heart wants. And right now, my heart wants a few more hours.

A few more hours to be with Hudson before we might lose each other forever.

A few more hours to hang with Macy and dance around to "Watermelon Sugar."

A few more hours to swap knock-knock jokes with Jaxon or go flying with Flint or do any of a million other things with Eden and Mekhi and the rest of our friends.

But before I can even get my hopes up, Tess enters the shop from a back room, her eyes meeting mine across the space.

She smiles a toothsome grin that reveals some seriously sharp teeth and takes a piece of taffy from her ornate-looking chalice on the counter. "I was beginning to think you weren't coming back," she says, toying with the wrapper. "Yet here you are in the middle of the night. Cute."

"We've had a lot on our plate," Jaxon answers for me.

She eyes him like he's a gnat buzzing around her head for several seconds before turning her gaze back to mine. "So you're in?"

I have to clear my throat to get the words out, but I say, "Yeah. We're in."

"Okay, then." She reaches under the counter and pulls out a binder. "We've got a few waivers for you to sign."

It's such a banal thing for her to say that, for a second, I don't even register it. By the time I do, Macy is already asking, "You want us to sign a waiver?"

"Several, actually. Covering everything from death to accidental dismemberment to inability to reverse magical spells." She pops open the cover. "Who's first?"

I look back at my friends, all of whom look both uneasy and determined. "I guess I'll sign first," I say, stepping up to the cash register where Tess is waiting.

But the second I get there, she laughs and slams the binder closed before I can see what's in it. "I'm just fucking with you, checking to see if you're really in this time. Who needs a waiver when you're probably going to die anyway?"

She shoves the binder back under the counter and turns away. "Follow me," she announces as she walks toward the door we went through last time.

"Wow. Isn't she nice?" Byron comments under his breath.

"Only if 'nice' and 'vicious' are actual synonyms," Dawud shoots back. But in typical Dawud fashion, they don't bother to lower their voice.

Which, in turn, has Tess turning around and smiling sweetly. "'Vicious' isn't on the program until later, but we can move it up a little, if you'd like."

They nearly choke on their tongue. She pushes open the storeroom door, and we walk into the arena. The ground is dirt and grass, almost like a sport pitch, with huge stone stands surrounding the perfectly round field. And in the middle, just like before, there is an ornate golden chalice crusted with diamonds atop a stone pedestal. When we got a glimpse of the arena the first time we'd visited the taffy shop, I had the impression the field was outdoors (which made no sense given it was in the back of a shop, but, well, there are a lot of things in this world that make no sense). But now that I get a better look at the sky, I can see it's not really a sky at all. There's some sort of dome over the arena, lit from within, giving it an almost glowing appearance. It's really quite beautiful.

"Yeah, that's what I thought." Her smile is as sharp as one of Izzy's daggers as she turns back around, her skirt swishing as she walks.

Today she's dressed all in crimson instead of black—crimson blouse, crimson skirt, crimson boots. Except for the belt she has wrapped three times around her waist, which is the same black one she wore earlier. I try not to take her outfit as an omen of how much of our blood we're about to spill on the arena ground, but it's hard not to think about it. Especially since the stands have already started to fill up with paranormals by the time we're outside.

"How did so many of them know we were coming to challenge?" I ask, shocked they'd all show up in the middle of the night.

"Magic," Tess deadpans to me, then winks. "Now, how many of you are competing?" she asks as the door closes behind us and the Florida heat hits us all over again.

"Twelve," I tell her. "I think you said that's okay?"

"Yup, that's the max. You sure you want that many dying today? We haven't really had that large of a group in a while, actually." She gets a pensive look on her face. "Which, come to think of it, also didn't go well."

She shrugs. "So, yeah. Twelve works for me if it works for you." She gestures to the chairs behind us. "Have a seat while we ready the course."

"We need to wait?" Dawud says, and I can hear the nerves in their voice.

Not that I blame them. Now that we're here, I want to get on with it, too. I'm pretty sure the longer we wait, the harder it's going to be to walk into that arena.

"It'll only be a few minutes," she tells them, and I think I see a flash of empathy in her eyes. But it disappears as quickly as it comes, and so does she, her boots clicking on the cement as she races down an impossibly long staircase.

122

I watch her go, my heart in my throat. And when she finally makes it down to the floor of the arena, I turn to the others. Because there's no way I could live with myself if I just let them walk into that arena with me if I didn't at least say something one last time. No matter what they told me earlier.

When leading your friends into certain death, it's never a bad thing to give everyone one more chance to hit the exits.

"You don't have to do this." The words come out before I know that I'm going to say them. It's not quite how I planned to start this conversation—I've been racking my brain for the last five minutes trying to figure that out—but it's good enough. More, the words say what they need to.

"Grace—" Macy starts, but I stop her with a raised hand.

"No," I tell her. "I need to say this.

"I have to do this," I tell them as I look from Flint and Byron to Dawud and Rafael and from Eden and Mekhi to Remy and Calder. "I'm the one who made the decision to steal the ring from Chastain and give it to Cyrus. I'm the one who made the entire Army turn to stone. I'm the gargoyle queen, responsible for saving them, the last of my kind. But you're not."

I don't bother looking at Hudson, Jaxon, or Macy, because I already know what their answers are going to be. They would never leave me here any more than I would leave them. But if I can save some of the others, then I have to try. I don't know how this is going to turn out, but I do know that all twelve of us dying is a huge waste.

"I appreciate you being here more than I can ever tell you. I really do. But this isn't your fight. You don't have to be here for it. I won't think less of you—and neither will anyone else—if you decide you don't want to go into that arena. We've already lost so much, I don't think it's fair to ask any of you to risk losing any more. And I need to be brutally honest here—I don't think we'll all make it. Do I think we're going to win? I do. I don't know why I feel this way, I just do. Probably because we've taken more hits than anyone can imagine, and yet we're still here. We've lost friends along the way, though, and I don't want to lose any more in my lifetime. And so, as much as I appreciate everyone for coming, I think maybe—maybe this is something I need to do by myself."

Hudson's at my back—one hand on my waist, the other on my shoulder—and I sink into him, reveling in the quiet strength and support he never fails to offer me. No matter what's happening around us or between us or even just in his own head, Hudson always, always has my back.

I don't know if I've ever thanked him for that, but I'm going to.

At first no one says anything, but I wait them out. Surely someone doesn't want to be here. Surely someone understands how foolhardy what we're about to do is.

A minute passes, maybe two, before Calder looks me straight in the eye and says, "You know you're not that special, right?"

Which is not exactly what I expected her to say, but oooookay. "Yeah, I know. Of course I know."

"Do you?" She narrows her big brown eyes at me. "Because it sure seems to me like you take everything on yourself."

"I d-don't—" I trip over the words, my brain going faster than my mouth as I try to figure out what I want to say here. "I mean—"

"What Calder is trying to say, *cher*"—Remy steps in smoothly, his green eyes warm and understanding—"is that we all have our reasons for being here. And loyalty to you is only part of it."

"That is *not* what I was trying to say, Mr. Big Old Mansplainer," Calder says, her claws suddenly gleaming. "What I was trying to say is that the world doesn't revolve around Grace. That I have my own reasons for being here."

Remy lifts a brow. "Isn't that what I just said?"

"No." She huffs before turning to me. "What I'm trying to say, Grace, is that I'm not leaving. And neither is Remy. So get over yourself, will you?"

"Yeah," Mekhi echoes with a wicked gleam in his eye. "Get over yourself, Grace."

I get what they're saying, but still I feel like I need to make one more plea for reason. "You guys—"

"Stop, Grace." This time it's Eden who speaks up. "All of us are here because we feel like we have to be. But none of us are here because we feel like we're forced to be. We're here because it's the right thing to do. We're here for you. But most of all, we're here because none of us want the people we love to live in this world if Cyrus is a fucking *god*. So let's go find that Tess chick and tell her to get this show on the road. We've got a fight to win."

123

Here Goes Nothing

As it turns out, "that Tess chick" comes back before we can even start to look for her. "You ready?" she asks, looking each of us in the face in turn.

"'Ready' is such a subjective word," Dawud says. But I notice they're the first one in line behind her.

"Let's do this," Flint says, his eyes meeting Jaxon's—and lingering—for just a second.

"Let's do it," I echo.

Hudson's hand stays on the small of my back all the way down the stairs, and never have I been more grateful for his support. My knees are shaking just enough that I'm honestly not sure I would have made it all the way to the arena floor without him by my side.

As we walk, I notice the huge screens all the way around the arena. They're twice as big as the jumbotrons at professional sporting events and there are twice as many—one to cover every side of the arena.

Spectators of all types have packed the seats, and I can't help wondering why they're here. Do they really want to watch people get the hell beat out of them and maybe even die, all in pursuit of an elixir that most of the world thinks is just a myth? Is that really what they think a fun evening would look like?

Judging from the screams and shouts all around us, my attitude is definitely in the minority. Everyone else here is acting like they're about to see a damn gladiator fight, and they can't wait to watch the lions tear us limb from limb.

Not that I think there's anything as tame as lions behind that wall in front of us, but still. The analogy stands, especially when Tess parades us out on the field in front of the entire stadium. She doesn't introduce us by name, but she does mention that the betting windows close in three minutes.

Because, apparently, betting on whether or not we will survive this monstrosity is an actual thing. And if the numbers on the jumbotron are any indication, the odds definitely don't look good.

"The rules are simple," Tess explains to the audience and to us as we wait for the betting to close down. The fact that she does so as she happily prances around doesn't endear her to any of us. Nor does the fact that I'm pretty sure she disappeared a little while ago because she wanted to place a bet against us. "Don't die."

"She's right," Hudson deadpans. "That is simple."

I elbow him in the stomach, but he just gives me an *am I wrong* look.

"There are four rounds between you and the Tears of Eleos. Get through them all and the Tears are yours. Fail and…"

She pauses to hold the microphone out to the crowd, all of whom scream, "Die!" at what feels like the top of their lungs. And continues to feel that way as they start to chant, "Die, die, die. Die, die, die."

"Who exactly are these people?" Macy asks, horrified.

"Crypt keepers, apparently," Hudson answers, though disgust is evident in his tone.

"Apparently," Calder echoes, her beautiful face hard as a diamond as she scans the crowd.

"What are you looking for?" Flint asks, curious.

"I'm not looking for anything," she replies with a toss of her hair. "I'm memorizing their faces for when we make it out of this. If they want death, I'm more than happy to show it to them." The fact that she makes the threat—promise?—in a super-sweet tone only makes it more disconcerting. As does the fact that Remy doesn't even look surprised.

"Are there any questions?" Tess asks when the betting clock runs out, interrupting Calder's attempt to memorize every face in the arena.

None of us has an actual question about the Trials, so we just wait for her to quit pandering to the crowd. Which doesn't take very long now that the bets have all been placed.

"Okay, then. When the buzzer sounds again, you have thirty seconds to get in through there."

She points to a four-foot-wide opening in the stone about a hundred yards away from where we are standing.

"Once your entire party is inside, the circle seals itself up, and it only opens again once you've completed all four rounds and you've earned the Tears. If you don't complete all four rounds and get far enough to claim them, the arena will lay claim to you."

I don't know what "lay claim" means, but it doesn't sound good. *Mental note to self—don't get claimed. And don't let any of your friends get claimed, either.*

"What happens if it takes longer than thirty seconds for all of us to get inside?" Dawud asks.

"Then the arena locks out whoever isn't inside," Tess answers. "And the Trials go on without them."

This just keeps getting better and better. *Another note to self—run really fast.*

"If there are no further questions..." Tess steps away from the rest of us. "Thank you for participating in the two thousandth, two hundred and sixty-fourth Impossible Trials. Let the countdown begin."

"Countdown?" Jaxon asks right before the people in the stands start to yell all over again.

"Ten. Nine. Eight." Tess joins the chant, her voice overlaying the frenzied nature of the crowd's as she counts down into the microphone.

"Ready to do this?" Hudson asks me. His voice is low and steady and, while it doesn't calm the nerves jangling in my stomach, it does make them a little easier to bear.

"Seven," the crowd roars.

"No," I say with an emphatic shake of my head. "You?"

He shrugs. "It's just one more thing we have to get through before I can take you back to our room at that lighthouse."

"Six!" Tess yells.

"Promise?" I ask. "When this is all over?"

"Five!" The crowd grows more frenzied.

He grins. "Oh, I promise."

Our conversation makes me think of my ring, and I rub my thumb across it for good luck.

"Maybe you should tell me what else you promised me," I say. "I'd hate to die without knowing what it is."

"Four!" Tess pumps her arms to encourage the crowd to get louder.

"You're not going to die in there," he tells me. "I won't let you."

"Three." The crowd members are on their feet now, cheering and stamping.

"Yeah, well, you better not die, either. I'm actually aiming for none of us to die."

"Two." Tess whoops and hollers right along with them.

"I love you," he tells me, his bright blue eyes burning into mine.

"I love *you*," I echo as the whole arena yells, "One!"

I squeeze his hand one last time, then let go.

The buzzer sounds. And I run like hell.

124

One Good Turn Deserves Another and Another and Another

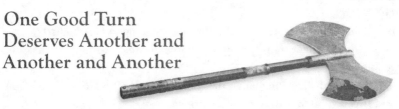

I've only gotten a couple of feet before Hudson picks me up and fades with me the hundred yards to the opening in the stone wall.

We're the first ones through, followed immediately by Jaxon and the rest of the Order.

In my head, I'm keeping a running tally of the seconds, and I know we've got about fifteen left when Dawud and Eden come crashing through the opening, right in front of Remy and Calder.

Flint and Macy rush in with about seven seconds to spare, and my heart is in my throat by the time they squeak through.

Relief swamps me, at least until the stones slide shut behind her, plunging our entire portion of the arena into total darkness.

"What do we do first?" Byron asks, unconcerned with the darkness, probably because he can see right through it.

"Light," I answer. "We need light first."

I'm barely done requesting it when Remy does something—I can't see what—and a spinning ring of light appears just to the left of us.

"I got you, *cher.*"

"Thanks," I tell him as I turn around in circles, trying to figure out what we're supposed to do now.

My friends are doing the exact same thing, all of us searching the dome we're locked inside for some clue as to what happens next.

Except nothing seems to be happening next. It's just the twelve of us spinning around, growing more and more bewildered.

"Are we being punked?" Macy finally asks. "Is this just some big joke to the crowd?"

I can hear them chanting outside, though the stone is so thick, I can't quite make out what they're saying. I can feel the ground shaking with their stomping, though.

"Nah," Rafael says, twisting his hair up into a bun on the top of his head. "That crowd is way too bloodthirsty for this to be a joke."

He's right, and I'm about to say so when the ground beneath our feet starts to rumble.

"Earthquake?" Remy suggests. "Is that what's going to happen first?"

"I hope not." Calder sighs heavily. "The dust it causes will totally mess up my eye glitter."

I bite back a disbelieving laugh that that's what she's worried about right now. But this is Calder, so is it really a surprise?

"You'll still be beautiful," Dawud tells her, and the puppy worship I saw earlier is definitely back in their eyes.

"Of course I will be," she tells them as she runs her fingers through her hair. "But I could get glitter in my eye and that doesn't feel good. Obviously."

"Obviously," they echo, looking just a little bewildered. Not that I blame them—Calder bewilders me sometimes, and I've had significantly more exposure to her than they have.

"We should spread out," Jaxon says when another minute passes and still nothing happens.

"Yeah," Eden agrees. "Let's look around and see if we can see something we need to do to activate this thing, because just waiting here like a sitting duck in a shooting gallery isn't really working for me."

"Good plan," Macy agrees and immediately starts moving toward the other side of the arena.

In a matter of seconds, we've all fanned out to check the ground, the walls, anything we can think of. Eden even turns into a dragon so she can fly up and check the top of the dome, just to be sure we aren't missing anything.

I don't see anything in my area and turn to Jaxon—who is to my right—to see if he's found anything, when suddenly, a loud groaning sound fills the arena. And the ground beneath our feet begins to spin.

125

We're Gonna Rock Around the Block Tonight

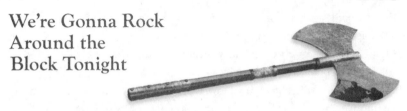

My heart explodes in my chest as memories of the gauntlet and the prison fill my head.

Fearing the worst, I plaster myself to the wall, but it turns out stone moves really, really slowly.

But what doesn't move slowly is the giant wall that comes up from the floor, dividing the room from floor to about two feet from the ceiling into two inequal sections, effectively cutting several of us off from the rest.

Jaxon and I end up together in a small section of the room that is shaped a lot like a quarter moon when everything is said and done. Thank God Remy's spinning light thingy ended up on this side with us, so at least we're not in the pitch dark.

"You okay?" Jaxon asks when the room stops spinning.

"I'm fine. It's not like that was fast enough to hurt anyone." I walk to the corner of our little section of the arena/moon and start looking to see if anything's changed. Nothing has, which has me baffled. Because, "What are we supposed to do in here?"

"I don't—" Jaxon breaks off as a loud scream comes from the other side, followed by snarling and hissing.

"Macy!" I yell, beating on the wall with my fists as I recognize my cousin as the one who screamed.

Another yell, this one from one of the guys—Mekhi, I think—followed by more snarling and a major thump, like someone has just been thrown against the stone wall.

"What do we do?" I ask Jaxon. "We can't just leave them—"

I break off as an oddly shaped brick falls from the sky and slams into my shoulder. It hurts, but more, it's red-hot, so it burns like hell.

"Oww," I gasp, bending down to look at what just hit me.

But Jaxon is already fading across our section of the arena and slamming into me. He takes me to the wall, shielding me with his body as an array of other blocks hit the ground, all in different shapes.

One falls and hits his arm, and he grinds his teeth together in pain. "Does it burn?" I ask, struggling to get out from behind him.

"It felt like an electric shock," he answers, and this time he tries to dodge as another block comes flying at him.

It hits his shoulder in a glancing blow, but it must shock him again, because his entire body convulses as he lets out an involuntary hiss of pain.

"That's it!" I tell him, pushing against his chest. "You trying to shield me isn't working."

He doesn't budge, and another brick slams into him. This one releases some kind of gas that has us both coughing and gasping for breath.

"Get off me!" I tell him, pushing more insistently this time as I struggle to get away from the noxious smoke.

He still doesn't move—he's too busy trying to protect me to figure out that he's actually killing both of us—and in the end, I shove him away as hard as I can, then duck under his arm while he's recovering from the shock of being pushed from me.

As soon as I get out from behind him, I realize we're in real trouble, because bricks are continuing to fall—and it's happening faster and faster.

"Duck!" I yell at him just as a large, cube-type white brick comes crashing toward the ground.

Jaxon whirls away as another scream sounds from the other side of the arena, followed by the sound of running water. A lot of running water.

But I only have a second to think about what's going on over there, because the cube block that just fell shoots arrows out in all four directions—and one of them hits Jaxon straight in the calf.

"What the fuck?" he growls, bending down to rip the arrow out of his leg, but as he does, several more bricks come careening down on top of us.

"We've got to try to shelter in place," I tell him. "Or we're not going to survive long enough to figure out what we need to do here."

I start coughing as I finish the sentence, trying to breathe through a new round of gas released from one of the bricks. It must not be actual poison because Jaxon and I are still breathing and functioning, but that doesn't make it pleasant, either.

My lungs feel like they're on fire.

I look up, then nearly moan in despair as I realize how many more pieces are raining down all over our section of the arena.

I dodge as another cube-shaped brick comes straight at us, but I forget about the darts and end up taking one to the upper thigh.

"We've got to do something," I tell Jaxon, gasping in pain as I pull the dart out of my leg. "Otherwise, we're going to die like this."

He reaches forward and knocks a brick away that was about to hit me in the head, as further proof that I'm right.

"Wait here," he tells me. "I'm going to fade to the other wall and see if I can—"

"I'm not waiting anywhere," I tell him as I knock two more bricks away from him—and end up with a brick to the temple for my trouble.

Fuck this. Just fuck this.

I reach inside me and grab on to the platinum string. Seconds later, I'm a gargoyle, and I'm flying through the air, trying to get a better look at the ground—and the ceiling where these things are falling from.

And nearly freak out as I realize the ground is so littered with the blocks that they're beginning to stack up on top of one another, Tetris-style. And if we don't figure out a way to stop them, we're going to end up drowning in blocks—or at least being crushed between them and the ceiling or a wall.

Down below me, Jaxon must be figuring out the same thing, because he's using his telekinesis to move the blocks to the side of the room nearly as fast as they're falling. But that just means he's more susceptible to the arrows and the caustic gas that keeps coming from some of these blocks.

"We've got to get ahead of this," I tell him as I land back on the ground. "Or we're going to end up buried. What if I—"

"That's what I'm trying to do," he interrupts. "I'm stacking them—"

He breaks off as a loud, bloodcurdling scream sounds from the other side. "What's happening over there?" he demands.

"The wall goes too close to the ceiling," I answer. "I couldn't see. But whatever it is, it's obviously even worse than—"

I break off as another brick slams into my shoulder hard enough to have me seeing stars, even in my gargoyle form.

"Damn it," Jaxon roars, and this time when he looks up, he uses his telekinesis to suspend all the falling blocks in midair.

Which seems like an excellent plan, as we're no longer getting hit, but it also causes another major problem. The bricks are now crashing into one another and into the stone walls as they start to stack up above us. And with each row that haphazardly stacks, the rows start getting closer and closer to our heads.

Forget being crushed against the ceiling. We're about to be crushed between the floor and row after row of heavy bricks.

Jaxon sees it too and raises his arm to stop them from floating around us.

"Wait," I tell him. "We have a few minutes before things get dire. We need to figure out what we're supposed to do with these blocks."

"No offense, but I think they're already dire," he says as he ducks just in time to avoid a dart to the cheek.

"Yeah," I agree, backing up to try to avoid the disgusting gas being issued continuously from one of the long, flat bricks that is hanging right near our heads. "But there has to be something we can do here, some way we can solve this puzzle."

"Puzzle," Jaxon repeats, looking stunned. "Is that what you think this is?"

"I mean, yeah. What else do you think it could— Ouch!" I don't duck in time to avoid a dart to the shoulder which, not going to lie, I'm shocked as hell can pierce solid stone.

Jaxon, in the meantime, must brush up against one of the shocking bricks because he jumps, then grinds his teeth together as he mutters a whole bunch of really vile curses. "I don't know, but we better figure it out. Quickly. Or we're not going to make it."

Suddenly, a series of loud thumps sounds from the other side, followed by a sickening crunching that chills my bones.

"And neither are they," he adds grimly.

126

Riddle Me Once,
Shame on You

Because I know he's right—and because I can't help thinking that the two sides are tied together in a way we don't understand—I take to the air again. And tell myself not to panic as I weave in and out of the small openings between the bricks and start to realize how dire our circumstances really are.

From the ground, it looks like the bricks are coming fast, but up here, past the beginning couple of layers, I realize they're filling up the sky so quickly that we won't stand a chance if we don't figure out how to eliminate the bricks. Fast. There are just too many of them, and the space we're in is just too small to accommodate them all.

Add to that whatever is happening over on the other side, and we are in a damn mess.

Jaxon is now standing on one end of our area of the arena, waving a hand left, then right, left, then right, and with each wave, blocks go flying to the side. That would be helpful except it doesn't stop the blocks from releasing darts or noxious gas. It just gains us a little time before death by block-phyxiation.

Determined to figure something out, I fly a little higher. It's harder now to weave between the blocks without getting a dart to the eye or stinging poison to the face, but I manage. At least until I run headfirst into a flat double brick that releases a gas that sets my entire face on fire.

It burns so badly that I gasp, tears streaming from my eyes as they try to clear themselves of the gas.

It's not working, and neither is rubbing at my face. The burning keeps getting worse, and I don't know what to do—until I remember the water bottle Macy packed in my backpack. Twisting in midair, trying to avoid touching any more of the bricks that are super close to me, I manage to get the bottle out and pour it all over my face and eyes.

It takes a few seconds, but the burning stops, thank God. It takes several seconds more before I can see anything, so I hover above the ground, waiting for my vision to clear enough that I can keep looking for a solution.

But it's as I'm hovering there, waiting for my eyes to come back to normal, that I look down at just the right angle and realize that there is an outline of a goblet etched into the ground. The shape is the same as the chalice sitting on the counter inside the taffy shop. I noticed it the last time we were here, and I noticed it today. It sits right next to the cash register and is filled to the brim with every colored taffy available.

This must be what we're looking for, I tell myself as I fly back down to Jaxon as fast as the crowded sky will let me. There's no other reason it would be here *and* in the shop—especially since we're probably looking for an elixir that would needs to be drunk out of a cup—just based on the fact that the mythos of the Fountain of Youth supposedly came from these Trials.

"I got it!" I tell Jaxon before I even land. "We need to fill up the outline of this cup right here with bricks."

"What cup?" he asks, looking at the ground around us with a baffled frown.

"This cup," I tell him, bending down and tracing the outline that is so clear to me now that I saw it from above. It takes up most of our floor space, though, so I can see how we missed it without an aerial view. From here, it just looks like a bunch of stones stuck together in a weird pattern.

"So what do we do?" Jaxon asks when he can finally see the cup.

"I don't know," I answer. "But I figure we need to fill it up, right? Like get the bricks to fit inside the cup like a puzzle."

Jaxon looks doubtful, but he doesn't have any better suggestions, so we drop down onto our knees and start grabbing whatever bricks we can find to try to fit them inside the puzzle's boundaries.

The main problem with that, though? The cup has a lot of rounded edges, and all the bricks that have fallen have straight edges.

Another problem with it? We have to touch each of the bricks to arrange them and every time we do, we set one off. Even moving it with Jaxon's telekinesis sets them off, so we are dealing constantly with electric shocks, darts, noxious gasses, and burning hot blocks—all while something is beating the hell out of our friends on the other side of this wall.

I've even heard Hudson yell a couple of times, and every time it happens, it turns my blood to ice.

Then again, if they're yelling, I'll take it as a sign that they're still alive. And right now, I'm afraid that's the best we can ask for.

"Give me the long brick," Jaxon tells me as he struggles to fit three bricks together at the base of the cup.

"It won't work," I tell him. "It's not wide enough—"

"It will," he tells me, even though the opening is obviously too big. "Just let me try—"

"Didn't you ever do puzzles as a kid?" I ask as he ignores my advice and tries the brick only to find out it doesn't work. "You need one of the shorter flat ones there. It's double in width so—"

"Then get it for me!" he snaps, and I swear if we weren't in such dire straits, I'd punch him in the face.

"Get it yourself," I snap back, pissed off that he's either been trying to protect me or yelling at me since we got trapped in here together. And I know it's just because we're both under stress that it's hitting me all the wrong ways, but he still needs to back off. I'm just as capable of doing this as he is—more, actually, considering he can't even get the squared-off base of the goblet right while I'm up here trying to make the pieces fit the rounded cup part.

He growls low in his throat, but he does, snatching the piece out of midair so violently that he ends up getting the same gas to his eye that I got to mine earlier.

At the same time, Hudson lets out a bellow of rage or fear—it's hard to tell when he's on the other side of the wall—that chills my blood.

A renewed sense of urgency to finish this damn puzzle fills me, but I still fumble the water bottle out of my backpack for Jaxon. I start to toss it to him, then realize he can't see shit with tears streaming from his red and irritated eyes, so I race over and dump whatever's left in the bottle on his face. And barely resist snarking that maybe I know what I'm doing after all, since he would have been screwed without me.

The second he's okay, we dive feverishly back into the puzzle. I end up finishing the cup part before he finishes the stem of the goblet—apparently, he really *didn't* play with any kind of puzzle as a kid—and I move down to help him finish up.

He growls at me a little when I try to adjust the pieces he's already laid, but this time I just ignore him as the banging and crashing on the other side of the wall gets even worse.

I haven't heard Hudson's or Macy's voices in a couple of minutes, and terror is a wild thing in my chest. What if something happened to them? What if whatever is over there got them? Or—

"Concentrate," Jaxon snarls as something else crashes into the wall—this one so hard that the entire floor vibrates beneath our feet. "The sooner we finish this, the sooner we can get to them."

"We hope," I mutter under my breath, but I know he's right, so I grab what I figure are the last two blocks—ignoring the stinging sensation that comes with touching one of them—and slide them into place.

The moment I do, everything stops.

There's no more sounds from the other side of the wall.

No more blocks fall from the sky over here.

Plus, the block I accidentally brushed against does nothing to me at all, and neither does the one Jaxon accidentally touches.

We stare at each other, eyes wide, and I know he's wondering the same thing I am—what's going to happen next?

It only takes a few more seconds before we get our answer, and the stone walls start to slide slowly back the way they came.

127

The Writhing's on the Wall

The next ten seconds are the most nerve-racking of my life as I wait to see if we're going to be reunited with the others.

Nearly everyone I care about in the world—besides Jaxon and my aunt and uncle—are on the other side of this partition, and I need them to be okay.

This whole Trials thing is awful—and no wonder it's so hard to win, if this was just the first level. Because it's not only about the pain Jaxon and I went through with the possessed bricks from hell that was so bad. It's what we could hear but couldn't see on the other side of the wall that made trying to solve that puzzle so distracting.

Every time I got in the groove, someone over there would scream. And all I could think about was what was happening to them, which made solving the puzzle a million times harder.

It was awful. More, that was only round one. I can't even imagine what's coming next.

Beside me, Jaxon is rocking up onto his toes over and over again. Apparently, I'm not the only one who's nervous about what we're going to find on the other side.

The arena finally clicks back into place so that we're all one big circle again. The moment it does, Jaxon and I take off running toward the others—who just kind of stand there looking at us, completely shell-shocked. And also covered pretty much from head to toe with mud.

But there's ten of them—I counted—which means they all survived whatever the hell happened over here.

I reach Hudson first—or, more precisely, he reaches me as he fades toward me the moment he realizes I'm running for him.

I throw myself into his arms and wrap myself around him, completely disregarding the mud. "You're okay," I repeat as I press my cheek to his. "You're okay, you're okay, you're okay."

He doesn't say anything, but he holds me like I'm his entire world, and I get it. I feel the exact same way.

"What happened to you?" he says when he finally pulls away. "I heard you yell and—"

"It was a puzzle. We had to do a puzzle with enchanted bricks. It was nothing." I look him over from head to toe to make sure he's all right. "What happened over here?"

"Nues," Macy says as she comes up to give me a hug. "Dozens and dozens of nues."

"What are they?" I ask, my knowledge of the paranormal world once again letting me down.

"Hybrid creatures," Eden answers. "Like manticores, but different."

"Excuse me, but no," Calder says, sounding highly insulted. "Manticores and nues are very different things. I mean, unless you want to say dragons and lizards are the same, too?"

Before Eden can respond, Calder turns her back on her and goes over to Macy. "Do you think you can help a girl out?" She bats her eyes at my cousin, which looks ridiculous considering every part of her is covered in mud—including her eyelids.

"Already way ahead of you," Macy answers as she steps back and does a group glamour.

It doesn't take off all the mud—there are a couple streaks on everybody's arms and faces—but they look, and probably feel, a million times better.

"What do we do now?" Mekhi asks as another minute passes without anything new happening.

"Figure out who we want on each side," Dawud suggests. "I'm good at puzzles—even dangerous ones—so I'll try to end up on that side of the arena this time. Does anyone else want to try to join me?" The way they try not to look at Calder is painful, especially since she's busy picking flecks of mud out of her hair.

As if the arena was just waiting for one of us to make a plan, the wall starts to slide again. "We'll go with you," Remy says, taking Calder by the arm and tugging her gently toward Dawud's side. She goes without an argument.

Hudson doesn't say anything, but he wraps an arm tightly around my waist—a very definite *you're coming with me this time* if I've ever felt one. Which works just fine for me. No way do I want to be separated from him or any of the other people in this room.

Then a thought occurs to me. "If the room divides into two pieces again—what happens if the second piece is even smaller than my and Jaxon's side last time? If we don't end up with *someone* in every piece, we could end up with no one able to solve the puzzle to stop the other side from fighting off whatever nightmare they dream up, right?"

Everyone stares at me for a beat, then Remy sighs and says, "She's right. Everybody, let's spread out and divide up the space. Stay near who you want to be sided with, but let's make sure we have every section covered."

We have about three seconds to follow Remy's directions, but there's a loud *SNAP* and another stone wall springs up from the ground. Too fast to jump on one side or the other, but at least this time it seems to be dividing the room exactly in half.

Dawud, Remy, Calder, and Rafael disappear behind the wall.

"Get ready," Hudson murmurs to me.

I want to tell him that I already am, but the truth is, I don't think any of us is ready. Not that that matters—this thing is coming for us, whether we're ready or not.

Sure enough, I've barely opened my mouth to answer my mate when the one source of light in this whole place—the circle of light Remy made for this side of the arena, too—goes dark. And plunges our area into total blackness.

128

Something slithers by me in the darkness. I feel it brush against my foot and nearly jump ten feet in the air.

"What was that?" I manage to squeak out.

"What was what?" Macy answers, sounding as freaked out as I feel even as she fumbles in her backpack for what I sincerely hope are the candles she put in there earlier.

Seconds later, she lets out a screech, which makes me think she just got to feel what I did.

"Hudson?" I ask, because what use is a vampire mate if he can't tell you what to be afraid of in the dark?

"I don't know." He sounds grim. "I can't see anything."

"Me neither," says Jaxon, who is soon echoed by the other members of the Order.

Fantastic. We're locked in the dark with something that slithers that even the vampires can't see. Nothing to worry about here, obviously.

Whatever it is brushes against me again, and it's cold. Really, really cold.

I shiver a little and move closer to Hudson. And yes, I know it's ridiculous to hide behind my boyfriend when I'm a bad-bitch gargoyle demigod who can take on whatever comes my way, but I'm becoming more and more afraid that we're in a pit of snakes. And I really, really hate snakes.

"How are those candles coming, Macy?"

"I found one," she answers. "I'm looking for—" She shrieks and stumbles backward, dropping her backpack.

"Fuck this," Flint says, and I hear him walking several feet away and shifting into his dragon form. "Stay back," he warns. And then he lights the place up, fire sweeping across the air in front of us.

Everything is stone in here, so nothing burns, but his flames give us light long enough for me to realize that there are no snakes at my feet. Thank God.

But as he breathes out another stream of fire, I realize that that might not be a good thing. Because I can't see *anything* at our feet at all, even though I keep feeling it.

I want to tell myself that it's just my imagination, but I don't believe it. Not when Macy obviously felt whatever it is, too.

"What's going on here?" Byron asks, and he sounds more than a little nervous himself.

"Haven't got a clue," Mekhi answers him, then stifles a shout as he jumps several feet in the air. "What the fuck was that?"

Second nail in the coffin of it being a figment of my imagination. Damn it.

"I've got the candles," Macy says, and with a sweep of her hand and a murmured spell, she lights all of them. Then she starts to hand them out. "I brought a few for everyone, so I have extras if anyone wants seconds."

"Thank God," I murmur fervently as my fingers close around one of the long white tapers. Not that I think a candle will defend me from whatever is in here, but once I see it, I can defend myself. And so can everyone else.

I almost ask for a second candle, but I need at least one hand free to fight, so I make do with one as we start to fan out across the stone semicircle, looking for God only knows what.

"We should probably put the candles around the room," Jaxon suggests. "So that we can see the whole arena."

It's a good idea, so I bend down and drip candle wax onto the stone until there is enough to hold the candle upright when it dries. I'm sad to have to let it go, but it's nice to have some light flickering around the arena—especially as Macy adds the extra candles.

Except as I start moving again and get closer to the middle, I realize the semicircle isn't empty anymore. Because sitting right in the center of this half of the arena is a statue.

"What is that?" I ask whoever's near me as I creep closer to get a better look. And damn if something doesn't slither across my feet again.

I jump back and stifle a shriek.

"You okay?" Hudson calls from a little bit away.

"Fine," I call back. And promise myself I'm not going to scream again, even if some paranormal snake slithers all the way up my leg.

It's a total and complete lie, but it makes me feel better, so I'm going with it.

I'm almost to the statue now, and as I look up at it, I realize it's an angel of some kind, with big wings and a feather in his hand, sitting on a large pile of rocks. Climbing up the rocks are carvings of people in various states of undress. Some are lounging on the rocks, some are trying to climb the rocks, and others look like they're struggling just to stay on the stones. Water from the large pool that surrounds the statue trickles down between the rocks.

It's a strange image, one rife with symbolism I'm not sure I can figure out, but there's something fascinating about it nonetheless. Without making the conscious decision to do so, I find myself walking closer to get a better look.

But the closer I get to the statue, the closer I want to get. The Crown on my palm burns hotter than it ever has before, and my fingers itch to touch the rocks, to feel the water cascade over my skin, to stroke the cool stone of the angel.

It's strange, but I'm mesmerized by it, enthralled, and though something deep inside me tells me to fight the urge, I can't help but walk straight toward it. I have to get to the statue. I have to—

"Grace, stop!" Hudson's voice—more serious and authoritative than I have ever heard it—hisses at me from across the arena.

I stumble a little in my quest, even start to answer him. But the statue is right here in front of me. Beautiful. Seductive. I walk closer, my arm fully outstretched now. I'm almost there, just a little farther.

I wade into the water, reaching a hand up, up, up in a futile attempt to touch the angel. And that's when Hudson fades across the square and slams into me so hard, it takes my breath away. We go flying and end up hitting the ground several feet away. We're going so fast when we hit, we skid across the stone and don't stop until we finally slam into the wall.

Hudson rolls off me the second we come to a stop and leaps to his feet. He tries to pull me up, but I can't breathe. He completely knocked the wind out of me with that body slam, and now my lungs are paralyzed.

"Grace, babe, I'm sorry. I'm so sorry, but you can't be near that." He starts to scoop me up, but I put a hand on his chest and push just hard enough for him to figure out that I mean business. I have absolutely no air in my body right now, and until I get some, I'm not going anywhere.

Again, I struggle to take a breath and again, my pancaked lungs refuse to expand. It's like a panic attack, only worse, because there is no rationalizing my way out of this inability to breathe. No way to calm myself down so I can get air. Right now, all I can do is gasp like a fish out of water and wait until my shell-shocked lungs finally decide to expand.

Hudson curses, long and low and British, but he doesn't try to pull me up again. Instead, he takes a deep breath and squats down next to me, his blue eyes wide and just a little wild as they stare into mine. If I didn't know better, I would say he's frightened.

But that doesn't make sense, because even when he's frightened, he almost never shows it. Annoyed, yes. Angry, of course. Resigned, all the bloody time. But scared? No, I don't think I've ever seen him show his fear like this.

He's scared now, though, and so are my other friends. Or at least, it looks like they are as they come racing across the square at us, waving their arms like they're at a concert or something.

"Breathe for me, Grace," Hudson says, and there's an urgency in his voice that has me struggling to pull air into my still depressed lungs. I make an ugly choking sound, but it's something, I suppose.

Hudson must think so, too, because he smiles as he rubs my back. "Good job. Do that a couple more times and we'll get up—"

He breaks off, a look of disgust flashing across his face that disappears as quickly as it comes. Then he's nearly pulling a lock of hair out of my head as he untangles something from it.

"What—" I manage to gasp out.

He doesn't say anything. Instead, he pulls me to my feet and starts brushing me off—my shoulders, my back, my hair. At first, I don't know what's happening, but then I look down and realize bugs—ugly, slimy, beetle-like black bugs—are crawling all over me.

It's the impetus my tortured lungs need to finally pull in a full breath. Which I do, right before I let it out in a startled shriek. One bug is one thing, but there are dozens, and they are *all over me*. I can feel them crawling on my arms and my back, can feel them brushing against my cheeks, can hear them chittering in my ears, and it's almost more than I can take.

I've done a lot of things since joining this world. From facing down Lia to surviving Cyrus's eternal bite to carrying a red-hot comet, but nothing—nothing—that I've had to do is as bad as this. How are we supposed to survive this level if we don't even know what to do?

A bug crawls out of my hair onto my cheek, and I lose it. I let out a long, loud, horrified scream and start flailing around as I try desperately to get them off me.

"Shhh!" Hudson clasps a hand over my mouth even as he moves so his face is right next to mine. "You can't scream, Grace," he whispers. "I know this is awful. I know it's beyond disgusting, but you cannot scream and draw their attention. Do you understand me?"

Draw whose attention? I shake my head wildly, trying to ignore the sharp little pinpricks I can feel from a bug crawling along my neck. No, no, I don't understand him at all.

"I finally figured out what's going on in here, and it's not safe," he whispers, his hands moving lightning-fast as he continues to pick bug after bug off me.

I give him a *no shit* look, because I swear I have never felt less safe in my life. And then scream into his hand as something bites my shoulder.

"Stop!" His whisper is harsh. "I'm going to take your hand and you're going to follow me to the corner of the arena—and so is everyone else. And you are not going to scream, okay? No matter how many bugs there are, you are not going to scream. Do you understand?"

No, I don't. I don't understand at all.

Panic wells up inside me, because something must be really, really wrong for my unflappable, irrepressible mate to be talking like this, looking like this. Hudson normally takes everything in stride, but he's shaken right now—seriously shaken—and that triggers my anxiety in pretty much every way it can be triggered.

I take another shallow breath—deep breaths are eluding me right now—and try to ignore the feel of legs scurrying across the back of my neck and down my spine. "Make it stop," I whisper to Hudson. "Please make it stop."

"I'm trying," he tells me. "But I have to get you out of here. It won't stop as long as we're this close to—"

He breaks off as another scream rends the air. This one doesn't come from me, though. It comes from Eden, who is jumping up and down and swatting herself as she screams and screams and screams.

She's nowhere near the water, but that doesn't seem to matter. Because the bugs have found her, too.

129

Throwing
all the Shade

"**H**ow do we kill these things?" I ask, horrified.

Before Hudson can answer, an eerie moaning fills the arena around us. It's like nothing I've ever heard before, and the sound has my blood chilling in my veins and the hair on the back of my neck standing straight up.

Even the bugs seem to be freaked out by the sound, because they start scurrying off me and back across the floor into the pool of water at the base of the statue. Nearby, Eden quiets, too, as bugs from everywhere rush into the water again.

"What was that?" Flint demands.

Hudson doesn't answer, because suddenly something starts tugging at his legs—and mine.

I kick out, barely able to stop myself from screaming as I try to break free of whatever's got me in its grasp.

"Bloody hell," Hudson mutters, scooping me up and laying on the speed in an effort to outrun whatever has a hold of us.

It hangs on for a second, its grip like iron around my ankles. I swallow my scream, kick out, and eventually it lets go, but not before it rakes its sharp talons down my calves.

The scratches burn like hellfire, and it takes every ounce of effort I have not to scream all over again. Especially when a random bug scurries out of my hair and across my cheek.

"Are you all right?" I ask Hudson, whose breathing has become increasingly labored. I know it has nothing to do with the running—he can fade for hundreds of miles without even getting winded—so it must be the thing that grabbed us. "Did it get you?"

"I'm fine," he bites out, but his jaw is tight, his face etched with pain.

I don't believe him. "Toss me in the air," I say.

He doesn't even slow down to ask why. He just does it. With his next step, he gives me an impressive throw into the air, and I immediately shift into my gargoyle, my giant wings catching my weight and pulling me high above the arena. Without the need to focus on me, Hudson is able to pull himself free of the last shadow's tendrils around his leg and really kick on the speed, and I let out a deep breath.

Just to be extra careful a shadow doesn't dart up to pluck me from the sky, I push myself to reach out as far as I can with my wings and then powerfully tuck them tight against my body, each stroke through the air exhilarating as I pick up more and more speed. God, I love flying. I just wish I didn't *have* to fly right now to stay alive. Sort of takes the fun out of it, I'll admit.

As I approach the wall of the arena, I tuck a wing and bank hard left, swooping around to fly across the entire space. We need to concentrate on staying alive long enough for the others to solve the puzzle, and getting a better sense of what is actually attacking us seems like a good plan right now.

Except, as I look around, I realize that's going to be a lot harder than it sounds. The strange black shadows have made a ring around the edges of the arena and are moving inward in a coordinated effort to corral us, to push us closer and closer to the statue in the center.

Macy screams next, and I whirl around just in time to see one of the shadows take her to the ground. "Hudson!" I yell, flipping midair and diving straight for her. "We need to get over there! We need to help her!"

But it's not just Macy now. Eden is being dragged down, too.

The shadows are winding their way up her body, wrapping themselves around her waist and rib cage, pressing against her mouth. Mekhi fades over to help her, but the minute he stops moving, a shadow gets him, too. The next thing I know, he's on the ground with the shadows spinning around him.

"Hudson!" I scream again as Jaxon and Byron go down right beside Mekhi.

But Hudson can't help them. He's too busy kicking out at the new shadow that has wrapped around his upper thighs. At least he's still on his feet, so I bank hard right and tuck my wings tight against my body as I try to get to him before he goes down. At the last second, I snap my wings open and fly up behind him, reaching under both of his arms to pull him up. I launch us both straight into the air with every ounce of strength and power I can muster.

The weird shadow thing shrieks and tries to keep its grip on his thigh, but we're moving too fast, flying too hard for it to hold on. I don't slow us down until we're near the top of the arena, at which point my arms start to tremble from the weight of carrying my six-foot-four boyfriend like a bag of chips.

"Drop me over there!" Hudson shouts, pointing to an area just past Eden where the shadows seem to be less concentrated.

My arms shaking hard now, I don't hesitate as I swoop right and use the last of my arm strength to toss him toward the area he pointed out. I don't even worry that we're more than a hundred feet off the ground. My mate does an impressive flip in the air and then lands in a power crouch that would give Black Widow a run for her money. I grin. *Show-off.*

I change directions again, putting on more speed, and take another pass over the statue in the center. Whatever is attacking us, I know it has something to do with that statue.

The shadows have dragged everyone except Hudson, who is fading now like his life depends on it in between brief stops to help pull our friends a few feet back away from the statue. It's a war of attrition, though, as for every foot he pulls them back, when he fades to someone else, the person he just saved gets yanked another two feet closer to the dark pool of water.

I glance over at Eden and Flint, who are both fully shifted and aiming giant breaths of ice at the shadows wrapped around their legs. At least they're no longer on their knees, instead hovering a foot off the ground, flapping their wings furiously to keep the shadows from pulling them back down. The ice seems to be slowing the shadows down, but it's by no means stopping them as they inch closer and closer to the statue as well.

I cross the arena once more and then decide I want to get a really close look at that statue. There's something about it that's very familiar. But to do that, I'm going to have to risk flying close enough that a shadow could more easily grab me.

Macy calls out, and I glance in her direction, my heart pounding in my chest. She's facedown on the stone floor, shadows wrapped around her waist now. I have to do something. Decision made, I pump my wings and pick up speed again as I climb as high in the arena as I can. Once at the top, I flip midair and tuck my wings tight against my body, diving straight for the statue.

I'm within thirty feet and about to extend my wings again so I can slow down enough to get a good look at the statue when Jaxon shouts, "Watch out!"

I glance over my shoulder—and scream.

130

Hundreds of translucent shadows in the form of ravens race across the arena straight for me. But I can't waste my opportunity to focus on them. Not yet.

Instead, I keep my wings tucked until I'm mere feet from the statue. At the last second, I snap them open and bring myself to a sudden and complete midair stop, the force causing pain to tear down one side of my back as though one of my wings were being torn from my body. Tears burst in my eyes, but I blink them back and continue to flap my wings, hovering in front of the statue. I've got seconds before the phantom birds have me, and I need to get a good look at this statue.

I reach up and swipe my hand across my eyes. With my vision clear, I blink and realize I'm staring directly into the stone eyes of the statue. And it's staring back. Calling to me, urging me to step into the fountain, to come to them and they will end my pain, make this all go away. And I want that so badly, I almost falter. But being this close, I notice something else. The statue is smirking at me, like they know I'm weak, telling me without words to give up fighting. Just give up.

"Grace!" Jaxon shouts, and it's enough of a distraction that I shake loose of the hold the statue has over me. The sound of a thousand birds' wings flapping is almost deafening as they reach me, and I don't have time to do more than flip around. I kick out at them, but I'm too late. They've caught me.

They tangle in my curls, peck at my wings, rake their talons down my arms and legs and back in a paranormal version of Hitchcock's *The Birds* that has bile churning in my stomach and terror clawing at my throat.

I try to fly away from them, but they pile on top of me and push me down, down, down.

"Hudson!" I shout, and he immediately reaches up with a hand and then makes a fist, trying to use his disintegration power on the flock. But despite their current bird form, the shadows are nebulous things. They must have no solid form because nothing happens, and without form, Hudson has nothing to disintegrate, nothing to "poof."

Terror claws at the back of my throat. If the shadows pull me to the ground, I know I'll never get back up again.

My mind races. I can't outfly them, Hudson can't destroy them, and judging from the way they're dragging Jaxon inexorably closer to the fountain at the center of the arena, his telekinesis isn't working against them, either. There's nothing we can do, no powers we can use to fight them off.

If Dawud, Remy, Calder, and Rafael don't solve the puzzle soon, they'll be the only ones left.

Panic is a wild thing within me now, fear and desperation making it nearly impossible for me to think or even breathe. Still, as the birds continue to peck away at my wings and face, I force myself to think past the pain, to focus on a solution.

I have to save my friends. I have to save Hudson.

There is no problem that's unsolvable, my mother used to tell me. You just have to find the solution. It's advice that has held me in good stead throughout my life—especially these last several months—but I'm beginning to think this might be the exception that proves the rule. I mean, solving my way out of being the main character in a horror movie isn't a normal problem to have.

But I've done it before. And damn it, I'm going to do it again. Because if I give up now, if I don't find a way to solve this problem, I'm not the only one who will suffer. Hudson will, too. As will Jaxon and Macy, Flint and Mekhi, and all our friends. And that is not okay with me.

Think, Grace. Think. If none of our regular powers can fight off these shadows, and we have to stay alive until the others solve the puzzle, what can delay the inevitable? Surely there's something I can do that will at least slow them down?

Water? No, they moved right through the fountain like it was nothing.

Earth? Dragging us down into the earth seems to be one of their game plans, so probably not.

Wind? They seem perfectly content to ride the air currents all around us, so no.

Fire? They don't have a corporeal form, so that won't do anything.

As Macy screams again below me, I remember what Remy said back at the Witch Court. Why am I trying so hard to have the right answer myself? Why aren't I thinking about my team, what they bring to the problem?

Flint? He can breathe fire...which creates light. What if we don't need to beat the shadows, we just need to drive them back? If so, maybe light is the answer. Eden can only breathe ice, so I've never been more happy that Flint can breathe both than right now.

I shout down at him frantically, "Flint! Breathe fire at the shadows, see if the light will chase them away."

He doesn't make a move to breathe fire for what feels like forever, but then he manages to get one knee under his body and pushes up. Just a little bit more, and then he lets out a massive bellow of fire, aiming it directly at the edges of the arena, from where the shadows seem to be crawling.

The shadows shimmy under the fire and light, but as soon as Flint takes another breath, they strengthen and seem to come after my friends with even more tendrils.

Well, hell, that made things worse, not better.

I bite my lip. Should I give up? There's an argument to be made for doing nothing in this situation—at least I can't accidentally make things worse.

But no, I've never been a quitter. Maybe two heads would be better than one, though?

The birds are still pecking at my wings and body, tearing pebble after pebble in their powerful beaks, and even though I'm managing to stay in the air, I'm getting dangerously close to the water below, which makes me frantically pump my wings harder and harder.

All of a sudden, something hard slams into my body, pain exploding in my hip and sending me flying halfway across the arena, flipping end over end as I try to catch myself with my wings to no avail.

At the last second, I feel Hudson's strong arms wrap around my waist and yank me against him, then he lands on his feet, my body tucked against his.

"Sorry about that," he says, breathing hard. "I couldn't see any other way."

"You mean other than swatting me across the arena like a fly?" I ask, but there's no censure in my voice. He probably just saved my life, although my hip is going to hurt for about a year.

"Hey." He gives me a quick smile. "I caught you."

"Yes, you did." I roll my eyes at him, then ask excitedly, "Did you see what happened when Flint blew fire on the shadows?"

"Yeah, they seemed to quiver." He raises a brow. "Then doubled in size. It was impressive."

Shadow tendrils are moving quickly across the arena toward us, so I know we don't have much time to solve this. "Which of our friends might have an ability to use against shadows? I think the answer is light, Hudson, but Flint's dragon fire wasn't enough."

Hudson narrows his eyes for a second, then his eyebrows shoot up. "Didn't Viola say Macy's mom was adept at shadow magic? I think she hinted Macy should have a similar talent."

Goddamn, this boy deserves the longest kiss ever if we make it out of here.

"I love you," I say and give him a quick peck before leaping into the air, my wings carrying me as fast as they can. Straight for Macy. I don't look back at Hudson, knowing he's likely already fading again to each of our friends, to do what he can to help. As soon as I get close to my cousin, I shout down, "Macy! Viola said your mom and you were able to use shadow magic! Could that be the potion your mom said would do what we needed it to?"

It's a long shot, but I have to believe if my mother were really good at a particular magic, she'd feel it important to always be prepared against that sort of attack. So surely Aunt Rowena prepared Macy as well.

"Maybe!" Macy yells up at us, but her voice is weaker than normal, her body coated in sweat and dirt from fighting off the shadows.

"Hurry, Macy! You can do this!" I shout down at her.

Macy grunts and then rolls over, laying on her back and breathing hard now. Ten more seconds pass before she reaches into her fanny pack and, with eyes closed, riffles around until her hand falls on one bottle. She glances down and nods, then grunts again, pushing herself to a kneeling position with great effort.

The shadows are closing in on Hudson now, the available space to stop fading for a breath shrinking with every second as the shadows have nearly covered the entire arena floor. Our friends aren't in the water yet, but they're very close. Flint keeps blowing fire all around the space, careful to not set anyone on fire but trying to keep the shadows from getting him on the ground again.

I let out a quick yelp as a shadow nearly latches on to my ankle. "Hurry!" I shout.

Macy reaches into her fanny pack again and grabs her wand, then tosses the potion in her other hand straight up into the air. She aims her wand at it and says something I can't hear—and then the potion bursts into a million tiny shards of brightness, bathing this entire half of the arena in light.

And all hell breaks loose.

131

Slip 'N Slime

I barely have a breath to celebrate that my idea worked and the shadows are shrinking before they let out an unholy screech that sends a shiver racing down my spine. And then, as though their fury opened a floodgate, bugs start to crawl from the water again.

With the brilliant light now coating the arena, I can see exactly how terrifying the bugs that were in my hair and crawled along my skin really are, and I almost throw up. In midair. Creepy jagged pincers and giant antennae that arch out like drooping flower stems, and the oh so many legs I remember crawling along my flesh, all attached to shiny black bodies broken into two distinct segments that allow the bugs to twist and turn this way and that as they crawl over rocks and grass.

Thousands and thousands of bugs crawling out of the water, heading straight for all my friends. Wave after wave, as though the statue were only toying with us earlier but all bets are off now. It only takes mere seconds before the entire floor vanishes beneath a living blanket of bugs—and heading straight for my friends, who've gotten back on their legs since the shadows receded.

Flint and Eden take to the skies while the vampires fade, Hudson carrying Macy. The sound of vampire feet crunching thousands and thousands of bugs' bodies against the stone floor echoes eerily around the arena. Eventually, the ground is more yellow than black with bug guts, and I shudder, so, so happy my kind has wings.

I know Hudson could disintegrate the bugs, but I don't even wonder why he hasn't. I can't imagine crawling into the minds of thousands of bugs. I shudder again.

But fading isn't a solution. Eventually, the vampires are going to tire, as Hudson taught the gargoyles in the frozen Court. I'm about to suggest the vampires jump on Flint's and Eden's dragon backs when Mekhi lets out a short yelp and then goes sliding across the ground now slick with smooshed insect guts. He slides all the way across the arena until he eventually loses momentum, like he was taking a turn on the world's worst Slip 'N Slide.

When he stops sliding, he just lays there for a few seconds, the wind clearly knocked out of him. My gaze darts to the water, but the bugs don't seem to notice that Mekhi is on the ground. They're still crawling out of the water, but no more in his direction than any other.

Then he groans and starts to get back on his feet and the bugs, as one, beat it in his direction. Within seconds, he's shouting and flicking his hands all over his body as he tries to get them off.

And then Byron trips. Hudson and Macy are next to go down. Then finally Jaxon.

Now that the vampires aren't running anymore, Flint and Eden circle lower and coat the ground around them with ice, which freezes the bugs not already on them, but that just makes even more bubble up out of the water around the statue.

Think, Grace! Think! We can't fight them. There are too many. And we can't outrun them. Maybe we can make them retreat like the light made the shadows leave? I shake my head. The bugs don't seem to be afraid of anything. They just keep coming and coming and coming, as though the fountain were a bottomless well of bugs.

And then it occurs to me. We don't need to beat the bugs—we need to cap the well.

I bank left and fly closer to Flint and Eden, who continue to breathe ice on the ground around our friends, taking out as many attacking bugs as possible.

Macy is screaming hysterically, pulling bug after bug from her hair as she jumps up and down in an effort to dislodge the bugs crawling up her legs. Byron, Jaxon, and Hudson are beating back the bugs as best they can, but it's a losing battle. But the person really struggling is Mekhi, who is on one knee and nearly covered in bugs. He must have hit the ground harder than I thought when he'd first tripped. Flint's icy breath is the only thing keeping the bugs from overcoming Mekhi entirely, so he shouldn't stop what he's doing. I flip around to Eden, who is on the other side near Macy.

"Eden! The fountain!" I shout. "Freeze the *fountain*!"

Eden pauses mid-breath for a second, maybe two, then takes off for the fountain. With a giant breath, she flies in a low circle around the base of the statue and freezes the water instantly. She flies around a couple more times, building a wall of ice nearly two feet thick at the base of the fountain before she widens her flight, freezing the remaining bugs on the ground, too.

Eventually, all the bugs are dead.

132

Drinking Outside the Juice Box

Suddenly, the entire stadium groans. Seconds later, the giant wall bisecting the arena lowers.

Thank God. Dawud, Calder, Remy, and Rafael have finally solved the puzzle.

They stumble toward us like they've seen a ghost—or ghosts. And maybe they have. Considering what we just battled, I'm not taking anything off the table.

"You're okay," Remy says, latching on to my hand. He looks more shaken than I've ever seen him, and his gaze keeps darting over to Macy. "I thought—"

He breaks off, shakes his head. "That last puzzle was a trip."

"More like a nightmare," Calder says, and she, too, looks a lot less animated than her normal self. "It's good to see you guys."

"It's good to see you, too." I give her a spontaneous hug, and the fact that she actually melts into it tells me just how upset she really is.

"Dawud solved the puzzle," Rafael comments after a second. "With a couple of marbles and an old key."

"That doesn't surprise me at all," Hudson tells Dawud. "Good job. You saved our lives."

Dawud doesn't answer right away. They're too busy cataloging the group, their gaze combing over every single one of us, much like mine did after Jaxon and I had to solve the first puzzle.

"We were really worried about you. Your screams were terrible," Dawud answers, glancing around at the bug slime coating the floor and most everyone's bodies.

Macy pulls out her wand and waves it, making short work of removing every hint of bugs, guts, and dead carapaces from the ground and us. I don't think even magic, though, can ever get the memory of bugs crawling in my hair from my mind, and I shudder.

Remy wraps an arm around my shoulder. "You okay?"

The look I give him says, *Not really*. But I nod. "Great advice earlier, by the way." And it's true. He gave me the idea to stop thinking of how I could save everyone and instead how we could save one another.

His eyes widen, and then he sighs for what feels like a minute straight. His hands are shaky as he pushes his dark hair out of his face.

I want to ask him if this is what he saw, but I'm not sure if I want to know. It would be great to confirm the fate he saw has been averted, but I'm definitely not interested in hearing if anyone dies—there's no way to get out of here except to go through the next two Trials. Knowing I was walking into one of the levels with someone who wouldn't be walking out... I can only imagine what that would do to me.

I honestly don't think I could make it through. Which gets me wondering how Remy does it. Everyone always makes it sound like seeing the future must be so great. But what's it like to know the things he does? And to not be able to stop the bad things from happening?

I'm pretty sure it would drive me mad. I know I'd have even more panic attacks than I do already.

"We need to get our heads in the game, or we're all going to end up dead," Eden says as the walls begin to rumble. We quickly spread out on the arena floor so we don't end up with no one on the right side to solve the puzzle.

I take a deep breath, blow it out slowly, and grab Hudson's hand. I don't know what's going to happen next, don't know what side of the level I'll be on. I just know that—whatever side it is—I want Hudson with me.

He must feel the same way because he wraps his arms around me and holds me so tightly, I can barely breathe. And when the walls finally stop adjusting, when the stone finally stops groaning, we're still together. For now, that's all I can ask for.

Well, that and some light as Macy's potion flickers and we're once again plunged into total darkness.

133

I'd Love to
Give Away
My Shot

"The dark? Again? Seriously?" Macy's plaintive voice cuts through the blackness surrounding us, telling me Hudson and I have at least one other person in here with us. "I can't even find the candles."

"Don't worry about that," Remy says from what feels like the other side of the arena. "I've got the lights."

Suddenly, his fist burns purple in the darkness as he swirls his arm to encompass the area all around us. As he does, light blooms in every section until there is a circle of violet light running all the way around the top of the arena.

Or, I realize as I get my first good look at the place, three-quarters of the arena. Because it's divided up again like a phase of the moon, same as it was during the first Trial. Only this time, I'm on the big side, along with Hudson, Remy, Mekhi, Macy, Calder, Flint, and Dawud. Which leaves Jaxon, Eden, and the rest of the Order to figure out the puzzle.

Now that the arena is lit up, I can see that the fountain is gone and in its place—directly in the center of the arena—is a table. And on the table is a box no more than a foot tall.

Just the sight of it has my palms going damp. I take a deep breath, blow it out slowly, and try to tell myself that this round will be okay. That we're not going to lose anyone.

But I'm not sure I believe it, and it's that doubt that makes it harder to walk toward the table than I ever imagined.

"What do you think is in the box?" Macy asks, and she sounds as tentative as I feel.

"Only one way to find out," Remy answers laconically.

"Yeah, but what if we don't want to find out?" Macy shoots back.

"Then I guess we can just stand here until we get tired of listening to the screams that I'm sure will be coming from the other side soon," Hudson says.

"Good point," Mekhi answers. Then looks at me like he thinks it's my job to open the box. Sigh.

I move forward to do it, a little squeamish about what might come out of it after everything we just went through, but Remy steps up before I can get there. After a quick look at the rest of us to make sure we're on board, he reaches forward and flips off the lid.

I brace myself for whatever it is—*please, please, please, no more bugs*—but nothing happens. The room doesn't shake, nothing jumps out of the box, no strange creatures ooze from the walls.

"There's another box inside," Remy informs us, pulling it out.

He opens this box, too, exposing a small crate with eight test tubes in it. Each test tube is filled with a different-colored liquid.

"What are we supposed to do with that?" I ask, a sinking feeling in my stomach telling me I already know the answer.

"Ooh, I call the red one," Calder says. "It matches my hair."

"I'm not sure that's going to matter," I tell her, "but have at it."

She rolls her eyes as she pulls the test tube in question out of the box. "Color coordination always matters, Grace." And with that, she pulls off the lid and drinks the whole thing down in one long swallow.

134

Long seconds pass with us staring at Calder, wondering what's going to happen, while she—blissfully unconcerned—pulls out a compact and stares at herself while she puts on another coat of lipstick.

"Mud is *so* good for the complexion," she says as she happily rubs her lips together. "We should do another mud bath sometime soon, Grace."

"Let's just get through tonight before we start making spa plans, hmm?" Remy tells her.

She sighs. "You're becoming a real party pooper, Remy. You know that, right?"

"It is a problem," he agrees easily. "Hey, you feeling weird or anything?"

"Why would I be feeling weird?" Calder asks doubtfully.

"I don't know. Maybe because you just put an unknown potion in your body?" Flint says.

Calder shrugs. "My body can handle it." She strikes a pose. "It's a work of art."

"It really is," Dawud agrees.

"Put your tongue back in your mouth, Dawud," Remy tells them. "She needs a partner who won't just roll over for her."

"I like people who roll over," Calder says after snapping her compact shut and shoving it back in her pocket. "Gives me easier access. Entrails are such tasty treats."

She smacks her newly painted lips together for emphasis while Dawud whimpers.

Hudson gives me a *what the hell are we supposed to do with this* look, and I just shrug. Because really, Calder is a whole bunch of laws unto herself, and Dawud seems perfectly okay living by every one of them. And perhaps even dying by them, entrails and all.

"Do you still feel okay?" I ask after about a minute passes, and Calder doesn't start vomiting uncontrollably or anything else.

"I feel fiiiiiiiiiiiiiiiiine," she answers as she very slowly tosses her hair back. In fact, the hair flip goes so slowly that she looks a little like a shampoo commercial, when they run the film in slow motion so everyone watching can see the shiny, healthy, beautiful hair fanned out all around the model's head. Except Calder's is still half crusted in mud, so not actually very shiny. Trust Calder to somehow look like a hair model anyway.

"Good." Remy looks at the seven potions left. "Anyone dying to go second?"

"We don't even know if we're supposed to drink those," I object. "Maybe we're supposed to throw them on the ground or something. We can't afford to do this wrong."

"Driiiiiiiiiiiiiink iiiiiiiiiiiiit," Calder says as she oh so slowly turns toward me. "Iiiiiiiiiiiiiiiit's deeeeeeeeeliiiiiiiiiiciooooooooous."

"Tastes like entrails, does it?" I comment, even as my heart sinks.

"Oh." Hudson's eyes go wide as he catches on to what's happening. "Calder, are you doing that on purpose?"

"Doooooooooooiiiiiiiiiiing whaaaaaaaaat?" It takes about five seconds for the words to come out—and about that same amount of time for her eyebrows to lift.

"Looks like we know what the red potion does," Macy says with a sigh.

"Apparently it slows you way down." I shake my head with a laugh.

"Waaaaaaaaaaay down," Remy agrees, then reaches in and grabs the green potion. "Anyone want this one?"

"I don't want any of them," I tell him.

"Yeah, well, I don't think that's really an option, *cher*," he says, then opens the tube and downs it like a shot.

Mekhi grins at Macy and me, clearly over being covered in bugs. More power to him, considering I'm pretty sure I'll hang on to that experience long enough for both of us. "I think that orange one has my name on it," he says. "I'll apologize now if it makes me even sexier, ladies."

And then, like he grew up in a frat house, he tosses the liquid straight back.

Macy rolls her eyes at him and reaches for the purple potion. "I'm leaving the hot-pink one for you, Grace. Since it's your favorite."

Of course she is. I am now 130 percent certain the hot-pink one is the worst of the eight potions, which is no less than what I deserve for lying to my cousin for the last seven months about my favorite color.

Hudson chokes back a laugh, and I give him a death glare even as Macy says, "Bottoms up!" and downs the purple potion.

"Any idea what your potion does?" Dawud asks Remy, who completely ignores them as he walks over to the edge of the wall and *bows*...which isn't even the *least* bit concerning. Seconds later, he waves his hand in the air and then takes off running—or as close as he can get, considering he's on his tiptoes while still wearing his work boots.

"Grace, careful!" Macy screams out of the blue as she points wildly above my head.

I duck as soon as she screams my name, but when I whirl around to confront whatever she's pointing at, there's nothing there.

"Grace!" she screams again. "It's coming! Get out of the way! It's coming!"

"What's coming?" I demand, looking at the ground for more of those damn shadow snake things. I can't imagine what else could make Macy sound so freaked out—especially since I can't see what she's pointing at.

"The monster!" She starts to cry. "Please, Grace. Run. You need to run."

"She's hallucinating," Hudson says, and it's his turn to look a little wild-eyed.

I think I can hear faint screams coming from our friends on the other side of the wall, but I can't focus on that right now. We need to survive the problems I can deal with here.

"Does anyone hear Tchaikovsky?" Dawud asks suddenly.

I tilt my head to the side and listen and sure enough, the very familiar strains of one of the songs from *The Nutcracker Suite* are playing. I recognize it immediately, as my mom used to take me to see it in L.A. every Christmas.

"I wonder if the music has something to do with the Trials," I murmur, praying to all the deities at once that we don't have to perform the *Nutcracker* ballet while under the influence of who knows what kind of potions. I can barely manage fifth position in the best of circumstances—or so my childhood dance teacher used to tell me.

I don't have to wonder for long, though, as Remy rushes over and does a fairly decent pirouette. If by "decent," I mean we were grading on a curve against a company of giraffes.

But his whole being seems enraptured by the music. With a flourish of his arm, he prepares to perform a jeté, and I have to give him points for commitment. At six foot four, he got some serious height on that leap. He also probably pulled a groin muscle as his legs attempted a midair split but fell short by about four feet.

Hudson whistles. "He really should have limbered up first."

But Remy doesn't seem to mind that his form is off—or that he didn't stick the landing. He simply incorporates a somersault into his movements and pops back up on his feet before continuing with his ballet, the wide grin splitting his face making it clear he is having the time of his life.

"I don't want to take a potion," I tell Hudson, and I can't help thinking suddenly that Calder is the lucky one. She had no idea what was going to happen when she swallowed that thing. Now that I do...now that I do, I'm even less inclined to put it in my mouth than I was when I first saw it, which is saying something.

He gives me a *no shit* look. "Yeah, me neither. But I don't think we have a choice. I don't think this level will start until we do."

"Start? You mean drinking the potion isn't enough?" I demand. "There are more things we have to do that might kill us?"

Hudson just sighs and hands me the test tube with the hot-pink liquid in it. Then turns to Dawud and Flint and holds out the last three. "Choose," he tells them.

Flint picks the blue one right away, while Dawud stands there looking a lot like I feel—like there is nothing in the world they want to do less than drink one of these things. But in the end, they choose the clear one, which leaves the yellow one for Hudson, who grimaces when he looks at it.

Not that I blame him. Bad enough he has to drink a potion. Does it actually have to look like urine when he does?

"Here goes nothing," I say, holding up my test tube in a macabre version of a toast.

Hudson, Flint, and Dawud do the same, then all four of us drink them down.

Dread settles in my stomach as Macy screams again and starts batting at something in front of her face while Calder backs away from the table in extreme slow motion. Remy is focused on a series of complicated jumps followed by a less complicated series of somersaults.

Then, suddenly, Dawud almost falls over.

Flint catches them and helps them steady themselves, but the second he lets go, Dawud starts to fall over again.

"I can't feel my right side," Dawud says, but it comes out all slurred because half their mouth suddenly doesn't work.

"Well, that's not good," I say to no one in particular, because everyone else is wrapped up in whatever symptom they're having.

My potion hasn't kicked in yet, so I rush over to see if I can help Dawud, but they seem fine. Except for the fact that half their body has gone completely limp, and they have absolutely no control over it.

I mean, what could go wrong in that equation?

"Yako era uoy?" Hudson asks me with worried eyes.

"I'm sorry?" I ask.

"Ecarg! Yako era uoy?" He reaches behind him and takes a step backward. Which makes both our eyes go wide.

"Oh shit!" It comes out half cry, half laugh. "You're backward?"

I think he's trying to nod, but his head shakes back and forth instead.

"Oh my God. You're backward! What are we going to do?" I start to laugh, because at this point, it's either laugh or cry.

On the plus side, still no potion effects for me. Looks like Macy was right all along—apparently hot pink really is my color. Or these Trials creators didn't account for a contestant with an immunity to magic.

Too bad none of my friends had the same luck.

I turn around to look at them and nearly crack up all over again.

Calder is strutting toward Remy, but she's going so slowly that she might as well be going backward. Which is a good thing, because if she reached him, she would interfere with the brisé volé he is currently attempting. He's doing it badly, but he is definitely attempting it. Hudson, in the meantime, keeps trying to get to me but he *actually* is moving backward every time he tries to take a step.

Meanwhile, Macy is cowering under the table, crying and batting at God only knows what, and Dawud is just kind of slumped over, like they have no idea what to do with their body. Mekhi, on the other hand, has the same *oh shit* expression on his face that I know is on mine. Although for very different reasons. He's currently sucking his thumb and walking in a circle, his head cocked as far over his shoulder as he can get it like he's trying to see what's wrong with his backside—and I'm suddenly beyond terrified that baby Mekhi might have soiled himself.

As for Flint, he seems to have just full-on decided that he's a chicken.

He clucks like a chicken.

He walks like a chicken.

He flaps his arms like a chicken.

He even runs away like a chicken the second anyone else gets too close to him, which should be really fun when we need to fight something.

Speaking of, I try my hardest not to freak out as the ground begins to creak beneath us.

Macy and Hudson must hear it, too, because both of them go on full alert with me. I turn around in a circle, trying to figure out where the threat is going to come from, but I can't find anything.

At least not until the floor starts to shake.

135

Ee I Ee I
Oh No

"Gnihtyna ees?" Hudson asks as he does his best to look around with me. He's finally figured out if he steps backward, he can get to me walking forward. It's a slow process, as his brain isn't used to it, but eventually he's by my side. Who knows what's going to happen when he tries to fight, though. Fingers and toes crossed backward that it doesn't mean beating the hell out of his friends instead of the enemy...

"Get ready, Calder!" I call.

"Iiiiiiiiiiii aaaaaaaaaaaaaam," she answers, then spends about ten seconds trying to turn in a half circle so that she's facing the same direction Remy, Hudson, and I are. Well, Remy was. Now he's on the other side of the arena spinning an imaginary ballerina before jumping into a full-blown cabriole that ends with him falling flat on his face.

I figure that should stop him for a while, but nope. He's back on his feet in seconds, nose bleeding and lip scraped to hell from the stone. I have to say, given the circumstances, I am impressed with the battement he performs. It could be way worse.

I glance at Hudson, who starts to say something, but then just rolls his eyes. Backward. Which might be one of the most bizarre things I've seen all day, and that is saying something.

In the meantime, Calder has tried shifting into her manticore form, but she's moving so slowly that it appears like she's caught halfway between her two selves. She's got most of a scorpion tail and part of her lion's mane, but everything else is human. And can I just say, it's definitely not a good look for her.

I start to go to her, to see if there is anything I can do to help. But before I can get more than three feet, my cousin screams for what feels like the hundredth time in the last fifteen minutes.

"Macy!" I call to her, trying to sound as patient as I possibly can. "Can you get out from under the table? There's nothing there."

"There is!" she tells me, tears in her voice. "Oh my God, it's so ugly, Grace! So ugly!"

"I need you to stand up, Mace. Just forget about whatever that is—I swear it won't hurt you—and come over to me. I need you."

"It's going to hurt you!" she screams. "No, don't hurt Grace!"

And suddenly she's firing a lightning spell straight at Hudson and me. I knock him out of the way—with my luck, he'd try to jump back and jump straight into it instead—and end up getting the bottom couple of inches of my hair singed off in the process. Luckily, she hits the side that wasn't already cut, so my hair is finally almost even again. Several inches shorter than it used to be, but even nonetheless.

My cousin whimpers, but I can hear her finally getting up. Or at least trying to, considering every time she gets too close to whatever she's currently hallucinating, she starts to scream again.

But I have bigger problems—we all do—because something else is happening. There is suddenly a loud whooshing sound sweeping through the arena.

I look around, trying to figure out where it's coming from, but no one else is paying attention to it. No one else but Hudson, that is, who is looking at me with a *here we go* look. At least until Flint jumps in front of him and starts trying to peck his eyes out.

And all I can think, as I watch Hudson punching and tripping backward in an effort to get away from him, is that if the Trial doesn't kill Flint, Hudson just might...if he can ever figure out how to work his limbs again.

136

Moonwalk-a-Doodle-Doo

"**W**hat's that noise?" I ask no one in particular as the whooshing sound grows louder.

"Grace! Look out!" Macy screams. "It's going to get you!" I don't even bother to look around.

"Mrotsdnas!" Hudson answers me. He's finally managed to get away from Flint, who is now in the corner clucking his displeasure as Hudson rushes toward me as fast as he can, considering he's only moving forward by putting one foot behind the other in a strangely uncoordinated version of the moonwalk.

"Mrotsdnas," I repeat, trying to put the sounds together in verse. "Mrots… stor—"

"Sandstorm!" Dawud yells as they somehow manage to drag Macy off the table that she must have just climbed onto using only their left arm. But when they try to turn it over—still using only their left arm—I give them a *what the hell* look.

"We need something to hide behind," they answer, and considering the kid spent most of their life in a pack in the Syrian Desert, I'm inclined to believe them.

So I leap into action and flip the table onto its side for them, then step back to let Remy—who was listening to the conversation even in the middle of a string of pirouettes—use a burst of magic to send it legs first against the wall, so that the tabletop provides a barrier against the sand that has just started blowing into the arena.

"We need to hide behind it," Dawud tells me.

"Can you try to get Macy?" I ask, pointing to where my cousin is firing spells at God only knows what. "I have to get the others."

"Pull your shirt over your mouth!" they call to me as I run. "It acts as a kind of filter for the sand."

I do as they say and race toward the center of the arena. Remy has pirouetted over to help Calder, who has finally shifted into a full manticore but can still only move in super slow motion, which—if the situation wasn't so dire—might be the funniest thing I've ever seen.

I trust Hudson to find a way to shuffle himself backward to the table, however bizarre-looking it may be, which leaves only baby Mekhi and Chicken Boy to save.

"Flint! Come on!" I yell to him as the wind kicks up in the arena, while I try to convince baby Mekhi to stop sucking his thumb and take my hand so I can lead him to safety.

This time, Flint's cock-a-doodle-do is all terror and no annoyance, so he doesn't even fight me when I drop off Mekhi behind the table and rush over and grab on to Flint and start herding him toward the table. Sand is flying through the air now, whipping against my face and hands and getting in my eyes.

"Pull your shirt up!" I tell him. But it's no use. The chicken is not okay with any kind of face mask.

I speed up, trying to keep my head down, but visibility is so bad in here that I have to look at least every once in a while to make sure we don't end up at the opposite end of the arena. With the way these winds are pushing at us, it's entirely possible that could happen.

And that's before a particularly strong gust of wind sweeps through the arena and nearly blows us off our feet. It freaks Flint out so much that he jumps in my arms before I have a clue what he's going to do, wrapping all six foot something inches of himself around me as he cock-a-doodle-dos at the top of his lungs—right next to my ear.

Which isn't a problem *at all*—especially considering I'm not in my gargoyle form at the moment—and this dragon-chicken is at least double my weight.

I stagger forward a few steps, but that's all I can manage before I end up dropping him right on his un-feathered butt. Flint isn't impressed, and he crows a few times to let me know it, then runs around me in circles, flapping his arms.

Through much coaxing—and a few threats to pop him in a stewpot for dinner—I finally manage to get Flint to the knocked-over table. He climbs in along with Macy, baby Mekhi, Calder, and Dawud, but when I tell Remy and Hudson to hurry up and get behind the table, too, they both look incredibly insulted.

"I don't have time for this!" I tell them. "Just get in there and let me deal with it."

Hudson gives me a *like that's going to happen* look while Remy just takes off doing fouettés across the arena. Or as close to a fouetté as he can manage, considering his utter lack of training or talent and the incredible wind currently blowing in here.

And damn it. Just damn it. Why do these men have to be so stubborn? I get that they want to help—and under normal circumstances, I would jump at the chance. But nothing about this is normal, and they are going to end up getting themselves, each other, or the rest of us killed with their stubbornness. And that I am *not* okay with.

Except as I turn around and see the sandstorm barreling toward me in all its full-blown glory, I have to admit I'm more than a little intimidated. The thing is taking up most of the arena by now, huge, billowing clouds heading straight for us as sand hits my skin hard enough to leave marks.

With some vague idea of being able to push the storm in on itself, I run to the opposite end of the arena from where Remy is. I'm halfway there when the storm overtakes me.

The shirt over my mouth is poor protection against the full brunt of the sandstorm, and I'm gasping for air as I try to make it through the roiling clouds. It's really hard to do, though. Not just because the wind keeps buffeting me backward, taking away at least half of any progress I make, but because what little I can see inside the storm is cast in an eerie red light that's completely disorienting.

I know what direction I was heading when I first started running, but between the wind and the sand and the enveloping clouds, I can only hope that I'm still pointing the same way.

I finally hit a wall—I can't see it, but I can feel the rough stone against my hand—so I can only hope that I'm in the right spot. I turn around, duck my head, close my streaming eyes against the onslaught of sand, and try to gather all the power and energy I have left inside me to fight this thing.

But just as I try to figure out where to start, the wind stops. It just stops, and the sand falls to the arena floor.

Which is either fortuitous or terrifying, and I'm not sure which one it is yet.

"Why'd it stop?" Remy asks as he does a pretty decent arabesque.

"I have no idea," I whisper, even while looking back and forth, desperate to figure it out. "Maybe they solved the puzzle?"

But even as I say it, there's a loud screeching sound on the other side of the wall, as though something heavy is being scraped across stone.

"Definitely not finished." Remy takes a bow.

For a second, I think he's finally done—that maybe the potion is finally wearing off. But then he does a lead-footed coupé jeté in his work boots, so maybe not.

"Dnas eht ta kool!" Hudson says suddenly. He points at the ground as I try to run the letter sounds in the opposite direction.

"What's wrong with the sand?" I ask as soon as I figure it out, terrified we're about to be swarmed by sand fleas or something even worse.

But it just looks like regular sand to me. The wind is completely gone, so it's not even blowing around. It's just lying there under our feet.

"Pu!" he says, bending down and sticking a finger into the sand. "Pu gniog sti, Ecarg!"

"Up? No it's not. My feet aren't moving at all."

But I look at his finger, still stuck in the sand, and realize he's right. Because the sand that was at his middle knuckle before is all the way to his palm now.

"Oh shit," I whisper as the truth finally hits me. The whole arena is filling up with sand. And we have no way out.

137

Give Me
a Sand

"We need to get to the others!" I shout as the truth sinks in.

Hudson shakes his head back and forth in what I'm pretty sure is supposed to be a nod. But when I take off running, all he does is move four quick steps back. Of course.

I turn back to help him, but he just nods and says, "Og! Og!"

So I do. Hudson figured out how to walk once in here; he'll be able to do it again. I'm not so sure about the chicken and baby, however. I'm pretty sure they'll end up buried in sand if I'm not around to stop it.

By the time I make it to the table they are all still crouched behind, the sand is up to my calves, which makes walking a lot of fun. Normally, I'd be able to move over the top of it, but it's pouring in so quickly now that it keeps covering my feet.

"Come on, guys!" I tell them as I grab the table and scoot it away—also harder than it should be because it's partially buried in sand. "We need to get you guys standing up."

Not that that's going to be enough with as fast as this stuff is coming. But it will at least buy me some time to figure out what to do.

What I'm deathly afraid of, though, is that there is nothing to do. The sand is rising, and there's no way out of here. If Jaxon and his group don't finish the puzzle soon, we're going to be completely screwed. I've always thought drowning was one of the worst ways to die. I can only imagine drowning in sand is a thousand times worse.

Flint must think so, too, because he is crowing loud enough to fill up the entire arena. In the meantime, baby Mekhi keeps trying to eat the stuff and Dawud keeps sinking into it.

What do I do? I rack my brain, trying to think of an answer as the sand pours in. It's up to my knees now and rising even faster than before.

I bend over to dig myself out and, for a second—standing on more than a foot of sand—I'm as tall as Flint, whose eyes go wide when he sees me looking at him eyeball to eyeball. He lets out a huge squawk and tries to run away, but he's buried, too—and can't dig himself out with his imaginary wings. He ends up falling face-first into the sand, which then starts rising over his back and legs.

Macy screams—and for once I'm actually with her. This is freaking terrifying. But then she's batting around her head like she's being dive-bombed by a prehistoric mosquito. Which means—

"Macy, no!" I jump for her, desperate to get to her before she starts shooting spells again, but I'm too late. Still, Macy doesn't even notice. She's too busy battling whatever she's hallucinating, and this time, she sends out an exploding spell that hits the sand and has it exploding up into the air in a giant cloud that ends up raining down on top of us. And makes baby Mekhi clap excitedly.

But that's not the worst part. Because Hudson has decided he wants to try to use his powers to disintegrate the sand. He's finally made it halfway across the arena, and when I turn to look at him, he holds out a hand.

And shit. His power is working backward. "Hudson, stop!" I scream, but it's too late. He closes his hand, and the whole arena shakes. And the amount of sand around us doubles.

I'm buried to my thighs now, and I have to work a lot harder to pull myself out.

As soon as I do, I turn to baby Mekhi—who is still sitting on his butt and is now covered up to his pecs—and start digging him out. At least until he grabs my hair and pulls on it.

"What are you— No, stop!" I tell him firmly, loosening my curls from one of his very large hands.

But he just laughs and claps and grabs another handful of my curls. And even better, he tries to stick them in his mouth.

I don't have time to fight him, so I just let him slobber all over my hair as I turn to help Dawud dig themselves out as well. They've got all their faculties about them, so they're digging as fast as they can, but with only one hand that works, it's slow going.

Flint cock-a-doodle-dos at the top of his lungs, over and over again, as I work to save the others—and keep myself dug out as well. Macy's screaming at some monster to let her go, but at least she's moving and keeping herself from getting buried in the sand.

Calder is back in her human form and trying to dig herself out as well, but she's moving so slowly that I'm afraid she's going to end up drowning in the sand before I can get to her. Remy, on the other hand, is lying down on the sand and rolling across, arms above his head in a classic ballerina pose.

And just when I think it can't get any worse, another loud rumbling fills the room. Then the floor starts to rise. Because apparently, we're not drowning in the sand quickly enough. The Trials are going to help us out.

We're not rising that fast, thankfully, but the sand is continuing to pour in all around us even as the floor creeps up to the ceiling. And damn it. Just damn it. I can't save everyone without help. I just can't. If Jaxon and the others don't finish that puzzle soon, we won't be here.

Mekhi finally gets tired of chewing on my hair and starts to cry. I don't know if he's hungry or scared or what, but I don't have time to do much but pat his head and tell him, "It's okay, baby. It's okay," before I have to go back to digging out Flint.

At this point, Mekhi is screaming, Flint is crowing, and *The Nutcracker Suite* is blasting through the air. I can barely hear myself think, let alone talk to any of the others, but a glance at the wall tells me we're running out of time faster than I anticipated. There is only about fifteen feet between us and the ceiling, whereas we originally started out with around two hundred feet separating us.

I can't wait for Jaxon and the others. I'm going to have to do something, fast. I just wish I had a clue what that was.

I glance around, frantically trying to figure it out. There has to be a way; there just has to be.

As I'm racking my brain, something occurs to me. It's a long shot—a real long shot, considering it involves me digging my way down through who knows how many feet of sand without suffocating. But with the floor lifting toward the ceiling, that means—theoretically—the space beneath the floor is empty. If I can somehow punch a big enough hole through the floor, the sand will pour in and buy us—and Jaxon's group—more time.

It seems like a ridiculous plan, considering Hudson can't help me. But the floor is stone, and I'm a gargoyle. I couldn't do anything with tile, but stone I might actually be able to move or absorb like the Unkillable Beast did for all those years.

"Remy, come here!" I shout to where he is now somersaulting over the sand. "Start digging for me!"

He looks confused, but he somersaults over to me, and that's something.

"Macy!" I yell my cousin's name, trying to get her attention away from whatever newest horror is haunting her. "I need you to dig, too. Just keep digging, no matter what comes at you. And you, Calder."

The manticore nods and starts digging. Or at least I think she does...

Hudson has made it over, and he must have figured out what I want to do because he yells, "Deaha og!" gesturing toward the sand. And then does some strange scooping-up motion with his hands that actually has him moving sand away from Mekhi instead of burying him in it.

I need them all to keep digging if we have any hope of keeping Mekhi, Flint, and Dawud alive. My friends digging might be a mess, but they're my mess, and I'm going to have to trust them with this.

Then, determined to do whatever I can to keep all of us alive, I take a deep breath and reach for my platinum string—and shift to solid stone.

It doesn't take long before the sand starts to settle, and I sink into the ground. By the time I've sunk so far that the sand is reaching my face, it's everything in me to push the panic down my throat. The idea that I could be buried alive, unable to shift back to human form, buried beneath the sand has my heart pounding in my stone chest.

The sand reaches my nose, and it's like I'm in a bad horror flick. And then the sand is over my head, and I can't see anything else. Just sand, sand, sand.

It feels like it takes forever but is probably no more than a minute before my stone feet finally reach the stone floor of the arena. I don't waste a second, calling on every ounce of earth magic I can muster and channeling it from the floor into my body.

At first, nothing happens, and I freak out. This is my one shot—our only shot—and I can't fail. I just can't. I can't let Hudson and Macy, Flint and baby Mekhi, Calder and Remy die. Not when they put their trust in me.

So I dig down deep, find every last drop of my power. Then I channel the earth magic into my body as hard as I can. I pull and pull and pull until there really is no more air in my lungs. And then I pull one more time as hard as I can.

There's an odd little popping sound, and then one of the large cobblestones springs free.

I absorb more of the rocks into my stone body, sand rushing in to fill the space where the rocks were. I absorb one more rock and suddenly, the sand is rushing past my body through the fairly large hole in the floor I've created.

It's not a perfect solution—sand is still filling the room and the floor is still rising—but it will buy us some time, and that is all that matters. Well, that and making sure Mekhi never chews on any part of me ever again.

138

A Nightmare to Remember

"Finally!" Eden says as soon as the arena arranges itself into one single room again.

After I made it back to the rest of my friends, the sand was filtering out of the room at a steady enough pace that no one was in danger of suffocating. Calder *very slowly* helped me flip the table up on its tallest side, and that kept the floor from continuing to rise as well.

We all just flopped onto the sandy floor and watched the end of Remy's spectacular *Nutcracker* ballet while I rocked Mekhi to sleep.

The potions wore off the instant the other side solved their puzzle, thank God, and Remy made short work of fixing his broken nose. He waved a hand at Mekhi as well, fist-bumping him and saying, "I'll never speak of this again if you won't."

"Do you think we still have enough time to get to Katmere before the blood moon?" I ask Hudson, panicked. "That last Trial felt like it took at least an hour."

"Hey, we solved that puzzle fast!" Jaxon says, a fair amount of pride in his voice.

"Are you serious?" I screech. *"Fast?"*

"He's actually right," Hudson says, checking his Vacheron Constantin watch. "That Trial only took about twenty minutes."

"Well, great," I grumble. "But the nightmares will last a lifetime."

"Hey, chill out, Grace, I'm just saying. We had to defeat some pretty serious taffy to solve our puzzle. We almost didn't complete it in time and had to defeat the taffy again, but we figured it out in the end."

"I'm sorry. Did you just say you defeated *taffy*?" I look from him to everyone who was on my side of the arena. "Guys, they defeated taffy and almost had to do it *twice*," I mock.

"If it helps, it was a lot of taffy," Byron tells me with his most charming grin.

"I don't give a shit if you defeated a world record amount of taffy. At least you don't have sand in places no one talks about at parties and at least no one in your group was a chicken."

Jaxon lifts a brow as he looks from Flint to Macy to Remy to Calder to Dawud to Hudson to Mekhi. "Do I get to guess which one of you was scared?"

"Not scared," I correct him. "A *chicken*."

Rafael bumps his shoulder into Byron. "I told you I heard a cock-a-doodle-do."

"Oh, there were several," I snarl, then whirl on Jaxon. "And I swear to God, if you laugh right now, I'm going to punch you in the junk."

"Of course not. I swear." He presses his lips together to keep the laughter in, even as he holds a hand up in surrender. "No amusement here at all."

I poke a finger in his face. "There better not be."

But the second I turn away, I hear him ask Hudson, "It was Flint, right? Flint was the chicken?"

"Fuck you, Vega," Flint growls.

"Yep," Byron agrees, and I can hear the struggle not to laugh in his voice. "Totally the chicken."

"I hate all of you," I say. "Taffy. You got *taffy*."

"Hey." Hudson holds out a hand—*that actually works*—to me. "That was intense. You did a great job."

And I don't know if it's his acknowledgment that holding that shit show together was really hard or if it's hearing him speak normally again but, just like that, the anger leaves me on a flood of relief.

He's okay. They're all okay. We didn't lose anyone this round, no matter how terrified I was that we would. No matter how terrified I was that it would be my fault because I couldn't hold everything together in there. My friends—my family—they're okay.

Out of nowhere, relieved tears bloom in my eyes, and I'm so embarrassed that I bury my head against Hudson's chest for a second. I don't need long, just enough time to take a breath or two and let the incredible amount of tension from the last hour leach out of my body.

But that's one of the many things that's great about Hudson. Somehow, he always knows exactly what I need.

He puts a hand on the small of my back and another behind my head and spins us gently around, so that I'm facing away from the group and his body is shielding me.

"One more," he tells me. "We only have one more to get through. And then this will all just be a nightmare for another time."

I nod, give a watery laugh. "We can add it to the collection. Not so Impossible after all, eh?"

"Isn't that the truth?" He shakes his head, a rueful grin on his too-beautiful face. "I'm pretty sure it's going to take a lot of years and therapy before I'm over the trauma of having Flint try to peck out my eyes."

"You and me both," I tell him. "You and me both."

"But hey, at least we're thinking about sand inside our clothes instead of bugs now," he says, and I shudder.

"Too soon. Way too soon," I mutter.

"Sorry," he says and chuckles, hugging me tight for the space of one more breath, then turns us back around.

"Still, I hope we can complete this last Trial quickly," I say. "We probably only have about a half hour left before we've missed the blood moon."

"Stop worrying, Grace. We got this," Calder says. "As long as I can move at normal speed in this next round, it shouldn't be a problem."

The others agree, and I don't have the heart to point out that none of us has any idea what's coming next or how quickly we might be able to beat it. But they're right about something. We're about to, so why borrow trouble?

As if on cue, the arena walls start to move, but instead of a wall bisecting the circle, the walls on the outside start to spin and move backward, making the space larger. And then they do it again. And again. And again.

"I don't know whether to be relieved or terrified," Dawud says as things continue to move.

"I'm going to go with terrified," Eden tells them, though she sounds more optimistic than scared. "Start with really low expectations, and then you can be pleasantly surprised if you were wrong."

"Yeah, but last is always the worst," Jaxon says. "So get your shit together and let's do this thing."

"You're right," I snark, not liking the way he's talking to Dawud. I know it's because Dawud is younger and bringing out Jaxon's protective instincts, but just no. "This time you might have to eat your way through taffy *and* cupcakes."

"That's not what most of us did," Byron says with a laugh, "though that sounds vaguely terrifying, too."

"To a vampire, maybe," Macy comments. "I've always loved taffy."

"We'll get you a big bag before we leave," Remy promises. "All the flavors you want."

Her face lights up for a second, but then she frowns. "Nah. I'm pretty sure I'm not going to want anything to remind me of this place ever again."

No one says anything after that, nerves getting the best of us as we wait for what feels like forever.

"Do you think they're ever going to stop?" Flint growls as the walls continue to move. In fact, the arena is now almost twice as large as it was before, and the walls are still spinning out.

"I'm pretty sure we're going to be screwed when they do," Hudson answers. "So I'm okay with them spinning a bit longer."

"I'm more terrified what they're going to throw at us that requires this much space," I add.

No one says anything to that, which says it all. The room isn't even trying to divide us into two groups anymore, like whatever is coming is going to take every single one of us to fight it back.

I glance around, realize pretty much everyone in the room is doing the same thing—including me. This is going to be bad. We all know it. The only question now is how bad.

Panic churns in my gut, has bile crawling up my throat. But I shove it back down, even go so far as to do the trick Hudson taught me and add numbers until my brain has to focus on them instead of the fear kicking around in every part of me.

It works again—and just in time, too. Because the walls finally stop. And a strange whirring noise fills the room.

"What's that?" Eden asks, spinning around to see where the sound is coming from.

Turns out, it's coming from a stone in the center of the arena. It's retracting slowly and as it does, a small stone podium rises up from the floor, the same podium we saw before the Trials began. And on the podium is the gold chalice ringed with diamonds.

"Oooh, pretty," Calder says.

"Oh my God," Macy whispers. "Is that it? Did we do it?"

We all look at one another in confusion because Tess had said four rounds. We've only done three.

Unless— "Do you think one of the rounds counted as two?" I ask. That bug round definitely felt like it should count as more than one. Or six.

"I wouldn't think so," Remy answers. "These don't exactly seem like the kind of people to skimp on the scary shit."

"And taffy doesn't seem scary enough to be a fourth round on its own," Calder says doubtfully.

"Jeez, let the taffy go, people," Rafael says with a roll of his eyes.

"We're never letting the taffy go," Macy tells him. "Get used to it."

Eden walks over to investigate. "It's empty," she says, reaching for the cup. "There's nothing in it, although...*pretty*."

"Nothing?" Flint asks, sounding confused. "Are you sure?"

She turns it over to show him and, sure enough, nothing comes out.

"So what does that mean?" Jaxon asks.

He's barely finished speaking when the lights snap off.

Dawud sighs. "I think that means round four's not done yet."

Yeah, me too.

"Again with the lights?" Macy sounds aggrieved and uses her wand to cast a small glow of light around us as Eden puts the cup back on the pedestal.

Suddenly, the pedestal starts slowly sinking into the ground like it's taking an elevator down, until it's completely gone and the floor closes up over it.

"Well that was interesting," Remy says. "Plus, the arena's intact. We're all in the same room this time."

"Do you think it's a mistake?" Eden asks.

"I think it's a chance for them to try to kill us all off at once," Jaxon answers.

"Thank you, Mr. Mary Sunshine," Calder tells him.

"Just calling it like I see it," he answers.

"Yeah, well, I'm guessing they think our odds aren't good with dividing us up," I mutter, and we all turn around, trying to figure out what the threat is in this round—and where it's going to come from. "Can you give us even more light, Remy?"

Remy does his magic thing again and, as I spin around, I realize that the arena is completely empty. With the pedestal and chalice now gone, there is nothing in here with us this time. No fountain, no puzzle grid, no table, nothing. It's just us and this big, empty stadium. Even the crowd has gone quiet.

The knowledge only makes me more nervous.

The others must feel the same, because unlike the earlier times, no one seems interested in striking out on their own to see what's happening. Instead, we all walk toward the center of the arena in a little huddle.

"There's really nothing?" Byron asks.

"There will be," Hudson answers confidently. "They didn't lock us in here just to hand us the elixir."

"It would be kind of cool if they did, though, huh?" Eden says.

"Very cool," I agree, even as I put my hand on my platinum string. Because like Hudson, I know something is coming, and I want to be ready for it, whatever it is.

"Do we need to—" Flint starts.

"Quiet!" Jaxon snaps, cocking his head to the side.

Flint looks like he's really freaking offended, but then he must hear something, too, because his eyes narrow, and he turns silently around so that he can watch the area right in back of us.

The other vampires and shifters are doing the same thing, their hearing better than the rest of ours.

"What is it?" I whisper as quietly as I can.

Hudson shakes his head to say he doesn't know.

And then suddenly, I hear it, too. The low, almost inaudible rhythm of something soft hitting the stone floor over and over again.

Like everyone else, I whirl around, trying to see where it's coming from. But there's nothing. No one is in here with us. At least no one we can see.

"Get ready," Remy breathes, turning so that his back is to the center of the room.

We all do the same, pressing our backs together in a circular arrangement so that nobody is left unprotected and we have a view of the entire room.

And then we wait. And wait. And wait.

Because the longer we stand here, the more apparent it becomes that we're being stalked.

139

This May Be
the Rune of Me

My heart is beating uncontrollably, and it's all I can do to stay where I am. My body wants to move, every survival instinct I have telling me that staying still like this is courting death.

But I've learned enough about survival these last few months to know that—unless you've got a firm strategy in mind—the person who moves first dies. Act, don't react.

So we wait, all of us. Breaths held, eyes watchful, bodies poised for fight or flight.

I hear the footfalls again, closer this time, and for a second I swear I catch a glimpse of something out of the corner of my eye. But when I turn my head to look, nothing's there. And Jaxon, who's on my left and has better eyesight than I do—particularly in the dark—never saw a thing.

And so we wait some more.

"This is ridiculous," Macy hisses at one point, but Dawud and Byron shush her right away. She listens to them but grumbles under her breath, and I'm sure it's because she doesn't know what's happening here. She doesn't get that the reason the hair on the back of her neck is standing up is because her subconscious recognizes something her conscious brain hasn't figured out.

For the first time in her life, she is actual prey.

The predators in our group know it—I can see it on their faces. Vampires, dragons, manticore, wolf. They all know what it is to hunt, so conversely, they know what it is to be hunted. Macy doesn't. She's never had to know.

I learned what it felt like for the first time when Cyrus looked in my eyes. And have felt it in every encounter since. That's why I know what's happening here.

All of a sudden, Dawud starts to growl, and it takes every ounce of willpower I have not to whirl around and try to see what set them off. But that's what it's counting on. One second of inattention, one momentary slip, and it'll be on us.

"What did you see?" Remy asks them calmly, but I notice he doesn't so much as move a muscle as we wait for the answer.

"I don't know. Something."

There's another flash in my peripheral vision—here, then gone superfast, just like last time.

More padding of feet, and they sound even closer than before.

"We need to move," I whisper to Hudson.

"I don't think we can," he answers me just as quietly.

"But it's getting closer."

"I know." He brushes my shoulder with his arm. "Be ready."

I don't think I can get any more ready, but I don't bother to tell him that. He already knows.

Long seconds pass, and I see the flash out of the corner of my eye again. From the way Jaxon and Hudson both stiffen, I can tell they saw it, too. Or maybe it's just the fact that the footfalls have gotten closer again.

I feel like whatever it is that's out there is closer than any of us expect, and I'm terrified that any second now, it's going to be on us and we're never going to have seen it coming.

"Grace." Remy's voice is as quiet as it is steady, but there is a note to it that warns me that I need to listen—and obey.

"Yes?"

"Step into the center of the circle so you're protected by the rest of us. Then open your bag and get out those protection runes."

Jaxon and Hudson are stepping in front of me—a little bit on each side—and easing me back into the center of the circle, where I can be protected by everyone while I'm looking for the runes.

I put them in the middle area of the pack so they're easy to find. Once I have my backpack zipped up again and over my shoulders, I whisper, "What do you want me to do with them now?"

"Hand them to me." He's slow and stealthy as he brings his left arm down and then reaches it back into the circle.

I put the box of runes in his hands, and as I do, I can't help praying that they'll all be in one piece when this is done. At the same time, though, if they're not because they've managed to save the life of one of my friends, then losing one—or even losing all of them—will be totally worth it.

I may hate to ruin a gift from my father, but I'll hate dying or losing one of my friends even more.

I press my right hand to Hudson's arm and my left one to Jaxon's, and they move back to their regular spots so that I can reclaim my position in the circle. I have a second, maybe two, to start looking around again, and then Remy does something I'm totally not expecting.

He takes the box of runes and throws it up in the air as hard as he can.

140

A Rune of One's Own

"W hat—" I yelp before I manage to cut myself off. Letting him use the runes to save us is one thing, but letting him just throw them away is something else entirely.

Remy doesn't answer. Instead, he heaves his arms over his head and spreads them wide. Then he starts to spin the right one in a circle over and over again. Every time he completes a rotation, he makes the circle bigger until it's as wide as his arms can reach.

I wait for the runes to come down, falling right in the middle of the circle he's making, but they don't. Instead, they get caught up in whatever power or magic he's generating, and as they fly out of the box, they arrange themselves in a circle that moves in tandem with Remy's hand.

Around and around they go, their circle widening until they are spinning above all of us—faster and faster—so quickly that they're practically a blur. And then, just when I'm getting used to them floating directly above our heads, Remy shouts and throws his arms out wide again.

And just like that, the runes fire themselves in all directions, speeding through the air like arrows loosed from a bow. All twenty of them hit the wall so hard that they embed themselves in the stone, where they give off a mystical flickering light.

Except one of them isn't embedded in a wall at all. It's moving up and down and round and round, like it's embedded in... I swallow my scream back as I realize it's embedded in the side of whatever is stalking us. And the invisible beast must be massive, given how high the rune is floating.

I don't have to wonder about its size for long, though, as the rune lets out an eerie glow and then whatever gave the creature invisibility ends and we can all see now exactly what's been stalking us around this arena.

As it whirls around, rears up on two feet, I can't help wishing that I'd never seen it. Because if I know nothing else, it's that I will see it in my nightmares every night for the rest of my life.

And that's before it leaps half the length of the stadium in one jump and lands directly in front of Hudson.

The rune is embedded in the creature's hide, and it does not look happy about it at all. It rears up on two feet again, more than sixty feet in the air and looming over us, as it releases a fearsome roar that sends shivers down my spine.

It turns out I'm not the only one horrified at the sight of the beast.

Macy gasps, Dawud moans, and Jaxon curses—long, low, and vicious. Flint lets out a shocked "what the fuck!" and everyone else just stares. Eyes wide, mouths open, fear in every line of their bodies.

"Bring the bugs back. Bring the bugs back," Macy whispers like a prayer, and honestly, I couldn't agree more.

Because I know now, I get it. I'd let myself think because we survived a few rounds with nothing more than bricks, bugs, or ballet, the Impossible Trials really weren't that bad. We were going to make it. Everything was going to be okay.

But as I stare into the eyes of this beast, I know how very wrong I was.

I was a child in the earlier rounds. My eyes have been opened now, and it's time to put aside childish thoughts.

We're all going to die.

141

No Skin
in the Game

"**W**hat the bloody hell is that?" Hudson asks.

And I don't know how to answer him.

To begin with, the thing is huge. Like eighteen-wheeler huge. It's got four legs and a snout, pointy ears, and a really long tail, and I think in an alternate universe, it could be classified as some kind of wolf creature. In this universe, though, I don't have a clue what to call it. I do know it looks nothing like Dawud or any other werewolf I've ever seen.

Besides being huge, it's also mostly...translucent? Not like I can see right through it or anything, but like it doesn't have any fur, at all. Instead, it has clear skin that shows off everything that normal skin and fur hide. And I mean *everything*. Its gigantic heart, its lungs and stomach and intestines. Its veins and bones and what I'm pretty sure is bright orange blood are all on full display for everyone to see.

It has a knobby gray spine, and each separate knob has bonelike spikes going out in all directions. Each paw has four sharp claws that measure at least eighteen inches each, and its tail is full of spikes long enough to impale a person with one well-placed swing.

Its face is even uglier—milky white eyes set in translucent skin, vicious-looking teeth as long as my arm, and a bizarrely twisted snout that does I'm not sure what...I mean, besides scare the hell out of anyone looking at it.

"Does it matter?" I finally answer as the creature whirls on us. It falls back down on all fours again with a powerful *thud* and paws at the ground like it wants nothing more than to eat the lot of us for a midafternoon snack. The fact that it's big enough to scoop us up—and gobble us down—like a colorful hand of M&M's is definitely not lost on me.

And neither is the fact that this really is the biggest, ugliest beast I've ever seen. Forget beetles by the thousands, forget shadow snakes from hell, forget anything and everything that I have ever had to fight—or will ever have to fight. This is the worst. I know, absolutely, that it can*not* get worse than this.

And Remy embedded a rune in its side and pissed it off.

Apparently, it wasn't bad enough that it's homicidal, smart enough to stalk us where we don't even see it coming, and creepy as fuck. Remy needed it angry, too.

This is what we have to fight to get the elixir? Worse, this is what we have to *beat*?

Part of me wants to hang it up now. To just say, *no thanks, bad idea, I'll come back another day with a rocket launcher and an entire missile system.*

But unfortunately, that's not an option for so many reasons. One, it's win or die in here—there is no going back. Two, I really need that elixir to cure the Gargoyle Army if I have any chance of saving my people. Three, I really need the Gargoyle Army if I have any chance of stopping Cyrus from becoming a god. And four, we've come so far and lost so much already. We just really, really need to get this shit done.

Which means it is past time for me to put my big-girl panties on and deal. So what if it's huge, ugly, terrifying, angry, and mean as all fuck. It's the one thing standing between me and saving everyone I care about, which means it's going down. Or I'm going to die trying.

I really hope it's the former, but at this point, it's pretty much up in the air.

"You ready?" I say, looking at Hudson on my right and Jaxon on my left.

"No," Macy says. But she's right behind me, and I know she's got my back.

Which is a good thing, because the creature looks more than ready to tear us limb from limb.

142

"**G**et to the sides of the arena!" Remy yells as we all scatter like bowling pins after a strike.

"Why?" Eden asks, even as we start to run.

"Trust me. And once you get there, run counterclockwise!"

"That's your big plan?" Flint demands. "What are we going to do? Run it to death?"

"I just want to see if it works," Remy tells him.

"*If* it works?" Macy says. She's running like her life depends on it, but suddenly she looks a lot less sure.

Not that I blame her. This thing has really freaking long legs, and I'm pretty sure it's going to be able to catch us. I mean, not the vampires or those of us who can fly maybe, but Macy, Calder, Dawud, and Remy are pretty much screwed.

No wonder my cousin doesn't sound impressed.

"Get to the side," Remy yells at Flint again.

Flint is hauling ass across the field, and his prosthetic isn't slowing him down at all, but the beast is gaining on him.

"What the fuck do you think I'm trying to do?" Flint snarls back. "Why don't you just change it into a rabbit or something?"

"You think I didn't try?" Macy calls to him. "It didn't work. It's immune or something."

"I couldn't do anything, either," Hudson tells him.

"Fuck this," Flint mutters before, in a spark of magic, shifting into his dragon.

The beast misses grabbing Flint's tail by about an inch—maybe less. And then Flint is soaring way up toward the arena dome, and the beast is looking for its next target.

Apparently, its next target is me, because it comes galloping toward me, snorting and slobbering as its bone claws scrape against the stone floor. It's a horrible sound, one that has me wincing even as I try to run faster. For a second, I think about doing what Flint did and taking to the air, but I'm trying to help lure him to the side like Remy wants.

Remy might not be the most forthcoming about his ideas, but if I learned nothing else in that prison, I learned that he always, *always* has a plan. I just hope whatever one he has for the beast is a good one.

I'm only about twenty yards from the side of the arena now, but the beast is gaining on me. I lay on more speed, try to make it, but a couple more feet and I can feel its hot breath against the back of my neck. And no, just no.

I don't even have time to take flight at this point, so instead, I grab my platinum string and change to solid stone on the fly, freezing with my arms and legs outstretched mid-run.

I was hoping it would be enough to dissuade the beast, but it's obviously more pissed than I thought because it chomps down around my midsection and starts dragging all two thousand pounds of me across the arena.

"Great plan, Remy," Jaxon snarls in the background, but I'm not paying attention to anyone but the beast at this point.

I need to get away from it before it breaks my arm off or decides to chow down like I'm an afternoon snack and pulverizes me completely, but I'm only going to have one shot at it. Which means I have to make it count.

Though it gets my anxiety way up, I let it drag me, waiting for its bite on me to loosen just the tiniest bit. Eventually it pauses, its jaws unclenching, and I partially release my grip on my platinum string, just enough to become animated but not enough to lose the stone completely.

I reach up and press one hand against one of the beast's giant teeth. I use it to whirl around and swing my other hand to punch it as hard as I can, right in the side of its snout.

It roars in surprise, which is all I need. I let go of the platinum string as I drop to the ground and roll away as fast as I can. As I do, I grab the string again and shift—this time into my animated form—and shoot straight up into the air, flapping my wings as hard as I can.

And still the damn beast nearly gets me. It would have, in fact, but Hudson comes racing out of nowhere and slams straight into the monster's side with all his strength.

The two of them go airborne, with the beast snarling and twisting around in an effort to get to Hudson and Hudson doing the same in an effort to keep away from it.

They land with a *thud* that shakes the arena, Hudson on the ground and the beast above him. He's holding the creature off with pure strength alone, but I can tell from his face that he's trying to use his power on the beast and persuade it to stand down and let us go. But like everything else we've tried, it's obviously not working. If possible, the beast looks *more* like it wants to kill Hudson instead of *less* after he's used his power of persuasion.

Which makes no sense to me. I know I'm not super well-versed in this world or anything, but everything I do know tells me that only gargoyles are immune to magic due to how we were created. And this thing, whatever it is, is definitely not a gargoyle—which means it shouldn't be immune to Remy's or Macy's or Hudson's power. But it obviously is, which means either there's another creature out there immune to magic or someone's done something to it to make it immune.

I just don't know enough about this world to be certain if that's even possible. And now isn't exactly the time to ask, considering my mate is currently trying to keep the thing from biting his head off.

Even worse, it looks like he's losing. And we're all too far away to help him.

143

Ring Around the Not-So-Rosie

"**H**udson!" I race toward him, flying faster than I've ever flown before in my life. And still I don't think it's going to matter. Still I don't think I'm going to be fast enough.

Hudson is managing to hold open the creature's jaws, using every ounce of strength he has to keep its sharp canines from chomping down. But the thing is stronger than a vampire, stronger even than one of the strongest vampires in existence, and there's not enough time.

Oh my God. Hudson. Hudson. "Hudson!"

His name is ripped from deep inside me, the horror of what's about to happen turning my stomach to dust. "No!" I scream as I barrel toward them. "No!"

All of a sudden, the ground starts to shake, a major earthquake ripping through the stadium. The beast screams in terror as the floor beneath it starts to split open and leaps away in an effort to save itself.

Hudson rolls away and jumps to his feet, fading straight to me as he calls out to his brother, "Thanks!"

Jaxon rolls his eyes, but there's a small smile on his face as he fades straight toward the beast, which I'm beginning to think is a very, very bad idea. After what almost happened to Hudson, I'd be happy if no one ever went near the thing again. But Jaxon never has had much of a sense of self-preservation, and he whips by the creature like it's nothing, pausing just long enough for it to catch his scent before fading several yards away.

That's all it takes. The beast is up and running, chasing him full-out now and leaping over the large crack Jaxon put in the stone with his power. More, Jaxon is letting it. In fact, I'm pretty sure he's encouraging the beast to chase him, using every ounce of strength he has to stay in front of the beast as he runs it *counterclockwise* around the arena, exactly as Remy requested.

"Okay, so he's got it running," Eden calls to Remy. "What do we do now?"

"We wait and see," he shoots back, which has all of us turning to stare at him.

"Wait and see?" I repeat. "That's your big plan? You saw what that thing almost did to Hudson. If he gets Jaxon now—"

"He's not going to get Jaxon," Calder tells me from where she's leaning against the wall watching the whole thing like she's at a Friday evening football game.

"How do you know that?" I ask, my heart in my throat.

"Because," she answers, nodding behind me. "It's already working."

"What's working?" Mekhi asks, looking confused.

But we turn back to Jaxon before Remy answers, and it's impossible not to see what's happening to the beast. The runes on the walls are all lit up, and every time the beast passes one, it grows a tiny bit smaller. A tiny bit calmer. And a hell of a lot less rabid-looking. So that by the time it passes the sixth one, it's still giant, but it's no longer the size of an actual eighteen-wheeler. Plus, suddenly, it looks more like it wants to play than like it wants to eat all of us.

"What is even happening?" I ask. "What are my father's runes *doing* to that thing?"

"Actually, they're *my* father's runes," Remy corrects me. "He gave them to your father to give to you so that—"

"I could give them to you when you needed them," I finish as the truth dawns on me. That's how Remy knew about them—they belong to him, and he knows what to do with them in a way I never will. I don't even have time to process the ache in my chest that my father hadn't actually left me something to remind me of the witch part of myself, like him.

Remy nods. "Exactly."

"You people who see the future are freaky," Mekhi tells him as he walks up to us.

Remy grins. "Definitely not the first time I've been told that."

"Maybe not," Flint says as he flies down and shifts next to us. "But I've got to ask. Did you see *that* coming?"

"See what?" Remy and I turn around to check out what he's looking at, and my heart almost stops all over again. Because the beast has suddenly stopped chasing Jaxon—and, more importantly, stopped running counterclockwise around the arena altogether.

"Did it figure it out?" I ask, astonished at the very idea.

"It must have," Hudson responds. "Because it just changed direction, and it sure as hell looks like it's doing it on purpose to me."

"Yeah, me too," I agree as the beast literally turns around and starts running in the opposite direction.

And gets bigger and bigger and bigger as it does.

Its arm-length teeth become leg-length. The bony spikes on its back become bigger and more involved. The spikes on its tail grow thicker and more curved until it looks ten times scarier and more dangerous than it did when we first got here.

"So, genius," Flint tells Remy. "What do we do with that?"

"Run," Macy says as it barrels toward us at top speed. "We run like hell."

144

You Really Want a
Pierce of Me?

We all do exactly what Macy suggests and run like hell.

Hudson fades across the arena straight toward the beast, trying to get it to follow him back the way he came, but the beast is having no part of that.

Remy gets to work in the center of the arena, building what I think might be a magical cage to hold the beast. But I'm not even sure that will work, considering it's immune to seemingly all other types of magic. So far, only the runes have worked.

The rest of us go back to scattering like scarab beetles, trying to run the beast to exhaustion.

I take to the air to get an aerial view of the arena, hoping against hope that there's something we missed. That there is something in here that we can use as a weapon, considering there's nothing we brought with us that will be long or sharp enough to penetrate the beast's thick skin.

I mean, the rune did it, but it didn't cut straight through to the muscle and organs below. Instead, it just embedded itself in the beast's hide.

I glance around at my friends all running, trying to figure out who to help first. Most are moving in counterclockwise circles, but Hudson and Jaxon are running clockwise now, trying to herd the beast to go in the other direction. Idly, I wonder why they're not getting larger, too. Why aren't the others getting smaller, too? Why does only the beast get smaller and larger based on the direction it runs in?

Which gives me an idea. I know optimally we herd it back in the counterclockwise direction and get it to become smaller and smaller again. But the fact of the matter is, this monster is smart, very smart, and there is no way it's going to do that again. I can see it already, considering everyone is running in that direction and it's not chasing any of them.

Instead, it's circling the other way, knowing it's going to run into them eventually on the other side—and when it does, it'll be twice its normal size.

Or maybe it's already twice its normal size. It was so big to begin with that it's hard to tell.

Which makes me think that there's only one thing to do at this point. Since it's dangerous as hell, I don't feel confident asking anyone else to do it. And I know Hudson will have a fit if I suggest it, so I...just don't suggest it.

Instead, I concentrate on gathering up as much speed as I possibly can and then flying straight at the beast from behind, hoping it won't notice me for a little while.

It seems to be working as Dawud and Calder have jumped into the fray, and they are taking turns zigzagging back and forth across the arena in an effort to tire it out. I mean, yeah, it's tiring them out, too, but there are twelve of us and only one of it. Surely we will win the stamina game in this situation.

The beast gets so close to Dawud, who is in their wolf form, that it actually leans down and nips their tail. Which has Dawud jumping five feet in the air and rolling under the beast to nip at its ankles in an effort to make it stumble.

The beast doesn't even notice them now that they're not in front of it, and it focuses all its attention on Calder. And on Macy, who is running behind it, trying to hit it with one magical spell after another.

Nothing works, of course, but my cousin doesn't let that stop her. She keeps trying, hoping one will stick.

And I—I'm getting ready to do maybe the most foolish thing of them all. If it keeps growing in size the longer it runs clockwise around the arena, pretty soon we're going to be dealing with a monster the size of the actual arena if we don't do something.

So praying this works, I fly right up to it from behind, reach out, and try to grab on to the rune embedded in its hide.

Only the beast is getting larger and smaller depending upon which direction it runs in—and only the beast has a rune embedded in its side. It has to be connected somehow, I just know it. So I grit my teeth and reach for the rune again.

My fingers dip around and grip the edges of the stone. I place my knees on the animal's side and, using my wings to flap in reverse to give me leverage, try to rip the rune from its hide.

It screams, whirling on me so fast, I don't have time to brace myself, and I end up flying straight off it. At first, I think I'm going to fall straight toward its mouth—which is going to be bye-bye for me when those teeth get ahold of me—but at the last minute, I manage to pull up just enough to run into one of the bony knobs on its neck.

It impales me, going straight through my upper thigh, making me scream in agony. On the plus side, though, I don't have to fight to keep up with it now. I'm well and truly stuck to it.

Deciding to take advantage of it despite the pain slamming through my body, I spread myself out along the side of its body and reach, reach, reach for the rune. But once again, my damn shortness does me no favors—plus the beast is so big now that even with my arms extended, I don't reach the side of its back hip, let alone all the way up to where the rune is embedded.

Which means I need to figure out a way to un-impale myself from this damn thing. But considering it's galloping at what feels like a hundred miles an hour and there's nothing good to grab on to save another one of the sharp, bony things sticking out of its back, I'm pretty sure I'm well and truly screwed.

Hudson and Remy are racing toward me, and I scream at them to get back. The beast is pissed as hell now, and I'm terrified it's going to rip them apart.

But before they can get here, Flint dives down in full dragon form and gets just close enough to the beast to distract it.

The beast goes nuts, leaping and snarling and twisting itself around in an effort to get to him. But Flint stays out of reach, occasionally dangling his tail or foot just close enough to make the beast think it has an actual chance to catch him.

Which only enrages it more.

Hudson, in the meantime, launches himself at the beast's back, grabbing on to the bony thing right behind the one I'm impaled on like it's a handle and pulling himself up onto its back. Which is a dangerous as fuck place to be, considering there are bones sticking up everywhere and the beast is bucking and jumping and doing everything imaginable to grab Flint and shake Hudson off at the exact same time.

I don't waste time telling him to get off the thing before he gets hurt—this is Hudson, after all, and he's not going anywhere without me. Instead, I ask, "What can I do to help?"

To which he answers, "Next time, don't get yourself bloody well impaled on an animal?"

"Yeah, it wasn't my plan."

"And yet here we are." He sounds mean, but he gives me a smile that lets me know he's just messing with me. And then, with no warning whatsoever, reaches over and breaks off the piece of the beast's bone that is protruding from my leg.

It tears up his hand while also enraging the beast beyond measure—I can only imagine how much it hurt for both of them—and suddenly I go from being stuck on the back of a bucking bronco to what feels like trying to bodysurf in the middle of a tsunami. Which feels really good on the leg that is still impaled on the bottom half of the beast's bony back thing.

"If you don't like that, then settle the fuck down, ya fooking wanker," Hudson snarls at the beast as it whirls around and tries to bite him. It is literally hopping around now, screaming at the top of its lungs as it twists a million different ways, trying to sink its teeth into one of us. And no matter how hard Flint tries to distract it, it's just not having it right now. It's out for blood, and only Hudson's and mine will do.

Jaxon comes racing across the arena now, along with Byron and Rafael, all of whom do what they can to get the beast's attention on them instead of us.

Jaxon jumps up in front of it and punches it in the face, much like I did earlier. It bellows in rage and tries to take his leg off, but Jaxon is fast.

Byron grabs one of its front legs while Rafael takes the other and they literally yank them out from under the beast so that when it comes down from a jump expecting to land on them, it hits its stone belly first instead.

It turns its head, tries to bite Byron, but the vampire has already faded twenty feet away and is taunting it, trying to get it to come after him.

Hudson, in the meantime, barely pays attention to any of them. Instead, he takes advantage of the beast's abrupt stop and tells me, "This is going to hurt."

145

Death and
Dis-Ordered

He's right, it does. Because with no more warning than that, he grabs my leg and yanks it straight off the bone it is currently impaled on. Before the scream dies on my lips, though, he's shouting at Jaxon and tossing me through the air like a sack of potatoes.

And I get it. I do. I can't shift into my stone form, I'm in too much pain and seeing stars. But he had to get me off the back of the monster fast before the bucking sent me in a direction he couldn't control where I'd land.

As Jaxon's strong arms snatch me out of the air, he fades as far from the beast as he can before setting me down. I partially shift to stanch the blood loss, but I feel dizzy. I look around, expecting Hudson to fade next to me, but when he doesn't, I blink around the arena. And find him still on its spiny back.

He jumps, turns in midair, and grabs the rune on the side of the beast. And my breath stalls in the back of my throat as I watch my mate hanging on to the side—and then he's falling, rune in his hand.

The monster roars as it immediately shrinks back to normal size, and I take my first breath in what feels like ten minutes. I mean, the beast is still eighteen-wheeler giant size, but at least it's not apartment-block size.

Hudson hits the ground and fades to me in a flash. "Can you stay here for a little while?" he asks as he pulls up short, breathing hard. "Just try to rest? I'll keep that thing away from you."

I give him a *you've got to be kidding me* look. "*I'll* keep it away from me," I tell him, grabbing my platinum string and becoming solid stone just long enough for the wound to superficially seal itself.

Then I'm back in my human form, and while I'm not up for running around like I was just a few minutes ago, I'm more than ready to get back in the fray.

Over Hudson's shoulder, I can see the Order fading around the arena, trying to keep the beast focused on them so the rest of us can come up with some kind of plan to destroy this thing once and for all.

The only problem is, I don't know what to do—and neither does anyone else.

Magic won't work.

We don't have any weapons that will work on it.

Nothing we do seems to penetrate its thick hide. Even the rune only embedded in the surface of its skin.

I don't have a clue how we're supposed to defeat this thing. No wonder no one ever wins the Trials. Even if they manage to survive everything else, how on earth do they survive this?

The only reason we've stayed alive this long is because of how many of us there are. But we can't outrun it forever. Eventually, something has to give, and I'm afraid it's going to be us.

"What can we do?" I ask Hudson.

"I don't know," he answers, looking grim. "If Jaxon and I bring the arena down and try to crush it, odds are I'm going to crush all of us, too."

"I know. But we've got to do something."

"Yeah."

All of a sudden, Macy darts to the center of the arena, right in the beast's current path.

"What's she doing?" I ask, my heart in my throat.

"I don't know," Hudson answers, and he takes off straight for my cousin, putting himself between her and the beast, and I take to the air to do the same thing.

But Macy is having none of it. "Get out of the way!" she shouts to him, so he does, just as I figure out what Macy's doing. She's building a portal.

"Is that going to work?" I ask no one in particular, but she must hear me, because she looks up and shrugs.

And I get it. At this point, anything is worth a shot. But where is she going to take it? I don't think any of us can actually leave this arena.

As it turns out, Macy doesn't plan on taking it far at all.

As the beast comes up on her, she dives into the portal, and it dives after her. Seconds later, she reappears at the other side of the arena, running like her life depends on it. Then again, I'm pretty sure it does.

"It works!" she shouts, but the monster is practically on her now, so I swoop down and pick her up by her arms, snatching her away right before its giant jaws close on her shoulder.

"What's your idea with the portals?" I ask as I fly her to the other side of the arena.

"I wanted to see if it worked—if the magic wasn't specifically directed at it, could it still access it. And it could—the portal worked for it."

"Yeah, but how are we going to use that to work for us?"

"What if I open one—" She breaks off with a scream as Flint flies too close to the beast. He and Eden have been taking turns flying around it, trying to tire it out and find a weakness while the Order does the same running on the ground.

But Flint miscalculated, and the beast has got its mouth around Flint's prosthetic leg, and it's not letting go. Instead, it's thrashing its head back and forth, whipping Flint in his giant dragon form around like he's nothing more than a bag of beans.

Flint tries kicking it in the face, he tries bending over and punching it in the snout, he even tries poking the beast in the eye, but it doesn't turn him loose. All it does is double down on the leg it does have, its powerful jaws squeezing so tightly, I can only be grateful that it isn't Flint's real leg that it managed to grab. Because I'm pretty sure if it had anything but his magical prosthetic, it would have crushed it beyond recognition already.

Because there's nothing it can do to hurt the leg, I try to calm down. Try to think our way through this. It's not an emergency because Flint's not being hurt, though I'm sure he's scared to death he's about to lose his other leg. God knows I would be.

We need to get him free. How do we get the beast to turn him loose? We have to give it something it wants to bite down on—something it wants to eat—more than it wants to eat Flint. But what is that?

I drop down and release Macy, then take to the air again and start to fly closer as I formulate a plan.

But the beast whirls around and slams Flint against the nearest wall hard enough to do some kind of damage, I'm sure.

And Jaxon freaks the fuck out. There's no other word for it.

He fades across the arena so fast, it's like he took a portal himself, and he jumps straight onto the beast's back. Unlike me, he is coordinated enough to not land on any of the bony knobs, thank God, as he pretty much walks across the monster's translucent back.

The beast goes apeshit, thrashing Flint like a shark with its prey, while at the same time ramming its back against the wall to try to shake Jaxon off—or, barring that, knock him off its back.

But Jaxon manages to stay on it somehow—sheer will, I think—and even makes it across its back to its head. Once there, he grabs on to its ears and pulls them back with all his vampire strength, trying to get the creature to let go of Flint.

The beast screams, the sound of its agony echoing through the empty arena. I feel it in my gut, the creature's rage and pain burrowing inside me, taking me back several months to the night Xavier died in the Unkillable Beast's cave.

We went to him. Attacked him. Tried to kill him when all he wanted to do was to be left alone. And suddenly, I can't help wondering if it's the same with this creature. If it's just trapped here, minding its own business until the next person wants to come along and kill it so they can get the elixir.

The thought makes me sick to my stomach, picturing this thing like Alistair, chained in a cave with no control over its own life. *Are we doing it again?* I wonder. *Are we making the same mistakes we made last time?*

I drop down lower, determined to tell Jaxon to back off. To give the beast the chance to drop Flint and go back to its corner without having to worry about us attacking it anymore. But before I can say anything to Jaxon, he must decide grabbing the ears isn't working, because he lets go. Then, grimacing, leaps up and lands on the beast's snout. He reaches lower and wraps his hand around the outer edges of the thing's nostrils and pulls back as hard as he can.

The beast roars in agony, its mouth flying open as its bellows of pain fill the arena. Orange blood streams from its nose as Flint flies away, and it throws itself on the ground in a desperate attempt to get Jaxon to let go.

Jaxon tries to do just that, but he doesn't get away in time and ends up trapped under the full weight of this screaming, fury-filled animal.

Hudson darts forward to try to save his brother, pushing at the animal's back to get it to move. And that's when the Order swoops in as one. They taunt it, poke at it, try to pick a fight with it—doing anything and everything they can to get it up and off Jaxon before it crushes him to death under its weight.

Eventually Byron lands a kick square in its sensitive, still-bleeding nose, and the beast leaps to its feet. Then, with a scream so high-pitched and filled with fury that it's hard to listen to it, it swings its sharp, bony tail like a club.

Hudson grabs Jaxon and jumps high enough that he clears the swinging tail. But the beast is out for blood now, and it whirls around, trying to get at someone, anyone.

And just like that, it does. Its tail swings in an upward arc and slams straight into Byron's chest, the spikes on it impaling him straight through the heart. Rafael runs for him, but the beast turns back around and grabs hold of him, its strong jaws closing over Rafael's head as it whips his body around.

There's a sickening crunching sound, and then he's flinging Rafael several feet away. But his skull is crushed, and he's dead before he even hits the floor.

I'm screaming, Macy's screaming, and Jaxon's beating the hell out of Hudson, who is using every ounce of strength he has to hold on to his brother and keep him from throwing himself into the path of the rampaging monster who now has Mekhi in its sights.

Flint and Eden barrel through the air trying to get to him, while Remy and Calder do the same on the ground. But it's already too late.

146

Any Portal
in a Storm

"No!" Jaxon's agonized screams tear through the auditorium. "No! No! No!"

The last is little more than a whimper as his legs go out from under him. The only thing that keeps him from hitting the ground is Hudson's arms around him.

The beast has Mekhi in its powerful jaws, bites down, and then shakes its head like it bit down on a lemon. With a flick of its head, the beast sends Mekhi's body flying across the arena to roll along the ground, once, twice, three times until he comes to a lifeless stop no more than twenty feet from us.

Hudson is trying to hold Jaxon up, but it's hard when Jaxon starts fighting to get to the corpses of his three best friends. He's mindless with pain, screaming and scratching and fighting Hudson with his last breath.

"Let me go!" Jaxon orders in a horror-filled voice. "Fucking let me go."

He's trying to claw his way over to Mekhi now, doing anything and everything he can to get to the Order.

Or at least what's left of them.

But Hudson still won't let go. He holds him tight even as he answers in a sorrow-filled voice, "I'm sorry, I can't. I'm not going to lose you again."

When he realizes Hudson isn't going to release him, Jaxon screams long and low. He screams and screams, until the screams eventually turn into broken sobs, until his legs give out completely, until he folds to the ground, his fists in his eyes as he rocks back and forth, keening like his soul is breaking all over again. And Hudson is right there with him, holding on like he'll never let his brother go again.

I swipe at my own tears coursing down my face, my gaze darting to the lifeless bodies of Byron, Rafael, and Mekhi. To anything but Jaxon.

And I suddenly don't know if I can do it. I don't know if I can keep going. The pain of losing my friends is almost unbearable—and I still have more friends

I am going to lose today. How can anyone keep fighting in the face of certain death? How can anyone be expected to prolong this agony?

Every minute the beast hasn't killed me is one more minute to mourn the loss of everyone I love.

My gaze seeks out Byron, Rafael, and Mekhi again. Over and over again. I can't look away. I can barely even see them now, my vision blurred by my tears, but I can't stop looking at their bodies, their crumpled and bloody bodies. They were all good men. Amazing. The best. And they didn't deserve to die like this. Oh God, it's all too much. Byron. Rafael. Mekhi...

But as my gaze passes over Mekhi's crumpled body, something catches my eye. His arm. Is his arm moving? I sniffle back my sobs and swipe frantically at my eyes, trying to get a clear view. I hold my breath and stare. And...there it is. His arm moved.

I take off at a dead run, sliding as I get close, and struggle with his weight to flip him over. His lashes flutter open, and I gasp. Jaxon and Hudson are by his side in a blink, Jaxon pulling him into his arms.

Mekhi groans. "Easy, easy. Some asshole just bit me."

Jaxon laughs, but it comes out sounding more like a sob, and he doesn't loosen his hold.

I reach out one hand to Mekhi and, meeting Jaxon's gaze and waiting for his answering nod, lay my other hand on Jaxon. I close my eyes and reach into Jaxon and pull as much power as I can, channeling it into Mekhi. I'm careful not to take too much, but I let my tattoo fill up and then release Jaxon, still channeling healing energy into Mekhi.

I vaguely hear Remy and Calder shouting to each other on the other side of the arena, working with Flint and Eden to keep the beast distracted, then someone screams and there's a *thud*, but I don't pay them any mind. I can't. Mekhi deserves my complete attention.

After a minute, his tense muscles loosen, his leg laying at an impossible angle straightens, and the massive gashes on his arms seal. When I've done as much as I can for now, I sigh as Jaxon helps him hobble to his feet.

I reach for the bottom of Mekhi's shirt, my eyes asking permission to look, and he nods, so I lift the fabric high above his chest and gasp.

Not because of the puncture wounds from the beast's teeth. I've channeled enough healing energy to close those up and stop the bleeding. Although the wounds are still rough-looking, they're not life-threatening. No, what has panic twisting in my stomach is a bite mark much smaller than the beast's. About the size of a beetle. And fanning out from it is a spidery dark web of tendrils just beneath the skin's surface.

No wonder the beast dropped him after taking a bite. Mekhi was somehow infected by one of the bugs from earlier.

I reach a hand out to try to heal it directly, but no amount of magic I send into the bite seems to have any effect. My gaze meets Jaxon's, and he just says, "Later. We'll deal with that later."

And he's right. We still have a beast that knows nothing else than we're in its cage with it and it wants us gone.

As if on cue, the beast lifts its bloody face and claws at the arena ground, its entire focus on Remy and Calder, who have stopped several feet from it. It starts toward them, bloodlust in its milky eyes.

"Oh my God!" Macy cries out, tears pouring down her face. "Oh my God. What do we do, Grace? What do we do?"

"I don't know," I answer, barely able to think past the horror and the devastation of what just happened. My brain is blank, the only thing inside it fear that Jaxon and Hudson will draw the beast's attention while helping Mekhi hobble to a corner in the arena.

I can't let that happen. I can't lose anybody else, and I can't, can't, *can't* lose them.

I glance over at the creature. It's pacing back and forth in front of the Order's bodies, snout dripping with blood and eyes glazed with rage. I know what it's doing—daring anyone to come near its prize, daring anyone to try to take it, and it requires every ounce of self-control I have not to throw up right here when I realize it doesn't just plan to kill them. It plans to feed on them as well.

I can't believe I thought it was like Alistair.

I can't believe I had sympathy for it.

It's a monster, pure and simple. It's designed to kill, and it revels in it. How could I possibly feel bad for that?

Remy, Calder, Dawud, Flint, and Eden are surrounding it now. They're not close enough for an immediate attack from it to work, but they're not far enough away for my liking, either. If it starts to run at them, the dragons are the only ones who aren't sitting ducks.

I turn to Macy. We're both still crying, but I do my best to wipe away the tears. I don't have time for them now. None of us do. We have to find our way out of here before the beast kills us all. "What was your idea with the portals?"

147

This Doesn't
Wing True

S he explains it to me using the Ludares tournament from months ago as an example. I don't know if her idea will work or not, but at this point, a plan that might work is better than no plan at all.

So I call Remy over, leave him and Macy chatting about how to build the portals while we fill the others in on the plan—all while also dodging the beast, who seems to have run out of patience with us as well.

"That's genius," Dawud says as I pick them up and fly them over the beast's snapping jaws, just as Calder slides in from behind to distract it.

It roars and changes direction, chasing after her until Eden dive-bombs it and kicks it right in the ass. It whirls around, snapping at her and trying to grab her tail in its teeth, but Eden is fast as hell when she wants to be. She's gone as quickly as she came, and Calder takes advantage of its distraction just long enough to sting it in the foot with her scorpion tail and then take off running.

The beast roars in pain and anger as it races after her. But it's favoring its back foot now, and though I know it will probably only take a few minutes for it to work out the pain and the poison she injected, I'm counting on taking advantage of it for as long as we can.

Flint, following the plan, swoops in and kicks it right in its swollen, bloody nose, then flies away while the beast screams.

And that's when Hudson races in and leaps over its back like a hurdler, pausing just long enough to grab one of the bony protrusions on its spine in each hand and break them off. And then he's running away.

The beast is nearly mindless with fury now. Its eyes roll back in its head and it's all but frothing at the mouth in its desperation to get to one of us. But that's what I need from it—to charge us haphazardly. It's too cunning, too smart, and too set on killing us all. If we give it any chance to think, my plan won't work. And soon enough more of us will be dead. And then Cyrus will kill everyone we ever loved.

Macy runs up to me and whispers, "We're ready," and I nod. Then I take to the air and fly around and around the beast, getting closer with each loop but still making sure to stay out of the range of its powerful jaws.

It lunges for me, tries to grab me and drag me down, and still I circle it. Still I get closer, hoping—

"You're too close!" Hudson growls at me as he fades in from across the arena.

"Look who's talking," I tell him as I dive in and punch as close to the beast's eye as I can get.

It snarls and snaps at me, nearly catching my fist in its sharp teeth. And now that I have all of its furious attention, I turn around and race toward one of the portals Macy set up.

The beast follows me, exactly as I intended, and I dive into it, hoping that it's pissed enough to forget self-preservation and follow me.

It doesn't. Instead, it whirls around and takes off after Hudson, its nails clicking on the ground as it races to catch up with my mate, who also dives into a portal.

I hold my breath the whole time he's in there, but Remy does some minor adjustment with his hand, and Hudson comes out twenty yards away.

Macy jumps in then, screaming to get the beast's attention—and then screaming for a whole different reason as it turns on a dime and comes after her. She, too, dives into a portal, but again, the beast doesn't follow her.

I don't know if it's because it's canny enough to have figured out our plan or if it just didn't like what it felt like to be in the portal it stepped into earlier. Either way, it sucks, because if we don't get it into one of these portals, there's no way Macy's plan can work. And I really, really need it to work.

It's pretty much the last shot we've got.

This time Flint goes in, kicking and hitting at the monster with the goal of getting it to follow him.

But instead of chasing after him, it just flicks its tail and catches Flint in the arm with one of its dangerous spikes.

Blood gushes everywhere, but Flint doesn't cry out—I guess because it's hard to look at that tail and not think of what happened to Byron. The wound on my leg or the one on his arm feel awfully small compared to that.

Flint slaps a clawed hand down on the puncture wound and dives away.

I expect the beast to turn and lunge for someone else, but there's something about the trail of blood Flint leaves that fascinates the creature. It follows it, licking up each drop—which only makes my uneasy stomach roll a little more.

But it's following Flint, who is injured, so I dive in front of it and grab its attention again. A little too close, though. It takes a swipe at me with its powerful tail, and I just barely shift and jump out of the way in time to not get impaled. But it does catch me across my midsection with the tip of its spike. My heart in my chest, I shift back to my human form and glance down at my stomach, fully expecting to see my entrails on my outside. I breathe a sigh of relief when it's just blood, no guts. I can live with that, I think.

And since blood is what it seems to like, I decide to use this to lure the beast exactly where we need it to go. I lay my hand against my stomach and pull it away coated in blood, then hold it up for the beast to smell.

The beast growls low in its throat and leaps, and I take off running.

It must work because I can feel it breathing down my neck as I race toward the closest portal. Macy is screaming at me to go faster, and a quick look at Hudson's face tells me it's taking every ounce of self-control he has to stand by and watch me do this. Normally he's all about letting me do my thing, but I can see how having a ten-ton monster—with sharp teeth, claws, and spikes—on my ass might arouse his protective instincts. I know it aroused mine when the thing was after him.

The portal is only a few feet away, though, and I need to make it. I need this thing to follow me in there. So I dig deep and find just a little more speed, and I push it as hard as I can.

And then, just like that, I'm there. The portal is right in front of me, and I dive in, praying with everything I have that the beast follows me in.

The blood must do it because it does, racing right through the portal entrance after me.

"Okay, Remy," I whisper to myself. "Don't let me down."

I count under my breath: *one, two, three.*

The portal should be very quick.

But it's not quick enough. The beast throws itself at me, catching my wing in its teeth, and I scream. My shoulder catches fire, like someone dipped it in kerosene and tossed a match at it, and I almost pass out from the pain. And then I'm tumbling out of the portal and plummeting straight through the air.

Because Macy's idea? The one she got from the Ludares tournament all those months ago? It was to put a portal a hundred feet in the air, near the very top of the dome.

I start to fly, spreading my wings out wide to catch as much air as I can. But it doesn't work—instead of flying I keep falling down, down, down no matter what I try, while the beast does the same right next to me.

And that's when it hits me. The beast didn't just bite my wing in that portal. He ripped it clean off.

148

No Time to Kill

I have about three seconds to figure out what to do—the ground is rushing up fast—but all I can think about is the terrifying pain in my shoulder and down my back. Hudson is fading straight to me, a horrified look on his face.

Out of the corner of my eye, I can see Eden doing the same thing, speeding toward me in dragon form. Vaguely I wonder if the beast lands on me, will the pain in my shoulder finally stop? That doesn't seem like a bad thing.

It's Hudson who gets to me first—not that that's a surprise—leaping twenty feet into the air and snatching me against him.

We hit the stone floor with a soft, controlled *thud*, and I watch in horror as the beast—my tattered wing still clutched in its mouth—hits with a sickening *thud* right next to us.

My friends race out from all directions to surround it. Calder, Remy, and Eden are all carrying as weapons one of the spikes Hudson broke off it earlier, but the beast doesn't get up.

"Is it dead?" I ask, even as Hudson rolls me over to look at my back.

"Grace," he says, sounding more shaken than I have ever heard him. "Grace, your wing—"

"I know," I interrupt because I don't want to hear him say it. I don't know why. Maybe because if he does, it will feel so much more real than it does right now.

"Oh my God, Grace." Suddenly Macy is behind me, whipping off her sweatshirt and pressing it against my back. "What are we going to do?"

I don't know if she's asking me or Hudson or the universe, but I don't have a clue what to tell her. Except I know there isn't time for this, not when that beast is still living.

I reach back and squeeze her hand, whispering, "I'm okay." And then I push to my feet.

Hudson is right there beside me. "Grace, stop. You need to rest that arm—"

"What I need is to see this through," I tell him. But I only take a couple of steps before my knees go out from under me, and I hit the ground.

Damn it. I ball my hand into a fist and slam it into the ground, hard, as frustration overwhelms me. I can't believe this is happening right now. I can't believe it. Not now, when everything else has already gone to shit.

Panic beats inside me, turns my lungs to fire and my blood to ice. I want to beat it back—need to beat it back—but it's so hard. Especially when the only thing I can think about is all the bad that has happened.

Yes, we're close to winning these Trials, close to getting the elixir and finding a way to defeat Cyrus. But to get here, we've lost so much. Almost the entire Order is dead. Jaxon is devastated. Everyone else has been through nightmares that will stay with us for the rest of our lives.

And now I don't have a wing. How can I be the gargoyle queen without a wing—or being able to fly? How can I fight Cyrus? More, how can I ask my friends to go into battle—to risk everything—when I'm in no shape to fight beside them? Not the way I need to be.

And yet I don't have a choice. We've come too far, burned too many bridges, lost too much.

We have to see this through, and somehow I have to figure out a way to do just that—even if I am just half a gargoyle.

The thought hurts like hell, but I shove it back down. I put it in that damn file deep inside my brain of shit I can't deal with today, and for now, focus on what I can.

I can't handle losing anyone else in this arena, which means we need to get the hell out of here. But to do that, we need to finish this. Right here, right now.

"Grace." Hudson drops down beside me. "Just rest. We've got this."

I know he's right, know that I can let my friends do this and they will get it done. But that's just taking the easy way out, and as I turn my head to look at the beast lying on the ground, I know I can't do that. Not after everything that's happened and everyone who has suffered.

"I'm okay," I say again, and this time it sounds stronger. It's not true—I'm a long way from being okay. But I can do this. I need to do this.

I walk toward the beast, whose strange white eyes are all but rolling in its head as it continues to lay on the ground, its body broken from the fall but still very much alive. And it makes me ill to think of what's coming next, of what I have to do. Which is absurd considering all the damage it's done here today, but it's the way I feel all the same.

I guess it's good that I feel like that, though. The idea of taking a life, even one as terrible as this one, should feel awful. It should hurt. It's why Hudson agonizes the way he does, why he beats himself up every time he has to use his power. Because life—no matter who it belongs to—is a precious gift. And that's not something I ever want to forget.

"What should we do now?" Macy asks as she and Hudson walk beside me. There are tears in her voice that make me think she must be feeling the same things I am.

"I think we have to finish it," Calder says. "Otherwise we don't win the round. And if we don't win the round..."

Her voice trails off, but I know what she's going to say.

If we don't win the round, then we did all this for nothing.

If we don't win the round, Byron and Rafael died in vain.

If we don't win the round, we'll never escape this place. The arena will take our lives as forfeit.

The beast tries to stand then, pushing up on its shaking legs. But the effort is too much, and it falls back to the ground and just lays there, waiting for us to do to it what it did to two people we love.

Waiting for us to kill it to spare ourselves.

"Let's get it over with," Hudson finally says, reaching for one of the spikes that broke off when the beast hit the ground.

I can see it weighing heavy on him, too, though—having to kill yet another being, even if he can't use his powers on this one.

I can't let him be the one to do it. I just can't. He's already made so many sacrifices for us—for me—that I can't let him make this one, too.

So I step between him and the beast and slowly, carefully take the spike from his hand. My shoulder aches from losing my wing, but I'm still strong enough to do this.

"I've got this," I tell him as he looks down at me with grave and shadowed eyes.

"No, Grace—"

"I've got this," I tell him again, and though everything inside me feels like it's shaking apart, I turn back to the beast.

It's watching me now, one milky white eye tracking my every movement, tears streaking down its cheek in obvious pain. My stomach is churning, churning, churning, and my heart feels like it's about to self-destruct in my chest.

You have to do this, Grace, I tell myself as I lean over it. *If you don't, how*

many other people will die because of Cyrus? If you don't, all your friends will
die, right here in this arena.

There is no other choice.

But as I bend down, the spike clutched in my hand, I watch one of its tears
slowly track down the side of its snout. And I remember why we're here. The
Tears of Eleos.

Is that what this was all about? Is this creature called Eleos? Do we have
to cause it pain to capture its tears? I gasp. Do they really mean for us to cause
this beast agony so we can take its tears to end someone else's pain?

That can't be right. It can't be.

And if it is, I want no part of it.

Another tear slides down its cheek, its eyes widening in fear as I walk closer,
its breaths coming in short pants, and a soft whimper bubbling up from the back
of its throat, wresting a sob from my chest.

What did this creature do to deserve this? If it were a wolf and I in its den,
would it not fight me with equal intensity to defend its home? And once I got it
on the ground and near death, would I relish taking its final breath?

I fall to my knees in front of the creature, and Hudson warns, "Grace.
Careful. It can still bite you."

But Hudson doesn't see what I see in the beast's eyes. Defeat.

And as I look, I see him. I really see him—ugly, terrible, hideous, murderous
beast that he is. And I realize that it's not his fault.

It's not his fault he looks like this.

It's not his fault he knows nothing else than to maim and kill.

It's not his fault he's been locked in this arena for millennia, just trying to
survive while everyone who walks in the door wants to kill him. He didn't ask
for it.

None of this is his fault.

But if I kill him right now, when he's lying helpless on the ground in front
of me, it will absolutely be my fault.

And that is not a sin I can live with.

Mercy is never wrong, and if the people who run these Trials don't understand
that, then we were never going to get out of here anyway.

I let the spike clatter to the floor.

"We can't kill him," I whisper, and when I turn around to look at my friends,
I realize they've all come to the same conclusion I have.

Even Calder, who thinks entrails are tasty, can't condemn this beast for doing what he was bred to do.

Even Jaxon, who has lost so much in this arena, can't take a life that doesn't need to be taken.

Only a second passes before Eden and Remy drop their spikes, too.

"He's in pain," Calder says.

"I know." Just like I know I can't leave him like this. "It's okay," I whisper to him as I stroke a hand down his neck. He's just as ugly from this angle as he is from all the others, but beauty doesn't equal worth. Look at Cyrus and Delilah.

He quivers under my hand, but I just make more soothing sounds as I close my eyes and channel all the healing energy I can muster from the earth straight into him.

It doesn't work.

Much like all the magic we tried against him, it can't get through.

The thought devastates me. I can't leave him like this in all this pain. I just can't. No animal should suffer like this.

"I'm sorry," I tell him, pulling back to get a better look at him.

And that's when it hits me—the harness he's wearing looks an awful lot like that belt Tess was wearing both times we saw her. I mean, it could be a coincidence, or—

I reach over and gingerly pick up one of the spikes we dropped just a couple of minutes ago.

"Grace—" Macy says, horrified.

"It's okay," I tell the beast, who starts to shake a little more. "I'll take care of you."

And then I lean forward and use the spike to slice the harness clean off.

Macy lets out a startled scream, then takes a long breath. "That's not what I thought you were going to do."

We're running out of time. I can feel it, so I don't bother to comment. Instead, I put my hand back on the beast's neck and once again try to heal him with earth magic, but it's very slow. Too slow.

He'll be dead before I can heal him, and I cry out, driving one of my hands into the earth, pulling at the dirt and grass, but it's not enough. I can't pull the magic fast enough—

The tattoo on my arm starts to fill up and glow. More and more magic enters my body, and I turn my head to find out where I'm getting this power from.

And that's when I see them. My friends.

One by one, they've fanned out and are laying their arm on the person next to them, one after another. Mekhi, Dawud, Flint, Jaxon, Eden, Calder, Remy, and Macy. My cousin is holding Hudson's hand and his other is placed on my shoulder that's numb from pain now. All of them offering their magic to save this creature.

And I've never been more in awe of the people I was lucky enough to have come into my life. My found family.

This time, when I turn back to the creature, I reach inside myself and channel as much healing energy as I can into this poor animal.

His whole body starts shaking as the energy goes through him, knitting together his broken bones and healing his damaged organs.

When I'm done, when I can feel nothing else broken within him, I take several steps back. My friends do the same.

And then we wait to find out if our mercy will save us or if it will end us all.

149

Lots of Tears for Fears

At first, nothing happens.

The walls don't move.

The lights don't go up.

The beast doesn't climb to his feet.

Nothing.

We didn't complete the round, so I'm assuming that means we don't get the elixir. At the same time, though, we're not dead. So what does that mean?

We're locked in here forever?

The beast is going to try to kill us again?

Something else is going to kill us?

What?

The not knowing is the worst part, and nerves crawl through my belly as we wait long, silent seconds for what comes next.

"Shouldn't the cup reappear?" Eden asks.

"We didn't finish," I tell her.

"I know, but…" Macy says. "We did all that for nothing? Rafael and Byron died for *nothing*?"

I want to tell her no, but I can't. At least not until we figure out what's going to happen next.

Eden looks shaken, too—hell, we're all shaken, I'm sure—but she still walks over to my cousin and wraps her in a hug.

"Should we try to get out?" Flint asks. He's standing next to Jaxon, and he looks more uncertain than I've ever seen him. Like he doesn't know what to do with the hollow-eyed, broken, silent man standing beside him.

And I get it. I've seen Jaxon broken before. I've seen him silent and hurt and alone. But I've never seen him like this. So shattered, so devastated, so lost. It reminds me of how I felt when I first got to Katmere, and I want nothing more than to pull this broken, broken boy into my arms and tell him that everything is going to be okay.

I glance at Hudson and realize he feels the same way. He's on Jaxon's other side, his arm wrapped around his baby brother's shoulders, and I realize—like earlier—he is the only thing keeping Jaxon upright at the moment.

Not for the first time, I'm grateful that—despite everything—they're slowly finding their way back to each other.

Suddenly, the walls start to spin, and I almost fall over but just manage to stay on my feet. The pedestal with the chalice rises again, but we can all see it's empty still. Then the arena opens, and I breathe a sigh of relief. We may not have gotten what we came here to get, but at least we're being allowed to leave.

The crowd in the stands is going wild. They apparently didn't expect any of us to make it out of here alive. Then again, at the end there, I'm not sure I did, either.

For a moment, I think about Rafael and Byron and what it means now that we've got to walk out of here carrying their bodies. Behind me, Jaxon makes a noise deep in his throat, and I know he's feeling the same failure I am.

But before I can say anything to him, the door at the end of the walkway bursts open, and Tess runs through it.

She looks nothing like the woman we first met in the taffy shop. This Tess is a mess. Her makeup is running, her hair is all over the place, and tears are pouring down her face. I brace myself for some kind of attack—we did break her Trials, after all—but she doesn't even seem to notice us.

Instead, she runs straight to the beast and wraps her arms around his neck. "My baby! My sweet baby!" She's sobbing hard now, her face pressed into the clear skin of the beast, and I feel just awful. Someone loved this animal, and I almost killed it.

As Tess holds on, though, the beast starts to shake. His whole body is trembling so badly, the floor of the arena is trembling as well. And then he starts to shrink.

His claws retract into his paws, then his paws start shrinking as well. His powerful snout is pulling inward, into his face, as his ears all but disappear. His translucent skin takes on a healthy glow as his body continues to shrink.

He shrinks and shrinks and shrinks, until there's no longer a beast there at all. There's a small boy. No older than five or six, with thick black hair and wide violet eyes. And Tess is covering his face in kisses.

I gasp, my stomach twisting so hard, I think I might vomit. We didn't almost kill a beast. We almost killed a *child*.

"Oh my God," Macy whispers, but it's not said with awe. Her voice is thick with guilt. The same guilt ricocheting through my own body right now.

Oblivious to our disgust, Tess picks up the boy and holds him close.

"Here you are!" she tells him as she spins him around and around and around. "Oh my God, Alwin. Finally, here you are!"

"Mom!" he shouts back, and he squeezes her just as tightly.

Tess buries her face in his neck and breathes him in while the rest of us look on. But just when I decide that we should go, she turns around and looks at me with a huge smile on her face. The tears are still on her cheeks, but there is an inner peace about her that was never there before. She's actually glowing.

"Thank you," she says, her eyes meeting each one of ours. "Thank you so much for giving my baby back to me. I've been waiting for him for fifteen hundred years."

Fifteen hundred years? I'm not sure if I'll ever get used to paranormal life expectancies. It just sounds so strange to hear anyone talk about living more than a century.

"Thank you, Grace," she says, and this time she walks right up to me, the boy balanced on her hip. "You saved my son, and that is a debt I can never repay."

Guilt swamps me at the joy in her voice, at the happiness on Alwin's face. I nearly killed this child, and I never would have known. It's a horrible thought and an even more horrible feeling.

"It's okay," Tess says, and I realize I said it out loud. "You never could have killed him. If you had plunged that spike into his body, you would have triggered his immortality and restored his full health. But because you showed mercy, you and your friends made it where no one ever has before. You beat the Trials and have earned the Tears of Eleos."

She looks down at the boy in her arms. "And you freed my son from the curse he's lived under for more than a millennium, all because of me."

"Because of you?" I whisper.

"I killed a god's son once, a long time ago. Because I didn't show his son mercy, my son was doomed to live as the most terrible beast to ever exist, cursed to fight and kill and suffer over and over again. He could only be free if someone stopped thinking only about themselves, as I had never done, and actually saw past his brutality to the pain and fear below.

"You did that, Grace, and now we're both free. Thank you, thank you, a million times thank you." Tess nods to the chalice on the pedestal. "And as promised, there is your prize. Use it wisely."

"What—" Dawud starts to ask, but then stops as they stare into the chalice. "There's some lavender liquid in it."

"But how?" Macy whispers.

Tess smiles gently. "Every tear Grace shed, offering my son mercy, took away his immortality and placed it in the cup, allowing my boy to finally shed his beast and come home to me."

"But they were just tears," I say, still not sure how my crying is a magical elixir that's going to save the Army.

"Grace," she says. "You think tears are weak. But to feel that much for someone else, for your enemy, that is true strength." She reaches over and squeezes my arm. Then winks. "Of course, that doesn't mean you shouldn't teach Cyrus a much-deserved lesson."

Tess looks down at her son again. He's fallen asleep in her arms, his little head pressed against her shoulder. They look good together, and I can't help thinking about my own mother. And what I would do to be able to wrap my arms around her, even one more time.

Because I don't want to dwell on that pain, I focus on Tess and Alwin again. "What are you going to do?" I ask. "Now that you're free?"

Tess grins. "I'm hanging up my taffy-making instruments and taking my son on a trip around the world. He's been locked up in that arena longer than anyone should ever have to be, and I want him to know that the world is a wide and beautiful place.

"I bet everything I had on you, Grace, and you didn't let me down. So thank you again."

Shock ricochets through me at her words. "Wait. You bet on me? You told me we didn't have a chance."

"And when you first came here, you didn't. But people change, and you definitely have. You've grown a lot since the day I first met you, and you've got more growing to do. But isn't that what life is for?"

Again, she looks down at her son. "More than anything, that's the gift I want to give Alwin."

She reaches out with her free hand then and shakes my hand. "Goodbye, Grace. We have a plane to catch, but I wish you and your friends strength, wisdom, and mercy in the battle ahead. May the gods be with you."

Her phone dings, and she grins. "That's my ride. Have a good life—and stay away from the taffy. It rots a lot more than your teeth."

And with that, she tosses her long black hair over her shoulder and carries her son out of the arena.

"Here it is," Macy says excitedly, picking up the chalice and bringing it over to me. "It's the elixir. We did it. You can save the Army now."

My stomach drops, and I turn to look at Hudson. He's still supporting Jaxon, but he looks straight at me. And gives me his patented *you've got this* nod.

I don't know if he's right. I don't feel like I've got this. At all.

I take a deep breath, anxiety eating at my stomach. Sitting on my chest. Making my palms sweat and my whole body shake. Because the one thing I hadn't allowed myself to think about, to consider if we were successful: what I'd have to do after that.

But we don't have time for me to freak out right now. Not even close.

I need to drink that elixir we fought so hard for, that we lost so much for. And then I need to grab that damn green string and make it work. Too much depends on me, and I can't fail.

Not this time.

I try to calm my beating heart by reminding myself that I don't have to push my demigod power through the gargoyles' strings. Just an elixir. I can do that. Right?

Hudson looks like he wants to come to me, but I shake my head. He's got Jaxon right now. I can do this.

So I pick up the cup, look deep into the lavender liquid at the bottom of the chalice. And pray that when I drink it, I don't become a beast with translucent skin, bony claws, and homicidal urges.

I know Hudson says he's in this mating-bond thing forever, but I'm not so sure he'd be okay with the threat of impalement every time he touches me.

But I've stalled long enough. The longer I stand here looking at this cup, the more reasons I'm going to come up with for why I shouldn't drink it. It's that thought more than any other that has me upending the cup and drinking the elixir down in one long swallow.

As soon as it's done, I lower the cup and wait to feel…something. Heat, cold, electricity, pain, *anything*.

But I don't. It felt just like drinking water, albeit a little saltier, as easy as breathing air—when I'm not having an anxiety attack.

My unease must show on my face, because all of a sudden, Hudson asks, "You okay?" and I realize that everyone is staring at me. Even Jaxon. I guess they're trying to figure out what happens next, too. Or maybe they just want to make sure I'm okay.

I smile at them and nod, fighting the urge to give a little *I'm okay* wave because it seems just over-the-top enough that they'll figure out how badly I'm freaking out.

And I am freaking out.

But freaking out isn't going to help anything, and it's definitely not going to save anyone. And we have a lot of people to save.

Besides, I am the gargoyle queen and the granddaughter of the God of Chaos. It's about time I start acting like it.

150

When Your Learning Curve Is a D-Cup

After Tess and Alwin take their leave, there's nothing for us to do but the same.

"We need to get Byron and Rafael," I say to Hudson softly.

But he just nods toward Jaxon, who is standing over his fallen friends. "Give him a minute," he answers.

Losing Byron and Rafael devastated all of us, but seeing Jaxon's grief over their loss hurts in a different way. I want to go to him, to tell him everything will be okay. But before I can take more than a step, Flint walks over and drops a hand on Jaxon's shoulder.

At first Jaxon stiffens, but then he seems to crumple, his whole body just collapsing in on itself. Flint wraps an arm around his shoulders then, holding him tightly as Jaxon falls apart.

He leans into Flint, who takes his weight, and while I'm not close enough to hear what they're saying to each other, I can see that whatever it is gives Jaxon comfort.

It goes a long way to helping me get over what a jerk Flint has been lately. And when he bends down and scoops up Byron's battered body like it's the most precious thing in the world, it's hard to hold anything against him.

Hudson joins them, too, picking up Rafael's body so that Jaxon has a chance to let his injuries heal just a little longer. Then the three of them head for the arena's exit so Remy can build a portal to bring the fallen members of the Order home.

As they walk away, I look inside myself for the elixir, and suddenly I can feel it coating all the strings inside me. I gather up the thousands upon thousands of silver gossamer ones.

I thought I'd have to force the elixir in, to use my power to push it out to every gargoyle all over the world. But that's not what's happening. It's doing the work for me, the lavender elixir coating all the strings and slowly, slowly seeping inside them—one drop at a time.

I help it along a little, pressing the liquid into every tiny, microscopic opening I can find in the strings, running my hand over them again and again, until all the elixir is gone, absorbed by the strings once and for all.

And then I brush my fingertips against the green string again, hoping it will help speed up the healing. I only hope that when it does, I'll be able to feel the Gargoyle Army coming back to life.

The others are discussing what to do next as Flint and Hudson lay the bodies on the pallets of flowers and branches Remy has conjured up for them. It's getting late, the clock ticking past eleven Alaska time, and the blood moon lunar eclipse starts at midnight, so it's not like we have a lot of time to waste. But we've got to make sure we get Byron and Rafael to their families so they can arrange a proper burial within twenty-four hours, and we also need to decide what to do about Cyrus. I don't know that any of us has a surefire answer—besides use the Gargoyle Army to kick his ass for good—but we need to figure it out and fast.

Because no one can afford Cyrus and the destruction he has planned, to human and paranormal alike, if we do nothing. We need to take a stand. I've lost too many people I love because of this man—all of us have—and I'm not going to do that anymore. He has to be stopped.

As my friends discuss our options, I feel one of the thin silver strings inside me coming to life for the first time ever. I duck inside myself, whisper, "Hello? Can you hear me?"

I know that Chastain and Alistair can talk to the entire Army anytime they want, but I've never been able to. I'm hoping that changes now that they're free from the poison—and from being frozen for a thousand years.

Another string starts to glow deep inside me, then another one and another one and another one. Soon the entire group of strings is glowing—thousands of them lighting me up from the inside, giving me hope, real hope, that somehow we're going to be able to do this.

We're going to be able to take Cyrus down.

"Hello?" I call again, wondering why I still haven't heard from anyone. "Are you there? Are you okay? Can you hear me?"

They can't hear you. Chastain's voice floods me loud and clear, and for a moment I'm so relieved that I don't process his words. When I do, confusion moves in, clouding some of the joy.

"Why not? I thought being queen means I can communicate with all gargoyles—"

If they accept you, he says. *But they won't. I'm making sure of it.*

His words hit like arrows, puncturing every fragile ounce of self-confidence I've gained regarding being gargoyle queen.

"I don't understand," I whisper. There's a part of me that wants nothing more than to turn tail and run, but I'm trying not to do that anymore. I'm trying to face even the awful things with honesty and grace so that I can figure out how to fix them.

Please, please let there be a way to fix this.

"I know you don't like me," I tell Chastain. "But is that really a reason to turn my people against me?"

Your people? he sneers, and suddenly he's not just a voice. I can see him standing in front of me. "You mean the ones you came to Court to lie to and use and steal from? Those people?"

"It wasn't like that. I was trying to help—"

"By stealing the ring that kept us safe?" He lifts a brow. "Or by assuming we were so horrible that we would let children die to save ourselves? We are protectors, Grace. It's who we are, who we have always been. And you are so out of touch with what it means to be a gargoyle that you couldn't even imagine that we would want to help you and those children."

He shakes his head. "You're weak. You're undisciplined. And you always take the easy way out. You'd rather lie and steal than be honest and face difficult situations the way a ruler should. So no, we're not going to follow you. And no, I'm not going to let you talk to the Army. You were willing to sacrifice us. So now we're going to find a new path, one that has nothing to do with some fake gargoyle queen."

The words fall like blows, each one harder and more painful. I have no idea what to say to him, no idea how to defend myself or make a case for why we have to fight Cyrus.

And before I can come up with one, Chastain continues. "I wish you luck growing up, Grace. This is a hard world, and it needs all the gargoyle protectors it can get. Maybe if you can figure out how to look inside yourself and see who you really are, you'll find your way back to us."

And just like that, he's gone—his voice, his very presence, disappearing from one moment to the next.

I don't know what to do. I don't know what to say. I don't know how to fix this. How can I when Chastain said that the problem is me?

I brought my friends here on the promise that we would free the Army and they would fight with us to defeat Cyrus once and for all. Xavier is dead. Luca is dead. Byron is dead. Rafael is dead. Liam is dead. Almost the entire Order—and I think Mekhi has been poisoned. Flint lost a leg. Nuri lost her dragon heart. I lost a wing. And Hudson, my strong, embattled Hudson has nearly lost his soul. And for what? A fake queen with delusions of grandeur?

It's humiliating. And more, it's devastating. Because without the Army, we can't end this. We've lost every single time we've gone up against Cyrus. We can't do that again. I can't be responsible for anyone else fighting—and dying—in a war I know we can't win.

My legs buckle, and I fall to the ground. Macy cries out, and Hudson dives for me.

"Grace!" he demands, his voice urgent. "What's wrong?"

"I failed," I tell him as the true horror of what just happened crashes down around me. "The Army won't follow me."

"What does that even mean?" Eden asks. "They *have* to follow you. You're their queen."

"It doesn't work like that. Chastain says—" I break off, too embarrassed and too heartbroken to tell my friends what he said to me. What he thinks of me—what all the gargoyles think of me.

Still, I have to tell them something. I owe them that much after getting them into this disaster. "He thinks I'm too weak, that I'm not a good leader. I won't be strong enough to command the Army."

"The bloody bastard doesn't know what he's talking about," Hudson growls, and the others chime in in agreement.

But it's hard to believe them when his words are still echoing inside me. "I think he might be right," I whisper. "Look at all the mistakes I've made. Look at all the people who have died, who've gotten hurt beyond repair."

"There you go again," Calder says from where she's leaning back against a pole. "Thinking you're responsible for everything and everyone."

"I brought you here—"

"We brought ourselves here, actually," she shoots back. "You think you're the only one who wants to kick Cyrus in his old, saggy meatballs? Besides, we don't follow you because we think you're the best fighter in the world." She makes a *tsk*ing sound. "As if."

"While I don't agree with her imagery or the attitude that comes with it," Flint says, crouching down beside me, "I do agree that we don't follow you for your fighting skills. I mean, everyone knows dragons are the best fighters."

Remy gives a disbelieving bark of laughter even as Eden says, "Hell yeah."

"Is this supposed to be a pep talk?" I ask him plaintively, tears that I refuse to shed burning the backs of my eyes.

"I'm getting there," he tells me with a shake of his head. "We don't follow you because you're a fighter. We follow you because you make us believe that we can do anything. You bring out the best in us, and you make us want to be better people. That's way more important than being able to cut someone in half with a sword."

"Plus, it doesn't ruin your outfit," Calder chimes in. "So I call it a win-win."

"She makes a good point," Hudson says, and there's a light in his eyes that tells me he doesn't give a shit what Chastain says. He loves me and trusts me and will follow me into battle any day. "So what do you say we get off these cobblestones and go do the right thing?"

The warmth of his words—and more, his belief in me—works its way through me. But that doesn't mean I can just forget everything that came before. "You know if we do this, I could be leading us all straight to our deaths." I can't help but look at Byron and Rafael.

"Or you could be saving us all," Remy tells me. "So why don't we go make sure their deaths aren't meaningless."

"It's not your fault they're dead," Macy says quietly. "It's Cyrus's. And he deserves to pay—for Luca, for Byron, for Rafael, for Liam, for Flint, for Nuri, for your parents, for Xavier, for my mother, for you. For everyone he's hurt."

She's right. I know she is. Just like I know we have to stop him before he can hurt—before he can destroy—anyone else.

"Okay," I reply, letting Hudson pull me to my feet as Remy opens two portals to bring Byron's and Rafael's bodies back to their parents where they belong. "I'll trust you guys that this is the right thing."

"And we'll trust you right back," Macy says.

But something else needs to be said. "Mekhi," I say, "when are you going to tell the others you've been poisoned by one of those disgusting bugs in the Trials?"

There's a hush in the group, and then everyone is talking at once.

Jaxon barks out, "Show me," and everyone goes silent.

"I'm fine. Really," Mekhi says with a smile, but Jaxon just raises one brow until Mekhi sighs and lifts up his shirt.

I gasp. The infection has spread, the spidery black lines reaching across nearly the entire side of his abdomen.

"You need to go back with Byron's and Rafael's bodies," Jaxon insists, and he's already scrolling on his phone. "I will send the best healers to your parents' house."

Mekhi places his hand on Jaxon's and stops him from typing on his phone. "I'm staying and fighting with my family. I feel fine, and when I don't, I'll let you know."

Jaxon starts to argue, but Mekhi cuts him off. "I have the right to fight for my fallen brothers, same as you."

Anguish moves across Jaxon's face as he says on a choked breath, "I can't lose you, too."

Mekhi just stares at his best friend, a grin slowly overtaking his face. "Then let's not fuck this up. Which means you'll need every fighter you can get."

After some good-natured ribbing on whether Mekhi is a lover or a fighter, Jaxon and Mekhi escort Byron's and Rafael's bodies through Remy's portal to Byron's parents' estate. We wait for them in a somber moment of silence, and both look a little worse for wear by the time they return.

Next, Remy opens another portal, this one to Katmere—to where it all began...to Cyrus—and I step up to the opening. Normally, I let the others go through first, but today I have no idea what we're going to be greeted with. Whatever it is, I'll meet it first.

"Ready?" Hudson asks.

"No, but let's do it anyway."

"Good plan," Jaxon says with as much of a smile as he can muster. "Oh, and Grace?"

"Yeah?"

"What happens when you fight a dinosaur?"

"Seriously?" I ask him even as I can't stop myself from smiling back. "That's what you want to say to me right now?"

"It is," he answers.

"Then I have no idea."

His grin gets a little wider. "You get jurasskicked."

"Well, I guess it's a good thing we're just fighting an old-ass vampire, then."

"Exactly," he agrees.

It turns out that stupid joke is exactly what I needed to get my head on straight. So now I take a deep breath and walk straight through the portal, knowing that whatever is on the other side, my friends—my family—and I will face it together.

151

Blood Mooning
Over Me

"**O**h my God." I'm trembling as we come out the other side of the portal, but how can I not be? We're on the top of a mountain peak above Katmere, and I'm looking down at the rubble that is left of the school I've come to love. It's devastating seeing the gorgeous castle with its ornate battlements and fancy spires reduced to nothing but a pile of rocks. Even more devastating to realize that there's so much more we can lose before this fight is done.

Hudson takes my hand then and nods toward the valley on the other side of the peak.

Damn. Cyrus and his army have definitely arrived. Thousands upon thousands of paranormals are standing in a clearing I've never seen before—and I realize that's because it's at the end of the path with the gnarly tree the Beast warned me not to go near my first week at Katmere. Big surprise that Cyrus went straight for the creepiest place on the grounds...

"How many do you think there are?" Macy whispers, leaning forward to get a better look.

"Thousands," Remy answers at the same time Hudson says, "At least ten thousand."

Too many, I want to say. There are too many for us to fight, too many for us to win. But we have to win. There is no other choice.

Staring down at the crowds, I can't help thinking that Hudson's estimate—terrible as it is—might be on the conservative side. There are a lot of paranormals in that clearing. Like, *a lot* a lot. I think most of them are vampires and werewolves, but there are quite a few dragons and witches here, too.

"True believers" who think Cyrus is going to deliver them to a whole new life. Zealots who believe he'll bring them out of the shadows and into the light where he promises they belong—ruling the humans.

He couldn't have assembled a more dangerous army. They're not fighting because they're afraid of Cyrus's wrath—they're fighting for what they believe.

And that makes them a million times more terrifying. Especially considering they're all here to see Cyrus become a god. To see him lead them on to victory.

I can't help wondering how long it will take them to understand that they are just a means to an end. That Cyrus doesn't care about them—he only cares about himself.

The only thing a man like him wants—the only thing a man who has spent his whole life trying to amass power wants—is more power. And he doesn't give a shit who he has to walk over, hurt, *kill* to get it.

His own sons and daughter are just pawns to get him what he desires. He'll hurt, torture, even destroy them if it means he'll have more power. More money. More everything. And if he's willing to sacrifice his own family on the altar of his ambition, what on earth makes all these people think he won't sacrifice them, too? I don't understand.

I don't think I'll ever understand.

"I didn't think there would be so many," I whisper as we continue to survey the area around us. We're walking into an absolute shit show. And if we're not very, very careful, also a massacre.

"I'm not sure what it says that there are," Mekhi murmurs, and I can't help agreeing with him. It's like Cyrus is expecting a fight. Expecting *us*?

"Delilah said there's an altar down that way"—he points to the path beside the giant, twisted tree—"so let's avoid the crowd and take the woods around back to reach it."

We all nod and creep through the woods as fast as we can. Doing our best not to make enough noise to alert all the paranormals with supernatural hearing. We're aiming to sound like a pack of wolves or deer so we don't arouse suspicion, but I think we sound closer to a pack of rhinos.

I breathe a giant sigh of relief when we finally reach the other side of the mountain where there's a large valley with a meadow and a small stream of water running through it. And in the center of the meadow is…

"What the hell? Is that *Stonehenge*?" Eden asks, and I point to her in the universal *what she said* motion.

Hudson studies the structure, a ring of stone pillars and capstones deliberately arranged around twelve other pillars in a horseshoe shape facing a giant sarsen stone altar, all of it on a large stone platform with three stairs leading to it. Then he replies, "It's similar but not exactly. Plus, the stones on this one don't appear broken at all."

And he's right. This structure looks like it could have been built five thousand years ago—or yesterday. Freaking *Stonehenge*—could Cyrus be more of an egomaniac? If I wasn't so worried about the people I love dying, I'd laugh at the absurdity of it all.

Speaking of, Cyrus is clearly visible from where we are hidden in the thick tree line, and I roll my eyes. He's stalking around the middle of Alaska in a full suit of armor like a conquering knight with delusions of king-dom. He's pointing at various stones and shouting stuff that we're too far away to hear, but with each order, his troops hustle to move large metal plates and strap them to the columns one by one. He's definitely preparing the site for something.

Delilah is beside him, *not* wearing magic-guarding armor, as is Izzy, who is leaning against a stone pillar and cleaning her nails. My heart tightens seeing my cousin in the middle of this mess, still doing whatever she can to please Cyrus.

Luckily, though, no one has spotted us yet, which seems unbelievable given the sheer number of troops he has assembled. They fill the field, more and more pouring from the path that runs by the tree, and I can't help wondering how we're going to do this.

How are we going to stop Cyrus from becoming the god he's always wanted to be—the god he believes he *should* be—without the Army or the use of my Crown? Each of us is strong, and we're even stronger together. But are we *more than ten thousand paranormals* strong?

It's a tall order.

"We should have used the witches after all," I whisper. They owe us their support, and originally I'd planned to call in their help to portal the gargoyles to the battle *after* I'd cured them. But it turns out that was a wasted favor because, well, the gargoyles aren't coming.

All because Chastain decided I'm not worthy to lead my own army.

For the briefest moment, I wonder if he's right, no matter what my friends say. A real general would have analyzed every aspect of the battle plan, moved their troops into position before engaging the enemy, and made damn sure there were contingency plans for their contingency plans.

But that's not how I've handled anything since this whole mess started. I've jumped feetfirst into every situation no matter how dire, made plans—bad plans, usually—on the fly and hoped like hell they worked. And it's finally bitten me in the ass.

I have no army. I left the only allies I have scattered around the world, doing nothing, while my friends—friends I don't even deserve after the shit I've put them through—are about to follow me into the middle of a war without an ounce of backup.

Yep, we're all going to die.

"They could still come, Grace," Macy whispers back, like she can hear my thoughts.

I shake my head. She didn't hear the absolute disgust in Chastain's voice at the thought of following me into an ill-planned battle. "They're not coming."

I glance at Hudson, trying to gauge what he's thinking. But his face is utterly blank—which is a surefire tell that whatever it is, it isn't good. A glance to the other side—where Remy and Jaxon are—reveals more poker faces. And more proof that this is a really, really bad idea.

Only the pain of everything we've lost—and the fear of how many Cyrus will ultimately hurt around the world—has me mentally moving forward when the only thing I want to do right now is get my friends as far away from this place as I can.

The only problem with that is this isn't a fight we can run from. If we do, we've already lost. And so has the rest of the world. But if we stay, Chastain was right about one thing...we're going to need a plan.

I say as much to my friends, all of whom look at one another. But none of them speak up.

"*Any* plan," I urge. And this time I look at Hudson. He's the smartest person I've ever met in my life. Surely he has some idea of what we should do here, even if he's still thinking.

For a second, it doesn't seem like he's going to say anything. But then he takes a deep breath, like he's shoring himself up, and says, "I think there's only one plan that makes sense."

And we all instantly know what he means, but before I can tell him *absolutely not*, Flint speaks up.

"No," Flint says. "That's not on you."

Flint holds Hudson's gaze, and I can feel my mate tremble beside me.

"I'm an asshole for what I said to you before," Flint continues. "No one should ever have to suffer what you do to save someone else. We all make our own choices. And Luca would be ashamed of how I've treated you, how I demeaned his choice to fight that day. And the sacrifice he made. I'm sorry, man."

Hudson doesn't say anything, just gives Flint a quick nod, but I can tell Flint's apology got to him. He's looking everywhere except at the big dragon—who looks more than ready to sob it out with him if Hudson makes even the slightest move.

And can I just say how nice it is that for once, it's not only Macy and me who like to hug shit out with tears?

"Am I missing something?" Calder asks, twirling her hair around her finger. "It sounds like Hudson is hiding his light under a bushel and you know I really don't recommend that." The look she gives him suggests she'd be more than happy to help him free his light—and anything else she might come across.

Remy chuckles even as he says, "Hudson can disintegrate people with his mind. He can make them disappear."

Calder stills, her beautiful face growing deadly serious. "He can't do that, Remy," she says, hair-twirling completely abandoned and real alarm in her voice. "Tell him he can't do that."

We all turn to Calder as one.

"Why?" I ask. "I mean, we all have our own opinions as to why it's a bad idea, but why do *you* think he can't?"

"Because no one should fight someone else's battle," she says, like it's the most obvious thing in the world. When it looks like we still don't understand, she adds, "A soul is only meant to carry the weight of one person. You try to carry more, and it'll just break." She fluffs her hair like she's about to take the most important selfie of her life and turns to Hudson. "So don't do that shit, okay?"

She tosses Remy a wink, too, for good measure, and I realize in some ways, he's not so different than Hudson. I've often wrestled with how Remy manages to carry everyone's fates in his head and not try to save every single person he can, and in a sentence, Calder schooled us all.

Remy leans over and pulls Calder against his big body in a bear hug.

"Damn, I love you, girl," he says roughly, and she accepts his embrace for a second, maybe two, then shoves him aside, complaining he'll wreck her hair. But when he turns to Hudson, she looks at Remy like he's her sun, and I smile. Our Calder might just have a crush on her best friend.

"Okay, so we all agree, we don't take out our nuclear weapon unless there is absolutely no other way, yes?" I ask, making eye contact with each person one by one. My heart swells as they each nod and pat Hudson on the back. In turn, my mate's eyes grow suspiciously glassy, and I give his hand a squeeze. "Other options?"

"I say we just go straight up to the asshole and take him out," Jaxon says. "I could crush his heart in my hands with telekinesis if I can get a little closer."

"As exciting as that visual sounds," Hudson says with a chuckle, "did you not notice the armor dear old Dad is sporting today?"

Jaxon arches a brow at his brother in question.

Hudson rolls his eyes. "It's the same metal as in the dungeon. At a guess, he had the Blacksmith make him armor that cancels magic."

"No offense, but your dad sure is a cowardly fucker," Flint mutters.

"Offense?" Hudson drawls. "I'm pretty sure that's the nicest thing that can be said about him."

The rest of us murmur in agreement.

"That wouldn't work even if he wasn't wearing armor," Remy says.

"What do you mean?" Macy starts, but he just gives a little chin nod toward the clearing below. He holds out a hand at Cyrus's weird rock altar, palm facing outward. Then he circles it, and his magic lets us see something we couldn't before.

There's some kind of weird force field surrounding him and the entire stone structure. It's made of a million strings of white light that form a dome over the whole platform and pillars, and I have no doubt it will light up anyone who goes near it. And connected to that dome about a hundred yards away, three much smaller domes are spread out. Circling the large dome are stationed hundreds of Cyrus's followers, with soldiers protecting the masses in a larger circle around them. Inside the smaller domes, one witch stands in the center, directing power to the stone circle where Cyrus is while about fifty witches surround her, hands outstretched.

"It's possible," Remy says, "that those witches are powering up the domes around the one witch, who is in turn sending more power to Cyrus's dome."

"Because this wasn't hard enough?" Eden complains. "Now the jerk has his own force field? What the hell?"

Eden's usually up for anything, and the discouraged look on her face has me checking out the rest of the group, trying to gauge where they're at.

The answer is nowhere good. Flint's jaw is working in that way it only does when he's really upset. Jaxon's scar is standing out in stark definition against his skin—a surefire tell that he's gritting his teeth. And even Dawud has stopped admiring Calder to stare at the ground where they are nervously shuffling their feet.

My friends are starting to see the hopelessness of the situation, and I don't blame them. For about the billionth time, I wonder if we're doing the right thing. But then I glance at Hudson, and there's an intensity in his eyes that I'd recognize anywhere. He's got an idea, just like he always does, and I can't help wondering why I haven't been utilizing him more. He's brilliant, *always* thinking sixteen steps ahead. I just need to know what those sixteen steps are.

But he's not the only one I should be seeking advice from. As I glance at each of my friends, I can't help but realize we all bring something special, and we need to start leaning into that more. We may not have magic-canceling armor and a ten-thousand-person army, but we aren't defenseless, either. Together, we can do some pretty amazing things.

I think everyone just needs a reminder of that—even me.

"We need to play to our strengths," I say.

"Do tell," Calder answers, batting her ridiculously long lashes. "What are those strengths—other than looking amazing?"

We all laugh, but I'm serious. "Hudson, you're the mastermind of this team, which means you come up with a plan."

Hudson's brows raise, but his chest puffs out a little with pride.

"Hey," Jaxon starts to argue, but we've got no time for that, so I continue in a rush. "Jaxon and Flint, you're the muscle."

Which makes Hudson's chest deflate, and now he's the one starting to protest, but I just pat his shoulder. "You're the backup muscle, babe, but we need your brains more." I turn to Macy and Remy. "You're the distraction element with spells and potions that can disorient and delay." I pivot to Eden. "You're the divider. You're fast, and your ice can create walls and segment groups from each other, making them easier to defeat."

Turning to my left, I continue. "Dawud, Calder, and Mekhi, you're cleanup crew. Jaxon and Flint knock the pins down, and you take out the stragglers." I look down at my own hands. "And me, well, I'm..." I don't know what I am. I can't fly anymore. I'm not particularly great at hand-to-hand combat. My gargoyle magic is better suited to healing than fighting. I'm not saying I can't bring something to help us fight; I just don't know that it's anything particularly special.

Hudson reaches out and tilts my chin up with his finger, until he's holding my gaze in his fathomless blue depths.

"You're our *heart*, Grace," he says, and tears flood my eyes.

I try to blink them away, but as each of my friends leans forward and places their hand on mine, more trickle out.

I sniffle. "Goddamn, you guys, we're supposed to be fighting, not crying."

Everyone laughs like I wanted, and I swipe the tears from my eyes and cheeks. I don't know what I did in my life to deserve these people, but I thank the universe every day I have the most amazing family in the world.

My gaze seeks out Hudson's again. "You *do* have a plan, don't you?"

"I do," he says. "But it's not a great one. We're grossly outnumbered, and"— he glances at his watch—"almost out of time. Honestly, we're probably all going to die, but this at least gives us a shot."

"Jesus, man," Flint grumbles. "This is why Grace should give all the motivational speeches."

"Yeah," Calder agrees. "I think I'd rather get my nails done. Is there a salon around here?"

I chuckle. "All right, let's hear this we're-all-going-to-die plan."

152

Plan A, Plan B, Plan See-If-We-All-Die

"We need to take down the force field surrounding the stone altar thing"—Hudson waves a hand at the circle of stone pillars in the middle of the field—"or whatever it is."

"Stonehenge," Mace says. "Let's just call it Stonehenge."

Hudson chuckles. "All right, Stonehenge Lite it is. I'm pretty sure those stone rings are some sort of machine that needs a God Stone to activate it during the lunar eclipse. We know the eclipse starts in an hour at midnight"—Hudson pulls his phone out of his knapsack, taps the screen a few times, and scrolls, then nods—"and the penumbral will be completely done near two a.m. Which gives him a little more than two hours to use the God Stone before the lunar eclipse is completely gone."

Mekhi whistles. "Two hours."

Hudson nods. "Yeah, that's the bad part of the plan."

"So there's a good part?" Flint asks, one eyebrow arched.

"Sort of," Hudson begins. "With the Gargoyle Army no longer frozen, Cyrus is mortal again."

Flint and Mekhi fist-bump, but Hudson rushes on. "Of course, with the Army no longer frozen, it also means his gift has likely been released. A gift we've never seen in action, so that's an unpredictable element."

"Well, fuck," Flint grumbles.

"The Bloodletter said his original ability was channeling energy, right?" I ask.

Hudson nods. "Likely, he can harness lightning, at a guess, which could prove extra cumbersome for our dragons." He looks from Eden to Flint, making sure they understand what he means. "I wouldn't be surprised if he could use that gift to do more, so be on guard."

They both nod, exchanging nervous looks. I know what they're thinking. If lightning were to hit one of their wings, it could be damaged beyond repair. My stomach sinks just thinking about my own missing wing, but I swallow and shove those thoughts aside. There will be plenty of time to mourn all our losses later—I hope.

Hudson continues. "His men are attaching metal to the stone pillars so…I'm thinking he needs more than just a God Stone to activate the machine. He needs power."

"Lightning?" I ask, and he nods.

"That's the most logical guess," Hudson says.

I'm loving a mortal Cyrus, but the rest of this doesn't sound like good news for our side, honestly. "What's your plan?"

Hudson turns to Remy. "You can punch through the magic of fifty witches, yes?"

Remy looks sheepish as he admits, "Yeah."

Everyone's eyebrows shoot up in surprise. *"Fifty?"* Macy asks.

Remy shrugs. "It'll take *some* effort." He turns to Hudson. "I'll be fairly weak if I have to do all three."

Hudson thinks for a minute, then says, "All right, so we'll have the element of surprise with the first witch dome. The dragons will clear a path around it, put up an ice wall to isolate it, and Remy will portal the rest of us over and punch through it. Then we make short work of those witches, which shouldn't be too difficult, as they've been using energy to project their dome and Cyrus's. That's the good news."

"Do I want to know the bad news?" Jaxon asks, and I couldn't agree more.

Hudson meets all our gazes. "The element of surprise will help us with the first dome. We won't have that with the second. They won't let the dragons isolate the next one. Plus, those troops protecting the first dome will move to reinforce the second dome."

"Twice as many enemies?" Mekhi jokes with a head shake. "This is starting to feel a little impossible."

"Yeah, I'm not seeing the 'brains' in this," Jaxon says, sounding worried.

"Well, we're not really going for the second dome." Hudson gives a half smile. "The dragons will make it seem like the next one is our target. Then Cyrus's army will move to reinforce that one, and when they do, we pivot to the third instead. Eden will lay down a wall to keep those troops from backtracking, but still… We won't have much time. We'll need to punch through that one and eliminate the witches before the troops can circle us."

"Ahh, so we wait to fight the *entire army* when we try to take the third dome?" Flint grumbles. "Seems like we might be just delaying the they-all-kill-us scenario."

"Well, *if* we actually went after the third dome…" Hudson crosses his arms over his chest, tilting his weight on the back of his feet. "The dragons will again make it seem like that's where we're headed, but Remy will portal us to the now-unprotected side of the big dome, and he'll punch through that one instead. It should actually be weaker than the third one now, with some of the witches' power going to reinforce their own dome."

"But won't the witches just put it back up as soon as we take it down?" I ask. I mean, I don't know how those witch domes work, didn't even know you could make one, but it seems like the witches should be able to just re-create it.

Hudson full-on smiles now, though. "If we cared, which we don't. Because as soon as Remy punches through the big dome, I'm going to disintegrate the machine. No machine, no god version of Cyrus."

"I would really like to avoid god Cyrus," I agree.

"What do you think, Remy?" Hudson asks. "Can you do it?"

Remy thinks for a minute. "You get me close enough, I can do it. I'll need to be touching it, though."

"We'll get you close enough," Jaxon says, and we all nod.

"So are we actually taking out Cyrus?" Eden asks.

"Yeah, it doesn't sound like this plan ends with Cyrus locked away," Dawud adds.

Hudson shrugs. "That'll depend on if we can get his armor off before his army attacks. I'm not liking our odds against ten thousand troops, so the better part of valor and all that. I think the immediate threat is the God Stone being used. What do you think, Grace?"

Everyone turns to look at me, like the final decision is mine. And can I just say, contemplating sending your best friends into battle where not all, if any, may return safely is an awful feeling. But how can we do nothing? So I say the truth. "The plan is solid, and I think it's our best shot. Odds aren't great but better than facing a god version of Cyrus any day."

"Look, we're not going to win if we fight his army head-on," Hudson says. "There are ten of us against ten thousand, maybe more if they bring in reinforcements. Instead of fighting an insurmountable force, let's avoid them and just fight one narcissistic vampire instead."

Remy grins and says, "Everybody keep calm. We're all going to die."

"*Shrek*?" Flint asks, and Remy fist-bumps him.

The conversation devolves into a discussion about how the second movie is an underrated masterpiece, and I wander off to the side to get a better look at the activity below.

While I agree that Hudson's plan has the best chance of success...that's not saying much when the odds are in the single digits in the first place.

153

If Wishes Were Roller Coasters, Gargoyles Would Ride

Down below us, the crowd starts chanting, and something about the complete adoration sets panic to churning in my stomach. But having a panic attack right now isn't an option—or so I tell myself as I take a series of deep breaths and try to name ten things I can see. But everything I see is scary as fuck, so maybe that's not the best mindfulness exercise for this moment.

"Hey," Hudson says, and then his face is next to mine. I know it's because he can see my anxiety, but that just makes me feel worse. One more sign that I'm weaker than I want to be.

"We've got this," he tells me.

I nod, because what else am I going to say? *No, we don't?*

Still, this is war, and things go wrong. "What if something happens? What if I d—"

"You won't," he says, his eyes glowing a fierce blue. "But if *something* happens, I've got this. And I've got them."

He means he'll use his power again. I can see it in the set of his jaw, in the way he squares his shoulders. "You don't need to do that. You can't—"

"I've got this," he repeats, and I can tell he means it. And that, whatever happens, he's solid.

The knowledge frees up the knots in my stomach, makes it a million times easier to breathe. And to accept whatever comes next.

And then, suddenly, everyone is crowding around, talking shit about Cyrus and planning our victory celebration. I know as well as they do that it's bullshit, that we may very well not feel like celebrating at the end of this—if there's even enough of us left to celebrate—but it feels good to say it. Almost as if speaking it into the universe gives us a chance of making it come true.

And I need that chance. We all do. Without it, I'd never be able to do what has to be done—especially when I'm terrified that this will be the last time

Hudson ever touches me.

"Hey," he whispers as he reaches for my hand.

"Hey, yourself," I answer.

He rubs his finger across our promise ring and asks, "Have you figured it out yet?"

I roll my eyes at him even as a fond grin creeps across my face. Because I know he's just trying to calm me down. "I have," I tell him with absolute conviction, just so I can see his eyes widen in surprise. "You promised to ride all the roller coasters at Disneyland with me—even the scary ones."

"Hudson on a roller coaster?" Jaxon mocks. "I'd rethink that one. He is a screamer, after all."

"I think Hudson *is* the roller coaster," Calder says with a hungry little lick of her lips.

"And on that note," Remy says with a wiggle of his brows, "maybe we should get this show on the road."

And then he looks at me. They all look at me, which isn't disconcerting at all. "Umm, is there something else?"

"I'm pretty sure this is your moment," Dawud says after clearing their throat.

"My moment?" Now I'm even more confused.

"I don't know about anybody else," Flint says, "but I could use one of your motivational speeches right about now."

"Maybe even two of them," Eden says slyly.

And shit. Just shit. Considering I'm pretty much with Hudson on the whole *we're all going to die* side of this situation, motivational speeches aren't exactly rolling off the tip of my tongue.

But they're all still looking at me, even Calder and Remy, like they expect words of wisdom to just fall from my lips. I sigh, searching my brain for something—anything—to say.

Finally, a glimmer of an idea comes to me, and I decide, what's the worst that can happen? They all run in the opposite direction? Turns out I'm okay with that. I could use a good night's sleep and a pedicure anyway.

I glance at Hudson, and he nods encouragingly, so I clear my throat. Take a deep breath. Clear my throat again. And begin.

"I know we've done this a lot of times now, guys. I know it's been hard. But we've got one more fight left in us, and I say we bring it all. We bring everything we've got straight to Cyrus's door, and we shove it down his throat. That way, even if we die, we know we've given this everything we have—and at least we die fighting for something we believe in.

"When things are good," I continue when I realize they're all nodding along with what I'm saying. "When things are good, we can go back to using our powers for midnight flights through the aurora borealis and kicking ass on the Ludares field. But now, now it's time to act like tigers."

Jaxon raises a brow as if to say, *Seriously, tigers?* and even Dawud doesn't seem impressed with being likened to a big cat, so I try something scarier. But it's hard to go there when I'm surrounded by the biggest, baddest monsters on the planet. Still, I need something, so I try, "No, not like tigers. Like *velociraptors*."

"Whoa, badass," Flint says, and he's leaning forward on the balls of his feet, really getting into the speech.

"Fuck yeah," Mekhi agrees. "That movie scared me."

"Word." Dawud raises their fist to Mekhi's for a knuckle bump.

"Yes, we'll be like that Indominus rex dinosaur—"

"Which one was that?" Macy whispers.

"The newest one," Dawud answers.

"Oh, I didn't see that one," she replies. "Maybe we can watch it once we're done here."

I raise my voice to bring their attention back to me. "We'll show Cyrus only our power and our fury. Our eyes will gleam with our lust for blood, and our brows will jut forth like cliffs over the wild, raging sea."

Macy looks a little traumatized as she reaches up to make sure her eyebrows are still as smooth as ever, but Eden is all in. Fists clenched, jaw tight, she looks ready to take the head off any vampire who gets too close.

"Now, tighten your jaw and take a deep breath. Draw on the most feverish wildness inside you and let it flow through your every cell, taking you to your fullest strength."

Calder snarls, then must take me at my word because seconds later, she's gone full manticore, her scorpion tail curling dangerously.

"We are descended from greatness," I continue, then add— "Well, except for Jaxon and Hudson," which has everyone nodding, even them. "Our parents have fought this battle before us, and we will not dishonor them as we pick up where they left off. We will prove we are worthy of the powers we have and the families we have come from. There is not one of you who doesn't have the magic of ages inside you and tonight, on this field, at this moment, we will let that magic loose. And we will win."

"Hell yeah!" Flint growls, pumping his fists. "We've got this."

"Fuck yeah, we do!" Jaxon yells.

Everyone is super pumped up and, as they clap one another on the back and walk over to the edge of the cliff, Hudson looks at me with a raised brow and whispers, "*Henry IV?*"

I shrug, then grin a little because of course my mate caught me. "I had nothing. Besides, who says it better than Shakespeare?"

He just shakes his head and laughs.

"Let's do this thing!" Eden says before transforming into a dragon. She takes a few steps away, then looks at Jaxon and Flint as if to say, *Ready, aerial support?*

Flint nods, and then everyone turns to Jaxon, who looks really, really small standing next to Eden's dragon.

"Think you can keep up with your telekinesis flying?" Hudson asks him. "The dragons are fast."

"True story," Flint agrees, which has Jaxon's eyes narrowing.

"Oh, I think I can manage," he says. And then, out of the blue, he shifts in a blaze of shimmering colors, evolving right before our eyes from a vampire into a gorgeous amber-colored dragon.

154

Imagine Dragons

"**B**loody hell!" Hudson's eyes are wide as he turns to Flint. "Did you know he could do that?"

"You mean, did I know that he's now some kind of weird vampire-dragon hybrid?" He gives Hudson an *are you serious right now* look. "Yeah, of course I knew that. I mean, who wouldn't?"

Jaxon, who manages to still look dark and broody even in his dragon form, just stares at Flint. But when he goes to give his patented snarl—or as close as he can get when he's a dragon—he belches a small shot of fire that nearly singes Flint's eyebrows off.

"What the hell!" Flint yelps as he jumps back about five feet.

Now Jaxon smiles just a little, and as he does, it's hard to miss that even as a dragon, his incisors are much longer than Flint's or Eden's.

Weird dragon-vampire hybrid indeed.

"Don't you think you should have probably mentioned this before?" Flint demands, swiping a wary hand over his eyebrows.

This time, Jaxon doesn't even bother to snarl. He just watches him in a way that seems to query, *Why didn't you ask?*

It's a question Flint obviously doesn't have an answer for because he sputters for several seconds while Macy just grins like a wild woman, glancing back and forth between the two.

Hudson gives me a *holy shit* look, but he's grinning, too. And he looks absolutely adorable.

"I love you," I tell him softly, because if I'm about to die, that's what I need him to remember. That no matter what, no matter how much shit we've been through, my love for him is something I did right.

The sky above is a startlingly dark navy that seems to glow a little more with each minute that ticks down. Which means we're getting closer to eclipse time, something I know Hudson is aware of from the way he keeps glancing at the horizon.

"I love you, too," he whispers to me. "And I will for an eternity. That's why we've got to do this, Grace. We've got forty minutes before the eclipse, and I want the chance to love you forever."

"That's what I want, too," I whisper, even as I step back. "Now let's go kick Cyrus's ass and make that future a reality."

"I'm all for that," Remy says, and he's obviously taken his magical Wheaties because the boy is practically glowing. Everything about him seems charged with power, and for the first time, I start to believe this plan can work.

"Okay, guys." I take a step back, recapping the plan. "This is it. First one to make a hole in the first witch wins. Now let's—"

"What do we win?" Calder asks after she shifts back into human form. "I hope it's a cupcake. With sprinkles."

It's exactly the tension breaker we need, and I crack up.

"If you get Remy through to that witch, I'll buy you a dozen cupcakes, and I'll make sure each one has a different kind of sprinkles," I say.

She grins. "That's good enough for me." And then she takes off running, shifting mid-step, her powerful lion legs eating up the ground between our group and the battlefield.

It's the signal everyone else seems to be waiting for, because Jaxon throws himself into the air seconds later.

I freak out and can tell that everyone else pretty much does, too. I remember how long it took me to feel comfortable with my gargoyle wings—trying to fly as a dragon has to be at least as hard. Trying to do so while surrounded by ten thousand soldiers who want you dead seems like a really bad idea.

But either Jaxon is way better at learning to fly than I was—a distinct possibility—or he's using his telekinesis to help him out. Either way, he looks good. Really, really good.

Flint must think so, too, because he just stares up at the sky, appearing totally and completely dazzled.

At least until Jaxon starts circling the field. I only have a moment to wonder what he's doing before he starts shooting fire down toward the ground.

"What the hell?" Flint exclaims again, right before he, too, shifts into his green dragon.

It happens in the blink of an eye—much faster than Jaxon managed it—and then he's flying up to meet Jaxon. At first, I think he's going to intercept him, but then he flies in the opposite direction until they're positioned on either side of the first witch, shooting fire at the paranormals all around the outside of the force field.

"Typical Jaxon," Hudson mutters, but he's grinning. "The kid just loves to make an entrance."

"Yeah, like he's the only one," I shoot back with a wink.

But Hudson's already gone, fading down to the battlefield with Mekhi.

Eden joins Jaxon and Flint, positioning herself in front of them so she can start shooting ice at the field, building a giant ice wall in the area Flint and Jaxon are clearing with their fire.

They back up a little once she starts to build, making sure their fire doesn't get close enough to melt her ice, which she is throwing down at an incredible rate.

Watching the field, I really hope Hudson was wrong about the first one being the easiest, because it looks like all hell has broken loose all around them. Dragons have launched themselves into the air to fight Flint, Jaxon, and Eden, while more vamps and werewolves rush in, trying to take the place of those being burned.

Some vamps and wolves have managed to scale the wall even as Eden builds it, but Hudson, Mekhi, and Calder are already there, kicking ass and not bothering to take names. They run along the inside of the wall, taking care of anyone who actually makes it into the space between the wall and the witches' force field.

All of a sudden, ice shoots in a totally different direction, and I look up to find that Eden's under attack. There are a lot of dragons in the air now—close to one hundred, I would guess—and they are determined to take Flint, Jaxon, and Eden down.

I start to shift into a gargoyle so I can go fight with my friends, but then it hits me all over again that I don't have a wing and that I won't be flying anywhere.

Not sure what else to do, I start hauling ass down the mountain with Macy and Dawud right beside me. But I've only gone about a hundred yards when Remy steps in front of me and says, "Need a lift?"

Before I can answer, a portal opens up, and he sweeps Macy, Dawud, and me into it. Seconds later, we walk onto the field—right in front of the first force field.

We're also only a few feet from Hudson, who whirls around with a violent look on his face—only to pause when he realizes it's just us.

"Took you long enough," he teases, but before I can answer, he jumps straight up above me and kicks out.

I watch as his foot connects with another vampire's face. The guy goes flying, and then Hudson is landing right next to me again. He drops a lightning-quick kiss on my lips before whirling around and capturing a wolf who made it over. He swings the wolf around by his tail before Hudson sends him soaring right over the wall.

"What do you need me to do?" I ask Remy as Dawud and Macy take off to help the others.

"Just watch my back," he answers as he holds his hands about a foot from each other.

"What are you going to—" I break off as the space between his hands starts to glow.

Remy's moving his hands around now, rotating them in a staggered circular pattern. As he does, the light grows bigger and bigger, hotter and hotter. And then it starts to pulse.

I lean forward, fascinated by what's happening, but before I can see what he does next, a werewolf comes over the wall right in front of Remy, fangs bared.

I shift and jump out from behind him, grabbing on to the wolf by her ears and yanking her backward.

The wolf snarls violently, lashing out with teeth and nails, but I turn to solid stone just as her mouth closes around my hand.

I feel her teeth strike my hand, hard, and then the wolf is screaming. She backs away, eyes wild and blood streaming from her mouth, and I reanimate enough to bring my foot up and deliver the roundhouse kick Artelya taught me when we were training together at the frozen Court.

The shock of hitting the wolf's hard jaw reverberates up my left foot, but it must work, because the wolf's eyes glaze over, and then she falls to the ground, out cold.

"Remind me not to piss you off," Remy says with a laugh.

When I glance back at him, the ball of light he'd been forming has dissipated, its light coating his fingers and hands and arms, all the way to his elbow so that he glows brightly.

Then, in front of my fascinated eyes, he pulls his right fist back and then plows it as hard as he can straight into the web of light that makes up the force field around the witches.

155

Some Things You Just Can't Force Field

The force field falls instantly, the witches' magic no match for Remy's power. As it sputters out, the giant force field around Stonehenge Lite flickers, but it holds. Which is a shame—I think there was a part of me that was hoping it would fall if one of the three domes holding it up fell.

But since that's not the case, we need to get to the second force field fast. But first we have fifty powerful, pissed-off witches converging on Remy and me, and they look like they're out for blood—in a purely non-vampire way, of course.

"What do we do now?" I whisper as Hudson and the others are currently on the other side of these witches.

Remy shoots me a cocky grin and says, "I'd get ready to put that roundhouse of yours to work again. But first, duck!"

He shoves me down just as a spell goes flying right at where my head would have been. It crashes into the ice wall behind me, and the wall makes an ominous *crack*.

It's followed by about twenty more spells, and they aren't even aimed at us. Now that the witches have figured out the ice wall is vulnerable, they're using their combined magic to try to bring it down. But that means the army on the other side of the wall will suddenly have access to us at the same time.

And since I don't relish taking on thousands of paranormals simultaneously, I figure we need to come up with a solution before that wall falls.

Remy must be thinking the same thing, because he throws his hand out and kicks up so much wind, I go flying against the ice wall. He steadies me with his other hand, even as he builds the wind around the witches higher and higher. They start bouncing off one another, the wind battering them from all directions even as it moves them closer and closer together.

"What are you going to do?" I ask as the wind currents tighten around them.

"I think this space will be a lot better if it's missing fifty witches, don't you, *cher*?"

"Absolutely."

He gives me another wicked grin and then, with a flick of his fingers, he sends the wind vortex he's creating barreling through the air. The last I see, it's literally flying over the top of the mountain. And as an extra bonus, Remy uses the wind tunnel he created to suck in a couple dozen of the dragons who had been attacking Flint, Jaxon, and Eden above our heads.

As they disappear over the mountain, he wipes his hands together as if the job is finished and says, "Hope they brought their broomsticks."

I know we're in the middle of a battle, and I know shit's about to get bad, but I can't help laughing. Only Remy would say something so ridiculous and so absolutely on point.

"Nice work," Hudson tells me as he fades up behind us and, for the first time, I realize just how fast Remy took care of our little witch infestation. Faster than Hudson could fade around the circle to get to me. I know some really powerful witches—Macy being one of them—but Remy really takes it to a whole new level.

"Right?" Mekhi agrees as he skids to a stop next to Hudson. "I've never seen anything like that."

"Yeah, well, he's just getting warmed up," Calder says with a quick little bat of her eyes. "Wait till he really decides to get his hands dirty."

Considering Remy just sent seventy-five or so paranormal beings careening over the side of a mountain, I'm a little concerned what *getting his hands dirty* might look like. But we've got a long night ahead of us, and something tells me I'm going to find out.

There's a familiar shadow above us, and I look up in time to see two dragons cut Eden off from Jaxon and Hudson and then sink their claws into her shoulders and back. A third flies up underneath her and sinks his teeth into her soft underbelly.

She screams again and starts tumbling ass over teakettle as she tries to shake him off. I scream for Jaxon and Flint to help her, but fire is flying as they fight off their own attackers.

"Oh, they can sod right off," Hudson growls, and then he's jumping twenty feet straight up into the air and ripping the dragon who is currently going for her entrails right off her. He keeps a hold on the jerk's tail all the way back down to the ground, where he spins him around like a discus and then lets him fly.

The dragon crashes into several other enemy dragons, and they all tumble to the ground.

"You're a better shot than I gave you credit for," Remy tells him.

Hudson rolls his eyes. "Remind me to be insulted about that later."

"Much later," Dawud interjects, "considering we've got another problem."

I start to ask what it is, but the second I turn around, I figure it out.

Some of the other witches on the field have caught on to the fact that spells can bring the ice wall down. It's starting to tumble, which means we're about to get a whole lot of extra attention—and none of it good.

"I think that's our cue to hit the road," Remy says, waving his hand to open another portal.

"What about the dragons?" Macy asks. "We can't just leave them."

She's right—more dragons have arrived and Flint, Jaxon, and Eden are under fire—figuratively and literally. If we don't get them out of this situation, and fast, I'm not sure how much longer any of them will last.

"Jaxon!" I scream, trying to get my best friend's attention.

He doesn't hear me, but Flint does. As he performs a barrel roll to get away from two attacking dragons, he shoots a stream of fire my way that I am pretty sure is his way of saying he gets it.

In the meantime, Macy shoots a spell at several of the dragons. They aren't paying attention to anyone but Flint, so they don't get the chance to dodge as it attacks them all at the same time. Seconds later, their wings are wrapped tightly in Bubble Wrap, and they are plummeting toward the ground.

But several more take their place, and Flint looks even more embattled.

"Do it again!" I tell Macy, but she just shakes her head.

"That's not a spell I can do more than once."

"What, all out of packing supplies?" Calder asks. "Next time, you should get the pink kind with white flowers. It's pretty, and I like flowers."

"I'll keep that in mind," Macy answers, and Calder grins. But when one of the dragons above her screams, Calder is the first to shift on the fly and jump up, raking her lion's claws against the sensitive skin of two of their necks.

The dragons bellow in rage and lunge for her, but she's already dropping back down to earth and shifting to her human form, yelling, "Let's go, let's go, let's go!"

Flint follows her down as fast as he can, determined to avoid the next wave of dragons coming at him.

At the same time, Dawud shifts on the run, then jumps up and bites the tail of one of the lower-flying dragons. She screams and tries to flick them off, but they hold on long enough to give Eden a chance to throw off another dragon before she, too, heads for the portal.

"Go!" Remy says as he herds Mekhi and Calder toward the portal.

Hudson, in the meantime, makes another jump, trying to reach the dragons who are all over Jaxon. But Jaxon's flying harder than Eden and Flint were, and he can't reach them.

I'm more frustrated than ever, desperate to fly so I can get to Jaxon. But flying isn't the only power I have, I remind myself, as I think back to my time at the Gargoyle Court.

I think about using the water I saw in the spring when we first got here, but the stream is on the other side of the clearing and too far away to get it here quickly. But there are other things I know how to channel, and I reach for the air before Jaxon even starts to buck against the dragon who's got his mouth wrapped around Jaxon's neck, his teeth locked against Jaxon's jugular.

Hudson jumps again, but again he misses Jaxon, and I know just what I need to do.

Throwing my arms out in front of me, I feel the wind against my palms and the warm summer air sliding against my skin. Then I cup my fingers together and punch forward as hard as I can, pushing out the air in front of me.

I do it so hard that it aggravates my wing injury, making my shoulder ache painfully. But throwing the wind must work, because about a second later, the dragon biting Jaxon squawks angrily and tumbles right off his neck.

I tried to focus it only on the dragon, but that must not have worked because Jaxon soars several feet backward, too. He also drops down a few feet, and thankfully, that is more than enough for Hudson to grab him on his second attempt.

But the other dragons who are attacking him come down with him. I start to punch air out at them as well, but Mekhi beats me to it.

He takes a running leap and jumps onto one of their backs, wrapping his arms around the dragon's neck and pulling back as hard as he can.

The dragon freaks out as Mekhi compresses her windpipe, and she jerks herself into the air. Mekhi drops back down to earth, and Calder goes after the third dragon with a quick leap and sting of her scorpion's tail right in the dragon's nose.

The dragon screams and flies away, and Jaxon's dragon—looking a little worse for wear but still all in one piece—shoots us a grateful look as he races straight into Remy's portal.

The rest of us follow right after him, and Remy closes it behind us.

Double, Double, Boil and Trouble

We walk through the portal—and again, Remy does the most amazing portals—and end up near the second group of witches. The dragons land beside us and shift.

"Are we sticking with the plan?" Eden asks as she wipes blood from her chest.

"As long as you're up for it," I tell her. And I know that's not the most general-like answer, but I'm not going to send my best friends into a battle with a high probability of death if they're already severely injured.

She makes a *tsk*ing sound. "This little scratch? I don't even need the first aid kit for this one."

Flint rolls his eyes. "God forbid Eden shows a little weakness."

"Oh, because you're ready to quit?" she asks archly.

It should be a valid question, considering he's got claw marks over his jugular and a whole lot of singed scales, but we all know Flint doesn't go down without a fight. Even before he says, "I haven't even gotten warmed up yet."

"Well, regardless, let me patch you up just a bit," I say, then lean forward and lay a hand on both of them and channel a little earth magic to seal up their wounds. It's nowhere near everything they need, but it'll at least keep them from bleeding out.

"Sorry to cut this short, but we need to move," Remy drawls.

"On it," Jaxon answers, but before he can shift again, I reach out for him.

"Do you mind?" I ask. He holds my gaze, then nods, so I place my hand on his shoulder and close up his wounds as well.

With a half smile when I pull away, he shifts back to his dragon form. The other two dragons do the same and take to the skies, being as obvious as they can be.

The whole battlefield turns toward us, running and yelling and looking like they're out for blood. Which, of course, they are.

"Good luck!" I call to the three dragons, but they're already swooping away.

Remy's gone ahead and built another portal—this one a lot smaller and less obvious than the last one. And as everyone focuses on the dragons, who are putting on quite a show—thank you, Flint—the rest of us slip quietly away to our real target, the third force field.

We used the element of surprise on the first one, and that worked really well. We can't surprise them again—they already know we're here—but we can try to even the playing field. Things are going to get ugly today, of that I have no doubt. But every chance I have to delay it, I'm going to take.

Which is why, when we exit Remy's portal in front of the third force field, we meet almost no resistance. Everyone has spent the last couple of minutes racing toward the force field near where the dragons are and leaving this one almost entirely undefended.

It won't stay that way, but Eden and Flint are already speeding through the air to build an ice wall to separate us from everyone else. It cuts us off from the rest of the field and gives us the breathing room we need before we have to take on a field of ten thousand paranormals.

Within seconds of exiting the portal, Remy's doing the energy thing again. Building up the ball of light, letting it spread along his hands and arms before once again slamming his fist through the force field.

But he's more tired now than he was the first time—he'd warned us that taking down these force fields would wear out even his formidable powers—but I still wince when it doesn't fall.

"What can we do to help?" I ask, but he just shakes his head. And then plows his second fist through the barrier as well.

This time, it falls. But Remy is wiped—I can see it on his face and in the sudden slump of his shoulders. Which means it's up to the rest of us to deal with the fifty witches inside, who come at us with everything they've got.

Spells go flying, and everyone except me has no choice but to duck—at least during the first round. I simply shift, and they have no effect on my gargoyle form at all. Not for the first time, I think gargoyle abilities are kick-ass.

As the witches converge on us, surrounding us on all sides, we prepare to fight our way out—or to die, depending on how things go. I'm really hoping for the former, but I'm afraid our luck might have run out.

Especially when one of the witches in front fires a spell that hits Mekhi square in the chest. For a second, he looks shocked, but then he falls to the ground, convulsing as if thousands of volts of electricity are tearing through his body.

Dawud goes down next, with a curse that has them itching everywhere. And since they are in their wolf form, they look particularly miserable—and like they have a really bad case of fleas.

The third curse hits Macy and has the ugliest, most painful-looking boils imaginable erupting all over her skin. "Are you fucking kidding me?" she snarls. "You used boils?"

Hudson steps forward then, starts whispering to the witches closest to us that they want to help us. That they want to stop the other witches. The others catch on to what's happening pretty quickly and must perform some kind of spell to block out his voice because they remain unaffected.

But the first witches who heard him have already turned on them.

The witches on our side take out a few of the other witches, but there are too many, and they're defeated in no time. The remaining witches turn to focus their attacks on us again.

They aren't our only problem, though. Eden's ice wall is holding off a lot of the horde, but a few hundred have managed to scale it. Others have finally gotten to the end and are pouring around the sides. It's only a matter of time before we have to deal with them, too.

But it's hard to formulate a plan about that when the next curse hits Remy and has him screaming in agony as he falls to his knees.

And damn it, just damn it. I have a lot of faith in Hudson, Calder, and myself, but these odds aren't looking good. I don't want Hudson to have to start disintegrating people, but I know if things get much more dire, that's where we're headed.

As the witches start sending another whole round of spells at us, I can see in his eyes that he knows that's what's coming, too. And that he's decided not to prolong the inevitable. He lifts a hand and holds it out in front of him. But before he can close it, all seven of us are suddenly flying through the air.

Up, Up, and Get Away

"**W**hat the hell? Are you doing this?" Calder asks Hudson.

"Yes, because I've been hiding a third power from all of you. Turns out if you think about enough wonderful things, anyone can fly." He rolls his eyes.

"What *is* happening?" Macy asks. "Remy, are you—"

"It's not Remy," I say as the truth finally dawns on me. I turn around in midair and find Jaxon watching us in his dragon form.

He's under attack, dragons coming at him from all sides, and still he managed to get us out of that mess.

I give him a look full of gratitude and awe, then turn back to the others just in time for him to gently drop us about fifty feet from the platform with Cyrus and the pillars. There are soldiers surrounding it, but if we can get through them, we'll be right next to the force field to bring it down.

I glance back to see if the witches are following us and realize Jaxon killed two birds with one stone—not only did he get us out of there, he did it so abruptly, he left the witches to accidentally curse one another with their spells.

Once we're on solid ground, Macy whirls around and whips out a few spells of her own. Within a minute, everyone is back to normal. Or almost. Mekhi looks more drained than I've ever seen him.

But that one minute is all the surcease we get. Because a giant pack of werewolves is racing across the clearing straight for us, with several vampires hot on their heels.

"Well, shite," Hudson grumbles even as he positions himself in the front of our group, to give the others a chance to recover from being spelled.

I move up to stand next to him—I know he wants to protect me, but I want to protect him right back. Besides, partners stand together against whatever comes their way, and that's what we are. Partners in every way.

"Remy is getting weaker. We need to get through that wall of soldiers so he can bring down the big dome before he's out of juice," I tell him.

"Right. On it, babe." He gives me a quick grin, then refocuses on the wolves racing toward us.

Right before they reach us, Hudson uses his power to carve the ground out in front of us. He just blasts a massive trench that's about thirty feet wide in between them and us.

The wolves howl their displeasure, but it doesn't slow them down for long. Instead, they leap as far into the divide as they can and then run the rest of the way.

Hudson meets the first two who come out of the trench. He grabs one by his neck and breaks it, then tosses him to the side. The second he picks up with his other hand and throws him back across the trench.

More are on us now, though, and I grab the dagger from my waist and whirl around, stabbing it into the chest of the wolf coming straight for me, fangs bared. Momentum carries him forward, and he tries to bite me even as the knife slices him all the way down to his belly.

Blood flows out of the wound onto my hand, and I stifle a scream as I pull my dagger out and push the wolf away. Tears flood my eyes—this is the first person I've ever killed, and it feels horrible. Not as horrible as dying myself, which is what the wolf intended, but definitely not good.

There's no time to dwell on it, though, because the other wolves are on us, and it's a fight for survival—for all of us.

The largest wolf in the group is in human form, but his hands are tipped with sharp claws that he's swinging wildly toward Calder. She's dodging them as best she can, considering she's got her own claws sunk into a vampire who made it across the trench and just tried to rip out her jugular.

The wolf howls with pain, but he's not giving up, either. His own fingers are wrapped around her biceps, twisting and squeezing her upper arm with every ounce of his wolf strength as he tries to drag her closer to his bared teeth.

Calder's face is drawn in pain, but she's not giving up, not giving in. Her scorpion tail is swinging wildly, trying to sting him while she strains away from him as hard as she can. But she can't keep this up, especially since there's another wolf right beside her, just waiting for a break in the tail swinging to dart toward her. If someone doesn't get in there and help her, she won't stand a chance.

Another wolf goes for me, but I turn to stone and hit him in the nose as hard as I can. The wolf goes down screaming, and I whirl around, slamming a foot into the stomach of an oncoming vampire. He snarls and lunges for me, but

Hudson gets between us.

Trusting my mate to take care of the vampire for me, I race toward Calder. As I do, I reach out for the earth and pull tree roots from beneath the surface. Then I lower my hand in a quick chop that slams the root across the back of the vampire's head.

He goes down hard, and Calder immediately whirls around to swipe at the wolf with her lion's claws. The wolf growls in response, and this time when he takes a swipe at her, he connects, his claw slicing across her beautiful face.

She gasps in outrage and throws herself at the wolf with a snarl. But he's ready for her, another claw slicing across her chest as she swings her tail around to sting him. The wolf is huge, so I use both hands to send roots after him.

But Remy turns around and rips the wolf off with his bare hands. He's bleeding and obviously much less powerful than usual, but he has just managed to fight off two vampires. And as the wolf lunges for him, Remy throws a spell at the wolf that turns him into a mouse.

Seconds later, another wolf gobbles him up. Remy lets the wolf eat his snack and then takes care of him, too, by transporting him to the top of the nearest tree.

I race toward Calder, determined to see how badly hurt she is, but another wolf gets there first. This one throws himself at her legs in the most awkward tackle of all time. It works, though, as she goes down. He hits her with a really painful-looking uppercut that sends her reeling backward.

Anger roars through me, and I go after him for real now, jumping into the air like I learned in training and kicking out as hard as I can. I hit him on the chin, and since he's not expecting the blow, he goes reeling backward. At which point, I shift to my full stone form and kick him in the face again. This time he goes down and stays down.

Calder's on the ground, and she's shifted back to her human form. She's cupping her wounded cheek in her hand as she tries to get up, but she's having a rough time. She can't seem to get her legs under her.

Trusting Hudson, Remy, Dawud, Mekhi, and Macy to keep the wolves off us for a few minutes, I drop down beside her, scooping up some of the earth as I go. Old Grace would never dream of rubbing dirt into a cut, but old Grace didn't have healing powers that come from the earth, so it's all relative.

Lowering her shaking hand, I look into Calder's beautiful brown eyes and press the soil into her wound. Then I cover it with my hand and channel a ton of energy from the earth below me and into her.

Compared to trying—and failing—to heal Flint's leg and Jaxon's heart during our last battle, this is a piece of cake. It only takes a minute or so before Calder's skin knits together and another minute before the scars are barely there pink lines that will fade on their own soon enough.

But that wound isn't her only one, and I spend another couple of minutes fixing the broken ribs and torn shoulder tendons. There's more damage, but it's smaller, and now that she's not hurting as badly, we're both raring to get back into the fight.

Which is a good thing, considering I've just pulled back from Calder when Jaxon comes skidding across the grass at our feet, landing in a pile of limp dragon scales and blood. I turn around, barely registering what just happened before the ground begins to shake.

158

Get Back
in Your
(Rib) Cage

"Jaxon!" I yell, half flying, half leapfrogging over a couple of pissed-off vampires in an effort to get to him as quickly as possible.

His dragon is laying on his side, his huge body trembling. I don't know if it's because he's severely injured or if it's just that he's had the wind knocked out of him, so I put a hand on his shuddering shoulder in an effort to figure it out.

"Jaxon?" I say as I crouch down next to him. "Are you okay? Where does it hurt?"

He doesn't answer, doesn't even open an eye or shake his head in an effort to let me know that he's heard me.

I don't know how to check the pulse on a dragon, but I can see that he's breathing. Or at least, I think he's breathing. It's a little hard to concentrate as Flint is tearing through every paranormal in his path in an effort to get to Jaxon.

Blocking out Flint's screams and his desperate fight to get here, I smooth a hand over Jaxon's side from his neck to his hip. He shudders again when I touch his ribs, so I go back and poke at the tender spot some more.

This time he all but convulses, jerking and folding in on himself in an effort to avoid the pain.

"It's okay," I soothe even as relief courses through me. I thought he was badly injured, was afraid it was like before on the Unkillable Beast's island. But he's okay. Hurt but okay. I lay my hand flat against his side, directly below the dragon's right front leg. "I'm going to take care of you, Jaxon. I promise."

He nods his dragon wearily—the first acknowledgment he's made of my presence that hasn't been shudders of pain.

"This rib hurts," I say, going over the area in question. "But do any of the others?" I move my hand lower, pressing it into his second rib and then running it along the length of the huge dragon bone.

He stiffens, a tiny little dragon cry escaping when I press on his second rib, too. The third and fourth ones bring no reaction. But I don't know what's going on on his other side, and right now I don't want to move him and make anything worse.

I glance up, see that Hudson has put himself between Jaxon and approaching enemies on one side and Remy has done the same on the other. They are dealing with any of Cyrus's army trying to come this way while Eden, Calder, Mekhi, Dawud, and Macy are distracting the ones farther away.

Flint, on the other hand, has single-handedly brought down ten members of the Vampire Guard and has burned everyone in his path in a nonstop quest to get to Jaxon.

He lands beside me in human form seconds later. "What can I do? What's wrong with him?"

Jaxon stiffens the second he hears Flint's voice, and then he's shifting back to human form in a shimmer of rainbow sparks.

"What hurts?" I ask the second he's human again. Because treating a dragon isn't impossible, but I much prefer trying to heal someone who can talk to me.

"My ribs," he grinds out, then laboriously pushes into a sitting position.

"What the fuck?" Flint growls as we get our first look at his other side. "Why didn't you—"

"Don't fucking start," Jaxon snaps back, then takes a deep breath, shifting so I can get a better look at the ugly gash that goes right between his ribs. He always has been a terrible patient.

"This looks like a puncture wound," I tell him as I reach into the earth and channel healing magic to close up the bleeding, oozing wound, but it's taking longer than with Calder because it's much deeper. It's all the way to the bone. "You're going to need the mother of all tetanus shots when we're done here," I say to distract him as I reach deeper to knit tissues together from the inside out.

"Vampires don't get tetanus," he tells me with a pained laugh.

"Seems to me like vampires have all the luck," I tease, trying to use the remnants of his shirt to sop up the blood. There's so much blood.

I don't think the wound is life-threatening, but I've never seen Jaxon willing to lay there and let someone tend to him—which, if I'm being honest, is scaring the fuck out of me. I pour more healing energy into him, searching for what beyond his ribs might be damaged as well.

Flint, who's been silent since Jaxon snapped at him, whips off his shirt and holds it out to me. "Here, use this."

Jaxon stiffens. "I'm fine—"

"You're not fine," I snap, pressing the shirt to his wound as delicately as I can considering I'm whisper-yelling at him. "Now knock off the macho bullshit and let me do my job."

"Yeah," Flint tells him with a smirk that is somehow both obnoxious and a little sweet. "Knock off the macho bullshit."

For a second, it looks like Jaxon's going to rip him a new one, but then he huffs out a breath and lays back down for me.

Thank you, I mouth to Flint, who shrugs uncomfortably. But I can see the tiny smile tipping the corners of his mouth and can't help shaking my head, even as I reach deep inside me for the energy that will help me heal Jaxon.

And I thought things between Jaxon and me were complicated once upon a time. Compared to this, we were as easy as breathing.

Jaxon winces as I start to heal the outside of the puncture wound now, but he doesn't say a word. Instead, he grits his teeth and looks away, trying to pretend it's no big deal. But the sweat rolling down his cheek says otherwise, as do the clenched fists.

"How does a vampire start a letter?" I ask, and Jaxon sends me a pained look.

He takes a shaky breath and asks, "Do I want to know?"

"Tomb it may concern," I say and grin.

It's definitely not the best joke in my repertoire, and he and Flint both groan—a lot—at the punch line. But it's also not my worst, so I stick my tongue out at both of them before glancing back at Jaxon's wounds.

I try to channel as much of the pain away from him as I can while using the rest of my magic to heal the wound. It's a delicate balance, though, because if I get too caught up in helping him manage the pain, I don't have enough magic available to heal him properly. And it's a deep wound, one that did a little damage to a couple of internal organs as well.

Once the wound is closed and at least partially healed on the inside, I turn my attention to knitting the two ribs on his other side back together. He winces again as I press on the broken spot, even groans a little.

"You've got this," Flint tells him in a low voice, leaning forward to press a hand on my shoulder. I'm already pulling energy from the earth, so I automatically pull from Flint, and my tattoo wrapping around my forearm that stores magic lights up.

Jaxon stiffens again, and at first I think he's about to object to Flint giving up some of his energy to heal him. But then I realize Flint has also dropped a hand onto Jaxon's clenched fist and is squeezing it gently.

Part of me expects Jaxon to shrug him off—especially considering the snarl on his face as he looks at his best friend. But in the end, he lets Flint's hand stay there and even relaxes into him a little so that their arms are brushing.

It's not much of a concession, especially since Flint has been studiously ignoring Jaxon when he's not snapping at him this last week. But it's something, and I can see from the way that Flint's shoulders relax that he recognizes it, too.

Closing my eyes now—trusting Hudson and Remy and Eden to keep us safe—I delve deep inside myself so that I can figure out where the two edges of the ribs should meet.

Jaxon yelps as I adjust them just slightly—he must have gotten one hell of a kick to do this kind of damage—and I feel Flint shift next to me. My eyes are closed, so I can't see what's happening, but seconds later, Jaxon relaxes into the pain, and the healing, just a little more.

I do the best I can in a couple of minutes—battlefield triage is a thing—then pull back and open my eyes.

Jaxon's mouth is still twisted in pain, but the gray cast is gone from his skin. "How's that feel?" I ask.

He twists a little, grimaces, then grins, even as he flashes me the first smile in what feels like forever. "About eighty-five percent better," he says. "Thanks."

I nearly sag in relief.

"Try not to get stabbed again, by talons or a sword," I tell Jaxon as I take Flint's hand and let him pull me to my feet.

"Because this was a choice," Jaxon grumbles, studiously ignoring the hand that Flint holds out to help him up. At least until Flint reaches in and grabs his hand anyway, yanking him to his feet in one smooth move.

I start to turn around, to give them as much privacy as I can in the middle of this crowded field, but before I can so much as move, one of Cyrus's personal guards drops in behind Hudson, who still has his hands full fighting several wolves at the same time.

The guard raises his sword, prepares to plunge it into Hudson's back, and I scream and take off running toward him, even though I know I won't make it in time.

159

Loyalty
Always Was
My Best Color

Mekhi turns to see what I'm screaming about and fades straight toward Hudson. I pray he gets there in time, but as the sword starts to come down, I don't think even a vampire could cover the distance.

But then, out of nowhere, a knife slices straight through the guard's back and—judging from where it's located and the way he falls to the ground, dead—into his heart.

Hudson, blissfully unaware of his very-near-death experience, tosses the attacking werewolf several yards away. As he does, I turn to look behind me, trying to figure out where the knife that saved him possibly could have come from, and lock eyes with Izzy.

She is still inside the force field, but she is standing right on the edge of it, looking straight out at us. And I realize she is somehow so good with a knife that she got it between the force field's narrowly woven web and across the field to save her brother's life, all within the blink of an eye.

Before I can consider what this means, a warlock in fancy purple robes with an insignia on the lapels is barreling down on Remy, his face contorted with rage. He fires a blast of power at Dawud, and I can immediately tell his spells are much more powerful than anything else we've seen on the battlefield today. The warlock nearly takes Dawud's head off and has them gasping for breath. Remy holds a hand out to Dawud, keeping the spell from fully taking over their body, but his hand is shaking.

The warlock sends another curse—or whatever you call the spell—after Dawud, and Remy blocks it with a spell that blows the warlock back several feet. It costs him, though.

Remy's losing color, his shoulders slumping, and the warlock is almost upon him again. I'm too far away to reach him in time, but I take off running anyway, praying Remy can hold on just a bit longer.

The warlock's eyes narrow on Remy. "You are done here."

Remy pales, even as he grits his teeth, clinging to the spell that's keeping Dawud breathing. But, like the rest of us, there's only so much power he can call on, and I can feel it.

He's out of time.

I cast a glance at Macy, but she's facing away from us and doesn't see that Remy is in danger. I pour on the speed, determined to get there in time.

The warlock draws back his hands, then slams them forward, sending a shock wave of power straight for Remy. I scream his name and plunge my hands into the ground, calling on magic that I know won't make it there in time.

Hudson's eyes go wide. He fades to Remy and shoves him as hard as he can, but I know it's too late. We aren't going to be able to save him—

Calder uses her powerful lion legs to jump over twenty feet in one leap and blocks Remy at the last moment, taking the blow herself.

She hangs in midair for one second, two, as the blow tears through her, then falls to the ground...lifeless.

160

Parting Is Such Sweet Sorrow

"**N**o!" The denial wrenches itself from Remy's chest as he crumples to the ground beside Calder, somehow managing to keep one hand out to Dawud as well.

Macy must have heard my scream, though, because she's beside Remy in seconds, taking over removing the spell keeping Dawud on the ground.

"No, no, no, no, no, please no," Remy begs the universe that seems determined to take away everyone we love. His hands rove frantically over Calder's hair, never quite touching, like he's trying to keep the still-beautiful locks fanned out around her in place. His whole body is shaking uncontrollably now.

Remy swipes at the tears on his cheeks, leaning down to pull her into his lap. "Wake up, Calder. I need you to wake up now, baby. You haven't swum with the dolphins yet. I know how much you love dolphins. And what about Paris, huh? We still haven't gotten to eat macarons at an outdoor café." His eyes are wild as he looks at us. "She wanted to bedazzle Flint's leg so badly. And she's still got the entire last season of *This Is Us* DVR'd because she said she didn't want to only watch the sad ones."

Macy chokes on a sob. Beside her, Eden and Mekhi cling to each other in horror. When Jaxon and Flint run up behind Remy, what little strength I'd been holding on to crumbles.

"She has a little sister, Grace," Remy says, turning his wide eyes on me. "What the hell am I going to tell her little sister?"

Tears flood my eyes instantly, and I want nothing more than to drop to the ground beside him and hold him while his whole world falls apart, the same way Heather held me when mine did, but there are hundreds of wolves and vampires closing in on us. So many, I don't know how we're not all about to join Calder in the grass. We're outnumbered and broken with loss.

And then Remy unleashes a scream, so raw and anguished, my heart breaks wide open.

Tears coursing down his own face, he slams his arms out with another scream and sends wave after wave of power around us in all directions, dropping every single enemy within a hundred yards to the ground, writhing in agony. Only when their screams eclipse his own, does Remy lower his arms and allow their bodies to collapse to the ground. Lifeless.

He scoops Calder back into his arms, rocking her against his chest.

Remy bought us some time, but there are thousands more soldiers racing toward us. And he's obviously too weak now to punch through the last barrier.

Cyrus has won.

161

I don't know what to do. I don't know how to get us out of this, not anymore. Calder is dead. Jaxon is injured. Remy is on the ground, destroyed by Calder's sacrifice. And Cyrus's evil masses are swarming all around us.

We make a circle, like we have so many times before. Backs toward the center so we can protect one another as we face whatever comes at us.

But right now, it's too much. No matter how many people we fight, no matter how many paranormals we kill, there's always more right behind them. More and more and more.

We don't stand a chance.

And more than anything, we don't want to give in. We don't want Cyrus to win. Not when he's proven over and over again just how evil he is. And not when we've already lost so many people. We can't let their deaths be in vain.

But as another nest of vampires swarms us, fangs bared and fingers curled into claws, I don't know how we're going to defeat them. How we're going to get out of this mess. Especially not when there's a coven of witches following hot on their heels.

I brace myself, start to turn to stone even as I'm terrified for Macy and Dawud and all the others. There are so many vampires in this wave—at least 150 or 160—and there's no way we can fight them all off.

The vampires attack as one, launching themselves at us, and I hold my breath, waiting for their teeth to scrape against me.

But their teeth never get close. They never land one blow. Because Hudson throws a hand out and, in the space from one heartbeat to the next, ends them all.

"You didn't have to do that—" I start, but he's not even listening.

He's focused on the coven of witches about to hit and the pack of werewolves behind them. And the giant flight of dragons that is even now soaring over our heads.

There's a part of me that expects him to just do it now. To disintegrate them all before they even have a chance—or a choice. But instead, he waits until they're close, until the witches are looking us in the eyes while their spells fly around us, before slipping inside them. And then, when they are so close I can practically feel their breath on my face, he closes his fist. And destroys them all in the most up-close-and-personal way possible. For Calder.

He falls to one knee, sweat breaking out on his forehead and his breath ragged.

"Don't," I whisper. "You can't."

But I know it doesn't matter what I say. This is endgame and we're losing. The nuclear option is our only remaining one.

It's our lives or Hudson's soul, and he's already made the impossible choice for us.

162

Losing Everything
but My Train
of Thought

I look at the carnage all around us and can't help thinking that we are totally fucked. We're just too stubborn to admit that we are tapped out.

Oh, we can continue fighting for a while longer. But if we do that, one of two things is going to happen. Either we are going to die one by one, or Hudson is going to end up killing everyone on this field and, in doing so, will lose his soul forever.

Neither of those outcomes is acceptable to me.

These are my friends, my family. The people who followed me into battle. I can't be too weak to defend them. I can't be too stubborn to save their lives.

Another wave of wolves comes at us, and I brace myself for their attack—or for Hudson disintegrating them. Whatever happens, I can't stop it. Not from where I am, back-to-back with my friends as we all wait to see what happens next.

We're so close to Cyrus's force field—barely fifty or seventy-five feet away—and there's a part of me that just wants to go for it. A part of me wants to say *to hell with everything else* and just storm the thing and make him pay for everything he's done.

It's a good fantasy, but that's all it is. Because even if I made it that seventy-five feet, it wouldn't change anything.

With Remy completely wiped out, there's absolutely no chance we'll ever make it past Cyrus's dome. And if we can't make it past the dome, there's no way we'll ever have a chance at stopping him. We'll just be on this field killing people—or dying ourselves—forever.

We really are totally fucked.

The next wave of witches comes at us, spells flying through the air. Hudson disintegrates them without a second thought, but this time I can see the way he trembles as he collapses onto both knees. Just like I can see the way the heaviness of what he's done weighs on him. It pulls him down, makes him smaller, makes him hurt in a way I don't think anything else ever has or ever will.

It's that thought that makes the decision for me, that thought that has me dropping my arms—dropping my position—and walking straight toward Cyrus. One way or another, this has to stop.

One way or another, I'm going to be the one to stop it.

"Grace!" Hudson calls. I can hear the confusion, and the worry, in his voice. But I can't turn back. I can't reassure him. If I do, Cyrus will be suspicious, and that is the last thing I want right now.

And so I keep my pace and keep the faith as I cover the distance to the stone circle in a few short seconds. As I do, I realize the sky is getting lighter, the super flower blood moon getting larger and larger above me.

It feels like a premonition, like a promise, but I ignore the skitter of nerves down my spine.

The massive clearing is spread out on either side of me, and it's filled with thousands and thousands of paranormals, the largest dome dead ahead of me.

As I get closer to Cyrus and the altar he has laid out in the middle of his little stone fantasy, it brings me kicking and screaming back to my first week at Katmere—when Lia strapped me to an altar and tried to human sacrifice me to bring back her lost love, Hudson. I know Cyrus has no plans to invoke Hudson tonight, but I'd be lying if I said I'm not afraid he might decide a little human sacrifice is exactly what he needs to shake this thing up.

But that absolutely, positively is not going to happen. Been there, done that, don't need a T-shirt or a repeat.

I'm at the border of the dome now, and more and more people on the field have caught on that something big is happening. I try to ignore the stares as much as I can, but the closer I get to the stone structure, the more people—and stares—there are. And then Cyrus is there, standing right in front of me.

"Well, well, well, look who's here," he says, his voice eerily projecting across the entire field, filling the bloodred sky above our heads. "Grace Foster. Did you come to help me celebrate my big night?"

"I came to surrender." The words nearly stick in my throat, but they have to be said. This really is the best option.

"No!" Hudson screams, and I should have known that his vampire hearing would pick up what I'm saying even this far away. "Grace, don't!"

I don't even look at him, don't look at any of my friends. I can't, not if I want to stay strong.

I need to stay strong.

"I'm sorry, Grace," Cyrus mocks, his voice booming across the clearing. "Can you repeat yourself? I thought it sounded like you said that you *surrender*."

I have one last-ditch idea that maybe, if we're lucky, will work. It won't give us a much-fought-for victory—but it could save my friends' lives. It only requires Cyrus being who he is—a lying, double-crossing narcissist. Well, and me being a good liar. It's that second one that has my voice quivering just a little bit.

"I did. But before I do, I want to make a deal." I look him dead in the eye and let him see just how broken I feel.

"A deal?" He raises a brow. "Do you actually think you're in any position to make a deal? There's very little fight left in your friends, and apparently none in you. So why would I make a deal when very soon you'll either be dead or once again my prisoner?"

Hearing him voice my worst fears makes them come to life inside me, writhing in my stomach like snakes in a frenzy. I ignore the feeling, even swallow down the bile that burns its way up my throat. And answer, "I have information you want."

The words have Cyrus rearing back. I've surprised him, maybe even made him curious. And as he tilts his head to the side and studies me, I can tell he's trying to decide what that information might be—and whether or not he wants it enough to strike a deal with me.

Eventually, though, the curiosity wins out. "What information could you possibly have for me?" he asks in the same tone as before. But his eyes are much more careful as his voice booms out across the valley. "I'm about to become a god."

As he says the last, the crowd of followers that is surrounding the dome goes wild. Ecstatic cheers fill the clearing, arms fly in the air, and there is so much whistling and hooting that I can barely hear my own thoughts. Which isn't terrifying at all.

It takes a minute or so before things die down enough that I can speak again. But once they do, I look him dead in the eye and lie. "I just got back from visiting the Crone, and all I can say is, I'd be careful if I were you."

That freezes Cyrus in his tracks for just a moment. His eyes narrow, his whole body growing so still, I'm not sure he even breathes. But then he seems to come back to himself, motioning with his head at two nearby guards inside the circle with him, both of whom are wearing the same magic-canceling armor that Cyrus is wearing. They rush over and grab me by my elbows.

Once they have me secured, my fragile neck in the hands of one of the elite Vampire Guard, the rest of my friends surrender as well, and soldiers rush to secure them. Remy creates his own force field around Calder's body, then surrenders as well.

After Cyrus is assured we're neutralized, he looks at the witches in the final force field bubble and nods to them. Seconds later, the electric dome around Cyrus falls.

Thank God.

We're one step closer to ending this thing, and right now, that's all that matters to me.

Fighting to keep my expression neutral, and maybe even a little afraid— which isn't very hard at the moment—I put up with being dragged before Cyrus like a criminal as his minions on the field shout with glee.

But as I get closer to him, I can see the very real suspicion in his eyes, and my stomach plummets to my knees. This whole plan rests on him believing the lies I'm feeding him. I'm guessing that a man who has double-crossed everyone he's ever worked with can't help but assume others are waiting for the chance to do the same to him.

I need to play this carefully, though. Cyrus needs to come to me, ask me what I know. If I have to give it out to him unsolicited—he'll know it isn't true.

More worried than I want to admit to myself, I glance toward the strange altar that he's erected in the middle of the Alaskan wilderness. Izzy is standing to the side of one of the largest stones.

"You went back to see my mother?" she asks, and there's just enough interest in her voice to have Cyrus turning around to stare at her in surprise.

"I did," I tell her, and this is where my voice breaks. Because now the lie just got a million times worse. It's one thing to tell Cyrus the Crone is brokenhearted over the loss of her child, but it's another to tell that child.

Izzy swore she didn't care about her mom and didn't want anything to do with her, but it's still hard to use someone's mother as a weapon—even if it's not against them.

"Well then, pray tell, my dear." Cyrus's British accent is on stark display. "What did my leftovers have to say? Apparently, Isadora would like to know."

"I think you need to know more than she does," I answer. "The Crone lied to you."

"Did she now?" His voice is more amused than ever, but something moves in his eyes that tells me he's listening. And more, he's rethinking everything the Crone ever told him.

Not that that's a surprise. Of course Cyrus is willing to believe the Crone double-crossed him. It's nothing he wouldn't, or hasn't, done a million times.

"So what exactly are you claiming the old hag lied about? Because the last thing I heard from her was her begging me to stay."

The crowd laughs—even the women—and my stomach pitches in disgust. How can people not see through him? More, how can they be amused by his cruelty? There's nothing funny about denigrating another person, especially if that person isn't around to defend themselves.

The Crone is far from my favorite person, but as Cyrus continues to mimic her as he panders to the crowd, I can't help wishing she'd show up and smite him. No one should talk about the mother of one of their children like this—especially in front of that child.

"It looks to me like you know everything you need to know. Although I guess I should warn you that some women don't take kindly to their children being stolen from them." I give him the coldest, most calculating smile I can muster—which isn't hard, because I learned it from watching him—and say, "So I suppose I'll be on my way."

I turn to walk away, shrugging my arms free of the guards, but I've only gone a step or two before Izzy says, "I don't know, Daddy. Grace is such a goody-goody, I can't believe she'd lie."

"Fine," says Cyrus, trying to project a very laissez-faire attitude, but I can tell I've got him on the line. Now all I have to do is reel him in. He turns to me. "Tell me what you came to say."

"I'd be happy to, but first I think we need to come to that agreement I mentioned."

"Money?" he sneers, then looks out at the crowd in a long-suffering manner. "Why do they *always* want money?"

The crowd boos and jeers and I rack my brain, trying to figure out the perfect thing to say next. "What I actually want is protection for my friends and myself. Promise me you and your army won't harm or kill us, ever, and I'll tell you everything the Crone told me about this little altar situation you have going on."

"You're really going to waste this opportunity on my worthless sons and a couple of mangy strays?"

"Yes," I say simply, "I am." Because if I say any more, he'll see just how angry I am that he referred to my friends like that. Who the hell is he to call my friends anything?

"If that's what you want," he says, walking forward with a slow, measured step. "Let's make a deal."

He extends his hand to shake mine, and the moment our palms clasp, a new tattoo blazes to life—this one the shape of a bloodred moon.

As it does, I can't help noticing just how many tattoos I have now—every one of them, except Remy's, representing a deal with a different kind of devil. I hope with all my heart that this is the last time I ever have to do this.

"So?" Cyrus demands impatiently. "What did that old bitch say about the God Stone?"

"Nothing," I answer, taking great delight in the look of rage that flares to life in his eyes now that he knows I got the better of him. "She told me absolutely nothing."

"You—" Cyrus leaps at me, and I know there's going to be hell to pay.

163

Rage Against the God Machine

Cyrus lands in front of me so fast, a snarl on his face and a clawed hand ready to slash my throat, that I don't even have time to scream.

But then he seems to catch himself, shakes his head, and his hand lowers. Probably the magical contract we just inked kicking in. I breathe a sigh of relief.

I watch as my friends, one after another, are dragged onto the platform.

As one of the guards grabs me and restrains me, I can tell now that all of Cyrus's guards in the circle with him, not just the Vampire Guard, are wearing the same magic-blocking armor. Not that Hudson or Jaxon would make a move now with my neck being held in a vampire's hands, especially since he brought out a knife and pressed it against my jugular.

I briefly consider shifting to solid stone, to give Hudson time to disintegrate the machine, but as I glance around at the pillars, also strapped in the same magic-blocking armor, I wonder if our plan to destroy the machine ever would have worked. I made a deal with Cyrus to spare our lives. That might be the best outcome any of us can hope for at this time.

I glance over at Izzy, who is leaning against a pillar near Delilah and watching everything with a bored expression—but her hands are clenched in fists. The vampire queen, for her part, looks like she's about to get everything she ever wanted, and a suspicion has the hairs on the back of my neck standing up.

"We didn't have to end up here, you know," I say, turning back to Cyrus. "You told Delilah to tell us about your plans, didn't you?"

"Of course." He looks at me like I'm daft. "You are here because I wanted you to be here. Everything I have done has been with this as an endgame. You were just too ignorant to figure it out. You are nothing if not predictable, Grace, and for that I thank you. You have made things so much easier for me."

His words suck the breath from my lungs as he confirms my suspicion.

We walked into another trap.

Worse, I *led* us into it. And this whole time I thought I was finally thinking three steps ahead. That this time, this one time, we had the advantage against Cyrus. I can't help but wonder how far back he's been planning his revenge.

The Bloodletter said he would know who I really was when he bit me on the Ludares field. Has he been plotting since then? Did he take one look at me and size me up in a breath? I'm rash. I rush in. I react when I should be reconsidering.

And when it was clear we were going to lose, I impulsively surrendered—and played right into Cyrus's hands. I thought as long as he didn't kill my friends, we would be okay. But as the guards drag each of them around the outside of the inner circle, I can't help wondering if I took everyone's choice to go down fighting away from them.

I've given him my friends and, worse, the means to become a god. At no point did I consider if we simply stayed away, Cyrus would fail on his own.

"You came like you always do, Grace. You can't seem to help yourself. All I had to do was plant a seed with Marise that I was draining children of their magic, and you couldn't wait to play avenger and rescue them, could you? All the while giving me exactly what I wanted—you. Which gave me the God Stone. So of course I knew you would be so sure of yourself that if you knew my plans here today, you would try to stop me. Every single time you thought someone was in jeopardy, you came running, didn't you, Grace?"

He's right. I did. I didn't even hesitate. Even when we knew it was only the ten of us against an army of ten thousand. Even when I knew the Gargoyle Army wouldn't have our backs. I still came. And I brought my friends with me.

My gaze bounces from Jaxon to Eden to Mekhi and Dawud, to Macy and Flint, Remy and Hudson. And with each one of them I look at, I grow a little taller. Because what I see shining in their eyes isn't anger or betrayal or even remorse. It's pride. Unwavering pride.

Yes, I came and I brought my friends with me—because I am their *heart*. My gargoyle heartstone knows no other way, and they love and follow me because of it. What Cyrus sees as my greatest weakness is why I have friends who will always have my back. That's something someone like Cyrus, who rules with fear and selfish goals, will never understand.

"I did," I agree. He's moved in front of me now, and as I look him in the eye—look him over from head to toe—I make no bones about the fact that I find him lacking. Feeling emboldened by our contract, I take a deep breath and tell him exactly why we are so different.

"You're right. I will always come." I square my shoulders, lift my chin. "But

I'm not ashamed of who I am. I am someone who will not cower. I will not look away. Every single time you try to take something from someone less powerful than you—*I will be there*. Because I am the *gargoyle queen*, and it is my *honor* to protect those defenseless against your evil. I'll always come. Because that is who I am, and it's in my *blood*.

"You are a monster, a king who thinks nothing of his subjects and everything of himself. A man who wants all the power he can get but will never know what it is to be truly powerful. And I am a gargoyle, defender of the innocent, protector of the defenseless. And as long as I live, I will never leave you in peace."

Several seconds pass while he looks at me like he can't believe he's hearing correctly—or, more accurately, like he can't believe I have the nerve to speak to him like this.

And maybe the old Grace, the one who showed up at Katmere Academy not so many months ago shattered and alone, would never have been able to say these things to him. But it's been a long seven months, and I'm not that girl anymore—and I never will be again.

He shakes his head, looks nearly sorrowful as he glances out over the field. "If you are truly the gargoyle queen"—he waves his arms out wide—"then where is your army, eh? Or do they know what I already know—that you are weak? That you would sacrifice every one of them to save your precious friends?"

I flinch and remember the day I told Chastain I would choose my mate over the Army every time. It feels like a lifetime ago.

My eyes search out Hudson, where a guard has finally wrestled him against one of the pillars across from me.

A smile touches my lips when I see his familiar face, such love and acceptance shining in his eyes. He told me not long ago that one day I would need to choose my people over him, and he understood then what I finally see now, too.

I give our mating bond a squeeze and then turn back to Cyrus. "I would sacrifice the Army for *any* of my friends; you are right, Cyrus. But the thing of it is, that's what my people would want me to do. That's who we are. We are protectors. And it is an honor to die protecting those in need. My friends would sacrifice their lives for the Army, if necessary, in return. That's what honor is. That's what *love* is. Sacrificing for those who need us the most."

I look out over the field of paranormals and continue. "And the Gargoyle Army would sacrifice their lives for anyone here, anyone in need. There is another way than following Cyrus. The Army will be your voice as well. We will find a way for humans and paranormals to live side by side—I give you my word."

As my gaze turns back to Cyrus's, though, I realize I've overplayed my hand.

Cyrus was willing to risk the Army coming before, because I think a part of him really believed they'd never follow such a "little girl." But I can see it in his eyes now—he's not taking the risk any longer.

"Enough!" Cyrus shouts, the fury he'd been so careful not to show the other paranormals coming off him in waves now. "Strap them to the machine!"

My eyes widen and I gasp. "But—but—" I don't know how to organize my thoughts. I don't even know what strapping us to the machine means, but I know it can't be good. "We have an agreement that you can't harm any of us!"

The smile that slides across his face like a serpent sends shivers along my spine. "My dear Grace, I simply need your power to activate the God Stone. You won't be *harmed*. You'll just become human after I drain your power."

164

What Doesn't
Cyrus Makes
Us Stronger

"There's no need to fight, Grace," Cyrus says. "This is how it was always going to end. I knew you would come, and I let you tire yourselves with my soldiers. Did you really think we couldn't have crushed you immediately? But everything is so much easier when the fight's been beaten out of you."

I watch in horror as my friends are each strapped to one of the metal-covered pillars. There's a leather strap around their shoulders, another around their waists, and a third that wraps around their legs. As I watch Hudson try to disintegrate them—and fail—I realize something horrible.

The metal we're strapped to—probably this entire machine—must have been made by the Blacksmith. And like the shackles for the Unkillable Beast—for Alistair—they are unbreakable by magic. Only a tool made by the Blacksmith himself will open them.

That doesn't keep my friends from trying. Either they haven't figured out what I have yet or, like the Unkillable Beast, they are determined to beat the magic.

Macy is casting spell after unsuccessful spell, Jaxon is shaking the ground all around us in an effort to dislodge the pillars without effect, Flint is straining against the bonds like he can use sheer brute strength to get him out, and Remy is completely still, which I'm pretty sure means he's focused internally on doing something to destroy the pillars.

Mekhi and Dawud are struggling, but they aren't making any progress, either.

As I watch them, my mind is desperately whirling, too, as I try to think of how I can help. I try to use my earth magic, to grab the roots beneath the ground and yank them to the surface. But the second the first root tip breaks the surface and crawls up the platform, the knife at my throat cuts deeper as the guard holding me snarls, "Stop."

The knife itself is dangerously close to my jugular and, for a second, I think about continuing to fight anyway. It's not that I want to die—I don't, at all. But there are three more pillars to this machine, and I have no doubt Cyrus plans for me to be on one of them. If he doesn't have me, if he can't use me to power whatever the hell this thing is, then maybe there's another chance to stop him.

Sure enough, the guard starts dragging me toward a pillar, and I begin to struggle in earnest. But as I do, Hudson screams my name, and when I look at him, his eyes are filled with a pleading I can't ignore. *Don't do this*, they say to me. *We'll find another way, no matter how hard it is.*

I can't leave Hudson, not again. And so I don't fight anymore, even as they strap me to a pillar. Instead, I focus on trying to figure out a plan to get us all out of this disaster.

As I do, Cyrus does perhaps the most Cyrus thing ever. He turns on Delilah and Izzy and shouts for the guards to seize them, too.

Delilah goes kicking and screaming—it takes three guards to control her— but Izzy just looks at him with steady, unblinking eyes as they drag her away.

Cyrus shakes his head, though. "I didn't intend to put you on this fence, daughter, but the manticore created an opening. And maybe I would have filled it with someone else if you hadn't chosen to use your knife skills to betray me. You know how I feel about betrayal."

Cyrus glances down at his watch, his eyes alighting with glee, and I know our time is up. The moon is behind us, facing Cyrus, but I can tell from his excitement that the lunar eclipse must be upon us. He's standing at the altar and sprinkling black sand from a pouch in a circle on the stone surface, then he reaches inside his breast pocket and pulls out the God Stone and sets it in the center. Like it's suspended from a thread, the God Stone rises up and hovers a foot above the altar.

I watch in awe and pure fear as the earth finally moves into position, and moonlight shines down in a perfect beam, red as blood, that moves across the altar. Like the hands of a clock, the light slowly moves until it reaches the God Stone.

The second the moonlight hits the Stone, it brings it to life. Its surface glows bright orange and red and starts to spin faster and faster until the entire altar is bathed in its eerie glow.

Like a despot receiving the ultimate adoration from the universe, Cyrus turns his face up to the moon and lets its rays wash over him. Then he raises his hands to the sky, and I hear a sizzling in the air before a sudden zap of lightning strikes one of the stone pillars. Flint calls out, and I turn to see the lightning ignite the metal plate, making it glow with incandescent white.

Oh my God. How can he do this? We have a contract!

But as I watch Flint writhe in pain, horror settles in my stomach. The lightning isn't so much harming Flint as causing pain. His skin isn't singed; there's no bruising or other sign that the lightning is causing any damage at all. But it *is* torturing him, burning the magic racing in his veins and drawing it into the glowing metal plate.

Another zap of lightning as Macy's metal plate is struck, and she screams out.

When her screams turn to broken sobs and whimpers, my whole body is shaking. Both for what's happening to my cousin, to all my friends, and in anticipation of what's about to happen to me.

Over and over, Cyrus calls down the lightning, and it strikes pillar after pillar. When it strikes mine, it's almost a welcome relief from focusing on the terror of my friends. The pain is almost unbearable, like every cell in my body is on fire, and I scream until my voice is raw and hoarse. And still Cyrus pulls more lightning down on us.

All of a sudden, the pillars on the outer ring of the stone circle start to rise up in the air and spin around us. The firelight from the God Stone follows them into the sky and makes it seem like the stones are encased in flames—their fiery light shining down directly on Cyrus, bathing him in a magical red glow.

And we all get to watch—some in jubilation, some in horror—as a monster becomes a god.

165

Fake Gods
and Very
Real Monsters

As more and more lightning strikes the metal behind me, I start to lose sense of the pain. Whimpers vaguely reach my ears as I sag against the restraints holding me upright. And as the fight slowly leaves my body...so does my magic.

I can feel it being pulled down into the machine, drawn to the stone pillars circling above us, and the God Stone giving it to Cyrus. I know I should fight it. I shouldn't give in and just let him take what he wants. But isn't that the way of those who want to steal others' power?

They just tear at you until you believe them, until the lies they're telling you make more sense than any truth that you know. Until you're so battered—so broken—that you let them take whatever they want because you don't have the energy or the will to hold on to it. To keep fighting when it all feels so pointless.

Cyrus is a master at this—I've seen what he's done to Izzy, to Delilah, what he tried to do to Hudson. And all so Cyrus could have more.

Now more and more power fills Cyrus until he starts to scream as though his skin is burning, making a shiver race down my spine. He screams and screams and, as much as I hate this man, I actually start to feel sorry for him. Thankfully, the screaming lasts only a minute, and the fire licking against his body hardens into crackly black ash—entombing him completely.

There's a hush across the meadow as we all stare at the spot where Cyrus used to be. The moonlight slowly moves past the God Stone, and as it does, the pillars stop burning and glide back to their original positions on the ground. Eventually, there's just the normal fat white moon shining its benign light across the platform and the ash encasing Cyrus's body like he's a statue.

There's no time to celebrate that the God Stone actually didn't work the way Cyrus hoped before the form of Cyrus begins to shake, small cracks opening and bright orange-red lava oozing out and dripping down his sides.

And then, with a *whoosh*, the hard shell explodes, and Cyrus is there again.

Living. And breathing. And most likely a god.

At first, nothing seems different. Nothing seems off. He didn't even get the gray streak of hair I was really kind of expecting—hello, too many superhero movies.

My shoulders start to sag. Maybe nothing happened. Maybe we're going to be okay.

But then he starts to grow. And grow. And grow.

All around us, people are cheering in the fields. Celebrating that their king has ascended and celebrating their erroneous belief that this means in some strange way they have, too.

As I watch, I can't help thinking of the day I earned the right to sit on the Circle as the gargoyle queen. I grew that day, just like he's growing now. I always thought it was because I had combined Hudson's power with mine, but now I know that it was probably the demigod inside me waking with Hudson's power.

It's funny how naive I was back then. How I had absolutely no idea what was in store for me in this world. I thought that losing Jaxon and then walking onto that Ludares field alone was the worst thing that could ever happen to me.

And now, now it seems like child's play.

I look over at my friends and gasp—Hudson, Jaxon, Macy, Mekhi, Flint, Dawud, Eden, Remy. They're all hanging on listlessly, their bindings the only thing holding them up. Bloody, broken, beaten in all the ways a person can be.

I can't help the sob that escapes my throat. My friends, my family, my everything, and they followed me through it all.

It's almost too much to even think about, and a buzzing in my ears is drowning out the sounds around me. A god-awful whirring sound, like the blood in my heart rushing in my ears.

Beating in my head over and over again that we lost. We lost.

Nearly everyone I love, the very essence of what it means to be their true self taken from them just so another person can have whatever he wants.

And I can do nothing to stop it. Nothing to change it. I've worked so hard, tried so hard. Done everything I know how to do, and still it wasn't enough.

Maybe it was never going to be enough. Maybe that's the lesson I need to learn from all this. You win some, you lose some.

I just never thought we'd lose this big.

166

Carpe Queen 'Em

I close my eyes, unable to watch Cyrus gloat for another moment as he turns to his crowd of followers and army and raises his giant hands for their praise.

I can't watch.

He's taken everything from me.

I can already tell—my gargoyle string is faded. My mating bond. Dull.

There's no magic at all left in me.

And as much as that hurts, and oh my God, I had no idea how much it would, imagining my friends who followed me into this battle feeling the same has my chest squeezing the breath from my lungs. I can't even bring myself to look at them again. I can't absorb that pain right now. Not yet. Maybe not ever.

So I just hang here, letting the straps hold me in place, the edges cutting into my flesh, reminding me that I'm only human.

I would give anything to unlock these restraints, to crawl away with my friends and lick our wounds.

But if I'm right, if these restraints were made by the Blacksmith, then it doesn't matter if I have the key or not. Just like in the Aethereum—there's no use fighting back. That place will take what it wants of your soul, and there's nothing you can do about it.

Except…it didn't take everything from me.

I never got pulled into the torture dreams like Jaxon and Flint and Calder.

There was something different about me.

My demigod string.

That tiny piece of me that came from my mother. And her mother before her. Passed down from generation to generation—an ancient power that cannot be contained by the magic of the Blacksmith.

I stir against my restraints.

Which means, I might still have a chance.

I look inside me, almost afraid at what I might find, and there it is. Still burning a brilliant bright green. Waiting for me to have the courage to grab it and set it free.

So I can stay here and let Cyrus take everything from me and everyone I love. Or I can grab my green string and take back everything he's stolen.

It turns out it's an easier decision than I ever imagined. Because no way am I going to let him hurt my family. And there's no way I'm going to let him hurt me. Not anymore.

It's that thought that gives me the courage to reach deep inside myself and grab my green string.

Electricity zaps along my hand and sets the nerve endings in my arm on fire. My hand starts to shake, the power in my string a wild and living thing beneath my fist, but I don't let go. I can't. It zings throughout my blood, burning up the oxygen in my veins, and my legs give out.

I remember Aunt Rowena telling me this part of me, my ancient magic, would be angry at being kept in a box for so long, and as the string whips and snaps in my hand, I would say "angry" was an understatement.

The two times I'd really grabbed my string before, in the lighthouse and the Bloodletter's cave, both times I'd had a purpose. I was trying to use the power. To push poison through my gargoyle strings. To control it.

But I'm done trying to keep that part of me locked away. I'm tired of being afraid of who I really am. I know who I am, and no matter how powerful I might become, no matter how much someone else might fear that power—I won't. It is a part of me, and I am amazing. *All* of me.

So I grip my string even harder. Not to control it but to let it know I'm here, and I'm ready to embrace that side of me. And as I squeeze, I swear I feel it *grow*.

Something starts to unfurl in my belly, and I feel a little dizzy, like looking over the side of a cliff at the ground far down below. The sensation almost has me letting go of my string, but then I remember the smirk on Cyrus's face after he knew he'd beaten me.

And I squeeze the string tighter in my hand.

I allow the sensation of falling to embrace me, let it take me where it wants me to go. And in letting go, my string wraps around my waist and gently lowers me to the ground. Right next to a brilliant green seed, the lavender Tears of Eleos elixir running down the sides of its hard shell. And in the center, the smallest of violet branches peeks out, a tiny leaf rolling open as I watch it reach for the moonlight.

It's so beautiful, I reflexively squeeze my green string in excitement, and the tiny violet branch grows even more, two more leaves bursting to life out of its narrow stem.

It's such a strange sensation, but I know now this is what the Bloodletter was referring to. This is my demigod magic, my chaos birthright, and it is beautiful. And fierce. And powerful.

And with a deep, steadying breath, I surrender to the promise of everything it should have become, that *I* should have become, had this side of me not been hidden away.

As electricity begins to zap along my skin, I spread my arms out wide, giving the power free rein to take all of me.

And that's when the leaf becomes a twig.

The twig becomes a branch.

And the branch becomes…everything.

Life exploding within me, following the curves and lines—the muscles and veins—of my body.

Twigs and branches scraping along the inside of my skin.

Leaves and flowers—so many glorious flowers—tickling the edges of my arteries as everything inside me blossoms.

As everything inside me becomes what it was always meant to be.

Underneath me, I feel the earth pulse with energy. With stories. With life. I tap into all of it, wrapping it around me. Pulling it inside me. Absorbing it into my every pore. Inhaling it with my every breath.

And sending power—so much unimaginable power—back out onto the land. Giving back to it what it so generously shares with me as I continue to bloom and bloom and bloom.

The first thing I do as the power grows inside me is to grab the dull blue string and send a blast of electricity racing down it to my mate. The magic was gone but the connection was so strong, it could withstand anything—and I breathe magic back into our bond.

I'm so connected now to Hudson, to the land, to the whole world around me that I actually feel it when it hits him. Feel his body arch and tremble. Feel the power soaking into every part of him.

I wait for him to absorb it, for it to sink into his shrinking, dying cells. And then I send some more. Filling him up. Using everything I have to save the man who has saved me so very many times before.

My mate.

My Hudson.

Love explodes through me at the thought, pours out over everything around me.

Love for Hudson, the strongest, kindest—and let's face it—the most sarcastic mate I could ever dream up.

And love for my friends, who are, even now, struggling to find a way up and through this nightmare that we have found ourselves in. Jaxon, Macy, Eden, Remy, Flint, Dawud, Mekhi. All these people who have come to mean everything to me in such a short time.

I send energy to all of them, grabbing their strings and sending pulses of electricity down every single one.

It doesn't deplete me like it used to, doesn't make me weak at all. In fact, the more energy I share, the stronger and more powerful I become.

I'd been sagging against my restraints, but I let that energy, that power, push me to my feet. God or vampire king, I will not kneel before a monster—a madman—for one moment longer. Not when who I am and who I have always been destined to become are finally merging into one.

I am the demigod of chaos.

I am a child of Mother Earth.

I am the gargoyle queen.

Bearer of the Crown.

Mated to a vampire.

And through it all—Grace. Always, always Grace.

And so I get up, one more time, to face the man who would take everything from me if I let him.

I get up for my mother, who never knew her own power and who died so that I could know mine.

I get up for my grandmother, who never knew who she was or what she had inside her.

I get up for my great-grandmother. For my great-great-grandmother. For ten generations of women before me, who had their power silenced. Who hid their very existence in order to survive. Who bound their power in order to placate someone else who was afraid of what they had inside them.

I am not afraid. And I will not hide anymore.

167

You're So Vine

I open my eyes now, ready to face Cyrus.

All around me, people are staring in shock at me. Cyrus. His guards. My friends. Even the cheering horde has quieted as they, too, see what I have created. My gaze bounces around the stone pillars, and I smile.

Everywhere I look, vines curve and twist and wrap around the sarsen stones. They grow through the metal lock, around and around until they pull the lock apart and my friends are free. And still the vines continue to grow, twisting around the metal plates on the stones until every single piece of evidence of what happened here is gone. And on the ends of the leafy green stems, thousands and thousands of violet flowers bloom.

Only Hudson seems unsurprised, and when our eyes meet, it's as if he's saying, *It's about time.* Like he knew all this was inside me even when I couldn't understand it. Or when I wouldn't accept it.

"Very—" Cyrus's voice breaks, so he clears his throat and tries again. "Very nice, Grace. Maybe this little show of power would be more effective if you weren't still strapped to that machine."

"Which machine?" I ask as I reach down and unlock my restraints like they're nothing more than a child's toy. "This one?"

The ground is alive with green vines, grass, moss, and a bunch of other things as trees sprout all around us. Flowers in shades of yellow and red and purple and yes, even hot pink, burst into life in front of me.

It's a beautiful sight, and I can feel the life, the power of it all calling to me as I cross to this fake vampire god. I don't stop until I'm right in front of him.

"You think a bunch of flowers make you powerful?" he sneers even as he grinds a perfect yellow bulb beneath his heel. "This is child's play, nothing more than a walk in the park. It's nothing compared to what I can do."

I lift a brow. "Oh yeah? And what is that exactly?"

And with that, he lashes out, slamming his hand into my chest as I reach for my platinum string and shoving me backward toward the sarsen stones so hard, it feels like he's cracked one of my ribs.

His face turns red, and he starts to step forward before freezing in his tracks. It's obvious he expected me to move back to let him through, to vacate the space he has no right to but wants to claim anyway. The only problem? I don't move. At all. Not for him. Not ever again.

He may be a god, but I've got more than a little power myself, and there is no way I am giving him an inch. Not when he's trying to take the whole damn world as the spoils in his war.

So instead of stepping backward, I step forward, right into his space. I don't shove him out of my way—partly because that's not my style and partly because he's waiting for any aggressive act on my part to blow the lid off this pressure cooker.

But I'm not backing down, either, and I'm not going away. He has to live with me and what his machinations have brought to life.

"I'm a god," he sneers. "I can do things you can't imagine."

"You're a fake god," I sneer back, even as I reach for my green demigod string again. But it's not there anymore—at least not the way it always has been. Instead, it's latched on to my gargoyle string, the two of them braided so tightly together that they can never be untangled. "Anything you can do, you've stolen from the universe. And I promise you, it won't take kindly to the theft."

His eyes flicker, and I can tell I'm getting to him. But then the vile posturing is back, as he looks down his nose at me and says, "Who are you to speak for the universe? Especially in reference to me?"

"I was *born* to be the demigod of chaos, you jackass, and I'm not the only demigod here."

I turn to Izzy, still standing on the platform with the others, and ask, "You want to help with this?"

She raises a brow, even as her eyes lock with her father's. "Does that mean we get to fuck his shit up?"

I laugh. "Baby, it means we get to fuck *all* the shit up."

168

Sometimes Lightning Strikes Twice

"I like the sound of that," Izzy says as she moves away from the pillar and walks over to me.

"Me too," I tell her, and it surprises me a little because it's true. There really must be more chaos in me than I thought.

Cyrus is scowling at his daughter now, but Izzy doesn't look away like she usually does. And she doesn't back down, either. Instead, she scowls right back, which only pisses him off more.

It's not just that we're refusing to bow and scrape to him—though I know that annoys him quite a bit. It's that we're doing it in front of all the people on the field. We're not afraid of him, at all. And we're not going to pretend we are. More, we're showing these people that they don't have to be afraid of him, either.

Something inside Cyrus must snap at our show of defiance, because once again, he reaches toward the sky like he plans on channeling the lightning again.

As if.

"You may have made yourself a false god," I tell him as I grab my newly braided string. "And you may be able to channel a few puny lightning bolts. But I *told* you that *I* am the demigod of chaos, and I *am* the lightning."

I move to hold Izzy's hand, then I, too, reach up for the sky. With every ounce of power I have inside me, I make a grab for the lightning.

And the entire sky explodes.

A thousand lightning strikes illuminate the fading red of the sky, then flash down to earth to strike the battlefield all around us.

People scream and run in all directions as the strikes hit the ground, creating more space between Cyrus and his followers and army, but I am nowhere close to done yet. I call down more lightning, and once again its electricity splits the sky wide open. This time, though, instead of dispersing it across the clearing, I pull it straight down into me.

It hits like an aftershock of the Big Bang, exploding through my every cell and making me vibrate with the power of the universe. Power Cyrus will never be able to even imagine, but that runs through Izzy's and my veins like quicksilver.

Once I have it all inside me, once I've used my own power to harness every last drop of it, I reach a hand out toward Cyrus. And slowly, carefully, inexorably begin to pull his ill-begotten god power out of him.

He screams, his face twisting in rage as he bellows for his troops to seize us. But for once, the Vampire Guard has absolutely no interest in following their king's orders. They are too busy gaping at me.

Good. Right now, I have more important things to do anyway.

I drop Izzy's hand and pivot to face my friends. Then, with one hand still reaching toward Cyrus and another reaching toward them, I pour every ounce of that stolen power back into them.

I sort it out first, finding each of their individual strands so I can give back what was taken from them.

They're so different that it's much easier than I expected it to be.

I find Hudson's formidable magic first, couched in his strength and intelligence.

Jaxon's is next, loaded with his power and his protectiveness.

Macy's is easy to sort out—it's all wrapped up in optimism and heart.

Mekhi comes fourth, his kindness and commitment to friends impossible not to recognize.

Dawud's clarity and trust are instantly recognizable as well, and as I funnel their power back, I realize they might just hide the heart of an alpha.

Eden's grit and kick-ass attitude cloak some serious abilities, and my fingertips feel like they're sizzling just a little as I send it all back to her.

Flint's joy and determination circle his fortuitous power, make a little bit of joy bloom inside me as I feed it back to him.

Remy's power is practically boundless and nearly impossible to hold, even cushioned as it is in his wisdom and sense of fun.

And Izzy...Izzy's power feels nearly limitless as it burns inside me.

I return all of it, every drop that was stolen from them. And then, begrudgingly, give what's left to Delilah. She may be a heinous person, but no one deserves to have their magic stolen from them against their will. No one.

Once everyone's magic is restored to what it was before Cyrus's little mad-scientist experiment, I take a deep breath and reach inside myself. Because the power of the lightning is still zinging around inside me, and I need to calm it down just a little so that I can do what still needs to be done.

Hoping to absorb it deep inside myself, I grab my green-and-platinum string one more time and start to funnel the power into it. As I do, warmth begins burning along the injured muscles of my back.

I gasp and wiggle my shoulders in an effort to figure out what is happening. But within seconds, the warmth has turned to a powerful heat—so powerful that I'm afraid it's going to burn me before it dissipates.

"Oh my God, Grace," Izzy gasps, her eyes wide as she stares at something right behind me.

I turn to look, and then I'm the one gasping in surprise.

"How is that possible?" I whisper, blood roaring in my ears.

"Your demigod and gargoyle have merged," Izzy says.

I know she's right. I can see it in my string, feel it deep inside me. The two very different parts of me finally coming together as one.

But never in my wildest dreams did it occur to me that in merging, my strings—my beautiful, braided, mixed-up strings—would find a way to give me back something that means so much to me. Somehow they have, though. Because attached to my left shoulder is a gorgeous, perfect, glowing bright green wing.

169

I Did It My Way

For a moment, I can do nothing but stare at my new wing in shock.

But then I shift, becoming fully gargoyle, just to see what happens. Just to see if the wing is real.

It is—or at least, it stays with me. But it doesn't look or feel like my other wing. No, this isn't a replacement wing, something to take the place of what I lost. This is something else entirely, and whatever it is, I will take it.

To prove to myself that I'm not dreaming in the middle of this nightmarish battlefield, I launch myself into the air. There's a part of me that expects to come crashing back down to earth, and I hold my breath, waiting to see. There must be a part of Hudson that feels the same way, though, because he fades to right underneath me, and I know it's so he can catch me if I fall.

But I don't fall. I fly. And nothing has ever felt so good.

I do a quick spin in the air, and no, the wing doesn't feel like my other wing, and it doesn't operate quite the same way, either. But I'm not earthbound anymore and that is more than good enough for me.

I dive back to the ground and flip at the last second to land next to Hudson, who is grinning at me wildly. I can't help it. I grin right back.

Cyrus, however, doesn't seem nearly as excited about the development. He freaks out, starts screaming at his troops to attack. Of course, without his god magic anymore, he's shrunken back down to his normal size, but I remind myself he was a formidable foe before he became a god. And now he is enraged.

I don't know how he wants his army to attack, considering all my friends are standing beside me now—and right next to him. The army seems confused as well.

But when Cyrus fades over to Hudson and tries to bite him, I decide enough is enough. I throw out an arm, and as I do, I use a whole lot of my power to call to the lightning again. But not just the lightning this time. I pull in the chaos of a storm. Thunderclouds roll in as well as a giant wall of wind rushing between

Cyrus and my mate.

Cyrus runs headlong into the gale of wind, and it knocks him back several steps. He tries again, using every ounce of his vampire strength, but it's not enough to beat a pissed-off demigod. Not even close.

To make sure I don't have to worry about him for a while, I swirl my hand in the air, and the wind turns into a cyclone, spinning around him fast enough to make it impossible for him to escape. And then, with a flick of my finger, I send the wind under his armor. I throw my hand out, and his armor snaps free of his body and lands just outside the wind vortex.

Once he no longer has protection from my mate's gift, from all of my friends' indomitable gifts, I drop the storm entirely.

"Move, and I will liquify your bones again," Hudson growls. "That was fun, wasn't it, asshole?"

Cyrus freezes, but that doesn't stop him from yelling to his troops, "Seize them!" For the first time in a while, they actually seem ready to listen to him, too.

The Vampire Guard starts to move toward Hudson, Izzy, and me, but before they can get to us, my other friends join the party. Suddenly, it's all ten of us squaring off against them and, for the first time all night, I like the odds. At least until I remember my friends have just been through an awful lot. And judging by the way Mekhi is swaying on his feet, they aren't fully recovered from it all.

I reach inside myself for Mekhi's beautiful yellow string and send him healing energy. I can see he feels it when he turns to me to toss out a half smile, but the minute I stop sending him energy, he starts to list again.

Nothing I've done so far today seems to have worked against his bugbite, and now that I've embraced my full demigodhood, well, if it's still not making a dent—we need to get him to a healer fast. I turn to tell Remy to open a portal for Mekhi, but Mekhi must get the sense of what I'm about to request and gives his head a hard shake.

A slow smile lifts one corner of his mouth and he says, "I think we all deserve the right to watch you hand Cyrus his ass, Grace. Don't let us down." Everyone starts fist-bumping, and he adds, "What's fighting a few thousand soldiers to see your final takedown?"

Everyone joins in with more smack talk, like we've got all day while Cyrus's army rushes toward us. My gaze holds Mekhi's as I give him a quick nod. He's right. If he wants to stay to see this through, he has the right to choose. If he seemed like he was going to fall over right now, I'd step in. But as long as he's still on his feet, I have to respect his wishes.

Besides, if I'm being honest, it's not like we don't need him. We only have nearly ten thousand trained soldiers about to reach us and, I don't know if it's that I'm not used to this demigod power or not, but my head is positively throbbing.

There's a steady *thump-thump-thump* pounding against my temples, and it's only getting louder. It's almost so loud now that I can't think past it.

It's filling up my ears, beating in my chest, pounding in my blood.

Even worse, as the sound gets faster, so does the feeling inside me. Now it's not just a drumbeat—it's the wild vibration of a hummingbird's wings. My whole body responds to it, my own wings and heart and soul vibrating at the same frequency.

When I can't take it anymore, I yell to Hudson to be heard over the noise. "Do you hear that?"

"Hear what?" he asks, looking around in confusion.

Which only freaks me out more...until I see them.

Giant wings rising up over the mountain behind the field. Thousands and thousands of gargoyles, huge swords and shields tight against their bodies as they head straight for us. And all around the meadow, portals open every few feet, on the ground and up in the sky. So many portals that I can barely see the trees or sky anymore. One after another, ripping open the sky as thousands upon thousands of gargoyles pour out.

I swallow a lump the size of Katmere in my throat, my chest squeezing impossibly tight, and I reach for Hudson's hand. His warm fingers curl around mine, and he gives my hand a squeeze, before dropping it and urging me in front of him.

Then he leans close and whispers in my ear, "Your Army has arrived, my queen."

170

Girlboss

For a second, I'm too stunned to move. Too stunned to do anything but stand there with my mouth open and watch as gargoyles of all shapes and sizes race over the battlefield.

They came. They really came.

My knees go weak and tears bloom in my eyes, but I blink them back. Now isn't the time for relief. It isn't the time for sentiment. It's the time for action.

How can it not be when the air above the battlefield is filled with gargoyles flying in formation? As they come closer, I move to get a better view of the front fliers, as I search for—There he is! Chastain himself leading the Army through the air and straight toward me.

They're flying fast, faster than I ever saw in training, and they're spreading out over the battlefield like a true force to be reckoned with.

It's awe-inspiring and terrifying at the same time, and I've never seen anything like it, even in movies.

They don't pause until they get to the edge of the battlefield, right before they make it to where we're standing in front of the stone circle. Only then does Chastain break off from the Army and head straight for me.

I expect the other gargoyles to land, but instead they stay exactly where they are, hovering above the battlefield like aircraft on a seek-and-destroy mission. While none of them makes a move against Cyrus's troops, it's impossible to miss the threat. And the fact that no matter how good the Vampire Guard is, this Army just might be able to eat them alive—pun absolutely intended.

Chastain drops down to the ground in front of me and takes a knee, his head bowed in a traditional pose of respect.

Shock tears through me. I'm already astonished that the Army is here, but to see Chastain behave in such a way to me? It's beginning to feel an awful lot like I tumbled into an alternate universe.

"My queen," he says, reaching for my ring, which he kisses.

"General." I incline my head to him.

There are a million questions I want to ask him, starting with why is he here when he told me just this morning that he would never serve me. But now isn't the time for questions, not with Cyrus screaming for his troops to attack my army.

And they are my army, every single troop my responsibility.

"I need my orders," Chastain says.

"Your first order is to stand back up," I tell him. And then I look over his shoulder where Cyrus's dragons have begun launching themselves into the air, racing toward the gargoyles.

It turns out I was right all along. My friends and I have just shown them that Cyrus is a total fraud, and yet they still follow him. They still fight for him. More, they are still willing to die for a man who cares about nothing but his own power.

So be it. Cyrus's reign needs to end tonight, and we are the army to end it.

"Your orders are to take that army. This fight is over, as is their leader. It is time they understand that."

My words only seem to galvanize Cyrus, though, who starts screaming even louder for his troops to "kill every last gargoyle on the field."

"I will disperse the troops," Chastain tells me, after sending Cyrus a particularly unimpressed look. "But I will leave a contingent here to protect you."

"That's not necessary," I tell him.

"It is our job to protect our queen. It has always been our job."

"Yes, but your queen can protect herself. And I don't want a single one of my people to get hurt protecting me. I will never ask you to fight a battle that I can fight myself."

"As you will it, my liege." Chastain bows once more, then returns to the Army.

We have our orders, he tells them as he takes to the air. *Tonight, we will vanquish the enemy.*

171

All Guts, No Glory

Ilearned when I was training with them that the Gargoyle Army takes nothing as seriously as they do their duty. Today, on this battlefield, I realize exactly what that means.

Because this army—my army—is brutal when they are unleashed.

Chastain takes some of his best sharpshooters and cuts a swath straight down the middle of the battlefield, immediately dividing the enemy into two smaller sections. In the meantime, Rodrigo takes a regiment of a thousand soldiers all the way to the left of the clearing while Artelya leads a regiment all the way to the right.

As soon as I see it, I understand exactly what they're doing. It's a standard pincer move, where Rodrigo crowds from one side and Artelya does the same from the other. Chastain, and his flyers and sharpshooters, will work down the middle so there is nowhere for these people to run.

The only possible escape is surrender.

And still Cyrus sends his troops into battle. Still, he screams for them to, "Attack, attack, attack!"

It's sickening. Then again, this entire battle has been horrific from beginning to end.

My friends and I move back onto the raised platform, forcing Cyrus to go with us, so that we don't get in the way of the Army. There's also a part of me that hopes if his troops can't hear Cyrus shout orders, they might finally give up. Hudson is right beside me on the left and Jaxon is on my right as we watch the Gargoyle Army get to work.

It's one of the most brutal things I've ever seen.

I know war is brutal. I've fought in enough battles—had enough people I love die horribly—to know that much. But this, this is something else entirely. This is a well-oiled war machine at work, honed by two thousand years of battles and nonstop training.

This is more than two thousand soldiers on the ground with broadswords taking down everything in their paths. It's wings flying off, heads actually rolling, limbs falling through the air in all directions.

This is one thousand soldiers in the air with arrows skewering anyone who attracts their attention. It's eyes being gouged from skulls, chests cracking open, entrails oozing onto the ground.

This is three thousand soldiers, laser-focused on vanquishing their enemy by any and all means necessary. It's a single-minded dedication to absolute destruction and nothing, nothing will survive.

As if to emphasize that fact, a red haze fills the air and, for a moment, the solar eclipse from earlier feels prophetic. Like the blood red of the sky and the moon was really just a preview of coming attractions. Of this moment when the skies rain blood and the battlefield flows with carnage.

It's slaughter, pure and simple, and I can't watch it any longer.

I know Cyrus's army is still fighting. I know they will follow him to their deaths. But this obsessive destruction is merciless, and it is wrong. More, it's not the kind of leader I want to be.

"I have to stop this," I whisper to myself as much as to my mate.

But Hudson hears me—of course he does—and answers, "Yes, we do." He sounds as disturbed as I feel.

I start to call the Army back, but that leaves them open to injury. If they pull back, if they try to leave, some of them might very well get hurt. And I can't have that, either, not when they are only doing what they have trained so long to do.

And so instead of that, I look inside myself. I'm not sure what I'm looking for, but I am certain I will know it when I see it.

I weave my fingers past the brilliant strings that usually attract my attention, past my mating-bond string, past the strings of my friends and parents, even past the gossamer strings of the Gargoyle Army. They are all important, all beautiful, but I know that there are more inside me. Know that what I want is out there.

And so I keep reaching, going deeper and deeper and deeper until I finally find them—a curtain of delicate threads in all different colors. An endless spool of life. And I know immediately what they are. The strings of every single person on this battlefield today.

Because war changes you.

And everyone who stepped on this field today made a connection with everyone else. The threads of our lives intertwined, and we changed one another forever. Friendship forged in a fire. Death carved in our souls. Jealousy. Anger. Support. Pain. Suffering. It's all there, shimmering in the thousands of multicolored strings.

I reach out and scoop every single string against my chest in a blink. And when I think I have every single string, I brush my hand against my green string—and freeze Cyrus and everyone in his army instantly.

172

Shoulda Put a Crown on It

It's the strangest thing in the world to see, an entire army frozen mid-swing, mid-spell, mid-some-other-destructive-thing. Just flat-out stopped in their tracks, like a volcano erupted and covered them in ash, and we're discovering them thousands of years later.

"What just happened?" Macy asks, staring at the battlefield wide-eyed.

Hudson whistles, low and long. "Got to hand it to you, babe. That's not the solution I was anticipating. But it's a good one."

"A very good one," Eden agrees. "Though I am curious what's going to happen when you unfreeze them."

"Nothing," I answer with a shrug. "Because we'll all be gone."

"A very good solution," Eden reiterates, even as the Gargoyle Army turns in circles on the field.

They look so confused, like they have no idea what could possibly have happened, despite having been frozen for a thousand years themselves. What's even funnier is they don't lower their weapons, like they're just waiting for everyone to leap back to life at any second.

I start to head toward Chastain, since he has the right to know what I did, but before I can take more than a couple of steps, Jikan appears.

And he. Is. Pissed. Like, really, really, really pissed.

"At least he wasn't on vacation this time," Flint comments.

"I'm not sure this is any better," Jaxon tells him.

And I have to agree with Jaxon. Because I'm pretty sure the only thing worse than interrupting a vacationing god is interrupting a sleeping one. And Jikan was very definitely asleep—at least if I take into account the way he's dressed.

He's got on light-blue pajamas with rubber duckies on them, yellow duck slippers with umbrella hats, and a tie-dye satin eye mask that is currently pushed up to his forehead. Add in the fact that his hair is sticking out in twenty different directions, and yeah. I definitely think I woke him up.

Whoops.

"What. Have. You. Done?" Jikan shouts in lieu of a greeting as he marches up to me, and I have to be honest, after the day I've had, I don't much care for it.

"Tone," I say, as though I'm scolding a child.

His eyebrows shoot up so fast that they knock his mask off, and his face goes rigid with rage. "What did you just say to me?"

"I said watch your tone," I answer with a roll of my eyes. "Today is not the day to yell at me for things I cannot control."

At this point, Jikan's grinding his molars so hard, it's pretty much a miracle that he hasn't broken one. Speaking of which, is it wrong that I'm praying for his teeth to hold up—if he's this mad now, I can't imagine what he'd be like with a toothache, especially one he is sure to attribute to me.

But to his credit, he takes a deep breath, blows it out slowly. And his tone is much more civil when he asks, "What do I have to do to make you stop messing with time?" like he genuinely wants to know the answer.

I'm pretty sure it's an act, but I decide to give him an honest answer anyway. "There's nothing you can do."

He blinks. "Excuse me? Nothing? I could send you to the Caribbean for twenty years to teach you a lesson. See how you like that."

"Dude," says Flint. "Not exactly a punishment."

Jikan's now-frigid gaze flashes toward the dragon. "Did I ask you?" he demands.

Flint doesn't answer, but he does duck behind Jaxon for protection. The coward.

"I could choose somewhere else." Jikan lifts a brow. "Antarctica, maybe?"

"Not my top choice," I tell him. "But well within your rights when I actually break some universal law or do something else wrong. But I haven't, so…"

"I'm here, aren't I?" He shakes his head, arms wide in the universal gesture for *what the everloving fuck*. "That basically means you did something wrong. I'm not in the habit of just showing up for no reason."

"Oh yeah?" I demand, because two can play at his game. "What did I do exactly?"

"You—you—" he sputters. But he never says anything else—because he *doesn't have an answer.*

"What I did was freeze everyone in this clearing who was fighting us." I wave a hand toward the field as if he needs me to point that out to him. "But then, I control the arrow of time, and that's my prerogative, is it not? When I mess with the timeline, though, I'll be sure and keep an eye out for that Caribbean island."

Jikan sputters again, practically tripping over his tongue as he tries to figure out how to answer me.

I'm pretty sure the old guy wants to tell me that I don't know my place or something, but that's the thing. I *do* know my place now. And I'm tired of worrying what other people think of me or letting them tell me what my boundaries should be.

I've lived by the rules my entire life. It's time I started making my own damn rules. And I'm going to start right here, right now.

"I'm the demigod of chaos, Jikan. I know exactly what I can and can't do, and right now, I need to teach this evil bastard"—I gesture to Cyrus's frozen body—"a lesson that takes him down a notch or twelve. Now, if you like, you are welcome to stay and watch what I do to someone who pisses me off. Otherwise, I lost someone—a lot of someones—very dear to me this week, and I'm really over people telling me how I'm supposed to live.

"However, if you do want to stick around and watch…" I point toward an area off to my left that currently only has about a dozen frozen vamps in it. "That's probably a good spot."

Without waiting to see what his response is, or even if he stays, I turn back to Cyrus—and my friends, all of whom are gaping at me open-mouthed.

"What now?" I ask, but they all just shake their heads.

In the meantime, Chastain has finally figured out what's going on, and he and Artelya are leading the Army straight toward us. Chastain is holding the left side of his chest, and I fear he took a pretty serious blow in the last skirmish.

"I see you've inherited your grandmother's gifts," Chastain drawls, but I can't tell if he's impressed or just stating a fact. "I assume you have a plan, Grace?"

"A plan might be overstating it," I tell him with a roll of my eyes. But I'm just joking and I'm pretty sure he knows it. "I need you to get the Army in position."

Chastain holds my gaze for several seconds, like he's trying to gauge if he wants to follow my orders or not. Which annoys me all over again.

"I'll unfreeze him and give him ten seconds to do his worst, if you prefer?" I ask, one eyebrow going up.

"You mistook my silence for judgment, my queen," Chastain answers, bowing low. "I was merely considering which angle would give me the best view of his face when he realizes what's happening to him."

"That's a really good question." I give him a half smile and gesture to the left where I sent Jikan—who actually took my suggestion and pulled up a chair out of thin air. He is currently scooping handfuls of popcorn and watching the show like we're the most interesting thing he's seen in a while. "However, perhaps you would like to give Artelya this honor instead while you keep our guest company?"

I'm not trying to take this away from him, but if he's badly injured, participating in what comes next is the last thing he needs.

He must know I'm giving him an injury out, too, because after one surprised second, he nods. Then says, "Artelya, are you ready to lead the Army today?"

Artelya nods, bowing to him before she turns back to the Army and barks out, "Fliers, circle formation," in the most commanding voice I've ever heard from her—or anyone.

The elite fliers—including Artelya and Rodrigo—move forward and form a circle around Cyrus, my friends, and me. In the meantime, all the other gargoyles form a larger double circle around us, encompassing all of Stonehenge Lite and beyond.

As they do, they line up perfectly so that only their wing tips touch. And as the last gargoyle closes formation—as the last wing tips touch—a powerful burst of electricity winds through the circles.

I can feel it as it whips through every single gargoyle on the field, and the overwhelming energy of it is incredible, all-consuming. Even before it arcs up over the inner circle and powers straight into me.

As the Army's wings touch, the Crown on my hand that has already been burning for hours suddenly feels like it has caught fire. And just like that, I know what I need to do.

Once my Army is in position, I sift through the strings in my embrace. There's one much larger than the other ones and dripping in gold. *Cyrus.* I release his string.

And that's when he realizes he has been played.

And he is *furious.*

173

I'll Take
the Check Mate

I walk toward Cyrus, who is suddenly turning around himself, trying desperately to find a way out of the circle of gargoyles. But the truth is, there is no way out. Everything that's happened, everything that he's done and everything that I've done—that *we've* done—has brought us here, to this moment.

I am calm in the face of Cyrus's panic and stoic in the face of his rage.

"You think you can beat me?" he snarls even as he retreats. "The world doesn't exist where some little slip of a girl can beat me."

"That's always been your problem," I tell him as I follow him, closing the gap between us as the room for him to flee runs out. "You see things how you think they should be, not how they really are."

I pause for a moment to look around the circles at all the gargoyles who answered the call and came to help. Then I look at my friends, bruised and battered, and I have never felt more proud in my life. Of all of us.

"Because the truth is, we've already won. We beat you. The fact that you don't know that yet only makes you look more pathetic." And then I reach out and place my hand on Cyrus's hand.

He tries to jerk away, but the second my palm touches him, he can't move. He can't speak. He can't do anything but stand there as I judge him.

"Cyrus Vega, you sought war when you should have fought for peace. You harmed those you should have kept safe. And you destroyed lives you could have lifted up. For your very many crimes, you will forfeit your power." My voice is steady.

And then I take a deep breath, and I pull every ounce of power from him.

I watch—we all watch—as before our eyes, he shrinks and shrinks and shrinks, in stature more than height. There's a moment in the middle when I start to pull away. I'd already drained everything his Descent gave him, already took back his eternal bite, too. I can step aside and let the Army have him. He won't last five minutes with them.

But a swift death isn't real justice for him or us—nor is killing ever justified. But a swift death would never be justice for Calder, for the thousand years my Army stayed frozen in time, for the thousands of gargoyles who died in the frozen Court.

It's not justice for the years of torment that Hudson and Jaxon and Izzy have lived through.

It's not justice for the so very many deaths he's caused.

It's not justice for Macy's mom or for Macy and Uncle Finn.

And it would never, ever be justice for everything he's done and all the pain he's caused to get us all to this point right here.

But I know what *would* be justice worthy of the pain Cyrus has caused.

So I don't lift my hand until every ounce of power inside him is gone, and he is nothing more than the thing that he has spent centuries whipping his followers into a hate-filled frenzy against.

Totally, completely, and utterly *human*—for one thousand years.

Because I left his immortality.

174

All Queened Up

It's over.
It's really over.

That's all I can think as relief sweeps through me and my shoulders slump, the weight of this entire world rolling off me for one blessed moment, as I walk along the battlefield and survey caring for the wounded and dead.

I know there's more to do and there's definitely more to deal with, but the worst is finally over, and I've never been more ready for anything in my life.

I take a deep breath, count to five, and then blow it out slowly as my stomach pitches and rolls with a seething combination of emotions. There's no joy in the mix—not yet, and maybe not ever. It's hard to stand here surrounded by this battlefield filled with the dead and feel anything resembling joy.

Solace, yes. Gratitude, absolutely. But joy, no. Not when the sadness twisting my insides is nearly overwhelming. Sadness at all the waste, at all the hurts that can't be undone, no matter what has happened here.

Artelya steps forward, breaking formation to come stand beside me.

She looks down at me from her formidable height and says, "You made a wise choice." Respect is evident in her tone at how I handled Cyrus as well as the battle, but I don't want to be respected for the carnage I see before me.

I stare at the field and murmur, "I can't help but think the minute we stepped onto the battlefield, we'd already lost, whether we left victorious or not, Artelya."

The warrior doesn't say anything at first, but then she faces me and bows deep. "It will be my greatest honor to serve you, my queen."

Like Chastain earlier, the fact that she just called me "queen" for the first time doesn't elude me.

One gargoyle down and… The sad truth is I don't actually know how many gargoyles remain, nor how many we lost today. The thought hits like a punch to my chest, has my heart hurting all over again.

"How many did we lose?" I ask, and everything inside me is trembling as I wait for her answer, though I strive to keep my voice steady. I don't know much about being a queen, but I know that I can't shy away from the tough questions—no matter how hard they are.

"We lost twenty-seven, though more have injuries."

Twenty-seven. It takes everything in me not to let my shoulders slump. It's too many. *Way* too many when you consider I'm the one who sent them into that battle.

I'm the one who put their lives at risk—and ultimately am the one responsible for the fact that those lives are now over. The weight of it all sits heavy.

"Do I—" I stop myself before I can ask if I knew any of them. I'm their queen. Each of them is my responsibility, and each one of them matters to me. "Can you please get me their next-of-kin information?" I ask after clearing my throat. "I'd like to give my condolences to their families."

"Of course," Artelya answers.

"We need to clear the battlefield," I say after a second. "Not just of our dead but of any who fought on our side."

"Of course." Artelya nods, her face solemn. "We've been looking for wounded, but we will start clearing the dead as well."

"Thank you." I look out over the field and realize that with Cyrus defeated, there is no one to clear *their* dead, either. Not when everyone alive has either fled or been taken prisoner—something else I need to deal with and feel totally ill-equipped for.

But thankfully, Artelya is already three steps ahead of me. "We will have the witches and wolves take care of their dead—on either side. And I'll speak to your mate regarding the others."

"That's a good idea," I agree. I hadn't even considered with Cyrus and Delilah no longer vampire king and queen, Hudson would be next in line. Of course, Izzy is technically the firstborn, if a bastard. I make a mental note to ask Hudson later about the protocol there.

Artelya says she must go oversee the clearing of the field, and then she turns and walks away.

I watch her go for one second, two, as I steel myself for everything I still have to do. Then I take a deep breath and look down at the tattoo that appeared on my arm after Cyrus was dealt with, and I know there's one last thing I have to deal with.

The Bloodletter.

175

"The End" Game

"**S**eriously?" Flint demands the second he exits Remy's portal and realizes where we are. "I thought we were done with this place forever?"

"We will be. I just have one more thing to do." I turn to Jaxon and Hudson. "Can you undo the safeguards for us?"

Jaxon laughs. "Yeah, I think I can manage that. Although—" He glances at his father and Delilah, who Chastain currently has chained up with a three-guard escort. "I'm still not sure why you decided to bring them along."

"Because I have a plan," I tell him. "So you're just going to have to trust me."

"I trust you," Hudson whispers in my ear.

I roll my eyes. "You're just trying to get some action."

"I'm always trying to get some action." He wraps an arm around my waist and pulls me close. And for a second, I let him. In fact, I lean into him, savoring the feel of him against me now that we both made it out alive from the worst battle of our lives.

"Where are we?" Chastain asks as we start down the icy trail that leads to the Bloodletter's Cave.

"I thought you might like to visit an old friend," I answer. At least I hope he's here. I can't imagine a world in which these two haven't found each other again, honestly.

We wind deeper and deeper into the cave, and I brace myself for my least favorite spot. But when we get to where the Bloodletter usually has her snacks hanging, the whole area is empty. Even the draining hooks and buckets are gone.

"What's up with that?" Flint asks, and Eden fist-bumps him. "I mean, not that I'm complaining."

"You'll see," I answer. And sure enough, as soon as we make the final turn, I realize that my intuition was right.

The Bloodletter is no longer alone in her icy prison. In fact, she's really, really not alone.

"Oh my God, my eyes!" Jaxon snarls, stumbling back as soon as we walk into her sitting room—which is a really pretty green this time.

Not that I—or anyone else, for that matter—am paying attention to her decor. How can we when the Bloodletter is currently feeding from Alistair's neck on her very pretty floral couch?

She pulls away with a start, and it's definitely the first time she didn't know we were here before we showed our faces. Then again, she was a little busy.

"What are you doing here?" she demands in an ugly tone. But it's not directed at us—it's directed at Cyrus, who is currently shrinking back as far away from her as his gargoyle guard will let him. Which really isn't very far at all.

"I've got a present for you," I tell her, as Hudson and I walk toward her.

"Is it him?" she asks, still eyeing Cyrus evilly. "Because that's a gift I can get behind."

"Not quite," I tell her, "but I think you'll like this one just as much. Your mate asked me to give it to you."

And then I reach out and touch her hand, passing the Crown from my palm to hers.

She gasps as the Crown emblazons itself onto her skin, then looks between Alistair and me with tears trickling down her cheeks.

To be honest, it's a little disconcerting to see the Bloodletter crying. She's such a badass, I didn't even know it was possible. But I guess freedom and her mate back after a thousand years will do that to a girl.

I think about what it would be like if I couldn't see Hudson for a thousand years, then banish the thought as quickly as it comes. It's too awful to entertain even for a second.

He must feel the same way, because his hand reaches out to take mine and he whispers, "I'm not going anywhere."

"Good, because now I have an army to track you down."

"Excuse me," the Bloodletter says as she reaches for her mate's hand. "I think we have somewhere to be."

"Where's that?" Macy asks curiously.

"Anywhere but here?" she answers, looking around what's about to be her former ice cave with distaste.

"A thousand years will do that to a person," Flint agrees.

"A thousand years will do a lot of things to a person," Hudson snarks. "Very little of it good."

"I can still smite you," the Bloodletter comments, but there's no heat behind the threat. Apparently, freedom has mellowed her… Or maybe it's being reunited with her mate that's done it. Either way, she seems happier than she ever has been before, and that can only be good for Hudson—and the rest of us.

"Not to interrupt your reunion tour," Delilah interjects, wiggling her fingers in the most condescending manner possible. "But I'm not sure what this little trip down memory lane has to do with the favor you owe me, Grace."

"Don't you?" I ask. "And here I thought the symmetry was obvious."

"It is," Jaxon interjects, and he sounds impressed with just how diabolical my plan is. "And it's perfect."

"What's perfect?" Flint asks, still looking confused.

I start to answer him, but before I can, Jaxon wraps an arm around his waist and leans in to whisper the answer in his ear. Which has the rest of us exchanging interested looks, especially since Flint sinks into him instead of pulling away.

There's very definitely a story there, and I plan on getting it—as soon as I'm done with this last, unpleasant task.

I turn to the Bloodletter. "I have a suspicion I know why Alistair made me promise to give you the Crown. Care to share?"

The Bloodletter is running her fingers along the edges of the tattoo, like she can't believe it's really on her hand finally. "When I froze the Gargoyle Army and hid the God Stone with them, I knew if Cyrus ever got a hold of me, eventually he could break me and release them." Tears well in her eyes as she turns to hold Alistair's gaze. "I could not let the Army fall while my mate was missing. Not on his honor. I didn't know where Cyrus had hidden him, and I had to make a quick decision. So I created this prison with my power—its strength the bounds of my soul. Therefore, I can never leave unless I suddenly have more power than is in my soul. There are only a few objects that can make a soul's power grow"—she looks down at the Crown again—"and this is one of them."

"You trapped yourself to protect the Army?" Flint asks, clearly not sure he heard correctly. I mean, we sort of knew this or guessed, but not in this detail.

"I would do anything for my mate," she says softly, and my gaze seeks out Hudson's.

"Of course," she continues, "keeping my sister imprisoned as well so she could stop harming our kind was just a nice added benefit."

"Good for you." Delilah looks unimpressed as she turns to me. "But how exactly does that live up to your promise to let me make him suffer?"

"Because you're going to be locked up with him, of course," I say. "Justice needs to be served—for the crimes both of you committed. And I don't believe *either* of your souls will ever be as powerful as my *grand-mère's*. However," I continue as she looks like she's about to protest. "There's a definite perk in your being locked up with him for a thousand years."

"And what is that?" she asks warily.

"He was still connected to the Gargoyle Army when I drank the elixir and cured their poisoning, which means he is immortal. And I did not strip him of that immortality. But he *is* only human now. Which means—"

"I know what it means," Delilah says, her eyes gleaming with avarice.

She's across the room in a second, her fangs sinking deep into Cyrus's neck before his guard can even undo his restraints.

"And on that note," Hudson says, "I think our work here is done."

"You can say that again," Macy comments as she watches Delilah's feeding frenzy with horrified fascination.

The Bloodletter snaps her fingers, and seconds later we're standing outside the cave in the early-morning sunlight—well, all of us except the Bloodletter herself, who insisted on walking out of the cave under her own volition.

A few seconds later, she, Alistair, and Chastain exit the ice cave together.

Alistair sees me and grins before turning to his old best friend. "I think that's our cue to take a walk," he tells him.

"You don't have to—" I start.

"It's all right, granddaughter," Alistair answers with a wink. "I've spent a thousand years missing the sunlight. I think it's time I catch up."

"You did well," the Bloodletter tells me after Alistair takes off across the summer meadow that has sprung up where usually there is only snow.

"I made a lot of mistakes."

"True," she agrees with a rueful tilt of her head. "But that's part of life. Being a demigod doesn't mean you're perfect. It just means that when you make a mistake, it's usually a big one."

"Well, doesn't that sound fabulous," I mutter.

"It's all about balance, Grace. It always has been."

"The good with the bad?" I ask.

She smiles. "Something like that."

"Is that why you did all this?"

"Did all what?"

"I know you're the one who planned out this whole chess game. Who put it all in motion."

"Me?" She shakes her head, but her eyes are sparkling with a joy I've never seen from her before. "I'm just an old woman, Grace. Besides, how can I be the mastermind when you're the one who ended up queen?"

She reaches out, quick as a lightning strike, and swipes her palm across mine. Seconds later, I feel the Crown emblazon itself back into my skin. Luckily, it's one of the tattoos I'm not so keen on getting rid of.

"Before you go…" I take a deep breath. "Are Izzy and I tied like you and the Crone? Meaning, if one of us dies, will the other die, too?"

"No, not in the same way. In fact, with the Crown, you're no longer tied at all." The Bloodletter smiles, and I can't help smiling back. Who knows. Maybe having the God of Chaos for a grandmother isn't as scary as that sounds.

She winks, then she takes a step back, snaps her fingers, and disappears.

"What now?" Eden asks. It's beginning to sink in that it's over. It's really over.

"Whatever we want," Macy answers, twirling around with her arms outstretched.

After everything that's led up to this moment, it's a shocking thought. And a welcome one.

"In case anyone's interested," I say with an apologetic glance at Hudson. "We do happen to have a lighthouse right on the ocean. It seems like the perfect place to relax and figure out what comes next."

Hudson gives me a *what the hell* look, and I shrug sheepishly. It doesn't quite seem time yet to go our separate ways. Not when we've come this far together.

"I'm very interested," Flint says, looking at Jaxon.

"Me too," Jaxon agrees.

"I'm in," Eden says with a grin. "I'll text Dawud and invite them and Amir."

"Me too!" Macy starts spinning a portal. "How about Remy? Should we text him an invite? And Mekhi?"

"I'll reach out, but Remy's with Calder's family right now," I answer quietly. "And Mekhi is getting looked at by the Vampire Court's healers."

"You're coming, too, right?" Hudson asks Izzy, and it's hard to tell which of them looks more uncomfortable with the invitation.

"I don't think so—" she starts, and I realize it's the first thing she's said since we left the battlefield. Still, I'm not having it. Hudson and Jaxon have spent their whole lives without their sister or each other. That stops now.

"You're coming," I tell her. "You don't have to stay the whole time, but you're definitely coming. Who else is going to help me keep Hudson and Jaxon in line?"

At first I think she's going to argue, but in the end she just shoves her hands in her pockets and shrugs. It's not a ringing endorsement, but it's progress, and I'll take it.

Apparently, so will the others, because Flint shoots her a wicked grin and says, "Race you to the ocean," right before he dives into Macy's portal.

Izzy squawks and jumps in after him, followed by Jaxon and Eden.

Hudson looks over at me with a huge grin and holds out his hand. I take it, of course I do, and we walk through the portal. Together.

Epilogue

It's fucking ridiculous what she does to me.

Right now, she's sitting under a tree with a cherry Pop-Tart in one hand and a bottle of water in the other, and I feel like a fucking debutante. I can barely catch my breath.

She's not doing anything special, not dressed any special way in her white shorts and turquoise tank top with her marine biology book open on her lap. But that doesn't matter because she's fucking perfect—or at least, perfect for me.

It's been a year since I met her.

Five months since she was crowned queen.

Three months since we moved to San Diego so she could get her undergrad degree in international politics and government to help her figure out how to be the best ruler she can be.

A gentle breeze blows by, whipping her glorious curls into her face, and she laughs a little as she pushes them away. As she does, she glances up, and our eyes meet across the quad.

She smiles then, a big, bold, brilliant smile that has my breath hitching in my chest even before she waves me over.

My mate, I think as I cross the grass to her. Grace Foster is my mate—which means she'll be taking my breath away every day for the rest of eternity.

I can't fucking wait.

"How was class?" she asks, leaning in for a quick kiss as I settle down on the ground beside her.

"A full-fledged argument broke out regarding differences between Chomsky, Chalmer, and Brandom's theories on language."

"Were any punches thrown?" she asks, brows lifted.

I laugh. "Not this time actually."

"So, all in all, a pretty mild day for graduate-level philosophy." She shoots me a wicked grin that makes me lean over and kiss her again—this time not so quickly.

"A very mild day," I agree when we finally come up for air. My heart is beating too fast, and I do my best to ignore the voice in the back of my head urging me to get her back to our town house—and, more specifically, *our bedroom*, ASAP.

"What are you working on?" I ask, glancing down at the book still in her lap.

She closes the book and shoves it into the hot-pink backpack she carries only because Macy gave it to her as a going-to-college present. "I've got a paper due in biology next week. Just trying to figure out what I want to write about."

"Biology, hmm?" I lean in for one more kiss. "I could probably help you with that."

"It's marine biology, not human anatomy," she answers with a roll of her eyes even as she leans forward and kisses me again.

But her phone buzzes a few seconds later, and she pulls back to check it. "Oh, wow!" she squeals after checking her messages. "The architect wants to set up a meeting! He's got preliminary plans ready for our new Gargoyle Court. Isn't that awesome?"

"Totally awesome," I agree. But it bothers me a little, her decision to move the Court here to San Diego because she knew I wanted to go to school here. I've let it go, waiting for a better time. But if the plans are ready, I'm pretty sure time has run out.

It's that thought that has me pulling away. "Are you sure you really want to do this?"

"Be gargoyle queen?" she asks, looking confused. "I'm pretty sure it's too late to change my mind. Also, considering you abdicated the vampire throne to join me as king." She pauses, her eyes going wide. "Why? Are you having second thoughts?"

"About you being queen? No. About moving the Court to San Diego. Maybe. I want to be sure you're not doing it just for me."

"Seriously? You're the only person I know who would worry about someone wanting to move permanently to San Diego." She throws her arms out in an effort to encompass the perfect seventy-five-degree day we're currently experiencing. "You do realize that most people consider this city paradise, right?"

"I do realize that, yes," I answer, and it's my turn to roll my eyes. "But I still want to make sure it's what you want. You are queen, after all, and your Court should be where you want it to be."

She sighs, leaning forward so that all those glorious curls fall into her face.

I reach forward, smoothing them back so I can see her eyes. This is important, and I need to be able to see what she's thinking.

"Well, soon-to-be-*Dr.* Vega, I'm pretty sure we both know you aren't going to be quitting school anytime soon. And since you're most interested in UCSD and UCLA, San Diego seems like a good fit for us."

That's exactly what I'm afraid of—that she's doing this for me and not for her. "Yes, but I don't want—"

She holds up a hand to stop me. "*And*, in case you haven't noticed, I love San Diego. It is my hometown, after all. Plus, after spending months in Alaska, I'm never going to take this weather for granted again. Besides, one of the best parts of having wings is that gargoyles can fly anywhere they want to be—so having the Court here doesn't limit any of us. Especially since you've got that daywalker ring from Remy." She blushes a little as she says it.

My fangs come down at the implication, my eyes lingering on the two tiny pinpricks at the base of her throat that I left there just this morning. Because, yes, I've made good use of the ring Remy gave me all those months ago. Very good use.

She sees where I'm looking and her blush deepens, even as her eyes turn a little hazy—a surefire sign that her mind is going the same place mine is. Lucky, lucky me.

"Want to head home?" I ask as casually as I can manage considering the thoughts currently racing through my head. Thoughts of touching, kissing, *tasting* Grace—

"Home?" She sounds confused, but the gleam in her eye tells me otherwise.

"Or we could take the boat out, cruise to Coronado for the afternoon."

As soon as I say the words, I like the sound of them. Grace spends so much time taking care of other people, but I'm the one who takes care of her. And after the tense meeting she had with the Circle last night where they were finalizing their secret delegation to the United Nations—Grace is making good on her promise to bring paranormals into the light—an afternoon cruising across the bay and then walking the little shops she loves so much sounds like a perfect fix.

The fact that our boat just happens to have a very comfortable stateroom— one that just happens to have a very comfortable bed—makes the idea even more appealing.

"Coronado?" She perks up at the mention of one of her favorite places in all of San Diego. "Can I get a cupcake from—"

"The little bakery you love?" I ask as I stand and then pull her to her feet.

"I was thinking more like a dozen cupcakes, with the little sprinkles on top."

She laughs. "And that's why I love you."

My whole freaking body lights up at the words. Grace loves me. She really loves me, even after everything I've done. Everything I put her through. It feels like a miracle, one I'll never take for granted.

I don't say anything back right away because I can't. Too many emotions—all of them good—are clogging my throat, making it hard to breathe, let alone talk. I feel like an arse, but I don't actually give a shite because I'm with Grace. And she loves me no matter how fucking sappy I get.

That doesn't keep her from rolling her eyes at the sappiness, though, even as she slips her dainty little hand into mine. "You're ridiculous. You know that, right?"

"You make me ridiculous," I answer, rubbing my thumb against her promise ring for good luck. "You have pretty much from the moment I laid eyes on you."

"So you say," she retorts. "But you still won't tell me what my ring means."

"What does that have to do with the fact that I'm crazy about you?" I ask as we start walking toward the university center. Grace has plans for lunch, and I know she hates to be late anywhere.

"I'm just saying, if you were really crazy about me, you would tell me what you promised me." She bats her eyes outrageously, but I just laugh at her even as I wonder how she'll react when I tell her the truth.

I know I owe her an explanation—it's been months since I slid that ring on her finger—but I can't help wondering how it will make her feel. There's a part of me that's still afraid she'll freak out at what I promised before I knew she would ever love me back, and that's the last thing I want now that things are finally good. Not just between us, but life in general.

It's never been like this for me—I've never had someone who loves me the way Grace does—and if she leaves…if she leaves, I don't know what the fuck I'll do.

But hiding it from her any longer doesn't work, either—unless my goal is to feel like a bloody coward.

"If you really want to know—" I start, but before I can finish, someone tugs on Grace's backpack from behind.

We both tense as memories of the last year flood through us. Bloody hell. I let my guard down for two minutes and—

"I'm early! Can you believe it?" Grace's best friend, Heather, says as she squeezes between us.

I order my rioting heart to calm the fuck down, can see that Grace is doing the same thing to hers.

"The shock is real," Grace deadpans.

Heather just snorts and shakes her head. Then tells me, "Nice fangs," before turning back to my mate. "My calculus class got out early, thank God. I swear, how many math problems can one woman be expected to do?"

"A question for the ages," I answer.

"Jeez, tough crowd." She bumps Grace's shoulder first, then mine. "I'm going to go back to being late."

"Maybe Hudson should buy you lunch—a little positive reinforcement never hurts," Grace tells her as I hold the door open for them both.

"I'll grab a table," I tell them, handing Grace my credit card as she and Heather head for the counter.

"I was just kidding," Grace starts, but I shake my head.

"Positive reinforcement's a thing," I tell her. "Besides, a deal's a deal."

Not that I need to make a deal to buy my mate and her friend lunch—I'd like nothing more than if Grace let me take care of all this kind of stuff for her. She's so strong, so sure of herself, that she doesn't let me do much to help her most days. Which is more than fine. I love her strength, love the power she continues to grow into.

But this I can do, and I have every intention of doing so.

Grace rolls her eyes, but she doesn't fight me over it. Instead, she loops an arm through Heather's and pulls her away. The last thing I hear her say as the cacophony of the university center rises up and swallows them is that they should get the biggest milkshakes in the place, on me.

I hope they do. I love making Grace smile, and as for Heather—I'll always be grateful to her for putting in an application to UCSD for Grace last November, when she was still grief-stricken and not thinking clearly. If she hadn't, we wouldn't be here right now, and here is a very good place to be.

Not to mention she's handled the whole vampire/gargoyle thing like a pro. She gets major points for that.

I snag a table near the windows and scroll through my phone as I wait for them to come back.

A text from Eden pops up, demanding to know where we are.

Me: Why? Need a tour of San Diego?

Eden: Maybe. But first I've got news

Me: Wait, you're here?

Eden: Keep up, vamp boy

Eden: Why else would I care where you were?

Me: Solid point

Me: We're in the UC

Eden: Gotcha

I have about two minutes to wonder what's up—she hasn't had a day off since she started at the academy—before she comes striding through the doors in her Dragon Guard in Training uniform.

She makes it to the table about the same time Grace and Heather do. And bloody hell. The look she gives Heather right before she grabs Grace in a bear hug is so scorching hot, it might burn the whole damn building down.

Especially since Heather returns the look with interest as she introduces herself.

Eden nods, gives her a very interested grin. But the grin fades the second she turns back to Grace and me. "We know how to reach the shadow queen—and how to get her to cure Mekhi."

"What? Seriously?" Grace grabs on to her arm. "Tell us everything."

Which she does, and it all sounds just bizarre enough to work. I start making plans to get out of class for the rest of the week, even before Eden concludes with, "So go pack. We need to swing by Galveston and spring Remy and Izzy from that shithole school. We're going to need them."

"I don't think Remy and Izzy are willing to be in the same room together, *still*. I don't know how their school is left standing, honestly," Grace says. "What about the others?"

"Already on board and waiting for you." She turns to me. "Speaking of which, Jaxon said to tell you that no self-respecting vampire actually settles down in one of the sunniest cities in the country. And that you're a real wanker for not inviting us onto that yacht of yours."

I lift a brow. "Oh really?"

"Okay, that last part was from me." She grins. "So how about it? We get the cure and pull Mekhi out of that fucking horrible Descent that's keeping that Shadow Curse from killing him—which I still can't believe the Bloodletter put him into—and celebrate with a cruise down to Mexico?"

"Only if I get to come," Heather says, twirling her hair around her finger as she bats her eyes at Eden.

"I'm counting on it," Eden responds.

"All right, then." Grace stands up and grabs her backpack. "Hudson and

I are going home to pack. Heather, why don't you buy Eden that milkshake while you wait?"

"Why don't I just?" Heather answers.

Grace and I don't wait around to see what comes next. But something tells me we're about to be seeing a whole lot more of Eden...

Now that we know where the shadow queen is, everything feels more urgent. So instead of our usual walk home, I fade with Grace back to our town house. But as we start to throw a few things into our backpacks—something that is far too familiar—Grace looks at me with a smile that somehow breaks my heart and puts it back together again at the same time.

And just like that, I realize there is no perfect moment to tell her about the ring. There is only this moment, and for once, I let myself believe that it's enough. That I'm enough.

Taking hold of her hand, I tug her close to me, then bring her hand to my lips. I kiss her palm first, then turn her hand over and kiss the ring I gave her all those months ago in the middle of a redwood forest.

Her eyes go wide. Her lips tremble. Her breath catches in her throat. And still, she doesn't ask. In fact, she doesn't say anything at all. She just waits and watches as eternity stretches between us.

"Years ago, I read an obscure poem by Bayard Taylor called 'Bedouin Love-Song' and, while I have forgotten most of the poem, a few lines at the end have stuck in my head for nearly a century. They're the lines that flashed through my mind the first time I saw you and the lines that continue to run through my head every time you smile at me," I say.

"Because, even then, my heart seemed to know that no matter what happened, whether you loved me or not—whether you chose me or not..." I pause, take a deep breath, then kiss her promise ring as I repeat what I promised her all those months ago.

"I will love you, Grace, till the sun grows cold and the stars are old," I murmur against her skin.

Grace lets out a startled cry as she stares at me with eyes that are suddenly filled with tears, shock coloring her features.

For a second, my stomach starts to sink—I was right. It was too much, too soon. But then she reaches up and cups my face in her trembling hands. And whispers, "I remember. Oh my God, Hudson. I remember *everything*."

But wait—there's more!

Read on for an exclusive look at two chapters from Hudson's point of view.

The end is just the beginning...

To Your
Heart's Malcontent
—Hudson—

"I thought you'd be sleeping." Jaxon's voice rings out behind me.

"I could say the same thing about you." It's not the most inviting answer, but I'm in a right foul mood at the moment. That's why I'm not in Grace's and my room. She has to get some sleep, which she will not do if I'm up there tossing and turning beside her.

And since the last thing I want is her worrying about me, I've set up camp in the living room of the lighthouse. I'd prefer to be outside, but the sun being up has pretty much nixed that idea. Well, the sun combined with my inability to keep my fangs out of Grace's various body parts.

I can't say that I'm sorry about the latter. How can I when everything about her feels like it was tailor-made for me—including her blood?

"You okay?" Jaxon asks, and the words sound awkward coming out of his mouth. Then again, when was the last time things *weren't* bloody awkward between us? We're a lot better than we used to be, but when life gets stressful, we tend to revert to old habits.

Or maybe it's just that neither of us is used to exposing our vulnerabilities— to each other or to anybody else.

"Shouldn't I be asking you that?" I turn around just enough to shoot a pointed look at his chest.

"It's all good," he answers with a cocky smirk on his face. But there's a flash in his eyes, something that makes me think whatever is going on with him isn't quite as fine as he's making it out to be. Or worse, that maybe *he's* not as fine.

And though there are a million things going on inside me, scores of thoughts chasing themselves around in my head as I try to figure out how to help Grace without losing myself to the darkness, I can't leave him alone with his misery.

Jaxon might be a wanker—and by *might be*, I mean *is*—but he's still my little brother, and I can't just ignore the way he's fronting, not when he's lost so much over the last few days—including one of the only people he's ever trusted or cared about in his life.

Of course, the fact that I feel guilty as bloody hell about Grace choosing me doesn't help the matter, either.

Not that I would change how things worked out—I wouldn't. Grace is mine. My mate, my heart, my very soul. And she always will be. I can never regret that, *will* never regret that she chose me.

But that doesn't mean I don't feel bad for Jaxon. I know what it's like to have Grace's love and then be forced to try to live without it. I could never get over Grace if I lost her, so if he needs time to come to grips with it, I totally understand.

Which is why I ask, "Are you sure everything's good?" as I turn around to face him.

Having a fucking heart-to-heart is the last thing I want to do right now, when the faces—the souls—of all those wolves I destroyed at Katmere are stalking me like prey, but for Jaxon I'll do it. I owe him that much.

"Yeah. I'm good." But he slumps on the couch, spinning a water bottle between his hands and tearing the wrapper off tiny piece by tiny piece.

"You hurting?" I ask.

His gaze shoots to mine, and once again there's just a flash of pain there before the bloody kid banishes it. "My heart's fine."

I don't know if he's referring to the fact that it's been a day since our father nearly ripped his heart out of his chest—and he got a dragon heart to replace it—or if he's talking about the more metaphysical part of his heart. The part that broke wide open when his and Grace's mating bond broke and nearly took his soul with it.

Instead of pushing for an answer that isn't a runaround, I settle for asking, "What's it feel like?"

"Nearly dying?" He lifts a brow.

I don't need him to tell me that—our dear, undeparted father made sure I understood that feeling before I saw five years of age. "Having a dragon heart."

There's a long ripping sound, and another piece of wrapper bites the dust. So maybe the tosser's not doing so bloody okay after all. Big fucking surprise.

"It's fine." Now he's rolling the bottle between his palms. "At least I'm alive. That's what matters, right?"

"If you're asking for confirmation..."

"Oh, fuck right off," he growls.

He sounds so British in that moment that he startles a laugh out of me.

Which just makes him more snarky.

"Are you laughing because I'm alive? Or because I almost died?"

I barely resist the urge to roll my eyes à la Grace. Always the drama with this kid. Always. "What do you think?"

"I think I'm a fucking mess, that's what I think." As soon as the words are out, he looks like he wants to take them back.

But I'm not about to let him. Not when it's the first real thing he's said to me today. "I think we're all fucking messes right now. It's been a rough few days."

I deliberately refuse to think about the moment the wolves went for Grace at Katmere and I ended them all in the blink of an eye. Refuse to think about who they were. If they had families or dreams or a mate waiting at home for them.

Jaxon snorts. "It's been a rough few months."

"I'm not going to deny that." I pause. "Getting murdered can be rough on a guy."

"Seriously?" He sits up, annoyance replacing the melancholy that had made me so uncomfortable earlier. "Are you still harping on that?"

"Harping on the fact that you tried to kill me?"

"Don't you mean *succeeded* in killing you?" He lifts a brow.

"Um, no. That's not what I mean at all. I let you think you killed me, but all you really did was put me back in that bloody fucking crypt for a year. Which is bad enough, you gormless prat."

"Seriously?" Jaxon searches my face. "Is *that* what happened?"

"Well, you didn't kill me, that's for sure." I smirk at him. "No matter how hard you tried."

"I didn't try that hard," he answers. "And if you hadn't gone around acting like a sociopath, I wouldn't have had to do it in the first place."

It's an old argument now, one we've gone round several times. But it hits differently today, after the wolves. Then again, everything hits differently after the wolves—and Flint's accusation that I let Luca die.

I try to hide my thoughts, but I must not be doing a good enough job because the sardonic grin slides off my brother's face. "I didn't mean it like that."

"I know you didn't." I force a grin I'm far from feeling.

"I would have done the same thing, you know. If I could have."

"No, you wouldn't. And that's a good thing—"

"Bullshit!" Jaxon explodes. "I was getting ready to bring the whole damn place down on our heads—"

"You did bring the whole place down on our heads," I remind him drily.

"You helped," he shoots back. "Plus, that's not what I meant and you know it."

I do know it, but yanking his chain about shite is too much fun to pass up. Especially since it deflects him from talking about me and what I'm feeling right now.

"I'm serious, Hudson. If I could—"

"I know what you're saying," I interrupt, because my brother's like a damn dog with a bone right now. Plus, ignoring it isn't getting the job done, so maybe acknowledging it will make him chill the fuck out.

"Do you?" he asks. "Because if I could do what you do, I would end anyone who went for Grace or F—" He breaks off abruptly, and everything inside me goes on red alert. Because this is a new fucking development, and a bloody interesting one at that.

"Or who?" I ask, brows raised. "Flint?"

But Jaxon just shakes his head, rubbing a hand up and down over the back of his hair. "I don't know."

"You don't know?" I query. "Or you don't want to know?"

"His mom gave me her fucking heart. She asked me to use it to protect him, and that's what I'm going to do, no matter what."

He's so frustrated, I'm a little surprised he hasn't brought the whole damn lighthouse down on top of us yet. Of course, I no sooner have the thought than the ground beneath us trembles just a little. He locks it down quick, though, and I pretend I didn't notice.

But I make sure to tread carefully when I ask, "I understand obligation. I understand doing something because you feel like it's your duty. But what you said earlier—when you were talking about Grace and Flint—it didn't sound like obligation. It sounded like something more."

Jaxon makes an annoyed sound deep in his throat, then lays his head back against the couch so that he's staring at the ceiling. "His boyfriend just died. His boyfriend who happened to be one of the best fucking friends I've ever had."

There's a lot rolled up in that sentence—a whole fucking lot. But I'm nothing if not persistent, so I say, "None of that actually tells me how you feel—"

"He was my best friend, okay? My best fucking friend. And I've destroyed his whole life. My brother killed his brother. Despite all my power, I couldn't save his boyfriend and I couldn't save his leg. And then I took his mother's heart—"

"She gave you her heart," I remind him.

He shrugs. "It's the same thing."

"It's not," I tell him again. "Not at all."

"Yeah, well, it sure feels like it. It feels like everything that's happened is my fault." He closes his eyes, swallows hard.

I know what he's saying. Because this whole mess feels like it's all my fault, too. I didn't kill Cyrus's forces on the island and all kinds of bad shite happened. I did kill the wolves at Katmere and even more bad shite happened. How can it *not* be my fault? Especially when I can feel broken pieces of them clawing away at me deep inside, burrowing straight through my defenses and into my soul.

"You know, everyone thinks it would be so great to be as powerful as we are," Jaxon says, and with his defenses down, he sounds as destroyed as I feel. "But sometimes it fucking sucks, man."

For me, there's no *sometimes* about it. It always fucking sucks to have these powers, which is why I keep thinking more and more about how I can get rid of them for good.

A sudden clomping outside the door has us both sitting up straighter.

"Who is that?" Jaxon asks, shooting to his feet. I can feel the fight in him, feel him getting ready to do whatever needs to be done.

But a quick glance out the window shows a delivery person walking back to his car, so I gesture for Jaxon to sit back down. "It's just breakfast for Grace and the others. I gave instructions to leave it on the porch so I can get it."

Jaxon shoots me a knowing look as he heads for the door anyway, to get the coffee and pastries I ordered from the fully closed-in porch. After collecting them, he puts a cup of coffee and a bag of food on the end table next to me before leaving the rest on the kitchen counter.

"I'll text the others, tell them to come get it."

"Thanks, I appreciate it."

He nods as I grab Grace's food and head for the stairs. But before I can do more than take a couple of steps, he asks, "Do you ever think about giving it all up?"

He doesn't have to say any more for me to know he's talking about our power. "Only every fucking day," I answer before continuing upstairs. "Only every fucking day."

"**A**re they skeletons?" Macy whispers, horror filling her voice. They don't look like skeletons. They look like something a whole lot fucking worse. I just don't know what that is yet.

Grace must think so, too, because she trembles beside me. I wrap an arm around her and pull her close as whatever the hell they are start climbing up the walls.

I've never seen anything like these things, all twisted, mismatched bones, splintered skulls, broken bodies. And if I have my way, I never will again.

They appear as if they might have been human once, but only if you look closely and ignore all the strange angles and missing parts. Plus the fact that they are totally and completely mindless, focused only on storming the castle, destroying whoever is in their path.

They're racing up the sides of the walls now, their bones making a sound I've never heard before. It's a strange clacking noise that gets inside you, that makes shivers race up your spine like nails on a chalkboard, only so much worse.

They're getting closer, and I glance around, trying to see what the gargoyles are doing. Surely Chastain isn't okay with these things—whatever they are— attacking the Gargoyle Court en masse. So why the fuck isn't anyone engaging with them? Yeah, they've got archers shooting burning arrows, but what's the point of all that sword training the gargoyles do every day if they aren't going to use it to defend themselves? It's baffling.

Especially since none of the flaming arrows flying by us seems to connect with the damn things. How hard can it be—there are thousands of them and they're all grouped together in a giant wave climbing up the side of the damn castle. Pure luck should have the archers hitting *something*.

Instead it seems like hours before—*finally*—an arrow strikes home and a bone creature lets out one of the most terrifying shrieks I've ever heard.

The scream goes on so long, it feels like it's become a permanent part of my brain, so that it takes a second for my mind to catch up when the sound finally dies away. Not that the silence lasts—seconds later, another arrow hits a different skeleton, who lets out an eerily similar sound.

The screams are followed by the sound of bones crunching, which is followed by more screams. It's a vicious cycle that keeps repeating itself as they make their way farther and farther up the wall.

More gargoyles are in the air now and I think they might make the difference, but then Grace stiffens behind me, a sound of terror ripping from her.

I follow her gaze and see one of the female gargoyles—Moira, I think her name is—being attacked by a bone creature. She's freaking out, screaming for someone to get it off. But no one moves to help her.

I start to do it—if the gargoyles choose not to protect their own, I'll do it for them. But then I see something that chills my blood, and has the other gargoyles' reticence making so much more sense.

The bone creature has sunk its teeth into her wrist, and her whole arm is dissolving. Her flesh is turning to dust in front of my eyes, blowing away in the wind like nothing. And the longer it holds her, the more flesh she loses.

It's the most disturbing thing I've ever seen, this strong, healthy gargoyle rotting piece by piece. Fingers, forearm, biceps, shoulder... These creatures take monstrous to a whole new level.

"We have to help her!" Grace shouts, pushing away from me. Then she's racing down the battlements toward Moira, and what's left of my heart stutters in my chest.

"Don't!" I yell, reaching out and yanking her back to me and away from whatever the hell those fucking things are.

"We have to help her!" she screams again. She's clawing me now, struggling hard to get free, but I don't let her go.

"We can't," I whisper, and she looks at me like I'm a coward. It slices deep, as does her lack of faith in me, but still I hold on tightly to her.

"There's still time!" she begs, her voice high-pitched and frantic. "We can save her!"

"No, we can't." I lean forward over one of the crenels, pulling her with me so her human eyes are close enough to see what I have all along.

"Oh my God," Grace whispers. "It's killing her. It's killing her!"

Her words, clear and terrified and more than a little painful—on every front—fill the air around us. And even before she turns to me, shoulders down, face wet with tears, eyes desperate for a miracle, I know what she wants me to do.

More, I know what she *needs* me to do.

I can't say no, not when she's hurting and panicked and desperate.

She's my mate. It's my job to take care of her. And that means when I know she needs something, she shouldn't even have to ask.

Her eyes meet mine, and I show her the answer before she even figures out the question.

She's crying in earnest now, and seeing her suffer destroys me. I start to turn away, to begin what has to be done. But then she whispers, "I'm sorry," and it breaks my heart all over again.

I cup her face in my hands, wipe her tears away with the pads of my thumbs. "I already told you, Grace. Don't ever apologize to me for wanting to save your people."

She makes a wild, panicked sound even as she shakes her head and reaches for me.

But this has gone on too long already. I need to end it before these people— before my *mate*—get hurt any worse.

I take a second to look down at the monstrosities below us, with their twisted, broken bones and their demented devotion to whatever destruction they can bring. *Monsters*, I tell myself. *They're just monsters.*

But even monsters have hearts—I know that better than anyone.

So I close my eyes and hold a hand out over the crenels. Then I open up my mind, let my power loose. And slowly, carefully separate the energy from each of the individual skeletons from everyone and everything else out here.

There are thousands of them, and each one is alive in some twisted, demented way. The realization is a fist to the gut, even if there's a part of me that expected it.

Each one has a mind. Each one has a soul. And I slide into every single one of them.

I feel the pain of splintered bone, the haze of bloodlust, the gnawing, ever-present ache to be real again. To be whole again.

It hurts more than I ever could have imagined, more than thirty thousand bony claws raking through me, shredding every tiny particle of my being. I try to block it off, try to concentrate only on what has to be done, but it's impossible. There are too many of them, and each one wants a piece of me. A tiny corner of my soul that I will never get back.

But this is for Grace. For her people.

Once I'm inside all 3,127 of them, once I can feel their hearts and bodies, their minds and souls, it nearly destroys me to know what's coming.

But Grace needs this, and that is all that matters. So I do what has to be done.

I close my hand.

And die 3,127 times.

Turn the page for an exclusive sneak peek of the upcoming epic fantasy about to take the YA reading community by storm.

THE LIAR'S CROWN

ONE BORN TO RULE—ONE TO FORFEIT...

1
A HOVEL AND A HAG

The moonlight filtering through my tiny glassless window creeps across my ceiling as I mark the time by the single star visible in the night sky, waiting.

I do this a lot. Waiting to sneak out. Waiting to fulfill my duties. Waiting for Omma to tell me what to do. Waiting to be anything but who and what I am.

Mereneith Evangeline XII of Sandes. Second-born princess of the royal line.

Only, my name was erased from the Book of Names so I can serve the dominion, the crown, and the greater good...in secret. Just another in a long line of hidden royal twins.

One born to rule—one to forfeit.

Guess which one I am.

My purpose is to stand in as a body double for Tabra when a situation is too dangerous to risk her life. Secretly, of course, because no one outside of my sister, our grandmother the queen, and our grandmother's own hidden twin, Omma, knows of my existence. My life is tied to my sister's until the day I have to save her life by sacrificing my own.

Quite a fate to hang over a girl's head.

All because King Eidolon sits on the throne in the icy dominion of Tyndra, a constant threat to the Sandes royal line. The stories Omma and Grandmother used to tell us about the seemingly immortal king are terrifying. He's been stealing and killing Sandes queens for centuries, though no one has figured out why. Only a few generations have escaped, Grandmother being one of them, which is why she's still on the throne instead of Omma.

He is always coming for us. We just don't know when. And that unpredictability is what scares me most.

I pull my knees to my chest, watching my star creep across the sky. I refuse to think about the king or his winter. Not tonight. Tonight is *mine*.

Or it will be, if I can get out of this damn house without the Hag catching me.

I've been sneaking out since I was a child, living for the days Omma leaves me behind to travel on her own to the palace in the capital city of Oaesys. Reckless? Yes. But worth it.

The desert is the only part of my life that is for me, not for Tabra, or the queen, or Sandes, or Omma, or anyone else. It's where I get to be Meren. Where my only real friend, Cain, teaches me things that Omma would never allow.

With a sigh, I stare at the shadows on the edges of the moonlight. They reach out for me like a cool caress. What I wouldn't give for a different life. One where a future of my own stretched out in front of me, full of possibilities. But that's not going to happen, so I shove the wish down deep.

The instant my star disappears, I'm on my feet, adjusting the disguise I put on earlier. My clothes—a black body-hugging top, breeches, and worn calfskin boots—are threadbare to keep up the appearance of Meren, poor city waif.

The last touch is a headscarf that makes me claustrophobic, but it hides most of my face, leaving only my eyes showing. I wear it any time I'm out of the house and in the city. Goddess forbid anyone mistakes me for Princess Tabra, heir apparent to the throne.

As Tabra's identical twin, I have the same long black hair, same sun-kissed skin, same unusual shade of amber eyes and stubborn chin. I am an exact copy, down to each mole and scar.

You don't want to know how I got the scars.

I climb out the window, hoping against hope that this will be unexpected and I'll actually make it out of the hovel without being seen. I haven't tried this way out before, for a good reason. As I swing my leg over, my stomach pitches, and I grip the windowsill hard. Heights and I do *not* get along.

I huff out an irritated breath. Princess Mereneith, Imperium and fearless body double to the future Queen of Sandes, afraid of falling to her death from only one story up.

Ridiculous.

Not looking down, I manage to scramble the rest of the way out and scoot across the tile-covered roof to the corner. There I grab the drainage pipe bolted to the wall. Is the air thinner up here? Black dots freckle the edges of my vision—or maybe I forgot to breathe. Ugh. Without letting myself think about it, I shimmy down to the alleyway below, sucking in a shuddering breath when my feet finally hit the ground.

I get lucky. The alley is empty. No sign of Omma's watchdog.

The small, weathered hovel where Omma and I live is tucked between two taller inns, like a tiny child squished between broad-shouldered men in a pew at temple. It always smells like piss out here. These are establishments for rough travelers, drunks, and whores. That's what Omma calls them, at least, though the women who work there have always been kind to me. Except for the selkie, but she's mean to everyone.

Ignoring my shaking hands, I pull out a pack from under a pile of trash where I'd hidden it earlier. Sand rats skitter resentfully out of my way, baring tiny, razor-sharp teeth. The menaces gnawed a hole in the side. Scowling, I check the contents, but it's sealed up tight.

Bag secure over one shoulder, I move quickly to the end of the alley and pause, peering down the street, which has yet to fill with people. The cool of night is when this city comes alive, and it helps if I get outside the walls before that happens.

But when I go to take a step, a gnarled hand wraps around my arm and tugs me back with surprising strength.

I grimace. Not so lucky then, which means I risked my life on that deathtrap of a roof for no good reason.

The Hag—I've never heard anyone call her anything else—glares in my general direction. For years, my great-aunt has paid this blind old beggar woman to watch the house—and me—when she's gone. But Omma is cheap, even when protecting the royal quasi-princess she's raised since infancy, and the Hag is only a Vex.

Her lack of powers doesn't make her any less intimidating, though.

"You shouldn't go out tonight," she says in a voice only a mother could love, her hooked fingers twitching.

No one is talking me out of this. "Listen—"

She holds up a hand to stop me and huffs out a sigh. "How are you from Sandes? Our goddess granted us patience, and yet you have none."

There's a lot about me that doesn't make sense in my dominion. I've never fit into any of the places or roles I've been forced into. Like filling an hourglass with rocks instead of sand and still expecting time to keep flowing—that's me.

"Just…watch yourself tonight, girl."

I frown. She's never bothered to warn me before. "Why?"

"I may be blind, but my ears work fine. Talk of more folk disappearing. Taken in the night." She pauses, then lowers her voice to a hush. "I think a Shadowraith walks among us."

Shadowraith. My breath stills at the whispered word.

I can only guess what kind of creature that is, but given the disappearances, it sounds pretty bad. Everyone in my city of Mierazh has heard of someone who knows someone who's gone missing. They call them the Vanished. The whispers have yet to reach the palace in Oaesys. Maybe it's time I mention it to Tabra. Grandmother isn't likely to bother with it, but a few well-placed murmurs in the viziers' ears from my sister might help.

The Hag's warning is one I'd be smart to listen to. Instead, I have to bury a spark of interest. I've never been frightened of shadows. I use shadows. More times than I can count, I've wished I could slide into them and let them take me anywhere but here.

Maybe I would feel differently if I came face-to-face with a Shadowraith. A girl of eighteen summer solstices, even an Imperium girl who came into her underwhelming powers way too early, probably couldn't do much. My ability to control sand wouldn't make a dent. I mean...sand isn't all that handy as a defense. I'm not supposed to use it in public anyway.

Hard rule. One of many.

I square my shoulders. I already have enough worries just getting out of the city, but the Hag's warning is more than most would do for me. Rather than hand over the tiny purse of coins I always bring in case she catches me—which she usually does—I pull out the last of the storm-asps I snuck out of the palace last time I was there. It was supposed to be a gift for Cain.

"Here," I say and place the sleek, pewter-scaled snake into her hand.

Her crow of delight follows me around the corner and into the darkened cobbled streets.

2
STRANGER IN THE NIGHT

I cut a careful path through the slowly awakening city. At night, it's harder to see the decay. Everything around here is chipped, broken, or falling apart. The deterioration isn't contained to the poorer parts of the city anymore, either.

During the day, these streets are full of people who remind me more and more of the sand rats, chewing through whatever and whoever they have to just to put food in their bellies. Vexillium, all of them, just like the Hag. Men and women stooped over, life etched into the crags of their faces, muck permanently worked under their fingernails. When Omma and I come back from trips to the palace, I have to scratch in the dirt or I look too clean.

Somewhere inside one of the buildings I pass, laughter tumbles out—a family, by the sound—and I smile.

Sandes at night always reminds me that under that decay are people who laugh, who love, and try to survive. Patience gets them through the heat of the day, and a world bathed in moonlight is their reward.

Sandes is the goddess of the three moons instead of the sun for a reason.

But there is still danger here, so I quicken my pace. The underbelly of Mierazh lurks in the cracks and crevices. Dealers, thieves, life stealers, and traffickers. But no one sees me, let alone tries to stop me, and no one follows. I know because I check over my shoulder so many times, I'm surprised I don't trip over my own feet.

Moving between dark patches and doorways, I near the south gate in the city walls. It's the least traveled gate because this is the way the Wanderers come in from the desert beyond. To trade...or, some would have you believe, to kill. I check over my shoulder one last time—

A man stands in the middle of the street, staring at me.

I stumble to a halt, shock and fear spiking in my veins. A series of thoughts tumble through my mind all at once. Should I run? Is he a Vex? He doesn't look like a Vex. He's too still. Too...controlled.

Which means he's an Imperium. Great.

But which kind?

A Corpori would be less of a threat. We control tangible, physical elements like sand or water or plants, depending on the person. But an Etheri... Their control over intangible things like emotions or souls or a person's mind can be terrifying.

King Eidolon is Etheri. Or so we've been told.

Omma is Etheri.

The last thing I want is to cross paths with an unfamiliar Etheri. *Please be pretty much anything else.*

I eye him. He's not just staring—he's watching. Intently.

Neither of us moves. I try to make out more of his sharp-edged face in the darkness. He's all shadow and hardness. Dressed in black, his clothes aren't those of a laborer or a waif, like me, but neither are they anything that speaks to wealth or privilege.

The strangest sense of recognition washes through me, but I can't pin it down, like trying to reach for a mirage.

Then a shaft of moonlight shifts, glinting over his features, and a wave of impressions strikes in rapid succession. A few summers older than I. Midnight black hair swept up off a high brow. A sharply set jaw. Slashing, thick brows over eyes that even in the silvery light are the color of the ocean. The turquoise is so clear and true, I'm reminded of the times I've stood on the protected side of our glass walls and watched the sun play on the shallow ocean waters beyond the narrow spit of sand. Sometimes, for a crazy, pulse-pounding instant, I've thought about risking a gruesome death just to know the feel of the translucent waves washing over my feet.

I feel that same pull now.

He is possibly the most harshly beautiful man I've ever seen, but that's not what captures my attention. It's the aura of leashed power that surrounds him... and the way he's studying me. Like he sees *me*.

And I'm just standing here, drinking in the sight of him like it's perfectly normal to come across beautiful, uncomfortably familiar men who all but appear from thin air in the middle of the night. An Imperium, no less. Omma would have my head. Tabra might even help.

I gather my wits and edge closer to the tunnel.

"Who are you?" he asks.

Goddess, what a voice. Velvet and iron. Another quiver of reaction fizzes through me, but then his question sinks in and dread wells up in its place. That is the *last* question I want anyone asking me. Especially an Etheri. What if his power is over truth?

Forget edging away. I bolt.

"Hey!" he calls after me.

I hesitate, glancing over my shoulder...and immediately get sucked into his gaze again. Dammit. At least I remember to deliberately lower my voice so I don't sound like my sister when I speak. "I'm no one."

His eyebrows slam down. *Oh, he didn't like that.* But then his expression shifts as he glances between me and the exit. "You shouldn't go out there alone."

As if he's trying to protect me.

For a man who looks like a criminal, that's a ridiculous idea. I lift my chin. "I do as I please." I hear the queen's imperious tone in my words, and I want to kick myself. A waif of Mierazh wouldn't sound so...royal. So entitled.

There's no flicker of recognition in his eyes, thank the goddesses. I've about convinced myself he's just a Vex criminal whose nighttime activities I interrupted when he gives a slight incline of his head.

I frown. A criminal with an authoritate's manners? Who *is* this man? Before I can ask, the stranger turns and melts into the shadows, leaving me alone. I stare at the spot he'd just been, wrestling with the strangest sense of disappointment and...emptiness.

I shake myself out of my stupor. *Emptiness?* I have no business feeling whatever that's about. No, I need to get out of the streets and into the desert. Lingering anywhere too long alone in Mierazh is never a good idea.

With one last glance at the shadows—what is *wrong* with me?—I scurry through the tunnel toward the sand on the other side. I pause at the end to be sure no one is hovering just outside the entry, then hurry into the rolling desert dunes.

Ten steps out, a tickling sense of being watched has me checking over my shoulder one last time, sure that I'm going to see the stranger standing at the gate.

No one is there.

All that lies behind me is Mierazh, all white, made of sand from the Crystaline Desert, that glows under the three full moons.

Muscles tensed, I walk quickly until I get to the towering glass wall that marks our dominion's farthest eastern border.

No one knows how high the glass walls go. Some think they're actually a dome, but if that were true, how do we still have air to breathe? Whatever magic lurks in that glass, I don't bother to question it. They protect us from a bigger threat.

On the other side, just beyond the narrow beach, the oceans that surround and separate all the dominions sleep in the darkness, seeming almost peaceful. I know better. The walls were made by our goddess to keep out the Devourers.

The monsters are violent and thirsty for human blood, and each is as different as the last. No one knows why our seas were damned with them, but each dominion has its own defenses, some more successful than others. This is ours.

Putting the water on my left, I keep moving south, away from the city.

In protecting us from the monsters, our goddess gave us an unexpected gift. The tendrils of Tyndra's winter are crawling beyond the borders of King Eidolon's lands, reaching for Sandes and the other dominions of Wildernyss, Savanah, Tropikis, and Mariana. The glass walls keep my people safe, but the brutal cold ravaging the other dominions is relentless.

The walls won't hold forever.

The more immediate problem is what's happening to the dominion itself. While the walls have kept out Tyndra's winter, they've also kept in the intense heat of summer. The desert has been eating away at anything that had once been lush and green, just as the decay has been eating our cities.

Too bad I'm the only one in the palace worried. And I technically don't exist.

The longer I walk without any sign of Cain, the more disappointment builds in my gut. No fires dot the dunes in the distance. No sounds of warm laughter float on the breeze. No horses' hooves scuff on the parched sand. Sighing, I unwrap my headscarf and drape it around my neck and shoulders. The closer I get to the well, the more the hope of seeing my friend shrivels.

It happens this way sometimes. Wanderers are, after all, a nomadic people who travel the deserts. But I'd heard in the city they were moving this way, and between his zariphate's movements and Omma's sharp eye keeping me in place, it's been so long since I've seen him. Ages.

Dropping to the sand with a small dune between me and the well, I sit and wait. Just in case. It's not like I have anywhere else to be. Out of sheer boredom, I reach for the small kernel of the power inside me I can't ever seem to fully grasp.

Warm tingles cascade through my skin like effervescent bubbles as the soft yellow glow of all Corpori illuminates my palm. Under me, the ground shivers. At a whisper of my direction, a small amount of sand lifts from the ground. I add heat and tiny golden sparks spray out, reminding me of fire sprites who lead people who are lost even deeper into the desert. The sand fuses, forming into a ball, then the individual grains melt and meld, becoming liquid.

With a flick of my fingers, I shape the small bubble into the start of a glass flower for Tabra. I make them for her as gifts, basing them off ancient drawings in rare books hidden away in Grandmother's personal library. A real flower hasn't been seen in eons, so I took to making poor imitations of them as practice.

My sister loves them so much she made a secret garden of them in the palace.

I don't finish, though. It's still just a bud when I decide I shouldn't stay here waiting any longer. He isn't coming. The zariphate isn't coming.

Wrestling with the disappointment dragging at me, I get to my feet, slipping the flower into a pocket to finish later.

But before I can turn back for the city, a pale-skinned, leanly muscled arm wraps around my chest and a knife blade digs into my throat.

3
CAIN

Shock pelts through me like a barrage of arrows. Merciful goddess. Did the stranger follow me after all? Did he see what I was doing with the sand?

"Move and you'll be breathing blood through your windhole," a low voice says close to my ear.

Not the stranger's voice.

The blade digs deeper and I flinch. I let myself get distracted and got caught. How could I have been so careless? The warm trickle oozing down my neck tells me whoever this is…he's deadly serious.

My mind splinters. If he isn't the stranger, then who in the hells is this? An Imperium would have used their power. A troll would be taller. Maybe an Outcast? Hopefully not the Shadowraith. The Hag's warning didn't help much if that's what I'm up against.

I catch a scent of sweat. Not my own, though—fouler, more pungent. Definitely a Vex.

Relief is sharp but brief. Now what?

I have a knife strapped to my ankle. It's the one valuable skill Omma ever taught me—only to protect Tabra, of course—but I can't reach it.

Which leaves me only one option.

Closing my eyes, I remain still and silent. As long as I don't pose a threat, maybe he'll let me go. Unless this guy is one of the "sacrifice her to the Pit of Bones" types. Being digested slowly over a hundred summers really isn't in my plans.

"I wondered how long it would take before we bumped into Cain's little pet," a familiar female voice purrs from behind me.

My eyes snap open. Despite the knife still at my neck, I don't bother to hide my irritation, my lips flattening.

Cain's half sister, Pella, moves the sleek black mare she sits atop around in front of me. Even though they don't look it with their smaller, fine-boned stature, the horses of the Wanderers have been bred to be hardy with incredible stamina. Survivors.

If I were a horse, I'd want to be like them.

Reins loose, hands casually draped over the high pommel of her saddle,

Pella sneers down at me. Sharp nosed and sharp tongued, Pella is a feminine version of Cain with skin the color of sand in the sunset. I always was jealous of that, since I have to protect my own to match my sister, who rarely leaves the shelter of the palace.

I've never liked Pella. The sneer I can handle. No one comes close to Omma—or even more so, my grandmother—for sneers. The court is riddled with judgment like the pox, so I've managed to grow a thick skin. But the fact that Pella always calls me Cain's little pet, despite me being a few months older than her, chafes like sand in my undergarments.

What's more, she knows it.

"Pella," I greet. "I wish I could say this was a nice surprise, but you clearly still haven't outgrown that bitchy phase. Shame."

Her sound of outrage is worth the sting of the knife pressed deeper into the flesh of my neck, earning me another oozing trickle of blood. "You dare insult the zariph's daughter?" the scout demands.

"Let her go," another familiar voice, deeper than the last time I saw him, commands from behind the well.

Cain.

He steps closer, the moonlight illuminating his face, and I blink. Lately, whenever I see him, I'm surprised. I can't help it. I guess I keep expecting to find the boy I grew up with—gangly and scrawny, with a head too big for his shoulders and coltish legs he hadn't known what to do with.

But that's not who he is anymore.

Laughing eyes, nearly onyx-colored in the night, are wide-set under a strong forehead. An even stronger jaw. Skin burnished by the sun to a rich, coppery-bronze, darker than his sister's. His form has filled out, broadened, and no doubt hardened under the looser clothing of the wandering desert peoples.

Made of cloth the exact hue of this desert, the clothes blend Cain's silhouette into his surroundings, sand the color of oats. It's difficult to see where one layer ends and another begins, but I know the outermost layer hides razor-thin armor strapped to his legs, torso, and shoulders.

The knife is removed from my neck, and the scout steps away. He pretends not to recognize me as he disappears into the desert, even though I know he does. Everyone in this zariphate knows me.

Cain is, after all, the eldest son of the zariph. Next in the line of succession.

Kind of like me, but legitimate.

He winks at me, and I try not to laugh.

Pella's expression curls into a scowl. She really would be strikingly beautiful if she'd stop doing that with her face.

I blow out a silent breath and turn my back to her. She has never, ever made me feel welcome among her people. Wanderers are naturally wary of strangers, but after so many years of me hanging around, Pella should be over it.

Behind me, she gives a little hiss. "Caught like the ignorant city-dweller she is."

If only she knew. In order to play the role I do in the palace, I've been educated the same as my sister. All the best tutors. Debates with philosophers and generals and government leaders. I'm the most educated waif in all of Sandes.

I wonder what the zariph would do if I knocked his only precious daughter off her horse with a rock?

"There's only so much I can protect you from," Cain murmurs softly as he steps nearer. "As much fun as your smart mouth is."

My response dies on my lips when a tremor deep in the ground catches my attention. A good distance away, a tiny plume rises into the air like smoke. It could be a dust devil, swirling and twisting spouts of wind.

It's not.

A zariphate of Wanderers, in number, is on the move and headed straight for the well. Still a league out at least.

Tracking my gaze, Pella suddenly sits straighter. "We'll see what Father has to say about your sand rat," she says, directing the words at Cain.

"Sand *snake*, don't you mean?" I glance pointedly at her.

Pella's hand goes to the small, puckered scar on her lip that I can't see but know is there. The last time she called me a sand snake, I'd cracked a whip at her. I'd meant it to be a warning. It caught her in the face instead. I can't say I'm sorry that I'm not all that great with whips.

Rather than pout, she grins at Cain. "Now that you're to be—"

"*Pella.*" Cain practically growls the word.

His sister blinks at him, all innocence, leaning forward to casually pat her horse's silky neck. "If you're going to be married, brother, I doubt your new heartmate will appreciate having *her* around."

A confusing swirl of emotions strikes with the force of a physical blow. Mostly, hurt rises to the top like curdled cream.

"Go tell Father I've purified the well," Cain says to his sister over my head.

"Yes," I say. "Run on back to daddy, little girl."

Hatred flashes through her eyes, but something else must pass between brother and sister because she huffs again, then turns away.

Leaving me alone with Cain.

I wait a beat before looking at him, searching his familiar face.

The first time I ran away from the hovel, I was six years old, and Cain, not much older, found me parched and barely alive under a lone tree in the desert. His father managed to have me returned to Omma in Mierazh.

You're lucky they didn't force you into servitude, Omma had scolded me.

I wasn't so sure "lucky" was the right word. Even at that tender age, being a servant who was wanted and useful sounded better than being what I was.

The second time I escaped, only a month later, thanks to the Hag turning a literal blind eye after I bribed her, Cain had been the one to find me again. That time, he'd taken responsibility for me, and his father didn't bother to send me back. Cain promised to teach me to live and survive in the desert as long as I promised to only venture out when I could find him near this well, the one closest to the city.

I've worshiped the ground he walks on ever since. But if he got married? I would lose my friend. My *only* friend.

Cain's eyes glint with something that might be amusement. "If I call you beautiful, will you cut out my tongue?"

For the first time in my life, I'm tempted to put a hand up to check my hair, which only adds another layer of confusion to go with my dry-as-dust mouth and no doubt dirt- and sweat-covered face. I shift awkwardly. "Is it true?" I ask. "What Pella said, I mean."

He grimaces. "She shouldn't have told you that way."

So, she *wasn't* lying.

"You're right." I suddenly want to lash out at him, hurt driving me. "*You* should have told me, Little Cainis."

I regret it the second the words are out. Cain hates his full name, but even more, he hates the patronizing tag of "little" some add to it. His father, for whom he'd been named, is called Mighty Cainis and is the leader of the largest zariphate in Sandes.

Cain shakes his head. "I'm sorry. I was going to—" He cuts himself off and starts over. "Father wants me to make a political match with an authoritate."

"Why?" My grandmother has been desperate to make an alliance with the Mighty Cainis for as long as I can remember, but the Wanderers have always spurned those who lived in cities.

"For access to resources," Cain says grimly.

Resources? The zariphates are self-sufficient. "What could you possibly need?"

"The wells are starting to dry." He takes a deep breath. "Tomorrow we'll travel to the city of Oaesys to barter for my...bride."

My mouth opens a few times without sound coming out. "You... You're going to the palace?"

Where Tabra is. Tabra, who looks exactly like me. *Don't panic.*

He steps closer, urgency in the tense motion of his body, the way his hands are clenching. "Yes. But it's not what *I* want."

I'm still stumbling over the whole palace thing. What if he gets a good look at my sister and puts it all together? Omma will kill me. No really. Because if my secret is uncovered, my existence revealed, what's the point of keeping me around?

Cain takes my hands in his. Touch in our dominion is important. Personal. Shock appears to be my only reaction tonight, because all I can do is stare at our linked hands. His are larger, stronger, and a couple shades deeper than mine.

"Come with me," he says.

I jerk my gaze up to eyes filled with a soft expression I've never seen before. Not from him. Tenderness and a question I can't possibly answer.

"Don't go back to Mierazh," he says. "Stay with the zariphate. And me."

What is he asking? That I go to Oaesys with him? That won't work on so many levels. I shake my head. "Pella's right. If you marry, your heartmate won't—"

"Meren." He sort of laughs and groans at the same time. Then digs in the loose pockets of his clothes before holding out a bracelet. A cuff made of pure, gleaming gold with the symbol of a sand fox—Cain's family sigil—etched into the center.

Oh.

"We could travel to the Sacred Tree, like we've always talked about...make our covenant there."

I've never even seen the Sacred Tree in Sandes, though Tabra got to for our sixteenth birthday as part of her entering the age of reason. But not me. That tree is on the other side of the dominion and never stops burning. Cain and I have talked all our lives of visiting all six sacred trees of the dominions. Together.

But that's not what he's asking now.

My skin goes tight all over, like part of me wants to jump right out of it. This is Cain—my friend, my protector, my hero—who has taught me so much and always treated me with kindness. As an equal.

I know who and what I am, but he doesn't. Even in the desert when I'm trying to escape my life, that knowing underlies every move I make, every word out of my mouth. That knowing hovers over everything I do. It has never once occurred to me that Cain could be more.

A different life. One where I'm not a secret, unwanted until I'm required to do my duty, where I get to always be part of the desert that has felt more like home than the palace or the hovel ever did.

The life he's offering is tempting, except for the odd, unsettled churning in my stomach. Even more unsettling is the sudden, sharp memory of turquoise eyes in the night.

Something cold and biting lands on my forehead. I still, then when it happens again in a different spot, pull my hand out of his to touch my face. My fingertip comes away wet.

"What in the dunes?" Cain mutters.

"You felt that, too?"

Only he's looking up. "Yeah."

I tip my head back and gasp. Delicate white crystals are floating out of the sky like fairy dust, catching the moonlight in a glittering array only to disappear when they hit the ground.

Snow.

Dread wraps an icy hand around my insides.

The eternal winter has breached the walls.

ACKNOWLEDGMENTS

Writing a series with as many moving parts as this one takes a whole village, so I have to start by thanking the two women who even made it possible: Liz Pelletier and Emily Sylvan Kim.

Liz, I know this was a rocky one, but I am grateful for all you do for me and the Crave series. You are a truly incredible editor and friend and I am so, so lucky to have you in my corner. Thank you for moving mountains to make sure this book happened.

Emily, I hit the agent jackpot. Sincerely. We're sixty-eight books in, and I couldn't be more grateful to have you in my corner. Your support, encouragement, friendship, determination, and joy for this series has kept me going when I wasn't sure I'd be able to make it. Thank you for everything you do for me. I am so, so, so lucky that you were willing to take me on all those years ago.

Stacy Cantor Abrams, I don't know how to thank you for everything you've done for me and for this book and this series. The fact that we are still working together after all these years is a matter of great pride and joy to me. I feel so lucky to have you in my corner.

To everyone else at Entangled who has played a part in the success of the Crave series, thank you, thank you, thank you, from the bottom of my heart. Heather Howland, for taking so much time from your busy schedule to solve plot problems and help make sure this behemoth makes sense. Jessica Turner, for your unfailing support. Bree Archer for making me ALL the beautiful covers and art all the time. Meredith Johnson for all your help with this series in all the different capacities. You make my job so much easier. To the fantastic proofreading team of Jessica, Greta, Debbie, Myshala, Lydia, and Richard, thank you for making my words shine! Toni Kerr for the incredible care you took with my baby. It looks amazing! Curtis Svehlak for making miracles happen on the production side over and over again—you are awesome! Katie Clapsadl for fixing my mistakes and always having my back, Riki Cleveland for being so lovely always, Heather Riccio for your attention to detail and your help with coordinating the million different things that happen on the business side of book publishing. A special thank-you to Jaime Bode and the amazing Macmillan sales team for all the support they've shown this series over the years and to Beth Metrick and Grainne Daly for working so extra hard to get these books into readers' hands.

Eden Kim, for being the best reader a writer could ever ask for. And for putting up with your mom's and my badgering of you ALL the time.

In Koo, Avery, and Phoebe Kim, thank you for lending me your wife and mom for all the late nights, early mornings, and breakfast/lunch/dinner/midnight conversations that went into making this book possible.

Stephanie Marquez, thank you for all your love, support, and enthusiasm as we navigate the fun but messy waters of this series (and our life). You are amazing.

For my three boys, who I love with my whole heart and soul. Thank you for understanding all the evenings I had to hide in my office and work instead of hanging out, for pitching in when I needed you most, for sticking with me through all the difficult years, and for being the best kids I could ever ask for.

And finally, for fans of Grace, Hudson, Jaxon, Flint, Macy, and the whole crew. Thank you, thank you, thank you for your unflagging support and enthusiasm for the Crave series. I can't tell you how much your emails and DMs and posts mean to me. I am so grateful that you've taken us into your hearts and chosen to go on this journey with me. I hope you enjoyed *Court* as much as I enjoyed writing it. I love and am grateful for every single one of you. xoxoxoxo

Author's Note: This book depicts issues of panic attacks, death and violence, emotional and psychological torture, insect-related situations, life-and-death situations, amputation, and sexual content. It is my hope that these elements have been handled sensitively, but if these issues could be considered triggering to you, please take note.

Let's be friends!

 @EntangledTeen

 @EntangledTeen

 @EntangledTeen

 bit.ly/TeenNewsletter

entangled teen

an imprint of Entangled Publishing LLC